The GOLDFINCH

The
GOLDFINCH

DONNA TARTT

Little, Brown

LITTLE, BROWN

First published in Great Britain in 2013 by Little, Brown
Reprinted 2013 (five times), 2014 (twice)

A CIP catalogue record for this book
is available from the British Library.

ISBN: 978-1-4087-0495-0

Printed and bound in Great Britain by
Clays Ltd, St Ives plc

Papers used by Little, Brown are from well-managed forests
and other responsible sources.

MIX
Paper from
responsible sources
FSC® C104740

Little, Brown
An imprint of
Little, Brown Book Group
100 Victoria Embankment
London EC4Y 0DY

An Hachette UK Company
www.hachette.co.uk

www.littlebrown.co.uk

For Mother,

For Claude

I.

The absurd does not liberate; it binds.

— ALBERT CAMUS

Chapter 1.

Boy with a Skull

i.

WHILE I WAS STILL in Amsterdam, I dreamed about my mother for the first time in years. I'd been shut up in my hotel for more than a week, afraid to telephone anybody or go out; and my heart scrambled and floundered at even the most innocent noises: elevator bell, rattle of the minibar cart, even church clocks tolling the hour, de Westertoren, Krijtberg, a dark edge to the clangor, an inwrought fairy-tale sense of doom. By day I sat on the foot of the bed straining to puzzle out the Dutch-language news on television (which was hopeless, since I knew not a word of Dutch) and when I gave up, I sat by the window staring out at the canal with my camel's-hair coat thrown over my clothes—for I'd left New York in a hurry and the things I'd brought weren't warm enough, even indoors.

Outside, all was activity and cheer. It was Christmas, lights twinkling on the canal bridges at night; red-cheeked *dames en heren,* scarves flying in the icy wind, clattered down the cobblestones with Christmas trees lashed to the backs of their bicycles. In the afternoons, an amateur band played Christmas carols that hung tinny and fragile in the winter air.

Chaotic room-service trays; too many cigarettes; lukewarm vodka from duty free. During those restless, shut-up days, I got to know every inch of the room as a prisoner comes to know his cell. It was my first time in Amsterdam; I'd seen almost nothing of the city and yet the room itself, in its bleak, drafty, sunscrubbed beauty, gave a keen sense of Northern Europe, a model of the Netherlands in miniature: whitewash and Protestant probity, co-mingled with deep-dyed luxury brought in merchant ships from the East. I spent an unreasonable amount of time scrutinizing a tiny pair of gilt-framed oils hanging over the bureau, one of peasants skating on an ice-pond by a church, the other a sailboat flouncing on a choppy winter sea: decorative copies, nothing special, though I studied them as if they held, encrypted, some key to the secret heart of the old Flemish masters. Outside, sleet tapped at the windowpanes and drizzled over the canal; and though the brocades were rich and the carpet was soft, still the winter light carried a chilly tone of 1943, privation and austerities, weak tea without sugar and hungry to bed.

Early every morning while it was still black out, before the extra clerks came on duty and the lobby started filling up, I walked downstairs for the newspapers. The hotel staff moved with hushed voices and quiet footsteps, eyes gliding across me coolly as if they didn't quite see me, the American man in 27 who never came down during the day; and I tried to reassure myself that the night manager (dark suit, crew cut, horn-rimmed glasses) would probably go to some lengths to avert trouble or avoid a fuss.

The *Herald Tribune* had no news of my predicament but the story was all over the Dutch papers, dense blocks of foreign print which hung, tantalizingly, just beyond the reach of my comprehension. *Onopgeloste moord. Onbekende.* I went upstairs and got back into bed (fully clad, because the room was so cold) and spread the papers out on the coverlet: photographs of police cars, crime scene tape, even the captions were impossible to decipher, and although they didn't appear to have my name, there was no way to know if they had a description of me or if they were withholding information from the public.

The room. The radiator. *Een Amerikaan met een strafblad.* Olive green water of the canal.

Because I was cold and ill, and much of the time at a loss what to do (I'd neglected to bring a book, as well as warm clothes), I stayed in bed most of the day. Night seemed to fall in the middle of the afternoon. Often — amidst the crackle of strewn newspapers — I drifted in and out of sleep, and my dreams for the most part were muddied with the same indeterminate anxiety that bled through into my waking hours: court cases, luggage burst open on the tarmac with my clothes scattered everywhere and endless airport corridors where I ran for planes I knew I'd never make.

Thanks to my fever I had a lot of weird and extremely vivid dreams, sweats where I thrashed around hardly knowing if it was day or night, but on the last and worst of these nights I dreamed about my mother: a quick, mysterious dream that felt more like a visitation. I was in Hobie's shop—

or, more accurately, some haunted dream space staged like a sketchy version of the shop—when she came up suddenly behind me so I saw her reflection in a mirror. At the sight of her I was paralyzed with happiness; it was her, down to the most minute detail, the very pattern of her freckles, she was smiling at me, more beautiful and yet not older, black hair and funny upward quirk of her mouth, not a dream but a presence that filled the whole room: a force all her own, a living otherness. And as much as I wanted to, I knew I couldn't turn around, that to look at her directly was to violate the laws of her world and mine; she had come to me the only way she could, and our eyes met in the glass for a long still moment; but just as she seemed about to speak—with what seemed a combination of amusement, affection, exasperation—a vapor rolled between us and I woke up.

ii.

THINGS WOULD HAVE TURNED out better if she had lived. As it was, she died when I was a kid; and though everything that's happened to me since then is thoroughly my own fault, still when I lost her I lost sight of any landmark that might have led me someplace happier, to some more populated or congenial life.

Her death the dividing mark: Before and After. And though it's a bleak thing to admit all these years later, still I've never met anyone who made me feel loved the way she did. Everything came alive in her company; she cast a charmed theatrical light about her so that to see anything through her eyes was to see it in brighter colors than ordinary—I remember a few weeks before she died, eating a late supper with her in an Italian restaurant down in the Village, and how she grasped my sleeve at the sudden, almost painful loveliness of a birthday cake with lit candles being carried in procession from the kitchen, faint circle of light wavering in across the dark ceiling and then the cake set down to blaze amidst the family, beatifying an old lady's face, smiles all round, waiters stepping away with their hands behind their backs—just an ordinary birthday dinner you might see anywhere in an inexpensive downtown restaurant, and I'm sure I wouldn't even remember it had she not died so soon after, but I thought about it again and again after her death and indeed I'll probably think about it all my life: that candlelit circle, a tableau vivant of the daily, commonplace happiness that was lost when I lost her.

She was beautiful, too. That's almost secondary; but still, she was. When she came to New York fresh from Kansas, she worked part-time as a model though she was too uneasy in front of the camera to be very good at it; whatever she had, it didn't translate to film.

And yet she was wholly herself: a rarity. I cannot recall ever seeing another person who really resembled her. She had black hair, fair skin that freckled in summer, china-blue eyes with a lot of light in them; and in the slant of her cheekbones there was such an eccentric mixture of the tribal and the Celtic Twilight that sometimes people guessed she was Icelandic. In fact, she was half Irish, half Cherokee, from a town in Kansas near the Oklahoma border; and she liked to make me laugh by calling herself an Okie even though she was as glossy and nervy and stylish as a racehorse. That exotic character unfortunately comes out a little too stark and unforgiving in photographs — her freckles covered with makeup, her hair pulled back in a ponytail at the nape of her neck like some nobleman in *The Tale of Genji* — and what doesn't come across at all is her warmth, her merry, unpredictable quality, which is what I loved about her most. It's clear, from the stillness she emanates in pictures, how much she mistrusted the camera; she gives off a watchful, tigerish air of steeling herself against attack. But in life she wasn't like that. She moved with a thrilling quickness, gestures sudden and light, always perched on the edge of her chair like some long elegant marsh-bird about to startle and fly away. I loved the sandalwood perfume she wore, rough and unexpected, and I loved the rustle of her starched shirt when she swooped down to kiss me on the forehead. And her laugh was enough to make you want to kick over what you were doing and follow her down the street. Wherever she went, men looked at her out of the corner of their eyes, and sometimes they used to look at her in a way that bothered me a little.

Her death was my fault. Other people have always been a little too quick to assure me that it wasn't; and yes, *only a kid, who could have known, terrible accident, rotten luck, could have happened to anyone,* it's all perfectly true and I don't believe a word of it.

It happened in New York, April 10th, fourteen years ago. (Even my hand balks at the date; I had to push to write it down, just to keep the pen moving on the paper. It used to be a perfectly ordinary day but now it sticks up on the calendar like a rusty nail.)

If the day had gone as planned, it would have faded into the sky unmarked, swallowed without a trace along with the rest of my eighth-grade year. What would I remember of it now? Little or nothing. But of course the texture of that morning is clearer than the present, down to the drenched, wet feel of the air. It had rained in the night, a terrible storm, shops were flooded and a couple of subway stations closed; and the two of us were standing on the squelching carpet outside our apartment building while her favorite doorman, Goldie, who adored her, walked backwards down Fifty-Seventh with his arm up, whistling for a taxi. Cars whooshed by in sheets of dirty spray; rain-swollen clouds tumbled high above the skyscrapers, blowing and shifting to patches of clear blue sky, and down below, on the street, beneath the exhaust fumes, the wind felt damp and soft like spring.

"Ah, he's full, my lady," Goldie called over the roar of the street, stepping out of the way as a taxi splashed round the corner and shut its light off. He was the smallest of the doormen: a wan, thin, lively little guy, light-skinned Puerto Rican, a former featherweight boxer. Though he was pouchy in the face from drinking (sometimes he turned up on the night shift smelling of J&B), still he was wiry and muscular and quick — always kidding around, always having a cigarette break on the corner, shifting from foot to foot and blowing on his white-gloved hands when it was cold, telling jokes in Spanish and cracking the other doormen up.

"You in a big hurry this morning?" he asked my mother. His nametag said BURT D. but everyone called him Goldie because of his gold tooth and because his last name, de Oro, meant "gold" in Spanish.

"No, plenty of time, we're fine." But she looked exhausted and her hands were shaky as she re-tied her scarf, which snapped and fluttered in the wind.

Goldie must have noticed this himself, because he glanced over at me (backed up evasively against the concrete planter in front of the building, looking anywhere but at her) with an air of slight disapproval.

"You're not taking the train?" he said to me.

"Oh, we've got some errands," said my mother, without much conviction, when she realized I didn't know what to say. Normally I didn't pay much attention to her clothes, but what she had on that morning (white trenchcoat, filmy pink scarf, black and white two-tone loafers) is so firmly burned into my memory that now it's difficult for me to remember her any other way.

I was thirteen. I hate to remember how awkward we were with each other that last morning, stiff enough for the doorman to notice; any other time we would have been talking companionably enough, but that morning we didn't have much to say to each other because I'd been suspended from school. They'd called her at her office the day before; she'd come home silent and furious; and the awful thing was that I didn't even know what I'd been suspended for, although I was about seventy-five percent sure that Mr. Beeman (en route from his office to the teachers' lounge) had looked out the window of the second-floor landing at exactly the wrong moment and seen me smoking on school property. (Or, rather, seen me standing around with Tom Cable while *he* smoked, which at my school amounted to practically the same offense.) My mother hated smoking. Her parents—whom I loved hearing stories about, and who had unfairly died before I'd had the chance to know them—had been affable horse trainers who travelled around the west and raised Morgan horses for a living: cocktail-drinking, canasta-playing livelies who went to the Kentucky Derby every year and kept cigarettes in silver boxes around the house. Then my grandmother doubled over and started coughing blood one day when she came in from the stables; and for the rest of my mother's teenage years, there had been oxygen tanks on the front porch and bedroom shades that stayed pulled down.

But—as I feared, and not without reason—Tom's cigarette was only the tip of the iceberg. I'd been in trouble at school for a while. It had all started, or begun to snowball rather, when my father had run off and left my mother and me some months before; we'd never liked him much, and my mother and I were generally much happier without him, but other people seemed shocked and distressed at the abrupt way he'd abandoned us (without money, child support, or forwarding address), and the teachers at my school on the Upper West Side had been so sorry for me, so eager to extend their understanding and support, that they'd given me—a scholarship student—all sorts of special allowances and delayed deadlines and second and third chances: feeding out the rope, over a matter of months, until I'd managed to lower myself into a very deep hole.

So the two of us—my mother and I—had been called in for a conference at school. The meeting wasn't until eleven-thirty but since my mother had been forced to take the morning off, we were heading to the West Side early—for breakfast (and, I expected, a serious talk) and so she could buy a birthday present for someone she worked with. She'd been up until two-thirty the night before, her face tense in the glow of the computer, writing emails and trying to clear the decks for her morning out of the office.

"I don't know about you," Goldie was saying to my mother, rather fiercely, "but I say enough with all this spring and damp already. Rain, rain—" He shivered, pulled his collar closer in pantomime and glanced at the sky.

"I think it's supposed to clear up this afternoon."

"Yeah, I know, but I'm ready for *summer.*" Rubbing his hands. "People leave town, they hate it, complain about the heat, but me—I'm a tropical bird. Hotter the better. Bring it on!" Clapping, backing on his heels down the street. "And—tell you what I love the best, is how it quietens out here, come July—? building all empty and sleepy, everyone away, you know?" Snapping his fingers, cab speeding by. "That's *my* vacation."

"But don't you burn up out here?" My standoffish dad had hated this about her—her tendency to engage in conversation with waitresses, doormen, the wheezy old guys at the dry cleaner's. "I mean, in winter, at least you can put on an extra coat—"

"Listen, you're working the door in winter? I'm telling you it gets *cold.* I don't care how many coats and hats you put on. You're standing out here, in January, February, and the wind is blowing in off the river? *Brrr.*"

Agitated, gnawing at my thumbnail, I stared at the cabs flying past Goldie's upraised arm. I knew that it was going to be an excruciating wait until the conference at eleven-thirty; and it was all I could do to stand still and not blurt out incriminating questions. I had no idea what they might spring on my mother and me once they had us in the office; the very word "conference" suggested a convocation of authorities, accusations and face-downs, a possible expulsion. If I lost my scholarship it would be catastrophic; we were broke since my dad had left; we barely had money for rent. Above all else: I was worried sick that Mr. Beeman had found out, somehow, that Tom Cable and I had been breaking into empty vacation houses when I went to stay with him out in the Hamptons. I say "breaking" though we hadn't forced a lock or done any damage (Tom's mother was a real estate agent; we let ourselves in with spare keys lifted from the rack in her office). Mainly we'd snooped through closets and poked around in dresser drawers, but we'd also taken some things: beer from the fridge, some Xbox games and a DVD (Jet Li, *Unleashed*) and money, about ninety-two dollars total: crumpled fives and tens from a kitchen jar, piles of pocket change in the laundry rooms.

Whenever I thought about this, I felt nauseated. It was months since I'd been out to Tom's but though I tried to tell myself that Mr. Beeman couldn't possibly know about us going into those houses—how could he know?—my imagination was flying and darting around in panicked zig-zags. I was determined not to tell on Tom (even though I wasn't so sure he hadn't told on me) but that left me in a tight spot. How could I have been so stupid? Breaking and entering was a crime; people went to jail for it. For hours the night before I'd lain awake tortured, flopping back and forth and watching the rain slap in ragged gusts against my windowpane and wondering what to say if confronted. But how could I defend myself, when I didn't even know what they knew?

Goldie heaved a big sigh, put his hand down and walked backward on his heels to where my mother stood.

"Incredible," he said to her, with one jaded eye on the street. "We got the flooding down in SoHo, you heard about that, right, and Carlos was saying they got some streets blocked off over by the UN."

Gloomily, I watched the crowd of workers streaming off the crosstown bus, as joyless as a swarm of hornets. We might have had better luck if we'd walked west a block or two, but my mother and I had enough experience of Goldie to know that he would be offended if we struck out on our own. But just then—so suddenly that we all jumped—a cab with its light on skidded across the lane to us, throwing up a fan of sewer-smelling water.

"Watch it!" said Goldie, leaping aside as the taxi plowed to a stop— and then observing that my mother had no umbrella. "Wait," he said, starting into the lobby, to the collection of lost and forgotten umbrellas that he saved in a brass can by the fireplace and re-distributed on rainy days.

"No," my mother called, fishing in her bag for her tiny candy-striped collapsible, "don't bother, Goldie, I'm all set—"

Goldie sprang back to the curb and shut the taxi door after her. Then he leaned down and knocked on the window.

"You have a blessed day," he said.

iii.

I LIKE TO THINK of myself as a perceptive person (as I suppose we all do) and in setting all this down, it's tempting to pencil a shadow gliding in overhead. But I was blind and deaf to the future; my single, crushing, worry was the meeting at school. When I'd called Tom to tell him I'd been suspended (whispering on the land line; she had taken away my cell phone) he hadn't seemed particularly surprised to hear it. "Look," he'd said, cutting me off, "don't be stupid, Theo, nobody knows a thing, just keep your fucking mouth shut"; and before I could get out another word, he said, "Sorry, I've got to go," and hung up.

In the cab, I tried to crack my window to get some air: no luck. It smelled like someone had been changing dirty diapers back there or maybe even taken an actual shit, and then tried to cover it up with a bunch of coconut air freshener that smelled like suntan lotion. The seats were greasy, and patched with duct tape, and the shocks were nearly gone. Whenever we struck a bump, my teeth rattled, and so did the religious claptrap dangling from the rear view mirror: medallions, a curved sword in miniature dancing on a plastic chain, and a turbaned, bearded guru who gazed into the back seat with piercing eyes, palm raised in benediction.

Along Park Avenue, ranks of red tulips stood at attention as we sped by. Bollywood pop — turned down to a low, almost subliminal whine — spiraled and sparkled hypnotically, just at the threshold of my hearing. The leaves were just coming out on the trees. Delivery boys from D'Agostino's and Gristede's pushed carts laden with groceries; harried executive women in heels plunged down the sidewalk, dragging reluctant kindergartners behind them; a uniformed worker swept debris from the gutter into a dustpan on a stick; lawyers and stockbrokers held their palms out and knit their brows as they looked up at the sky. As we jolted up the avenue (my mother looking miserable, clutching at the armrest to brace herself) I stared out the window at the dyspeptic workaday faces (worried-looking people in raincoats, milling in grim throngs at the cross-walks, people drinking coffee from cardboard cups and talking on cell phones and glancing furtively side to side) and tried hard not to think of all the unpleasant fates that might be about to befall me: some of them involving juvenile court, or jail.

The cab swung into a sharp sudden turn, onto Eighty-Sixth Street. My mother slid into me and grabbed my arm; and I saw she was clammy and pale as a cod.

"Are you carsick?" I said, forgetting my own troubles for the moment. She had a woeful, fixed expression that I recognized all too well: her lips were pressed tight, her forehead was glistening and her eyes were glassy and huge.

She started to say something—and then clapped her hand to her mouth as the cab lurched to a stop at the light, throwing us forward and then back hard against the seat.

"Hang on," I said to her, and then leaned up and knocked on the greasy plexiglass, so that the driver (a turbaned Sikh) started in surprise.

"Look," I called through the grille, "this is fine, we'll get out here, okay?"

The Sikh—reflected in the garlanded mirror—gazed at me steadily. "You want to stop here."

"Yes, please."

"But this is not the address you gave."

"I know. But this is good," I said, glancing back at my mother—mascara-smeared, wilted-looking, scrabbling though her bag for her wallet.

"Is she all right?" said the cabdriver doubtfully.

"Yes, yes, she's fine. We just need to get out, thanks."

With trembling hands, my mother produced a crumple of damp-looking dollars and pushed them through the grille. As the Sikh slid his hand through and palmed them (resignedly, looking away) I climbed out, holding the door open for her.

My mother stumbled a little stepping onto the curb, and I caught her arm. "Are you okay?" I said to her timidly as the cab sped away. We were on upper Fifth Avenue, by the mansions facing the park.

She took a deep breath, then wiped her brow and squeezed my arm. "Phew," she said, fanning her face with her palm. Her forehead was shiny and her eyes were still a little unfocused; she had the slightly ruffled aspect of a sea-bird blown off course. "Sorry, still got the wobblies. Thank God we're out of that cab. I'll be fine, I just need some air."

People streamed around us on the windy corner: schoolgirls in uniform, laughing and running and dodging around us; nannies pushing elaborate prams with babies seated in pairs and threes. A harried, lawyerly father brushed past us, towing his small son by the wrist. "No, Braden," I heard him say to the boy, who trotted to keep up, "you shouldn't think that way, it's more important to have a job you *like* —"

We stepped aside to avoid the soapsuds that a janitor was dumping from a pail on the sidewalk in front of his building.

"Tell me," said my mother — fingertips at her temple — "was it just me, or was that cab *unbelievably* —"

"Nasty? Hawaiian Tropic and baby poo?"

"Honestly —" fanning the air in front of her face — "it would have been okay if not for all the stopping and starting. I was perfectly fine and then it just hit me."

"Why don't you ever just ask if you can sit in the front seat?"

"You sound just like your father."

I looked away, embarrassed — for I'd heard it too, a hint of his annoying know-it-all tone. "Let's walk over to Madison and find some place for you to sit down," I said. I was starving to death and there was a diner over there I liked.

But — with a shudder almost, a visible wave of nausea — she shook her head. "Air." Dashing mascara smudges from under her eyes. "The air feels good."

"Sure," I said, a bit too quickly, anxious to be accommodating. "Whatever."

I was trying hard to be agreeable but my mother — fitful and woozy — had picked up on my tone; she looked at me closely, trying to figure out what I was thinking. (This was another bad habit we'd fallen into, thanks to years of life with my father: trying to read each other's minds.)

"What?" she said. "Is there someplace you want to go?"

"Um, no, not really," I said, taking a step backwards and looking around in my consternation; even though I was hungry, I felt in no position to insist on anything.

"I'll be fine. Just give me a minute."

"Maybe—" blinking and agitated, what did she want, what would please her? — "how about we go sit in the park?"

To my relief, she nodded. "All right then," she said, in what I thought of as her Mary Poppins voice, "but just till I catch my breath," and we started down toward the crosswalk at Seventy-Ninth Street: past topiaries in baroque planters, ponderous doors laced with ironwork. The light had faded to an industrial gray, and the breeze was as heavy as teakettle steam. Across the street by the park, artists were setting up their stalls, unrolling their canvases, pinning up their watercolor reproductions of St. Patrick's Cathedral and the Brooklyn Bridge.

We walked along in silence. My mind was whirring busily on my own troubles (had Tom's parents got a call? Why hadn't I thought to ask him?) as well as what I was going to order for breakfast as soon as I could get her to the diner (Western omelet with home fries, side of bacon; she would have what she always had, rye toast with poached eggs and a cup of black coffee) and I was hardly paying attention where we were going when I realized she had just said something. She wasn't looking at me but out over the park; and her expression made me think of a famous French movie I didn't know the name of, where distracted people walked down windblown streets and talked a lot but didn't actually seem to be talking to each other.

"What did you say?" I asked, after a few confused beats, walking faster to catch up with her. "Try more—?"

She looked startled, as if she'd forgotten I was there. The white coat— flapping in the wind—added to her long-legged ibis quality, as if she were about to unfurl her wings and sail away over the park.

"Try more what?"

"Oh." Her face went blank and then she shook her head and laughed quickly in the sharp, childlike way she had. "No. I said *time warp.*"

Even though it was a strange thing to say I knew what she meant, or thought I did—that shiver of disconnection, the missing seconds on the sidewalk like a hiccup of lost time, or a few frames snipped out of a film.

"No, no, puppy, just the neighborhood." Tousling my hair, making me smile in a lopsided, half-embarrassed way: *puppy* was my baby name, I didn't like it any more nor the hair-tousling either, but sheepish though I felt, I was glad to see her in a better mood. "Always happens up here. Whenever I'm up here it's like I'm eighteen again and right off the bus."

"Here?" I said doubtfully, permitting her to hold my hand, not normally something I would have done. "That's weird." I knew all about my mother's early days in Manhattan, a good long way from Fifth Avenue — on Avenue B, in a studio above a bar, where bums slept in the doorway and bar fights spilled out on the street and a crazy old lady named Mo kept ten or twelve illegal cats in a blocked-off stairwell on the top floor.

She shrugged. "Yeah, but up here it's still the same as the first day I ever saw it. Time tunnel. On the Lower East Side — well, you know what it's like down there, always something new, but for me it's more this Rip van Winkle feeling, always further and further away. Some days I'd wake up and it was like they came in and rearranged the storefronts in the night. Old restaurants out of business, some trendy new bar where the dry cleaner's used to be...."

I maintained a respectful silence. The passage of time had been much on her mind lately, maybe because her birthday was coming up. *I'm too old for this routine,* she'd said a few days before as we'd scrambled together over the apartment, rummaging under the sofa cushions and searching in the pockets of coats and jackets for enough change to pay the delivery boy from the deli.

She dug her hands in her coat pockets. "Up here, it's more stable," she said. Though her voice was light I could see the fog in her eyes; clearly she hadn't slept well, thanks to me. "Upper Park is one of the few places where you can still see what the city looked like in the 1890s. Gramercy Park too, and the Village, some of it. When I first came to New York I thought this neighborhood was Edith Wharton and *Franny and Zooey* and *Breakfast at Tiffany's* all rolled into one."

"*Franny and Zooey* was the West Side."

"Yeah, but I was too dumb to know that. All I can say, is, it was pretty different from the Lower East, homeless guys starting fires in trash cans. Up here on the weekends it was magical — wandering the museum — lolloping around Central Park on my own —"

"Lolloping?" So much of her talk was exotic to my ear, and *lollop* sounded like some horse term from her childhood: a lazy gallop maybe, some equine gait between a canter and a trot.

"Oh, you know, just loping and sloping along like I do. No money, holes in my socks, living off oatmeal. Believe it or not I used to *walk* up here, some weekends. Saving my train fare for the ride home. That was when they still had tokens instead of cards. And even though you're supposed to pay to get in the museum? The 'suggested donation'? Well, I guess I must have had a lot more nerve back then, or maybe they just felt sorry for me because — Oh no," she said, in a changed tone, stopping cold, so that I walked a few steps by her without noticing.

"What?" Turning back. "What is it?"

"Felt something." She held out her palm and looked at the sky. "Did you?"

And just as she said it, the light seemed to fail. The sky darkened rapidly, darker every second; the wind rustled the trees in the park and the new leaves on the trees stood out tender and yellow against black clouds.

"Jeez, wouldn't you know it," said my mother. "It's about to pour." Leaning over the street, looking north: no cabs.

I caught her hand again. "Come on," I said, "we'll have better luck on the other side."

Impatiently we waited for the last few blinks on the Don't Walk sign. Bits of paper were whirling in the air and tumbling down the street. "Hey, there's a cab," I said, looking up Fifth; and just as I said it a businessman ran to the curb with his hand up, and the light popped off.

Across the street, artists ran to cover their paintings with plastic. The coffee vendor was pulling down the shutters on his cart. We hurried across and just as we made it to the other side, a fat drop of rain splashed on my cheek. Sporadic brown circles — widely spaced, big as dimes — began to pop up on the pavement.

"Oh, *drat!*" cried my mother. She fumbled in her bag for her umbrella — which was scarcely big enough for one person, let alone two.

And then it came down, cold sweeps of rain blowing in sideways, broad gusts tumbling in the treetops and flapping in the awnings across the street. My mother was struggling to get the cranky little umbrella up, without much success. People on the street and in the park were holding newspapers and briefcases over their heads, scurrying up the stairs to the portico of the museum, which was the only place on the street to get out of the rain. And there was something festive and happy about the two of us, hurrying up the steps beneath the flimsy candy-striped umbrella, quick

quick quick, for all the world as if we were escaping something terrible instead of running right into it.

iv.

THREE IMPORTANT THINGS HAD happened to my mother after she arrived in New York on the bus from Kansas, friendless and practically penniless. The first was when a booking agent named Davy Jo Pickering had spotted her waiting tables in a coffee shop in the Village: an underfed teenager in Doc Martens and thrift-shop clothes, with a braid down her back so long she could sit on it. When she'd brought him his coffee, he'd offered her seven hundred and then a thousand dollars to fill in for a girl who hadn't shown up for work at the catalogue shoot across the street. He'd pointed out the location van, the equipment being set up in Sheridan Square park; he'd counted out the bills, laid them on the counter. "Give me ten minutes," she'd said; she'd brought out the rest of her breakfast orders, then hung up her apron and walked out.

"I was only a mail-order model," she always took pains to explain to people — by which she meant she'd never done fashion magazines or couture, only circulars for chain stores, inexpensive casuals for junior misses in Missouri and Montana. Sometimes it was fun, she said, but mostly it wasn't: swimsuits in January, shivering from flu; tweeds and woolens in summer heat, sweltering for hours amid fake autumn leaves while a studio fan blew hot air and a guy from makeup darted in between takes to powder the sweat off her face.

But during those years of standing around and pretending to be in college — posing in mock campus settings in stiff pairs and threes, books clutched to her chest — she'd managed to sock away enough money to send herself to college for real: art history at NYU. She'd never seen a great painting in person until she was eighteen and moved to New York, and she was eager to make up for lost time — "pure bliss, perfect heaven," she'd said, up to the neck in art books and poring over the same old slides (Manet, Vuillard) until her vision started to blur. ("It's crazy," she'd said, "but I'd be perfectly happy if I could sit looking at the same half dozen paintings for the rest of my life. I can't think of a better way to go insane.")

College was the second important thing that had happened to her in

New York—for her, probably the most important. And if not for the third thing (meeting and marrying my father—not so lucky as the first two) she would almost certainly have finished her master's and gone on for her PhD. Whenever she had a few hours to herself she always headed straight to the Frick, or MoMA, or the Met—which is why, as we stood under the dripping portico of the museum, gazing out across hazy Fifth Avenue and the raindrops jumping white in the street, I was not surprised when she shook her umbrella out and said: "Maybe we should go in and poke around for a bit till it stops."

"Um—" What I wanted was breakfast. "Sure."

She glanced at her watch. "Might as well. We're not going to get a cab in all this."

She was right. Still, I was starving. *When are we going to eat?* I thought grumpily, following her up the stairs. For all I knew, she was going to be so mad after the meeting she wouldn't take me out to lunch at all, I would have to go home and eat a bowl of cereal or something.

Yet the museum always felt like a holiday; and once we were inside with the glad roar of tourists all around us, I felt strangely insulated from whatever else the day might hold in store. The Great Hall was loud, and rank with the smell of wet overcoats. A drenched crowd of Asian senior citizens surged past, after a crisp stewardessy guide; bedraggled Girl Scouts huddled whispering near the coat check; beside the information desk stood a line of military-school cadets in gray dress uniforms, hats off, clasped hands behind their backs.

For me—a city kid, always confined by apartment walls—the museum was interesting mainly because of its immense size, a palace where the rooms went on forever and grew more and more deserted the farther in you went. Some of the neglected bedchambers and roped-off drawing rooms in the depths of European Decorating felt bound-up in deep enchantment, as if no one had set foot in them for hundreds of years. Ever since I'd started riding the train by myself I'd loved to go there alone and roam around until I got lost, wandering deeper and deeper in the maze of galleries until sometimes I found myself in forgotten halls of armor and porcelain that I'd never seen before (and, occasionally, was unable to find again).

As I hung behind my mother in the admissions line, I put my head back and stared fixedly into the cavernous ceiling dome two stories above:

if I stared hard enough, sometimes I could make myself feel like I was floating around up there like a feather, a trick from early childhood that was fading as I got older.

Meanwhile my mother—red-nosed and breathless from our dash through the rain—was grappling for her wallet. "Maybe when we're done I'll duck in the gift shop," she was saying. "I'm sure the last thing Mathilde wants is an art book but it'll be hard for her to complain much about it without sounding stupid."

"Yikes," I said. "The present's for Mathilde?" Mathilde was the art director of the advertising firm where my mother worked; she was the daughter of a French fabric-importing magnate, younger than my mother and notoriously fussy, apt to throw tantrums if the car service or the catering wasn't up to par.

"Yep." Wordlessly, she offered me a stick of gum, which I accepted, and then threw the pack back in her purse. "I mean, that's Mathilde's whole thing, the well-chosen gift shouldn't cost a lot of money, it's all about the perfect inexpensive paperweight from the flea market. Which would be fantastic, I guess, if any of us had time to go downtown and scour the flea market. Last year when it was Pru's turn—? She panicked and ran into Saks on her lunch hour and ended up spending fifty bucks of her own money on top of what they gave her, for sunglasses, Tom Ford I think, and Mathilde still had to get her crack in about Americans and consumer culture. Pru isn't even American, she's Australian."

"Have you discussed it with Sergio?" I said. Sergio—seldom in the office, though often in the society pages with people like Donatella Versace—was the multimillionaire owner of my mother's firm; "discussing things with Sergio" was akin to asking: "What would Jesus do?"

"Sergio's idea of an art book is Helmut Newton or maybe that coffee-table book that Madonna did a while back."

I started to ask who Helmut Newton was, but then had a better idea. "Why don't you get her a MetroCard?"

My mother rolled her eyes. "Believe me, I ought to." There had recently been a flap at work when Mathilde's car was held up in traffic, leaving her stranded in Williamsburg at a jeweler's studio.

"Like—anonymously. Leave one on her desk, an old one without any money on it. Just to see what she'd do."

"I can tell you what she'd do," said my mother, sliding her membership card through the ticket window. "Fire her assistant and probably half the people in Production as well."

My mother's advertising firm specialized in women's accessories. All day long, under the agitated and slightly vicious eye of Mathilde, she supervised photo shoots where crystal earrings glistened on drifts of fake holiday snow, and crocodile handbags—unattended, in the back seats of deserted limousines—glowed in coronas of celestial light. She was good at what she did; she preferred working behind the camera rather than in front of it; and I knew she got a kick out of seeing her work on subway posters and on billboards in Times Square. But despite the gloss and sparkle of the job (champagne breakfasts, gift bags from Bergdorf's) the hours were long and there was a hollowness at the heart of it that—I knew—made her sad. What she really wanted was to go back to school, though of course we both knew that there was little chance of that now my dad had left.

"Okay," she said, turning from the window and handing me my badge, "help me keep an eye on the time, will you? It's a massive show"—she indicated a poster, PORTRAITURE AND NATURE MORTE: NORTHERN MASTERWORKS OF THE GOLDEN AGE—"we can't see it all on this visit, but there are a few things…"

Her voice drifted away as I trailed behind her up the Great Staircase—torn between the prudent need to stick close and the urge to slink a few paces back and try to pretend I wasn't with her.

"I hate to race through like this," she was saying as I caught up with her at the top of the stairs, "but then again it's the kind of show where you need to come two or three times. There's *The Anatomy Lesson,* and we do have to see that, but what I really want to see is one tiny, rare piece by a painter who was Vermeer's teacher. Greatest Old Master you've never heard of. The Frans Hals paintings are a big deal, too. You know Hals, don't you? *The Jolly Toper?* And the almshouse governors?"

"Right," I said tentatively. Of the paintings she'd mentioned, *The Anatomy Lesson* was the only one I knew. A detail from it was featured on the poster for the exhibition: livid flesh, multiple shades of black, alcoholic-looking surgeons with bloodshot eyes and red noses.

"Art One-oh-one stuff," said my mother. "Here, take a left."

Upstairs it was freezing cold, with my hair still wet from the rain.

"No, no, this way," said my mother, catching my sleeve. The show was complicated to find, and as we wandered the busy galleries (weaving in and out of crowds, turning right, turning left, backtracking through labyrinths of confusing signage and layout) large gloomy reproductions of *The Anatomy Lesson* appeared erratically and at unexpected junctures, baleful signposts, the same old corpse with the flayed arm, red arrows beneath: *operating theater, this way.*

I was not very excited at the prospect of a lot of pictures of Dutch people standing around in dark clothes, and when we pushed through the glass doors — from echoing halls into carpeted hush — I thought at first we'd gone into the wrong hall. The walls glowed with a warm, dull haze of opulence, a generic mellowness of antiquity; but then it all broke apart into clarity and color and pure Northern light, portraits, interiors, still lifes, some tiny, others majestic: ladies with husbands, ladies with lapdogs, lonely beauties in embroidered gowns and splendid, solitary merchants in jewels and furs. Ruined banquet tables littered with peeled apples and walnut shells; draped tapestries and silver; trompe l'oeils with crawling insects and striped flowers. And the deeper we wandered, the stranger and more beautiful the pictures became. Peeled lemons, with the rind slightly hardened at the knife's edge, the greenish shadow of a patch of mold. Light striking the rim of a half-empty wine glass.

"I like this one too," whispered my mother, coming up alongside me at a smallish and particularly haunting still life: a white butterfly against a dark ground, floating over some red fruit. The background — a rich chocolate black — had a complicated warmth suggesting crowded storerooms and history, the passage of time.

"They really knew how to work this edge, the Dutch painters — ripeness sliding into rot. The fruit's perfect but it won't last, it's about to go. And see here especially," she said, reaching over my shoulder to trace in the air with her finger, "this passage — the butterfly." The underwing was so powdery and delicate it looked as if the color would smear if she touched it. "How beautifully he plays it. Stillness with a tremble of movement."

"How long did it take him to paint that?"

My mother, who'd been standing a bit too close, stepped back to regard the painting — oblivious to the gum-chewing security guard whose attention she'd attracted, who was staring fixedly at her back.

"Well, the Dutch invented the microscope," she said. "They were jewelers, grinders of lenses. They want it all as detailed as possible because even the tiniest things mean something. Whenever you see flies or insects in a still life — a wilted petal, a black spot on the apple — the painter is giving you a secret message. He's telling you that living things don't last — it's all temporary. Death in life. That's why they're called natures mortes. Maybe you don't see it at first with all the beauty and bloom, the little speck of rot. But if you look closer — there it is."

I leaned down to read the note, printed in discreet letters on the wall, which informed me that the painter — Adriaen Coorte, dates of birth and death uncertain — had been unknown in his own lifetime and his work unrecognized until the 1950s. "Hey," I said, "Mom, did you see this?"

But she'd already moved on. The rooms were chilly and hushed, with lowered ceilings, and none of the palatial roar and echo of the Great Hall. Though the exhibition was moderately crowded, still it had the sedate, meandering feel of a backwater, a certain vacuum-sealed calm: long sighs and extravagant exhalations like a room full of students taking a test. I trailed behind my mother as she zigzagged from portrait to portrait, much faster than she usually went through an exhibition, from flowers to card tables to fruit, ignoring a great many of the paintings (our fourth silver tankard or dead pheasant) and veering to others without hesitation ("Now, Hals. He's so corny sometimes with all these tipplers and wenches but when he's on, he's *on*. None of this fussiness and precision, he's working wet-on-wet, slash, slash, it's all so *fast*. The faces and hands — rendered really finely, he knows that's what the eye is drawn to but look at the clothes — so loose — almost sketched. Look how open and modern the brushwork is!"). We spent some time in front of a Hals portrait of a boy holding a skull ("Don't be mad, Theo, but who do you think he looks like? Somebody" — tugging the back of my hair — "who could use a haircut?") — and, also, two big Hals portraits of banqueting officers, which she told me were very, very famous and a gigantic influence on Rembrandt. ("Van Gogh loved Hals too. Somewhere, he's writing about Hals and he says: *Frans Hals has no less than twenty-nine shades of black!* Or was it twenty-seven?") I followed after her with a sort of dazed sense of lost time, delighted by her preoccupation, how oblivious she seemed of the minutes flying. It seemed that our half hour must be almost up; but still I wanted to dawdle and distract her, in the infantile hope that time would slip away and we would miss the meeting altogether.

"Now, Rembrandt," my mother said. "Everybody always says this painting is about reason and enlightenment, the dawn of scientific inquiry, all that, but to me it's creepy how polite and formal they are, milling around the slab like a buffet at a cocktail party. Although—" she pointed—"see those two puzzled guys in the back there? They're not looking at the body—they're looking at *us*. You and me. Like they see us standing here in front of them—two people from the future. Startled. 'What are *you* doing here?' Very naturalistic. But then"—she traced the corpse, midair, with her finger—"the body isn't painted in any very natural way at all, if you look at it. Weird glow coming off it, do you see? Alien autopsy, almost. See how it lights up the faces of the men looking down at it? Like it's shining with its own light source? He's painting it with that radioactive quality because he wants to draw our eye to it—make it jump out at us. And here"—she pointed to the flayed hand—"see how he calls attention to it by painting it so big, all out of proportion to the rest of the body? He's even turned it around so the thumb is on the wrong side, do you see? Well, he didn't do that by mistake. The skin is off the hand—we see it immediately, something very wrong—but by reversing the thumb he makes it look even *more* wrong, it registers subliminally even if we can't put our finger on it, something really out of order, not right. Very clever trick." We were standing behind a crowd of Asian tourists, so many heads that I could see the picture scarcely at all, but then again I didn't care that much because I'd seen this girl.

She'd seen me, too. We'd been eyeing each other as we were going through the galleries. I wasn't quite even sure what was so interesting about her, since she was younger than me and a little strange-looking— nothing at all like the girls I usually got crushes on, cool serious beauties who cast disdainful looks around the hallway and went out with big guys. This girl had bright red hair; her movements were swift, her face sharp and mischievous and strange, and her eyes were an odd color, a golden honeybee brown. And though she was too thin, all elbows, and in a way almost plain, yet there was something about her too that made my stomach go watery. She was swinging and knocking a battered-looking flute case around with her—a city kid? On her way to a music lesson? Maybe not, I thought, circling behind her as I followed my mother into the next gallery; her clothes were a little too bland and suburban; she was probably a tourist. But she moved with more assurance than most of the girls I knew; and the sly, composed glance that she slid over me as she brushed past drove me crazy.

I was trailing along behind my mother, only half paying attention to what she was saying, when she stopped in front of a painting so suddenly that I almost ran into her.

"Oh, sorry —!" she said, without looking at me, stepping back to make room. Her face was like someone had turned a light into it.

"*This* is the one I was talking about," she said. "Isn't it amazing?"

I inclined my head in my mother's direction, in an attitude of attentive listening, while my eyes wandered back to the girl. She was accompanied by a funny old white-haired character who I guessed from his sharpness of face was related to her, her grandfather maybe: houndstooth coat, long narrow lace-up shoes as shiny as glass. His eyes were close-set, and his nose beaky and birdlike; he walked with a limp — in fact, his whole body listed to one side, one shoulder higher than the other; and if his slump had been any more pronounced, you might have said he was a hunchback. But all the same there was something elegant about him. And clearly he adored the girl from the amused and companionable way he hobbled at her side, very careful where he put his feet, his head inclined in her direction.

"This is just about the first painting I ever really loved," my mother was saying. "You'll never believe it, but it was in a book I used to take out of the library when I was a kid. I used to sit on the floor by my bed and stare at it for hours, completely fascinated — that little guy! And, I mean, actually it's incredible how much you can learn about a painting by spending a lot of time with a reproduction, even not a very good reproduction. I started off loving the bird, the way you'd love a pet or something, and ended up loving the way he was painted." She laughed. "*The Anatomy Lesson* was in the same book actually, but it scared the pants off me. I used to slam the book shut when I opened it to that page by mistake."

The girl and the old man had come up next to us. Self-consciously, I leaned forward and looked at the painting. It was a small picture, the smallest in the exhibition, and the simplest: a yellow finch, against a plain, pale ground, chained to a perch by its twig of an ankle.

"He was Rembrandt's pupil, Vermeer's teacher," my mother said. "And this one little painting is really the missing link between the two of them — that clear pure daylight, you can see where Vermeer got his quality of light from. Of course, I didn't know or care about any of that when I was a kid, the historical significance. But it's there."

I stepped back, to get a better look. It was a direct and matter-of-fact little creature, with nothing sentimental about it; and something about the neat, compact way it tucked down inside itself—its brightness, its alert watchful expression—made me think of pictures I'd seen of my mother when she was small: a dark-capped finch with steady eyes.

"It was a famous tragedy in Dutch history," my mother was saying. "A huge part of the town was destroyed."

"What?"

"The disaster at Delft. That killed Fabritius. Did you hear the teacher back there telling the children about it?"

I had. There had been a trio of ghastly landscapes, by a painter named Egbert van der Poel, different views of the same smouldering wasteland: burnt ruined houses, a windmill with tattered sails, crows wheeling in smoky skies. An official looking lady had been explaining loudly to a group of middle-school kids that a gunpowder factory exploded at Delft in the 1600s, that the painter had been so haunted and obsessed by the destruction of his city that he painted it over and over.

"Well, Egbert was Fabritius's neighbor, he sort of lost his mind after the powder explosion, at least that's how it looks to me, but Fabritius was killed and his studio was destroyed. Along with almost all his paintings, except this one." She seemed to be waiting for me to say something, but when I didn't, she continued: "He was one of the greatest painters of his day, in one of the greatest ages of painting. Very very famous in his time. It's sad though, because maybe only five or six paintings survived, of all his work. All the rest of it is lost—everything he ever did."

The girl and her grandfather were loitering quietly to the side, listening to my mother talk, which was a bit embarrassing. I glanced away and then—unable to resist—glanced back. They were standing very close, so close I could have reached out and touched them. She was batting and plucking at the old man's sleeve, tugging his arm to whisper something in his ear.

"Anyway, if you ask me," my mother was saying, "this is the most extraordinary picture in the whole show. Fabritius is making clear something that he discovered all on his own, that no painter in the world knew before him—not even Rembrandt."

Very softly — so softly I could barely hear her — I heard the girl whisper: "It had to live its whole life like that?"

I'd been wondering the same thing; the shackled foot, the chain was terrible; her grandfather murmured some reply but my mother (who seemed totally unaware of them, even though they were right next to us) stepped back and said: "Such a mysterious picture, so simple. Really tender — invites you to stand close, you know? All those dead pheasants back there and then this little living creature."

I allowed myself another stealthy glimpse in the girl's direction. She was standing on one leg, with her hip swung out to the side. Then — quite suddenly — she turned and looked me in the eye; and in a heart-skip of confusion, I looked away.

What was her name? Why wasn't she in school? I'd been trying to make out the scribbled name on the flute case but even when I leaned in as far as I dared without being obvious, still I couldn't read the bold spiky marker strokes, more drawn than written, like something spray-painted on a subway car. The last name was short, only four or five letters; the first looked like R, or was it P?

"People die, sure," my mother was saying. "But it's so heartbreaking and unnecessary how we lose *things*. From pure carelessness. Fires, wars. The Parthenon, used as a munitions storehouse. I guess that anything we manage to save from history is a miracle."

The grandfather had drifted away, a few paintings over; but she was loitering a few steps behind, the girl, and kept casting glances back at my mother and me. Beautiful skin: milky white, arms like carved marble. Definitely she looked athletic, though too pale to be a tennis player; maybe she was a ballerina or a gymnast or even a high diver, practicing late in shadowy indoor pools, echoes and refractions, dark tile. Plunging with arched chest and pointed toes to the bottom of the pool, a silent *pow*, shiny black swimsuit, bubbles foaming and streaming off her small, tense frame.

Why did I obsess over people like this? Was it normal to fixate on strangers in this particular vivid, fevered way? I didn't think so. It was impossible to imagine some random passer-by on the street forming quite such an interest in *me*. And yet it was the main reason I'd gone in those houses with Tom: I was fascinated by strangers, wanted to know what food they ate and what dishes they ate it from, what movies they watched and what music they listened to, wanted to look under their beds and in their secret drawers and night tables and inside the pockets of their coats. Often I saw interesting-looking people on the street and thought about them restlessly for days, imagining their lives, making up stories about them on the subway or the crosstown bus. Years had passed, and I still hadn't stopped thinking about the dark-haired children in Catholic school uniforms—brother and sister—I'd seen in Grand Central, literally trying to pull their father out the door of a seedy bar by the sleeves of his suit jacket. Nor had I forgotten the frail, gypsyish girl in a wheelchair out in front of the Carlyle Hotel, talking breathlessly in Italian to the fluffy dog in her lap, while a sharp character in sunglasses (father? bodyguard?) stood behind her chair, apparently conducting some sort of business deal on his phone. For years, I'd turned those strangers over in my mind, wondering who they were and what their lives were like, and I knew I would go home and wonder about this girl and her grandfather the same way. The old man had money; you could tell from how he was dressed. Why was it just the two of them? Where were they from? Maybe they were part of some big old complicated New York family—music people, academics, one of those large, artsy West Side families that you saw up around Columbia or at Lincoln Center matinees. Or, maybe—homely, civilized old creature that he was—maybe he wasn't her grandfather at all. Maybe he was a music teacher, and she was the flute prodigy he had discovered in some small town and brought to play at Carnegie Hall—

"Theo?" my mother said suddenly. "Did you hear me?"

Her voice brought me back to myself. We were in the last room of the show. Beyond lay the exhibition shop—postcards, cash register, glossy stacks of art books—and my mother, unfortunately, had not lost track of the time.

"We should see if it's still raining," she was saying. "We've still got a little while"—(looking at her watch, glancing past me at the Exit sign)—"but I think I'd better go downstairs if I'm going to try to get something for Mathilde."

I noticed the girl observing my mother as she spoke—eyes gliding curiously over my mother's sleek black ponytail, her white satin trenchcoat cinched at the waist—and it thrilled me to see her for a moment as the girl saw her, as a stranger. Did she see how my mother's nose had the tiniest bump at the top, where she'd broken it falling out of a tree as a child? or how the black rings around the light blue irises of my mother's eyes gave her a slightly wild quality, as of some steady-eyed hunting creature alone on a plain?

"You know—" my mother looked over her shoulder—"if you don't mind, I just might run back and take another quick look at *The Anatomy Lesson* before we leave. I didn't get to see it up close and I'm afraid I might not make it back before it comes down." She started away, shoes clacking busily—and then glanced at me as if to say: *are you coming?*

This was so unexpected that for a split second I didn't know what to say. "Um," I said, recovering, "I'll meet you in the shop."

"Okay," she said. "Buy me a couple of cards, will you? I'll be back in a sec."

And off she hurried, before I had a chance to say a word. Heart pounding, unable to believe my luck, I watched her walking rapidly away from me in the white satin trenchcoat. This was it, my chance to talk to the girl; *but what can I say to her,* I thought furiously, *what can I say?* I dug my hands in my pockets, took a breath or two to compose myself, and— excitement fizzing bright in my stomach—turned to face her.

But, to my consternation, she was gone. That is to say, she wasn't gone; there was her red head, moving reluctantly (or so it seemed) across the room. Her grandpa had slipped his arm through hers and—whispering to her, with great enthusiasm—was towing her away to look at some picture on the opposite wall.

I could have killed him. Nervously, I glanced at the empty doorway. Then I dug my hands deeper in my pockets and—face burning— walked conspicuously across the length of the gallery. The clock was ticking; my mother would be back any second; and though I knew I didn't have the nerve to barge up and actually say something, I could at the very least get a last good look at her. Not long before, I had stayed up late with my mother and watched *Citizen Kane,* and I was very taken with the idea that a person might notice in passing some bewitching stranger and remember her for the rest of his life. Someday I too might be like the old man in the movie, leaning back in my chair with a far-off look in my eyes, and saying: "You know, that was sixty years ago, and I never saw that girl with the red hair again, but you know what? Not a month has gone by in all that time when I haven't thought of her."

I was more than halfway across the gallery when something strange happened. A museum guard ran across the open doorway of the exhibition shop beyond. He was carrying something in his arms.

The girl saw it, too. Her golden-brown eyes met mine: a startled, quizzical look.

Suddenly another guard flew out of the museum shop. His arms were up and he was screaming.

Heads went up. Someone behind me said, in an odd flat voice: oh! The next instant, a tremendous, earsplitting blast shook the room.

The old man—with a blank look on his face—stumbled sideways. His outstretched arm—knotty fingers spread—is the last thing I remember seeing. At almost exactly the same moment there was a black flash, with debris sweeping and twisting around me, and a roar of hot wind slammed into me and threw me across the room. And that was the last thing I knew for a while.

V.

I DON'T KNOW HOW long I was out. When I came to, it seemed as if I was flat on my stomach in a sandbox, on some dark playground—someplace I didn't know, a deserted neighborhood. A gang of tough, runty boys was bunched around me, kicking me in the ribs and the back of the head. My neck was twisted to the side and the wind was knocked out of me, but that wasn't the worst of it; I had sand in my mouth, I was breathing sand.

The boys muttered, audibly. *Get up, asshole.*

Look at him, look at him.

He don't know dick.

I rolled over and threw my arms over my head and then—with an airy, surreal jolt—saw that nobody was there.

For a moment I lay too stunned to move. Alarm bells clanged in a muffled distance. As strange as it seemed, I was under the impression that I was lying in the walled-in courtyard of some godforsaken housing project.

Somebody had beaten me up pretty good: I ached all over, my ribs were sore and my head felt like someone had hit me with a lead pipe. I was working my jaw back and forth and reaching for my pockets to see if I had train fare home when it came over me abruptly that I had no clue where I was. Stiffly I lay there, in the growing consciousness that something was badly out of joint. The light was all wrong, and so was the air: acrid and sharp, a chemical fog that burned my throat. The gum in my mouth was gritty, and when—head pounding—I rolled over to spit it out, I found myself blinking through layers of smoke at something so foreign I stared for some moments.

I was in a ragged white cave. Swags and tatters dangled from the ceiling. The ground was tumbled and bucked-up with heaps of a gray substance like moon rock, and blown about with broken glass and gravel and a hurricane of random trash, bricks and slag and papery stuff frosted with a thin ash like first frost. High overhead, a pair of lamps beamed through the dust like off-kilter car lights in fog, cock-eyed, one angled upward and the other rolled to the side and casting skewed shadows.

My ears rang, and so did my body, an intensely disturbing sensation: bones, brain, heart all thrumming like a struck bell. Faintly, from somewhere far away, the mechanical shriek of alarms rang steady and impersonal. I could hardly tell if the noise was coming from inside me or outside me. There was a strong sense of being alone, in wintry deadness. Nothing made sense in any direction.

In a cascade of grit, my hand on some not-quite-vertical surface, I stood, wincing at the pain in my head. The tilt of the space where I was had a deep, innate wrongness. On one side, smoke and dust hung in a still, blanketed layer. On the other, a mass of shredded materials slanted down in a tangle where the roof, or the ceiling, should have been.

My jaw hurt; my face and knees were cut; my mouth was like sandpaper. Blinking around at the chaos I saw a tennis shoe; drifts of crumbly matter, stained dark; a twisted aluminum walking stick. I was swaying there, choked and dizzy, not knowing where to turn or what to do, when all of a sudden I thought I heard a phone going off.

For a moment I wasn't sure; I listened, hard; and then it spieled off again: faint and draggy, a little weird. Clumsily I grappled around in the wreckage—upending dusty kiddie purses and day packs, snatching my hands back at hot things and shards of broken glass, more and more troubled by the way the rubble gave under my feet in spots, and by the soft, inert lumps at the edge of my vision.

Even after I became convinced I'd never heard a phone, that the ringing in my ears had played a trick on me, still I kept looking, locked into the mechanical gestures of searching with an unthinking, robot intensity. Among pens, handbags, wallets, broken eyeglasses, hotel key cards, compacts and perfume spray and prescription medications (Roitman, Andrea, alprazolam .25 mg) I unearthed a keychain flashlight and a non working phone (half charged, no bars), which I threw in a collapsible nylon shopping bag I'd found in some lady's purse.

I was gasping, half-choked with plaster dust, and my head hurt so badly I could hardly see. I wanted to sit down, except there was no place to sit.

Then I saw a bottle of water. My eyes reverted, fast, and strayed over the havoc until I saw it again, about fifteen feet away, half buried in a pile of trash: just a hint of a label, familiar shade of cold-case blue.

With a benumbed heaviness like moving through snow, I began to slog and weave through the debris, rubbish breaking under my feet in sharp, glacial-sounding cracks. But I had not made it very far when, out of the corner of my eye, I saw movement on the ground, conspicuous in the stillness, a stirring of white-on-white.

I stopped. Then I waded a few steps closer. It was a man, flat on his back and whitened head to toe with dust. He was so well camouflaged in the ash-powdered wreckage that it was a moment before his form came clear: chalk on chalk, struggling to sit up like a statue knocked off his pedestal. As I drew closer, I saw that he was old and very frail, with a misshapen hunchback quality; his hair — what he had — was blown straight up from his head; the side of his face was stippled with an ugly spray of burns, and his head, above one ear, was a sticky black horror.

I had made it over to where he was when — unexpectedly fast — he shot out his dust-whitened arm and grabbed my hand. In panic I started back, but he only clutched at me tighter, coughing and coughing with a sick wetness.

Where—? he seemed to be saying. Where—? He was trying to look up at me, but his head dangled heavily on his neck and his chin lolled on his chest so that he was forced to peer from under his brow at me like a vulture. But his eyes, in the ruined face, were intelligent and despairing.

—Oh, God, I said, bending to help him, wait, wait—and then I stopped, not knowing what to do. His lower half lay twisted on the ground like a pile of dirty clothes.

He braced himself with his arms, gamely it seemed, lips moving and still struggling to raise himself. He reeked of burned hair, burned wool. But the lower half of his body seemed disconnected from the upper half, and he coughed and fell back in a heap.

I looked around, trying to get my bearings, deranged from the crack on the head, with no sense of time or even if it was day or night. The grandeur and desolation of the space baffled me — the high, rare, loft of it, layered with gradations of smoke, and billowing with a tangled, tent-like effect where the ceiling (or the sky) ought to be. But though I had no idea where I was, or why, still there was a half-remembered quality about the wreckage, a cinematic charge in the glare of the emergency lamps. On the Internet I'd seen footage of a hotel blown up in the desert, where the honeycombed rooms at the moment of collapse were frozen in just such a blast of light.

Then I remembered the water. I stepped backwards, looking all around, until with a leap of my heart I spotted the dusty flash of blue.

— Look, I said, edging away. I'm just —

The old man was watching me with a gaze at once hopeful and hopeless, like a starved dog too weak to walk.

— No — wait. I'm coming back.

Like a drunk, I staggered through the rubbish — weaving and plowing, stepping high-kneed over objects, muddling through bricks and concrete and shoes and handbags and a whole lot of charred bits I didn't want to see too closely.

The bottle was three quarters full and hot to the touch. But at the first swallow my throat took charge and I'd gulped more than half of it — plastic-tasting, dishwater warm — before I realized what I was doing and forced myself to cap it and put it in the bag to take back to him.

Kneeling beside him. Rocks digging into my knees. He was shivering, breaths rasping and uneven; his gaze didn't meet mine but strayed above it, fixed fretfully on something I didn't see.

I was fumbling for the water when he reached his hand to my face. Carefully, with his bony old flat-pad fingers, he brushed the hair from my eyes and plucked a thorn of glass from my eyebrow and then patted me on the head.

"There, there." His voice was very faint, very scratchy, very cordial, with a ghastly pulmonary whistle. We looked at each other, for a long strange moment that I've never forgotten, actually, like two animals meeting at twilight, during which some clear, personable spark seemed to fly up through his eyes and I saw the creature he really was—and he, I believe, saw me. For an instant we were wired together and humming, like two engines on the same circuit.

Then he lolled back again, so limply I thought he was dead. — "Here," I said, awkwardly, slipping my hand under his shoulder. "That's good." I held up his head as best I could, and helped him drink from the bottle. He could only take a little and most of it ran down his chin.

Again falling back. Effort too much.

"Pippa," he said thickly.

I looked down at his burnt, reddened face, stirred by something familiar in his eyes, which were rusty and clear. I had seen him before. And I had seen the girl too, the briefest snapshot, an autumn-leaf lucidity: rusty eyebrows, honey-brown eyes. Her face was reflected in his. Where was she?

He was trying to say something. Cracked lips working. He wanted to know where Pippa was.

Wheezing and gasping for breath. "Here," I said, agitated, "try to lie still."

"She should take the train, it's so much faster. Unless they bring her in a car."

"Don't worry," I said, leaning closer. I wasn't worried. Someone would be in to get us shortly, I was sure of it. "I'll wait till they come."

"You're so kind." His hand (cold, dry as powder) tightening on mine. "I haven't seen you since you were a little boy again. You were all grown up the last time we spoke."

"But I'm Theo," I said, after a slightly confused pause.

"Of course you are." His gaze, like his handclasp, was steady and kind. "And you've made the very best choice, I'm sure of it. The Mozart is so much nicer than the Gluck, don't you think?"

I didn't know what to say.

"It'll be easier the two of you. They're so hard on you children in the auditions—" Coughing. Lips slick with blood, thick and red. "No second chances."

"Listen—" It felt wrong, letting him think I was someone else.

"Oh, but you play it so beautifully, my dear, the pair of you. The

G major. It keeps running through my mind. Lightly, lightly, touch and go—"

Humming a few shapeless notes. A song. It was a song.

"...and I must have told you, how I went for piano lessons, at the old Armenian lady's? There was a green lizard that lived in the palm tree, green like a candy drop, I loved to watch for him...flashing on the windowsill...fairy lights in the garden...*du pays saint*...twenty minutes to walk it but it seemed like miles..."

He faded for a minute; I could feel his intelligence drifting away from me, spinning out of sight like a leaf on a brook. Then it washed back and there he was again.

"And you! How old are you now?"

"Thirteen."

"At the Lycée Français?"

"No, my school's on the West Side."

"And just as well, I should think. All these French classes! Too many vocabulary words for a child. *Nom et pronom,* species and phylum. It's only a form of insect collecting."

"Sorry?"

"They always spoke French at Groppi's. Remember Groppi's? With the striped umbrella and the pistachio ices?"

Striped umbrella. It was hard to think through my headache. My glance wandered to the long gash in his scalp, clotted and dark, like an axe wound. More and more, I was becoming aware of dreadful bodylike shapes slumped in the debris, dark hulks not clearly seen, pressing in silently all around us, dark everywhere and the ragdoll bodies and yet it was a darkness you could drift away upon, something sleepy about it, frothy wake churned and vanished on a cold black ocean

Suddenly something was very wrong. He was awake, shaking me. Hands flapping. He wanted something. He tried to press himself up on a whistling in-breath.

"What is it?" I said, shaking myself alert. He was gasping, agitated, tugging at my arm. Fearfully I sat up and looked around, expecting to see some fresh danger rolling in: loose wires, a fire, the ceiling about to collapse.

Grabbing my hand. Squeezing it tight. "Not there," he managed to say.

"What?"

"Don't leave it. No." He was looking past me, trying to point at something. "Take it away from there."

Please, lie down —

"No! They mustn't see it." He was frantic, gripping my arm now, trying to pull himself up. "They've stolen the rugs, they'll take it to the customs shed —"

He was, I saw, pointing over at a dusty rectangle of board, virtually invisible in the broken beams and rubbish, smaller than my laptop computer at home.

"That?" I said, looking closer. It was blobbed with drips of wax, and pasted with an irregular patchwork of crumbling labels. "That's what you want?"

"I beg of you." Eyes squeezed tight. He was upset, coughing so hard he could barely speak.

I reached out and picked the board up by the edges. It felt surprisingly heavy, for something so small. A long splinter of broken frame clung to one corner.

Drawing my sleeve across the dusty surface. Tiny yellow bird, faint beneath a veil of white dust. *The Anatomy Lesson was in the same book actually but it scared the pants off me.*

Right, I answered drowsily. I turned, painting in hand, to show it to her, and then realized she wasn't there.

Or — she was there and she wasn't. Part of her was there, but it was invisible. The invisible part was the important part. This was something I had never understood before. But when I tried to say this out loud the words came out in a muddle and I realized with a cold slap that I was wrong. Both parts had to be together. You couldn't have one part without the other.

I rubbed my arm across my forehead and tried to blink the grit from my eyes and, with a massive effort, like lifting a weight much too heavy for me, tried to shift my mind where I knew it needed to be. Where was my mother? For a moment there had been three of us and one of these — I was pretty sure — had been her. But now there were only two.

Behind me, the old man had begun to cough and shudder again with an uncontrollable urgency, trying to speak. Reaching back, I tried to hand the picture over to him. "Here," I said, and then, to my mother — in the spot where she had seemed to be — "I'll be back in a minute."

But the painting wasn't what he wanted. Fretfully he pushed it back at me, babbling something. The right side of his head was such a sticky drench of blood I could hardly see his ear.

"What?" I said, mind still on my mother — where was she? "Sorry?"

"Take it."

"Look, I'll be back. I have to —" I couldn't get it out, not quite, but my mother wanted me to go home, immediately, I was supposed to meet her there, that was the one thing she had made very clear

"Take it with you!" Pressing it on me. "Go!" He was trying to sit up. His eyes were bright and wild; his agitation frightened me. "They took all the light bulbs, they've smashed up half the houses in the street —"

A drip of blood ran down his chin.

"Please," I said, hands flustering, afraid to touch him. "Please lie down —"

He shook his head, and tried to say something, but the effort broke him down hacking with a wet, miserable sound. When he wiped his mouth, I saw a bright stripe of blood on the back of his hand.

"Somebody's coming." Not sure I believed it, not knowing what else to say.

He looked straight into my face, searching for some flicker of understanding, and when he didn't find it he clawed to sit up again.

"Fire," he said, in a gargling voice. "The villa in Ma'adi. *On a tout perdu.*"

He broke off coughing again. Red-tinged froth bubbling at his nostrils. In the midst of all that unreality, cairns and broken monoliths, I had a dreamlike sense of having failed him, as if I'd botched some vital fairy-tale task through clumsiness and ignorance. Though there wasn't any visible fire anywhere in that tumble of stone, I crawled over and put the painting in the nylon shopping bag, just to get it out of his sight, it was upsetting him so.

"Don't worry," I said. "I'll —"

He had calmed down. He put a hand on my wrist, eyes steady and bright, and a chill wind of unreason blew over me. I had done what I was supposed to do. Everything was going to be all right.

As I was basking in the comfort of this notion, he squeezed my hand reassuringly, as if I'd spoken the thought aloud. We'll get away from here, he said.

"I know."

"Wrap it in newspapers and pack it at the very bottom of the trunk, my dear. With the other curiosities."

Relieved that he'd calmed down, exhausted with my headache, all memory of my mother faded to a mothlike flicker, I settled down beside him and closed my eyes, feeling oddly comfortable and safe. Absent, dreamy. He was rambling a bit, under his breath: foreign names, sums and numbers, a few French words but mostly English. A man was coming to look at the furniture. Abdou was in trouble for throwing stones. And yet it all made sense somehow and I saw the palmy garden and the piano and the green lizard on the tree trunk as if they were pages in a photograph album.

Will you be all right getting home by yourself, my dear? I remember him asking at one point.

"Of course." I was lying on the floor beside him, my head level with his rickety old breastbone, so that I could hear every catch and wheeze in his breath. "I take the train by myself every day."

"And where did you say you were living now?" His hand on my head, very gently, the way you'd rest your hand on the head of a dog you liked.

"East Fifty-Seventh Street."

"Oh, yes! Near Le Veau d'Or?"

"Well, a few blocks." Le Veau d'Or was a restaurant where my mother had liked to go, back when we had money. I had eaten my first escargot there, and tasted my first sip of Marc de Bourgogne from her glass.

"Towards Park, you say?"

"No, closer to the river."

"Close enough, my dear. Meringues and caviare. How I loved this city the first time I saw it! Still, it's not the same, is it? I miss it all terribly, don't you? The balcony, and the..."

"Garden." I turned to look at him. Perfumes and melodies. In my swamp of confusion, it had come to seem that he was a close friend or family member I'd forgotten about, some long-lost relative of my mother's....

"Oh, your mother! The darling! I'll never forget the first time she came to play. She was the prettiest little girl I ever saw."

How had he known I was thinking about her? I started to ask him but he was asleep. His eyes were closed but his breath was fast and hoarse like he was running from something.

I was fading out myself—ears ringing, inane buzz and a metallic taste in my mouth like at the dentist's—and I might have drifted back into unconsciousness and stayed there had he not at some point shaken me, hard, so I awoke with a buck of panic. He was mumbling and tugging at his index finger. He'd taken his ring off, a heavy gold ring with a carved stone; he was trying to give it to me.

"Here, I don't want that," I said, shying away. "What are you doing that for?"

But he pressed it into my palm. His breath was bubbled and ugly. "Hobart and Blackwell," he said, in a voice like he was drowning from the inside out. "Ring the green bell."

"Green bell," I repeated, uncertainly.

He lolled his head back and forth, punch-drunk, lips quivering. His eyes were unfocused. When they slid over me without seeing me they gave me a shiver.

"Tell Hobie to get out of the store," he said thickly.

In disbelief, I watched the blood trickling bright from the corner of his mouth. He'd loosened his tie by yanking at it; "here," I said, reaching over to help, but he batted my hands away.

"He's got to close the register and get out!" he rasped. "His father's sending some guys to beat him up—"

His eyes rolled up; his eyelids fluttered. Then he sank down into himself, flat and collapsed-looking like all the air was out of him, thirty seconds, forty, like a heap of old clothes but then—so harshly I flinched—his chest swelled on a bellows-like rasp, and he coughed a percussive gout of blood that spewed all over me. As best he could, he hitched himself up on his elbows—and for thirty seconds or so he panted like a dog, chest pumping frantically, up and down, up and down, his eyes fixed on something I couldn't see and all the time gripping my hand like maybe if he held on tight enough he'd be okay.

"Are you all right?" I said—frantic, close to tears. "Can you hear me?"

As he grappled and thrashed—a fish out of water—I held his head up, or tried to, not knowing how, afraid of hurting him, as all the time he clutched my hand like he was dangling off a building and about to fall. Each breath was an isolated, gargling heave, a heavy stone lifted with terrible effort and dropped again and again to the ground. At one point he looked at me directly, blood welling in his mouth, and seemed to say something, but the words were only a burble down his chin.

Then—to my intense relief—he grew calmer, quieter, his grasp on my hand loosening, melting, a sense of sinking and spinning almost like he was floating on his back away from me, on water.—Better? I asked, and then—

Carefully, I dripped a bit of water on his mouth—his lips worked, I saw them moving; and then, on my knees, like a servant boy in a story, I wiped some of the blood off his face with the paisley square from his pocket. As he drifted—cruelly, by degrees and latitudes—into stillness, I rocked back on my heels and looked hard into his wrecked face.

Hello? I said.

One papery eyelid, half shut, twitched, a blue-veined tic.

"If you can hear me, squeeze my hand."

But his hand in mine was limp. I sat there and looked at him, not knowing what to do. It was time to go, well past time—my mother had made that perfectly clear—and yet I could see no path out of the space where I was and in fact in some ways it was hard to imagine being any-where else in the world—that there was another world, outside that one. It was like I'd never had another life at all.

"Can you hear me?" I asked him, one last time, bending close and put-ting my ear to his bloodied mouth. But there was nothing.

vi.

NOT WANTING TO DISTURB him, in case he was only resting, I was as quiet as I could be, standing up. I hurt all over. For some moments I stood looking down at him, wiping my hands on my school jacket—his blood was all over me, my hands were slick with it—and then I looked at the moonscape of rubble trying to orient myself and figure the best way to go.

When—with difficulty—I made my way into the center of the space, or what seemed like the center of the space, I saw that one door was obscured by rags of hanging debris, and I turned and began to work in the other direction. There, the lintel had fallen, dumping a pile of brick almost as tall as I was and leaving a smoky space at the top big enough to drive a car through. Laboriously I began to climb and scramble for it—over and around the chunks of concrete—but I had not got very far when I realized that I was going to have to go the other way. Faint traces of fire licked down the far walls of what had been the exhibition shop, spitting and sparkling in the dim, some of it well below the level where the floor should have been.

I didn't like the looks of the other door (foam tiles stained red; the toe of a man's shoe protruding from a pile of gravel) but at least most of the material blocking the door wasn't very solid. Blundering back through, ducking some wires that sparked from the ceiling, I hoisted the bag over my shoulder and took a deep breath and plunged into the wreckage headlong.

Immediately I was choked by dust and a sharp chemical smell. Coughing, praying there were no more live wires hanging loose, I patted and groped in the dark as all sorts of loose debris began to patter and shower down in my eyes: gravel, crumbs of plaster, shreds and chunks of god-knows-what.

Some of the building material was light, and some of it was not. The further I worked in, the darker it got, and the hotter. Every so often my way dwindled or closed up unexpectedly and in my ears a roaring crowd noise, I wasn't sure where it came from. I had to squeeze around things; sometimes I walked, sometimes I crawled, bodies in the wreckage more sensed than seen, a disturbing soft pressure that gave under my weight but worse than this, the smell: burnt cloth, burnt hair and flesh and the tang of fresh blood, copper and tin and salt.

My hands were cut and so were my knees. I ducked under things and went around things, feeling my way as I went, edging with my hip along the side of some sort of long lathe, or beam, until I found myself blocked in by a solid mass that felt like a wall. With difficulty—the spot was narrow—I worked around so I could reach into the bag for a light.

I wanted the keychain light—at the bottom, under the picture—but my fingers closed on the phone. I switched it on—and almost immediately dropped it, because in the glow I'd caught sight of a man's hand protruding between two chunks of concrete. Even in my terror, I remember feeling grateful that it was only a hand, although the fingers had a meaty, dark, swollen look I've never been able to forget; every now and then I still start back in fear when some beggar on the street thrusts out to me such a hand, bloated and grimed with black around the nails.

There was still the flashlight—but I wanted the phone. It cast a weak glimmer up into the cavity where I was, but just as I recovered myself enough to stoop for it, the screen went dark. An acid-green afterburn floated before me in the blackness. I got down on my knees and crawled around in the dark, grabbling with both hands in rocks and glass, determined to find it.

I thought I knew where it was, or about where it was, and I kept looking for it probably longer than I should have; and it was when I'd given up hope and tried to get up again that I realized I'd crawled into a low spot where it was impossible to stand, with some solid surface about three inches above my head. Turning around didn't work; going backwards didn't work; so I decided to crawl forward, hoping that things would open up, and soon found myself inching along painfully with a smashed, desperate feeling and my head turned sharply to one side.

When I was about four, I'd gotten partially stuck inside a Murphy bed in our old apartment on Seventh Avenue, which sounds like a humorous predicament but wasn't really; I think I would have suffocated if Alameda, our housekeeper back then, hadn't heard my muffled cries and pulled me out. Trying to maneuver in that airless space was somewhat the same, only worse: with glass, hot metal, the stink of burned clothes, and an occasional soft something pressing in on me that I didn't want to think about. Debris was pattering down on me heavily from above; my throat was filling with dust and I was coughing hard and starting to panic when I realized I could see, just barely, the rough texture of the broken bricks that surrounded me. Light—the faintest gleam imaginable—crept in subtly from the left, about six inches from floor level.

I ducked lower, and found myself looking over into the dim terrazzo floor of the gallery beyond. A disorderly pile of what looked like rescue equipment (ropes, axes, crowbars, an oxygen tank that said FDNY) lay harum-scarum on the floor.

"Hello?" I called—not waiting for an answer, dropping to wriggle through the hole as fast as I could.

The space was narrow; if I'd been a few years older or a few pounds heavier I might not have got through. Partway, my bag caught on something, and for a moment I thought I might have to slip free of it, painting or no painting, like a lizard shedding its tail, but when I gave it one last pull it finally broke free with a shower of crumbled plaster. Above me was a beam of some sort, which looked like it was holding up a lot of heavy building material, and as I twisted and squirmed beneath it, I was light-headed with fear that it would slip and cut me in two until I saw that somebody had stabilized it with a jack.

Once clear, I climbed to my feet, watery and stunned with relief. "Hello?" I called again, wondering why there was so much equipment around and not a fireman in sight. The gallery was dim but mostly undamaged, with gauzy layers of smoke that thickened the higher they rose, but you could tell that a tremendous force of some sort had blown through the room just from the lights and the security cameras, which were knocked askew and facing the ceiling. I was so happy to be out in open space again that it was a moment or so before I realized the strange-ness of being the only person standing up in a room full of people. Every-body else was lying down except me.

There were at least a dozen people on the floor — not all of them intact. They had the appearance of having been dropped from a great height. Three or four of the bodies were partially covered with firemen's coats, feet sticking out. Others sprawled glaringly in the open, amidst explosive stains. The splashes and bursts carried a violence, like big blood sneezes, an hysterical sense of movement in the stillness. I remember par-ticularly a middle aged lady in a bloodspattered blouse that had a pattern of Fabergé eggs on it, like a blouse she might have bought in the museum gift shop, actually. Her eyes — lined with black makeup — stared blankly at the ceiling; and her tan was obviously sprayed on since her skin had a healthy apricot glow even though the top of her head was missing.

Dim oils, dulled gilt. Taking tiny steps, I walked out into the middle of the room, swaying, slightly off balance. I could hear my own breath rasping in and out and there was a strange shallowness in the sound, a nightmare lightness. I didn't want to look and yet I had to. A small Asian man, pathetic in his tan windbreaker, curled in a bellying pool of blood. A guard (his uniform the most recognizable thing about him, his face was burned so badly) with an arm twisted behind his back and a vicious spray where his leg should have been.

But the main thing, the important thing: none of the lying-down peo-ple was her. I made myself look at them all, each separately, one by one — even when I couldn't force myself to look at their faces, I knew my mother's feet, her clothes, her two-tone black and white shoes — and long after I was sure of it I made myself stand in their midst, folded deep inside myself like a sick pigeon with its eyes closed.

In the gallery beyond: more dead. Three dead. Fat Argyll-vest man; cankered old lady; a milky duckling of a little girl, red abrasion at her temple but otherwise hardly a mark on her. But then, there were no more. I walked through several galleries littered with equipment but despite the bloodstains on the floor, there were no dead at all. And when I walked into the far-seeming gallery where she'd been, where she'd gone, the gallery with *The Anatomy Lesson* — eyes closed tight, wishing hard — there were only the same stretchers and equipment and there, as I walked through, in the oddly screaming silence, the only two observers were the same two puzzled Dutchmen who had stared at my mother and me from the wall: what are *you* doing here?

Then something snapped. I don't even remember how it happened; I was just in a different place and running, running through rooms that were empty except for a haze of smoke that made the grandeur seem insubstantial and unreal. Earlier, the galleries had seemed fairly straightforward, a meandering but logical sequence where all tributaries flowed into the gift shop. But coming back through them fast, and in the opposite direction, I realized that the path wasn't straight at all; and over and over I turned into blank walls and veered into dead-end rooms. Doors and entrances weren't where I expected them to be; freestanding plinths loomed out of nowhere. Swinging around a corner a little too sharply I almost ran headlong into a gang of Frans Hals guardsmen: big, rough, ruddy-cheeked guys, bleary from too much beer, like New York City cops at a costume party. Coldly they stared me down, with hard, humorous eyes, as I recovered, backed off, and began to run again.

Even on a good day, I sometimes got turned around in the museum (wandering aimlessly in galleries of Oceanic Art, totems and dugout canoes) and sometimes I had to go up and ask a guard to point the way out. The painting galleries were especially confusing since they were rearranged so often; and as I ran around in the empty halls, in the ghostly half-light, I was growing more and more frightened. I thought I knew my way to the main staircase, but soon after I was out of the Special Exhibitions galleries things started looking unfamiliar and after a minute or two running light-headed through turns I was no longer quite sure of, I realized I was thoroughly lost. Somehow I'd gone right through the Italian

masterworks (crucified Christs and astonished saints, serpents and embattled angels) ending up in England, eighteenth century, a part of the museum I had seldom been in before and did not know at all. Long elegant
lines of sight stretched out before me, mazelike halls which had the feel of
a haunted mansion: periwigged lords, cool Gainsborough beauties, gazing
superciliously down at my distress. The baronial perspectives were infuriating, since they didn't seem to lead to the staircase or any of the main corridors but only to other stately baronial galleries exactly like them; and I
was close to tears when suddenly I saw an inconspicuous door in the side
of the gallery wall.

You had to look twice to see it, this door; it was painted the same color
as the gallery walls, the kind of door which, in normal circumstances,
looked like it would be kept locked. It had only caught my attention
because it wasn't completely closed—the left side wasn't flush with the
wall, whether because it hadn't caught properly or because the lock wasn't
working with the electricity out, I didn't know. Still, it was not easy to get
open—it was heavy, steel, and I had to pull with all my strength.
Suddenly—with a pneumatic gasp—it gave so capriciously I stumbled.

Squeezing through, I found myself in a dark office hallway under a
much lower ceiling. The emergency lights were much weaker than in the
main gallery, and it took my eyes a moment to adjust.

The hallway seemed to stretch for miles. Fearfully I crept along, peering into the offices where the doors happened to stand ajar. *Cameron
Geisler, Registrar. Miyako Fujita, Assistant Registrar.* Drawers were open
and chairs were pushed away from desks. In the doorway of one office a
woman's high-heeled shoe lay on its side.

The air of abandonment was unspeakably eerie. It seemed that far in
the distance I could hear police sirens, maybe even walkie-talkies and
dogs, but my ears were ringing so hard from the explosion that I thought I
might well be hearing things. It was starting to unnerve me more and
more that I had seen no firemen, no cops, no security guards—in fact not
a single living soul.

It wasn't dark enough for the keychain flashlight in the Staff Only
area, but neither was there nearly enough light for me to see well. I was in
some sort of records or storage area. The offices were lined with filing
cabinets floor to ceiling, metal shelves with plastic mailroom crates and
cardboard boxes. The narrow corridor made me feel edgy, closed in, and

my footsteps echoed so crazily that once or twice I stopped and turned
around to see if somebody was coming down the hall after me.

"Hello?" I said, tentatively, glancing into some of the rooms as I passed.
Some of the offices were modern and spare; others were crowded and
dirty-looking, with untidy stacks of paper and books.

*Florens Klauner, Department of Musical Instruments. Maurice Orabi-
Roussel, Islamic Art. Vittoria Gabetti, Textiles.* I passed a cavernous dark
room with a long workshop table where mismatched scraps of cloth were
laid out like pieces of a jigsaw puzzle. In the back of the room was a jumble of rolling garment racks with lots of plastic garment bags hanging off
them, like racks by the service elevators at Bendel's or Bergdorf's.

At the T-junction I looked this way and that, not knowing where to
turn. I smelled floor wax, turpentine and chemicals, a tang of smoke.
Offices and workshops stretched out to infinity in all directions: a contained geometrical network, fixed and featureless.

To my left, light flickered from a ceiling fixture. It hummed and
caught, in a staticky fit, and in the trembling glow, I saw a drinking fountain down the hall.

I ran for it—so fast my feet almost slid out from underneath me—
and gulped with my mouth pressed against the spigot, so much cold water,
so fast, that a spike of pain slid into my temple. Hiccupping, I rinsed the
blood from my hands and splashed water in my sore eyes. Tiny splinters of
glass—almost invisible—tinkled to the steel tray of the fountain like
needles of ice.

I leaned against the wall. The overhead fluorescents—vibrating, spitting on and off—made me feel queasy. With effort, I pulled myself up
again; on I walked, wobbling a bit in the unstable flicker. Things were
looking decidedly more industrial in this direction: wooden pallets, a flat-
bed pushcart, a sense of crated objects being moved and stored. I passed
another junction, where a slick shadowy passageway receded into darkness, and I was just about to walk past it and keep going when I saw a red
glow at the end that said EXIT.

I tripped; I fell over my feet; I got up again, still hiccupping, and ran
down the endless hall. Down at the end of the corridor was a door with a
metal bar, like the security doors at my school.

It pushed open with a bark. Down a dark stairwell I ran, twelve
steps, a turn at the landing, then twelve steps to the bottom, my fingertips

skimming on the metal rail, shoes clattering and echoing so crazily that it sounded like half a dozen people were running with me. At the foot of the steps was a gray institutional corridor with another barred door. I threw myself against it, pushed it open with both hands—and was slapped hard in the face by rain and the deafening wail of sirens.

I think I might have screamed out loud, I was so happy to be outside, though nobody could have heard me in all that noise: I might as well have been trying to scream over jet engines on the tarmac at LaGuardia during a thunderstorm. It sounded like every fire truck, every cop car, every ambulance and emergency vehicle in five boroughs plus Jersey was howling and caterwauling out on Fifth Avenue, a deliriously happy noise: like New Year's and Christmas and Fourth of July fireworks rolled into one.

The exit had spat me out in Central Park, through a deserted side door between the loading docks and the parking garage. Footpaths stood empty in the gray-green distance; treetops plunged white, tossing and foaming in the wind. Beyond, on the rainswept street, Fifth Avenue was blocked off. Through the downpour, from where I stood, I could just see the great bright bombardment of activity: cranes and heavy equipment, cops pushing the crowds back, red lights, yellow and blue lights, flares that beat and whirled and flashed in quicksilver confusion.

I put my elbow up to keep the rain out of my face and took off running through the empty park. Rain drove in my eyes and dripped down my forehead, melting the lights on the avenue to a blur that pulsed in the distance.

NYPD, FDNY, parked city vans with the windshield wipers going: K-9, Rescue Operations Battalion, NYC Hazmat. Black rain slickers flapped and billowed in the wind. A band of yellow crime scene tape was stretched across the exit of the park, at the Miners' Gate. Without hesitation, I lifted it up and ducked underneath it and ran out into the midst of the crowd.

In all the welter, nobody noticed me. For a moment or two, I ran uselessly back and forth in the street, rain peppering in my face. Everywhere I looked, images of my own panic dashed past. People coursed and surged around me blindly: cops, firemen, guys in hard hats, an elderly man cradling a broken elbow and a woman with a bloody nose being shooed toward Seventy-Ninth Street by a distracted policeman.

Never had I seen so many fire trucks in one place: Squad 18, Fighting 44, New York Ladder 7, Rescue One, 4 Truck: Pride of Midtown. Pushing through the sea of parked vehicles and official black raincoats, I spotted a Hatzolah ambulance: Hebrew letters on the back, a little lighted hospital room visible through the open doors. Attendants were bending over a woman, trying to press her down as she struggled to sit up. A wrinkled hand with red fingernails clawed at the air.

I beat on the door with my fist. "You need to go back inside," I yelled. "People are still in there—"

"There's another bomb," yelled the attendant without looking at me. "We had to evacuate."

Before I had time to register this, a gigantic cop swooped down on me like a thunderclap: a thickheaded, bulldoggish guy, with pumped-up arms like a weightlifter's. He grabbed me roughly by the upper arm and began to hustle and shove me to the other side of the street.

"What the fuck are you doing over here?" he bellowed, drowning out my protests, as I tried to wrench free.

"Sir—" A bloody-faced woman coming up, trying to get his attention—"Sir, I think my hand is broken—"

"Get back from the building!" he screamed at her, throwing her arm off and then, at me—"Go!"

"But—"

With both hands, he shoved me so hard I staggered and nearly fell. "GET BACK FROM THE BUILDING!" he screamed, throwing up his arms with a flap of his rain slicker. "NOW!" He wasn't even looking at me; his small, bearish eyes were riveted on something going on over my head, up the street, and the expression on his face terrified me.

In haste, I dodged through the crowd of emergency workers to the opposite sidewalk, just above Seventy-Ninth Street—keeping an eye out for my mother, though I didn't see her. Ambulances and medical vehicles galore: Beth Israel Emergency, Lenox Hill, NY Presbyterian, Cabrini EMS Paramedic. A bloody man in a business suit lay flat on his back behind an ornamental yew hedge, in the tiny, fenced yard of a Fifth Avenue mansion. A yellow security tape was strung up, snapping and popping in the wind—but the rain-drenched cops and firemen and guys in hard hats were lifting it up and ducking back and forth under it as if it weren't even there.

All eyes were turned uptown, and only later would I learn why; on Eighty-Fourth Street (too far away for me to see) the Hazmat cops were in the process of "disrupting" an undetonated bomb by shooting it with a water cannon. Intent on talking to someone, trying to find out what had happened, I tried to push my way towards a fire truck but cops were charging through the crowds, waving their arms, clapping their hands, beating people back.

I caught hold of a fireman's coat—a young, gum-chewing, friendly-looking guy. "Somebody's still in there!" I screamed.

"Yeah, yeah, we know," shouted the fireman without looking at me. "They ordered us out. They're telling us five minutes, they're letting us back in."

A swift push in the back. "Move, move!" I heard somebody scream.

A rough voice, heavily accented: "Get your hands off me!"

"NOW! Everybody get moving!"

Somebody else pushed me in the back. Firemen leaned off the ladder trucks, looking up towards the Temple of Dendur; cops stood tensely shoulder to shoulder, impassive in the rain. Stumbling past them, swept along by the current, I saw glazed eyes, heads nodding, feet unconsciously tapping out the countdown.

By the time I heard the crack of the disrupted bomb, and the hoarse football-stadium cheer rising from Fifth Avenue, I had already been swept well along towards Madison. Cops—traffic cops—were windmilling their arms, pushing the stream of stunned people back. "Come on people, move it, move it." They plowed through the crowd, clapping their hands. "Everybody east. Everybody east." One cop—a big guy with a goatee and an earring, like a professional wrestler—reached out and shoved a delivery guy in a hoodie who was trying to take a picture on his cell phone, so that he stumbled into me and nearly knocked me over.

"Watch it!" screamed the delivery man, in a high, ugly voice; and the cop shoved him again, this time so hard he fell on his back in the gutter.

"Are you deaf or what, buddy?" he yelled. "Get going!"

"Don't touch me!"

"How 'bout I bust your head open?"

Between Fifth and Madison, it was a madhouse. Whap of helicopter rotors overhead; indistinct talking on a bullhorn. Though Seventy-Ninth Street was closed to traffic, it was packed with cop cars, fire trucks, cement barricades, and throngs of screaming, panicky, dripping-wet people. Some of them were running from Fifth Avenue; some were trying to muscle and press their way back toward the museum; many people held cell phones aloft, attempting to snap pictures; others stood motionless with their jaws dropped as the crowds surged around them, staring up at the black smoke in the rainy skies over Fifth Avenue as if the Martians were coming down.

Sirens; white smoke billowing from the subway vents. A homeless man wrapped in a dirty blanket wandered back and forth, looking eager and confused. I looked around hopefully for my mother in the crowd, fully expecting to see her; for a short time I tried to swim upstream against the cop-driven current (standing on my toes, craning to see) until I realized it was hopeless to push back up and try to look for her in that torrential rain, that mob. *I'll just see her at home,* I thought. Home was where we were supposed to meet; home was the emergency arrangement; she must have realized how useless it would be, trying to find me in all that crush. But still I felt a petty, irrational pang of disappointment—and, as I walked home (skull-cracking headache, practically seeing double) I kept looking for her, scanning the anonymous, preoccupied faces around me. She'd gotten out; that was the important thing. She'd been rooms away from the worst part of the explosion. None of the bodies was her. But no matter what we had agreed upon beforehand, no matter how much sense it made, somehow I still couldn't quite believe she had walked away from the museum without me.

Chapter 2.

The Anatomy Lesson

WHEN I WAS LITTLE, four or five, my greatest fear was that some day my mother might not come home from work. Addition and subtraction were useful mainly insofar as they helped me track her movements (how many minutes till she left the office? how many minutes to walk from office to subway?) and even before I'd learned to count I'd been obsessed with learning to read a clock face: desperately studying the occult circle crayoned on the paper plate that, once mastered, would unlock the pattern of her comings and goings. Usually she was home just when she said she'd be, so if she was ten minutes late I began to fret; any later, and I sat on the floor by the front door of the apartment like a puppy left alone too long, straining to hear the rumble of the elevator coming up to our floor.

Almost every day in elementary school I heard things on the Channel 7 news that worried me. What if some bum in a dirty fatigue jacket pushed my mother onto the tracks while she was waiting for the 6 train? Or muscled her into a dark doorway and stabbed her for her pocketbook? What if she dropped her hair dryer in the bathtub, or got knocked in front of a car by a bicycle, or was given the wrong medicine at the dentist's and died, as had happened to the mother of a classmate of mine?

To think of something happening to my mother was especially frightening because my dad was so unreliable. *Unreliable* I guess is the diplomatic way of putting it. Even when he was in a good mood he did things like lose his paycheck and fall asleep with the front door to the apartment open, because he drank. And when he was in a bad mood—which was much of the time—he was red-eyed and clammy-looking, his suit so rumpled it looked like he'd been rolling on the floor in it and an air of unnatural stillness emanating from him as from some pressurized article about to explode.

Though I didn't understand why he was so unhappy, it was clear to me that his unhappiness was our fault. My mother and I got on his nerves. It was because of us he had a job he couldn't stand. Everything we did was irritating. He particularly didn't enjoy being around me, not that he often was: in the mornings, as I got ready for school, he sat puffy-eyed and silent over his coffee with the *Wall Street Journal* in front of him, his bathrobe open and his hair standing up in cowlicks, and sometimes he was so shaky that the cup sloshed as he brought it to his mouth. Warily he eyed me when I came in, nostrils flaring if I made too much noise with the silverware or the cereal bowl.

Apart from this daily awkwardness, I didn't see him much. He didn't eat dinner with us or attend school functions; he didn't play with me or talk to me a lot when he was at home; in fact, he was seldom home at all until after my bedtime, and some days — paydays, especially, every other Friday — he didn't come clattering in until three or four in the morning: banging the door, dropping his briefcase, crashing and bumping around so erratically that sometimes I bolted awake in terror, staring at the glow-in-the-dark planetarium stars on the ceiling and wondering if a killer had broken into the apartment. Luckily, when he was drunk, his footsteps slowed to a jarring and unmistakable cadence — Frankenstein steps, as I thought of them, deliberate and clumping, with absurdly long pauses between each footfall — and as soon as I realized it was only him thudding around out there in the dark and not some serial murderer or psychopath, I would drift back into a fretful doze. The following day, Saturday, my mother and I would contrive to be out of the apartment before he woke from his sweaty, tangled sleep on the sofa. Otherwise we would spend the whole day creeping around, afraid of shutting the door too loudly or of disturbing him in any way, while he sat stony-faced in front of the television with a Chinese beer from the takeout place and a glassy look in his eye, watching news or sports with the sound off.

Consequently, neither my mother nor I had been overly troubled when we woke up one Saturday and found he hadn't come home at all. It was Sunday before we started getting concerned, and even then we didn't worry the way you normally would; it was the start of the college football season; it was a pretty sure thing that he had money on some of the games, and we thought he'd gotten on the bus and gone to Atlantic City without telling us. Not until the following day, when my father's secretary Loretta called because he hadn't shown up at work, did it start to appear that something was seriously wrong. My mother, fearing he'd been robbed or killed coming out drunk from a bar, phoned the police; and we spent several tense days waiting for a phone call or a knock on the door. Then, towards the end of the week, a sketchy note from my dad arrived (postmarked Newark, New Jersey) informing us in a high-strung scrawl that he was heading off to "start a new life" in an undisclosed location. I remember pondering the phrase "new life" as if it actually might reveal some hint of where he'd gone; for after I'd badgered and clamored and pestered my mother for about a week, she'd finally consented to let me see the letter myself ("well, all right," she said resignedly, as she opened her desk drawer and fished it out, "I don't know what he expects me to tell you, you might as well hear it from him"). It was written on stationery from a Doubletree Inn near the airport. I'd believed it might contain valuable clues to his whereabouts, but instead I was struck by its extreme brevity (four or five lines) and its speedy, careless, go-to-hell sprawl, like something he'd dashed off before running out to the grocery store.

In many respects it was a relief to have my father out of the picture. Certainly I didn't miss him much, and my mother didn't seem to miss him either, though it was sad when she had to let our housekeeper, Cinzia, go because we couldn't afford to pay her (Cinzia had cried, and offered to stay and work for free; but my mother had found her a part time job in the building, working for a couple with a baby; once a week or so, she stopped in to visit my mother for a cup of coffee, still in the smock she wore over her clothes when she cleaned.) Without fanfare, the photo of a younger, suntanned dad atop a ski slope came down from the wall, and was replaced by one of my mother and me at the rink in Central Park. At night my mother sat up late with a calculator, going over bills. Even though the apartment was rent stabilized, getting by without my dad's salary was a month-by-month adventure, since whatever new life he'd fashioned for himself elsewhere did not include sending money for child support. Basically we were content enough doing our own laundry down in the basement, going to matinees instead of full-price movies, eating day-old baked goods and cheap Chinese carry-out (noodles, egg foo yung) and counting out nickels and dimes for bus fare. But as I trudged home

from the museum that day — cold, wet, with a tooth-crunching headache —
it struck me that with my dad gone, no one in the world would be particularly worried about my mother or me; no one was sitting around
wondering where we'd been all morning or why they hadn't heard from
us. Wherever he was, off in his New Life (tropics or prairie, tiny ski town
or Major American City) he would certainly be riveted to the television;
and it was easy to imagine that maybe he was even getting a little frantic
and wound-up, as he sometimes did over big news stories that had absolutely nothing to do with him, hurricanes and bridge collapses in distant
states. But would he be worried enough to call and check on us? Probably
not — no more than he would be likely to call his old office to see what
was happening, though certainly he would be thinking of his ex-col-
leagues in midtown and wondering how all the bean counters and pencil-
pushers (as he referred to his co-workers) were faring at 101 Park. Were
the secretaries getting scared, gathering their pictures off their desks and
putting on their walking shoes and going home? Or was it turning into a
subdued party of sorts on the fourteenth floor, people ordering in sandwiches and gathering around the television in the conference room?

Though the walk home took forever, I don't remember much about it
except a certain gray, cold, rain-shrouded mood on Madison Avenue —
umbrellas bobbing, the crowds on the sidewalk flowing silently downtown, a sense of huddled anonymity like old black and white photos I'd
seen of bank crashes and bread lines in the 1930s. My headache, and the
rain, constricted the world to such a tight sick circle that I saw little more
than the hunched backs of people ahead of me on the sidewalk. In fact,
my head hurt so badly that I could hardly see where I was going at all; and
a couple of times I was nearly hit by cars when I plowed into the crosswalk without paying attention to the light. Nobody appeared to know
exactly what had happened, though I overheard "North Korea" blaring
from the radio of a parked cab, and "Iran" and "al-Qaeda" muttered by a
number of passersby. And a scrawny black man with dreadlocks —
drenched to the bone — was pacing back and forth out in front of the
Whitney museum, jabbing at the air with his fists and shouting to nobody
in particular: "Buckle up, Manhattan! Osama bin Laden is *rockin* us
again!"

Though I felt faint, and wanted to sit down, somehow I kept hobbling
along with a hitch in my step like a partially broken toy. Cops gestured;

cops whistled and beckoned. Water dripped off the end of my nose. Over and over, blinking the rain from my eyes, the thought coursed through my mind: I had to get home to my mother as soon as I could. She would be waiting frantically for me at the apartment; she would be tearing her hair out with worry, cursing herself for having taken my phone. Everyone was having problems getting calls through and pedestrians were lined ten and twenty deep at the few pay phones on the street. *Mother,* I thought, *Mother,* trying to send her a psychic message that I was alive. I wanted her to know I was all right but at the same time I remember telling myself it was okay I was walking instead of running; I didn't want to pass out on the way home. How lucky that she had walked away only a few moments before! She had sent me directly into the heart of the explosion; she was sure to think that I was dead.

And to think of the girl who'd saved my life made my eyes smart. Pippa! An odd, dry name for a rusty, wry little redhead: it suited her. Whenever I thought of her eyes on mine, I felt dizzy at the thought that she — a perfect stranger — had saved me from walking out of the exhibition and into the black flash in the postcard shop, nada, the end of everything. Would I ever get to tell her she'd saved my life? As for the old man: the firemen and rescue people had rushed the building only minutes after I got out, and I still had hopes that someone had made it back in to rescue him — the door was jacked, they knew he was in there. Would I ever see either of them again?

When I finally made it home, I was chilled to the bone, punch-drunk and stumbling. Water streamed from my sodden clothes and wound behind me in an uneven trail across the lobby floor.

After the crowds on the street, the air of desertion was unnerving. Though the portable television was going in the package room, and I heard walkie talkies spluttering somewhere in the building, there was no sign of Goldie or Carlos or Jose or any of the regular guys.

Farther back, the lighted cabinet of the elevator stood empty and waiting, like a stage cabinet in a magic act. The gears caught and shuddered; one by one, the pearly old deco numbers blinked past as I creaked up to the seventh floor. Stepping into my own, drab hallway, I was overwhelmed with relief — mouse-brown paint, stuffy carpet-cleaner smell and all.

The key turned noisily in the lock. "Hello?" I called, stepping into the dimness of the apartment: shades down, all quiet.

In the silence, the refrigerator hummed. *God,* I thought, with a terrible jolt, *isn't she home yet?*

"Mother?" I called again. With rapidly sinking heart, I walked fast through the foyer, and then stood confused in the middle of the living room.

Her keys weren't on the peg by the door; her bag wasn't on the table. Wet shoes squelching in the stillness, I walked through to the kitchen — which wasn't much of a kitchen, only an alcove with a two-burner stove, facing an airshaft. There sat her coffee cup, green glass from the flea market, with a lipstick print on the rim.

I stood staring at the unwashed coffee cup with an inch of cold coffee at the bottom and wondered what to do. My ears were ringing and whooshing and my head hurt so badly I could scarcely think: waves of blackness on the edge of my vision. I'd been so fixed on how worried she would be, on making it home to tell her that I was okay, that it had never occurred to me that she might not be home herself.

Wincing with every step, I walked down the hallway to my parents' bedroom: essentially unchanged since my father had left but more cluttered and feminine-looking now that it was hers alone. The answering machine, on the table by the tumbled and mussed-up bed, was dark: no messages.

Standing in the doorway, half-reeling with pain, I tried to concentrate. A jarring sensation of the day's movement jolted through my body, as if I'd been riding in a car for far too long.

First things first: find my phone, check my messages. Only I didn't know where my phone was. She had taken it away after I was suspended; the night before, when she was in the shower, I'd tried to find it by calling the number but apparently she'd turned it off.

I remember plunging my hands in the top drawer of her bureau and clawing through a bewilderment of scarves: silks and velvets, Indian embroideries.

Then, with immense effort (even though it wasn't very heavy) I dragged over the bench at the end of her bed and climbed on it so I could look on the top shelf of her closet. Afterwards, I sat on the carpet in a semi-stupor, with my cheek leaning against the bench and an ugly white roar in my ears.

Something was wrong. I remember raising my head with a sudden blaze of conviction that gas was seeping out of the kitchen stove, that I was being poisoned from a gas leak. Except I couldn't smell any gas.

I might have gone into the little bathroom off her bedroom and looked in the medicine cabinet for an aspirin, something for my head, I don't know. All I know for sure is that at some point I was in my room, not knowing how I got there, bracing myself with one hand against the wall by the bed and feeling like I was going to be sick. And then everything was so confused I can't give a clear account of it at all until I sat up disoriented on the living room sofa at the sound of something like a door opening.

But it wasn't the front door, only somebody else down the hall. The room was dark and I could hear afternoon traffic, rush-hour traffic, out on the street. In the dimness, I was still for a heartstopping moment or two as the noises sorted themselves out and the familiar lines of table lamp, lyre-shaped chair backs grew visible against the twilight window. "Mom?" I said, and the crackle of panic was plainly audible in my voice.

I had fallen asleep in my gritty wet clothes; the sofa was damp too, with a clammy, body-shaped depression where I'd been lying down on it. A chilly breeze rattled in the venetian blinds, through the window my mother had left partly open that morning.

The clock said 6:47 p.m. With growing fear, I walked stiffly around the apartment, turning on all the lights — even the overhead lights in the living room, which we generally didn't use because they were so stark and bright.

Standing in the doorway of my mother's bedroom, I saw a red light blinking in the dark. A delicious wave of relief washed over me: I darted around the bed, fumbled for the button on the answering machine, and it was several seconds before I realized that the voice was not my mother at all but a woman my mother worked with, sounding unaccountably cheerful. "Hi, Audrey, Pru here, just checking in. Crazy day, eh? Listen, the galley proofs are in for Pareja and we need to talk but the deadline's been postponed so no worries, for now anyway. Hope you're holding up, love, give a call when you've got a chance."

I stood there for a long time, looking down at the machine after the message beeped off. Then I lifted up the edge of the blinds and peeked out at the traffic.

It was that hour: people coming home. Horns honked faintly down on the street. I still had a splitting headache and the feeling (new to me then, but now unfortunately all too familiar) of waking up with a nasty hangover, of important things forgotten and left undone.

I went back to her bedroom, and with trembling hands, punched in the number of her cell phone, so fast that I got it wrong and had to dial again. But she didn't answer; the service picked up. I left a message (*Mom, it's me, I'm worried, where are you?*) and sat on the side of her bed with my head in my hands.

Cooking smells had begun to drift from the lower floors. Indistinct voices floated in from neighboring apartments: abstract thumps, somebody opening and shutting cabinets. It was late: people were coming home from work, dropping their briefcases, greeting their cats and dogs and children, turning on the news, getting ready to go out for dinner. Where was she? I tried to think of all the reasons why she might have been held up and couldn't really come up with any — although, who knew, maybe a street somewhere had been closed off so she couldn't get home. But wouldn't she have called?

Maybe she dropped her phone? I thought. Maybe she broke it? Maybe she gave it to someone who needed it more?

The stillness of the apartment unnerved me. Water sang in the pipes, and the breeze clicked treacherously in the blinds. Because I was just sitting uselessly on the side of her bed, feeling like I needed to do something, I called back and left yet another message, this time unable to keep the quaver out of my voice. *Mom, forgot to say, I'm at home. Please call, the second you get a chance, okay?* Then I called and left a message on the voice mail at her office just in case.

With a deadly coldness spreading in the center of my chest, I walked back into the living room. After standing there for a few moments, I went to the bulletin board in the kitchen to see if she had left me a note, though I already knew very well she hadn't. Back in the living room, I peered out the window at the busy street. Could she have run to the drugstore or the deli, not wanting to wake me? Part of me wanted to go out on the street and look for her, but it was crazy to think I would spot her in rush-hour crowds and besides if I left the apartment, I was scared I'd miss her call.

It was past time for the doormen to change shifts. When I phoned downstairs, I was hoping for Carlos (the most senior and dignified of the doormen) or even better Jose: a big happy Dominican guy, my favorite.

But nobody answered at all, for ages, until finally a thin, halting, foreign-sounding voice said: "Hello?"

"Is Jose there?"

"No," said the voice. "No. You cah back."

It was, I realized, the frightened-looking Asian guy in safety goggles and rubber gloves who ran the floor waxer and managed the trash and did other odd jobs around the building. The doormen (who didn't appear to know his name any more than I did) called him "the new guy," and griped about management bringing in a houseman who spoke neither English nor Spanish. Everything that went wrong in the building, they blamed on him: the new guy didn't shovel the walks right, the new guy didn't put the mail where it was supposed to go or keep the courtyard clean like he should.

"You cah back later," the new guy was saying, hopefully.

"No, wait!" I said, as he was about to hang up. "I need to talk to somebody."

Confused pause.

"Please, is anybody else there?" I said. "It's an emergency."

"Okay," said the voice warily, in an open-ended tone that gave me hope. I could hear him breathing hard in the silence.

"This is Theo Decker," I said. "In 7C? I see you downstairs a lot? My mother hasn't come home and I don't know what to do."

Long, bewildered pause. "Seven," he repeated, as if it were the only part of the sentence he understood.

"My mother," I repeated. "Where's Carlos? Isn't anybody there?"

"Sorry, thank you," he said, in a panicky tone, and hung up.

I hung up the phone myself, in a state of high agitation, and after a few moments standing frozen in the middle of the living room went and switched on the television. The city was a mess; the bridges to the outer boroughs were closed, which explained why Carlos and Jose hadn't been able to get in to work, but I saw nothing at all that made me understand what might be holding my mother up. There was a number to call, I saw, if someone was missing. I copied it down on a scrap of newspaper and made a deal with myself that if she wasn't home in exactly one half hour, I would call.

Writing the number down made me feel better. For some reason I felt sure that the act of writing it down was going to magically make her walk through the door. But after forty-five minutes passed, and then an hour, and still she hadn't turned up, I finally broke down and called it (pacing back and forth, keeping a nervous eye on the television the whole time I was waiting for somebody to pick up, the whole time I was on hold, commercials for mattresses, commercials for stereos, fast free delivery and no credit required). Finally a brisk woman came on, all business. She took my mother's name, took my phone number, said my mother wasn't "on her list" but I would get a call back if her name turned up. Not until after I hung up the phone did it occur to me to ask what sort of list she was talking about; and after an indefinite period of misgiving, walking in a tormented circuit through all four rooms, opening drawers, picking up books and putting them down, turning on my mother's computer and seeing what I could figure out from a Google search (nothing), I called back again to ask.

"She's not listed among the dead," said the second woman I spoke to, sounding oddly casual. "Or the injured."

My heart lifted. "She's okay, then?"

"I'm saying we've got no information at all. Did you leave your number earlier so we can give you a call back?"

Yes, I said, they had told me I would get a call back.

"Free delivery and set up," the television was saying. "Be sure and ask about our six months' free financing."

"Good luck then," said the woman, and hung up.

The stillness in the apartment was unnatural; even the loud talking on the television didn't drive it away. Twenty-one people were dead, with "dozens more" injured. In vain, I tried to reassure myself with this number: twenty-one people wasn't so bad, was it? Twenty-one was a thin crowd in a movie theatre or even on a bus. It was three people less than my English class. But soon fresh doubts and fears began to crowd around me and it was all I could do not to run out of the apartment yelling her name.

As much as I wanted to go out on the street and look for her, I knew I was supposed to stay put. We were supposed to meet at the apartment; that was the deal, the ironclad agreement ever since elementary school, when I'd been sent home from school with a Disaster Preparedness Activity Book, featuring cartoon ants in dust masks gathering supplies and preparing for some unnamed emergency. I'd completed the crosswords and dim questionnaires ("What is the best clothing to pack in a Disaster

Supply Kit? A. Bathing suit B. Layers C. Hula Skirt D. Aluminum foil")
and — with my mother — devised a Family Disaster Plan. Ours was simple: we would meet at home. And if one of us couldn't get home, we would call. But as time crawled by, and the phone did not ring, and the death toll on the news rose to twenty-two and then twenty-five, I phoned the city's emergency number again.

"Yes," said the woman who answered, in an infuriatingly calm voice, "I see here that you've phoned in already, we've got her down on our list."

"But — maybe she's in the hospital or something?"

"She might be. I'm afraid I can't confirm that, though. What did you say your name was? Would you like to speak to one of our counselors?"

"What hospital are they taking people to?"

"I'm sorry, I really can't —"

"Beth Israel? Lenox Hill?"

"Look, it depends on the type of injury. People have got eye trauma, burns, all sorts of stuff. There are people undergoing surgery all over the city —"

"What about those people that were reported dead a few minutes ago?"

"Look, I understand, I'd like to help you, but I'm afraid there's no Audrey Decker on my list."

My eyes darted nervously around the living room. My mother's book (*Jane and Prudence,* Barbara Pym) face-down on the back of the sofa; one of her thin cashmere cardigans over the arm of a chair. She had them in all colors; this one was pale blue.

"Maybe you should come down to the Armory. They've set up something for families there — there's food, and lots of hot coffee, and people to talk to."

"But what I'm asking you, are there any dead people that you don't have names for? Or injured people?"

"Listen, I understand your concern. I really, really wish I could help you with this but I just can't. You'll get a call back as soon as we have some specific information."

"I need to find my mother! Please! She's probably in a hospital somewhere. Can't you give me some idea where to look for her?"

"How old are you?" said the woman suspiciously.

After a shocked silence, I hung up. For a few dazed moments I stared at the telephone, feeling relieved but also guilty, as if I'd knocked something over and broken it. When I looked down at my hands and saw them shaking, it struck me in a wholly impersonal way, like noticing the battery was drained on my iPod, that I hadn't eaten in a while. Never in my life except when I had a stomach virus had I gone so long without food. So I went to the fridge and found my carton of leftover lo mein from the night before and wolfed it at the counter, standing vulnerable and exposed in the glare from the overhead bulb. Though there was also egg foo yung, and rice, I left it for her in case she was hungry when she came in. It was nearly midnight: soon it would be too late for her to order in from the deli. After I was finished, I washed my fork and the coffee things from that morning and wiped down the counter so she wouldn't have anything to do when she got home: she would be pleased, I told myself firmly, when she saw I had cleaned the kitchen for her. She would be pleased too (at least I thought so) when she saw I'd saved her painting. She might be mad. But I could explain.

According to the television, they now knew who was responsible for the explosion: parties that the news was alternately calling "right wing extremists" or "home-grown terrorists." They had worked with a moving and storage company; with help from unknown accomplices inside the museum, they had concealed the explosives within the hollow, carpenter-built display platforms in the museum shops where the postcards and art books were stacked. Some of the perpetrators were dead; some of them were in custody, others were at large. They were going into the particulars in some detail, but it was all too much for me to take in.

I was now working with the sticky drawer in the kitchen, which had been jammed shut since long before my father left; nothing was in it but cookie cutters and some old fondue skewers and lemon zesters we never used. She'd been trying for well over a year to get someone from the building in to fix it (along with a broken doorknob and a leaky faucet and half a dozen other annoying little things). I got a butter knife, pried at the edges of the drawer, careful not to chip the paint any more than it was chipped already. The force of the explosion still rang deep in my bones, an inner echo of the ringing in my ears; but worse than this, I could still smell blood, taste the salt and tin of it in my mouth. (I would be smelling it for days, though I didn't know that then.)

While I worked and worried at the drawer, I wondered if I should call somebody, and, if so, who. My mother was an only child. And though,

technically I had a set of living grandparents—my father's dad and stepmother, in Maryland—I didn't know how to get in touch with them.
Relations were barely civil between my dad and his stepmother, Dorothy,
an immigrant from East Germany who had cleaned office buildings for a
living before marrying my grandfather. (Always a clever mimic, my dad
did a cruelly funny imitation of Dorothy: a sort of battery-operated haus-
frau, all compressed lips and jerky movements, and an accent like Curt
Jurgens in *Battle of Britain*.) But though my dad disliked Dorothy enough,
his chief enmity was for Grandpa Decker: a tall, fat, frightening-looking
man with ruddy cheeks and black hair (dyed, I think) who wore lots of
waistcoats and loud plaids, and believed in belt beatings for children. *No
picnic* was the primary phrase I associated with Grandpa Decker—as in
my dad saying "Living with that bastard was no picnic" and "Believe me,
dinnertime was never any picnic at our house." I had met Grandpa Decker
and Dorothy only twice in my life, tense charged occasions where my
mother leaned forward on the sofa with her coat on and her purse in her
lap and her valiant efforts to make conversation all stumbled and sank
into quicksand. The main thing I remembered were the forced smiles, the
heavy smell of cherry pipe tobacco and Grandpa Decker's not-very-
friendly warning to keep my sticky little mitts off his model train set (an
Alpine village which took up an entire room of their house and according
to him was worth tens of thousands of dollars).

I'd managed to bend the blade of the butter knife by stabbing it too
hard into the side of the stuck drawer—one of my mother's few good
knives, a silver knife that had belonged to her mother. Gamely, I tried to
bend it back, biting my lip and concentrating all my will on the task, as all
the time ugly flashes of the day kept flying up and hitting me in the face.
Trying to stop thinking about it was like trying to stop thinking of a purple cow. The purple cow was all you could think of.

Unexpectedly the drawer popped open. I stared down at the mess:
rusty batteries, a broken cheese grater, the snowflake cookie cutters my
mother hadn't used since I was in first grade, jammed in with ragged old
carry-out menus from Viand and Shun Lee Palace and Delmonico's. I left
the drawer wide open—so it would be the first thing she saw when she
walked in—and wandered over to the couch and wrapped myself up in a
blanket, propped up so I could keep a good eye on the front door.

My mind was churning in circles. For a long time I sat shivering and red-eyed in the glow of the television, as the blue shadows flickered uneasily in and out. There was no news, really; the picture kept returning to night shots of the museum (looking perfectly normal now, except for the yellow police tape still strung up on the sidewalk, the armed guards out front, rags of smoke blowing up sporadically from the roof into the Klieg-lit sky).

Where was she? Why hadn't she come home yet? She would have a good explanation; she would make this into nothing, and then it would seem completely stupid how worried I'd been.

To force her from my mind I concentrated hard on an interview they were running again, from earlier in the evening. A bespectacled curator in tweed jacket and bow tie—visibly shaken—was talking about what a disgrace it was that they weren't letting specialists into the museum to care for the artwork. "Yes," he was saying, "I understand that it's a crime scene, but these paintings are very sensitive to changes in air quality and temperature. They may have been damaged by water or chemicals or smoke. They may be deteriorating as we speak. It is of vital importance that conservators and curators be allowed into the crucial areas to assess the damage as soon as possible—"

All of a sudden the telephone rang—abnormally loud, like an alarm clock waking me from the worst dream of my life. My surge of relief was indescribable. I tripped and nearly fell on my face in my headlong dive to grab it. I was certain it was my mother, but the caller ID stopped me cold: NYDoCFS.

New York Department of—what? After half a beat of confusion, I snatched up the phone. "Hello?"

"Hello there," said a voice of hushed and almost creepy gentleness. "To whom am I speaking?"

"Theodore Decker," I said, taken aback. "Who is this?"

"Hello, Theodore. My name is Marjorie Beth Weinberg and I'm a social worker in the Department of Child and Family Services?"

"What is it? Are you calling about my mother?"

"You're Audrey Decker's son? Is that correct?"

"My mother! Where is she? Is she all right?"

A long pause—a terrible pause.

"What's the matter?" I cried. "Where is she?"

"Is your father there? May I speak to him?"

"He can't come to the phone. What's wrong?"

"I'm sorry, but it's an emergency. I'm afraid it's really very important that I speak to your father right now."

"What about my mother?" I said, rising to my feet. "Please! Just tell me where she is! What happened?"

"You're not by yourself, are you, Theodore? Is there an adult with you?"

"No, they've gone out for coffee," I said, looking wildly around the living room. Ballet slippers, askew beneath a chair. Purple hyacinths in a foil-wrapped pot.

"Your father, too?"

"No, he's asleep. Where's my mother? Is she hurt? What's happened?"

"I'm afraid I'll have to ask you to wake your dad up, Theodore."

"No! I can't!"

"I'm afraid it's very important."

"He can't come to the phone! Why can't you just tell me what's wrong?"

"Well then, if your dad's not available, maybe it's best if I just leave my contact information with you." The voice, while soft and sympathetic, was reminiscent to my ear of Hal the computer in *2001: A Space Odyssey*. "Please tell him to get in touch with me as soon as possible. It's really very important that he returns the call."

After I got off the telephone, I sat very still for a long time. According to the clock on the stove, which I could see from where I sat, it was two-forty-five in the morning. Never had I been alone and awake at such an hour. The living room—normally so airy and open, buoyant with my mother's presence—had shrunk to a cold, pale discomfort, like a vacation house in winter: fragile fabrics, scratchy sisal rug, paper lamp shades from Chinatown and the chairs too little and light. All the furniture seemed spindly, poised at a tiptoe nervousness. I could feel my heart beating, hear the clicks and ticks and hisses of the large elderly building slumbering around me. Everyone was asleep. Even the distant horn-honks and the occasional rattle of trucks out on Fifty-Seventh Street seemed faint and uncertain, as lonely as a noise from another planet.

Soon, I knew, the night sky would turn dark blue; the first tender, chilly gleam of April daylight would steal into the room. Garbage trucks would roar and grumble down the street; spring songbirds would start singing in the park; alarm clocks would be going off in bedrooms all over the city. Guys hanging off the backs of trucks would toss fat whacking bundles of the *Times* and the *Daily News* to the sidewalks outside the newsstand. Mothers and dads all over the city would be shuffling around wild-haired in underwear and bathrobes, putting on the coffee, plugging in the toaster, waking their kids up for school.

And what would I do? Part of me was immobile, stunned with despair, like those rats that lose hope in laboratory experiments and lie down in the maze to starve.

I tried to pull my thoughts together. For a while, it had almost seemed that if I sat still enough, and waited, things might straighten themselves out somehow. Objects in the apartment wobbled with my fatigue: halos shimmered around the table lamp; the stripe of the wallpaper seemed to vibrate.

I picked up the phone book; I put it down. The idea of calling the police terrified me. And what could the police do anyway? I knew only too well from television that a person had to be missing twenty-four hours. I had just about convinced myself that I ought to go uptown and look for her, middle of the night or no, and the hell with our Family Disaster Plan, when a deafening buzz (the doorbell) shattered the silence and my heart leaped up for joy.

Scrambling, skidding harum-scarum to the door, I fumbled with the lock. "Mom?" I called, sliding the top bolt, throwing open the door — and then my heart plunged, a six-story drop. Standing on the doormat were two people I had never seen in my life: a chubby Korean woman with a short, spiky haircut, a Hispanic guy in shirt and tie who looked a lot like Luis on *Sesame Street*. There was nothing at all threatening about them, quite the contrary; they were reassuringly dumpy and middle-aged, dressed like a pair of substitute school teachers, but though they both had kindly expressions on their faces, I understood the instant I saw them that my life, as I knew it, was over.

Chapter 3.

Park Avenue

i.

THE SOCIAL WORKERS PUT me in the back seat of their compact car and drove me to a diner downtown, near their work, a fake-grand place glittering with beveled mirrors and cheap Chinatown chandeliers. Once we were in the booth (both of them on one side, with me facing) they took clipboards and pens from their briefcases and tried to make me eat some breakfast while they sat sipping coffee and asking questions. It was still dark outside; the city was just waking up. I don't remember crying, or eating either, though all these years later I can still smell the scrambled eggs they ordered for me; the memory of that heaped plate with the steam coming off it still ties my stomach in knots.

The diner was mostly empty. Sleepy busboys unpacked boxes of bagels and muffins behind the counter. A wan cluster of club kids with smudged eyeliner were huddled in a nearby booth. I remember staring over at them with a desperate, clutching attention — a sweaty boy in a Mandarin jacket, a bedraggled girl with pink streaks in her hair — and also at an old lady in full make-up and a fur coat much too warm for the weather who was sitting by herself at the counter, eating a slice of apple pie.

The social workers — who did everything but shake me and snap their fingers in my face to get me to look at them — seemed to understand how unwilling I was to absorb what they were trying to tell me. Taking turns, they leaned across the table and repeated what I did not want to hear. My mother was dead. She had been struck in the head by flying debris. She had died instantly. They were sorry to be the ones who broke the news, it was the worst part of their job, but they really really needed me to understand what had happened. My mother was dead and her body was at New York Hospital. Did I understand?

"Yes," I said, in the long pause where I realized they were expecting me to say something. Their blunt, insistent use of the words *death* and *dead* was impossible to reconcile with their reasonable voices, their polyester business clothes, the Spanish pop music on the radio and the peppy signs behind the counter (*Fresh Fruit Smoothie, Diet Delite, Try Our Turkey Hamburger!*).

"*¿Fritas?*" said the waiter, appearing at our table, holding aloft a big plate of french fries.

Both social workers looked startled; the man of the pair (first names only: Enrique) said something in Spanish and pointed a few tables over, where the club kids were gesturing to him.

Sitting red-eyed in my shock, before my rapidly cooling plate of scrambled eggs, I could scarcely grasp the more practical aspects of my situation. In light of what had happened, their questions about my father seemed so wholly beside the point that I had a hard time understanding why they kept asking so insistently about him.

"So when's the last time you saw him?" said the Korean lady, who'd asked me several times to call her by her first name (I've tried and tried to recall it, and can't). I can still see her plumpish hands folded on the table, though, and the disturbing shade of her nail polish: an ashen, silvery color, something between lavender and blue.

"A guesstimate?" prompted the man Enrique. "About your dad?"

"Ballpark will do," the Korean lady said. "When do you think you last saw him?"

"Um," I said—it was an effort to think—"sometime last fall?" My mother's death still seemed like a mistake that might be straightened out somehow if I pulled myself together and cooperated with these people.

"October? September?" she said, gently, when I didn't respond.

My head hurt so badly I felt like crying whenever I turned it, although my headache was the least of my problems. "I don't know," I said. "After school started."

"September, would you say then?" asked Enrique, glancing up as he made a note on his clipboard. He was a tough-looking guy—uneasy in his suit and tie, like a sports coach gone to fat—but his tone conveyed a reassuring sense of the nine-to-five world: office filing systems, industrial carpeting, business as usual in the borough of Manhattan. "No contact or communication since then?"

"Who's a buddy or close friend who might know how to reach him?" said the Korean lady, leaning forward in a motherly way.

The question startled me. I didn't know of any such person. Even the suggestion that my father had close friends (much less "buddies") conveyed a misunderstanding of his personality so profound I didn't know how to respond.

It was only after the plates had been taken away, in the edgy lull after the meal was finished but no one was getting up to leave, that it crashed down on me where all their seemingly irrelevant questions about my father and my Decker grandparents (in Maryland, I couldn't remember the town, some semi-rural subdivision behind a Home Depot) and my nonexistent aunts and uncles had so plainly been leading. I was a minor child without a guardian. I was to be removed immediately from my home (or "the environment," as they kept calling it). Until my father's parents were contacted, the city would be stepping in.

"But what are you going to do with me?" I asked for the second time, pushing back in my chair, a crackle of panic rising in my voice. It had all seemed very informal when I'd turned off the television and left the apartment with them, for a bite to eat as they'd said. Nobody had said a word about removing me from my home.

Enrique glanced down at his clipboard. "Well, Theo—" he kept pronouncing it Teo, they both did, which was wrong—"you're a minor child in need of immediate care. We're going to need to place you in some kind of emergency custody."

"Custody?" The word made my stomach crawl; it suggested courtrooms, locked dormitories, basketball courts ringed with barbed-wire fence.

"Well, let's say *care* then. And only until your grandpa and grandma—"

"Wait," I said—overwhelmed at exactly how fast things were spinning out of control, at the false assumption of warmth and familiarity in the way he'd said the words *grandpa* and *grandma*.

"We'll just need to make some temporary arrangements until we reach them," said the Korean lady, leaning close. Her breath smelled minty but also had the slightest underbite of garlic. "We know how sad you must be, but there's nothing to worry about. Our job is just to keep you safe until we reach the people who love you and care about you, okay?"

It was too awful to be real. I stared at the two strange faces across the booth, sallow in the artificial lights. Even the proposition that Grandpa Decker and Dorothy were people who cared about me was absurd.

"But what's going to happen to me?" I said.

"The main concern," said Enrique, "is that you're in a capable foster situation for the time being. With someone that'll work hand in hand with Social Services to implement your care plan."

Their combined efforts to soothe me — their calm voices and sympathetic, reasonable expressions — made me increasingly frantic. "Stop it!" I said, jerking away from the Korean lady, who had reached over the table and was attempting to clasp my hand in a caring way.

"Look, Teo. Let me explain something. Nobody's talking about detention or a juvenile facility —"

"Then what?"

"Temporary custody. All that means, is that we take you to a safe place with people who will act as guardians for the state —"

"What if I don't want to go?" I said, so loudly that people turned to stare.

"Listen," Enrique said, leaning back and signalling for more coffee. "The city has certified crisis homes for youth in need. Fine places. And right now, that's just one option we're looking at. Because in a lot of cases like yours —"

"I don't want to go to a foster home!"

"Kid, you sure don't," the pink-haired club girl said audibly at the next table. Recently, the *New York Post* had been full of Johntay and Keshawn Divens, the eleven-year-old twins who had been raped by their foster father and starved nearly to death, up around Morningside Heights.

Enrique pretended not to hear this. "Look, we're here to help," he said, refolding his hands on the tabletop. "And we'll also consider other alternatives if they keep you safe and address your needs."

"You never told me I couldn't go back to the apartment!"

"Well, city agencies are overburdened — *sí, gracias,*" he said to the waiter who'd come to refill his cup. "But sometimes other arrangements can be made if we get provisional approval, especially in a situation like yours."

"What he's saying?" The Korean lady tapped her fingernail on the Formica to get my attention. "It's not set in stone you go into the system if there's somebody who can come stay with you for a little while. Or vice versa."

"A little while?" I repeated. It was the only part of the sentence that had sunk in.

"Like maybe there's somebody else we could call, that you might be comfortable staying with for a day or two? Like a teacher, maybe? Or a family friend?"

Off the top of my head, I gave them the telephone number of my old friend Andy Barbour — the first number that came to me, maybe because it was the first phone number besides my own I'd learned by heart. Though Andy and I had been good friends in elementary school (movies, sleepovers, summer classes in Central Park in map and compass skills), I'm still not quite sure why his name was the first to fall out of my mouth, since we weren't such good friends any more. We'd drifted apart at the start of junior high; I'd hardly seen him in months.

"Barbour with a u," said Enrique as he wrote the name down. "Who are these people? Friends?"

Yes, I replied, I'd known them all my life, practically. The Barbours lived on Park Avenue. Andy had been my best friend since third grade. "His dad has a big job on Wall Street," I said — and then I shut up. It had just occurred to me that Andy's dad had spent some unknown amount of time in a Connecticut mental hospital for "exhaustion."

"What about the mother?"

"She and my mom are good friends." (Almost true, but not quite; though they were on perfectly friendly terms, my mother wasn't nearly rich or connected enough for a social-pages lady like Mrs. Barbour.)

"No, I mean, what does she do for a living?"

"Charity work," I said, after a disoriented pause. "Like the Antiques Show at the Armory?"

"So she's a stay-at-home mom?"

I nodded, glad she'd supplied the phrase so handily, which though technically true was not how anyone who knew Mrs. Barbour would ever think to describe her.

Enrique signed his name with a flourish. "We'll look into it. Can't promise anything," he said, clicking his pen and sticking it back in his pocket. "We can certainly drop you over with these folks for the next few hours, though, if they're who you want to be with."

He slid out of the booth and walked outside. Through the front window, I could see him walking back and forth on the sidewalk, talking on the phone with a finger in one ear. Then he dialed another number, for a much shorter call. There was a quick stop at the apartment—less than five minutes, just long enough for me to grab my school bag and a few impulsive and ill-considered articles of clothing—and then, in their car again ("Are you buckled up back there?") I leaned with my cheek to the cold glass and watched the lights go green all up the empty dawn canyon of Park Avenue.

Andy lived in the upper Sixties, in one of the great old white-glove buildings on Park where the lobby was straight from a Dick Powell movie and the doormen were still mostly Irish. They'd all been there forever, and as it happened I remembered the guy who met us at the door: Kenneth, the midnight man. He was younger than most of the other doormen: dead-pale and poorly shaven, often a bit slow on the draw from working nights. Though he was a likable guy—had sometimes mended soccer balls for Andy and me, and dispensed friendly advice on how to deal with bullies at school—he was known around the building for having a bit of a drinking problem; and as he stepped aside to usher us in through the grand doors, and gave me the first of the many *God, kid, I'm so sorry* looks I would be receiving over the next months, I smelled the sourness of beer and sleep on him.

"They're expecting you," he said to the social workers. "Go on up."

ii.

IT WAS MR. BARBOUR who opened the door: first a crack, then all the way. "Morning, morning," he said, stepping back. Mr. Barbour was a tiny bit strange-looking, with something pale and silvery about him, as if his treatments in the Connecticut "ding farm" (as he called it) had rendered him incandescent; his eyes were a queer unstable gray and his hair was pure white, which made him seem older than he was until you noticed that his face was young and pink—boyish, even. His ruddy cheeks and his long, old-fashioned nose, in combination with the prematurely white hair, gave him the amiable look of a lesser founding father, some minor member of the Continental Congress teleported to the twenty-first century. He was wearing what appeared to be yesterday's office clothes: a rumpled dress shirt and expensive-looking suit trousers that looked like he had just grabbed them off the bedroom floor.

"Come on in," he said briskly, rubbing his eyes with his fist. "Hello there, dear," he said to me — the *dear* startling, from him, even in my disoriented state.

Barefoot, he padded ahead of us, through the marble foyer. Beyond, in the richly decorated living room (all glazed chintz and Chinese jars) it felt less like morning than midnight: silk-shaded lamps burning low, big dark paintings of naval battles and drapes drawn against the sun. There — by the baby grand, and a flower arrangement the size of a packing case — stood Mrs. Barbour in a floor-sweeping housecoat, pouring coffee into cups on a silver tray.

As she turned to greet us, I could feel the social workers taking in the apartment, and her. Mrs. Barbour was from a society family with an old Dutch name, so cool and blonde and monotone that sometimes she seemed partially drained of blood. She was a masterpiece of composure; nothing ever ruffled her or made her upset, and though she was not beautiful her calmness had the magnetic pull of beauty — a stillness so powerful that the molecules realigned themselves around her when she came into a room. Like a fashion drawing come to life, she turned heads wherever she went, gliding along obliviously without appearing to notice the turbulence she created in her wake; her eyes were spaced far apart, her ears were small, high-set, and very close to her head, and her body was long-waisted and thin, like an elegant weasel's. (Andy had these features as well, but in ungainly proportions, without her slinky ermine grace.)

In the past, her reserve (or coldness, depending how you saw it) had sometimes made me uncomfortable, but that morning I was grateful for her sang froid. "Hi there. We'll be putting you in the room with Andy," she said to me without beating around the bush. "I'm afraid he's not up for school yet, though. If you'd like to lie down for a while, you're perfectly welcome to go to Platt's room." Platt was Andy's older brother, away at school. "You know where it is, of course?"

I said that I did.

"Are you hungry?"

"No."

"Well, then. Tell us what we can do for you."

I was aware of them all looking at me. My headache was bigger than anything else in the room. In the bull's-eye mirror above Mrs. Barbour's head, I could see the whole scene replicated in freakish miniature: Chinese jars, coffee tray, awkward-looking social workers and all.

In the end, it was Mr. Barbour who broke the spell. "Come along, then, let's get you squared away," he said, clapping his hand on my shoulder and firmly steering me out of the room. "No — back here, this way — aft, aft. Right back here."

The only time I'd ever set foot in Platt's room, several years before, Platt — who was a champion lacrosse player and a bit of a psychopath — had threatened to beat the everliving crap out of Andy and me. When he'd lived at home, he'd stayed in there all the time with the door locked (and, Andy told me, smoked pot). Now all his posters were gone and the room was very clean and empty-looking, since he was away at Groton. There were free weights, stacks of old *National Geographics*, an empty aquarium. Mr. Barbour, opening and closing drawers, was babbling a bit. "Let's see what's in here, shall we? Bedsheets. And ... more bedsheets. I'm afraid I never come in here, I do hope you'll forgive me — ah. Swimming trunks! Won't be needing those this morning, will we?" Scrabbling around in yet a third drawer, he finally produced some new pyjamas with the tags still on, ugly as hell, reindeer on electric blue flannel, no mystery why they'd never been worn.

"Well then," he said, running a hand through his hair and cutting his eyes anxiously towards the door. "I'll leave you now. Hell of a thing that's happened, good Lord. You must be feeling awfully rough. A good solid sleep will be the best thing in the world for you. Are you tired?" he said, looking at me closely.

Was I? I was wide awake, and yet part of me was so glassed-off and numb I was practically in a coma.

"If you'd rather have company? Perhaps if I build a fire in the other room? Tell me what you want."

At this question, I felt a sharp rush of despair — for as bad as I felt there was nothing he could do for me, and from his face, I realized he knew that, too.

"We're only in the next room if you need us — that is to say, I'll be leaving soon for work but *some*one will be here...." His pale gaze darted around the room, and then returned to me. "Perhaps it's incorrect of me, but in the circumstances I wouldn't see the harm in pouring you what my father used to call a minor nip. *If* you should happen to want such a thing. Which of course you don't," he added hastily, noting my confusion. "Quite unsuitable. Never mind."

He stepped closer, and for an uncomfortable moment I thought he might touch me, or hug me. But instead he clapped his hands and rubbed them together. "In any case. We're perfectly happy to have you and I hope you'll make yourself as comfortable as you can. You'll speak right up if you need anything, won't you?"

He had hardly stepped out when there was whispering outside the door. Then a knock. "Someone here to see you," Mrs. Barbour said, and withdrew.

And in plodded Andy: blinking, fumbling with his glasses. It was clear that they had woken him up and hauled him out of bed. With a noisy creak of bedsprings, he sat beside me on the edge of Platt's bed, looking not at me but at the wall opposite.

He cleared his throat, pushed his glasses up on the bridge of his nose. There followed a long silence. Urgently the radiator clanked and hissed. Both his parents had gotten out of there so fast it was like they'd heard the fire alarm.

"Wow," he said, after some moments, in his eerie flat voice. "Disturbing."

"Yeah," I said. And together we sat in silence, side by side, staring at the dark green walls of Platt's room and the taped squares where his posters had once been. What else was there to say?

iii.

EVEN NOW, TO REMEMBER that time fills me with a choking, hopeless sensation. Everything was terrible. People offered me cold drinks, extra sweaters, food I couldn't eat: bananas, cupcakes, club sandwiches, ice cream. I said yes and no when I was spoken to, and spent a lot of time staring at the carpet so people wouldn't see I'd been crying.

Though the Barbours' apartment was enormous by New York standards, it was on a low floor and practically lightless, even on the Park Avenue side. Though it was never quite night there, or exactly day, still the glow of lamplight against burnished oak gave off an air of conviviality and safety like a private club. Friends of Platt's called it "the creepatorium" and my father, who'd come there once or twice to pick me up after sleepovers, had referred to it as "Frank E. Campbell's" after the funeral home. But I found a solace in the massive, opulent, pre-war gloom, which was easy to retreat into if you didn't feel like talking or being stared at.

People stopped by to see me — my social workers of course, and a pro-bono psychiatrist who'd been sent to me by the city, but also people from my mother's work (some of whom, like Mathilde, I'd been expert at imitating in order to make her laugh), and loads of friends from NYU and her fashion days. A semi-famous actor named Jed, who sometimes spent Thanksgiving with us ("Your mother was the Queen of the Universe, as far as I was concerned"), and a slightly punked-out woman in an orange coat, named Kika, who told me how she and my mother — dead broke in the East Village — had thrown a wildly successful dinner party for twelve people for less than twenty dollars (featuring, among other things, cream and sugar packets lifted from a coffee bar, and herbs picked surreptitiously from a neighbor's windowbox). Annette — a fireman's widow, in her seventies, my mother's former neighbor down on the Lower East Side — showed up with a box of cookies from the Italian bakery around where she and my mother used to live, the same butter cookies with pine nuts she always brought us when she visited at Sutton Place. Then there was Cinzia, our old housekeeper, who burst into tears when she saw me, and asked me for a picture of my mother to keep in her wallet.

Mrs. Barbour broke up these visits if they dragged on too long, on the grounds that I got tired easily, but also — I suspect — because she couldn't handle people like Cinzia and Kika monopolizing her living room for indefinite periods of time. After forty-five minutes or so she would come and stand quietly in the door. And if they didn't take the hint, she would speak up and thank them for coming — perfectly polite, but in such a way that people realized that the time was getting on and rose to their feet. (Her voice, like Andy's, was hollow and infinitely far away; even when she was standing right next to you she sounded as if she were relaying transmissions from Alpha Centauri.)

Around me, over my head, the life of the household went on. Every day, the doorbell rang many times: housekeepers, nannies, caterers, tutors, the piano instructor, social-pages ladies and tassel-loafer business guys connected with Mrs. Barbour's charities. Andy's younger siblings, Toddy and Kitsey, raced through the gloomy halls with their school friends. Often, in the afternoons, perfume-smelling women with shopping bags dropped by for coffee and tea; in the evenings, couples dressed for dinner congregated over wine and fizzy water in the living room, where the flower arrangements were delivered every week from a swanky Madison Avenue florist and the newest issues of *Architectural Digest* and the *New Yorker* were fanned just so on the coffee table.

If Mr. and Mrs. Barbour were terribly inconvenienced to have an extra kid dumped on them, at scarcely a moment's notice, they were graceful enough not to show it. Andy's mother, with her understated jewelry and her not-quite-interested smile — the kind of woman who could get on the phone with the mayor if she needed a favor — seemed to operate somehow above the constraints of New York City bureaucracy. Even in my confusion and grief, I had a sense that she was managing things behind the scenes, making it all easier for me, shielding me from the rougher aspects of the Social Services machinery — and, I'm now fairly sure, the press. Calls were forwarded from the insistently ringing telephone directly to her cell phone. There were conversations in low voices, instructions to the doormen. After coming in on one of Enrique's many tireless interrogations about my father's whereabouts — interrogations that often brought me close to tears; he might as well have been grilling me about the location of missile sites in Pakistan — she sent me out of the room and then in a controlled monotone put a stop to it ("Well I mean, *obviously* the boy doesn't know where he is, the mother didn't know either... yes, I know you'd like to find him but clearly the man doesn't *want* to be found, he's taken *measures* not to be found... he wasn't paying child support, he left a lot of debts, he more or less flew town without a word so frankly I'm not quite sure what you mean to accomplish by contacting this stellar parent and fine citizen and... yes, yes, all well and good, but if the man's creditors can't run him down and your agency can't either then I'm not sure what's to be gained from continuing to badger the child, are you? Can we agree to put a stop to this?")

Certain elements of the martial law imposed since my arrival had inconvenienced the household: no longer, for instance, were the housemaids permitted to listen to Ten Ten WINS, the news station, while they worked ("No, no," said Etta the cook, with a warning glance at me, when one of the cleaners tried to turn the radio on) and in the mornings, the *Times* was taken immediately to Mr. Barbour and not left out for the rest of the family to read. Clearly, this was not the usual custom — "Somebody's carried the paper off *again*," Andy's little sister Kitsey would wail before falling into guilty silence after a look from her mother — and I soon gathered that the newspaper had begun vanishing into Mr. Barbour's study because there were things in it that it was thought preferable for me not to see.

Thankfully Andy, who had been my companion in adversity before, understood that the last thing I wanted was to talk. Those first few days, they let him stay home from school with me. In his musty plaid room with the bunk beds, where I had spent many a Saturday night in elementary school, we sat over the chessboard, Andy playing for both of us, since in my fog I scarcely remembered how to move the pieces. "Okay," he said, pushing his glasses up on the bridge of his nose. "Right. Are you absolutely sure you want to do that?"

"Do what?"

"Yes, I see," said Andy, in the wispy, irritating voice which had driven so many bullies to shove him to the sidewalk out in front of our school over the years. "Your rook is in danger, that's perfectly correct, but I would suggest you take a closer look at your queen — no, no, your *queen*. D5."

He had to say my name to get my attention. Over and over, I was reliving the moment where my mother and I had run up the museum steps. Her striped umbrella. Rain peppering and driving in our faces. What had happened, I knew, was irrevocable, yet at the same time it seemed there had to be some way I could go back to the rainy street and make it all happen differently.

"The other day," said Andy, "somebody, I really believe it was Malcolm whats-his-name or some other supposedly respected writer — anyway, he made a big production the other day in the *Science Times* of pointing out that there are more potential games of chess than there are grains of sand in the entire world. It's ridiculous that a science writer for a major newspaper would feel compelled to belabor a fact so obvious."

"Right," I said, returning with effort from my thoughts.

"Like who doesn't know that grains of sand on the planet, however numerous, are finite? It's absurd that someone would even comment on such a non-issue, you know, like, *Breaking News Story!* Just throwing it out there, you know, as a supposedly arcane fact."

Andy and I, in elementary school, had become friends under more or less traumatic circumstances: after we'd been skipped ahead a grade because of high test scores. Everyone now appeared to agree that this had been a mistake for both of us, though for different reasons. That year— bumbling around among boys all older and bigger than us, boys who tripped us and shoved us and slammed locker doors on our hands, who tore up our homework and spat in our milk, who called us *maggot* and *faggot* and *dickhead* (sadly, a natural for me, with a last name like Decker)—during that whole year (our Babylonian Captivity, Andy called it, in his faint glum voice) we'd struggled along side by side like a pair of weakling ants under a magnifying glass: shin-kicked, sucker-punched, ostracized, eating lunch huddled in the most out-of-the-way corner we could find in order to keep from getting ketchup packets and chicken nuggets thrown at us. For almost two years he had been my only friend, and vice versa. It depressed and embarrassed me to remember that time: our Autobot wars and Lego spaceships, the secret identities we'd assumed from classic *Star Trek* (I was Kirk, he was Spock) in an effort to make a game of our torments. *Captain, it would appear that these aliens are holding us captive in some simulacrum of your schools for human children, on Earth.*

Before I'd been tossed in with a tight, competitive bunch of older boys, with a label reading "gifted" tied around my neck, I'd never been especially reviled or humiliated at school. But poor Andy—even before he was skipped ahead a grade—had always been a chronically picked-upon kid: scrawny, twitchy, lactose-intolerant, with skin so pale it was almost transparent, and a penchant for throwing out words like 'noxious' and 'chthonic' in casual conversation. As bright as he was, he was clumsy; his flat voice, his habit of breathing through his mouth due to a chronically blocked nose, gave him the appearance of being mildly stupid instead of excessively smart. Among the rest of his kittenish, sharp-toothed, athletic siblings—racing around between their friends and their sports teams and their rewarding after-school programs—he stood out like a random pastehead who had wandered out onto the lacrosse field by mistake.

Whereas I'd managed to recover, somewhat, from the catastrophe of fifth grade, Andy had not. He stayed home on Friday and Saturday nights;

he never got invited to parties or to hang out in the park. As far as I knew, I was still his only friend. And though thanks to his mother he had all the right clothes, and dressed like the popular kids—even wore contact lenses some of the time—no one was fooled: hostile jock types who remembered him from the bad old days still pushed him around and called him "Threepio" for his long-ago mistake of wearing a Star Wars shirt to school.

Andy had never been overly talkative, even in childhood, except in occasional pressured bursts (much of our friendship had consisted of wordlessly passing comic books back and forth). Years of harassment at school had rendered him even more close-tongued and uncommunicative—less apt to employ Lovecraftian vocabulary words, more prone to entomb himself in advanced-placement math and science. Math had never interested me much—I was what they called a high verbal—but while I'd fallen short of my early academic promise, in every area, and had no interest in good grades if I had to work for them, Andy was in AP everything and at the very top of our class. (Certainly he would have been sent off to Groton like Platt—a prospect that had terrified him, as far back as third grade—had not his parents worried with some justification about sending away to school a son so persecuted by his classmates that he had once been nearly suffocated at recess by a plastic bag thrown over his head. And there were other worries as well; the reason I knew about Mr. Barbour's time in the "ding farm" was that Andy had told me, in his matter-of-fact way, that his parents were afraid he might have inherited something of the same vulnerability, as he put it.)

During his time home from school with me, Andy apologized for having to study, "but unfortunately it's necessary," he said, sniffling and wiping his nose on his sleeve. His course load was incredibly demanding ("AP Hell on wheels") and he couldn't afford to fall even a day behind. While he labored over what seemed endless amounts of schoolwork (Chem and Calculus, American History, English, Astronomy, Japanese) I sat on the floor with my back against the side of his dresser, counting silently to myself: this time only three days ago she was alive, this time four days, a week. In my mind, I went over all the meals we'd eaten in the days leading up to her death: our last visit to the Greek diner, our last visit to Shun Lee Palace, the last dinner she'd cooked for me (spaghetti carbonara) and the last dinner before that (a dish called chicken Indienne, which she'd learned to make from her mother back in Kansas). Sometimes, to look occupied, I turned through old volumes of *Fullmetal Alchemist* or an illustrated H. G. Wells he had in his room, but even the pictures were more than I could absorb. Mostly I stared out at the pigeons flapping on the window ledge as Andy filled out endless grids in his hiragana workbook, his knee bouncing under the desk as he worked.

Andy's room — originally one large bedroom that the Barbours had divided in half — faced Park Avenue. Horns cried in the crosswalk at rush hour and the light burned gold in the windows across the street, dying down around the same time as the traffic began to thin. As the night wore on (phosphorescent in the streetlamps, violet city midnights that never quite faded to black) I turned from side to side, the low ceiling over the bunk pressing down on me so heavily that sometimes I woke convinced I was lying underneath the bed instead of on top of it.

How was it possible to miss someone as much as I missed my mother? I missed her so much I wanted to die: a hard, physical longing, like a craving for air underwater. Lying awake, I tried to recall all my best memories of her — to freeze her in my mind so I wouldn't forget her — but instead of birthdays and happy times I kept remembering things like how a few days before she was killed she'd stopped me halfway out the door to pick a thread off my school jacket. For some reason, it was one of the clearest memories I had of her: her knitted eyebrows, the precise gesture of her reaching out to me, everything. Several times too — drifting uneasily between dreaming and sleep — I sat up suddenly in bed at the sound of her voice speaking clearly in my head, remarks she might conceivably have made at some point but that I didn't actually remember, things like *Throw me an apple, would you?* and *I wonder if this buttons up the front or the back?* and *This sofa is in a terrible state of disreputableness.*

Light from the street flew in black bands across the floor. Hopelessly, I thought of my bedroom standing empty only a few blocks away: my own narrow bed with the worn red quilt. Glow-in-the-dark stars from the planetarium, a picture postcard of James Whale's *Frankenstein*. The birds were back in the park again, the daffodils were up; this time of year, when the weather got nice, sometimes we woke up extra early in the mornings and walked through the park together instead of taking the bus to the West Side. If only I could go back and change what had happened, keep it from happening somehow. Why hadn't I insisted we get breakfast instead of going to the museum? Why hadn't Mr. Beeman asked us to come in on Tuesday, or Thursday?

Either the second night after my mother died or the third — some time at any rate after Mrs. Barbour took me to the doctor to get my headache seen to — the Barbours were throwing a big party at the apartment that it was too late for them to cancel. There was whispering, a flurry of activity that I could scarcely take in. "I think," said Mrs. Barbour when she came back to Andy's room, "you and Theo might enjoy staying back here." Despite her light tone, clearly it was not a suggestion but an order. "It'll be such a bore, and I really don't think you'll enjoy yourselves at all. I'll ask Etta to bring you a couple of plates from the kitchen."

Andy and I sat side by side on the lower bunk of his bed, eating cocktail shrimp and artichoke canapés from paper plates — or, rather, he ate, while I sat with the plate on my knees, untouched. He had on a DVD, some action movie with exploding robots, showers of metal and flame. From the living room: clinking glasses, smells of candle wax and perfume, every now and then a voice rising brilliantly in laughter. The pianist's sparkling, up-tempo arrangement of "It's All Over Now, Baby Blue" seemed to be floating in from an alternate universe. Everything was lost, I had fallen off the map: the disorientation of being in the wrong apartment, with the wrong family, was wearing me down, so I felt groggy and punch-drunk, weepy almost, like an interrogated prisoner prevented from sleeping for days. Over and over, I kept thinking *I've got to go home* and then, for the millionth time, *I can't.*

iv.

AFTER FOUR DAYS, OR maybe it was five, Andy loaded his books in his stretched-out backpack and returned to school. All that day, and the next, I sat in his room with his television turned to Turner Classic Movies, which was what my mother watched when she was home from work. They were showing movies adapted from Graham Greene: *Ministry of Fear, The Human Factor, The Fallen Idol, This Gun for Hire.* That second evening, while I was waiting for *The Third Man* to come on, Mrs. Barbour (all Valentino-ed up and on her way out the door to an event at the Frick) stopped by Andy's room and announced that I was going back to school the next day. "*Any*body would feel out of sorts," she said. "Back here by yourself. It isn't good for you."

I didn't know what to say. Sitting around on my own watching movies was the only thing I'd done since my mother's death that had felt even vaguely normal.

"It's high time for you to get back into some sort of a routine. Tomorrow. I know it doesn't seem so, Theo," she said when I didn't answer, "but keeping busy is the only thing in the world that'll make you feel better."

Resolutely I stared at the television. I hadn't been at school since the day before my mother died and as long as I stayed away her death seemed unofficial somehow. But once I went back it would be a public fact. Worse: the thought of returning to any kind of normal routine seemed disloyal, wrong. It kept being a shock every time I remembered it, a fresh slap: she was gone. Every new event—everything I did for the rest of my life—would only separate us more and more: days she was no longer a part of, an ever-growing distance between us. Every single day for the rest of my life, she would only be further away.

"Theo."

Startled, I looked up at her.

"One foot after the other. There's no other way to get through this."

The next day, they were having a World War II spy marathon (*Cairo, The Hidden Enemy, Code Name: Emerald*) that I really wanted to stay home and see. Instead, I dragged myself out of bed when Mr. Barbour stuck his head in to wake us ("Up and at 'em, hoplites!") and walked to the bus stop with Andy. It was a rainy day, and cold enough that Mrs. Barbour had forced me into wearing an embarrassing old duffel coat of Platt's over my clothes. Andy's little sister, Kitsey, danced ahead of us in her pink raincoat, skipping through puddles and pretending she didn't know us.

I knew it was going to be horrible and it was, from the second I stepped into the bright hall and smelled the familiar old school smell: citrus disinfectant and something like old socks. Hand-lettered signs in the hallway: sign-up sheets for tennis lab and cooking classes, tryouts for *The Odd Couple,* field trip to Ellis Island and tickets still available for the Swing into Spring concert, hard to believe that the world had ended and yet somehow these ridiculous activities kept grinding on.

The strange thing: the last day I'd been in the building, she was alive. I kept on thinking it, and every time it was new: last time I opened this locker, last time I touched this stupid fucking *Insights in Biology* book, last time I saw Lindy Maisel putting on lip gloss with that plastic wand. It seemed hardly credible that I couldn't follow these moments back to a world where she wasn't dead.

"Sorry." People I knew said it, and people who had never spoken to me in my life. Other people—laughing and talking in the hallways—fell silent when I walked by, throwing grave or quizzical looks my way. Others still ignored me completely, as playful dogs will ignore an ill or injured dog in their midst: by refusing to look at me, by romping and frolicking around me in the hallways as if I weren't there.

Tom Cable, in particular, avoided me as assiduously as if I were a girl he'd dumped. At lunch, he was nowhere to be found. In Spanish (he sauntered in well after class started, missing the awkward scene where everyone crowded somberly around my desk to say they were sorry) he didn't sit by me as usual but up front, slouched down with his legs thrown out to the side. Rain drummed on the windowpanes as we translated our way through a series of bizarre sentences, sentences that would have done Salvador Dalí proud: about lobsters and beach umbrellas, and Marisol with the long eyelashes taking the lime-green taxi to school.

After class, on the way out, I made a point of going up and saying hi as he was getting his books.

"Oh, hey, how's it going," he said—distanced, leaning back with a smart-ass arch to the brow. "I heard an' all."

"Yeah." This was our routine: too cool for everyone else, always in on the same joke.

"Tough luck. That really bites."

"Thanks."

"Hey—shoulda played sick. Told you! My mom blew up over all that shit too. Hit the fucking ceiling! Well, er," he said, half-shrugging in the stunned moment that followed this, looking up, down, around, with a *who, me?* look, like he'd thrown a snowball with a rock in it.

"Anyway. So," he said in a moving-right-along voice. "What's with the costume?"

"What?"

"Well"—ironic little back-step, eyeing the plaid duffel coat—"first place, *definitely,* in the Platt Barbour Look-Alike Contest."

And despite myself — it was a shock, after days of horror and numbness, an eruptive Tourette's-like spasm — I laughed.

"Excellent call, Cable," I said, adopting Platt's hateful drawl. We were good mimics, both of us, and often conducted entire conversations in other people's voices: dumb newscasters, whiny girls, wheedling and fatuous teachers. "Tomorrow I'm coming dressed as you."

But Tom didn't reply in kind or pick up the thread. He'd lost interest. "Errr — maybe not," he said, with a half-shrug, a little smirk. "Later."

"Right, later." I was annoyed — what the fuck was his problem? Yet it was part of our ongoing dark-comedy act, amusing only to us, to abuse and insult each other; and I was pretty sure he'd come find me after English or that he'd catch up with me on the way home, running up behind me and bopping me on the head with his algebra workbook. But he didn't. The next morning before first period he didn't even look at me when I said hi, and his blanked-out expression as he shouldered past stopped me cold. Lindy Maisel and Mandy Quaife turned at their lockers to stare at each other, giggling in a half-shocked way: *oh my God!* Next to me my lab partner, Sam Weingarten, was shaking his head. "What a dick," he said, in a loud voice, so loud everybody in the hall turned. "You're a real dick, Cable, you know that?"

But I didn't care — or, at least, I wasn't hurt or depressed. Instead I was furious. My friendship with Tom had always had a wild, manic quality, something unhinged and hectic and a little perilous about it, and though all the same old high energy was still there, the current had reversed, voltage humming in the opposite direction so that now instead of horsing around with him in study hall I wanted to push his head in the urinal, yank his arm out of the socket, beat his face bloody on the sidewalk, make him eat dogshit and garbage off the curb. The more I thought about it, the more enraged I grew, so mad sometimes that I walked back and forth in the bathroom muttering to myself. If Cable hadn't fingered me to Mr. Beeman ("I know, now, Theo, those cigarettes weren't yours")...if Cable hadn't got me suspended...if my mom hadn't taken the day off...if we hadn't been at the museum at exactly the wrong time...well, even Mr. Beeman had apologized for it, sort of. Because, sure, there were issues with my grades (and plenty of other stuff Mr. Beeman didn't know about) but the inciting incident, the thing that had got me called in, the whole business with the cigarettes in the courtyard—whose fault was that? Cable's. It wasn't like I expected him to apologize. In fact it wasn't like I would have said anything to him about it, ever. Only—now I was a pariah? Persona non grata? He wouldn't even talk to me? I was smaller than Cable but not by a lot, and whenever he cracked wise in class, as he couldn't prevent himself from doing, or ran past me in the hall with his new best friends Billy Wagner and Thad Randolph (the way we'd once raced around together, always in overdrive, that urge to danger and craziness)—all I could think was how much I wanted to beat the shit out of him, girls laughing as he cowered from me in tears: *oooh, Tom! boo hoo hoo! are you crying?* (Doing my best to provoke a fight, I cracked him in the nose accidentally on purpose by swinging the bathroom door in his face, and shoved him into the drinks dispenser so he dropped his disgusting cheese fries on the floor, but instead of jumping on me—as I longed for him to do—he only smirked and walked off without a word.)

Not everyone avoided me, of course. Lots of people put notes and gifts in my locker (including Isabella Cushing and Martina Lichtblau, the most popular girls in my year) and my old enemy Win Temple from fifth grade surprised me by coming up and giving me a bear hug. But most people responded to me with a cautious, half-terrified politeness. It wasn't as if I went around crying or even acting disturbed but still they'd stop in the middle of their conversations if I sat down with them at lunch.

Grown-ups, on the other hand, paid me an uncomfortable amount of attention. I was advised to keep a journal, talk with my friends, make a "memory collage" (crackpot advice, as far as I was concerned; other kids were uneasy around me no matter how normally I acted, and the last thing I wanted was to call attention to myself by sharing my feelings with people or doing therapeutic crafts in the Arts room). I seemed to spend an inordinate amount of time standing in empty classrooms and offices (staring at the floor, nodding my head senselessly) with concerned teachers who asked me to stay after class or pulled me aside to talk. My English teacher, Mr. Neuspeil, after sitting on the side of his desk and delivering a tense account of his own mother's horrifying death at the hands of an incompetent surgeon, had patted me on the back and given me a blank notebook to write in; Mrs. Swanson, the school counselor, showed me a couple of breathing exercises and suggested that I might find it helpful to discharge my grief by going outside and throwing ice cubes against a tree;

and even Mr. Borowsky (who taught math, and was considerably less bright-eyed than most of the other teachers) took me aside out in the hall and—talking very quietly, with his face about two inches away from mine—told me how guilty he'd felt after his brother had died in a car accident. (Guilt came up a lot in these talks. Did my teachers believe, as I did, that I was guilty of causing my mother's death? Apparently so.) Mr. Borowsky had felt so guilty for letting his brother drive home drunk from the party that night that he'd even thought for a brief while about killing himself. Maybe I'd thought about suicide too. But suicide wasn't the answer.

I accepted all this counsel politely, with a glassy smile and a glaring sense of unreality. Many adults seemed to interpret this numbness as a positive sign; I remember particularly Mr. Beeman (an overly clipped Brit in a dumb tweed motoring cap, whom despite his solicitude I had come to hate, irrationally, as an agent of my mother's death) complimenting me on my maturity and informing me that I seemed to be "coping awfully well." And maybe I *was* coping awfully well, I don't know. Certainly I wasn't howling aloud or punching my fist through windows or doing any of the things I imagined people might do who felt as I did. But sometimes, unexpectedly, grief pounded over me in waves that left me gasping; and when the waves washed back, I found myself looking out over a brackish wreck which was illumined in a light so lucid, so heartsick and empty, that I could hardly remember that the world had ever been anything but dead.

V.

QUITE HONESTLY, MY DECKER grandparents were the last thing on my mind, which was just as well since Social Services was unable to run them down right away on the scanty information I had given them. Then Mrs. Barbour knocked at the door of Andy's room and said, "Theo, may we speak for a moment, please?"

Something in her manner spoke distinctly of bad news, though in my situation it was hard to imagine how things could possibly be worse. When we were seated in the living room—by a three foot tall arrangement of pussy willow and blossoming apple branches fresh from the florist—she crossed her legs and said: "I've had a call from the Social Services. They've contacted your grandparents. Unfortunately it seems that your grand-mother is unwell."

For a moment I was confused. "Dorothy?"

"If that's what you call her, yes."

"Oh. She's not really my grandmother."

"I see," said Mrs. Barbour, as if she didn't actually see and didn't want to. "At any rate. It seems she's not well — a back ailment, I believe — and your grandfather is looking after her. So the thing is, you see, I'm sure they're very sorry, but they say it's not practical for you to be down there right now. Not to stay with them in their home, anyway," she added, when I didn't say anything. "They've offered to pay for you to stay in a Holiday Inn near their house, for the time being, but that seems a bit impractical, doesn't it?"

There was an unpleasant buzzing in my ears. Sitting there under her level, ice-gray gaze, I felt for some reason terribly ashamed of myself. I had dreaded the thought of going to Grandpa Decker and Dorothy so much that I'd blocked them almost completely from my mind, but it was quite another thing to know they didn't want me.

A flicker of sympathy passed over her face. "You mustn't feel bad about it," she said. "And in any case you mustn't worry. It's been settled that you'll stay with us for the next few weeks and at the very least, finish your year at school. Everyone agrees that's best. By the way," she said, leaning closer, "that's a lovely ring. Is that a family thing?"

"Um, yes," I said. For reasons I would have found hard to explain, I had taken to carrying the old man's ring with me almost everywhere I went. Mostly I toyed around with it while it was in my jacket pocket, but every now and then I slipped it on my middle finger and wore it, even though it was too big and slid around a bit.

"Interesting. Your mother's family, or your father's?"

"My mother's," I said, after a slight pause, not liking the way the con-versation was going.

"May I see it?"

I took it off and dropped it in her palm. She held it up to the lamp. "Lovely," she said, "carnelian. And this intaglio. Greco-Roman? Or a family crest?"

"Um, crest. I think."

She examined the clawed, mythological beast. "It looks like a griffin.

Or maybe a winged lion." She turned it sideways into the light and looked inside of the ring. "And this engraving?"

My expression of puzzlement made her frown. "Don't tell me you never noticed it. Hang on." She got up and went to the desk, which had lots of intricate drawers and cubbyholes, and returned with a magnifying glass.

"This will be better than my reading glasses," she said, peering through it. "Still this old copperplate is hard to see." She brought the magnifying glass close, then farther away. "Blackwell. Does that ring a bell?"

"Ah—" In fact it did, something beyond words, but the thought had blown away and vanished before it fully materialized.

"I see some Greek letters, too. Very interesting." She dropped the ring back in my hand. "It's an old ring," she said. "You can tell by the patina on the stone and by the way it's worn down—see there? Americans used to pick up these classical intaglios in Europe, back in the Henry James days, and have them set as rings. Souvenirs of the Grand Tour."

"If they don't want me, where am I going to go?"

For a blink, Mrs. Barbour looked taken aback. Almost immediately she recovered herself and said: "Well, I wouldn't worry about that now. It's probably best anyway for you to stay here a bit longer and finish out your year at school, don't you agree? Now"—she nodded—"be careful with that ring and mind that you don't lose it. I can see how loose it is. You might want to put it someplace safe instead of wearing it around like that."

vi.

BUT I DID WEAR IT. Or—rather—I ignored her advice to put it in a safe place, and continued to carry it around in my pocket. When I hefted it in my palm, it was very heavy; if I closed my fingers around it, the gold got warm from the heat of my hand but the carved stone stayed cool. Its weighty, antiquated quality, its mixture of sobriety and brightness, were strangely comforting; if I fixed my attention on it intensely enough, it had a strange power to anchor me in my drifting state and shut out the world around me, but for all that, I really didn't want to think about where it had come from.

Nor did I want to think about my future—for though I had scarcely been looking forward to a new life in rural Maryland, at the chill mercies of my Decker grandparents, I now began to seriously worry about what was going to happen to me. Everyone seemed profoundly shocked at the Holiday Inn idea, as if Grandpa Decker and Dorothy had suggested I move into a shed in their back yard, but to me it didn't seem so bad. I'd always wanted to live in a hotel, and even if the Holiday Inn wasn't the kind of hotel I'd imagined, certainly I would manage: room service hamburgers, pay-per-view, a pool in summer, how bad could it be?

Everyone (the social workers, Dave the shrink, Mrs. Barbour) kept telling me again and again that I could not possibly live on my own at a Holiday Inn in suburban Maryland, that no matter what, it would never actually come to that—not seeming to realize that their supposedly comforting words were only increasing my anxiety a hundredfold. "The thing to remember," said Dave, the psychiatrist who had been assigned to me by the city, "is that you'll be taken care of no matter what." He was a thirtyish guy with dark clothes and trendy eyeglasses who always looked as if he'd just come from a poetry reading in the basement of some church. "Because there are tons of people looking out for you who only want what's best for you."

I had grown suspicious of strangers talking about what was best for me, as it was exactly what the social workers had said before the subject of the foster home came up. "But—I don't think my grandparents are so wrong," I said.

"Wrong about what?"

"About the Holiday Inn. It might be an okay place for me to be."

"Are you saying that things are not okay for you at your grandparents' home?" said Dave, without missing a beat.

"No!" I hated this about him—how he was always putting words in my mouth.

"All right then. Maybe we can phrase it another way." He folded his hands, and thought. "Why would you rather live at a hotel than with your grandparents?"

"I didn't say that."

He put his head to the side. "No, but from the way you keep bringing up the Holiday Inn, like it's a viable choice, I'm hearing you say that's what you prefer to do."

"It seems a lot better than going into a foster home."

"Yes—" he leaned forward—"but please hear me say this. You're only thirteen. And you just lost your primary caregiver. Living alone right now is really not an option for you. What I'm trying to say is that it's too bad your grandparents are dealing with these health issues, but believe me, I'm sure we can work out something much better once your grandmother is up and around."

I said nothing. Clearly he had never met Grandpa Decker and Dorothy. Though I hadn't been around them very much myself, the main thing I remembered was the complete absence of blood feeling between us, the opaque way they looked at me as if I was some random kid who'd wandered over from the mall. The prospect of going to live with them was almost literally unimaginable and I'd been racking my brains trying to remember what I could about my last visit to their house — which wasn't very much, as I'd been only seven or eight years old. There had been hand-stitched sayings framed and hanging on the walls, a plastic countertop contraption that Dorothy used to dehydrate foods in. At some point — after Grandpa Decker had yelled at me to keep my sticky little mitts off his train set — my dad had gone outside for a cigarette (it was winter) and not come back inside the house. "Jesus God," my mother had said, once we were out in the car (it had been her idea that I should get to know my father's family), and after that we never went back.

Several days after the Holiday Inn offer, a greeting card arrived for me at the Barbours'. (An aside: is it wrong to think that Bob and Dorothy, as they signed themselves, should have picked up the telephone and called me? Or got in their car and driven to the city to see about me themselves? But they did neither of these things — not that I exactly expected them to rush to my side with wails of sympathy, but still, it would have been nice if they'd surprised me with some small, if uncharacteristic, gesture of affection.)

Actually, the card was from Dorothy (the "Bob," plainly in her hand, had been squeezed in alongside her own signature as an afterthought). The envelope, interestingly, had the look of having been steamed open and resealed — by Mrs. Barbour? Social Services? — although the card itself was definitely in Dorothy's stiff up-and-down European handwriting that appeared exactly once a year on our Christmas cards, writing that — as my father had once commented — looked as if it ought to be on the chalkboard at La Goulue listing the daily fish specials. On the front of

the card was a drooping tulip, and—underneath—a printed slogan:
THERE ARE NO ENDINGS.

Dorothy, from the very little I remembered of her, was not one to
waste words, and this card was no exception. After a perfectly cordial
opening—sorry for my tragic loss, thinking of me in this time of
sorrow—she offered to send me a bus ticket to Woodbriar, MD, while
simultaneously alluding to vague medical conditions that made it difficult
for her and Grandpa Decker to "meet the demands" for my care.

"Demands?" said Andy. "She makes it sound as if you're asking for ten
million in unmarked notes."

I was silent. Oddly, it was the picture on the greeting card that had
troubled me. It was the kind of thing you'd see in a drugstore card rack,
perfectly normal, but still a photograph of a wilted flower—no matter
how artistically done—didn't seem quite the thing to send to somebody
whose mother had just died.

"I thought she was supposed to be so sick. Why's she the one
writing?"

"Search me." I had wondered the same thing; it did seem weird that
my actual grandfather hadn't included a message or even bothered to sign
his own name.

"Maybe," said Andy gloomily, "your grandfather has Alzheimer's and
she's holding him prisoner in his own home. To get his money. That happens quite frequently with the younger wives, you know."

"I don't think he has that much money."

"Possibly not," said Andy, clearing his throat ostentatiously. "But one
can never rule out the thirst for power. 'Nature red in tooth and claw.' Perhaps she doesn't want you edging in on the inheritance."

"Chum," said Andy's father, looking up rather suddenly from the
Financial Times, "I don't think this is a terribly productive line of
conversation."

"Well, quite honestly, I don't see why Theo can't stay on with us," said
Andy, voicing my own thoughts. "I enjoy the company and there's plenty
of space in my room."

"Well certainly we'd all like to keep him for ourselves," said Mr. Barbour, with a heartiness not as full or convincing as I would have liked.
"But what would his family think? The last I heard, kidnapping was still
against the law."

"Well, I mean, Daddy, that hardly seems to be the situation here," said Andy, in his irritating, faraway voice.

Abruptly Mr. Barbour got up, with his club soda in his hand. He wasn't allowed to drink because of the medicine he took. "Theo, I forget. Do you know how to sail?"

It took me a moment to realize what he'd asked me. "No."

"Oh, that's too bad. Andy had *the* most outstanding time at his sailing camp up in Maine last year, didn't you?"

Andy was silent. He had told me, many times, that it was the worst two weeks of his life.

"Do you know how to read nautical flags?" Mr. Barbour asked me.

"Sorry?" I said.

"There's an excellent chart in my study I'd be happy to show you. Don't make that face, Andy. It's a perfectly handy skill for any boy to know."

"Certainly it is, if he needs to hail a passing tugboat."

"These smart remarks of yours are very tiresome," said Mr. Barbour, although he looked more distracted than annoyed. "Besides," he said, turning to me, "I think you'd be surprised how often nautical flags pop up in parades and movies and, I don't know, on the stage."

Andy pulled a face. "*The stage*," he said derisively.

Mr. Barbour turned to look at him. "Yes, *the stage*. Do you find the term amusing?"

"Pompous is a lot more like it."

"Well, I'm afraid I fail to see what you find so pompous about it. Certainly it's the very word your great-grandmother would have used." (Mr. Barbour's grandfather had been dropped from the Social Register for marrying Olga Osgood, a minor movie actress.)

"My point exactly."

"Then what would you have me call it?"

"Actually, Daddy, what I would really like to know is the last time you saw nautical flags showcased in *any* theatrical production."

"*South Pacific*," said Mr. Barbour swiftly.

"Besides *South Pacific*."

"I rest my case."

"I don't believe you and Mother even saw *South Pacific*."

"For God's sake, Andy."

"Well, even if you did. One example doesn't sufficiently establish your case."

"I refuse to continue this absurd conversation. Come along, Theo."

vii.

FROM THIS POINT ON, I began trying especially hard to be a good guest: to make my bed in the mornings; to always say thank you and please, and to do everything I knew my mother would want me to do. Unfortunately the Barbours didn't exactly have the kind of household where you could show your appreciation by babysitting the younger siblings or pitching in with the dishes. Between the woman who came to look after the plants — a depressing job, since there was so little light in the apartment the plants mostly died — and Mrs. Barbour's assistant, whose main job seemed to be rearranging the closets and the china collection — they had somewhere in the neighborhood of eight people working for them. (When I'd asked Mrs. Barbour where the washing machine was, she'd looked at me as if I'd asked for lye and lard to boil up for soap.)

But though nothing was required of me, still the effort to blend into their polished and complicated household was an immense strain. I was desperate to vanish into the background — to slip invisibly among the Chinoiserie patterns like a fish in a coral reef — and yet it seemed I drew unwanted attention to myself hundreds of times a day: by having to ask for every little item, whether a wash cloth or the Band-Aids or the pencil sharpener; by not having a key, always having to ring when I came and went — even by my well-intentioned efforts to make my own bed in the morning (it was better just to let Irenka or Esperenza do it, Mrs. Barbour explained, as they were used to doing it and did a better job with the corners). I broke off a finial on an antique coat stand by throwing open a door; twice managed to set off the burglar alarm by mistake; and even blundered into Mr. and Mrs. Barbour's room one night when I was looking for the bathroom.

Luckily, Andy's parents were around so little that my presence didn't seem to inconvenience them very much. Unless Mrs. Barbour was entertaining, she was out of the apartment from about eleven a.m. — popping in for a couple of hours before dinner, for a gin and lime and what she called "a bit of a tub" — and then not home again until we were in bed. Of Mr. Barbour I saw even less, except on weekends and when he was sitting around after work with his napkin-wrapped glass of club soda, waiting for Mrs. Barbour to dress for their evening out.

By far the biggest issue I faced was Andy's siblings. Though Platt, luckily, was off terrorizing younger children at Groton, still Kitsey and the youngest brother, Toddy, who was only seven, clearly resented having me around to usurp what minor attention they got from their parents. There were a lot of tantrums and pouting, a lot of eye rolling and hostile giggling on Kitsey's part, as well as a baffling (to me) upset — never fully resolved — where she complained to her friends and the housekeepers and anyone who would listen that I'd been going in her room and messing around with the piggy-bank collection on the shelf above her desk. As for Toddy, he grew more and more disturbed as the weeks went by and still I was there; at breakfast, he gaped at me unashamed and frequently asked questions that made his mother reach under the table and pinch him. Where did I live? How much longer was I going to stay with them? Did I have a dad? Then where was he?

"Good question," I said, provoking horrified laughter from Kitsey, who was popular at school and — at nine — as pretty in her white-blonde way as Andy was plain.

viii.

PROFESSIONAL MOVERS WERE COMING, at some point, to pack my mother's things and put them in storage. Before they came, I was to go to the apartment and pick out anything I wanted or needed. I was aware of the painting in a nagging but vague way which was entirely out of proportion to its actual importance, as if it were a school project I'd left unfinished. At some point I was going to have to get it back to the museum, though I still hadn't quite figured out how I was going to do that without causing a huge fuss.

Already I had missed one chance to give it back — when Mrs. Barbour had turned away some investigators who had shown up at the apartment looking for me. That is: I understood they were investigators or even police from what Kellyn, the Welsh girl who looked after the younger children, told me. She had been bringing Toddy home from day care when the strangers showed up asking for me. "Suits, you know?" she said, raising a significant eyebrow. She was a heavy, fast-talking girl with cheeks so flushed she always looked like she'd been standing next to a fire. "They had that look."

I was too afraid to ask what she meant by *that look;* and when I went in, cautiously, to see what Mrs. Barbour had to say about it, she was busy. "I'm sorry," she said, without quite looking at me, "but can we please talk about this later?" Guests were arriving in half an hour, among them a well-known architect and a famous dancer with the New York City Ballet; she was fretting over the loose catch to her necklace and upset because the air conditioner wasn't working properly.

"Am I in trouble?"

It slipped out before I knew what I was saying. Mrs. Barbour stopped. "Theo, don't be ridiculous," she said. "They were perfectly nice, very considerate, it's just that I can't have them sitting around just now. Turning up, without telephoning. Anyway, I told them it wasn't the best time, which of course they could see for themselves." She gestured at the caterers darting back and forth, the building engineer on a ladder, examining inside the air-conditioning vent with a flashlight. "Now run along. Where's Andy?"

"He'll be home in an hour. His astronomy class went to the planetarium."

"Well, there's food in the kitchen. I don't have a lot of the miniature tarts to spare, but you can have all the finger sandwiches you want. And after the cake's cut, you're welcome to have some of that too."

Her manner had been so unconcerned that I forgot about the visitors until they showed up at school three days later, at my geometry class, one young, one older, indifferently dressed, knocking courteously at the open door. "We see Theodore Decker?" the younger, Italian-looking guy said to Mr. Borowsky as the older one peered cordially inside the classroom.

"We just want to talk to you, is that okay?" said the older guy as we walked down to the dreaded conference room where I was to have had the meeting with Mr. Beeman and my mother on the day she died. "Don't be scared." He was a dark-skinned black man with a gray goatee — tough-looking but nice-seeming too, like a cool cop on a television show. "We're just trying to piece together a lot of things about that day and we hope you can help us."

I had been frightened at first, but when he said *don't be scared,* I believed him — until he pushed open the door of the conference room. There sat my tweed-cap nemesis Mr. Beeman, pompous as ever with his waistcoat and watch chain; Enrique my social worker; Mrs. Swanson the school counselor (the same person who had told me I might feel better if I threw some ice cubes against a tree); Dave the psychiatrist in his customary black Levi's and turtleneck — and, of all people, Mrs. Barbour, in heels and a pearl-gray suit that looked like it cost more money than all the other people in the room made in a month.

My panic must have been written plainly on my face. Maybe I wouldn't have been quite so alarmed if I'd understood a little better what wasn't clear to me at the time: that I was a minor, and that my parent or guardian had to be present at an official interview — which was why anyone even vaguely construed as my advocate had been called in. But all I understood, when I saw all those faces and a tape recorder in the middle of the table, was that the official parties had convened to judge my fate and dispose of me as they saw fit.

Stiffly I sat and endured their warm-up questions (did I have any hobbies? Did I play any sports?) until it became clear to everyone that the preliminary chit-chat wasn't loosening me up very much.

The bell rang for the end of class. Bang of lockers, murmur of voices out in the hall. "You're *dead,* Thalheim," some boy shouted gleefully.

The Italian guy — Ray, he said his name was — pulled up a chair in front of me, knee to knee. He was young, but heavy, with the air of a good-natured limo driver, and his downturned eyes had a moist, liquid, sleepy look, as if he drank.

"We just want to know what you remember," he said. "Probe around in your memory, get a general picture of that morning, you know? Because maybe by remembering some of the little things, you might remember something that will help us."

He was sitting so close I could smell his deodorant. "Like what?"

"Like what you ate for breakfast that morning. That's a good place to start, huh?"

"Um —" I stared at the gold ID bracelet on his wrist. This wasn't what

I'd been expecting them to ask. The truth was: we hadn't eaten breakfast at all that morning because I was in trouble at school and my mother was mad at me, but I was too embarrassed to say that.

"You don't remember?"

"Pancakes," I burst out desperately.

"Oh yeah?" Ray looked at me shrewdly. "Your mother make them?"

"Yes."

"What'd she put in them? Blueberries, chocolate chips?"

I nodded.

"Both?"

I could feel everybody looking at me. Then Mr. Beeman said— as loftily as if he were standing in front of his Morals in Society class—"There's no reason to invent an answer, if you don't remember."

The black guy—in the corner, with a notepad—gave Mr. Beeman a sharp warning glance.

"Actually, there seems to be some memory impairment," interjected Mrs. Swanson in a low voice, toying with the glasses that hung from a chain around her neck. She was a grandmother who wore flowing white shirts and had a long gray braid down her back. Kids who got sent to her office for guidance called her "the Swami." In her counseling sessions with me at school, besides dispensing the advice about the ice cubes, she had taught me a three-part breath to help release my emotions and made me draw a mandala representing my wounded heart. "He hit his head. Didn't you, Theo?"

"Is that true?" said Ray, glancing up at me frankly.

"Yes."

"Did you get it checked out by a doctor?"

"Not right away," said Mrs. Swanson.

Mrs. Barbour crossed her ankles. "I took him to the emergency room at New York–Presbyterian," she said coolly. "When he got to my house, he was complaining of a headache. It was a day or so before we had it seen to. Nobody seems to have thought to ask him if he was hurt or not."

Enrique, the social worker, began to speak up at this, but after a look from the older black cop (whose name has just come back to me: Morris) fell silent.

"Look, Theo," said the guy Ray, tapping me on the knee. "I know you want to help us out. You do want to help us, don't you?"

I nodded.

"That's great. But if we ask you something and you don't know? It's okay to say you don't know."

"We just want to throw a whole lot of questions out there and see if we can draw your memory out about anything," Morris said. "Are you cool with that?"

"You need anything?" said Ray, eyeing me closely. "A drink of water, maybe? A soda?"

I shook my head—no sodas were allowed on school property—just as Mr. Beeman said: "Sorry, no sodas permitted on school property."

Ray made a *give me a break* face that I wasn't sure if Mr. Beeman saw or not. "Sorry, kid, I tried," he said, turning back to me. "I'll run out and get you a soda at the deli if you feel like it later on, how about it? Now." He clapped his hands together. "How long do you think you and your mother were in the building prior to the first explosion?"

"About an hour, I guess."

"You guess or you know?"

"I guess."

"You think it was more than an hour? Less than an hour?"

"I don't think it was more than an hour," I said, after a long pause.

"Describe to us your recollection of the incident."

"I didn't see what happened," I said. "Everything was fine and then there was a loud flash and a bang—"

"A loud flash?"

"That's not what I meant. I meant the bang was loud."

"You said a bang," said the guy Morris, stepping forward. "Do you think you might be able to describe to us in a little more detail what the bang sounded like?"

"I don't know. Just...loud," I added, when they kept on looking at me like they expected something more.

In the silence that followed, I heard a stealthy clicking: Mrs. Barbour, with her head down, discreetly checking her BlackBerry for messages.

Morris cleared his throat. "What about a smell?"

"Excuse me?"

"Did you notice any particular smell in the moments prior?"

"I don't think so."

"Nothing at all? You sure?"

As the questioning wore on—the same stuff over and over, switched around a little to confuse me, with every now and then something new thrown in—I steeled myself and waited hopelessly for them to work around to the painting. I would simply have to admit it and face the consequences, no matter what the consequences were (probably fairly dire, since I was well on my way to becoming a Ward of the State). At a couple of points, I was on the verge of blurting it out, in my terror. But the more questions they asked (where was I when I'd hit my head? Who had I seen or spoken to on my way downstairs?) the more it dawned on me that they didn't know a thing about what had happened to me—what room I'd been in when the bomb exploded, or even what exit I'd taken out of the building.

They had a floor plan; the rooms had numbers instead of names, Gallery 19A and Gallery 19B, numbers and letters in a mazelike arrangement all the way up to 27. "Were you here when the initial blast occurred?" Ray said, pointing. "Or here?"

"I don't know."

"Take your time."

"I don't know," I repeated, a bit frantically. The diagram of the rooms had a confusing, computer-generated quality, like something from a video game or a reconstruction of Hitler's bunker that I'd seen on the History Channel, that in truth didn't make any sense or seem to represent the space as I remembered it.

He pointed to a different spot. "This square?" he said. "That's a display plinth, with paintings on it. I know these rooms all look alike, but maybe you can remember where you were in relation to that?"

I stared hopelessly at the diagram and didn't answer. (Part of the reason it looked so unfamiliar was that they were showing me the area where my mother's body was found—rooms away from where I'd been when the bomb went off—although I didn't realize that until later.)

"You didn't see anybody on your way out," said Morris encouragingly, repeating what I'd already told them.

I shook my head.

"Nothing you remember at all?"

"Well, I mean—bodies covered up. Equipment lying around."

"Nobody coming in or out of the area of the explosion."

"I didn't see anybody," I repeated doggedly. We had been over this.

"So you never saw firemen or rescue personnel."

"No."

"I suppose we can establish, then, that they'd been ordered out of the building by the time you came to. So we're talking about a time lapse of forty minutes to an hour and a half after the initial explosion. Is that a safe assumption?"

I shrugged, limply.

"Is that a yes or a no?"

Staring at the floor. "I don't know."

"What don't you know?"

"I don't know," I said again, and the silence that followed was so long and uncomfortable I thought I might break down crying.

"Do you recall hearing the second blast?"

"Pardon me for asking," said Mr. Beeman, "but is this really necessary?"

Ray, my questioner, turned. "Excuse me?"

"I'm not sure I see the purpose of putting him through this."

With careful neutrality, Morris said: "We're investigating a crime scene. It's our job to find out what happened in there."

"Yes, but surely you must have other means of doing so for such routine matters. I would think they had all manner and variety of security cameras in there."

"Sure they do," said Ray, rather sharply. "Except cameras can't see through dust and smoke. Or if they're blown up to face the ceiling. Now," he said, settling back in his chair with a sigh. "You mentioned smoke. Did you smell it or see it?"

I nodded.

"Which one? Saw or smelled?"

"Both."

"What direction do you think it was coming from?"

I was about to say I didn't know again, but Mr. Beeman had not finished making his point. "Forgive me, but I entirely fail to see the purpose in security cameras if they don't operate in an emergency," he said, to the room in general. "With technology today, and all that artwork —"

Ray turned his head as if to say something angry, but Morris, standing in the corner, raised his hand and spoke up.

"The boy's an important witness. The surveillance system isn't designed to withstand an event like this. Now, I'm sorry, but if you can't stop it with the comments we'll have to ask you to leave, sir."

"I'm here as this child's advocate. I've the right to ask questions."

"Not unless they pertain directly to the child's welfare."

"Oddly enough, I was under the impression that they did."

At this Ray, in the chair in front of me, turned around. "Sir? If you continue to obstruct the proceedings?" he said. "You *will* have to leave the room."

"I have no intention of obstructing you," said Mr. Beeman in the tense silence that followed. "Nothing could be further from my mind, I assure you. Go on, please continue," he said, with an irritated flick of the hand. "Far be it from me to stop you."

On the questioning dragged. What direction had the smoke come from? What color was the flash? Who went in and out of the area in the moments prior? Had I noticed anything unusual, anything at all, before or after? I looked at the pictures they showed me—innocent vacation faces, nobody I recognized. Passport photos of Asian tourists and senior citizens, moms and acned teenagers smiling against blue studio backgrounds—ordinary faces, unmemorable, yet all somehow smelling of tragedy. Then we went back to the diagram. Could I maybe just try, just one more time, to pinpoint my location on this map? Here, or here? What about here?

"I don't remember." I kept on saying it: partly because I really wasn't sure, partly because I was frightened and anxious for the interview to come to a close, but also because there was an air of restlessness and distinct impatience in the room; the other adults seemed already to have agreed silently among themselves that I didn't know anything, and should be left alone.

And then, before I knew it, it was over. "Theo," said Ray, standing up and placing a meaty hand on my shoulder, "I want to thank you, buddy, for doing what you could for us."

"That's okay," I said, jarred by how abruptly it had all come to an end.

"I know exactly how hard this was for you. Nobody but nobody wants to relive this type of stuff. It's like—" he made a picture frame with his hands—"we're putting together pieces of a jigsaw puzzle, trying to figure out what went on in there, and you've maybe got some pieces of the puzzle that nobody else has got. You really helped us a lot by letting us talk to you."

"If you remember anything else," said Morris, leaning in to give me a card (which Mrs. Barbour quickly intercepted and tucked in her purse), "you'll call us, won't you? You'll remind him, won't you, miss," he said to Mrs. Barbour, "to phone us if he has anything else to say? The office number's right on that card but—" he took a pen from his pocket—"you don't mind, can I have it back for a second, please?"

Without a word, Mrs. Barbour opened her bag and handed the card back to him.

"Right, right." He clicked the pen out and scribbled a number on the back. "That's my cell phone there. You can always leave a message at my office, but if you can't reach me there, phone me on my cell, all right?"

As everyone was milling around the entrance, Mrs. Swanson floated up and put her arm around me, in the cozy way she had. "Hi there," she said, confidentially, as if she were my tightest friend in the world. "How's it going?"

I looked away, made an *okay, I guess* face.

She stroked my arm like I was her favorite cat. "Good for you. I know that must have been tough. Would you like to go to my office for a few minutes?"

With dismay, I noticed Dave the psychiatrist hovering in the background, and behind him Enrique, hands on hips, with an expectant half-smile on his face.

"Please," I said, and my desperation must have been audible in my voice, "I want to get back to class."

She squeezed my arm, and—I noticed—threw a glance at Dave and Enrique. "Sure," she said. "Where are you this period? I'll walk you down."

ix.

BY THEN IT WAS English—last class of the day. We were studying the poetry of Walt Whitman:

Jupiter shall emerge, be patient, watch again another night, the Pleiades
shall emerge,

They are immortal, all those stars both silvery and golden shall shine out
again

Vacant faces. The classroom was hot and drowsy in the late afternoon, windows open, traffic noises floating up from West End Avenue. Kids leaned on their elbows and drew pictures in the margins of their spiral notebooks.

I stared out the window, out at the grimy water tank on the roof opposite. The interrogation (as I thought of it) had disturbed me greatly, kicking up a wall of the disjointed sensations that crashed over me at unexpected moments: a choking burn of chemicals and smoke, sparks and wires, the blanched chill of emergency lights, overpowering enough to blank me out. It happened at random times, at school or out on the street—frozen in mid-step as it washed over me again, the girl's eyes locked on mine in the queer, skewed instant before the world blew apart. Sometimes I'd come to, uncertain what had just been said to me, to find my lab partner in biology staring at me, or the guy whose way I was blocking in front of the cold-drinks case at the Korean market saying *look kid, move it, I aint got all day.*

Then dearest child mournest thou only for Jupiter?
Considerest thou alone the burial of the stars?

They had shown me no photographs I recognized of the girl—or of the old man either. Quietly, I put my left hand in my jacket pocket and felt around for the ring. On our vocabulary list a few days before we'd had the word *consanguinity:* joined in blood. The old man's face had been so torn up and ruined I couldn't even say exactly what he'd looked like, and yet I remembered all too well the warm slick feel of his blood on my hands— especially since in some way the blood was still there, I could still smell it and taste it in my mouth, and it made me understand why people talked about blood brothers and how blood bound people together. My English class had read *Macbeth* in the fall, but only now was it starting to make sense why Lady Macbeth could never scrub the blood off her hands, why it was still there after she washed it away.

X.

BECAUSE, APPARENTLY, SOMETIMES I woke Andy by thrashing and crying out in my sleep, Mrs. Barbour had started giving me a little green pill called Elavil that she explained would keep me from being scared at night. This was embarrassing, especially since my dreams weren't even full-blown nightmares but only troubled interludes where my mother was working late and stranded without a ride—sometimes upstate, in some burned-out area with junked cars and chained dogs barking in the yards. Uneasily I searched for her in service elevators and abandoned buildings, waited for her in the dark at strange bus stops, glimpsed women who looked like her in the windows of passing trains and just missed grabbing up the telephone when she called me at the Barbours' house—disappointments and near-misses that thumped me around and woke me with a sharp hiss of breath, lying queasy and sweaty in the morning light. The bad part wasn't trying to find her, but waking up and remembering she was dead.

With the green pills, even these dreams faded into airless murk. (It strikes me now, though it didn't then, that Mrs. Barbour was well out of line by giving me unprescribed medication on top of the yellow capsules and tiny orange footballs Dave the Shrink had prescribed me.) Sleep, when it came, was like tumbling into a pit, and often I had a hard time waking up in the morning.

"Black tea, that's the ticket," said Mr. Barbour one morning when I was nodding off at breakfast, pouring me a cup from his own well-stewed pot. "Assam Supreme. As strong as Mother makes it. It'll flush the medication right out of your system. Judy Garland? Before shows? Well, my grandmother told me that Sid Luft used to always phone down to the Chinese restaurant for a big pot of tea to knock all the barbs out of her system, this was London, I believe, the Palladium, and strong tea was the only thing that did the trick, sometimes they'd have a hard time waking her up, you know, just getting her out of bed and dressed—"

"He can't drink that, it's like battery acid," said Mrs. Barbour, dropping in two sugar cubes and pouring in a heavy slug of cream before she handed the cup over to me. "Theo, I hate to keep harping on this, but you really must eat something."

"Okay," I said sleepily, but without moving to take a bite of my blueberry muffin. Food tasted like cardboard; I hadn't been hungry in weeks.

"Would you rather have cinnamon toast? Or oatmeal?"

"It's completely ridiculous that you won't let us have coffee," said Andy, who was in the habit of buying himself a huge Starbucks on the way to school and on the way home every afternoon, without his parents' knowledge. "You're very behind the times on this."

"Possibly," Mrs. Barbour said coldly.

"Even half a cup would help. It's unreasonable for you to expect me to go into Advanced Placement Chemistry at 8:45 in the morning with no caffeine."

"Sob, sob," said Mr. Barbour, without looking up from the paper.

"Your attitude is very unhelpful. Everyone else is allowed to drink it."

"I happen to know that's not true," said Mrs. Barbour. "Betsy Ingersoll told me—"

"Maybe Mrs. Ingersoll doesn't let *Sabine* drink coffee, but it would take a whole lot more than a cup of coffee to get Sabine Ingersoll into Advanced Placement anything."

"That's uncalled for, Andy, and very unkind."

"Well, it's only the truth," said Andy coolly. "Sabine is as dumb as a post. I suppose she may as well safeguard her health since she has so little else going for her."

"Brains aren't everything, darling. Would you eat an egg if Etta poached you one?" Mrs. Barbour said, turning to me. "Or fried? Or scrambled? Or whatever you like?"

"I like scrambled eggs!" Toddy said. "I can eat four!"

"No you can't, pal," said Mr. Barbour.

"Yes I can! I can eat six! I can eat the whole box!"

"It's not as if I'm asking for Dexedrine," Andy said. "Although I could get it at school if I felt like it."

"Theo?" said Mrs. Barbour. Etta the cook, I noticed, was standing in the door. "What about that egg?"

"Nobody ever asks *us* what *we* want for breakfast," Kitsey said; and even though she said it in a very loud voice, everyone pretended not to hear.

xi.

ONE SUNDAY MORNING, I climbed up to the light from a weighty and complicated dream, nothing of it left but a ringing in my ears and the ache of something slipped from my grasp and fallen into a crevasse where I would not see it again. Yet somehow — in the midst of this profound sinking, snapped threads, fragments lost and untrackable — a sentence stood out, ticking across the darkness like a news crawler at the bottom of a TV screen: *Hobart and Blackwell. Ring the green bell.*

I lay staring at the ceiling, not wanting to stir. The words were as clear and crisp as if someone had handed them to me typed on a slip of paper. And yet — most wonderfully — an expanse of forgotten memory had opened up and floated to the surface with them, like one of those paper pellets from Chinatown that bloom and swell into flowers when dropped into a glass of water.

Adrift in an air of charged significance, doubt struck me: was it a real memory, had he really spoken those words to me, or was I dreaming? Not long before my mother died, I'd woken convinced that a (nonexistent) schoolteacher named Mrs. Malt had put ground glass in my food because I had no discipline — in the world of my dream, a perfectly logical series of events — and I'd lain in a muddle of worry for two or three minutes before I came to my senses.

"Andy?" I said, and then leaned over and peered at the lower bunk, which was empty.

After lying wide-eyed for several moments, staring at the ceiling, I climbed down and retrieved the ring from the pocket of my school jacket and held it up to the light to look at the inscription. Then, quickly, I put it away and dressed. Andy was already up with the rest of the Barbours, at breakfast — Sunday breakfast was a big deal for them, I could hear them all in the dining room, Mr. Barbour rambling on indistinctly as he sometimes did, holding forth a bit. After pausing in the hall, I walked the other way, to the family room, and got the White Pages in its needlepoint cover from the cabinet under the telephone.

Hobart and Blackwell. There it was — clearly a business, though the listing didn't say what sort. I felt a bit dizzy. Seeing the name in black and white gave me a strange thrill, as of unseen cards falling into place.

The address was in the Village, West Tenth Street. After some hesitation, and with a great deal of anxiety, I dialed the number.

As the phone rang, I stood fiddling with a brass carriage clock on the table in the family room, chewing my lower lip, looking at the framed prints of water birds over the telephone table: Noddy Tern, Townsend's Cormorant, Common Osprey, Least Water Rail. I wasn't quite sure how I was going to explain who I was or ask what I needed to know.

"Theo?"

I jumped, guiltily. Mrs. Barbour—in gossamer-gray cashmere—had come in, coffee cup in hand.

"What are you doing?"

The phone was still ringing away on the other end. "Nothing," I said.

"Well, hurry up. Your breakfast is getting cold. Etta's made French toast."

"Thanks," I said, "I'll be right there," just as a mechanical voice from the phone company came on the line and told me to try my call again later.

I joined the Barbours, preoccupied—I had hoped that at least a machine would pick up—and was surprised to see none other than Platt Barbour (much bigger and redder in the face than the last time I'd seen him) in the place where I usually sat.

"Ah," said Mr. Barbour—interrupting himself mid-sentence, blotting his lips with his napkin and jumping up—"here we are, here we are. Good morning. You remember Platt, don't you? Platt, this is Theodore Decker—Andy's friend, remember?" As he was speaking, he had wandered off and returned with an extra chair, which he wedged in awkwardly for me at the sharp corner of the table.

As I sat down on the outskirts of the group—three or four inches lower than everyone else, in a spindly bamboo chair that didn't match the others—Platt met my gaze without much interest and looked away. He had come home from school for a party, and he looked hung over.

Mr. Barbour had sat down again and resumed talking about his favorite topic: sailing. "As I was saying. It all boils down to lack of confidence. You're unsure of yourself on the keelboat, Andy," he said, "and there's just no darn reason you should be, except you're short of experience on single-hand sailing."

"No," said Andy, in his faraway voice. "The problem essentially is that I despise boats."

"Horsefeathers," said Mr. Barbour, winking at me as if I were in on the joke, which I wasn't. "I don't buy that ho-hum attitude! Look at that picture on the wall in there, down in Sanibel two springs ago! That boy wasn't bored by the sea and the sky and the stars, no sir."

Andy sat contemplating the snow scene on the maple syrup bottle while his father rhapsodized in his dizzying, hard-to-follow way about how sailing built discipline and alertness in boys, and strength of character as in mariners of old. In past years, Andy had told me, he hadn't minded going on the boat quite so much because he'd been able to stay down in the cabin, reading and playing card games with his younger siblings. But now he was old enough to help crew — which meant long, stressful, sun-blinded days toiling on deck alongside the bullying Platt: ducking beneath the boom, completely disoriented, doing his best to keep from getting tangled in the lines or knocked overboard as their father shouted orders and rejoiced in the salt spray.

"God, remember the light on that Sanibel trip?" Andy's father pushed back in his chair and rolled his eyes at the ceiling. "Wasn't it *glorious?* Those red and orange sunsets? Fire and embers? Atomic, almost? Pure flame just *ripping* and *pouring* out of the sky? And remember that fat, smacking moon with the blue mist around it, off Hatteras — is it Maxfield Parrish I'm thinking of, Samantha?"

"Sorry?"

"Maxfield Parrish? That artist I like? Does those very grand skies, you know —" he threw his arms out — "with the towering clouds? Excuse me there, Theo, didn't mean to knock you in the snoot."

"Constable does clouds."

"No, no, that's not who I mean, this painter is much more satisfying. Anyway — my word, *what* skies we had out on the water that night. Magical. *Arcadian.*"

"Which night was that?"

"Don't tell me you don't remember! It was absolutely the highlight of the trip."

Platt — slouched back in his chair — said maliciously: "The highlight of Andy's trip was when we stopped for lunch that time at the snack bar."

Andy said, in a thin voice: "Mother doesn't care for sailing either."

"Not madly, no," said Mrs. Barbour, reaching for another strawberry. "Theo, I really do wish you would eat at least a small bite of your breakfast. You can't go on starving yourself like this. You're starting to look very peaked."

Despite Mr. Barbour's impromptu lessons from the flag chart in his study, I had not found much to engage me in the topic of sailing, either. "Because the greatest gift my own father ever gave to me?" Mr. Barbour was saying very earnestly. "Was the sea. The love for it—the *feel*. Daddy *gave me the ocean*. And it's a tragic loss for you, Andy—Andy, look at me, I'm talking to you—it's a terrible loss if you've made up your mind to turn your back on the very thing that gave me my *freedom*, my—"

"I have tried to like it. I have a natural hatred of it."

"*Hatred?*" Astonishment; dumbfoundment. "Hatred of what? Of the stars and the wind? Of the sky and the sun? Of *liberty?*"

"Insofar as any of those things have to do with boating, yes."

"Well—" looking around the table, including me in the appeal—"now he's just being pigheaded. The sea—" to Andy—"deny it all you may but it's your *birthright*, it's in your blood, back to the Phoenicians, the ancient *Greeks*—"

But as Mr. Barbour went on about Magellan, and celestial navigation, and *Billy Budd* ("I remember Taff the Welshman when he sank/And his cheek it was the budding pink"), I found my own thoughts drifting back to Hobart and Blackwell: wondering who Hobart and Blackwell were, and what exactly they did. The names sounded like a pair of musty old lawyers, or even stage magicians, business partners shuffling about in candle-lit darkness.

It seemed a hopeful sign that the telephone number was still in service. My own home phone had been disconnected. As soon as I could decently slip away from breakfast and my untouched plate, I went back to the telephone in the family room, with Irenka flustering around and running the vacuum and dusting the bric-a-brac all around me, and Kitsey across the room on the computer, determined not to even look at me.

"Who are you calling?" said Andy—who, in the manner of all his family, had come up behind me so quietly that I didn't hear him.

I might not have told him anything, except I knew that I could trust him to keep his mouth shut. Andy never talked to anybody, certainly not his parents.

"These people," I said quietly — stepping back a little bit, so I was out of the sight line of the doorway. "I know it sounds weird. But you know that ring I have?"

I explained about the old man, and I was trying to think how to explain about the girl, too, the connection I'd felt with her and how much I wanted to see her again. But Andy — predictably — had already leapt ahead, away from personal aspects to the logistics of the situation. He eyed the White Pages, open on the telephone table. "Are they in the city?"

"West Tenth."

Andy sneezed, and blew his nose; spring allergies had hit him very hard. "If you can't get them on the phone," he said, folding up his handkerchief and putting it in his pocket, "why don't you just go down there?"

"Really?" I said. It seemed creepy not to call first, just show up. "You think so?"

"That's what I would do."

"I don't know," I said. "Maybe they don't remember me."

"If they see you in person, they'll be more likely to remember," said Andy reasonably. "Otherwise you could just be any weirdo calling and pretending. Don't worry," he said, glancing over his shoulder, "I won't tell anybody if you don't want me to."

"A weirdo?" I said. "Pretending what?"

"Well, I mean, you get lots of strange people calling you here," said Andy flatly.

I was silent, not knowing how to absorb this.

"Besides, they're not picking up, what else are you going to do? You won't be able to get down there again until next weekend. Also, is this a conversation you want to have —" he cast his eyes down the hallway, where Toddy was jumping up and down in some kind of shoes that had springs on them, and Mrs. Barbour was interrogating Platt about the party at Molly Walterbeek's.

He had a point. "Right," I said.

Andy pushed his glasses up on the bridge of his nose. "I'll go with you if you want."

"No, that's okay," I said. Andy, I knew, was doing Japanese Experience for extra credit that afternoon — a study group at the Toraya teahouse, then on to see the new Miyazaki at Lincoln Center; not that Andy needed extra credit but class outings were as much as he had of a social life.

"Well here," he said, digging around in his pocket and coming up with his cell phone. "Take this with you. Just in case. Here—" he was punching stuff on the screen—"I've taken off the security code for you. Good to go."

"I don't need this," I said, looking at the sleek little phone with an anime still of Virtual Girl Aki (naked, in porny thigh-high boots) on the lock screen.

"Well, you might. Never know. Go ahead," he said, when I hesitated. "Take it."

xii.

AND SO IT WAS that around half past eleven, I found myself riding down to the Village on the Fifth Avenue bus with the street address of Hobart and Blackwell in my pocket, written on a page from one of the mono-grammed notepads Mrs. Barbour kept by the telephone.

Once I got off the bus at Washington Square, I wandered for about forty-five minutes looking for the address. The Village, with its erratic layout (triangular blocks, dead-end streets angling this way and that) was an easy place to get lost, and I had to stop and ask directions three times: in a news shop full of bongs and gay porn magazines, in a crowded bakery blasting opera, and of a girl in white undershirt and overalls who was outside washing the windows of a bookstore with a squeegee and bucket.

When finally I found West Tenth—which was deserted—I walked along, counting the numbers. I was on a slightly shabby part of the street that was mainly residential. A group of pigeons strutted ahead of me on the wet sidewalk, three abreast, like small officious pedestrians. Many of the numbers weren't clearly posted, and just as I was wondering if I'd missed it and ought to double back, I suddenly found myself looking at the words *Hobart and Blackwell* painted in a neat, old-fashioned arch upon the window of a shop. Through the dusty windows I saw Staffordshire dogs and majolica cats, dusty crystal, tarnished silver, antique chairs and settees upholstered in sallow old brocade, an elaborate faience birdcage, miniature marble obelisks atop a marble-topped pedestal table and a pair of alabaster cockatoos. It was just the kind of shop my mother would have liked — packed tightly, a bit dilapidated, with stacks of old books on the floor. But the gates were pulled down and the place was closed.

Most of the stores didn't open until noon, or one. To kill some time I walked over to Greenwich Street, to the Elephant and Castle, a restaurant where my mother and I ate sometimes when we were downtown. But the instant I stepped in, I realized my mistake. The mismatched china elephants, even the ponytailed waitress in a black T-shirt who approached me, smiling: it was too overwhelming, I could see the corner table where my mother and I had eaten lunch the last time we were there, I had to mumble an excuse and back out the door.

I stood on the sidewalk, heart pounding. Pigeons flew low in the sooty sky. Greenwich Avenue was almost empty: a bleary male couple who looked like they'd been up fighting all night; a rumple-haired woman in a too-big turtleneck sweater, walking a dachshund toward Sixth Avenue. It was a little weird being in the Village on my own because it wasn't a place where you saw many kids on the street on a weekend morning; it felt adult, sophisticated, slightly alcoholic. Everybody looked hung over or as if they had just rolled out of bed.

Because nothing much was open, because I felt a bit lost and I didn't know what else to do, I began to wander back over in the direction of Hobart and Blackwell. To me, coming from uptown, everything in the Village looked so little and old, with ivy and vines growing on the buildings, herbs and tomato plants in barrels on the street. Even the bars had handpainted signs like rural taverns: horses and tomcats, roosters and geese and pigs. But the intimacy, the smallness, also made me feel shut out; and I found myself hurrying past the inviting little doorways with my head down, very aware of all the convivial Sunday-morning lives unrolling around me in private.

The gates on Hobart and Blackwell were still down. I had the feeling that the shop hadn't been open in a while; it was too cold, too dark; there was no sense of vitality or interior life like the other places on the street.

I was looking in the window and trying to think what I should do next when suddenly I saw motion, a large shape gliding at the rear of the shop. I stopped, transfixed. It moved lightly, as ghosts are said to move, without looking to either side, passing quickly before a doorway into darkness.

Then it was gone. With my hand to my forehead, I peered into the murky, crowded depths of the shop, and then knocked on the glass.

Hobart and Blackwell. Ring the green bell.

A bell? There wasn't a bell; the entrance to the shop was enclosed by an iron gate. I walked to the next doorway — number 12, a modest apartment building — and then back to number 8, a brownstone. There was a stoop, going up to the first floor, but this time, I saw something I hadn't seen before: a narrow doorwell, tucked halfway between number 8 and number 10, half-hidden by a rack of old-fashioned tin garbage cans. Four or five steps led down to an anonymous-looking door about three feet below the level of the sidewalk. There was no label, no sign — but what caught my eye was a flash of kelly green: a flag of green electrical tape, pasted beneath a button in the wall.

I went down the stairs; I rang the bell and rang it, wincing at the hysterical buzz (which made me want to run away) and taking deep breaths for courage. Then — so suddenly I started back — the door opened, and I found myself gazing up at a large and unexpected person.

He was six foot four or six five, at least: haggard, noble-jawed, heavy, something about him suggesting the antique photos of Irish poets and pugilists that hung in the midtown pub where my father liked to drink. His hair was mostly gray, and needed cutting, and his skin an unhealthy white, with such deep purple shadows around his eyes that it was almost as if his nose had been broken. Over his clothes, a rich paisley robe with satin lapels fell almost to his ankles and flowed massively around him, like something a leading man might wear in a 1930s movie: worn, but still impressive.

I was so surprised that all my words left me. There was nothing impatient in his manner, quite the opposite. Blankly he looked at me, with dark-lidded eyes, waiting for me to speak.

"Excuse me —" I swallowed; my throat was dry. "I don't want to bother you —"

He blinked, mildly, in the silence that followed, as if of course he understood this perfectly, would never dream of suggesting such a thing.

I fumbled in my pocket; I held out the ring to him, on my open palm. The man's large, pallid face went slack. He looked at the ring, and then at me.

"Where did you get this?" he said.

"He gave it to me," I said. "He told me to bring it here."

He stood and looked at me, hard. For a moment, I thought he was going to tell me he didn't know what I was talking about. Then, without a word, he stepped back and opened the door.

"I'm Hobie," he said, when I hesitated. "Come in."

Chapter 4.

Morphine Lollipop

A WILDERNESS OF GILT, gleaming in the slant from the dust-furred windows: gilded cupids, gilded commodes and torchieres, and—undercutting the old-wood smell—the reek of turpentine, oil paint, and varnish. I followed him through the workshop along a path swept in the sawdust, past pegboard and tools, dismembered chairs and claw-foot tables sprawled with their legs in the air. Though a big man he was graceful, "a floater," my mother would have called him, something effortless and gliding in the way he carried himself. With my eyes on the heels of his slippered feet, I followed him up some narrow stairs and into a dim room, richly carpeted, where black urns stood on pedestals and tasseled draperies were drawn against the sun.

At the silence, my heart went cold. Dead flowers stood rotting in the massive Chinese vases and a shut-up heaviness overweighed the room: the air almost too stale to breathe, the exact, suffocating feel of our apartment when Mrs. Barbour took me back to Sutton Place to get some things I needed. It was a stillness I knew; this was how a house closed in on itself when someone had died.

All at once I wished I hadn't come. But the man—Hobie—seemed to sense my misgiving, because he turned quite suddenly. Though he wasn't a young man he still had something of a boy's face; his eyes, a childish blue, were clear and startled.

"What's the matter?" he said, and then: "Are you all right?"

His concern embarrassed me. Uncomfortably I stood in the stagnant, antique-crowded gloom, not knowing what to say.

He didn't seem to know what to say either; he opened his mouth; closed it; then shook his head as if to clear it. He seemed to be around fifty or sixty, poorly shaven, with a shy, pleasant, large-featured face neither

handsome nor plain — a man who would always be bigger than most of
the other men in the room, though he also seemed unhealthy in some
clammy, ill-defined way, with black-circled eyes and a pallor that made
me think of the Jesuit martyrs depicted in the church murals I'd seen on
our school trip to Montreal: large, capable, death-pale Europeans, staked
and bound in the camps of the Hurons.

"Sorry, I'm in a bit of a tip...." He was looking around with a vague,
unfocused urgency, as my mother did when she'd misplaced something. His
voice was rough but educated, like Mr. O'Shea my History teacher who'd
grown up in a tough Boston neighborhood and ended up going to Harvard.

"I can come back. If that's better."

At this he glanced at me, mildly alarmed. "No, no," he said — his cufflinks were out, the cuff fell loose and grubby at the wrist — "just give me
a moment to collect myself, sorry — here," he said distractedly, pushing
the straggle of gray hair out of his face, "here we go."

He was leading me towards a narrow, hard-looking sofa, with scrolled
arms and a carved back. But it was tossed with pillow and blankets and
we both seemed to notice at the same time that the tumble of bedding
made it awkward to sit.

"Ah, sorry," he murmured, stepping back so fast we almost bumped
into each other, "I've set up camp in here as you can see, not the best
arrangement in the world but I've had to make do since I can't hear properly with all the goings-on..."

Turning away (so that I missed the rest of the sentence) he sidestepped
a book face-down on the carpet and a teacup ringed with brown on the
inside, and ushered me instead to an ornate upholstered chair, tucked and
shirred, with fringe and a complicated button-studded seat — a Turkish
chair, as I later learned; he was one of the few people in New York who
still knew how to upholster them.

Winged bronzes, silver trinkets. Dusty gray ostrich plumes in a silver
vase. Uncertainly, I perched on the edge of the chair and looked around. I
would have preferred to be on my feet, the easier to leave.

He leaned forward, clasping his hands between his knees. But instead
of saying a word he only looked at me and waited.

"I'm Theo," I said in a rush, after much too long a silence. My face was
so hot I felt about to burst into flames. "Theodore Decker. Everybody calls
me Theo. I live uptown," I added doubtfully.

"Well, I'm James Hobart, but everyone calls me Hobie." His gaze was bleak and disarming. "I live downtown."

At a loss I glanced away, unsure if he was making fun.

"Sorry." He closed his eyes for a moment, then opened them. "Don't mind me. Welty —" he glanced at the ring in his palm — "was my business partner."

Was? The moon-dial clock — whirring and cogged, chained and weighted, a Captain Nemo contraption — burred loudly in the stillness before gonging on the quarter hour.

"Oh," I said. "I just. I thought —"

"No. I'm sorry. You didn't know?" he added, looking at me closely.

I looked away. I had not realized how much I'd counted on seeing the old man again. Despite what I'd seen — what I knew — somehow I'd still managed to nurture a childish hope that he'd pulled through, miraculously, like a murder victim on TV who after the commercial break turns out to be alive and recovering quietly in the hospital.

"And how do you happen to have this?"

"What?" I said, startled. The clock, I noticed, was way off: ten a.m., ten p.m., nowhere even near the correct time.

"You said he gave it to you?"

I shifted uncomfortably. "Yes. I —" The shock of his death felt new, as if I'd failed him a second time and it was happening all over again from a completely different angle.

"He was conscious? He spoke to you?"

"Yes," I began, and then fell silent. I felt miserable. Being in the old man's world, among his things, had brought the sense of him back very strongly: the dreamy underwater mood of the room, its rusty velvets, its richness and quiet.

"I'm glad he wasn't alone," said Hobie. "He would have hated that." The ring was closed in his fingers and he put his fist to his mouth and looked at me.

"My. You're just a cub, aren't you?" he said.

I smiled uneasily, not sure how I was meant to respond.

"Sorry," he said, in a more businesslike tone that I could tell was meant to reassure me. "It's just — I know it was bad. I saw. His body —" he seemed to grasp for words — "before they call you in, they clean them up as best they can and they tell you that it won't be pleasant, which of course you know but—well. You can't prepare yourself for something like that. We had a set of Mathew Brady photographs come through the shop a few years ago—Civil War stuff, so gruesome we had a hard time selling it."

I said nothing. It was not my habit to contribute to adult conversation apart from a 'yes' or 'no' when pressed, but all the same I was transfixed. My mother's friend Mark, who was a doctor, had been the one who'd gone in to identify her body and no one had had very much to say to me about it.

"I remember a story I read once, a soldier, was it at Shiloh?" He was talking to me but not with his whole attention. "Gettysburg? a soldier so mad with shock that he started burying birds and squirrels on the battle-field. You had a lot of little things killed too, in the crossfire, little animals. Many tiny graves."

"24,000 men died at Shiloh in two days," I blurted.

His eyes reverted to me in alarm.

"50,000 at Gettysburg. It was the new weaponry. Minié balls and repeating rifles. That was why the body count was so high. We had trench warfare in America way before World War I. Most people don't know that."

I could see he had no idea what to do with this.

"You're interested in the Civil War?" he said, after a careful pause.

"Er—yes," I said brusquely. "Kind of." I knew a lot about Union field artillery, because I'd written a paper on it so technical and fact-jammed that the teacher had made me write it again, and I also knew about Brady's photographs of the dead at Antietam: I'd seen the pictures online, pin-eyed boys black with blood at the nose and mouth. "Our class spent six weeks on Lincoln."

"Brady had a photography studio not far from here. Have you ever seen it?"

"No." There had been a trapped thought about to emerge, something essential and unspeakable, released by the mention of those blank-faced soldiers. Now it was all gone but the image: dead boys with limbs akimbo, staring at the sky.

The silence that followed this was excruciating. Neither of us seemed to know how to move forward. At last Hobie recrossed his legs. "I mean to say—I'm sorry. To press you," he said falteringly.

I squirmed. Coming downtown, I'd been so filled with curiosity that I'd failed to anticipate that I might be expected to answer any questions myself.

"I know it must be difficult to talk about. It's just — I never thought —"

My shoes. It was interesting how I'd never really looked at my shoes. The toe scuffs. The frayed laces. *We'll go to Bloomingdale's Saturday and buy you a new pair.* But that had never happened.

"I don't want to put you on the spot. But — he was aware?"

"Yes. Sort of. I mean —" his alert, anxious face made some remote part of me want to burst out with all kinds of stuff he didn't need to know and it wasn't right to tell him, splattered insides, ugly repetitive flashes that broke in on my thoughts even while I was awake.

Murky portraits, china spaniels on the mantelpiece, golden pendulum swinging, tockety-tock, tockety-tock.

"I heard him calling." Rubbing my eye. "When I woke up." It was like trying to explain a dream. You couldn't. "And I went over to him and I was with him and — it wasn't that bad. Or, not like you'd think," I added, since this had come out sounding like the lie it was.

"He spoke to you?"

Swallowing hard, I nodded. Dark mahogany; potted palms.

"He was conscious?"

Again I nodded. Bad taste in my mouth. It wasn't something you could summarize, stuff that didn't make sense and didn't have a story, the dust, the alarms, how he'd held my hand, a whole lifetime there just the two of us, mixed-up sentences and names of towns and people I hadn't heard of. Broken wires sparking.

His eyes were still on me. My throat was dry and I felt a bit sick. The moment wasn't moving on to the next moment like it was supposed to and I kept waiting for him to ask more questions, anything, but he didn't.

At last he shook his head as if to clear it. "This is —" He seemed as confused as I was; the robe, the gray hair loose gave him the look of a crownless king in a costume play for children.

"I'm sorry," he said, shaking his head again. "This is all so new."

"Excuse me?"

"Well, you see, it's just —" he leaned forward and blinked, quick and agitated — "It's all very different from what I was told, you see. They said he died instantly. Very, very emphatic on that point."

"But —" I stared, astonished. Did he think I was making it up?

"No, no," he said hastily, putting a hand up to reassure me. "It's just — I'm sure it's what they say to everyone. 'Died instantly'?" he said bleakly, when still I stared at him. "'Perfectly painless'? 'Never knew what hit him'?"

Then—all at once—I did see, the implications slithering in on me with a chill. My mother too had "died instantly." Her death had been "perfectly painless." The social workers had harped on it so insistently that I'd never thought to wonder how they could be quite so sure.

"Although, I do have to say, it was difficult to imagine him going that way," Hobie said, in the abrupt silence that had fallen. "The flash of lightning. Falling over unawares. Had a sense, you do sometimes, that it wasn't like they said, you know?"

"Sorry?" I said, glancing up, disoriented by the vicious new possibility I'd stumbled into.

"A goodbye at the gate," said Hobie. He seemed to be talking partly to himself. "That's what he would have wanted. The parting glimpse, the death haiku—he wouldn't have liked to leave without stopping to speak to someone along the way. 'A teahouse amid the cherry blossoms, on the way to death.' "

He had lost me. In the shadowy room, a single blade of sun pierced between the curtains and struck across the room, where it caught and blazed up in a tray of cut glass decanters, casting prisms that flickered and shifted this way and that and wavered high on the walls like paramecia under a microscope. Though there was a strong smell of wood smoke, the fireplace was burnt-out and black looking and the grate choked with ashes, as if the fires hadn't been lit in a while.

"The girl," I said timidly.

His glance came back to me.

"There was a girl too."

For a moment, he did not seem to understand. Then he sat back in his chair and blinked rapidly as if water had been flicked in his face.

"What?" I said—startled. "Where is she? She's okay?"

"No—" rubbing the bridge of his nose—"no."

"But she's alive?" I could hardly believe it.

He raised his eyebrows in a way that I understood to mean yes. "She was lucky." But his voice, and his manner, seemed to say the opposite.

"Is she here?"

"Well—"

"Where is she? Can I see her?"

He sighed, with something that looked like exasperation. "She's meant to be quiet and not have visitors," he said, rummaging in his pockets. "She's not herself—it's hard to know how she'll react."

"But she's going to be all right?"

"Well, let us hope so. But she's not out of the woods yet. To employ the highly unclear phrase the doctors insist on using." He'd taken cigarettes from the pocket of his bathrobe. With uncertain hands he lit one then with a flourish threw the pack on the painted Japanese table between us.

"What?" he said, waving the smoke from his face, when he caught me staring at the crumpled packet, French, like people smoked in old movies. "Don't tell me you want one too."

"No thank you," I said, after an uneasy silence. I was pretty sure he was joking although I wasn't a hundred per cent sure.

He, in return, was blinking at me sharply through the tobacco haze with a sort of worried look, as though he had just realized some crucial fact about me.

"It's you, isn't it?" he said unexpectedly.

"Excuse me?"

"You're the boy, aren't you? Whose mother died in there?"

I was too stunned to say anything for a moment.

"What," I said, meaning *how do you know,* but I couldn't quite get it out.

Uncomfortably, he rubbed an eye and sat back suddenly, with the fluster of a man who's spilled a drink on the table. "Sorry. I don't—I mean—that didn't come out right. God. I'm—" vaguely he gestured as if to say I'm exhausted, not thinking straight.

Not very politely, I looked away—blindsided by a queasy, unwelcome swell of emotion. Since my mother's death, I had cried hardly at all and certainly not in front of anyone—not even at her memorial service, where people who barely knew her (and one or two who had made her life Hell, such as Mathilde) were sobbing and blowing their noses all around me.

He saw I was upset; started to say something; reconsidered.

"Have you eaten?" he said unexpectedly.

I was too surprised to answer. Food was the last thing on my mind.

"Ah, I thought not," he said, rising creakily to his big feet. "Let's go rustle up something."

"I'm not hungry," I said, so rudely I was sorry. Since my mother's death, all anyone seemed to think of was shovelling food down my throat.

"No, no, of course not." With his free hand he fanned away a cloud of smoke. "But come along, please. Humor me. You're not vegetarian, are you?"

"No!" I said, offended. "Why would you think that?"

He laughed — short, sharp. "Easy! Lots of her friends are veg, so is she."

"Oh," I said faintly, and he looked down at me with a sort of lively, unhurried amusement.

"Well, just so you know, I'm not a vegetarian either," he said. "I'll eat any old sort of ridiculous thing. So I suppose we'll manage all right."

He pushed open a door, and I followed him down a crowded hallway lined with tarnished mirrors and old pictures. Though he was walking ahead of me fast, I was anxious to linger and look: family groupings, white columns, verandahs and palm trees. A tennis court; a Persian carpet spread on a lawn. Male servants in white pyjamas, solemnly abreast. My eye landed on Mr. Blackwell — beaky and personable, dapperly dressed in white, back hunched even in youth. He was lounging by a seaside retaining wall in some palmy locale; beside him — atop the wall, hand on his shoulder and standing a head taller — smiled a kindergarten-aged Pippa. As tiny as she was, the resemblance sounded: her coloring, her eyes, her head cocked at the same angle and hair as red as his.

"That's her, isn't it?" I said — at the same instant I realized it couldn't possibly be her. This photo, with its faded colors and outmoded clothes, had been taken long before I was born.

Hobie turned, came back to look. "No," he said quietly, hands behind his back. "That's Juliet. Pippa's mother."

"Where is she?"

"Juliet —? Dead. Cancer. Six years last May." And then, seeming to realize he'd spoken too curtly: "Welty was Juliet's big brother. Half brother, rather. Same father — different wives — thirty years apart. But he brought her up like his own child."

I stepped in for a closer look. She was leaning against him, cheek inclined sweetly against the sleeve of his jacket.

Hobie cleared his throat. "She was born when their father was in his sixties," he said quietly. "Far too old to interest himself in a small child, particularly since he'd had no weakness for children to start with."

A door in the opposite side of the hallway stood ajar; he pushed it open and stood looking into darkness. On tiptoe, I craned behind, but almost immediately he backed away and clicked the door shut.

"Is that her?" Though it had been too dark to see very much, I had caught the unfriendly glow of animal eyes, an unnerving greenish sheen from across the room.

"Not now." His voice was so low I could barely hear him.

"What's that in there with her?" I whispered—lingering by the doorway, reluctant to move along. "A cat?"

"Dog. The nurse doesn't approve, but she wants him in the bed with her and honestly, I can't keep him out—he scratches at the door and whines—Here, this way."

Moving slowly, creakily, with an old person's forward-leaning quality, he pushed open a door into a crowded kitchen with a ceiling skylight and a curvaceous old stove: tomato red, with svelte lines like a 1950s spaceship. Books stacked on the floor—cookbooks, dictionaries, old novels, encyclopedias; shelves closely packed with antique china in half a dozen patterns. Near the window, by the fire escape, a faded wooden saint held up a palm in benediction; on the sideboard alongside a silver tea set, painted animals straggled two by two into a Noah's Ark. But the sink was piled with dishes, and on the countertops and windowsills stood medicine bottles, dirty cups, alarming drifts of unopened mail, and plants from the florist's dry and brown in their pots.

He sat me down at the table, pushing away Con Ed bills and back issues of *Antiques* magazine. "Tea," he said, as if remembering an item on a grocery list.

As he busied himself at the stove, I stared at the coffee rings on the tablecloth. Restlessly, I pushed back in my chair and looked around.

"Er—" I said.

"Yes?"

"Can I see her later?"

"Maybe," he said, with his back to me. Whisk beat against blue china bowl: *tap tap tap*. "If she's awake. She's in a good deal of pain and the medicine makes her sleepy."

"What happened to her?"

"Well—" His tone was both brisk and subdued and I recognized it at once since it was much the tone I employed when people asked about my mother. "She's had a bad crack on the head, a skull fracture, to tell you the truth she was in a coma for a while and her left leg was broken in so many pieces she came near to losing it. 'Marbles in a sock,'" he said, with a mirthless laugh. "That's what the doctor said when he looked at the x-ray. Twelve breaks. Five surgeries. Last week," he said, half-turning, "she had the pins out, and she begged so to come home they said she could. As long as we had a nurse part time."

"Is she walking yet?"

"Goodness, no," he said, bringing his cigarette up for a drag; he was somehow managing to cook with one hand and smoke with the other, like some tugboat captain or lumber camp cook in an old movie. "She can hardly sit up more than half an hour."

"But she'll be fine."

"Well, that's what we hope," he said, in what did not seem an overly hopeful tone. You know," he said, glancing back at me, "if you were in there too, it's remarkable that you're okay."

"Well." I never knew how to respond when people commented, as they often did, on my being "okay."

Hobie coughed, and put out the cigarette. "Well." I could see, from his expression, that he knew he'd disturbed me, and was sorry. "I suppose they spoke to you too? The investigators?"

I looked at the tablecloth. "Yes." The less said about this, I felt, the better.

"Well, I don't know about you, but I found them very decent — very informed. This one Irishman — he'd seen a lot of these things, he was telling me about suitcase bombs in England and in the Paris airport, some sidewalk café thing in Tangier, you know, dozens dead and the person right next to the bomb isn't hurt at all. He said they see some pretty strange effects, you know, in older buildings especially. Enclosed spaces, uneven surfaces, reflective materials — very unpredictable. Just like acoustics, he said. The blast waves are like sound waves — they bounce and deflect. Sometimes you have shop windows broken miles off. Or —" he pushed the hair out of his eyes with his wrist — "sometimes, closer to hand, there's what he called a shielding effect. Things very close to the detonation remain intact — the unbroken teacup in the blown-out IRA cottage or what have you. It's the flying glass and debris that kills most people, you know, often at pretty far range. A pebble or a piece of glass at that speed is as good as a bullet."

I traced my thumb along the flower pattern of the tablecloth. "I —"

"Sorry. Maybe not the right thing to talk about."

"No no," I said hurriedly; it was actually a huge relief to hear someone speak directly, and in an informed way, about what most people tied themselves in knots to avoid. "That's not it. It's just —"

"Yes?"

"I was wondering. How'd she get out?"

"Well, it was a stroke of luck. She was trapped under a lot of rubbish — the firemen wouldn't have found her if one of the dogs hadn't alerted. They worked partway in, jacked up the beam — I mean, the amazing thing too, she was awake, talked to them the whole time, though she doesn't remember a bit of it. The miracle of it was they got her out before the call came to evacuate — how long were you knocked out, did you say?"

"I don't remember."

"Well, you were lucky. If they'd had to go off and leave her there, still pinned, which I understand *did* happen to some people — Ah, here we go," he said as the kettle whistled.

The plate of food, when he set it before me, was nothing to look at — puffy yellow stuff on toast. But it smelled good. Cautiously, I tasted it. It was melted cheese, with chopped-up tomato and cayenne pepper and some other things I couldn't figure out, and it was delicious.

"Sorry, what is this?" I said, taking another careful bite.

He looked a bit embarrassed. "Well, it doesn't really have a name."

"It's good," I said, slightly astonished how hungry I really was. My mother had made a cheese-on-toast very similar which we ate sometimes on Sunday nights in winter.

"You like cheese? I should have thought to ask."

I nodded, mouth too full to answer. Even though Mrs. Barbour was always pressing ice cream and sweets on me, somehow it felt as if I'd hardly eaten a normal meal since my mother died — at least, not the kind of meals that had been normal for us, stir fry or scrambled eggs or macaroni and cheese from the box, while I sat on the kitchen step-ladder and told her about my day.

As I ate, he sat across the table with his chin in his big white hands. "What are you good at?" he asked rather suddenly. "Sports?"

"Sorry?"

"What are you interested in? Games and all that?"

"Well — video games. Like Age of Conquest? Yakuza Freakout?"

He seemed nonplussed. "What about school, then? Favorite subjects?"

"History, I guess. English too," I said when he didn't answer. "But English is going to be really boring for the next six weeks—we stopped doing literature and went back to the grammar book and now we're diagramming sentences."

"Literature? English or American?"

"American. Right now. Or we were. American history too, this year. Although it's been really boring lately. We're just getting off the Great Depression but it'll be good again once we get to World War II."

It was the most enjoyable conversation I'd had in a while. He asked me all kinds of interesting questions, like what I'd read in literature and how middle school was different from elementary school; what was my hardest subject (Spanish) and what was my favorite historical period (I wasn't sure, anything but Eugene Debs and the History of Labor, which we'd spent way too much time on) and what did I want to be when I grew up? (no clue)—normal stuff, but still it was refreshing to converse with a grown-up who seemed interested in me apart from my misfortune, not prying for information or running down a checklist of Things to Say to Troubled Kids.

We'd gotten off on the subject of writers—from T. H. White and Tolkien to Edgar Allan Poe, another favorite. "My dad says Poe's a second-rate writer," I said. "That he's the Vincent Price of American Letters. But I don't think that's fair."

"No, it isn't," said Hobie, seriously, pouring himself a cup of tea. "Even if you don't like Poe—he invented the detective story. And science fiction. In essence, he invented a huge part of the twentieth century. I mean—honestly, I don't care as much for him as I did when I was a boy, but even if you don't like him you can't dismiss him as a crank."

"My dad did. He used to go around reciting 'Annabel Lee' in a stupid voice, to make me mad. Because he knew I liked it."

"Your dad's a writer then."

"No." I didn't know where he'd gotten that. "An actor. Or he was." Before I was born, he'd played guest roles on several TV shows, never the star but the star's spoiled playboy friend or corrupt business partner who gets killed.

"Would I have heard of him?"

"No. Now he works in an office. Or he did."

"And what's he doing now, then?" he asked. He had slipped the ring over his little finger, and from time to time he twisted it between thumb and forefinger of his other hand, as if to make sure it was still there.

"Who knows? He ditched us."

To my surprise, he laughed. "Good riddance?"

"Well—" I shrugged—"I don't know. Sometimes he was okay. We'd watch sports and cop shows and he'd tell me how they did the special effects with the blood and all. But, it's like—I don't know. Like, sometimes he was drunk when he came to pick me up from school?" I hadn't really talked about this with Dave the Shrink or Mrs. Swanson or anyone. "I was scared to tell my mother but then one of the other mothers told her. And then—" it was a long story, I was feeling embarrassed, I wanted to cut it short—"he got his hand broken in a bar, he was fighting somebody in a bar, he had this bar he liked to go to every day only we didn't know that's where he was because he said he was working late, and he had this whole set of friends we didn't know about and they sent him postcards when they went on vacation to places like the Virgin Islands? to our home address? which was how we found out about it? and my mother tried to make him go to AA but he wouldn't go. Sometimes the doormen used to come and stand in the hall outside the apartment and make a lot of noise so he could hear them—so he knew they were out there, you know? So he didn't get too out of hand."

"Out of hand?"

"There was a lot of yelling and stuff. It was mostly him doing it. But—" uncomfortably aware that I'd said more than I meant to—"it was mainly him making a bunch of noise. Like—oh, I don't know, like when he had to stay with me, when she had to work? He was always in a really bad mood. I couldn't talk to him when he was watching news or sports, that was the rule. I mean—" I paused, unhappily, feeling I'd talked myself into a corner. "Anyway. That was a long time ago."

He sat back in his chair and looked at me: a big, self-contained, guarded man, though his eyes were the worried blue of boyishness.

"And now?" he said. "Do you like the people you're staying with?"

"Um—" I paused, with full mouth, at a loss how to explain the Barbours. "They're nice, I guess."

"I'm glad. I mean, I can't say I know Samantha Barbour, although I've done some work for her family in the past. She has a good eye."

At this, I stopped eating. "You know the Barbours?"

"Not him. Her. Though his mother was quite a collector—I gather it all went to the brother, though, due to some family quarrel. Welty would have been able to tell you more about it. Not that he was a gossip," he added hastily, "Welty was very discreet, buttoned up to here, but people confided in him, he was that sort, you know? Strangers opened up to him—clients, people he hardly knew, he was the kind of man people liked to entrust with their sadnesses.

"But yes." He folded his hands. "Every art dealer and *antiquario* in New York knows Samantha Barbour. She was a Van der Pleyn before she married. Not a great buyer, though Welty saw her at auction sometimes, and she certainly has some pretty things."

"Who told you I was staying with the Barbours?"

He blinked, rapidly. "It was in the paper," he said. "You didn't see it?"

"The paper?"

"The *Times.* You didn't read it? No?"

"There was something in the paper about me?"

"No, no," he said quickly. "Not about *you.* About children who had lost family members in the museum. Most of them were tourists. There was one little girl...a baby, really...diplomat's child from South America—"

"What did they say about me in the paper?"

He made a face. "Oh, an orphan's plight...charity-minded socialite steps in...that kind of thing. You can imagine."

I stared into my plate, feeling embarrassed. Orphan? Charity?

"It was a very nice piece. I gather you protected one of her sons from bullies?" he said, lowering his large gray head to catch my eye. "At school? The other gifted boy who was put ahead?"

I shook my head. "Sorry?"

"Samantha's son? Whom you defended from a group of older boys at school? Took beatings for him—that kind of thing?"

Again I shook my head—completely bewildered.

He laughed. "Such modesty! You shouldn't be embarrassed."

"But—it wasn't like that," I said, baffled. "We both got picked on and beaten up. Every day."

"So the story said. Which made it all the more remarkable that you stood up for him. A broken bottle?" he said, when I didn't respond. "Someone was trying to cut Samantha Barbour's son with a broken bottle, and you—"

"Oh, that," I said, embarrassed. "That was nothing."

"You were cut yourself. When you tried to help him."

"That's not how it happened! Cavanaugh jumped on both of us! There was a piece of broken glass on the sidewalk."

Again he laughed — a big man's laugh, rich and rough and at odds with his carefully cultivated voice. "Well, however it happened," he said, "you've certainly tipped up in an interesting family." Standing, he went to the cupboard, where he retrieved a bottle of whiskey and poured a couple of fingers in a not-very-clean glass.

"Samantha Barbour doesn't seem the warmest and most welcoming of hearts — at least that's not the impression," he said. "Yet she seems to do an awful lot of good in the world with the foundations and fundraising, doesn't she?"

I kept quiet as he put the bottle back in the cupboard. Above, through the skylight, the light was gray and opalescent; a fine rain peppered at the glass.

"Are you going to open the shop again?" I said.

"Well —" he sighed. "Welty handled all that end of it — the clients, the sales. Me — I'm a cabinet maker, not a businessman. *Brocanteur, bricoleur.* Barely set foot up there — I'm always below stairs, sanding and polishing. Now he's gone — well, it's still very new. People calling for things he sold, things still being delivered I never knew he bought, don't know where the paperwork is, don't know who any of it's for . . . there are a million things I need to ask him, I'd give anything if I could talk to him for five minutes. Particularly — well, particularly as regards Pippa. Her medical care and — well."

"Right," I said, aware how lame I sounded. We were heading into the clumsy territory of my mother's funeral, stretched-out silences, wrong smiles, the place where words didn't work.

"He was a lovely man. Not many like him. Gentle, charming. People always felt sorry for him because of his back, though I've never met anyone so naturally gifted with a happy disposition, and of course the customers loved him . . . outgoing fellow, very sociable, always was . . . 'the world won't come to me,' he used to say, 'so I must go to it' —"

Quite suddenly, Andy's iPhone chimed: text message coming in.

Hobie — glass halfway to his mouth — started, violently. "What was that?"

"Wait a second," I said, digging in my pocket. The text was from Phil Lefkow, one of the kids in Andy's Japanese class: Hi Theo, Andy here, are you ok? Hastily, I switched the phone off and stuck it back in my pocket.

"Sorry?" I said. "What were you saying?"

"I forget." He stared into space for a moment or two, then shook his head. "I never thought I'd see this again," he said, looking down at the ring. "So like him to ask you to bring it here — to put it in my hand. I — well, I didn't say anything but I thought for sure someone had pocketed it at the morgue—"

Again the phone chimed its annoying, high-pitched note. "Gosh, sorry!" I said, scrambling for it. Andy's text read:

Just making sure your not being killed!!!!

"Sorry," I said — holding the button down, just to make sure — "it really is off this time."

But he only smiled, and looked into his glass. Rain tapped and dripped at the skylight, casting watery shadows that streamed down the wall. Too shy to say anything, I waited for him to pick up the thread again — and when he didn't, we sat there peacefully, while I sipped my cooling tea (Lapsang Souchong, smoky and peculiar) and felt the strangeness of my life, and where I was.

I pushed my plate aside. "Thank you," I said dutifully, eyes wandering round the room, "that was really good" — speaking (as had become my habit) for my mother's benefit, in case she was listening.

"Oh, how polite!" he said — laughing at me but not unkindly, in a way that felt friendly. "Do you like it?"

"What?"

"My Noah's Ark." He nodded at the shelf. "You were looking at it over there, I thought." The worn wooden animals (elephants, tigers, oxen, zebras, all the way down to a tiny pair of mice) stood patiently in line, waiting to board.

"Is it hers?" I asked, after a fascinated silence; for the animals were so lovingly positioned (the big cats ignoring each other; the male peacock turned away from his hen to admire his reflection in the toaster) I could imagine her spending hours arranging them and trying to get them exactly right.

"No—" his hands came together on the table — "it was one of the first antiques I ever bought, thirty years ago. In an American Folk sale. I'm not a great one for the folk art, never have been — this piece, not of the first quality, doesn't fit with anything else I own, and yet isn't it always the inappropriate thing, the thing that doesn't quite work, that's oddly the dearest?"

I pushed back in my chair, unable to keep my feet still. "Can I see her now?" I said.

"If she's awake —" he pursed his lips — "well, don't see the harm. But only for a minute, mind." When he stood, his bulky, stoop-shouldered height took me by surprise all over again. "I warn you, though — she's a bit muddled. Oh —" he turned in the doorway — "and best not to bring up Welty if you can help it."

"She doesn't know?"

"Oh yes —" his voice was brisk — "she knows, but sometimes when she hears it she gets upset all over again. Asks when it happened and why nobody told her."

ii.

WHEN HE OPENED THE door, the shades were down, and it took my eyes a moment to adjust to the dark, which was aromatic and perfume-smelling, with an undertone of sickness and medicine. Over the bed hung a framed poster from the movie *The Wizard of Oz*. A scented candle guttered in a red glass, among trinkets and rosaries, sheet music, tissue-paper flowers and old valentines — along with what looked like hundreds of get-well cards strung up on ribbons, and a bunch of silver balloons hovering ominously at the ceiling, metallic strings hanging down like jellyfish stingers.

"Someone here to see you, Pip," said Hobie, in a loud and cheerful tone.

I saw the coverlet stir. An elbow went up. "Umn?" said a sleepy voice.

"It's so dark, my dear. Won't you let me open the curtains?"

"No, please don't, the light hurts my eyes."

She was smaller than I remembered, and her face — a blur in the gloom — was very white. Head shaven, all but a single lock in front. As I drew closer, a bit fearfully, I saw a glint of metal at her temple — a barrette or hairpin, I thought, before I made out the steel medical staples in a vicious coil above one ear.

"I heard you in the hallway," she said, in a small, raspy voice, looking from me to Hobie.

"Heard what, pigeon?" said Hobie.

"Heard you talking. Cosmo did too."

At first I didn't see the dog, and then I did — a gray terrier curled alongside her, amidst the pillows and stuffed toys. When he raised his head, I saw from his grizzled face and cataract-clouded eyes that he was very old.

"I thought you were asleep, pigeon," Hobie was saying, reaching out to scratch the dog's chin.

"You always say that, but I'm always awake. Hi," she said, looking up at me.

"Hi."

"Who are you?"

"My name's Theo."

"What's your favorite piece of music?"

"I don't know," I said, and then, so as not to appear stupid: "Beethoven."

"That's great. You look like somebody who would like Beethoven."

"I do?" I said, feeling overwhelmed.

"I meant that in a nice way. I can't listen to music. Because of my head. It's completely horrible. No," she said to Hobie, who was clearing books and gauze and Kleenex packets out of the bedside chair so I could sit down in it, "let him sit here. You can sit here," she said to me, shifting over slightly in the bed to make room.

After a glance back at Hobie to make sure it was okay, I sat down, gingerly, with one hip, careful not to disturb the dog, who raised his head and glared.

"Don't worry, he won't bite. Well, sometimes he bites." She looked at me with drowsy eyes. "I know you."

"You remember me?"

"Are we friends?"

"Yes," I said without thinking, and then glanced back at Hobie, embarrassed I'd lied.

"I forgot your name, I'm sorry. I remember your face though." Then — stroking the dog's head — she said: "I didn't remember my room when I came home. I remembered my bed, and all my stuff, but the room was different."

Now that my eyes had adjusted to the dark, I saw the wheelchair in the corner, the bottles of medicine on the table by her bed.

"What Beethoven do you like?"

"Uh—" I was staring at her arm, resting atop the coverlet, the tender skin on the inside of her arm with a Band-Aid in the crook of the elbow.

She was pushing up in bed—looking past me, to Hobie, silhouetted in the bright doorway. "I'm not supposed to talk too much, am I?" she said.

"No, pigeon."

"I don't think I'm too tired. But I can't tell. Do you get tired during the day?" she asked me.

"Sometimes." After my mother's death, I had developed a tendency to fall asleep in class and conk out in Andy's room after school. "I never used to."

"I do, too. I feel sleepy all the time now. I wonder why? I think it's so boring."

Hobie—I noticed, looking back at the lighted doorway—had stepped away for a moment. Although it was very unlike me, for some strange reason I had been itching to reach out and take her hand, and now that we were alone, I did.

"You don't mind, do you?" I asked her. Everything seemed slow like I was moving through deep water. It was very strange to be holding some-body's hand—a girl's hand—and yet oddly normal. I had never done anything of the sort before.

"Not at all. I think it's nice." Then, after a brief pause—during which I could hear the little terrier snoring—she said: "You don't mind if I close my eyes for a few seconds, do you?"

"No," I said, running a thumb over her knuckles, tracing the bones.

"I know it's rude, but I just absolutely have to."

I looked down at her shaded eyelids, chapped lips, pallor and bruises, the ugly hashmark of metal over one ear. The strange combination of what was exciting about her, and what wasn't supposed to be, made me feel light-headed and confused.

Guilty, I glanced back, and noticed Hobie standing in the door. After tiptoeing out to the hall again, I closed the door quietly behind me, grate-ful that the hall was so dark.

Together, we walked back through to the parlor. "How does she seem to you?" he said, in a voice so low I could hardly hear him.

What was I supposed to say to that? "Okay, I guess."

"She's not herself." He paused, unhappily, with his hands dug deep into the pockets of the bathrobe. "That is — she is, and she isn't. She doesn't recognize a lot of people who were close to her, speaks to them very formally, and yet sometimes she's very open with strangers, very chatty and familiar, people she's never seen before, treats them like old friends. Quite common, I'm told."

"Why isn't she supposed to listen to music?"

He raised an eyebrow. "Oh, she does, sometimes. But sometimes, late in the day especially, it tends to upset her — she thinks she has to practice, that she has to prepare a piece for school, she gets distraught. Very difficult. As far as playing on some amateur level, that's perfectly possible someday, or so they tell me —"

Quite suddenly, the doorbell rang, startling us both.

"Ah," said Hobie — looking distressed, glancing at what I noticed was an extremely beautiful old wristwatch, "that'll be her nurse."

We looked at each other. We weren't finished talking; there was so much still to say.

Again the doorbell rang. Down the hall, the dog was barking. "She's early," said Hobie — hurrying through, looking a bit desperate.

"Can I come back? To see her?"

He stopped. He seemed appalled that I had even asked. "But of *course* you can come back," he said. "*Please* come back —"

Again the doorbell.

"Any time you like," said Hobie. "Please. We're always glad to see you."

iii.

"So, what happened down there?" said Andy as we were dressing for dinner. "Was it weird?" Platt had left to catch the train back to school; Mrs. Barbour had a supper with the board of some charity; and Mr. Barbour was taking the rest of us out to dinner at the Yacht Club (where we only went on nights when Mrs. Barbour had something else to do).

"He knew your mother, the guy."

Andy, knotting his necktie, made a face: everybody knew his mother.

"It was a little weird," I said. "But it's good I went. Here," I said, fishing in my jacket pocket, "thanks for your phone."

Andy checked it for messages, then switched it off and slipped it in his pocket. Pausing, with his hand still in the pocket, he looked up, not straight at me.

"I know things are bad," he said unexpectedly. "I'm sorry everything is so fucked up for you now."

His voice — as flat as the robot voice on an answering machine — kept me for a moment from realizing quite what he'd said.

"She was awfully nice," he said, still without looking at me. "I mean —"

"Yeah, well," I muttered, not anxious to continue the conversation.

"I mean, *I* miss her," Andy said, meeting my eye with a sort of half-terrified look. "I never knew anybody that died before. Well, my grandpa Van der Pleyn. Never anybody I liked."

I said nothing. My mother had always had a soft spot for Andy, patiently drawing him out about his home weather station, teasing him about his Galactic Battlegrounds scores until he went bright red with pleasure. Young, playful, fun-loving, affectionate, she had been everything his own mother wasn't: a mother who threw Frisbees with us in the park and discussed zombie movies with us and let us lie around in her bed on Saturday mornings to eat Lucky Charms and watch cartoons; and it had annoyed me sometimes, a little, how goofy and exhilarated he was in her presence, trotting behind her babbling about Level 4 of whatever game he was on, unable to tear his eyes from her rear end when she was bending to get something from the fridge.

"She was the coolest," said Andy, in his faraway voice. "Do you remember when she took us on the bus to that horror-fan convention way out in New Jersey? And that creep named Rip who kept following us around trying to get her to be in his vampire movie?"

He meant well, I knew. But it was almost unbearable for me to talk about anything to do with my mother, or Before, and I turned my head away.

"I don't think he was even a horror person," Andy said, in his faint, annoying voice. "I think he was some kind of fetishist. All that dungeon stuff with the girls strapped to the laboratory tables was pretty much straight-up bondage porn. Do you remember him begging her to try on those vampire teeth?"

"Yeah. That was when she went up to talk to the security guard."

"Leather pants. All those piercings. I mean, who knows, maybe he really was making a vampire film but he was definitely a huge perv, did you notice that? Like, that sneaky smile? And the way he kept trying to look down her top?"

I gave him the finger. "Come on, let's go," I said. "I'm hungry."

"Oh, yes?" I'd lost nine or ten pounds since my mother died—enough weight that Mrs. Swanson (embarrassingly) had started weighing me in her office, on the scale she used for girls with eating disorders.

"What, you're not?"

"Yeah, but I thought you were watching your weight. So you'd fit in your prom dress."

"Fuck you," I said good-naturedly as I opened the door—and walked straight into Mr. Barbour, who had been standing right outside, whether eavesdropping or about to knock it was hard to say.

Mortified, I began to stammer—swearing was seriously against the rules at the Barbours' house—but Mr. Barbour didn't seem greatly perturbed.

"Well, Theo," he said dryly, looking over my head, "I'm certainly glad to hear that you're feeling better. Come along now, and let's go get a table."

iv.

DURING THE NEXT WEEK, everyone noticed that my appetite had improved, even Toddy. "Are you done with your hunger strike?" he asked me curiously, one morning.

"Toddy, eat your breakfast."

"But I thought that was what it was called. When people don't eat."

"No, a hunger strike is for people in prison," Kitsey said coolly.

"*Kitten*," said Mr. Barbour, in a warning tone.

"Yes, but he ate three waffles yesterday," said Toddy, looking eagerly between his uninterested parents in an attempt to engage them. "I only ate two waffles. And this morning he ate a bowl of cereal and six pieces of bacon, but you said five pieces of bacon was too much for me. Why can't I have five pieces, too?"

V.

"WELL, HELLO THERE, GREETINGS," said Dave the psychiatrist as he closed the door and took a seat across from me in his office: kilim rugs, shelves filled with old textbooks (*Drugs and Society; Child Psychology: A Different Approach*); and beige draperies that parted with a hum when you pushed a button.

I smiled, awkwardly, eyes going all around the room, potted palm tree, bronze statue of the Buddha, everywhere but him.

"So." The faint traffic drone floating up from First Avenue made the silence between us seem vast, intergalactic. "How's everything today?"

"Well—" I dreaded my sessions with Dave, a twice-weekly ordeal not incomparable to dental surgery; I felt guilty for not liking him more since he made such an effort, always asking what movies I enjoyed, what books, burning me CDs, clipping articles from *Game Pro* he thought I'd be interested in—sometimes he even took me over to EJ's Luncheonette for a hamburger—and yet whenever he started with the questions I froze stiff, as if I'd been pushed onstage in a play where I didn't know the lines.

"You seem a little distracted today."

"Um..." It had not escaped me that a number of the books on Dave's shelves had titles with the word *sex* in them: *Adolescent Sexuality, Sex and Cognition, Patterns of Sexual Deviance* and—my favorite: *Out of the Shadows: Understanding Sexual Addiction*. "I'm okay, I guess."

"You guess?"

"No, I'm fine. Things are good."

"Oh yeah?" Dave leaned back in his chair, Converse sneaker bobbing. "That's great." Then: "Why don't you bring me up to speed a little bit on what's been going on?"

"Oh—" I scratched my eyebrow, looked away—"Spanish is still pretty difficult—I have another make-up test, I'll probably take that Monday. But I got an A on my Stalingrad paper. So it looks like that'll bring my B minus in history up to a B."

He was quiet so long, looking at me, that I began to feel cornered and started casting around for something else to say. Then: "Anything else?"

"Well—" I looked at my thumbs.

"How has your anxiety been?"

"Not so bad," I said, thinking how uneasy it made me that I didn't know a thing about Dave. He was one of those guys who wore a wedding ring that didn't really look like a wedding ring—or maybe it wasn't a wedding ring at all and he was just super-proud of his Celtic heritage. If I'd had to guess, I would have said he was newly married, with a baby— he gave off a glazed vibe of exhausted young fatherhood, like he might have to get up and change diapers in the night—but who knew?

"And your medication? What about the side effects?"

"Uh—" I scratched my nose—"better I guess." I hadn't even been taking my pills, which made me so tired and headachey I'd started spitting them down the plughole of the bathroom sink.

Dave was quiet for a moment. "So—would it be out of line to say that you're feeling better generally?"

"I guess not," I said, after a silence, staring at the wall hanging behind his head. It looked like a lopsided abacus made of clay beads and knotted rope, and I had spent what felt like a massive portion of my recent life staring at it.

Dave smiled. "You say that like it's something to be ashamed of. But feeling better doesn't mean you've forgotten about your mother. Or that you loved her any less."

Resenting this supposition, which had never occurred to me, I looked away from him and out the window, at his depressing view of the white brick building across the street.

"Do you have any idea why you might be feeling better?"

"No, not really," I said curtly. *Better* wasn't even the word for how I felt. There wasn't a word for it. It was more that things too small to mention—laughter in the hall at school, a live gecko scurrying in a tank in the science lab—made me feel happy one moment and the next like crying. Sometimes, in the evenings, a damp, gritty wind blew in the windows from Park Avenue, just as the rush hour traffic was thinning and the city was emptying for the night; it was rainy, trees leafing out, spring deepening into summer; and the forlorn cry of horns on the street, the dank smell of the wet pavement had an electricity about it, a sense of crowds and static, lonely secretaries and fat guys with bags of carry-out, everywhere the ungainly sadness of creatures pushing and struggling to live. For weeks, I'd been frozen, sealed-off; now, in the shower, I would turn up the water as hard as it would go and howl, silently. Everything was raw and painful and confusing and wrong and yet it was as if I'd been dragged from freezing water through a break in the ice, into sun and blazing cold.

"Where did you go just now?" said Dave, attempting to catch my eye.

"Sorry?"

"What were you just thinking about?"

"Nothing."

"Oh yeah? Pretty hard to think about absolutely nothing."

I shrugged. Aside from Andy, I'd told no one about going down on the bus to Pippa's house, and the secret colored everything, like the afterglow of a dream: tissue-paper poppies, dim light from a guttering candle, the sticky heat of her hand in mine. But though it was the most resonant and real-seeming thing that had happened in a long time, I didn't want to spoil it by talking about it, especially not with him.

We sat there for another long moment or two. Then Dave leaned forward with a concerned expression and said: "You know, when I ask you where you go during these silences, Theo, I'm not trying to be a jerk or put you on the spot or anything."

"Oh, sure! I know," I said uneasily, picking at the tweed upholstery on the arm of the sofa.

"I'm here to talk about whatever you want to talk about. Or —" creak of wood as he shifted in his chair — "we don't have to talk at all! Only I wonder if you have something on your mind."

"Well," I said, after another never-ending pause, resisting the temptation to peek sideways at my watch. "I mean I just" — how many more minutes did we have? *Forty?*

"Because I hear, from some of the other adults in your life, that you've had a noticeable upswing of late. You've been participating in class more," he said, when I didn't answer. "Engaging socially. Eating normal meals again." In the stillness, an ambulance siren floated up faintly from the street. "So I guess I'm wondering if you could help me understand what's changed."

I shrugged, scratched the side of my face. How were you supposed to explain this kind of thing? It seemed stupid to try. Even the memory was starting to seem vague and starry with unreality, like a dream where the details get fainter the harder you try to grasp them. What mattered more was the feeling, a rich sweet undertow so commanding that in class, on the school bus, lying in bed trying to think of something safe or pleasant, some environment or configuration where my chest wasn't tight with anxiety, all I had to do was sink into the blood-warm current and let myself spin away to the secret place where everything was all right. Cinnamon-colored walls, rain on the windowpanes, vast quiet and a sense of depth and distance, like the varnish over the background of a nineteenth-century painting. Rugs worn to threads, painted Japanese fans and antique valentines flickering in candlelight, Pierrots and doves and flower-garlanded hearts. Pippa's face pale in the dark.

vi.

"LISTEN," I SAID TO Andy several days later, as we were coming out of Starbucks after school, "can you cover for me this afternoon?"

"Certainly," said Andy, taking a greedy swallow of his coffee. "How long?"

"Don't know." Depending on how long it took me to change trains at Fourteenth Street, it might take forty-five minutes to get downtown; the bus, on a weekday, would be even longer. "Three hours?"

He made a face; if his mother was at home, she would ask questions. "What shall I tell her?"

"Tell her I had to stay late at school or something."

"She'll think you're in trouble."

"Who cares?"

"Yes, but I don't want her to phone school to check on you."

"Tell her I went to a movie."

"Then she'll ask why I didn't go too. Why don't I say you're at the library."

"That's so lame."

"All right, then. Why don't we tell her that you have a terribly pressing engagement with your parole officer. Or that you stopped in to have a couple of Old Fashioneds at the bar of the Four Seasons."

He was imitating his father; the impression was so dead-on, I laughed. "*Fabelhaft,*" I replied, in Mr. Barbour's voice. "Very funny."

He shrugged. "The main branch is open tonight until seven," he said, in his own bland and faint-ish voice. "But I don't have to know which branch you went to, if you forget to tell me."

vii.

THE DOOR OPENED QUICKER than I'd expected, while I was staring down the street and thinking of something else. This time, he was clean-shaven, smelling of soap, with his long gray hair neatly combed back and tucked behind his ears; and he was just as impressively dressed as Mr. Blackwell had been when I'd seen him.

His eyebrows came up; clearly he was surprised to see me. "Hello!"

"Have I come at a bad time?" I said, eyeing the snowy cuff of his shirt, which was embroidered with a tiny cypher in Chinese red, block letters so small and stylized they were nearly invisible.

"Not at all. As a matter of fact I was hoping you'd stop by." He was wearing a red tie with a pale yellow figure; black oxford brogues; a beautifully tailored navy suit. "Come in! Please."

"Are you going somewhere?" I said, regarding him timidly. The suit made him seem a different person, less melancholy and distracted, more capable — unlike the Hobie of my first visit, with his bedraggled aspect of an elegant but mistreated polar bear.

"Well — yes. But not now. Quite frankly, we're in a bit of a tip. But no matter."

What did that mean? I followed him inside — through the forest of the workshop, table legs and unsprung chairs — and up through the gloomy parlor into the kitchen, where Cosmo the terrier was pacing fretfully back and forth and whimpering, his toenails clicking on the slate. When we came in, he took a few steps backwards and glared up at us aggressively.

"Why's he in here?" I asked, kneeling to stroke his head, and then pulling my hand back when he shied away.

"Hmn?" said Hobie. He seemed preoccupied.

"Cosmo. Doesn't he like to be with her?"

"Oh. Her aunt. She doesn't want him in there." He was filling the teakettle at the sink; and — I noticed — the kettle shook in his hands as he did it.

"Aunt?"

"Yes," he said, putting the kettle on to boil, then stooping to scratch the dog's chin. "Poor little toad, you don't know what to make of it, do you? Margaret's got very strong opinions on the subject of dogs in the sickroom.

No doubt she's right. And here *you* are," he said, glancing over his shoulder with an odd bright look. "Washing up on the strand again. Pippa's been talking of you ever since you were here."

"Really?" I said, delighted.

"'Where's that boy.' 'There was a boy here.' She told me yesterday that you were coming back and *presto,*" he said, with a warm and young-sounding laugh, "here you are." He stood, knees creaking, and wiped the back of his wrist against his knobbly white brow. "If you wait a bit, you can go in and see her."

"How is she doing?"

"*Much* better," he said, crisply, without looking at me. "Lots of goings-on. Her aunt is taking her to Texas."

"Texas?" I said, after a stunned pause.

"Afraid so."

"When?"

"Day after tomorrow."

"No!"

He grimaced—a twinge that vanished the moment I saw it. "Yes, I've been packing her up to go," he said, in a cheerful voice that did not match the flash of unhappiness that he'd let slip. "People have been in and out. Friends from school—in fact, this is the first quiet moment we've had in a while. It's been quite a busy week."

"When is she coming back?"

"Well—not for a while, actually. Margaret's taking her down there to live."

"Forever?"

"Oh no! Not *forever,*" he said, in a voice that made me realize that *forever* was exactly what he meant. "It's not as if anyone's leaving the planet," he added, when he saw my face. "Certainly I'll be going down to see her. And certainly she'll be back for visits."

"But—" I felt like the ceiling had collapsed on top of me. "I thought she lived here. With you."

"Well, she did. Until now. Although I'm sure she'll be much better off down there," he added, without conviction. "It's a big change for us all, but in the long run I'm sure it's all for the best."

I could tell he didn't believe a word of what he was saying. "But why can't she stay here?"

He sighed. "Margaret is Welty's half sister," he said. "His *other* half sister. Pippa's nearest relative. Blood, in any case, which I am not. She thinks that Pippa will be better off in Texas, now that she's well enough to move."

"I wouldn't want to live in Texas," I said, taken aback. "It's too hot."

"I don't think the doctors are as good there either," said Hobie, dusting his hands off. "Although Margaret and I disagree about that."

He sat down, and looked at me. "Your glasses," he said. "I like them."

"Thanks." I didn't want to talk about my new eyeglasses, an unwelcome development, although they did actually help me to see better. Mrs. Barbour had picked out the frames for me at E. B. Meyrowitz after I'd failed an eye test with the school nurse. They were round tortoiseshell, a little too grown-up and expensive-looking, and adults had been going a little too far out of their way to assure me how great they looked.

"How are things uptown?" said Hobie. "You can't imagine the stir your visit has caused. As a matter of fact, I was thinking of coming uptown to see you myself. The only reason I didn't was that I hated to leave Pippa since she's going away so soon. This has all happened very fast, you see. The business with Margaret. She's like their father, old Mr. Blackwell— she gets something in her head and off she goes, it's done."

"Is he going to Texas too? Cosmo?"

"Oh no—he'll be fine here. He's lived here in this house since he was twelve weeks old."

"Won't he be unhappy?"

"I hope not. Well—quite honestly—he'll miss her. Cosmo and I get on fairly well, though he's been in a terrible slump since Welty died. He was Welty's dog really, he's only taken up with Pippa quite recently. These little terriers like Welty always had aren't always so crazy about children, you understand—Cosmo's mother Chessie was a holy terror."

"But why does Pippa have to move down there?"

"Well," he said, rubbing his eye, "it's really the only thing that makes sense. Margaret is the technical nearest of kin. Though Margaret and Welty scarcely spoke while Welty was alive—not in recent years, anyway."

"Why not?"

"Well—" I could tell he didn't want to explain it. "It's all very complicated. Margaret was quite against Pippa's mother, you see."

Just as he said this, a tall, sharp-nosed, capable-looking woman walked into the room, the age of a young-ish grandmother, with a thin, patrician-harpy face and iron-rust hair going gray. Her suit and shoes reminded me of Mrs. Barbour, only they were a color that Mrs. Barbour would never have worn: lime green.

She looked at me; she looked at Hobie. "What is this?" she said coldly.

Hobie exhaled audibly; he looked exasperated. "Never mind, Margaret. This is the boy who was with Welty when he died."

She peered over her half-glasses at me — and then laughed sharply, a high self-conscious laugh.

"But hello," she said — all charm all of a sudden, holding out to me her thin red hands covered with diamonds. "I'm Margaret Blackwell Pierce. Welty's sister. *Half* sister," she corrected herself, with a glance over my shoulder at Hobie, when she saw my eyebrows go down. "Welty and I had the same father, you see. My mother was Susie Delafield."

She said the name as if it ought to mean something. I looked at Hobie to see what he thought about it. She saw me doing it, and glanced at him sharply before she returned her attention — all sparkle — to me.

"And what an adorable little boy you are," she said to me. Her long nose was slightly pink at the end. "I'm awfully glad to meet you. James and Pippa have been telling me all about your visit — *the* most extraordinary thing. We've all been abuzz about it. Also—" she clasped my hand — "I have to thank you from the bottom of my heart for returning my grandfather's ring to me. It means an awful lot to me."

Her ring? Again, in confusion, I looked at Hobie.

"It would have meant a lot to my father, as well." There was a deliberate, practiced quality to her friendliness ("buckets of charm," as Mr. Barbour would have said); and yet her coppery tang of resemblance to Mr. Blackwell, and Pippa, drew me in despite myself. "You know how it was lost before, don't you?"

The kettle whistled. "Would you like some tea, Margaret?" said Hobie.

"Yes please," she replied briskly. "Lemon and honey. A tiny bit of scotch in it." To me, in a more friendly voice, she said: "I'm terribly sorry, but I'm afraid we have some grown-up business to attend to. We're to meet with the lawyer shortly. As soon as Pippa's nurse arrives."

Hobie cleared his throat. "I don't see any harm if—"

"May I go in and see her?" I said, too impatient for him to finish the sentence.

"Of course," said Hobie quickly, before Aunt Margaret could intervene — turning expertly away to evade her annoyed expression. "You remember the way, don't you? Just through there."

viii.

THE FIRST THING SHE said to me was: "Will you please turn off the light?" She was propped in bed with the earbuds to her iPod in, looking blinded and disoriented in the light from the overhead bulb.

I switched it off. The room was emptier, cardboard boxes stacked against the walls. A thin spring rain was hitting at the windowpanes; outside, in the dark courtyard, the foamy white blossoms of a flowering pear were pale against wet brick.

"Hello," she said, folding her hands a little tighter on the coverlet.

"Hi," I said, wishing I didn't sound quite so awkward.

"I knew it was you! I heard you talking in the kitchen."

"Oh, yeah? How'd you know it was me?"

"I'm a musician! I have very sharp ears."

Now that my eyes had adjusted to the dim, I saw that she seemed less frail than she had on my previous visit. Her hair had grown back in a bit and the staples were out, though the puckered line of the wound was still visible.

"How do you feel?" I said.

She smiled. "Sleepy." The sleep was in her voice, rough and sweet at the edges. "Do you mind sharing?"

"Sharing what?"

She turned her head to the side and removed one of the earbuds, and handed it to me. "Listen."

I sat down by her on the bed, and put it in my ear: aethereal harmonies, impersonal, piercing, like a radio signal from Paradise.

We looked at each other. "What is it?" I said.

"Umm —" she looked at the iPod — "Palestrina."

"Oh." But I didn't care what it was. The only reason I was even hearing it was because of the rainy light, the white tree at the window, the thunder, her.

The silence between us was happy and strange, connected by the cord and the icy voices thinly echoing. "You don't have to talk," she said. "If you don't feel like it." Her eyelids were heavy and her voice was drowsy and like a secret. "People always want to talk but I like being quiet."

"Have you been crying?" I said, looking at her a bit more closely.

"No. Well—a little."

We sat there, not saying anything, and it didn't feel clumsy or weird.

"I have to leave," she said presently. "Did you know?"

"I know. He told me."

"It's awful. I don't want to go." She smelled like salt, and medicine, and something else, like the chamomile tea my mother bought at Grace's, grassy and sweet.

"She seems nice," I said, cautiously. "I guess."

"I guess," she echoed gloomily, trailing a fingertip along the border of the coverlet. "She said something about a swimming pool. And horses."

"That should be fun."

She blinked, in confusion. "Maybe."

"Do you ride?"

"No."

"Me neither. My mother did though. She loved horses. She always stopped to talk to the carriage horses on Central Park South. Like—" I didn't know how to say it—"it was almost like they'd talk to *her*. Like, they'd try to turn their heads, even with their blinkers on, to where she was walking."

"Is your mother dead too?" she said timidly.

"Yes."

"My mother's been dead for—" she stopped and thought—"I can't remember. She died after my spring holidays from school one year, so I had spring holidays off and the week after spring holidays too. And there was a field trip we were supposed to go on, to the Botanical Gardens, and I didn't get to go. I miss her."

"What'd she die of?"

"She got sick. Was your mother sick too?"

"No. It was an accident." And then—not wanting to venture more upon this subject: "Anyway, she loved horses a lot, my mother. When she was growing up she had a horse she said got lonely sometimes? and he liked to come right up to the house and put his head in at the window to see what was going on."

"What was his name?"

"Paintbox." I'd loved it when my mother told me about the stables back in Kansas: owls and bats in the rafters, horses nickering and blowing. I knew the names of all her childhood horses and dogs.

"Paintbox! Was he all different colors?"

"He was spotted, sort of. I've seen pictures of him. Sometimes — in the summer — he'd come and look in on her while she was having her afternoon nap. She could hear him breathing, you know, just inside the curtains."

"That's so nice! I like horses. It's just —"

"What?"

"I'd rather stay here!" All at once she seemed close to tears. "I don't know why I have to go."

"You should tell them you want to stay." When did our hands start touching? Why was her hand so hot?

"I did tell them! Except everyone thinks it'll be better there."

"Why?"

"I don't know," she said fretfully. "Quieter, they said. But I don't like the quiet, I like it when there's lots of stuff to hear."

"They're going to make me leave, too."

She pushed up on her elbow. "No!" she said, looking alarmed. "When?"

"I don't know. Soon, I guess. I have to go live with my grandparents."

"Oh," she said longingly, falling back on the pillow. "I don't have any grandparents."

I threaded my fingers through hers. "Mine aren't very nice."

"I'm sorry."

"That's okay," I said, in as normal a voice as I could, though my heart was pounding so hard that I could feel my pulse jumping in my fingertips. Her hand, in mine, was velvety and fever-hot, just the slightest bit sticky.

"Don't you have any other family?" Her eyes were so dark in the wan light from the window that they looked black.

"No. Well—" Did my father count? "No."

There followed a long silence. We were still connected by the earbuds: one in her ear, one in mine. Seashells singing. Angel choirs and pearls. Things had gotten way too slow all of a sudden; it was as if I'd forgotten how to breathe properly; over and over I found myself holding my breath, then exhaling raggedly and too loud.

"What did you say this music was?" I asked, just for something to say.

She smiled sleepily, and reached for a pointed, unappetizing-looking lollipop that lay atop a foil wrapper on her nightstand.

"Palestrina," she said, around the stick in her mouth. "High mass. Or something. They're all a lot alike."

"Do you like her?" I said. "Your aunt?"

She looked at me for several long beats. Then she put the lollipop carefully back on the wrapper and said: "She seems nice. I guess. Only I don't really know her. It's weird."

"Why do you? Have to go?"

"It's about money. Hobie can't do anything—he isn't my real uncle. My pretend uncle, she calls him."

"I wish he was your real uncle," I said. "I want you to stay."

Suddenly she sat up, and put her arms around me, and kissed me; and all the blood rushed from my head, a long sweep, like I was falling off a cliff.

"I—" Terror struck me. In a daze, by reflex, I reached to wipe the kiss away—only this wasn't soggy, or gross, I could feel a trace of it glowing all along the back of my hand.

"I don't want you to go."

"I don't want to, either."

"Do you remember seeing me?"

"When?"

"Right before."

"No."

"I remember you," I said. Somehow my hand had found its way to her cheek, and clumsily I pulled it back and forced it to my side, making a fist, practically sitting on it. "I was there." It was then I realized that Hobie was in the door.

"Hello, old love." And though the warmth in the voice was mostly for her, I could tell a little was for me. "I told you he'd be back."

"You did!" she said, pushing herself up. "He's here."

"Well, will you listen to me next time?"

"I was *listening* to you. I just didn't *believe* you."

The hem of a sheer curtain brushed a windowsill. Faintly, I heard traffic singing on the street. Sitting there on the edge of her bed, it felt like the waking-up moment between dream and daylight where everything merged and mingled just as it was about to change, all in the same, fluid, euphoric slide: rainy light, Pippa sitting up with Hobie in the doorway, and her kiss (with the peculiar flavor of what I now believe to have been a morphine lollipop) still sticky on my lips. Yet I'm not sure that even morphine would account for how lightheaded I felt at that moment, how smilingly wrapped-up in happiness and beauty. Half-dazed, we said our goodbyes (there were no promises to write; it seemed she was too ill for that) and then I was in the hallway, with the nurse there, Aunt Margaret talking loud and bewilderingly and Hobie's reassuring hand on my shoulder, a strong, comforting pressure, like an anchor letting me know that everything was okay. I hadn't felt a touch like that since my mother died—friendly, steadying in the midst of confusing events—and, like a stray dog hungry for affection, I felt some profound shift in allegiance, blood-deep, a sudden, humiliating, eyewatering conviction of *this place is good, this person is safe, I can trust him, nobody will hurt me here.*

"Ah," cried Aunt Margaret, "are you crying? Do you see that?" she said to the young nurse (nodding, smiling, eager to please, clearly under her spell). "How sweet he is! You'll miss her, won't you?" Her smile was wide and assured of itself, of its own rightness. "You'll have to come down and visit, *absolutely* you will. I'm always happy to have guests. My parents...they had one of the biggest Tudor houses in Texas..."

On she prattled, friendly as a parrot. But my loyalties were elsewhere. And the flavor of Pippa's kiss—bittersweet and strange—stayed with me all the way back uptown, swaying and sleepy as I sailed home on the bus, melting with sorrow and loveliness, a starry ache that lifted me up above the windswept city like a kite: my head in the rainclouds, my heart in the sky.

ix.

I HATED TO THINK of her leaving. I couldn't stand thinking of it. On the day she was going, I woke feeling heartsick. Looking at the sky over Park Avenue, blue-black and threatening, a roiling sky straight from a painting of Calvary, I imagined her looking out at the same dark sky from her airplane window; and — as Andy and I walked to the bus stop, the downcast eyes and the sober mood on the street seemed to reflect and magnify my sadness at her departure.

"Well, Texas is boring, all right," said Andy, between sneezes; his eyes were pink and streaming from pollen so he looked even more like a lab rat than usual.

"You went there?"

"Yes — Dallas. Uncle Harry and Aunt Tess lived there for a while. There's nothing to do but go to the movies and you can't walk anywhere, people have to drive you. Also they have rattlesnakes, and the death penalty, which I think is primitive and unethical in ninety-eight per cent of cases. But it'll probably be better for her there."

"Why?"

"The climate, primarily," said Andy, swiping his nose with one of the pressed cotton handkerchiefs he plucked every morning from the stack in his drawer. "Convalescents do better in warm weather. That's why my grandpa Van der Pleyn moved to Palm Beach."

I was silent. Andy, I knew, was loyal; I trusted him, I valued his opinion, and yet his conversation sometimes made me feel as though I was talking to one of those computer programs that mimic human response.

"If she's in Dallas she should definitely go to the Nature and Science Museum. Although I think she'll find it small and somewhat dated. The IMAX I saw there wasn't even 3-D. Also they ask for extra money to get into the planetarium, which is ridiculous considering how inferior it is to Hayden."

"Huh." Sometimes I wondered exactly what it might take to break Andy out of his math-nerd turret: a tidal wave? Decepticon invasion? Godzilla tromping down Fifth Avenue? He was a planet without an atmosphere.

X.

HAD ANYONE EVER FELT so lonely? Back at the Barbours', amidst the clamor and plenitude of a family that wasn't mine, I now felt even more alone than usual—especially since, as the end of the school year neared, it wasn't clear to me (or Andy either, for that matter) if I would be accompanying them to their summer house in Maine. Mrs. Barbour, with her characteristic delicacy, managed to skirt the topic even in the midst of the cardboard boxes and open suitcases that were appearing all over the house; Mr. Barbour and the younger siblings all seemed excited but Andy regarded the prospect with frank horror. "Sun and fun," he said contemptuously, pushing his glasses (like mine, only a lot thicker) up on the bridge of his nose. "At least with your grandparents you'll be on dry land. With hot water. An Internet connection."

"I don't feel sorry for you."

"Well, if you do have to go with us, see how you like it. It's like *Kidnapped*. The part where they sell him into slavery on that boat."

"What about the part where he has to go to his creepy relative in the middle of nowhere that he doesn't even know?"

"Yes, I was thinking that," said Andy seriously, turning in his desk chair to look at me. "Although at least they aren't scheming to kill you—it's not as if there's an inheritance at stake."

"No, there's certainly not."

"Do you know what my advice to you is?"

"No, what?"

"My advice," said Andy, scratching his nose with the eraser of his pencil, "is to work as hard as you possibly can when you get to your new school in Maryland. You've got an advantage—you're ahead a year. That means you'll graduate when you're seventeen. If you apply yourself, you can be out of there in four years, maybe even three, with a scholarship anywhere you want to go."

"My grades aren't that good."

"No," said Andy seriously, "but only because you don't work. Also I think it fair to assume that your new school, wherever it is, won't be quite as demanding."

"I pray to God not."

"I mean—public school," said Andy. "Maryland. No disrespect to Maryland. I mean, they do have the Applied Physics Laboratory and the Space Telescope Science Institute at Johns Hopkins, to say nothing of the Goddard Space Flight Center in Greenbelt. Definitely it's a state with some serious NASA commitment. You tested in what percentile back in junior high?"

"I don't remember."

"Well, it's fine if you don't want to tell me. My point is, you can finish with good marks when you're seventeen—maybe sixteen, if you bear down hard—and then you can go to college wherever you want."

"Three years is a long time."

"It is to us. But in the scheme of things—not at all. I mean," said Andy reasonably, "look at some poor dumb bunny like Sabine Ingersoll or that idiot James Villiers. Forrest fucking Longstreet."

"Those people aren't poor. I saw Villiers's father on the cover of the *Economist*."

"No, but they're as dumb as a set of sofa cushions. I mean—Sabine can barely put one foot in front of the other. If her family didn't have money and she had to manage on her own, she'd have to be, I don't know, a prostitute. Longstreet—he'd probably just crawl in the corner and starve. Like a hamster you forgot to feed."

"You're depressing me."

"All I'm saying is—you're smart. And grownups like you."

"What?" I said doubtfully.

"Sure," said Andy, in his wan, irritating voice. "You remember names, do the eye-contact stuff, shake hands when you're supposed to. At school they all tie themselves in knots for you."

"Yeah, but—" I didn't want to say it was because my mother was dead.

"Don't be stupid. You get away with murder. You're smart enough to figure it out on your own."

"Why haven't you figured out this sailing business then?"

"Oh, I've figured it out, all right," said Andy grimly, returning to his hiragana workbook. "I've figured that I have four summers of Hell, at absolute worst. Three if Daddy lets me go to early college when I'm sixteen. Two if I bite the bullet junior year and go to that summer program at the Mountain School and learn organic farming. And after that, I'm never setting foot on a boat again."

xi.

"IT'S DIFFICULT TO TALK to her on the phone, alas," said Hobie. "I wasn't anticipating that. She doesn't do well at all."

"Doesn't do well?" I said. Scarcely a week had passed, and though I'd had no thought of returning to see Hobie somehow I was down there again: sitting at his kitchen table and eating my second dish of what had, upon first glance, appeared to be a black lump of flowerpot mud but was actually some delicious mess of ginger and figs, with whipped cream and tiny, bitter slivers of orange peel on top.

Hobie rubbed his eye. He'd been repairing a chair in the basement when I'd arrived. "It's all very frustrating," he said. His hair was tied back from his face; his glasses were around his neck on a chain. Under his black work smock, which he'd removed and hung on a peg, he was wearing old corduroys stained with mineral spirit and beeswax, and a thin-washed cotton shirt with the sleeves rolled above the elbow. "Margaret said she cried for three hours after she got off the telephone with me on Sunday night."

"Why can't she just come back?"

"Honestly, I wish I knew how to make things better," said Hobie. Capable-looking and morose, his knobbly white hand flat on the table, there was something in the set of his shoulder that suggested a good-natured draft horse, or maybe a workman in the pub at the end of a long day. "I'd thought I might fly down and see about her, but Margaret says no. That she won't settle in properly if I'm hovering about."

"I think you should go anyway."

Hobie raised his eyebrows. "Margaret's hired a therapist—someone famous, apparently, who uses horses to work with injured children. And yes, Pippa loves animals, but even if she was perfectly well she wouldn't want to be outdoors and riding horses the whole time. She's spent most of her life in music lessons and practice halls. Margaret's full of enthusiasm about the music program at her church but an amateur children's choir can hardly hold much interest for her."

I pushed the glass dish—scraped clean—aside. "Why did Pippa not know her before?" I said timidly, and then, when he didn't answer: "Is it about money?"

"Not so much. Although—yes. You're right. Money always has

something to do with it. You see," he said, leaning forward with his big, expressive hands on the table, "Welty's father had three children. Welty, Margaret, and Pippa's mother, Juliet. All with different mothers."

"Oh."

"Welty—the eldest. And I mean—eldest son, you'd think, wouldn't you? But he contracted a tuberculosis of the spine when he was about six, when his parents were up in Aswan—the nanny didn't recognize how serious it was, he was taken to the hospital too late—he was a very bright boy, so I understand, personable too, but old Mr. Blackwell wasn't a man tolerant of weakness or infirmity. Sent him to America to live with relatives and barely gave him another thought."

"That's awful," I said, shocked at the unfairness of this.

"Yes. I mean—you'll get quite a different picture from Margaret, of course—but he was a hard man, Welty's father. At any rate, after the Blackwells were expelled from Cairo—*expelled* isn't the best term, perhaps. When Nasser came in, all the foreigners had to leave Egypt— Welty's father was in the oil business, luckily for him he had money and property elsewhere. Foreigners weren't allowed to take money or anything of much value out of the country.

"At any rate." He reached for another cigarette. "I've gone off track a little. The point is that Welty scarcely knew Margaret, who was a good twelve years younger. Margaret's mother was Texan, an heiress, with plenty of money of her own. That was the last and longest of old Mr. Blackwell's marriages—the great love affair, to hear Margaret tell it. Prominent couple in Houston—lots of drinking and chartered airplanes, African safaris—Welty's father loved Africa, even after he had to leave Cairo, he could never stay away.

"At any rate—" The match flared up, and he coughed as he exhaled a cloud of smoke. "Margaret was their father's princess, apple of his eye, all that. But still and all, throughout the marriage, he carried on with coat check girls, waitresses, the daughters of friends—and at some point, when he was in his sixties, he fathered a baby with a girl who cut his hair. And that baby was Pippa's mother."

I said nothing. In second grade there had been a huge fuss (documented, daily, in the gossip pages of the *New York Post*) when the father of one of my classmates had a baby with a woman not Eli's mother, which had meant that a lot of the mothers took sides and stopped speaking to each other out in front of school while they were waiting to pick us up in the afternoons.

"Margaret was in college, at Vassar," said Hobie fitfully. Though he was speaking to me as if I were a grownup (which I liked), he didn't seem particularly comfortable with the subject. "I think she didn't speak to her father for a couple of years. Old Mr. Blackwell tried to pay the hairdresser off but his cheapness got the better of him, his cheapness where his dependents were concerned, anyway. And so you see Margaret — Margaret and Pippa's mother Juliet never even met, except in the courtroom, when Juliet was practically still a babe in arms. Welty's father had grown to hate the hairdresser so much that he'd made it plain in the will that neither she nor Juliet was to get a cent, apart from whatever mingy child support was required by law. But Welty —" Hobie stubbed out his cigarette — "Old Mr. Blackwell had some second thoughts where Welty was concerned, and did the right thing by him in the will. And throughout all this legal fracas, which went on for years, Welty grew to be terribly disturbed by how the baby was shunted off and neglected. Juliet's mother didn't want her; none of the mother's relatives wanted her; old Mr. Blackwell had certainly never wanted her, and Margaret and her mother, frankly, would have been happy enough to see her on the street. And, in the meantime, there was the hairdresser, leaving Juliet alone in the apartment when she went to work . . . bad situation all around.

"Welty had no obligation to put his foot in but he was an affectionate man, without family, and he liked children. He invited Juliet here for a holiday when she was six years old, or 'JuleeAnn' as she was then —"

"Here? In this house?"

"Yes, here. And when the summer was over and it was time to send her back and she was crying about having to leave and the mother wasn't answering her telephone, he cancelled the plane tickets and phoned around to see about enrolling her in first grade. It was never an official arrangement — he was afraid to rock the boat, as they say — but most people assumed she was his child without inquiring too deeply. He was in his mid-thirties, plenty old enough to be her father. Which, in all the essential respects, he was.

"But, no matter," he said, looking up, in an altered tone. "You said you wanted to look around the workshop. Would you like to go down?"

"Please," I said. "That would be great." When I'd found him down there working on his up-ended chair, he'd stood and stretched and said he was ready for a break but I hadn't wanted to come upstairs at all, the workshop was so rich and magical: a treasure cave, bigger on the inside than it looked on the outside, with the light filtering down from the high windows, fretwork and filigree, mysterious tools I didn't know the names of, and the sharp, intriguing smells of varnish and beeswax. Even the chair he'd been working on — which had goat's legs in front, with cloven hooves — had seemed less like a piece of furniture than a creature under enchantment, like it might up-end itself and hop down from his work bench and trot away down the street.

Hobie reached for his smock and put it back on. For all his gentleness, his quiet manner, he was built like a man who moved refrigerators or loaded trucks for a living.

"So," he said, leading me downstairs. "The shop-behind-the-shop."

"Sorry?"

He laughed. "The arrière-boutique. What the customers see is a stage set — the face that's displayed to the public — but down here is where the important work happens."

"Right," I said, looking down at the labyrinth at the foot of the stairs, blond wood like honey, dark wood like poured molasses, gleams of brass and gilt and silver in the weak light. As with the Noah's Ark, each species of furniture was ranked with its own kind: chairs with chairs, settees with settees; clocks with clocks, desks and cabinets and highboys standing in stiff ranks opposite. Dining tables, in the middle, formed narrow, maze-like paths to be edged around. At the back of the room a wall of tarnished old mirrors, hung frame to frame, glowed with the silvered light of old ballrooms and candlelit salons.

Hobie looked back at me. He could see how pleased I was. "You like old things?"

I nodded — it was true, I did like old things, though it was something I'd never realized about myself before.

"It must be interesting for you at the Barbours', then. I expect that some of their Queen Anne and Chippendale is as good as anything you'll see in a museum."

"Yes," I said, hesitantly. "But here it's different. Nicer," I added, in case he didn't understand.

"How so?"

"I mean—" I squeezed my eyes shut, trying to collect my thoughts—"down here, it's great, so many chairs with so many other chairs...you see the different personalities, you know? I mean, that one's kind of—" I didn't know the word—"well, silly almost, but in a good way—a comfortable way. And that one's more nervous sort of, with those long spindly legs—"

"You have a good eye for furniture."

"Well—" compliments threw me, I was never sure how to respond except to act like I hadn't heard—"when they're lined up together you see how they're made. At the Barbours'—" I wasn't sure how to explain it—"I don't know, it's more like those scenes with the taxidermy animals at the Natural History Museum."

When he laughed, his air of gloom and anxiety evaporated; you could feel his good-nature, it radiated off him.

"No, I mean it," I said, determined to plow on and make my point. "The way she has it set up, a table on its own with a light on it, and all the stuff arranged so you're not supposed to touch it—it's like those dioramas they place around the yak or whatever, to show its habitat. It's nice, but I mean—" I gestured at the chair backs lined against the wall. "That one's a harp, that one's like a spoon, that one—" I imitated the sweep with my hand.

"Shield back. Although, I'll tell you, the nicest detail on that one is the tasselled splats. You may not realize it," he said, before I could ask what a splat was, "but it's an education in itself seeing that furniture of hers every day—seeing it in different lights, able to run your hand along it when you like." He fogged his glasses with his breath, wiped them with a corner of his apron. "Do you need to head back uptown?"

"Not really," I said, though it was getting late.

"Come along then," he said. "Let's put you to work. I could use a hand with this little chair down here."

"The goat foot?"

"Yes, the goat's foot. There's another apron on the peg—I know, it's too big, but I just coated this thing with linseed oil and I don't want you to spoil your clothes."

xii.

Dave the Shrink had mentioned more than once that he wished I would develop a hobby — advice I resented, as the hobbies he suggested (racquetball, table tennis, bowling) all seemed incredibly lame. If he thought a game or two of table tennis was going to help me get over my mother, he was completely out to lunch. But — as evidenced by the blank journal I'd been given by Mr. Neuspeil, my English teacher; Mrs. Swanson's suggestion that I start attending art classes after school; Enrique's offer to take me down to watch basketball at the courts on Sixth Avenue; and even Mr. Barbour's sporadic attempts to interest me in chart markers and nautical flags — a lot of adults had the same idea.

"But what do you like to *do* in your spare time?" Mrs. Swanson had asked me in her spooky, pale gray office that smelled like herb tea and sagebrush, issues of *Seventeen* and *Teen People* stacked high on the reading table and some kind of silvery Asian chime music floating in the background.

"I don't know. I like to read. Watch movies. Play Age of Conquest II and Age of Conquest: Platinum Edition. I don't know," I said again, when she kept on looking at me.

"Well, all those things are fine, Theo," she said, looking concerned. "But it would be nice if we could find some group activity for you. Something with teamwork, something you could do with other kids. Have you ever thought about taking up a sport?"

"No."

"I practice a martial art called Aikido. I don't know if you've heard of it. It's a way of using the opponent's own movements as a form of self-defense."

I looked away from her and at the weathered-looking panel board of Our Lady of Guadalupe hanging behind her head.

"Or perhaps photography." She folded her turquoise-ringed hands on her desk. "If you're not interested in art classes. Although I have to say, Mrs. Sheinkopf showed me some of the drawings you did last year — that series of rooftops, you know, water towers, the views from the studio window? Very observant — I know that view and you caught some really interesting line and energy, I think kinetic was the word she used, really nice quickness about it, all those intersecting planes and the angle of the

fire escapes. What I'm trying to say is that it's not so much *what* you do —
I just wish that we could find a way for you to be more connected."

"Connected to what?" I said, in a voice that came out sounding far too
nasty.

She looked nonplussed. "To other people! And —" she gestured at the
window — "the world around you! Listen," she said, in her gentlest, most
hypnotically-soothing voice, "I know that you and your mother had an
incredibly close bond. I spoke to her. I saw the two of you together. And I
know exactly how much you must miss her."

No you don't, I thought, staring her insolently in the eye.

She gave me an odd look. "You'd be surprised, Theo," she said, leaning back in her shawl-draped chair, "what small, everyday things can lift
us out of despair. But nobody can do it for you. You're the one who has to
watch for the open door."

Though I knew she meant well, I'd left her office head down, tears of
anger stinging my eyes. What the hell did she know about it, the old bat?
Mrs. Swanson had a gigantic family — about ten kids and thirty grand-
kids, to judge from the photos on her wall; Mrs. Swanson had a huge
apartment on Central Park West and a house in Connecticut and zero
idea what it was like for a plank to snap so it was all gone in a minute.
Easy enough for her to sit back comfortably in her hippie armchair and
ramble about extracurricular activities and open doors.

And yet, unexpectedly, a door *had* opened, and in a most unlikely
quarter: Hobie's workshop. "Helping" with the chair (which had basically
involved me standing by while Hobie ripped the seat up to show me the
worm damage, slapdash repairs, and other hidden horrors under the
upholstery) had rapidly turned into two or three oddly absorbing afternoons a week, after school: labeling jars, mixing rabbit-skin glue, sorting
through boxes of drawer fittings ("the fiddly bits") or sometimes just
watching him turn chair legs on the lathe. Though the upstairs shop
stayed dark, with the metal gates down, still, in the shop-behind-the-shop,
the tall-case clocks ticked, the mahogany glowed, the light filtered in a
golden pool on the dining room tables, the life of the downstairs menag-
erie went on.

Auction houses all over the city called him, as well as private clients; he
restored furniture for Sotheby's, for Christie's, for Tepper, for Doyle. After
school, amidst the drowsy tick of the tall-case clocks, he taught me the

pore and luster of different woods, their colors, the ripple and gloss of tiger maple and the frothed grain of burled walnut, their weights in my hand and even their different scents — "sometimes, when you're not sure what you have, it's easiest just to take a sniff" — spicy mahogany, dusty-smelling oak, black cherry with its characteristic tang and the flowery, amber-resin smell of rosewood. Saws and counter-sinks, rasps and rifflers, bent blades and spoon blades, braces and mitre-blocks. I learned about veneers and gilding, what a mortise and tenon was, the difference between ebonized wood and true ebony, between Newport and Connecticut and Philadel-phia crest rails, how the blocky design and close-cropped top of one Chip-pendale bureau rendered it inferior to another bracket-foot of the same vintage with its fluted quarter columns and what he liked to call the "exalted" proportions of the drawer ratio.

Downstairs — weak light, wood shavings on the floor — there was something of the feel of a stable, great beasts standing patiently in the dim. Hobie made me see the creaturely quality of good furniture, in how he talked of pieces as "he" and "she," in the muscular, almost animal quality that distinguished great pieces from their stiff, boxy, more mannered peers and in the affectionate way he ran his hand along the dark, glowing flanks of his sideboards and lowboys, like pets. He was a good teacher and very soon, by walking me through the process of examination and com-parison, he'd taught me how to identify a reproduction: by wear that was too even (antiques were always worn asymmetrically); by edges that were machine-cut instead of hand-planed (a sensitive fingertip could feel a machine edge, even in poor light); but more than that by a flat, dead qual-ity of wood, lacking a certain glow: the magic that came from centuries of being touched and used and passed through human hands. To contem-plate the lives of these dignified old highboys and secretaries — lives lon-ger and gentler than human life — sank me into calm like a stone in deep water, so that when it was time to go I walked out stunned and blinking into the blare of Sixth Avenue, hardly knowing where I was.

More than the workshop (or the "hospital," as Hobie called it) I enjoyed Hobie: his tired smile, his elegant big-man's slouch, his rolled sleeves and his easy, joking manner, his workman's habit of rubbing his forehead with the inside of his wrist, his patient good humor and his steady good sense. But though our talk was casual and sporadic there was never anything simple about it. Even a light "How are you" was a nuanced question, without it seeming to be; and my invariable answer ("Fine") he could read easily enough without my having to spell anything out. And though he seldom pried, or questioned, I felt he had a better sense of me than the various adults whose job it was to "get inside my head" as Enrique liked to put it.

But—more than anything—I liked him because he treated me as a companion and conversationalist in my own right. It didn't matter that sometimes he wanted to talk about his neighbor who had a knee replacement or a concert of early music he'd seen uptown. If I told him something funny that happened at school, he was an attentive and appreciative audience; unlike Mrs. Swanson (who froze and looked startled when I made a joke) or Dave (who chuckled, but awkwardly, and always a beat too late), he liked to laugh, and I loved it when he told me stories of his own life: raucous late-marrying uncles and busybody nuns of his childhood, the third-rate boarding school on the Canadian border where his teachers had all been drunks, the big house upstate that his father kept so cold there was ice on the inside of the windows, gray December afternoons reading Tacitus or Motley's *Rise of the Dutch Republic.* ("I loved history, *always.* The road not taken! My grandest boyhood ambition was to be a professor of history at Notre Dame. Although what I do now is just a different way of working with history, I suppose.") He told me about his blind-in-one-eye canary rescued from a Woolworth's who woke him singing every morning of his boyhood; the bout of rheumatic fever that kept him in bed for six months; and the queer little antique neighborhood library with frescoed ceilings ("torn down now, alas") where he'd gone to get away from his house. About Mrs. De Peyster, the lonely old heiress he'd visited after school, a former Belle of Albany and local historian who clucked over Hobie and fed him Dundee cake ordered from England in tins, who was happy to stand for hours explaining to Hobie every single item in her china cabinet and who had owned, among other things, the mahogany sofa—rumored to have belonged to General Herkimer—that got him interested in furniture in the first place. ("Although I can't quite picture General Herkimer lounging on that decadent old Grecian-looking article.") About his mother, who had died shortly after his three-days-old sister, leaving Hobie an only child; and about the young Jesuit father, a football coach, who—telephoned by a panicky Irish housemaid when Hobie's father was beating Hobie "to flinders practically" with a belt—had dashed to the house, rolled up his sleeves, and punched Hobie's father to the ground. ("Father Keegan! He was the one who came to the house that time when I had rheumatic fever, to give me communion. I was his altar boy—he knew what the story was, he'd seen the stripes on my back. There've been so many priests lately naughty with the boys, but he was so good to me—I always wonder what happened to him, I've tried to find him and I can't. My father telephoned the archbishop and next thing you knew, done and dusted, they'd shipped him off to Uruguay.") It was all very different from the Barbours', where—despite the general atmosphere of kindness—I was either lost in the throng or else the uncomfortable subject of formal inquiry. I felt better knowing he was only a bus ride away, a straight shot down Fifth Avenue; and in the night when I woke up jarred and panicked, the explosion plunging through me all over again, sometimes I could lull myself back to sleep by thinking of his house, where without even realizing it you slipped away sometimes into 1850, a world of ticking clocks and creaking floorboards, copper pots and baskets of turnips and onions in the kitchen, candle flames leaning all to the left in the draft of an opened door and tall parlor windows billowing and swagged like ball gowns, cool quiet rooms where old things slept.

It was becoming increasingly difficult to explain my absences, however (dinnertime absences, often), and Andy's powers of invention were being taxed. "Shall I go up there with you and talk to her?" said Hobie one afternoon when we were in the kitchen eating a cherry tart he'd bought at the farmers' market. "I'm happy to go up and meet her. Or maybe you'd like to ask her here."

"Maybe," I said, after thinking about it.

"She might be interested to see that Chippendale chest-on-chest—you know, the Philadelphia, the scroll-top. Not to buy—just to look at. Or, if you'd like, we could invite her out to lunch at La Grenouille—" he laughed "—or even some little joint down here that might amuse her."

"Let me think about it," I said; and went home early on the bus, brooding. Quite apart from my chronic duplicity with Mrs. Barbour—constant late nights at the library, a nonexistent history project—it would be embarrassing to admit to Hobie that I'd claimed Mr. Blackwell's ring was a family heirloom. Yet, if Mrs. Barbour and Hobie were to meet, my lie was sure to emerge, one way or another. There seemed no way around it.

"Where have you been?" said Mrs. Barbour sharply, dressed for dinner but without her shoes on, emerging from the back of the apartment with her gin and lime in her hand.

Something in her manner made me sense a trap. "Actually," I said, "I was downtown visiting a friend of my mother's."

Andy turned to stare at me blankly.

"Oh yes?" said Mrs. Barbour suspiciously, with a sideways glance at Andy. "Andy was just telling me that you were working at the library again."

"Not tonight," I said, so easily that it surprised me.

"Well, I must say I'm relieved to hear that," said Mrs. Barbour coolly. "Since the main branch is closed on Mondays."

"I didn't say he was at the main branch, Mother."

"I think you might actually know him," I said, anxious to draw fire from Andy. "Know of him, anyway."

"Who?" said Mrs. Barbour, her gaze coming back to me.

"The friend I was visiting. His name is James Hobart. He runs a furniture shop downtown — well, doesn't run it. He does the restorations."

She brought her eyebrows down. "Hobart?"

"He works for lots of people in the city. Sotheby's, sometimes."

"You wouldn't mind if I gave him a call, then?"

"No," I said defensively. "He said we should all go out to lunch. Or maybe you'd like to come down to his shop sometime."

"Oh," said Mrs. Barbour, after a beat or two of surprise. Now she was the one thrown off-balance. If Mrs. Barbour ever went south of Fourteenth Street, for any reason whatsoever, I didn't know about it. "Well. We'll see."

"Not to buy anything. Just to look. He has some nice things."

She blinked. "Of course," she said. She seemed strangely disoriented — something fixed and distracted about the eyes. "Well, lovely. I'm sure I would enjoy meeting him. *Have* I met him?"

"No, I don't think so."

"In any case. Andy, I'm sorry. I owe you an apology. You too, Theo."

Me? I didn't know what to say. Andy — sucking furtively at the side of his thumb — gave a one-shouldered shrug as she spun out of the room.

"What's the matter?" I asked him quietly.

"She's upset. It's nothing to do with you. Platt's home," he added.

Now that he mentioned it, I was aware of muffled music emanating from the rear of the apartment, a deep, subliminal thump. "Why?" I said. "What's wrong?"

"Something happened at school."

"Something bad?"

"God knows," he said tonelessly.

"He's in trouble?"

"I assume so. No one will talk about it."

"But what happened?"

Andy made a face: *who knows.* "He was here when we got home from school — we heard his music. Kitsey was excited and ran back to tell him hello but he screamed and slammed the door in her face."

I winced. Kitsey idolized Platt.

"Then Mother came home. She's been back in his room. Then she was on the telephone for a while. I *slightly* think Daddy's on his way home now. They were supposed to have dinner with the Ticknors tonight but I think that's been cancelled."

"What about supper?" I said, after a brief pause. Normally on school nights we ate in front of the television while doing our homework — but with Platt home, Mr. Barbour on his way, and the evening's plans abandoned, it was starting to look more like a family dinner in the dining room.

Andy straightened his glasses, in the fussy, old-womanish way he had. Although my hair was dark and his was light, I was only too aware how the identical eyeglasses Mrs. Barbour had chosen for us made me look like Andy's egghead twin — especially since I'd overheard some girl at school calling us "the Goofus Brothers" (or maybe "the Doofus brothers" — whatever, it wasn't a compliment).

"Let's walk over to Serendipity and get a hamburger," he said. "I'd really rather not be here when Daddy gets home."

"Take me, too," said Kitsey unexpectedly, galloping in and stopping just short of us, flushed and breathless.

Andy and I looked at each other. Kitsey didn't even like to be seen standing in line next to us at the bus stop.

"Please," she wailed, looking back and forth between us. "Toddy's doing soccer practice, I have my own money, I don't want to be by myself with them, *please.*"

"Oh, come on," I said to Andy, and she flashed me a grateful look.

Andy put his hands in his pockets. "All right, then," he said to her expressionlessly. They were a pair of white mice, I thought — only Kitsey was a spun-sugar, fairy-princess mouse whereas Andy was more the kind of luckless, anemic, pet-shop mouse you might feed to your boa constrictor.

"Get your stuff. *Go,*" he said, when she still stood there staring. "I'm not waiting for you. And don't forget your money because I'm not paying for you either."

xiii.

I DIDN'T GO DOWN to Hobie's for the next few days, out of loyalty to Andy, although I was greatly tempted in the atmosphere of tension that hung over the household. Andy was right: it was impossible to figure out what Platt had done, since Mr. and Mrs. Barbour behaved as if absolutely nothing were wrong (only you could tell that something was) and Platt himself wouldn't say a word, only sat sullenly at meals with his hair hanging in his face.

"Believe me," said Andy, "it's better when you're around. They talk, and make more of an effort to be normal."

"What do you think he did?"

"Honestly, I don't know. I don't *want* to know."

"Sure you do."

"Well, yes," said Andy, relenting. "But I really don't have the foggiest."

"Do you think he cheated? Stole? Chewed gum in chapel?"

Andy shrugged. "The last time he was in trouble, it was for hitting somebody in the face with a lacrosse stick. But *that* wasn't like *this.*" And then, out of the blue: "Mother loves Platt the best."

"You think?" I said evasively, though I knew very well this was true.

"Daddy loves Kitsey best. And Mother loves Platt."

"She loves Toddy a lot too," I said, before realizing quite how this sounded.

Andy grimaced. "I would think I'd been switched at birth," he said. "If I didn't look so much like Mother."

xiv.

FOR SOME REASON, DURING this strained interlude (possibly because Platt's mysterious trouble reminded me of my own) it occurred to me that maybe I ought to tell Hobie about the painting, or—at the very least—broach the subject in some oblique manner, to see what his reaction would be. The difficulty was how to bring it up. It was still in the apartment, exactly where I'd left it, in the bag I'd brought out of the museum. When I'd seen it leaning against the sofa in the front room, on the dreadful afternoon I'd gone back in to get some school things I needed, I'd walked right past it, skirting it as assiduously as I would have a grasping bum on the sidewalk, and all the time feeling Mrs. Barbour's cool pale eye on my back, on our apartment, on my mother's things, as she stood in the door with her arms folded.

It was complicated. Every time I thought of it my stomach squirmed, so that my first instinct was to slam the lid down hard and think of something else. Unfortunately, I'd waited so long to say anything to anybody that it was starting to feel like it was too late to say anything at all. And the more time I spent with Hobie—with his crippled Hepplewhites and Chippendales, the old things he took such diligent care of—the more I felt it was wrong to keep silent. What if someone found the picture? What would happen to me? For all I knew, the landlord might have gone into the apartment—he had a key—but even if he did go in, I didn't think he would necessarily happen upon it. Yet I knew I was tempting fate by leaving it there while I put off deciding what to do.

It wasn't that I minded giving it back; if I could have returned it magically, by wishing, I would have done it in a second. It was just that I couldn't think how to return it in a way that wouldn't endanger either me or the painting. Since the museum bombing, there were notices all over the city saying that packages left unattended for any reason would be destroyed, which did away with most of my brilliant ideas for returning it anonymously. Any suspicious suitcase or parcel would be blown up, no questions asked.

Of all the adults I knew, there were only two I considered taking into my confidence: Hobie, or Mrs. Barbour. Of these, Hobie seemed by far the more sympathetic and less terrifying prospect. It would be much easier to explain to Hobie how I had happened to take the painting out of the

museum in the first place. That it was a mistake, sort of. That I'd been following Welty's instruction; that I'd had a concussion. That I hadn't fully
considered what I was doing. That I hadn't meant to let it sit around so
long. Yet in my homeless limbo, it seemed insane to step up and admit to
what I knew a lot of people were going to view as very serious wrongdo-
ing. Then, by coincidence — just as I was realizing I really couldn't wait
much longer before I did something — I happened to see a tiny black and
white photo of the painting in the business section of the *Times*.

Due perhaps to the unease that had overtaken the household in the
wake of Platt's disgrace, the newspaper now occasionally found its way out
of Mr. Barbour's study, where it dis-assembled itself and re-appeared a
page or two at a time. These pages, awkwardly folded, were scattered near
a napkin-wrapped glass of club soda (Mr. Barbour's calling card) on
the coffee table in the living room. It was a long, boring article, toward the
back of the section, having to do with the insurance industry — about
the financial difficulties of mounting big art shows in a troubled economy,
and especially the difficulty in insuring travelling artworks. But what had
caught my eye was the caption under the photo: **The Goldfinch, Carel
Fabritius's 1654 masterpiece, destroyed.**

Without thinking, I sat down in Mr. Barbour's chair and began scanning the dense text for any further mention of my painting (already I'd
begun to think of it as *mine;* the thought slid into my head as if I'd owned
it all my life)

> Questions of international law come into play in cultural terrorism such
> as this, which has sent a chill through the financial community as well as
> the artistic world. "The loss of even one of these pieces is impossible to
> quantify," said Murray Twitchell, a London-based insurance-risk analyst.
> "Along with the twelve pieces lost and presumed destroyed, another 27
> works were badly damaged, although restoration, for some, is possible."
> In what may seem a futile gesture to many, the Art Loss Database

The story was continued on the next page; but just then Mrs. Barbour
came into the room and I had to put the newspaper down.

"Theo," she said. "I have a proposal for you."

"Yes?" I said, warily.

"Would you like to come up to Maine with us this year?"

For a moment I was so overjoyed that I went completely blank. "Yes!" I said. "Wow. That'd be great!"

Even she couldn't help but smile, a bit. "Well," she said, "Chance will certainly be happy to put you to work on the boat. It seems that we're going out somewhat earlier this year—well, Chance and the children will be going early. I'll be staying in the city to take care of some things, but I'll be up in a week or two."

I was so happy I couldn't think of a single thing to say.

"We'll see how you like sailing. Perhaps you'll like it better than Andy does. Let us hope so, at any rate."

"You think it's going to be fun," said Andy gloomily, when I ran back to the bedroom (ran, not walked) to give him the good news. "But it's not. You'll hate it." All the same, I could tell exactly how pleased he was. And that night—before bed—he sat down with me on the edge of the bottom bunk to talk about what books we would bring, what games, and what the symptoms of seasickness were, so that I could get out of helping on deck, if I felt like it.

XV.

THIS TWO-FOLD NEWS — good on both fronts—left me limp and dazed with relief. If my painting was destroyed—if that was the official story—there was plenty of time to decide what to do. By the same magic, Mrs. Barbour's invitation seemed to extend beyond the summer and far into the horizon, as if the entire Atlantic Ocean lay between me and Grandpa Decker; the lift was dizzying, and all I could do was exult in my reprieve. I knew that I should give the painting to either Hobie or Mrs. Barbour, throw myself on their mercy, tell them everything, beg them to help me— in some bleak, lucid corner of my mind I knew I would be sorry if I didn't—but my mind was too full of Maine and sailing to think about anything else; and it was starting to occur to me that it might even be smart to keep the painting for a while, as a sort of insurance for the next three years, against having to go live with Grandpa Decker and Dorothy. It is a hallmark of my stunning naïveté that I thought I might even be able to sell it, if I had to. So I kept quiet, looked at maps and chart markers with Mr. Barbour, and let Mrs. Barbour take me to Brooks Brothers to buy some deck shoes and some light cotton sweaters to wear on the water when it got cool at night. And said nothing.

xvi.

"Too much education, was my problem," said Hobie. "Or so my father thought." I was in the workshop with him and helping sort through end-less pieces of old cherry-wood, some redder, some browner, all salvaged from old furniture, to get the exact shade he needed to patch the apron of the tall-case clock he was working on. "My father had a trucking com-pany" (this I already knew; the name was so famous that even I was famil-iar with it), "and in the summers and over Christmas vacation he had me loading trucks—I'd have to work up to driving one, he said. The men on the loading docks all went dead silent the moment I walked out there. Boss's son, you know. Not their fault, because my father was a holy bastard to work for. Anyway he had me doing that from fourteen, after school and on weekends—loading boxes in the rain. Sometimes I worked in the office too—dismal, dingy place. Freezing in winter and hot as blazes in summer. Shouting over the exhaust fans. At first, it was only in the sum-mers and over Christmas vacation. But then, after my second year of col-lege, he announced he wasn't paying my tuition any more."

I had found a piece of wood that looked like a good match for the bro-ken piece, and I slid it over to him. "Did you have bad grades?"

"No—I did all right," he said, picking up the wood and holding it to the light, then putting it in the stack with possible matches. "The thing was, he hadn't gone to college himself and he'd done fine, hadn't he? Did I think I was better than him? But more than that—well, he was the kind of man who had to bully everyone around him, you know the type, and I think it must have dawned on him, what better way to keep me under his thumb and working for free? At first—" he deliberated several moments over another piece of veneer, then put it in the maybe pile—"at first he told me I'd have to take a year off—four years, five, however long it took—and earn the rest of my college money the hard way. Never saw a penny I made. I lived at home, and he was putting it all into a special account, you see, for my own good. Rough enough but fair, I thought. But then—after I'd worked full-time for him for about three years—the game changed. Suddenly—" he laughed—"well, hadn't I understood the deal? I was paying him back for my first two years of college. He hadn't set aside anything at all."

"That's awful!" I said, after a shocked pause. I didn't see how he could laugh about something so unfair.

"Well—" he rolled his eyes—"I was still a bit green, but I realized at that rate I'd be perishing of old age before I ever got out of there. But—no money, nowhere to live—what was I to do? I was trying hard to figure something out when lo and behold, Welty happened into the office one day while my father was going off at me. He loved to berate me in front of his men, my dad—swaggering around like a Mafia boss, saying I owed him money for this and that, taking it out of my quote unquote 'salary.' Withholding my alleged paycheck for some imaginary infraction. That kind of thing.

"Welty—it wasn't the first time I'd seen him. He'd been in the office to arrange for shipping from estate sales—he always claimed that with his back he had to work harder to make a good impression, make people see past the deformity and all that, but I liked him from the start. Most people did—my father even, who shall I say wasn't a man who took kindly to people. At any rate, Welty, having witnessed this outburst, telephoned my father the next day and said he could use my help packing the furniture for a house he'd bought the contents of. I was a big strong kid, hard worker, just the ticket. Well—" Hobie stood and stretched his arms over his head—"Welty was a good customer. And my father, for whatever reason, said yes.

"The house I helped him pack was the old De Peyster mansion. And as it happened I'd known old Mrs. De Peyster quite well. From the time I was a kid I'd liked to wander down and visit her—funny old woman in a bright yellow wig, font of information, papers everywhere, knew everything about local history, incredibly entertaining storyteller—anyway, it was quite a house, packed with Tiffany glass and some very good furniture from the 1800s, and I was able to help with the provenance of a lot of the pieces, better than Mrs. De Peyster's daughter, who hadn't the slightest interest in the chair President McKinley had sat in or any of that.

"The day I finished helping him with the house—it was about six o'clock in the afternoon, I was head-to-toe with dust—Welty opened a bottle of wine and we sat around on the packing cases and drank it, you know, bare floors and that empty house echo. I was exhausted—he'd paid me directly, cash, leaving my father out of it—and when I thanked him and asked if he knew of any more work, he said: Look, I've just opened a shop in New York, and if you want a job, you've got it. So we clinked glasses on it, and I went home, packed a suitcase full of books mostly, said goodbye to the housekeeper, and hitched a ride on the truck to New York the next day. Never looked back."

A lull ensued. We were still sorting through the veneer: clicking fragments, paper-thin, like counters in some ancient game from China maybe, an eerie lightness in the sound which made you feel lost in some much larger silence.

"Hey," I said, spotting a piece and snatching it up, passing it to him triumphantly: exact color match, closer than any of the pieces he'd set aside in his pile.

He took it from me, looked at it under the lamp. "It's all right."

"What's wrong with it?"

"Well, you see—" he put the veneer up to the clock's apron—"this kind of work, it's the grain of the wood you really have to match. That's the trick of it. Variations in tone are easier to fudge. Now this—" he held up a different piece, visibly several shades off—"with a little beeswax and a bit of the right coloring—maybe. Bichromate of potash, touch of Vandyke brown—sometimes, with a grain really difficult to match, certain kinds of walnut especially, I've used ammonia to darken a bit of new wood. But only when I was desperate. It's always best to use wood of the same vintage as the piece you're repairing, if you have it."

"How'd you learn how to do all this?" I said, after a timid pause.

He laughed. "The same way you're learning it now! Standing around and watching. Making myself useful."

"Welty taught you?"

"Oh, no. He understood it—knew how it was done. You have to in this business. He had a very reliable eye and often I'd bob up and fetch him when I wanted a second opinion. But before I joined the enterprise usually he'd pass on a piece that needed restoration. It's time-consuming work—takes a certain mind-set—he didn't have the temperament nor the physical hardiness for it. He much preferred the acquisitions end—you know, going to auction—or being in the shop and chatting up the customers. Every afternoon around five, I'd pop up for a cup of tea.

'Scourged from your dungeons.' It really was pretty foul down here in the old days with the mold and damp. When I came to work for Welty—" he laughed—"he had this old fellow named Abner Mossbank. Bad legs, arthritis in his fingers, could barely see. It would take him a year sometimes to finish a piece. But I stood at his back and watched him work. He was like a surgeon. Couldn't ask questions. Utter silence! But he knew absolutely everything—work that other people didn't know how to do or care to learn any more—it hangs by a thread, this trade, generation to generation."

"Your dad never gave you the money you earned?"

He laughed, warmly. "Not a penny! Never spoke to me again, either. He was a bitter old sod—fell down dead of a heart attack in the middle of firing one of his oldest employees. One of the most poorly attended funerals you'd ever care to see. Three black umbrellas in the sleet. Hard not to think of Ebenezer Scrooge."

"You never went back to college?"

"No. Didn't want to. I'd found what I liked to do. So—" he put both hands in the small of his back, and stretched; his out-at-elbows jacket, loose and a bit dirty, made him look like a good-natured groom on his way to the stables—"moral of the story is, who knows where it all will take you?"

"All what?"

He laughed. "Your sailing holiday," he said, moving to the shelf where the jars of pigment were arrayed like potions in an apothecary; ocherous earths, poisonous greens, powders of charcoal and burnt bone. "Might be the decisive moment. It takes some people that way, the sea."

"Andy gets seasick. He has to carry a baggie on the boat to throw up in."

"Well—" reaching for a jar of lampblack—"must admit, it never took *me* that way. When I was a kid—'Rime of the Ancient Mariner,' those Doré illustrations—no, the ocean gives me the shivers but then I've never been on an adventure like yours. You never know. Because—" brow furrowed, tapping out a bit of soft black powder on his palette—"I never dreamed that all that old furniture of Mrs. De Peyster's would be the thing that decided my future. Maybe you'll get fascinated by hermit crabs and study marine biology. Or decide you want to build boats, or be a marine painter, or write the definitive book about the *Lusitania*."

"Maybe," I said, hands behind my back. But what I really hoped I didn't dare articulate. Even to think of it practically made me tremble. Because, the thing was: Kitsey and Toddy had started being much, much nicer to me, as if someone had drawn them aside; and I'd seen glances, subtle cues, between Mr. and Mrs. Barbour that made me hopeful — more than hopeful. In fact, it was Andy who'd put the thought in my head. "They think being around you is good for me," he'd said on the way to school the other day. "That you're drawing me out of my shell and making me more social. I'm thinking they might make a family announcement once we get up to Maine."

"Announcement?"

"Don't be a dunce. They've grown quite fond of you — Mother, especially. But Daddy, too. I believe they may want to keep you."

xvii.

I RODE UPTOWN ON the bus, slightly drowsy, swaying comfortably back and forth and watching the wet Saturday streets flash by. When I stepped inside the apartment — chilled from walking home in the rain — Kitsey ran into the foyer to stare at me, wild-eyed and fascinated, as if I were an ostrich who had wandered into the apartment. Then, after a few blank seconds, she darted off into the living room, sandals clattering on the parquet floor, crying: "Mum? He's here!"

Mrs. Barbour appeared. "Hello, Theo," she said. She was perfectly composed but there was something constrained in her manner, though I couldn't quite put my finger on it. "Come in here. I've got a surprise for you."

I followed her into Mr. Barbour's study, gloomy in the overcast afternoon, where the framed nautical charts and the rain streaming down the gray windowpanes were like a theatrical set of a ship's cabin on a storm-tossed sea. Across the room, a figure rose from a leather club chair. "Hi, buddy," he said. "Long time no see."

I stood frozen in the doorway. The voice was unmistakable: my father.

He stepped forward into the weak light from the window. It was him, all right, though he'd changed since I'd seen him: he was heavier, tanned, puffy in the face, with a new suit and a haircut that made him look like a downtown bartender. In my dismay, I glanced back to Mrs. Barbour, and she gave me a bright but helpless smile as if to say: *I know, but what can I do?*

While I still stood speechless with shock, another figure rose and elbowed forward, in front of my father. "Hi, I'm Xandra," said a throaty voice.

I found myself confronted by a strange woman, tan and very fit-looking: flat gray eyes, lined coppery skin, and teeth that went in, with a split between them. Although she was older than my mother, or at any rate older-looking, she was dressed like someone younger: red platform sandals; low-slung jeans; wide belt; lots of gold jewelry. Her hair, the color of caramel straw, was very straight and tattered at the ends; she was chewing gum and a strong smell of Juicy Fruit was coming off her.

"It's Xandra with an X," she said in a gravelly undertone. Her eyes were clear and colorless, with spikes of dark mascara around them, and her gaze was powerful, confident, unwavering. "Not Sandra. And, *God* knows, not Sandy. I get that one a lot, and it drives me up the wall."

As she spoke, my astonishment was growing by the moment. I couldn't quite take her in: her whiskey voice, her muscular arms; the Chinese character tattooed on her big toe; her long square fingernails with the white tips painted on; her earrings shaped like starfish.

"Um, we just got into LaGuardia about two hours ago," said my dad, clearing his throat, as if this explained everything.

Was this who my dad had left us for? In stupefaction, I looked back to Mrs. Barbour again—only to see that she had vanished.

"Theo, I'm out in Las Vegas now," my father said, looking at the wall somewhere over my head. He still had the controlled, assertive voice of his actorly training but though he sounded as authoritative as ever, I could see that he wasn't any more comfortable than I was. "I guess I should have called, but I thought it would be easier if we just came on out to get you."

"Get me?" I said, after a long pause.

"Tell him, Larry," said Xandra, and then, to me: "You should be proud of your Pops. He's on the wagon. How many days' sobriety now? Fifty-one? Did it all on his own too—didn't even check himself into the joint—detoxed on the sofa with a basket of Easter candy and a bottle of Valium."

Because I was too embarrassed to look at her, or my father, I looked back at the doorway again—and saw Kitsey Barbour standing in the hall listening to all this with big round eyes.

"Because, I mean, *I* just couldn't put up with it," said Xandra, in a tone suggesting that my mother had condoned, and encouraged, my dad's alcoholism. "I mean—my Moms was the kind of lush who would throw up in her glass of Canadian Club and then drink it anyway. And one night I said to him: Larry, I'm not going to say to you 'never drink again,' and frankly I think that AA is way too much for the level of problem you have—"

My father cleared his throat and turned to me with a genial face he usually reserved for strangers. Maybe he *had* stopped drinking; but still he had a bloated, shiny, slightly stunned look, as if he'd been living for the past eight months off rum drinks and Hawaiian party platters.

"Um, son," he said, "we're right off the plane, and we came over because—we wanted to see you right away, of course..."

I waited.

"...we need the key to the apartment."

This was all moving a little too fast for me. "The key?" I said.

"We can't get in over there," said Xandra bluntly. "We tried already."

"The thing is, Theo," my dad said, his tone clear and cordial, running a businesslike hand over his hair, "I need to get in over at Sutton Place and see what's what. I'm sure things are a mess over there, and somebody needs to get in and start taking care of stuff."

If you didn't leave things such a goddamned mess... These were words I'd heard my father scream at my mother when—about two weeks before he vanished—they'd had the biggest fight I ever heard them have, when the diamond-and-emerald earrings that belonged to her mother vanished from the dish on her bedside table. My father (red in the face, mocking her in a sarcastic falsetto) had said it was *her* fault, Cinzia had probably taken them or who the hell knew, it wasn't a good idea to leave jewelry lying out like that, and maybe this would teach her to look after her things better. But my mother—ash-white with anger—had pointed out in a cold still voice that she'd taken the earrings off on Friday night, and that Cinzia hadn't been in to work since.

What the hell are you trying to say? bellowed my father.

Silence.

So I'm a thief now, is that it? You're accusing your own husband of stealing jewelry from you? What the hell kind of sick irrational thing is that? You need help, you know that? You really need professional help—

Only it wasn't just the earrings that had vanished. After he vanished himself, it turned out that some other things including cash and some antique coins belonging to her father had vanished as well; and my mother had changed the locks and warned Cinzia and the doormen not to let him in if he showed up when she was at work. And of course now everything was different, and there was nothing to stop him from going in the apartment and going through her belongings and doing with them what he liked; but as I stood looking at him and trying to think what the hell to say, half a dozen things were running through my mind and chief among them was the painting. Every day, for weeks, I'd told myself that I would go over and take care of it, figure it out somehow, but I'd kept putting it off and putting it off and now here he was.

My dad was still smiling at me fixedly. "Okay, buddy? Think you might want to help us out?" Maybe he wasn't drinking any more, but all the old late afternoon wanting-a-drink edge was still there, scratchy as sandpaper.

"I don't have the key," I said.

"That's okay," my dad returned swiftly. "We can call a locksmith. Xandra, give me the phone."

I thought fast. I didn't want them to go in the apartment without me. "Jose or Goldie might let us in," I said. "If I go over there with you."

"Fine then," said my dad, "let's go." From his tone, I suspected he knew I was lying about the key (safely hidden, in Andy's room). I knew too he didn't like the sound of involving the doormen, as most of the guys who worked in the building didn't care that much for my father, having seen him the worse for drink a few too many times. But I met his eye as blankly as I could until he shrugged and turned away.

xviii.

"*¡Hola, Jose!*"

"*¡Bomba!*" cried Jose, doing a happy step backward when he saw me on the sidewalk; he was the youngest and most buoyant of the doormen, always trying to sneak away before his shift was over to play soccer in the park. "Theo! *¿Qué lo que, manito?*"

His uncomplicated smile threw me back hard to the past. Everything was the same: green awning, sallow shade, same furry brown puddle collecting in the sunken place in the sidewalk. Standing before the art-deco doors — nickel-bright, rayed with abstract sunbursts, doors that urgent news guys in fedoras might push through in a 1930s movie — I remembered all the times I'd stepped inside to find my mother sorting the mail, waiting for the elevator. Fresh from work, heels and briefcase, with the flowers I'd sent for her birthday. *Well what do you know. My secret admirer has struck again.*

Jose, looking past me, had spotted my father, and Xandra, hanging back slightly. "Hello, Mr. Decker," he said, in a more formal tone, reaching around me to take my dad's hand: politely, but no love lost. "Is nice to see you."

My father, with his Personable Smile, started to answer but I was too nervous and interrupted: "Jose—" I'd been racking my brains for the Spanish on the way over, rehearsing the sentence in my mind — "*mi papá quiere entrar en el apartamento, le necesitamos abrir la puerta.*" Then, quickly, I slipped in the question I'd worked out earlier, on the way over: "*¿Usted puede subir con nosotros?*"

Jose's eyes went quickly to my father and Xandra. He was a big, handsome guy from the Dominican Republic, something about him reminiscent of the young Muhammad Ali — sweet-tempered, always kidding around, but you didn't want to mess with him. Once, in a moment of confidence, he had pulled up his uniform jacket and shown me a knife scar on his abdomen, which he said he'd gotten in a street fight in Miami.

"Happy to do it," he said in English, in an easy voice. He was looking at them but I knew he was talking to me. "I'll take you up. Everything is okay?"

"Yep, we're fine," said my dad curtly. He was the very one who'd insisted that I study Spanish as my foreign language instead of German ("so at least one person in the family can communicate with these fucking doormen").

Xandra, who I was starting to think was a real dingbat, laughed nervously and said in her stuttery quick voice: "Yeah, we're fine, but the flight really took it out of us. It's a long way from Vegas and we're still a little—" and here she rolled her eyes and waggled her fingers to indicate wooziness.

"Oh yeah?" said Jose. "Today? You flew into LaGuardia?" Like all the doormen he was a genius at small talk, especially if it was about traffic or weather, the best route to the airport at rush hour. "I heard big delays out there today, some problem with the baggage handlers, the union, right?"

All the way up in the elevator, Xandra kept up a steady but agitated stream of chatter: about how dirty New York was compared to Las Vegas ("Yeah, I admit it, everything's cleaner out west, I guess I'm spoiled"), about her bad turkey sandwich on the airplane and the flight attendant who "forgot" (Xandra, with her fingertips, inserting the quotations manually) to bring Xandra the five dollars change from the wine she ordered.

"Oh, ma'am!" said Jose, stepping in the hallway, wagging his head in the mock-serious way he had. "Airplane food, it's the worst. These days you're lucky if they feed you at all. Tell you one thing in New York, though. You going to find you some good food. You got good Vietnamese, good Cuban, good Indian—"

"I don't like all that spicy stuff."

"Good whatever you want, then. We got it. *Segundito,*" he said, holding up a finger as he felt around on the ring for the passkey.

The lock tumbled with a solid *clunk,* instinctive, blood-deep in its rightness. Though the place was stuffy from being shut up, still I was leveled by the fierce smell of home: books and old rugs and lemon floor cleaner, the dark myrrh-smelling candles she bought at Barney's.

The bag from the museum was propped on the floor by the sofa— exactly where I'd left it, how many weeks before? Feeling light-headed, I darted around and inside to grab it as Jose—slightly blocking my irritated father's path, without quite appearing to—stood just outside the door listening to Xandra, arms folded. The composed but slightly absent-minded look on his face reminded me of the way he'd looked when he'd had to practically carry my dad upstairs one freezing night, my dad so drunk he'd lost his overcoat. — Happens in the best of families, he'd said with an abstract smile, refusing the twenty-dollar bill that my father— incoherent, vomit on his suit jacket, scratched-up and dirty like he'd been rolling on the sidewalk — was trying hard to push into his face.

"Actually, I'm *from* the East Coast?" Xandra was saying. "From Florida?" Again that nervous laugh—stuttery, sputtering. "West Palm, to be specific."

"Florida you say?" I heard Jose remark. "Is beautiful down there."

"Yeah, it's great. At least in Vegas we've got the sunshine—I don't know if I could take the winters out here, I'd turn into a Popsicle—"

The instant I picked the bag up, I realized it was too light—almost empty. Where the hell was the painting? Though I was nearly blind with panic, I didn't stop but kept going, down the hallway, on autopilot, back to my bedroom, mind whirring and grinding as I walked—

Suddenly—through my disconnected memories of that night—it came back to me. The bag had been wet. I hadn't wanted to leave the picture in a wet bag, to mildew or melt or who knew what. Instead—how could I have forgotten?—I'd set it on my mother's bureau, the first thing she'd see when she came home. Quickly, without stopping, I dropped the bag in the hallway outside the closed door of my bedroom and turned into my mother's room, light-headed with fear, hoping that my father wasn't following but too afraid to look back and see.

From the living room, I heard Xandra say: "I bet you see a lot of celebrities on the street here, huh?"

"Oh, yeah. LeBron, Dan Aykroyd, Tara Reid, Jay-Z, Madonna..."

My mother's bedroom was dark and cool, and the faint, just-detectable smell of her perfume was almost more than I could bear. There sat the painting, propped among silver-framed photographs—her parents, her, me at many ages, horses and dogs galore: her father's mare Chalkboard, Bruno the Great Dane, her dachshund Poppy who'd died when I was in kindergarten. Steeling myself against her reading glasses on the bureau and her black tights stiff where she'd draped them to dry and her handwriting on her desk calendar and a million other heart-piercing sights, I picked it up and tucked it under my arm and walked quickly into my own room across the hall.

My room—like the kitchen—faced the airshaft, and was dark without the lights on. A dank bath towel lay crumpled where I'd thrown it after my shower that last morning, atop a heap of dirty clothes. I picked it up—wincing at the smell—with the idea of throwing it over the painting while I found a better place to hide it, maybe in the—

"What are you doing?"

My father stood in the doorway, a darkish silhouette with the light shining behind him.

"Nothing."

He stooped and picked up the bag I'd dropped in the hall. "What's this out here?"

"My book bag," I said, after a pause—though the thing was clearly a mom's collapsible shopping tote, nothing I, or any kid, would ever take to school.

He tossed it in the open door, crinkling his nose at the smell. "Phew," he said, waving his hand in front of his face, "it smells like old hockey socks in here." As he reached inside the door and flipped the light switch, I managed with a complex but spasmodic movement to throw the towel over the picture so (I hoped) he couldn't see it.

"What's that you've got there?"

"A poster."

"Well look, I hope you're not planning to haul a lot of junk out to Vegas. No need to pack your winter clothes—you won't need them, except maybe some ski stuff. You won't believe the skiing in Tahoe—not like these icy little mountains upstate."

I felt that I needed to make a reply, especially since it was the longest and friendliest-seeming thing he'd said since he'd shown up, but somehow I couldn't quite pull my thoughts together.

Abruptly, my father said: "Your mother wasn't so easy to live with either, you know." He picked up something that looked like an old math test from my desk, examined it, and then threw it back down. "She played her cards way too close to the vest. You know how she used to do. Clamming up. Freezing me out. Always had to take the high road. It was a power thing, you know—really controlling. Quite honestly, and I really hate to say this, it got to the point where it was hard for me to even be in the same room with her. I mean, I'm not saying she was a bad person. It's just one minute everything's fine, and the next, *bam,* what did I do, the old silent treatment..."

I said nothing—standing there awkwardly with the mildewy towel draped over the painting and the light shining into my eyes, wishing that I were anywhere else (Tibet, Lake Tahoe, the moon) and not trusting myself to reply. What he'd said about my mother was perfectly true: often she was uncommunicative, and when she was upset it was difficult to tell what she was thinking, but I wasn't interested in a discussion of my mother's faults and at any rate they seemed like fairly minor faults compared to my father's.

My father was saying: "...because I've got nothing to prove, see? Every game has two sides. It's not an issue of who's right and who's wrong. And sure, I'll admit, I'm to blame for some of it too, although I'll say this, and

I'm sure you know it too, she sure did have a way of re-writing history in her own favor." It was strange to be in the room with him again, especially as he was so different: he gave off a different smell almost, and there was a different heaviness and weight to him, a sleekness, as though he were padded all over with a smooth half-inch of fat. "I guess a lot of marriages run into problems like ours—she'd just gotten so bitter, you know? And withholding? Honestly, I just didn't feel like I could live with her any longer, though God knows she didn't deserve *this*...."

She sure didn't, I thought.

"Because you know what this was really about, don't you?" said my dad, leaning on the door frame with one elbow and looking at me shrewdly. "Me leaving? I had to withdraw some money from our bank account to pay taxes and she flipped her lid, like I'd stolen it." He was watching me very carefully, looking for my response. "Our *joint* bank account. I mean basically, when the chips were down, she didn't trust me. Her own husband."

I didn't know what to say. It was the first I'd heard about the taxes, although it was certainly no secret that my mother didn't trust my dad where money was concerned.

"God, but she could hold on to a grievance," he said, with a half-humorous wince, wiping his hand down the front of his face. "Tit for tat. Always looking to even the score. Because, I mean it—she never forgot anything. If she had to wait twenty years, she was going to get you back. And sure, *I'm* the one who always looks like the bad guy and maybe I *am* the bad guy..."

The painting, though small, was getting heavy, and my face felt frozen with the effort of concealing my discomfort. In order to block his voice out I started counting to myself in Spanish. *Uno dos tres, cuatro cinco seis...*

By the time I reached twenty-nine, Xandra had appeared.

"Larry," she said, "you and your wife had a really nice place here." The way she said it made me feel bad for her without liking her any better.

My dad put his arm around her waist and drew her to him with a sort of kneading motion that made me sick. "Well," he said modestly, "it's really more hers than mine."

You can say that again, I thought.

"Come in here," said my dad, catching her by the hand and leading her away towards my mother's bedroom, all thought of me forgotten. "I want you to see something." I turned and watched them go, queasy at the prospect of Xandra and my father pawing through my mother's things but so glad to see them go I didn't care.

With one eye on the empty doorway, I walked around to the far side of my bed and placed the painting out of sight. An old *New York Post* lay on the floor—the same newspaper that she'd thrown in to me, in a flap, on our last Saturday together. *Here, kiddo,* she'd said, sticking her head in at the door, *pick a movie.* Though there were several movies we both would have liked, I'd chosen a matinee at the Boris Karloff film festival: *The Body Snatcher.* She had accepted my choice without a word of complaint; we'd gone down to Film Forum, watched the movie, and after it was over walked to Moondance Diner for a hamburger—a perfectly pleasant Saturday afternoon, apart from the fact that it was her last on Earth, and now I felt rotten whenever I thought about it, since (thanks to me) the last movie she'd ever seen was a corny old horror flick about corpses and graverobbing. (If I'd picked the movie I knew she wanted to see—the well-reviewed one about Parisian children during World War I—might she have lived, somehow? My thoughts often ran along such dark, superstitious faultlines.)

Though the newspaper felt sacrosanct, an historical document, I turned it to the middle and took it apart. Grimly, I wrapped the painting, sheet by sheet, and taped it up with the same tape I'd used a few months before to wrap my mother's Christmas present. *Perfect!* she'd said, in a storm of colored paper, leaning in her bathrobe to kiss me: a watercolor set she would never be carrying to the park, on Saturday mornings in summer she would never see.

My bed—a brass camp bed from the flea market, soldierly and reassuring—had always seemed like the safest place in the world to hide something. But now, looking around (beat-up desk, Japanese Godzilla poster, the penguin mug from the zoo that I used as a pencil cup), I felt the impermanence of it all strike me hard; and it made me dizzy to think of all our things flying out of the apartment, furniture and silver and all my mother's clothes: sample-sale dresses with the tags still on them, all those colored ballet slippers and tailored shirts with her initials on the cuffs. Chairs and Chinese lamps, old jazz records on vinyl that she'd bought down in the Village, jars of marmalade and olives and sharp German mustard in the refrigerator. In the bathroom, a bewilderment of perfumed oils and moisturizers, colored bubble bath, half-empty bottles of over-priced shampoo crowded on the side of the tub (Kiehl's, Klorane, Kérastase, my mother always had five or six kinds going). How could the apartment have seemed so permanent and solid-looking when it was only a stage set, waiting to be struck and carried away by movers in uniform?

When I walked into the living room, I was confronted by a sweater of my mother's lying across the chair where she'd left it, a sky-blue ghost of her. Shells we'd picked up on the beach at Wellfleet. Hyacinths, which she'd bought at the Korean market a few days before she died, with the stems draped dead-black and rotten over the side of the pot. In the waste-basket: catalogues from Dover Books, Belgian Shoes; a wrapper from a pack of Necco Wafers, which had been her favorite candy. I picked it up and sniffed it. The sweater — I knew — would smell of her too if I picked it up and put it to my face, yet even the sight of it was unendurable.

I went back in my bedroom and stood on my desk chair and got down my suitcase — which was soft-sided and not too big — and packed it full of clean underwear, clean school clothes, and folded shirts from the laundry. Then I put in the painting, with another layer of clothes on top.

I zipped the suitcase — no lock, but it was only canvas — and stood very still. Then I went out into the hall. I could hear drawers opening and shutting in my mother's bedroom. A giggle.

"Dad," I said in a loud voice, "I'm going downstairs and talk to Jose."

Their voices went dead silent.

"You bet," said my father, through the closed door, in an unnaturally cordial tone.

I went back and got the suitcase and walked out of the apartment with it, leaving the front door cracked so I could get in again. Then I rode the elevator down, staring into the mirror that faced me, trying hard not to think about Xandra in my mother's bedroom pawing through her clothes. Had he been seeing her before he left home? Didn't he feel even a bit creepy about permitting her to root around in my mother's things?

I was walking to the front door where Jose was on duty when a voice called: "Wait a sec!"

Turning, I saw Goldie, hurrying from the package room.

"Theo, my God, I'm sorry," he said. We stood looking at each other for an uncertain moment and then — in an impulsive, what-the-hell move-ment, so awkward it was almost funny, he reached around and hugged me.

"So sorry," he repeated, shaking his head. "My God, what a thing." Goldie, since his divorce, often worked nights and holidays, standing at the doors with his gloves off and an unlit cigarette in his hand, looking out at the street. My mother had sometimes sent me down with coffee and doughnuts for him when he was in the lobby by himself, no company but the lighted tree and the electric menorah, sorting out the newspapers by himself at 5:00 a.m. on Christmas Day, and the expression on his face reminded me of those dead holiday mornings, empty-looking stare, his face ashy and uncertain, in the unguarded moment before he saw me and put on his best *hi kid* smile.

"I been thinking about you and your mother so much," he said, wiping his brow. "*Ay bendito.* I can't—I don't even know what you must be going through."

"Yeah," I said, looking away, "it's been hard"—which was for whatever reason the phrase I constantly fell back upon when people told me how sorry they were. I'd had to say it so much that it was starting to come out sounding glib and a bit phony.

"I'm glad you stopped by," said Goldie. "That morning—I was on duty, you remember? Right out front there?"

"Sure I do," I said, wondering at his urgency, as if he thought I might *not* remember.

"*Oh,* my God." He passed his hand over his forehead, a little wild-looking, as if he himself had suffered only a narrow escape. "I think about it every single day. I still see her face, you know, getting into that cab? Waving goodbye, so happy."

Confidentially, he leaned forward. "When I heard she died?" he said, as if telling me a big secret. "I called up my ex-wife, that's how upset I was." He pulled back and looked at me with raised eyebrows, as if he didn't expect me to believe him. Goldie's battles with his ex-wife were epic.

"I mean, we hardly talk," he said, "but who I'm gonna tell? I gotta tell somebody, you know? So I called her up and told her: 'Rosa, you can't believe it. We lost such a beautiful lady from the building.'"

Jose—spotting me—had strolled back from the front door to join our conversation, in his distinctive springy walk. "Mrs. Decker," he said— shaking his head fondly, as if there had never been anyone like her. "Always say hello, always such a nice smile. Considerate, you know."

"Not like some of these people in the building," said Goldie, glancing over his shoulder. "You know—" he leaned closer, and mouthed the word—"snobby. The kind of person stands there empty-handed with no packages or nothing and waits for you to open the door, is what I'm saying."

"She wasn't like that," said Jose, still shaking his head—big head movements, like a somber child saying no. "Mrs. Decker was Class A."

"Say, will you wait here a second?" Goldie said, holding up his hand. "I'll be right back. Don't leave. Don't let him leave," he said to Jose.

"You want me to get you a cab, *manito*?" said Jose, eyeing the suitcase.

"No," I said, glancing back at the elevator. "Listen, Jose, will you keep this for me until I come back and get it?"

"Sure," he said, picking it up and hefting it. "Happy to."

"I'll come back for it myself, okay? Don't let anybody else have it."

"Sure, I get it," said Jose pleasantly. I followed him into the package room, where he tagged the bag and hoisted it onto a top shelf.

"You see?" he said. "Out of the way, baby. We don't keep nothing up high there except some packages people got to sign for and our own personal stuff. Nobody's going to release that bag to you without your personal signature, you understand? Not to your uncle, your cousin, nobody. And I'll tell Carlos and Goldie and the other guys, don't give that bag to nobody but you. Okay?"

I was nodding, about to thank him, when Jose cleared his throat. "Listen," he said, in a lowered voice. "I don't want to worry you or nothing but there've been some guys coming around lately asking after your dad."

"Guys?" I said, after a disjointed silence. "Guys," coming from Jose, meant only one thing: men that my dad owed money to.

"Don't worry. We told them nothing. I mean, your dad's been gone for what, like a year? Carlos told them none of you lived here no more and they aint been back. But—" he glanced at the elevator—"maybe your dad there, he don't want to be spending a lot of time in the building just now, you know what I'm saying?"

I was thanking him when Goldie returned with what looked to me like a gigantic wad of cash. "This is for you," he said, a bit melodramatically.

For a minute I thought I'd heard him wrong. Jose coughed and looked away. On the package room's tiny black and white television (its screen no bigger than a CD case) a glamorous woman in long jangling earrings brandished her fists and shouted abusive Spanish at a cowering priest.

"What's going on?" I said to Goldie, who was still holding the money out.

"Your mother, she didn't tell you?"

I was mystified. "Tell me what?"

It seemed that—one day shortly before Christmas—Goldie had ordered a computer and had it delivered to the building. The computer was for Goldie's son, who needed it for school, but (Goldie was hazy about this part) Goldie hadn't actually paid for it, or had only paid for part of it, or his ex-wife had been supposed to pay for it instead of him. At any rate, the delivery people were hauling the computer out the door again and loading it back into their van when my mother happened to come downstairs and see what was going on.

"And she paid herself, that beautiful lady," Goldie said. "She saw what was happening, and she opened her bag and she took out her checkbook. She said to me, 'Goldie, I know your son needs this computer for his schoolwork. Please let me do this thing for you, my friend, and you pay me when you can.'"

"You see?" said Jose, unexpectedly fierce, glancing back from the television, where the woman was standing in a graveyard now, arguing with a tycoon-looking guy in sunglasses. "That's your mother that did that." He nodded at the money, almost angrily. "*Sí, es verdad,* she was Class A. She cared about people you know? Most women? They spend that money on gold earrings or perfume or some things for themselves like that."

I felt strange taking the money, for all sorts of reasons. Even in my shock, something about the story felt dodgy (what kind of store would deliver a computer that wasn't paid for?). Later, I wondered: did I look that destitute, that the doormen had taken up a collection for me? I still don't know where the money came from; and I wish I had asked more questions, but I was so stunned by everything that had happened that day (and more than anything by the sudden appearance of my dad, and Xandra) that if Goldie had confronted me and tried to give me a piece of old chewing gum he'd scraped off the floor I would have held out my hand and taken it just as obediently.

"None of my business, you know," Jose said, looking over my head as he said it, "but if I was you, I wouldn't tell anybody about that money. You know what I'm saying?"

"Yeah, put it in your pocket," said Goldie. "Don't walk around waving it out in your hand like that. Plenty of people on the street would kill you for that much cash."

"Plenty of people in this building!" said Jose, overcome with sudden laughter.

"Ha!" said Goldie, cracking up himself, and then said something in Spanish I didn't understand.

"*Cuidado,*" said Jose — wagging his head in the way he did, mock-serious, but unable to keep from smiling. "That's why they don't let Goldie and me work on the same floor," he said to me. "They got to keep us separated. We have too good a time."

xix.

ONCE DAD AND XANDRA showed up, things started moving fast. At dinner that night (at a touristy restaurant I was surprised my dad had chosen), he took a call at the table from somebody at my mother's insurance company — which, even all these years later, I wish I'd been able to hear better. But the restaurant was loud and Xandra (between gulps of white wine — maybe *he'd* quit drinking, but she sure hadn't) was alternately complaining because she couldn't smoke and telling me in a sort of unfocused way how she'd learned to practice witchcraft out of a library book when she was in high school, somewhere in Fort Lauderdale. ("Actually, Wicca it's called. It's an earth religion.") With anyone else, I would have asked exactly what it involved, being a witch (spells and sacrifices? deal with the devil?) but before I had a chance she'd moved on, how she'd had the opportunity to go to college and was sorry she hadn't done it ("I'll tell you what I was interested in. English history and like that. Henry the Eighth, Mary Queen of Scots"). But she'd ended up not going to college at all because she'd been too obsessed with this guy. "*Obsessed,*" she hissed, fixing me with her sharp, no-color eyes.

Why being obsessed with the guy kept Xandra from going to college, I never found out, because my dad got off the phone. He ordered (and it gave me a funny feeling) a bottle of champagne.

"I can't drink this whole damn thing," said Xandra, who was into her second glass of wine. "It'll give me a headache."

"Well, if I can't have champagne, you might as well have some," my father said, leaning back in his chair.

Xandra nodded at me. "Let *him* have some," she said. "Waiter, bring another glass."

"Sorry," said the waiter, a hard-edged Italian guy who looked like he was used to dealing with out-of-control tourists. "No alcohol if he's under eighteen."

Xandra started scrabbling in her purse. She was wearing a brown halter dress, and she had blusher, or bronzer, or some brownish powder brushed under her cheekbones in such a strong line that I had an urge to smudge it in with my fingertip.

"Let's go outside and have a smoke," she said to my father. There was a long moment where they exchanged a smirky look that made me cringe. Then Xandra pushed her chair back and—dropping her napkin in the chair—looked around for the waiter. "Oh, good, he's gone," she said, reaching for my (mostly) empty water glass and slopping some champagne into it.

The food had arrived and I'd poured myself another large but surreptitious glass of champagne before they returned. "Yum!" said Xandra, looking glazed and a bit shiny, tugging her short skirt down, edging around and slithering back into her seat without bothering to pull her chair out all the way. She flapped her napkin into her lap and pulled her massive, bright-red plate of manicotti towards her. "Looks awesome!"

"So does mine," said my dad, who was picky about his Italian food, and whom I'd often known to complain about overly tomatoey, marinara-drenched pasta dishes exactly like the plate in front of him.

As they tucked into their food (which was probably fairly cold, judging by how long they'd been gone), they resumed their conversation in mid-stream. "Well, anyway, didn't work out," he said, leaning back in his chair and toying rakishly with a cigarette he was unable to light. "That's how it goes."

"I bet you were great."

He shrugged. "Even when you're young," he said, "it's a tough game. It's not just talent. It has a lot to do with looks and luck."

"But still," said Xandra, blotting the corner of her lip with a napkin-wrapped fingertip. "An actor. I can so totally see it." My dad's thwarted acting career was one of his favorite subjects and — though she seemed interested enough — something told me that this wasn't the very first time she had heard about it either.

"Well, do I wish I'd kept going with it?" My dad contemplated his non-alcoholic beer (or was it three percent? I couldn't see from where I was sitting). "I have to say yes. It's one of those lifelong regrets. I would have loved to do something with my gift but I didn't have the luxury. Life has a funny way of intervening."

They were deep in their own world; for all the attention they were paying to me I might as well have been in Idaho but that was fine with me; I knew this story. My dad, who'd been a drama star in college, had for a brief while earned his living as an actor: voice-overs in commercials, a few minor parts (a murdered playboy, the spoiled son of a mob boss) in television and movies. Then — after he'd married my mother — it had all fizzled out. He had a long list of reasons why he hadn't broken through, though as I'd often heard him say: if my mother had been a little more successful as a model or worked a little harder at it, there would have been enough money for him to concentrate on acting without worrying about a day job.

My dad pushed his plate aside. I noticed that he hadn't eaten very much — often, with my dad, a sign that he was drinking, or about to start.

"At some point, I just had to cut my losses and get out," he said, crumpling his napkin and throwing it on the table. I wondered if he had told Xandra about Mickey Rourke, whom he viewed apart from me and my mother as the prime villain in derailing his career.

Xandra took a big drink of her wine. "Do you ever think about going back to it?"

"I *think* about it, sure. But —" he shook his head as if refusing some outrageous request — "no. Essentially the answer is no."

The champagne tickled the roof of my mouth — distant, dusty sparkle, bottled in a happier year when my mother was still alive.

"I mean, the *second* he saw me, I knew he didn't like me," my dad was saying to her quietly. So he had told her about Mickey Rourke.

She tossed her head, drained the rest of her wine. "Guys like that can't stand competition."

"It was all Mickey this, Mickey that, Mickey wants to meet you, but the minute I walked in there I knew it was over."

"Obviously the guy's a freak."

"Not then, he wasn't. Because, tell you the truth, there really was a resemblance back in the day—not just physically, but we had similar acting styles. Or, let's say, I was classically trained, I had a range, but I could do the same kind of stillness as Mickey, you know, that whispery quiet thing—"

"Oooh, you just gave me chills. *Whispery.* Like the way you *said* that."

"Yeah, but Mickey was the star. There wasn't room enough for two."

As I watched them sharing a piece of cheesecake like lovebirds in a commercial, I sank into a ruddy, unfamiliar free-flow of mind, the dining room lights too bright and my face flaming hot from the champagne, thinking in a disordered but heated way about my mother after her parents died and she had to go live with her aunt Bess, in a house by the train tracks with brown wallpaper and plastic covers on the furniture. Aunt Bess—who fried everything in Crisco, and had cut up one of my mother's dresses with scissors because the psychedelic pattern disturbed her—was a chunky, embittered, Irish-American spinster who had left the Catholic Church for some tiny, insane sect that believed it was wrong to do things like drink tea or take aspirin. Her eyes—in the one photograph I'd seen—were the same startling silver-blue as my mother's, only pink-rimmed and crazed, in a potato-plain face. My mother had spoken of those eighteen months with Aunt Bess as the saddest of her life—the horses sold, the dogs given away, long weeping goodbyes by the side of the road, arms around the necks of Clover and Chalkboard and Paintbox and Bruno. Back in the house, Aunt Bess had told my mother she was spoiled, and that people who didn't fear the Lord always got what they deserved.

"And the producer, you see—I mean, they all knew how Mickey was, everyone did, he was already starting to get a reputation for being difficult—"

"She didn't deserve it," I said aloud, interrupting their conversation.

Dad and Xandra stopped talking and looked at me as if I'd turned into a Gila monster.

"I mean, why would anybody say that?" It wasn't right that I was speaking aloud, and yet the words were tumbling unbidden out of my mouth as if someone had pushed a button. "She was so great and why was everybody so horrible to her? She never deserved any of the stuff that happened to her."

My dad and Xandra exchanged a glance. Then he signalled for the check.

XX.

By the time we left the restaurant, my face was on fire and there was a bright roar in my ears, and when I got back to the Barbours' apartment, it wasn't even terribly late but somehow I tripped over the umbrella stand and made a lot of noise coming in and when Mrs. Barbour and Mr. Barbour saw me, I realized (from their faces, more than the way I felt) that I was drunk.

Mr. Barbour flicked off the television with the remote control. "Where have you been?" he said, in a firm but good-natured voice.

I reached for the back of the sofa. "Out with Dad and—" But her name had slipped my mind, everything but the X.

Mrs. Barbour raised her eyebrows at her husband as if to say: *what did I tell you?*

"Well, take it on in to bed, pal," said Mr. Barbour cheerfully, in a voice that managed, in spite of everything, to make me feel a little bit better about life in general. "But try not to wake Andy up."

"You don't feel sick, do you?" Mrs. Barbour said.

"No," I said, though I did; and for a large part of the night I lay awake in the upper bunk, miserable and tossing as the room spun around me, and a couple of times starting up in heart-thudding surprise because it seemed that Xandra had walked in the room and was talking to me: the words indistinct, but the rough, stuttery cadence of her voice unmistakable.

xxi.

"So," said Mr. Barbour at breakfast the next morning, clapping a hand on my shoulder as he pulled out the chair beside me, "festive dinner with old Dad, eh?"

"Yes, sir." I had a splitting headache, and the smell of their French toast made my stomach twist. Etta had unobtrusively brought me a cup of coffee from the kitchen with a couple of aspirins on the saucer.

"Out in Las Vegas, do you say?"

"That's right."

"And how does he bring in the bacon?"

"Sorry?"

"How does he keep himself busy out there?"

"Chance," said Mrs. Barbour, in a neutral voice.

"Well, I mean…that is to say," Mr. Barbour said, realizing that the question had perhaps been indelicately phrased, "what line of work is he in?"

"Um—" I said—and then stopped. What *was* my dad doing? I hadn't a clue.

Mrs. Barbour—who seemed troubled by the turn the conversation had taken—appeared about to say something; but Platt—next to me—spoke up angrily instead. "So who do I have to blow to get a cup of coffee around this place?" he said to his mother, pushing back in his chair with one hand on the table.

There was a dreadful silence.

"*He* has it," said Platt, nodding at me. "*He* comes home drunk, and *he* gets coffee?"

After another dreadful silence, Mr. Barbour said—in a voice icy enough to put even Mrs. Barbour to shame—"That's quite enough, Pard."

Mrs. Barbour brought her pale eyebrows together. "Chance—"

"No, you won't take up for him this time. Go to your room," he said to Platt. "Now."

We all sat staring into our plates, listening to the angry thump of Platt's footsteps, the deafening slam of his door, and then—a few seconds later—the loud music starting up again. No one said much for the rest of the meal.

xxii.

MY DAD — WHO LIKED TO do everything in a hurry, always itching to "get the show on the road" as he liked to say—announced that he planned to get everything wrapped up in New York and the three of us in Las Vegas within a week. And he was true to his word. At eight o'clock that Monday morning, movers showed up at Sutton Place and began to dismantle the apartment and pack it in boxes. A used-book dealer came to look at my mother's art books, and somebody else came in to look at her furniture — and, almost before I knew it, my home began to vanish before my eyes with sickening speed. Watching the curtains disappear and the pictures taken down and the carpets rolled up and carried away, I was reminded of an animated film I'd once seen where a cartoon character with an eraser rubbed out his desk and his lamp and his chair and his window with a scenic view and the whole of his comfortably appointed office until — at last — the eraser hung suspended in a disturbing sea of white.

Tormented by what was happening, yet unable to stop it, I hovered around and watched the apartment vanishing piece by piece, like a bee watching its hive being destroyed. On the wall over my mother's desk (among numerous vacation snaps and old school pictures) hung a black and white photo from her modelling days taken in Central Park. It was a very sharp print, and the tiniest details stood out with almost painful clarity: her freckles, the rough texture of her coat, the chickenpox scar above her left eyebrow. Cheerfully, she looked out into the disarray and confusion of the living room, at my dad throwing out her papers and art supplies and boxing up her books for Goodwill, a scene she probably never dreamed of, or at least I hope she didn't.

xxiii.

MY LAST DAYS WITH the Barbours flew by so fast that I scarcely remember them, apart from a last-minute flurry of laundry and dry cleaning, and several hectic trips to the wine shop on Lex for cardboard boxes. In black marker, I wrote the address of my exotic-sounding new home:

Theodore Decker c/o Xandra Terrell
6219 Desert End Road
Las Vegas, NV

Glumly, Andy and I stood and contemplated the labeled boxes in his bedroom. "It's like you're moving to a different planet," he said.

"More or less."

"No I'm serious. That address. It's like from some mining colony on Jupiter. I wonder what your school will be like."

"God knows."

"I mean—it might be one of those places you read about. With gangs. Metal detectors." Andy had been so mistreated at our (supposedly) enlightened and progressive school that public school, in his view, was on a par with the prison system. "What will you do?"

"Shave my head, I guess. Get a tattoo." I liked that he didn't try to be upbeat or cheerful about the move, unlike Mrs. Swanson or Dave (who was clearly relieved that he wasn't going to have to negotiate any more with my grandparents). Nobody else at Park Avenue said much about my departure, though I knew from the strained expression Mrs. Barbour got when the subject of my father and his "friend" came up that I wasn't totally imagining things. And besides, it wasn't that the future with Dad and Xandra seemed bad or frightening so much as incomprehensible, a blot of black ink on the horizon.

xxiv.

"WELL, A CHANGE OF scenery may be good for you," said Hobie when I went down to see him before I left. "Even if the scene isn't what you'd choose." We were having dinner in the dining room for a change, sitting together at the far end of the table, long enough to seat twelve, silver ewers and ornaments stretching off into opulent darkness. Yet somehow it still felt like the last night in our old apartment on Seventh Avenue, my mother and father and I sitting atop cardboard boxes to eat our Chinese take-out dinner.

I said nothing. I was miserable; and my determination to suffer in secret had made me uncommunicative. All during the anxiety of the previous week, as the apartment was being stripped and my mother's things were folded and boxed and carted off to be sold, I'd yearned for the darkness and repose of Hobie's house, its crowded rooms and old-wood smell, tea leaves and tobacco smoke, bowls of oranges on the sideboard and candlesticks scalloped with puddled beeswax.

"I mean, your mother—" He paused delicately. "It'll be a fresh start."

I studied my plate. He'd made lamb curry, with a lemon-colored sauce that tasted more French than Indian.

"You're not afraid, are you?"

I glanced up. "Afraid of what?"

"Of going to live with him."

I thought about it, gazing off into the shadows behind his head. "No," I said, "not really." For whatever reason, since his return my dad seemed looser, more relaxed. I couldn't attribute it to the fact that he'd stopped drinking, since normally when my dad was on the wagon he grew silent and visibly swollen with misery, so prone to snap that I took good care to stay an arm's reach away.

"Have you told anyone else what you told me?"

"About —?"

In embarrassment, I put my head down and took a bite of the curry. It was actually pretty good once you got used to the fact it wasn't curry.

"I don't think he's drinking any more," I said, in the silence that followed. "If that's what you mean? He seems better. So…" Awkwardly, I trailed away. "Yeah."

"How do you like his girlfriend?"

I had to think about that one too. "I don't know," I admitted.

Hobie was amiably silent, reaching for his wine glass without taking his eyes off me.

"Like, I don't really know her? She's okay, I guess. I can't understand what he likes about her."

"Why not?"

"Well —" I didn't know where to begin. My dad could be charming to 'the ladies' as he called them, opening doors for them, lightly touching their wrists to make a point; I'd seen women fall apart over him, a spectacle I watched coldly, wondering how anyone could be taken in by such a transparent act. It was like watching small children being fooled by a cheesy magic show. "I don't know. I guess I thought she'd be better looking or something."

"Pretty doesn't matter if she's nice," said Hobie.

"Yeah, but she's not all that nice."

"Oh." Then: "Do they seem happy together?"

"I don't know. Well — yes," I admitted. "Like, he doesn't seem constantly so mad all the time?" Then, feeling the weight of Hobie's un-asked question pressing in on me: "Also, he came to get me. I mean, he didn't have to. They could have stayed gone if they didn't want me."

Nothing more was said on the subject, and we finished the dinner talking of other things. But as I was leaving, as we were walking down the photograph-lined hallway — past Pippa's room, with a night light burning, and Cosmo sleeping on the foot of her bed — he said, as he was opening the front door for me: "Theo."

"Yes?"

"You have my address, and my telephone."

"Sure."

"Well then." He seemed almost as uncomfortable as I was. "I hope you have a good trip. Take care of yourself."

"You too," I said. We looked at each other.

"Well."

"Well. Good night, then."

He pushed open the door, and I walked out of the house — for the last time, as I thought. But though I had no idea I'd ever be seeing him again, about this I was wrong.

II.

When we are strongest — who draws back?
Most merry — who falls down laughing?
When we are very bad, — what can they do to us?
— Arthur Rimbaud

Chapter 5.

Badr al-Dine

i.

THOUGH I HAD DECIDED to leave the suitcase in the package room of my old building, where I felt sure Jose and Goldie would look after it, I grew more and more nervous as the date approached until, at the last minute, I determined to go back for what now seems a fairly dumb reason: in my haste to get the painting out of the apartment, I'd thrown a lot of random things in the bag with it, including most of my summer clothes. So the day before my dad was supposed to pick me up at the Barbours', I hurried back over to Fifty-Seventh Street with the idea of unzipping the suitcase and taking a couple of the better shirts off the top.

Jose wasn't there, but a new, thick-shouldered guy (Marco V, according to his nametag) stepped in front of me and cut me off with a blocky, obstinate stance less like a doorman's than a security guard's. "Sorry, can I help you?" he said.

I explained about the suitcase. But after perusing the log — running a heavy forefinger down the column of dates — he didn't seem inclined to go in and get it off the shelf for me. "An' you left this here why?" he said doubtfully, scratching his nose.

"Jose said I could."

"You got a receipt?"

"No," I said, after a confused pause.

"Well, I can't help you. We got no record. Besides, we don't store packages for non-tenants."

I'd lived in the building long enough to know that this wasn't true, but I wasn't about to argue the point. "Look," I said, "I used to live here. I know Goldie and Carlos and everybody. I mean — come on," I said, after a frigid, ill-defined pause, during which I felt his attention drifting. "If you take me back there, I can show you which one."

"Sorry. Nobody but staff and tenants allowed in back."

"It's canvas with ribbon on the handle. My name's on it, see? Decker?" I was pointing out the label still on our old mailbox for proof when Goldie strolled in from his break.

"Hey! look who's back! This one's my kid," he said to Marco V. "I've known him since he was this high. What's up, Theo my friend?"

"Nothing. I mean — well, I'm leaving town."

"Oh, yeah? Out to Vegas already?" said Goldie. At his voice, his hand on my shoulder, everything had become easy and comfortable. "Some crazy place to live out there, am I right?"

"I guess so," I said doubtfully. People kept telling me how crazy things were going to be for me in Vegas although I didn't understand why, as I was unlikely to be spending much time in casinos or clubs.

"You *guess?*" Goldie rolled his eyes up and shook his head, with a drollery that my mother in moments of mischief had been apt to imitate. "Oh my God, I'm telling you. That city? The unions they got…I mean, restaurant work, hotel work…*very* good money, anywhere you look. And the weather? Sun — every day of the year. You're going to love it out there, my friend. When did you say you're leaving?"

"Um, today. I mean tomorrow. That's why I wanted to—"

"Oh, you came for your bag? Hey, sure thing." Goldie said something sharp-sounding in Spanish to Marco V, who shrugged blandly and headed back into the package room.

"He's all right, Marco," said Goldie to me in an undertone. "But, he don't know anything about your bag here because me and Jose didn't enter it down in the book, you know what I'm saying?"

I did know what he was saying. All packages had to be logged in and out of the building. By not tagging the suitcase, or entering it into the official record, they had been protecting me from the possibility that somebody else might show up and try to claim it.

"Hey," I said awkwardly, "thanks for looking out for me…"

"No problemo," said Goldie. "Hey, thanks, man," he said loudly to Marco as he took the bag. "Like I said," he continued in a low voice; I had to walk close beside him in order to hear — "Marco's a good guy, but we had a lot of tenants complaining because the building was understaffed during the, you know." He threw me a significant glance. "I mean, like Carlos couldn't get in to work for his shift that day, I guess it wasn't his fault, but they fired him."

"Carlos?" Carlos was the oldest and most reserved of the doormen, like an aging Mexican matinee idol with his pencil moustache and greying temples, his black shoes polished to a high gloss and his white gloves whiter than everyone else's. "They fired Carlos?"

"I know—unbelievable. Thirty-four years and—" Goldie jerked a thumb over his shoulder—"pfft. And now—management's all like security-conscious, new staff, new rules, sign everybody in and out and like that—

"Anyway," he said, as he backed into the front door, pushing it open. "Let me get you a cab, my friend. You're going straight to the airport?"

"No—" I said, putting out a hand to stop him—I'd been so preoccupied, I hadn't really noticed what he was doing—but he brushed me aside with a *naah* motion.

"No, no," he said—hauling the bag to the curb—"it's all right, my friend, I got it," and I realized, in consternation, that he thought I was trying to stop him taking the bag outside because I didn't have money to tip.

"Hey, wait up," I said—but at the same instant, Goldie whistled and charged into the street with his hand up. "Here! Taxi!" he shouted.

I stopped in the doorway, dismayed, as the cab swooped in from the curb. "Bingo!" said Goldie, opening the back door. "How's that for timing?" Before I could quite think how to stop him without looking like a jerk, I was being ushered into the back seat as the suitcase was hoisted into the trunk, and Goldie was slapping the roof, the friendly way he did.

"Have a good trip, amigo," he said—looking at me, then up at the sky. "Enjoy the sunshine out there for me. You know how I am about the sunshine—I'm a tropical bird, you know? I can't wait to go home to Puerto Rico and talk to the bees. *Hmmn...*" he sang, closing his eyes and putting his head to the side. "My sister has a hive of tame bees and I sing them to sleep. Do they got bees in Vegas?"

"I don't know," I said, feeling quietly in my pockets to see if I could tell how much money I had.

"Well if you see any bees, tell 'em Goldie says hi. Tell 'em I'm coming."

"*¡Hey! ¡Espera!*" It was Jose, hand up—still dressed in his soccer-playing clothes, coming to work straight from his game in the park—swaying towards me with his head-bobbing, athletic walk.

"Hey, *manito,* you taking off?" he said, leaning down and sticking his head in the window of the cab. "You gotta send us a picture for down-stairs!" Down in the basement, where the doormen changed into their uniforms, there was a wall papered with postcards and Polaroids from Miami and Cancun, Puerto Rico and Portugal, which tenants and door-men had sent home to East Fifty-Seventh Street over the years.

"That's right!" said Goldie. "Send us a picture! Don't forget!"

"I—" I was going to miss them, but it seemed gay to come out and say so. So all I said was: "Okay. Take it easy."

"You too," said Jose, backing away with his hand up. "Stay away from them blackjack tables."

"Hey, kid," the cabdriver said, "you want me to take you somewhere or what?"

"Hey, hey, hold your horses, it's cool," said Goldie to him. To me he said: "You gonna be fine, Theo." He gave the cab one last slap. "Good luck, man. See you around. God bless."

ii.

"Don't tell me," my dad said, when he arrived at the Barbours' the next morning to pick me up in the taxi, "that you're carrying *all that shit* on the plane." For I had another suitcase beside the one with the painting, the one I'd originally planned to take.

"I think you're going to be over your baggage allowance," said Xandra a bit hysterically. In the poisonous heat of the sidewalk, I could smell her hair spray even where I was standing. "They only let you carry a certain amount."

Mrs. Barbour, who had come down to the curb with me, said smoothly: "Oh, he'll be fine with those two. I go over my limit all the time."

"Yes, but it costs money."

"Actually, I think you'll find it quite reasonable," said Mrs. Barbour. Though it was early and she was without jewelry or lipstick, somehow even in her sandals and simple cotton dress she still managed to give the impression of being immaculately turned out. "You might have to pay twenty dollars extra at the counter, but that shouldn't be a problem, should it?"

She and my dad stared each other down like two cats. Then my father looked away. I was a little ashamed of his sports coat, which made me think of guys pictured in the *Daily News* under suspicion of racketeering.

"You should have told me you had two bags," he said, sullenly, in the silence (welcome to me) that followed her helpful remark. "I don't know if all this stuff is going to fit in the trunk."

Standing at the curb, with the trunk of the cab open, I almost considered leaving the suitcase with Mrs. Barbour and phoning later to tell her what it contained. But before I could make up my mind to say anything, the broad-backed Russian cab driver had taken Xandra's bag from the trunk and hoisted my second suitcase in, which—with some banging and mashing around—he made to fit.

"See, not very heavy!" he said, slamming the trunk shut, wiping his forehead. "Soft sides!"

"But my carry-on!" said Xandra, looking panicked.

"Not a problem, madame. It can ride in front seat with me. Or in the back with you, if you prefer."

"All sorted, then," said Mrs. Barbour—leaning to give me a quick kiss, the first of my visit, a ladies-who-lunch air kiss that smelled of mint and gardenias. "Toodle-oo, you all," she said. "Have a fantastic trip, won't you?" Andy and I had said our goodbyes the day before; though I knew he was sad to see me go, still my feelings were hurt that he hadn't stayed to see me off but instead had gone with the rest of the family up to the supposedly detested house in Maine. As for Mrs. Barbour: she didn't seem particularly upset to see the last of me, though in truth I felt sick to be leaving.

Her gray eyes, on mine, were clear and cool. "Thank you so much, Mrs. Barbour," I said. "For everything. Tell Andy I said goodbye."

"Certainly I will," she said. "You were an awfully good guest, Theo." Out in the steamy morning heat haze on Park Avenue, I stood holding her hand for a moment longer—slightly hoping that she would tell me to get in touch with her if I needed anything—but she only said, "Good luck, then," and gave me another cool little kiss before she pulled away.

...
iii.

I COULDN'T QUITE FATHOM that I was leaving New York. I'd never been out of the city in my life longer than eight days. On the way to the airport, staring out the window at billboards for strip clubs and personal-injury lawyers that I wasn't likely to see for a while, a chilling thought settled over me. What about the security check? I hadn't flown much (only twice, once when I was in kindergarten) and I wasn't even sure what a security check involved: x-rays? A luggage search?

"Do they open up everything in the airport?" I asked, in a timid voice—and then asked again, because nobody seemed to hear me. I was sitting in the front seat in order to ensure Dad and Xandra's romantic privacy.

"Oh, sure," said the cab driver. He was a beefy, big-shouldered Soviet: coarse features, sweaty red-apple cheeks, like a weightlifter gone to fat. "And if they don't open, they x-ray."

"Even if I check it?"

"Oh, yes," he said reassuringly. "They are wiping for explosives, everything. Very safe."

"But—" I tried to think of some way to formulate what I needed to ask, without betraying myself, and couldn't.

"Not to worry," said the driver. "Lots of police at airport. And three-four days ago? *Roadblocks.*"

"Well, all I can say is, I can't fucking wait to get out of here," Xandra said in her husky voice. For a perplexed moment, I thought she was talking to me, but when I looked back, she was turned toward my father.

My dad put his hand on her knee and said something too low for me to hear. He was wearing his tinted glasses, leaning with his head lolled back on the rear seat, and there was something loose and young-sounding in the flatness of his voice, the secret something that passed between them as he squeezed Xandra's knee. I turned away from them and looked out at the no-man's-land rushing past: long low buildings, bodegas and body shops, car lots simmering in the morning heat.

"See, I don't mind sevens in the flight number," Xandra was saying quietly. "It's eights freak me out."

"Yeah, but eight's a lucky number in China. Take a look at the international board when we get to McCarran. All the incoming flights from Beijing? Eight eight eight."

"You and your Wisdom of the Chinese."

"Number pattern. It's all energy. Meeting of heaven and earth."

"'Heaven and earth.' You make it sound like magic."

"It is."

"Oh yeah?"

They were whispering. In the rear view mirror, their faces were goofy, and too close together; when I realized they were about to kiss (something that still shocked me, no matter how often I saw them do it), I turned to stare straight ahead. It occurred to me that if I didn't already know how my mother had died, no power on earth could have convinced me they hadn't murdered her.

iv.

WHILE WE WERE WAITING to get our boarding passes I was stiff with fear, fully expecting Security to open my suitcase and discover the painting right then, in the check-in line. But the grumpy woman with the shag haircut whose face I still remember (I'd been praying we wouldn't have to go to her when it was our turn) hoisted my suitcase on the belt with hardly a glance.

As I watched it wobble away, towards personnel and procedures unknown, I felt closed-in and terrified in the bright press of strangers — conspicuous too, as if everyone was staring at me. I hadn't been in such a dense mob or seen so many cops in one place since the day my mother died. National Guardsmen with rifles stood by the metal detectors, steady in fatigue gear, cold eyes passing over the crowd.

Backpacks, briefcases, shopping bags and strollers, heads bobbing down the terminal as far as I could see. Shuffling through the security line, I heard a shout — of my name, as I thought. I froze.

"Come on, come *on*," said my dad, hopping behind me on one foot, trying to get his loafer off, elbowing me in the back, "don't just stand there, you're holding up the whole damn line —"

Going through the metal detector, I kept my eyes on the carpet — rigid with fear, expecting any moment a hand to fall on my shoulder.

Babies cried. Old people puttered by in motorized carts. What would they do to me? Could I make them understand it wasn't quite how it looked? I imagined some cinder-block room like in the movies, slammed doors, angry cops in shirtsleeves, *forget about it, you're not going anywhere, kid.*

Once out of security, in the echoing corridor, I heard distinct, purposeful steps following close behind me. Again I stopped.

"Don't tell me," said my dad — turning back with an exasperated roll of his eyes. "You left something."

"No," I said, looking around. "I —" There was no one behind me. Passengers coursed around me on every side.

"Jeez, he's white as a fucking sheet," said Xandra. To my father, she said: "Is he all right?"

"Oh, he'll be fine," said my father as he started down the corridor again. "Once he's on the plane. It's been a tough week for everybody."

"Hell, if I was him, I'd be freaked about getting on a plane too," said Xandra bluntly. "After what he's been through."

My father — tugging his rolling carry-on behind him, a bag my mother had bought him for his birthday several years before — stopped again.

"Poor kid," he said — surprising me by his look of sympathy. "You're not scared, are you?"

"No," I said, far too fast. The last thing I wanted to do was attract anybody's attention or look like I was even one quarter as wigged-out as I was.

He knit his brows at me, then turned away. "Xandra?" he said to her, lifting his chin. "Why don't you give him one of those, you know."

"Got it," said Xandra smartly, stopping to fish in her purse, producing two large white bullet-shaped pills. One she dropped in my father's outstretched palm, and the other she gave to me.

"Thanks," said my dad, slipping it into the pocket of his jacket. "Let's go get something to wash these down with, shall we? Put that away," he said to me as I held the pill up between thumb and forefinger to marvel at how big it was.

"He doesn't need a whole," Xandra said, grasping my dad's arm as she leaned sideways to adjust the strap of her platform sandal.

"Right," said my dad. He took the pill from me, snapped it expertly in half, and dropped the other half in the pocket of his sports coat as they strolled ahead of me, tugging their luggage behind them.

V.

THE PILL WASN'T STRONG enough to knock me out, but it kept me high and happy and somersaulting in and out of air-conditioned dreams. Passengers whispered in the seats around me as a disembodied air hostess announced the results of the in-flight promotional raffle: dinner and drinks for two at Treasure Island. Her hushed promise sent me down into a dream where I swam deep in greenish-black water, some torchlit competition with Japanese children diving for a pillowcase of pink pearls. Throughout it all the plane roared bright and white and constant like the sea, though at some strange point — wrapped deep in my royal-blue blanket, dreaming somewhere high over the desert — the engines seemed to shut off and go silent and I found myself floating chest upward in zero gravity while still buckled into my chair, which had somehow drifted loose from the other seats to float freely around the cabin.

I fell back into my body with a jolt as the plane hit the runway and bounced, screaming to a stop.

"*And* ... welcome to Lost Wages, Nevada," the pilot was saying over the intercom. "Our local time in Sin City is 11:47 a.m."

Half-blind in the glare, plate glass and reflecting surfaces, I trailed after Dad and Xandra through the terminal, stunned by the chatter and flash of slot machines and by the music blaring loud and incongruous so early in the day. The airport was like a mall-sized version of Times Square: towering palms, movie screens with fireworks and gondolas and showgirls and singers and acrobats.

It took a long time for my second bag to come off the carousel. Chewing my fingernails, I stared fixedly at a billboard of a grinning Komodo dragon, an ad for some casino attraction: "Over 2,000 reptiles await you." The baggage-claim crowd was like a group of colorful stragglers in front of some third-rate nightclub: sunburns, disco shirts, tiny bejeweled Asian ladies with giant logo sunglasses. The belt was circling around mostly empty and my dad (itching for a cigarette, I could tell) was starting to stretch and pace and rub his knuckles against his cheek like he did when he wanted a drink when there it came, the last one, khaki canvas with the red label and the multicolored ribbon my mother had tied around the handle.

My dad, in one long step, lunged forward and grabbed it before I could get to it. "About time," he said jauntily, tossing it onto the baggage cart. "Come on, let's get the hell out of here."

Out we rolled through the automatic doors and into a wall of breathtaking heat. Miles of parked cars stretched around us in all directions, hooded and still. Rigidly I stared straight ahead—chrome knives glinting, horizon shimmering like wavy glass—as if looking back, or hesitating, might invite some uniformed party to step in front of us. Yet no one collared me or shouted at us to stop. No one even looked at us.

I was so disoriented in the glare that when my dad stopped in front of a new silver Lexus and said: "Okay, this is us," I tripped and nearly fell on the curb.

"This is yours?" I said, looking between them.

"What?" said Xandra coquettishly, clumping around to the passenger side in her high shoes as my dad beeped the lock open. "You don't like it?"

A Lexus? Every day, I was struck by all sorts of matters large and small that I urgently needed to tell my mother and as I stood dumbly watching my dad hoist the bags in the trunk my first thought was: *wow, wait until she hears about this.* No wonder he hadn't sent money home.

My dad threw aside his half-smoked Viceroy with a flourish. "Okay," he said, "hop in." The desert air had magnetized him. Back in New York, he had looked a bit worn-out and seedy but out in the rippling heat his white sportcoat and his cult-leader sunglasses made sense.

The car—which started with the push of a button—was so quiet that at first I didn't realize we were moving. Away we glided, into depthlessness and space. Accustomed as I was to jolting around in the backs of taxis, the smoothness and chill of the ride was sealed off, eerie: brown sand, vicious glare, trance and silence, blown trash whipping at the chain-link fence. I still felt numbed and weightless from the pill, and the crazy façades and superstructures of the Strip, the violent shimmer where the dunes met sky, made me feel as if we had touched down on another planet.

Xandra and my dad had been talking quietly in the front seat. Now she turned to me—snapping gum, robust and sunny, her jewelry blazing in the strong light. "So, whaddaya think?" she said, exhaling a strong breath of Juicy Fruit.

"It's wild," I said—watching a pyramid sail past my window, the Eiffel Tower, too overwhelmed to take it in.

"You think it's wild now?" said my dad, tapping his fingernail on the steering wheel in a manner I associated with frayed nerves and late-night quarrels after he got home from the office. "Just wait until you see it lit up at night."

"See there — check it out," said Xandra, reaching over to point out the window on my dad's side. "There's the volcano. It really works."

"Actually, I think they're renovating it. But in theory, yeah. Hot lava. On the hour, every hour."

"Exit to the left in point two miles," said a woman's computerized voice.

Carnival colors, giant clown heads and XXX signs: the strangeness exhilarated me, and also frightened me a little. In New York, everything reminded me of my mother — every taxi, every street corner, every cloud that passed over the sun — but out in this hot mineral emptiness, it was as if she had never existed; I could not even imagine her spirit looking down on me. All trace of her seemed burned away in the thin desert air.

As we drove, the improbable skyline dwindled into a wilderness of parking lots and outlet malls, loop after faceless loop of shopping plazas, Circuit City, Toys "R" Us, supermarkets and drugstores, Open Twenty-Four Hours, no saying where it ended or began. The sky was wide and trackless, like the sky over the sea. As I fought to stay awake — blinking against the glare — I was ruminating in a dazed way over the expensive-smelling leather interior of the car and thinking of a story I'd often heard my mother tell: of how, when she and my dad were dating, he'd turned up in a Porsche he'd borrowed from a friend to impress her. Only after they were married had she learned that the car wasn't really his. She'd seemed to think this was funny — although given other, less amusing facts that came to light after their marriage (such as his arrest record, as a juvenile, on charges unknown), I wondered that she was able to find anything very entertaining about the story.

"Um, you've had this car how long?" I said, speaking up over their conversation in front.

"Oh — gosh — little over a year now, isn't that right, Xan?"

A year? I was still chewing this over — this figure meant my dad had acquired the car (and Xandra) before he'd disappeared — when I looked up and saw that the strip malls had given way to an endless-seeming grid of small stucco homes. Despite the air of boxed, bleached sameness — row on row, like stones in a cemetery — some of the houses were painted in festive pastels (mint green, rancho pink, milky desert blue) and there was something excitingly foreign about the sharp shadows, the spiked desert plants. Having grown up in the city, where there was never enough space, I was if anything pleasantly surprised. It would be something new to live in a house with a yard, even if the yard was only brown rocks and cactus.

"Is this still Las Vegas?" As a game, I was trying to pick out what made the houses different from each other: an arched doorway here, a swimming pool or a palm tree there.

"You're seeing a whole different part now," my dad said — exhaling sharply, stubbing out his third Viceroy. "This is what tourists never see."

Though we'd been driving a while, there were no landmarks, and it was impossible to say where we were going or in which direction. The skyline was monotonous and unchanging and I was fearful that we might drive through the pastel houses altogether and out into the alkali waste beyond, into some sun-beaten trailer park from the movies. But instead — to my surprise — the houses began to grow larger: with second stories, with cactus gardens, with fences and pools and multi-car garages.

"Okay, this is us," said my dad, turning into a road that had an imposing granite sign with copper letters: *The Ranches at Canyon Shadows*.

"You live *here?*" I said, impressed. "Is there a canyon?"

"No, that's just the name of it," said Xandra.

"See, they have a bunch of different developments out here," said my dad, pinching the bridge of his nose. I could tell by his tone — his scratchy old needing-a-drink voice — that he was tired and not in a very good mood.

"Ranch communities is what they call them," said Xandra.

"Right. Whatever. Oh, shut the fuck up," snapped my dad, reaching over to turn the volume down as the lady on the navigation system piped up with instructions again.

"They all have different themes, sort of," said Xandra, who was dabbing on lip gloss with the pad of her little finger. "There's Pueblo Breeze, Ghost Ridge, Dancing Deer Villas. Spirit Flag is the golf community? And Encantada is the fanciest, lots of investment properties — Hey, turn here, sweet pea," she said, clutching his arm.

My dad kept driving straight and did not answer.

"Shit!" Xandra turned in her seat to look at the road receding behind us. "Why do you always have to go the long way?"

"Don't start with the shortcuts. You're as bad as the Lexus lady."

"Yeah, but it's faster. By fifteen minutes. Now we're going to have to drive all the way around Dancing Deer."

My dad blew out an exasperated breath. "Look —"

"What's so hard about cutting over to Gitana Trails and making two lefts and a right? Because that's all it is. If you get off on Desatoya —"

"Look. You want to drive the car? Or you want to let me drive the fucking car?"

I knew better than to challenge my dad when he took that tone, and apparently Xandra did too. She flounced around in her seat and — in a deliberate manner that seemed calculated to annoy him — turned up the radio very loud and started punching through static and commercials.

The stereo was so powerful I could feel it thumping through the back of my white leather seat. *Vacation, all I ever wanted* . . . Light climbed and burst through the wild desert clouds — never-ending sky, acid blue, like a computer game or a test pilot's hallucination.

"Vegas 99, serving up the Eighties and Nineties," said the fast, excited voice on the radio. "And here's Pat Benatar coming up for you, in our Ladies of the Eighties Lapdance lunch."

In Desatoya Ranch Estates, on 6219 Desert End Road, where lumber was stacked in some of the yards and sand blew in the streets, we turned into the driveway of a large Spanish-looking house, or maybe it was Moorish, shuttered beige stucco with arched gables and a clay-tiled roof pitched at various startling angles. I was impressed by the aimlessness and sprawl of it, its cornices and columns, the elaborate ironwork door with its sense of a stage set, like a house from one of the Telemundo soap operas the doormen always had going in the package room.

We got out of the car and were circling around to the garage entrance with our suitcases when I heard an eerie, distressing noise: screaming, or crying, from inside the house.

"Gosh, what's that?" I said, dropping my bags, unnerved.

Xandra was leaning sideways, stumbling a bit in her high shoes and grappling for her key. "Oh, shut up, shut up, shutthefuckup," she was muttering under her breath. Before she'd opened the door all the way, a hysterical stringy mop shot out, shrieking, and began to hop and dance and caper all around us.

"Get down!" Xandra was yelling. Through the half-opened door, safari music (trumpeting elephants, chattering monkeys) was playing so loud that I could hear it all the way out in the garage.

"Wow," I said, peering inside. The air inside smelled hot and stale: old cigarette smoke, new carpet, and—no question about it—dog shit.

"For the zookeeper, big cats pose a unique series of challenges," the voice on the television boomed. "Why don't we follow Andrea and her staff on their morning rounds."

"Hey," I said, stopping in the door with my bag, "you left the television on."

"Yes," said Xandra—brushing past me—"that's Animal Planet, I left it on for him. For Popper. I said get down!" she snapped at the dog, who was scrabbling at her knees with his claws as she hobbled in on her platforms and switched the television off.

"He stayed by himself?" I said, over the dog's shrieks. He was one of those long-haired girly dogs who would have been white and fluffy if he was clean.

"Oh, he's got a drinking fountain from Petco," said Xandra, wiping her forehead with the back of her hand as she stepped over the dog. "And one of those big feeder things?"

"What kind is he?"

"Maltese. Pure bred. I won him in a raffle. I mean, I know he needs a bath, it's a pain to keep them groomed. That's right, just look what you did to my pants," she said to the dog. "White jeans."

We were standing in a large, open room with high ceilings and a staircase that ran up to a sort of railed mezzanine on one side—a room almost as big as the entire apartment I'd grown up in. But when my eyes adjusted from the bright sun, I was taken aback by how bare it was. Bone-white walls. Stone fireplace, with sort of a fake hunting-lodge feel. Sofa like something from a hospital waiting room. Across from the glass patio doors stretched a wall of built-in shelves, mostly empty.

My dad creaked in, and dropped the suitcases on the carpet. "Jesus, Xan, it smells like shit in here."

Xandra—leaning over to set down her purse—winced as the dog began to jump and climb and claw all over her. "Well, Janet was supposed to come and let him out," she said over his high-pitched screams. "She had the key and everything. God, Popper," she said, wrinkling her nose, turning her head away, "you stink."

The emptiness of the place stunned me. Until that moment, I had never questioned the necessity of selling my mother's books and rugs and antiques, or the need of sending almost everything else to Goodwill or the garbage. I had grown up in a four-room apartment where closets were packed to overflowing, where every bed had boxes beneath it and pots and pans were hung from the ceiling because there wasn't room in the cupboards. But—how easy it would have been to bring some of her things, like the silver box that had been her mother's, or the painting of a chestnut mare that looked like a Stubbs, or even her childhood copy of *Black Beauty*! It wasn't as if he couldn't have used a few good pictures or some of the furniture she'd inherited from her parents. He had gotten rid of her things because he hated her.

"Jesus Christ," my father was saying, his voice raised angrily over the shrill barks. "This dog has destroyed the place. Quite honestly."

"Well, I don't know—I mean, I know it's a mess but Janet said—"

"I *told* you, you should have kennelled this dog. Or, I don't know, taken him to the pound. I don't like having him in the house. Outdoors is the place for him. Didn't I tell you this was going to be a problem? Janet is such a fucking flake—"

"So he went on the rug a few times? So what? And—what the hell are *you* looking at?" said Xandra angrily, stepping over the shrieking dog—and with a bit of a start, I realized it was me she was glaring at.

vi.

MY NEW ROOM FELT so bare and lonely that, after I unpacked my bags, I left the sliding door of the closet open so I could see my clothes hanging inside. From downstairs, I could still hear Dad shouting about the carpet. Unfortunately, Xandra was shouting too, getting him more wound up, which (I could have told her, if she'd asked) was exactly the wrong way to handle him. At home, my mother had known how to suffocate my dad's anger by growing silent, a low, unwavering flame of contempt that sucked all the oxygen out of the room and made everything he said and did seem ridiculous. Eventually he would whoosh out with a thunderous slam of the front door and when he returned — hours later, with a quiet click of the key in the lock — he would walk around the apartment as if nothing had happened: going to the refrigerator for a beer, asking in a perfectly normal voice where his mail was.

Of the three empty rooms upstairs I'd chosen the largest, which like a hotel room had its own tiny bathroom to the side. Floor heavily carpeted in steel blue plush. Bare mattress, with a plastic package of bedsheets at the foot. Legends Percale. Twenty percent off. A gentle mechanical hum emanated from the walls, like the hum of an aquarium filter. It seemed like the kind of room where a call girl or a stewardess would be murdered on television.

With an ear out for Dad and Xandra, I sat on the mattress with the wrapped painting on my knees. Even with the door locked, I was hesitant to take the paper off in case they came upstairs, and yet the desire to look at it was irresistible. Carefully, carefully, I scratched the tape with my thumbnail and peeled it up by the edges.

The painting slid out more easily than I'd expected, and I found myself biting back a gasp of pleasure. It was the first time I'd seen the painting in the light of day. In the arid room — all sheetrock and whiteness — the muted colors bloomed with life; and even though the surface of the painting was ghosted ever so slightly with dust, the atmosphere it breathed was like the light-rinsed airiness of a wall opposite an open window. Was this why people like Mrs. Swanson went on about the desert light? She had loved to warble on about what she called her "sojourn" in New Mexico — wide horizons, empty skies, spiritual clarity. Yet as if by some trick of the light the painting seemed transfigured, as the dark roofline view of water tanks from my mother's bedroom window sometimes stood gilded and electrified for a few strange moments in the stormlight of late afternoon, right before a summer cloudburst.

"Theo?" My dad, knocking briskly at the door. "You hungry?"

I stood up, hoping he wouldn't try the door and find it locked. My new room was as bare as a jail cell; but the closet had high shelves, well above my dad's eye level, very deep.

"I'm going to pick up some Chinese. Want me to get you something?"

Would my dad know what the painting was, if he saw it? I hadn't thought so — but looking at it in the light, the glow it threw off, I realized that any fool would. "Um, be right there," I called, my voice false-sounding and hoarse, slipping the painting into an extra pillowcase and hiding it under the bed before hurrying out of the room.

vii.

IN THE WEEKS IN Las Vegas before school started, loitering around downstairs with the earphones of my iPod in but the sound off, I learned a number of interesting facts. For starters: my dad's former job had not involved nearly as much business travel to Chicago and Phoenix as he had led us to believe. Unbeknownst to my mother and me, he had actually been flying out to Vegas for some months, and it was in Vegas—in an Asian-themed bar at the Bellagio—that he and Xandra had met. They had been seeing each other for a while before my dad vanished—a bit over a year, as I gathered; it seemed that they had celebrated their "anniversary" not long before my mother died, with dinner at Delmonico Steakhouse and the Jon Bon Jovi concert at the MGM Grand. (Bon Jovi! Of all the many things I was dying to tell my mother—and there were thousands of them, if not millions—it seemed terrible that she would never know this hilarious fact.)

Another thing I figured out, after a few days in the house on Desert End Road: what Xandra and my dad really meant when they said my dad had "stopped drinking" was that he'd switched from Scotch (his beverage of choice) to Corona Lights and Vicodin. I had been puzzled by how frequently the peace sign, or V for Victory, was flashed between them, in all sorts of incongruous contexts, and it might have gone on being a mystery for a lot longer if my dad hadn't just come out and asked Xandra for a Vicodin when he thought I wasn't listening.

I didn't know anything about Vicodin except that it was something that a wild movie actress I liked was always getting her picture in the tabloids about: stumbling from her Mercedes as police lights flashed in the background. Several days later, I came across a plastic bag with what looked like about three hundred pills in it—sitting on the kitchen counter, alongside a bottle of my dad's Propecia and a stack of unpaid bills— which Xandra snatched up and threw in her purse.

"What are those?" I said.

"Um, vitamins."

"Why are they in that baggie like that?"

"I get them from this bodybuilder guy at work."

The weird thing was — and this was something else I wished I could have discussed with my mother — the new, drugged-out Dad was a much more pleasant and predictable companion than the Dad of old. When my father drank, he was a twist of nerves — all inappropriate jokes and aggressive bursts of energy, right up until the moment he passed out — but when he stopped drinking, he was worse. He blasted along ten paces ahead of my mother and me on the sidewalk, talking to himself and patting his suit pockets as if for a weapon. He brought home stuff we didn't want and couldn't afford, like crocodile Manolos for my mother (who hated high heels) and not even in the right size. He lugged piles of paper home from the office and sat up past midnight drinking iced coffee and punching in numbers on the calculator, sweat pouring off him like he'd just done forty minutes on the StairMaster. Or else he would make a big deal of going to some party way the hell over in Brooklyn ("What do you mean, 'maybe I shouldn't go'? You think I should live like a fucking hermit, is that it?") and then — after dragging my mother there — storm out ten minutes later after insulting someone or mocking them to their face.

This was a different, more affable energy, with the pills: a combination of sluggishness and brightness, a bemused, goofy, floating quality. His walk was looser. He napped more, nodded agreeably, lost the thread of his arguments, ambled about barefoot with his bathrobe halfway open. From his genial cursing, his infrequent shaving, the relaxed way he talked around the cigarette in the corner of his mouth, it was almost as if he were playing a character: some cool guy from a fifties noir or maybe *Ocean's Eleven,* a lazy, sated gangster with not much to lose. Yet even in the midst of his new laid-backness he still had that crazed and slightly heroic look of schoolboy insolence, all the more stirring since it was drifting towards autumn, half-ruined and careless of itself.

In the house on Desert End Road, which had the super-expensive cable television package my mother would never let us get, he drew the blinds against the glare and sat smoking in front of the television, glassy as an opium addict, watching ESPN with the sound off, no sport in particular, anything and everything that came on: cricket, jai alai, badminton, croquet. The air was overly chilled, with a stale, refrigerated smell; sitting motionless for hours, the filament of smoke from his Viceroy floating to the ceiling like a thread of incense, he might as well have been contemplating the Buddha, the Dharma, and the Sangha as the leaderboard at the PGA or whatever.

What wasn't clear was if my dad had a job—or, if he did, what kind of job it was. The phone rang all hours of the day and night. My dad went in the hallway with the handset, his back to me, bracing his arm against the wall and staring at the carpet as he talked, something in his posture suggesting the attitude of a coach at the end of a tough game. Usually he kept his voice well down but even when he didn't, it was tough to understand his end of the conversation: vig, moneyline, odds-on favorite, straight up and against the spread. He was gone much of the time, on unexplained errands, and a lot of nights he and Xandra didn't come home at all. "We get comped a lot at the MGM Grand," he explained, rubbing his eyes, sinking back into the sofa cushions with an exhausted sigh—and again I got a sense of the character he was playing, moody playboy, relic of the eighties, easily bored. "I hope you don't mind. It's just when she's working the late shift, it's easier for us to crash on the Strip."

viii.

"WHAT ARE ALL THESE papers everywhere?" I asked Xandra one day while she was in the kitchen making her white diet drink. I was confused by the pre-printed cards I kept finding all over the house: grids pencilled in with row after monotonous row of figures. Vaguely scientific-looking, they had a creepy feel of DNA sequences, or maybe spy transmissions in binary code.

She switched the blender off, flicked the hair out of her eyes. "Excuse me?"

"These work sheets or whatever."

"Bacca-*rat!*" said Xandra—rolling the r, doing a tricky little fillip with her fingers.

"Oh," I said after a flat pause, though I'd never heard the word before.

She stuck her finger in the drink, and licked it off. "We go to the baccarat salon at the MGM Grand a lot?" she said. "Your dad likes to keep track of his played games."

"Can I go some time?"

"No. Well yeah—I guess you *could,*" she said, as if I'd inquired about vacation prospects in some unstable Islamic nation. "Except they're not super-welcoming of kids in the casinos? You're not really allowed to come and watch us play."

So what, I thought. Standing around and watching Dad and Xandra gamble was scarcely my idea of fun. Aloud, I said: "But I thought they had tigers and pirate boats and things like that."

"Yeah, well. I guess." She was reaching up for a glass on the shelf, exposing a quadrangle of blue-inked Chinese characters between her T-shirt and her low-slung jeans. "They tried to sell this whole family-friendly package a few years ago, but it didn't wash."

ix.

I MIGHT HAVE LIKED Xandra in other circumstances—which, I guess, is sort of like saying I might have liked the kid who beat me up if he hadn't beat me up. She was my first inkling that women over forty—women maybe not all that great-looking to start with—could be sexy. Though she wasn't pretty in the face (bullet eyes, blunt little nose, tiny teeth) still she was in shape, she worked out, and her arms and legs were so glossy and tan that they looked almost sprayed, as if she anointed herself with lots of creams and oils. Teetering in her high shoes, she walked fast, always tugging at her too-short skirt, a forward-leaning walk, weirdly alluring. On some level, I was repelled by her—by her stuttery voice, her thick, shiny lip gloss that came in a tube that said Lip Glass; by the multiple pierce holes in her ears and the gap in her front teeth that she liked to worry with her tongue—but there was something sultry and exciting and tough about her too: an animal strength, a purring, prowling quality when she was out of her heels and walking barefoot.

Vanilla Coke, vanilla Chapstick, vanilla diet drink, Stoli Vanilla. Off from work, she dressed like sort of a rapped-up tennis mom, short white skirts, lots of gold jewelry. Even her tennis shoes were new and spanking white. Sunbathing by the pool, she wore a white crocheted bikini; her back was wide but thin, lots of ribs, like a man without his shirt on. "Uh-oh, wardrobe malfunction," she said when she sat up from the lounge chair without remembering to fasten her top, and I saw that her breasts were as tan as the rest of her.

She liked reality shows: *Survivor, American Idol.* She liked to shop at Intermix and Juicy Couture. She liked to call her friend Courtney and "vent," and a lot of her venting, unfortunately, was on the subject of me. "Can you believe it?" I heard her saying on the telephone when my dad was out of the house one day. "I didn't sign on for this. A kid? Hello?

"Yeah, it's a pain in the ass, all right," she continued, inhaling lazily on her Marlboro Light — pausing by the glass doors that led to the pool, staring down at her freshly painted, honeydew-green toenails. "No," she said after a brief pause. "I don't know how long for. I mean, what does he expect me to think? I'm not a freaking soccer mom."

Her complaints seemed routine, not particularly heated or personal. Still it was hard to know just how to make her like me. Previously, I had operated on the assumption that mom-aged women loved it when you stood around and tried to talk to them but with Xandra I soon learned that it was better not to joke around or inquire too much about her day when she came home in a bad mood. Sometimes, when it was just the two of us, she switched the channel from ESPN and we sat eating fruit cocktail and watching movies on Lifetime peacefully enough. But when she was annoyed with me, she had a cold way of saying "Apparently" in answer to almost anything I said, making me feel stupid.

"Um, I can't find the can opener."

"Apparently."

"There's going to be a lunar eclipse tonight."

"Apparently."

"Look, sparks are coming out of the wall socket."

"Apparently."

Xandra worked nights. Usually she breezed off around three thirty in the afternoon, dressed in her curvy work uniform: black jacket, black pants made of some stretchy, tight-fitting material, with her blouse unbuttoned to her freckled breastbone. The nametag pinned to her blazer said XANDRA in big letters and underneath: *Florida*. In New York, when we'd been out at dinner that night, she'd told me that she was trying to break into real estate but what she really did, I soon learned, was manage a bar called "Nickels" in a casino on the Strip. Sometimes she came home with plastic platters of bar snacks wrapped in cellophane, things like meatballs and chicken teriyaki bites, which she and my dad carried in front of the television and ate with the sound off.

Living with them was like living with roommates I didn't particularly get along with. When they were at home, I stayed in my room with the door shut. And when they were gone — which was most of the time — I prowled through the farther reaches of the house, trying to get used to its openness. Many of the rooms were bare of furniture, or almost bare, and the open space, the uncurtained brightness — all exposed carpet and parallel planes — made me feel slightly unmoored.

And yet it was a relief not to feel constantly exposed, or onstage, the way I had at the Barbours'. The sky was a rich, mindless, never-ending blue, like a promise of some ridiculous glory that wasn't really there. No one cared that I never changed my clothes and wasn't in therapy. I was free to goof off, lie in bed all morning, watch five Robert Mitchum movies in a row if I felt like it.

Dad and Xandra kept their bedroom door locked — which was too bad, as that was the room where Xandra kept her laptop, off-limits to me unless she was home and she brought it down for me to use in the living room. Poking around when they were out of the house, I found real estate leaflets, new wineglasses still in the box, a stack of old *TV Guides*, a cardboard box of beat-up trade paperbacks: *Your Moon Signs, The South Beach Diet, Caro's Book of Poker Tells, Lovers and Players* by Jackie Collins.

The houses around us were empty — no neighbors. Five or six houses down, on the opposite side of the street, there was an old Pontiac parked out front. It belonged to a tired-looking woman with big boobs and ratty hair whom I sometimes saw standing barefoot out in front of her house in the late afternoon, clutching a pack of cigarettes and talking on her cell phone. I thought of her as "the Playa" as the first time I'd seen her, she'd been wearing a T-shirt that said DON'T HATE THE PLAYA, HATE THE GAME. Apart from her, the Playa, the only other living person I'd seen on our street was a big-bellied man in a black sports shirt way the hell down at the cul-de-sac, wheeling a garbage can out to the curb (although I could have told him: no garbage pickup on our street. When it was time to take the trash out, Xandra made me sneak out with the bag and throw it in the dumpster of the abandoned-under-construction house a few doors down). At night — apart from our house, and the Playa's — complete darkness reigned on the street. It was all as isolated as a book we'd read in the third grade about pioneer children on the Nebraska prairie, except with no siblings or friendly farm animals or Ma and Pa.

The hardest thing, by far, was being stuck in the middle of nowhere — no movie theaters or libraries, not even a corner store. "Isn't there a bus or something?" I asked Xandra one evening when she was in the kitchen unwrapping the night's plastic tray of Atomic Wings and blue cheese dip.

"Bus?" said Xandra, licking a smear of barbecue sauce off her finger.

"Don't you have public transportation out here?"

"Nope."

"What do people do?"

Xandra cocked her head to the side. "They drive?" she said, as if I was a retard who'd never heard of cars.

One thing: there was a pool. My first day I'd burned myself brick red within an hour and suffered a sleepless night on scratchy new sheets. After that, I only went out after the sun started going down. The twilights out there were florid and melodramatic, great sweeps of orange and crimson and Lawrence-in-the-desert vermilion, then night dropping dark and hard like a slammed door. Xandra's dog Popper — who lived, for the most part, in a brown plastic igloo on the shady side of the fence — ran back and forth along the side of the pool yapping as I floated on my back, trying to pick out constellations I knew in the confusing white spatter of stars: Lyra, Cassiopeia the queen, whiplash Scorpius with the twin stings in his tail, all the friendly childhood patterns that had twinkled me to sleep from the glow-in-the-dark planetarium stars on my bedroom ceiling back in New York. Now, transfigured — cold and glorious like deities with their disguises flung off — it was as if they'd flown through the roof and into the sky to assume their true, celestial homes.

x.

MY SCHOOL STARTED THE second week of August. From a distance, the fenced complex of long, low, sand-colored buildings, connected by roofed walkways, made me think of a minimum security prison. But once I stepped through the doors, the brightly colored posters and the echoing hallway were like falling back into a familiar old dream of school: crowded stairwells, humming lights, biology classroom with an iguana in a piano-sized tank; locker-lined hallways that were familiar like a set from some much-watched television show—and though the resemblance to my old school was only superficial, on some strange wavelength it was also comforting and real.

The other section of Honors English was reading *Great Expectations*. Mine was reading *Walden;* and I hid myself in the coolness and silence of the book, a refuge from the sheet-metal glare of the desert. During the morning break (where we were rounded up and made to go outside, in a chain-fenced yard near the vending machines), I stood in the shadiest corner I could find with my mass-market paperback and, with a red pencil, went through and underlined a lot of particularly bracing sentences: "The mass of men lead lives of quiet desperation." "A stereotyped but unconscious despair is concealed even under what are called the games and amusements of mankind." What would Thoreau have made of Las Vegas: its lights and rackets, its trash and daydreams, its projections and hollow façades?

At my school, the sense of transience was unsettling. There were a lot of army brats, a lot of foreigners—many of them the children of executives who had come to Las Vegas for big managerial and construction jobs. Some of them had lived in nine or ten different states in as many years, and many of them had lived abroad: in Sydney, Caracas, Beijing, Dubai, Taipei. There were also a good many shy, half-invisible boys and girls whose parents had fled rural hardship for jobs as hotel busboys and chambermaids. In this new ecosystem money, or even good looks, did not seem to determine popularity; what mattered most, as I came to realize, was who'd lived in Vegas the longest, which was why the knock-down Mexican beauties and itinerant construction heirs sat alone at lunch while the bland, middling children of local realtors and car dealers were the cheerleaders and class presidents, the unchallenged elite of the school.

The days were clear and beautiful; and, as September rolled around, the hateful glare gave way to a certain luminosity, a dusty, golden quality. Sometimes I ate lunch at the Spanish Table, to practice my Spanish; sometimes I ate lunch at the German Table even though I didn't speak German because several of the German II kids—children of Deutsche Bank and Lufthansa executives—had grown up in New York. Of my classes, English was the only one I looked forward to, yet I was disturbed by how many of my classmates disliked Thoreau, railed against him even, as if he (who claimed never to have learned anything of value from an old person) was an enemy and not a friend. His scorn of commerce — invigorating to me — nettled a lot of the more vocal kids in Honors English. "Yeah, right," shouted an obnoxious boy whose hair was gelled and combed stiff like a Dragon Ball Z character — "some kind of world it would be if *every-body* just dropped out and moped around in the woods —"

"*Me, me, me,*" whined a voice in the back.

"It's antisocial," a loudmouth girl interjected eagerly over the laughter that followed this — shifting in her seat, turning back to the teacher (a limp, long-boned woman named Mrs. Spear, who always wore brown sandals and earthtone colors, and looked as if she was suffering from major depression). "Thoreau is always just sitting around on his can telling us how good he has it —"

"—*Because,*" said the Dragon Ball Z boy — his voice rising gleefully, "if everybody dropped out, like he's saying to do? What kind of community would we have, if it was just people like him? We wouldn't have hospitals and stuff. We wouldn't have roads."

"Twat," mumbled a welcome voice — just loud enough for everybody around to hear.

I turned to see who had said this: the burnout-looking boy across the aisle, slouched and drumming his desk with his fingers. When he saw me looking at him, he raised a surprisingly lively eyebrow, as if to say: *can you believe these fucking idiots?*

"Did someone have something to say back there?" said Mrs. Spear.

"Like Thoreau gave a toss about roads," said the burnout boy. His accent took me by surprise: foreign, I couldn't place it.

"Thoreau was the first environmentalist," said Mrs. Spear.

"He was also the first vegetarian," said a girl in back.

"Figures," said someone else. "Mr. Crunchy-chewy."

"You're all totally missing my point," the Dragon Ball Z boy said excitedly. "Somebody has to build roads and not just sit in the woods looking at ants and mosquitoes all day. It's called civilization."

My neighbor let out a sharp, contemptuous bark of a laugh. He was pale and thin, not very clean, with lank dark hair falling in his eyes and the unwholesome wanness of a runaway, callused hands and black-circled nails chewed to the nub — not like the shiny-haired, ski-tanned skate rats from my school on the Upper West Side, punks whose dads were CEOs and Park Avenue surgeons, but a kid who might conceivably be sitting on a sidewalk somewhere with a stray dog on a rope.

"Well, to address some of these questions? I'd like for everybody to turn back to page fifteen," Mrs. Spear said. "Where Thoreau is talking about his experiment in living."

"Experiment how?" said Dragon Ball Z. "Why is living in the woods like he does any different from a caveman?"

The dark-haired boy scowled and sank deeper in his seat. He reminded me of the homeless-looking kids who stood around passing cigarettes back and forth on St. Mark's Place, comparing scars, begging for change — same torn-up clothes and scrawny white arms; same black leather bracelets tangled at the wrists. Their multi-layered complexity was a sign I couldn't read, though the general import was clear enough: *different tribe, forget about it, I'm way too cool for you, don't even try to talk to me.* Such was my mistaken first impression of the only friend I made when I was in Vegas, and — as it turned out — one of the great friends of my life.

His name was Boris. Somehow we found ourselves standing together in the crowd that was waiting for the bus after school that day.

"Hah. Harry Potter," he said, as he looked me over.

"Fuck you," I said listlessly. It was not the first time, in Vegas, I'd heard the Harry Potter comment. My New York clothes — khakis, white oxford shirts, the tortoiseshell glasses which I unfortunately needed to see — made me look like a freak at a school where most people dressed in tank tops and flip flops.

"Where's your broomstick?"

"Left it at Hogwarts," I said. "What about you? Where's your board?"

"Eh?" he said, leaning in to me and cupping his hand behind his ear with an old-mannish, deaf-looking gesture. He was half a head taller than me; along with jungle boots and bizarre old fatigues with the knees busted out, he was wearing a ratted-up black T-shirt with a snowboarding logo, 𝔑𝔢𝔳𝔢𝔯 𝔖𝔲𝔪𝔪𝔢𝔯 in white gothic letters.

"Your shirt," I said, with a curt nod. "Not much boarding in the desert."

"Nyah," said Boris, pushing the stringy dark hair out of his eyes. "I don't know how to snowboard. I just hate the sun."

We ended up together on the bus, in the seat closest to the door — clearly an unpopular place to sit, judging from the urgent way other kids muscled and pushed to the rear, but I hadn't grown up riding a school bus and apparently neither had he, as he too seemed to think it only natural to fling himself down in the first empty seat up front. For a while we didn't say much, but it was a long ride and eventually we got talking. It turned out that he lived in Canyon Shadows too—but farther out, the end that was getting reclaimed by the desert, where a lot of the houses weren't finished and sand stood in the streets.

"How long have you been here?" I asked him. It was the question all the kids asked each other at my new school, like we were doing jail time.

"Dunno. Two months maybe?" Though he spoke English fluently enough, with a strong Australian accent, there was also a dark, slurry undercurrent of something else: a whiff of Count Dracula, or maybe it was KGB agent. "Where are you from?"

"New York," I said—and was gratified at his silent double-take, his lowered eyebrows that said: *very cool.* "What about you?"

He pulled a face. "Well, let's see," he said, slumping back in his seat and counting off the countries on his fingers. "I've lived in Russia, Scotland which was maybe cool but I don't remember it, Australia, Poland, New Zealand, Texas for two months, Alaska, New Guinea, Canada, Saudi Arabia, Sweden, Ukraine—"

"Jesus Christ."

He shrugged. "Mostly Australia, Russia, and Ukraine, though. Those three places."

"Do you speak Russian?"

He made a gesture that I took to mean *more or less.* "Ukrainian too, and Polish. Though I've forgotten a lot. The other day, I tried to remember what was the word for 'dragonfly' and couldn't."

"Say something."

He obliged, something spitty and guttural.

"What does that mean?"

He chortled. "It means 'Fuck you up the ass.' "

"Yeah? In Russian?"

He laughed, exposing grayish and very un-American teeth. "Ukrainian."

"I thought they spoke Russian in the Ukraine."

"Well, yes. Depends what part of Ukraine. They're not so different languages, the two. Well—" click of the tongue, eye roll—"not so very much. Numbers are different, days of the week, some vocabulary. My

name is spelled different in Ukrainian but in North America it's easier to
use Russian spelling and be Boris, not B-o-r-y-s. In the West everybody
knows Boris Yeltsin…" he ticked his head to one side — "Boris Becker—"

"Boris Badenov—"

"Eh?" he said sharply, turning as if I'd insulted him.

"Bullwinkle? Boris and Natasha?"

"Oh, yes. Prince Boris! *War and Peace.* I'm named like him. Although
the surname of Prince Boris is Drubetskóy, not what you said."

"So what's your first language? Ukrainian?"

He shrugged. "Polish maybe," he said, falling back in his seat, slinging
his dark hair to one side with a flip of his head. His eyes were hard and
humorous, very black. "My mother was Polish, from Rzeszów near the
Ukrainian border. Russian, Ukrainian — Ukraine as you know was satel-
lite of USSR, so I speak both. Maybe not Russian quite so much — it's best
for swearing and cursing. With Slavic languages — Russian, Ukrainian,
Polish, even Czech — if you know one, you sort of get drift in all. But for
me, English is easiest now. Used to be the other way around."

"What do you think about America?"

"Everyone always smiles so big! Well — most people. Maybe not so
much you. I think it looks stupid."

He was, like me, an only child. His father (born in Siberia, a Ukrainian national from Novoagansk) was in mining and exploration. "Big
important job — he travels the world." Boris's mother — his father's second wife — was dead.

"Mine too," I said.

He shrugged. "She's been dead for donkey's years," he said. "She was
an alkie. She was drunk one night and she fell out a window and died."

"Wow," I said, a bit stunned by how lightly he'd tossed this off.

"Yah, it sucks," he said carelessly, looking out the window.

"So what nationality are you?" I said, after a brief silence.

"Eh—?"

"Well, if your mother's Polish, and your dad's Ukrainian, and you
were born in Australia, that would make you—"

"Indonesian," he said, with a sinister smile. He had dark, devilish, very
expressive eyebrows that moved around a lot when he spoke.

"How's that?"

"Well, my passport says Ukraine. And I have part citizenship in

Poland too. But Indonesia is the place I want to get back to," said Boris, tossing the hair out of his eyes. "Well — PNG."

"What?"

"Papua, New Guinea. It's my favorite place I've lived."

"New Guinea? I thought they had headhunters."

"Not any more. Or not so many. This bracelet is from there," he said, pointing to one of the many black leather strands on his wrist. "My friend Bami made it for me. He was our cook."

"What's it like?"

"Not so bad," he said, glancing at me sideways in his brooding, self-amused way. "I had a parrot. And a pet goose. And, was learning to surf. But then, six months ago, my dad hauled me with him to this shaddy town in Alaska. Seward Peninsula, just below Arctic Circle? And then, middle of May — we flew to Fairbanks on a prop plane, and then we came here."

"Wow," I said.

"*Dead* boring up there," said Boris. "Heaps of dead fish, and bad Internet connection. I should have run away — I wish I had," he said bitterly.

"And done what?"

"Stayed in New Guinea. Lived on the beach. Thank God anyway we weren't there all winter. Few years ago, we were up north in Canada, in Alberta, this one-street town off the Pouce Coupe River? Dark the whole time, October to March, and fuck-all to do except read and listen to CBC radio. Had to drive fifty klicks to do our washing. Still —" he laughed — "loads better than Ukraine. Miami Beach, compared."

"What does your dad do again?"

"Drink, mainly," said Boris sourly.

"He should meet my dad, then."

Again the sudden, explosive laugh — almost like he was spitting over you. "Yes. Brilliant. And whores?"

"Wouldn't be surprised," I said, after a small, startled pause. Though not too much my dad did shocked me, I had never quite envisioned him hanging out in the Live Girls and Gentlemen's Club joints we sometimes passed on the highway.

The bus was emptying out; we were only a few streets from my house. "Hey, this is my stop up here," I said.

"Want to come home with me and watch television?" said Boris.

"Well—"

"Oh, come on. No one's there. And I've got *S.O.S. Iceberg* on DVD."

xi.

THE SCHOOL BUS DIDN'T actually go all the way out to the edge of Canyon Shadows, where Boris lived. It was a twenty minute walk to his house from the last stop, in blazing heat, through streets awash with sand. Though there were plenty of Foreclosure and "For Sale" signs on my street (at night, the sound of a car radio travelled for miles)—still, I was not aware quite how eerie Canyon Shadows got at its farthest reaches: a toy town, dwindling out at desert's edge, under menacing skies. Most of the houses looked as if they had never been lived in. Others—unfinished—had raw-edged windows without glass in them; they were covered with scaffolding and grayed with blown sand, with piles of concrete and yellowing construction material out front. The boarded-up windows gave them a blind, battered, uneven look, as of faces beaten and bandaged. As we walked, the air of abandonment grew more and more disturbing, as if we were roaming some planet depopulated by radiation or disease.

"They built this shit way too far out," said Boris. "Now the desert is taking it back. And the banks." He laughed. "Fuck Thoreau, eh?"

"This whole town is like a big Fuck You to Thoreau."

"I'll tell you who's fucked. People who own these houses. Can't even get water out to a lot of them. They all get taken back because people can't pay—that's why my dad rents our place so bloody cheap."

"Huh," I said, after a slight, startled pause. It had not occurred to me to wonder how my father had been able to afford quite such a big house as ours.

"My dad digs mines," said Boris unexpectedly.

"Sorry?"

He raked the sweaty dark hair out of his face. "People hate us, everywhere we go. Because they promise the mine won't harm the environment, and then the mine harms the environment. But here—" he shrugged in a fatalistic, Russianate way—"my God, this fucking sand pit, who cares?"

"Huh," I said, struck by the way our voices carried down the deserted street, "it's *really empty* down here, isn't it?"

"Yes. A graveyard. Only one other family living here — those people, down there. Big truck out front, see? Illegal immigrants, I think."

"You and your dad are legal, right?" It was a problem at school: some of the kids weren't; there were posters about it in the hallways.

He made a *pfft, ridiculous* sound. "Of course. The mine takes care of it. Or somebody. But those people down there? Maybe twenty, thirty of them, all men, all living in one house. Drug dealers maybe."

"You think?"

"Something very funny going on," said Boris darkly. "That's all I know."

Boris's house — flanked by two vacant lots overflowing with garbage — was much like Dad and Xandra's: wall-to-wall carpet, spanking-new appliances, same floor plan, not much furniture. But indoors, it was much too warm for comfort; the pool was dry, with a few inches of sand at the bottom, and there was no pretense of a yard, not even cactuses. All the surfaces — the appliances, the counters, the kitchen floor — were lightly filmed with grit.

"Something to drink?" said Boris, opening the refrigerator to a gleaming rank of German beer bottles.

"Oh, wow, thanks."

"In New Guinea," said Boris, wiping his forehead with the back of his hand, "when I lived there, yah? We had a bad flood. Snakes...very dangerous and scary...unexploded mine shells from Second World War floating up in the yard...many geese died. Anyway —" he said, cracking open a beer — "all our water went bad. Typhus. All we had was beer — Pepsi was all gone, Lucozade was all gone, iodine tablets gone, three whole weeks, my dad and me, even the Muslims, nothing to drink but beer! Lunch, breakfast, everything."

"That doesn't sound so bad."

He made a face. "Had a headache the whole time. Local beer, in New Guinea — very bad tasting. This is the good stuff! There's vodka in the freezer too."

I started to say yes, to impress him, but then I thought of the heat and the walk home and said, "No thanks."

He clinked his bottle against mine. "I agree. Much too hot to drink it in the day. My dad drinks it so much the nerves are gone dead in his feet."

"Seriously?"

"It's called —" he screwed up his face, in an effort to get the words out — "peripheral neuropathy" (pronounced, by him, as "peri*pher*al neu-ro*pathy*"). "In Canada, in hospital, they had to teach him to walk again. He stood up — he fell on the floor — his nose is bleeding — hilarious."

"Sounds entertaining," I said, thinking of the time I'd seen my own dad crawling on his hands and knees to get ice from the fridge.

"Very. What does yours drink? Your dad?"

"Scotch. When he drinks. Supposedly he's quit now."

"Hah," said Boris, as if he'd heard this one before. "My dad should switch — good Scotch is very cheap here. Say, want to see my room?"

I was expecting something on the order of my own room, and I was surprised when he opened the door into a sort of ragtag tented space, reeking of stale Marlboros, books piled everywhere, old beer bottles and ashtrays and heaps of old towels and unwashed clothes spilling over on the carpet. The walls billowed with printed fabric — yellow, green, indigo, purple — and a red hammer-and-sickle flag hung over the batik-draped mattress. It was as if a Russian cosmonaut had crashed in the jungle and fashioned himself a shelter of his nation's flag and whatever native sarongs and textiles he could find.

"You did this?" I said.

"I fold it up and put it in a suitcase," said Boris, throwing himself down on the wildly-colored mattress. "Takes only ten minutes to put it up again. Do you want to watch *S.O.S. Iceberg*?"

"Sure."

"Awesome movie. I've seen it six times. Like when she gets in her plane to rescue them on the ice?"

But somehow we never got around to watching *S.O.S. Iceberg* that afternoon, maybe because we couldn't stop talking long enough to go downstairs and turn on the television. Boris had had a more interesting life than any person of my own age I had ever met. It seemed that he had only infrequently attended school, and those of the very poorest sort; out in the desolate places where his dad worked, often there were no schools for him to go to. "There are tapes?" he said, swigging his beer with one eye on me. "And tests to take. Except you have to be in a place with Internet and sometimes like far up in Canada or Ukraine we don't have that."

"So what do you do?"

He shrugged. "Read a lot, I guess." A teacher in Texas, he said, had pulled a syllabus off the Internet for him.

"They must have had a school in Alice Springs."

Boris laughed. "Sure they did," he said, blowing a sweaty strand of hair out of his face. "But after my mum died, we lived in Northern Territory for a while — Arnhem Land — town called Karmeywallag? Town, so called. Miles in the middle of nowhere — trailers for the miners to live in and a petrol station with a bar in back, beer and whiskey and sandwiches. Anyway, wife of Mick that ran the bar, Judy her name was? All I did —" he took a messy slug of his beer — "all I did, every day, was watch soaps with Judy and stay behind the bar with her at night while my dad and his crew from the mine got thrashed. Couldn't even get television during monsoon. Judy kept her tapes in the fridge so they wouldn't get ruined."

"Ruined how?"

"Mold growing in the wet. Mold on your shoes, on your books." He shrugged. "Back then I didn't talk so much as I do now, because I didn't speak English so well. Very shy, sat alone, stayed always to myself. But Judy? She talked to me anyway, and was kind, even though I didn't understand a lick of what she said. Every morning I would go to her, she would cook me my same nice fry. Rain rain rain. Sweeping, washing dishes, helping to clean the bar. Everywhere I followed like a baby goose. This is cup, this is broom, this is bar stool, this pencil. That was my school. Television — Duran Duran tapes and Boy George — everything in English. *McLeod's Daughters* was her favorite programme. Always we watched together, and when I didn't know something? She explained to me. And we talked about the sisters, and we cried when Claire died in the car wreck, and she said if she had a place like Drover's? she would take me to live there and be happy together and we would have all women to work for us like the McLeods. She was very young and pretty. Curly blonde hair and blue stuff on her eyes. Her husband called her slut and horse's arse but I thought she looked like Jodi on the show. All day long she talked to me and sang — taught me the words of all the jukebox songs. 'Dark in the city, the night is alive…' Soon I had developed quite proficiency. Speak English, Boris! I had a little English from school in Poland, hello excuse me thank you very much, but two months with her I was chatter chatter chatter! Never stopped talking since! She was very nice and kind to me always. Even though she went in the kitchen and cried every day because she hated Karmeywallag so much."

It was getting late, but still hot and bright out. "Say, I'm starving," said Boris, standing up and stretching so that a band of stomach showed between his fatigues and ragged shirt: concave, dead white, like a starved saint's.

"What's to eat?"

"Bread and sugar."

"You're kidding."

Boris yawned, wiped red eyes. "You never ate bread with sugar poured on it?"

"Nothing else?"

He gave a weary-looking shrug. "I have a coupon for pizza. Fat lot of good. They don't deliver this far out."

"I thought you had a cook where you used to live."

"Yah, we did. In Indonesia. Saudi Arabia too." He was smoking a cigarette — I'd refused the one he offered me; he seemed a little trashed, drifting and bopping around the room like there was music on, although there wasn't. "Very cool guy named Abdul Fataah. That means 'Servant of the Opener of the Gates of Sustenance.'"

"Well, look. Let's go to my house, then."

He flung himself down on the bed with his hands between his knees. "Don't tell me the slag cooks."

"No, but she works in a bar with a buffet. Sometimes she brings home food and stuff."

"Brilliant," said Boris, reeling slightly as he stood. He'd had three beers and was working on a fourth. At the door, he took an umbrella and handed me one.

"Um, what's this for?"

He opened it and stepped outside. "Cooler to walk under," he said, his face blue in the shade. "And no sunburn."

xii.

BEFORE BORIS, I HAD borne my solitude stoically enough, without real-izing quite how alone I was. And I suppose if either of us had lived in an even halfway normal household, with curfews and chores and adult supervision, we wouldn't have become quite so inseparable, so fast, but almost from that day we were together all the time, scrounging our meals and sharing what money we had.

In New York, I had grown up around a lot of worldly kids—kids who'd lived abroad and spoke three or four languages, who did summer programs at Heidelberg and spent their holidays in places like Rio or Inns-bruck or Cap d'Antibes. But Boris—like an old sea captain—put them all to shame. He had ridden a camel; he had eaten witchetty grubs, played cricket, caught malaria, lived on the street in Ukraine ("but for two weeks only"), set off a stick of dynamite by himself, swum in Australian rivers infested with crocodiles. He had read Chekhov in Russian, and authors I'd never heard of in Ukrainian and Polish. He had endured midwinter darkness in Russia where the temperature dropped to forty below: endless blizzards, snow and black ice, the only cheer the green neon palm tree that burned twenty-four hours a day outside the provincial bar where his father liked to drink. Though he was only a year older than me—fifteen—he'd had actual sex with a girl, in Alaska, someone he'd bummed a cigarette off in the parking lot of a convenience store. She'd asked him if he wanted to sit in her car with her, and that was that. ("But you know what?" he said, blowing smoke out of the corner of his mouth. "I don't think she liked it very much."

"Did you?"

"God, yes. Although, I'm telling you, I know I wasn't doing it right. I think was too cramped in the car.")

Every day, we rode home on the bus together. At the half-finished Community Center on the edge of Desatoya Estates, where the doors were padlocked and the palm trees stood dead and brown in the planters, there was an abandoned playground where we bought sodas and melted candy bars from the dwindling stock in the vending machines, sat around outside on the swings, smoking and talking. His bad tempers and black moods, which were frequent, alternated with unsound bursts of hilarity;

he was wild and gloomy, he could make me laugh sometimes until my sides ached, and we always had so much to say that we often lost track of time and stayed outside talking until well past dark. In Ukraine, he had seen an elected official shot in the stomach walking to his car — just happened to witness it, not the shooter, just the broad-shouldered man in a too-small overcoat falling to his knees in darkness and snow. He told me about his tiny tin-roof school near the Chippewa reservation in Alberta, sang nursery songs in Polish for me ("For homework, in Poland, we are usually learning a poem or song by heart, a prayer maybe, something like that") and taught me to swear in Russian ("This is the true *mat* — from the gulags"). He told me too how, in Indonesia, he had been converted to Islam by his friend Bami the cook: giving up pork, fasting during Ramadan, praying to Mecca five times a day. "But I'm not Muslim any more," he explained, dragging his toe in the dust. We were lying on our backs on the merry-go-round, dizzy from spinning. "I gave it up a while back."

"Why?"

"Because I drink." (This was the understatement of the year; Boris drank beer the way other kids drank Pepsi, starting pretty much the instant we came home from school.)

"But who cares?" I said. "Why does anybody have to know?"

He made an impatient noise. "Because is wrong to profess faith if I don't observe properly. Disrespectful to Islam."

"Still. 'Boris of Arabia.' It has a ring."

"Fuck you."

"No, seriously," I said, laughing, raising up on my elbows. "Did you really believe in all that?"

"All what?"

"You know. Allah and Muhammad. 'There is no God but God' —?"

"No," he said, a bit angrily, "my Islam was a political thing."

"What, you mean like the shoe bomber?"

He snorted with laughter. "Fuck, no. Besides, Islam doesn't teach violence."

"Then what?"

He came up off the merry-go-round, alert gaze: "What do you mean, what? What are you trying to say?"

"Back off! I'm asking a question."

"Which is —?"

"If you converted to it and all, then what did you believe?"

He fell back and chortled as if I'd let him off the hook. "Believe? Ha! I don't believe in *anything*."

"What? You mean now?"

"I mean never. Well—the Virgin Mary, a little. But Allah and God...? not so much."

"Then why the hell did you want to be Muslim?"

"Because—" he held out his hands, as he did sometimes when he was at a loss—"such wonderful people, they were all so friendly to me!"

"That's a start."

"Well, it was, really. They gave me an Arabic name—Badr al-Dine. *Badr* is moon, it means something like moon of faithfulness, but they said, 'Boris, you are *badr* because you light everywhere, being Muslim now, lighting the world with your religion, you shine wherever you go.' I loved it, being Badr. Also, the mosque was brilliant. Falling-down palace—stars shining through at night—birds in the roof. An old Javanese man taught us the Koran. And they fed me too, and were kind, and made sure I was clean and had clean clothes. Sometimes I fell asleep on my prayer rug. And at salah, near dawn, when the birds woke up, always the sound of wings beating!"

Though his Australo-Ukrainian accent was certainly very odd, he was almost as fluent in English as I was; and considering what a short time he'd lived in America he was reasonably conversant in *amerikanskii* ways. He was always poring through his torn-up pocket dictionary (his name scrawled in Cyrillic on the front, with the English carefully lettered beneath: BORYS VOLODYMYROVYCH PAVLIKOVSKY) and I was always finding old 7-Eleven napkins and bits of scratch paper with lists of words and terms he'd made:

> *bridle and domesticate*
> *celerity*
> *trattoria*
> *wise guy = крутой пацан*
> *propinquity*
> *Dereliction of duty.*

When his dictionary failed him, he consulted me. "What is Sophomore?" he asked me, scanning the bulletin board in the halls at school.

"Home Ec? Poly Sci?" (pronounced, by him, as "politzei"). He had never heard of most of the food in the cafeteria lunch: fajitas, falafel, turkey tetrazzini. Though he knew a lot about movies and music, he was decades behind the times; he didn't have a clue about sports or games or television, and—apart from a few big European brands like Mercedes and BMW— couldn't tell one car from another. American money confused him, and sometimes too American geography: in what province was California located? Could I tell him which city was the capital of New England?

But he was used to being on his own. Cheerfully he got himself up for school, hitched his own rides, signed his own report cards, shoplifted his own food and school supplies. Once every week or so we walked miles out of our way in the suffocating heat, shaded beneath umbrellas like Indonesian tribesmen, to catch the poky local bus called the CAT, which as far as I could tell no one rode out our way except drunks, people too poor to have a car, and kids. It ran infrequently, and if we missed it we had to stand around for a while waiting for the next bus, but among its stops was a shopping plaza with a chilly, gleaming, understaffed supermarket where Boris stole steaks for us, butter, boxes of tea, cucumbers (a great delicacy for him), packages of bacon—even cough syrup once, when I had a cold—slipping them in the cutaway lining of his ugly gray raincoat (a man's coat, much too big for him, with drooping shoulders and a grim Eastern Bloc look about it, a suggestion of food rationing and Soviet-era factories, industrial complexes in Lviv or Odessa). As he wandered around I stood lookout at the head of the aisle, so shaky with nerves I sometimes worried I would black out—but soon I was filling my own pockets with apples and chocolate (other favored food items of Boris's) before walking up brazenly to the counter to buy bread and milk and other items too big to steal.

Back in New York, when I was eleven or so, my mother had signed me up for a Kids in the Kitchen class at my day camp, where I'd learned to cook a few simple meals: hamburgers, grilled cheese (which I'd sometimes made for my mother on nights she worked late), and what Boris called "egg and toasts." Boris, who sat on the countertop kicking the cabinets with his heels and talking to me while I cooked, did the washing-up. In the Ukraine, he told me, he'd sometimes picked pockets for money to eat. "Got chased, once or twice," he said. "Never caught, though."

"Maybe we should go down to the Strip sometime," I said. We were standing at the kitchen counter at my house with knives and forks, eating our steaks straight from the frying pan. "If we were going to do it, that'd be the place. I never saw so many drunk people and they're all from out of town."

He stopped chewing; he looked shocked. "And why should we? When so easy to steal here, from so big stores!"

"Just saying." My money from the doormen — which Boris and I spent a few dollars at a time, in vending machines and at the 7-Eleven near school that Boris called "the magazine" — would hold out a while, but not forever.

"Ha! And what will I do if you are arrested, Potter?" he said, dropping a fat piece of steak down to the dog, whom he had taught to dance on his hind legs. "Who will cook the dinner? And who will look after Snaps here?" Xandra's dog Popper he'd taken to calling 'Amyl' and 'Nitrate' and 'Popchik' and 'Snaps' — anything but his real name. I'd started bringing him in even though I wasn't supposed to because I was so tired of him always straining at the end of his chain trying to look in at the glass door and yapping his head off. But inside he was surprisingly quiet; starved for attention, he stuck close to us wherever we went, trotting anxiously at our heels, upstairs and down, curling up to sleep on the rug while Boris and I read and quarrelled and listened to music up in my room.

"Seriously, Boris," I said, pushing the hair from my eyes (I was badly in need of a haircut, but didn't want to spend the money), "I don't see much difference in stealing wallets and stealing steaks."

"*Big* difference, Potter." He held his hands apart to show me just how big. "Stealing from working person? And stealing from big rich company that robs the people?"

"Costco doesn't rob the people. It's a discount supermarket."

"Fine then. Steal essentials of life from private citizen. This is your so-smart plan. Hush," he said to the dog, who'd barked sharply for more steak.

"I wouldn't steal from some poor working person," I said, tossing Popper a piece of steak myself. "There are plenty of sleazy people walking around Vegas with wads of cash."

"Sleazy?"

"Dodgy. Dishonest."

"Ah." The pointed dark eyebrow went up. "Fair enough. But if you steal money from sleazy person, like gangster, they are likely to hurt you, *nie?*"

"You weren't scared of getting hurt in Ukraine?"

He shrugged. "Beaten up, maybe. Not shot."

"Shot?"

"Yes, *shot*. Don't look surprised. This cowboy country, who knows? Everyone has guns."

"I'm not saying a cop. I'm saying drunk tourists. The place is crawling with them Saturday night."

"Ha!" He put the pan down on the floor for the dog to finish off. "Likely you will end up in jail, Potter. Loose morals, slave to the economy. Very bad citizen, you."

xiii.

BY THIS TIME — OCTOBER or so — we were eating together almost every night. Boris, who'd often had three or four beers before dinner, switched over at mealtimes to hot tea. Then, after a post-dinner shot of vodka, a habit I soon picked up from him ("It helps you digest the food," Boris explained), we lolled around reading, doing homework, and sometimes arguing, and often drank ourselves to sleep in front of the television.

"Don't go!" said Boris, one night at his house when I stood up toward the end of *The Magnificent Seven* — the final gunfight, Yul Brynner rounding up his men. "You'll miss the best part."

"Yeah, but it's almost eleven."

Boris — lying on the floor — raised himself on an elbow. Long-haired, narrow-chested, weedy and thin, he was Yul Brynner's exact opposite in most respects and yet there was also an odd familial resemblance: they had the same sly, watchful quality, amused and a bit cruel, something Mongol or Tatar in the slant of the eyes.

"Call Xandra to come collect you," he said with a yawn. "What time does she get off work?"

"Xandra? Forget it."

Again Boris yawned, eyes heavy-lidded with vodka. "Sleep here, then," he said, rolling over and scrubbing his face with one hand. "Will they miss you?"

Were they even coming home? Some nights they didn't. "Doubtful," I said.

"Hush," said Boris—reaching for his cigarettes, sitting up. "Watch now. Here come the bad guys."

"You saw this movie before?"

"Dubbed into Russian, if you can believe it. But very weak Russian. Sissy. Is *sissy* the word I want? More like schoolteachers than gunfighters, is what I'm trying to say."

xiv.

THOUGH I'D BEEN MISERABLE with grief at the Barbours', I now thought longingly of the apartment on Park Avenue as a lost Eden. And though I had access to email on the computer at school, Andy wasn't much of a writer, and the messages I got in reply were frustratingly impersonal. (*Hi, Theo. Hope you enjoyed your summer. Daddy got a new boat* [*the* Absalom]. *Mother will not set foot upon it but unfortunately I was compelled. Japanese II is giving me some headaches but everything else is fine.*) Mrs. Barbour dutifully answered the paper letters I sent—a line or two on her monogrammed correspondence cards from Dempsey and Carroll—but there was never anything personal. She always asked *how are you?* and closed with *thinking about you,* but there was never any *we miss you* or *we wish we could see you.*

I wrote to Pippa, in Texas, though she was too ill to answer—which was just as well, since most of the letters I never sent.

Dear Pippa,

How are you? How do you like Texas? I've thought about you a lot. Have you been riding that horse you like? Things are great here. I wonder if it's hot there, since it's so hot here.

That was boring; I threw it away, and started again.

Dear Pippa,

How are you? I've been thinking about you and hoping you are okay. I
hope that things are ~~going okay~~ wonderful for you in Texas. I have to
say, I sort of hate it here, but I've made some friends and am getting
used to it a bit, I guess.

I wonder if you get homesick? I do. I miss New York a lot. I wish
we lived closer together. How is your head now? Better, I hope. I'm
sorry that

"Is that your girlfriend?" said Boris — crunching an apple, reading
over my shoulder.

"Shove off."

"What happened to her?" he said and then, when I didn't reply: "Did
you hit her?"

"What?" I said, only half listening.

"Her head? That's why you're apologizing? You hit her or something?"

"Yeah, right," I said — and then, from his earnest, intent expression,
realized he was perfectly serious.

"You think I beat girls up?" I said.

He shrugged. "She might have deserved it."

"Um, we don't hit women in America."

He scowled, and spit out an apple seed. "No. Americans just persecute
smaller countries that believe different from them."

"Boris, shut up and leave me alone."

But he had rattled me with his comment and rather than start a new
letter to Pippa, I began one to Hobie.

Dear Mr. Hobart,

Hello, how are you? Well, I hope. I have never written to thank you
for your kindness during my last weeks in New York. I hope that you
and Cosmo are okay, though I know you both miss Pippa. How is she?
I hope she's been able to go back to her music. I hope too

But I didn't send that one either. Hence I was delighted when a letter
arrived — a long letter, on real paper — from none other than Hobie.

"What've you got there?" said my father suspiciously — spotting the New York postmark, snatching the letter from my hand.

"What?"

But my dad had already torn the envelope open. He scanned it, quickly, and then lost interest. "Here," he said, handing it back to me. "Sorry, kiddo. My mistake."

The letter itself was beautiful, as a physical artifact: rich paper, careful penmanship, a whisper of quiet rooms and money.

Dear Theo,

I've wanted to hear how you are and yet I'm glad I haven't, as I hope this means you are happy and busy. Here, the leaves have turned, Washington Square is sodden and yellow, and it's getting cold. On Saturday mornings, Cosmo and I mooch around the Village — I pick him up and carry him into the cheese shop — not sure that's entirely legal but the girls behind the counter save him bits and bobs of cheese. He misses Pippa as much as I do but — like me — still enjoys his meals. Sometimes we eat by the fireplace now that Jack Frost is on us.

I hope that you're settling in there a bit and have made some friends. When I talk to Pippa on the telephone she doesn't seem very happy where she is, though her health is certainly better. I am going to fly down there for Thanksgiving. I don't know how pleased Margaret will be to have me, but Pippa wants me so I'll go. If they allow me to carry Cosmo on the plane I might bring him, too.

I'm enclosing a photo that I thought you might enjoy — of a Chippendale bureau that has just arrived, very bad repair, I was told it was stored in an unheated shed up around Watervliet, New York. Very scarred, very nicked, and the top's in two pieces — but — look at those swept-back, weight-bearing talons on that ball-and-claw! the feet don't come out well in the photo, but you can really see the pressure of the claws digging in. It's a masterpiece, and I only wish it had been better looked after. I don't know if you can see the remarkable graining on the top — extraordinary.

As for the shop: I open it a few times a week by appointment, but mostly I keep myself busy below stairs with things sent to me by private clients. Mrs. Skolnik and several people in the neighborhood have asked about you—everything's much the same here, except Mrs. Cho at the Korean market had a little stroke (*very* little, she's back at work now). Also that coffee shop on Hudson that I liked so much has gone out of business—very sad. I walked by this morning and it looks as if they're turning it into a—well, I don't know what you'd call it. Some sort of Japanese novelty store.

I see that as usual I've gone on too long and that I'm running out of room, but I do hope that you are happy and well, and it's all a little less lonely out there than you may have feared. If there's anything I can do for you back here, or if I can help you in any way, please know that I will.

XV.

THAT NIGHT, AT BORIS'S—lying drunk on my half of the batik-draped mattress—I tried to remember what Pippa had looked like. But the moon was so large and clear through the uncurtained window that it made me think instead of a story my mother had told me, about driving to horse shows with her mother and father in the back seat of their old Buick when she was little. "It was a lot of travelling—ten hours sometimes through hard country. Ferris wheels, rodeo rings with sawdust, everything smelled like popcorn and horse manure. One night we were in San Antonio, and I was having a bit of a melt-down—wanting my own room, you know, my dog, my own bed—and Daddy lifted me up on the fairgrounds and told me to look at the moon. 'When you feel homesick,' he said, 'just look up. Because the moon is the same wherever you go.' So after he died, and I had to go to Aunt Bess—I mean, even now, in the city, when I see a full moon, it's like he's telling me not to look back or feel sad about things, that home is wherever *I* am." She kissed me on the nose. "Or where *you* are, puppy. The center of my earth is you."

A rustle, next to me. "Potter?" said Boris. "You awake?"

"Can I ask you something?" I said. "What does the moon look like in Indonesia?"

"What are you on about?"

"Or, I don't know, Russia? Is it just the same as here?"

He rapped me lightly on the side of the head with his knuckles—a gesture of his that I had come to know, meaning *idiot*. "Same everywhere," he said, yawning, propping himself up on his scrawny braceleted wrist. "And why?"

"Dunno," I said, and then, after a tense pause: "Do you hear that?"

A door had slammed. "What's that?" I said, rolling to face him. We looked at each other, listening. Voices downstairs—laughter, people knocking around, a crash like something had been knocked over.

"Is that your dad?" I said, sitting up—and then I heard a woman's voice, drunken and shrill.

Boris sat up too, bony and sickly-pale in the light through the window. Downstairs, it sounded like they were throwing things and pushing furniture around.

"What are they saying?" I whispered.

Boris listened. I could see all the bolts and hollows in his neck. "Bullshit," he said. "They're drunk."

The two of us sat there, listening—Boris more intently than me.

"Who's that with him then?" I said.

"Some whore." He listened for a moment, brow furrowed, his profile sharp in the moonlight, and then lay back down. "Two of them."

I rolled over, and checked my iPod. It was 3:17 in the morning.

"Fuck," groaned Boris, scratching his stomach. "Why don't they shut up?"

"I'm thirsty," I said, after a timid pause.

He snorted. "Ha! You don't want to go out there now, trust me."

"What are they doing?" I asked. One of the women had just screamed—whether in laughter or fright, I couldn't tell.

We lay there, stiff as boards, staring at the ceiling, listening to the ominous crashing and bumping-around.

"Ukrainian?" I said, after a bit. Though I couldn't understand a word of what they were saying, I'd been around Boris enough that I was beginning to differentiate the intonations of spoken Ukrainian from Russian.

"Top marks, Potter." Then: "Light me a cigarette."

We passed it back and forth, in the dark, until another door slammed somewhere and the voices died down. At last, Boris exhaled, a final smoky sigh, and rolled over to stub it out in the overflowing ashtray beside the bed. "Good night," he whispered.

"Good night."

He fell asleep almost immediately—I could tell from his breathing—but I lay awake a lot longer, with a scratchy throat, feeling light-headed and sick from the cigarette. How had I fetched up into this strange new life, where drunk foreigners shouted around me in the night, and all my clothes were dirty, and nobody loved me? Boris—oblivious—snored beside me. At last, towards dawn, when I finally fell asleep, I dreamed of my mother: sitting across from me on the 6 train, swaying slightly, her face calm in the flickering artificial lights.

What are you doing here? she said. *Go home! Right now! I'll meet you at the apartment.* Only the voice wasn't quite right; and when I looked more closely I saw it wasn't her at all, only someone pretending to be her. And with a gasp and a start, I woke up.

xvi.

BORIS'S FATHER WAS A mysterious figure. As Boris explained it: he was often on site in the middle of nowhere, at his mine, where he stayed with his crew for weeks at a time. "Doesn't wash," said Boris austerely. "Stays filthy drunk." The beaten-up short wave radio in the kitchen belonged to him ("From Brezhnev era," said Boris; "he won't throw it away"), and so were the Russian-language newspapers and *USA Today*s I sometimes found around. One day I'd walked into one of the bathrooms at Boris's house (which were fairly grim—no shower curtain or toilet seat, upstairs or down, and black stuff growing in the tub) and got a bad start from one of his dad's suits, soaking wet and smelly, dangling like a dead thing from the shower rod: scratchy, misshapen, of lumpy brown wool the color of dug roots, it dripped horribly on the floor like some moist-breathing golem from the old country or maybe a garment dredged up in a police net.

"What?" said Boris, when I emerged.

"Your dad washes his own suits?" I said. "In the sink in there?"

Boris—leaning against the frame of the door, gnawing the side of his thumb nail—shrugged evasively.

"You've got to be kidding," I said, and then, when he kept on looking at me: "What? They don't have dry cleaning in Russia?"

"He has plenty of jewelry and posh," growled Boris around the side of his thumb. "Rolex watch, Ferragamo shoes. He can clean his suit however he wants."

"Right," I said, and changed the subject. Several weeks passed with no thought of Boris's dad at all. But then came the day when Boris slid in late to Honors English with a wine colored bruise under his eye.

"Ah, got it in the face with a football," he said in a cheery voice when Mrs. Spear ('Spirsetskaya,' as he called her) asked him, suspiciously, what had happened.

This, I knew, was a lie. Glancing over at him, across the aisle, I wondered throughout our listless class discussion of Ralph Waldo Emerson how he'd managed to black his eye after I'd left him the previous night to go home and walk Popper—Xandra left him tied up outside so much that I was starting to feel responsible for him.

"What'd you do?" I said when I caught up with him after class.

"Eh?"

"How'd you get that?"

He winked. "Oh, come on," he said, bumping his shoulder against mine.

"What? Were you drunk?"

"My dad came home," he said, and then, when I didn't answer: "What else, Potter? What did you think?"

"Jesus, why?"

He shrugged. "Glad you'd gone," he said, rubbing his good eye. "Couldn't believe when he showed up. Was sleeping on the couch downstairs. At first I thought it was you."

"What happened?"

"Ah," said Boris, sighing extravagantly; he'd been smoking on the way to school, I could smell it on his breath. "He saw the beer bottles on the floor."

"He hit you because you were drinking?"

"Because he was fucking plastered, is why. He was drunk as a log—I don't think he knew it was me he was hitting. This morning—he saw my face, he cried and was sorry. Anyway, he won't be back for a while."

"Why not?"

"He's got a lot going on out there, he said. Won't be back for three weeks. The mine is close to one of those places where they have the state-run brothels, you know?"

"They aren't state-run," I said — and then found myself wondering if they were.

"Well, you know what I mean. One good thing though — he left me moneys."

"How much?"

"Four thousand."

"You're kidding."

"No, no —" he slapped his forehead — "thinking in roubles, sorry! About two hundred dollars, but still. Should have asked for more but I didn't have the nerve."

We'd reached the juncture of the hallway where I had to turn for algebra and Boris had to turn for American Government: the bane of his existence. It was a required course — easy even by the desultory standards of our school — but trying to get Boris to understand about the Bill of Rights, and the enumerated versus implied powers of the U.S. Congress, reminded me of the time I'd tried to explain to Mrs. Barbour what an Internet server was.

"Well, see you after class," said Boris. "Explain again, before I go, what's the difference between Federal Bank and Federal Reserve?"

"Did you tell anybody?"

"Tell what?"

"You know."

"What, you want to report me?" said Boris, laughing.

"Not *you*. Him."

"And why? Why is that a good idea? Tell me. So I can get deported?"

"Right," I said, after an uncomfortable pause.

"So — we should eat out tonight!" said Boris. "In a restaurant! Maybe the Mexican." Boris, after initial suspicion and complaint, had grown to like Mexican food — unknown in Russia, he said, not bad when you got used to it, though if it was too spicy he wouldn't touch it. "We can take the bus."

"The Chinese is closer. And the food is better."

"Yah, but — remember?"

"Oh, yeah, right," I said. The last time we'd eaten there we'd slipped out without paying. "Forget that."

xvii.

Boris liked Xandra a lot better than I did: leaping forward to open doors for her, saying he liked her new haircut, offering to carry things. I'd teased him about her ever since I'd caught him looking down her top when she leaned to reach her cell phone on the kitchen counter.

"God, she's hot," said Boris, once we were up in my room. "Think your dad would mind?"

"Probably wouldn't notice."

"No, serious, what do you think your dad would do to me?"

"If what?"

"If me and Xandra."

"I dunno, probably call the police."

He snorted, derisively. "What for?"

"Not you. Her. Statutory rape."

"I wish."

"Go on and fuck her if you want," I said. "I don't care if she goes to jail."

Boris rolled over on his stomach and looked at me slyly. "She takes cocaine, do you know that?"

"What?"

"Cocaine." He mimed sniffing.

"You're kidding," I said, and then, when he smirked at me: "How can you tell?"

"I just know. From the way she talks. Also she's grinding her teeth. Watch her sometime."

I didn't know what to watch for. But then one afternoon we came in when my dad wasn't home and saw her straightening up from the coffee table with a sniff, holding her hair behind her neck with one hand. When she threw her head back, and her eyes landed on us, there was a moment where nobody said anything and then she turned away as if we weren't there.

We kept walking, up the stairs to my room. Though I'd never seen anybody snorting drugs before, it was clear even to me what she was doing.

"God, sexy," said Boris, after I shut the door. "Wonder where she keeps it?"

"Dunno," I said, flopping down on my bed. Xandra was just leaving; I could hear her car in the driveway.

"Think she'll give us some?"

"She might give *you* some."

Boris sank down to sit on the floor by the bed, with his knee up and his back against the wall. "Do you think she's selling it?"

"No way," I said, after a slight, disbelieving pause. "You think?"

"Ha! Good for you, if she is."

"How's that?"

"Cash around the house!"

"Fat lot of good that does me."

He swung his shrewd, appraising gaze over to me. "Who pays the bills here, Potter?" he said.

"Huh." It was the first time that this question, which I immediately recognized as of great practical importance, had even occurred to me. "I don't know. My dad, I think. Though Xandra puts in some too."

"And where does he get it? His moneys?"

"No clue," I said. "He talks to people on the telephone and then he leaves the house."

"Any checkbooks lying around? Any cash?"

"No. Never. Chips, sometimes."

"As good as cash," Boris said swiftly, spitting a bitten-off thumbnail on the floor.

"Right. Except you can't cash them in the casino if you're under eighteen."

Boris chortled. "Come on. We figure out something, if we have to. We dress you up in that poncy school jacket with the coat of arms, send you to the window, '*Excuse me,* miss —'"

I rolled over and punched him hard, in the arm. "Fuck you," I said, stung by his drawling, snobbish rendering of my voice.

"Can't be talking like that, Potter," said Boris gleefully, rubbing his arm. "They won't give you a fucking cent. All I'm saying is, I know where my dad's checkbook is, and if there's an emergency —" he held out his open palms — "right?"

"Right."

"I mean, if I have to write bad check, I write bad check," said Boris philosophically. "Good to know I can. I'm not saying, break in their room and go through their things, but still, good idea to keep your eye open, yes?"

xviii.

BORIS AND HIS FATHER didn't celebrate Thanksgiving, and Xandra and my dad had reservations for a Romantic Holiday Extravaganza at a French restaurant in the MGM Grand. "Do you want to come?" said my father when he saw me looking at the brochure on the kitchen counter: hearts and fireworks, tricolor bunting over a plate of roast turkey. "Or do you have something of your own to do?"

"No thanks." He was being nice, but the thought of being with Dad and Xandra on their Romantic Holiday Whatever made me uneasy. "I've got plans."

"What are you doing then?"

"I'm having Thanksgiving with somebody else."

"Who with?" said my dad, in a rare burst of parental solicitude. "A friend?"

"Let me guess," said Xandra—barefoot, in the Miami Dolphins jersey she slept in, staring into the fridge. "The same person who keeps eating these oranges and apples I bring home."

"Oh, come on," said my dad sleepily, coming up behind her and putting his arms around her, "you like the little Russki—what's his name—Boris."

"Sure I like him. Which is good, I guess, since he's here pretty much all the time. Shit," she said—twisting away from him, slapping her bare thigh—"who let this mosquito inside? Theo, I don't know why you can't remember to keep that door to the pool shut. I've told you and told you."

"Well, you know, I could always have Thanksgiving with you guys, if you'd rather," I said blandly, leaning back against the kitchen counter. "Why don't I."

I had intended this to annoy Xandra, and with pleasure I saw that it did. "But the reservation's for two," said Xandra, flicking her hair back and looking at my dad.

"Well, I'm sure they can work something out."

"We'll need to call ahead."

"Fine then, call," said my dad, giving her a slightly stoned pat on the back and ambling on in to the living room to check on his football scores.

Xandra and I stood looking at each other for a moment, and then she looked away, as if into some bleak and untenable vision of the future. "I need coffee," she said listlessly.

"It wasn't me who left that door open."

"I don't know who keeps doing it. All I know is, those weird Amway-selling people over there didn't drain their fountain before they moved and now there's a jillion mosquitoes everywhere I look—I mean, there goes another one, shit."

"Look, don't be mad. I don't have to come with you guys."

She put down the box of coffee filters. "So, what are you saying?" she said. "Should I change the reservation or not?"

"What are you two going on about?" called my father faintly from the next room, from his nest of beringed coasters, old cigarette packs, and marked-up baccarat sheets.

"Nothing," called Xandra. Then, a few minutes later, as the coffee maker began to hiss and pop, she rubbed her eye and said in a sleep-roughened voice: "I never said I didn't want you to come."

"I know. I never said you did." Then: "Also, just so you know, it's not me that leaves the door open. It's Dad, when he goes out there to talk on the phone."

Xandra—reaching in the cabinet for her Planet Hollywood coffee mug—looked back at me over her shoulder. "You're not really having dinner at his house?" she said. "The little Russki or whatever?"

"Nah. We'll just be here watching television."

"Do you want me to bring you something?"

"Boris likes those cocktail sausages you bring home. And I like the wings. The hot ones."

"Anything else? What about those mini taquito things? You like those too, don't you?"

"That would be great."

"Fine. I'll hook you guys up. Just stay out of my cigarettes, that's all I ask. I don't care if you smoke," she said, raising a hand to hush me, "it's not like I'm busting you, but somebody's been stealing packs out of the carton in here and it's costing me like twenty-five bucks a week."

xix.

EVER SINCE BORIS HAD shown up with the bruised eye, I had built Boris's father up in my mind to be some thick-necked Soviet with pig eyes and a buzz haircut. In fact—as I was surprised to see, when I did finally meet him—he was as thin and pale as a starved poet. Chlorotic, with a sunken chest, he smoked incessantly, wore cheap shirts that had grayed in the wash, drank endless cups of sugary tea. But when you looked him in the eye you realized that his frailty was deceptive. He was wiry, intense, bad temper shimmering off him—small-boned and sharp-faced, like Boris, but with an evil red-rimmed gaze and tiny, brownish sawteeth. He made me think of a rabid fox.

Though I'd glimpsed him in passing, and heard him (or a person I presumed was him) bumping around Boris's house at night, I didn't actually meet him face-to-face until a few days before Thanksgiving. Then we walked into Boris's house one day after school, laughing and talking, to find him hunched at the kitchen table with a bottle and a glass. Despite his shabby clothes, he was wearing expensive shoes and lots of gold jewelry; and when he looked up at us with reddened eyes we shut up talking immediately. Though he was a small, slightly built man, there was something in his face that made you not want to get too close to him.

"Hi," I said tentatively.

"Hello," he said—stony-faced, in a much thicker accent than Boris—and then turned to Boris and said something in Ukrainian. A brief conversation followed, which I observed with interest. It was interesting to see the change that came over Boris when he was speaking another language—a sort of livening, or alertness, a sense of a different and more efficient person occupying his body.

Then—unexpectedly—Mr. Pavlikovsky held out both hands to me. "Thank you," he said thickly.

Though I was afraid to approach him—it felt like approaching a wild animal—I stepped forward anyway and held out both my hands, awkwardly. He took them in his own, which were hard-skinned and cold.

"You are good person," he said. His gaze was bloodshot and way too intense. I wanted to look away, and was ashamed of myself.

"God be with you and bless you always," he said. "You are like a son to me. For letting my son come into your family."

My family? In confusion, I glanced over at Boris.

Mr. Pavlikovsky's eyes went to him. "You told him what I said?"

"He said you are part of our family here," said Boris, in a bored voice, "and if there is anything ever he can do for you..."

To my great surprise, Mr. Pavlikovsky pulled me close and caught me in a solid embrace, while I closed my eyes and tried hard to ignore his smell: hair cream, body odor, alcohol, and some sort of sharp, disagreeably pungent cologne.

"What was that about?" I said quietly when we were up in Boris's room with the door shut.

Boris rolled his eyes. "Believe me. You don't want to know."

"Is he that loaded all the time? How does he keep his job?"

Boris cackled. "High official in the company," he said. "Or something."

We stayed up in Boris's murky, batik-draped room until we heard his dad's truck start up in the driveway. "He won't be back for a while," Boris said, as I let the curtain fall back over the window. "He feels bad for leaving me so much alone. He knows is a holiday coming up, and he asked if I could stay at your house."

"Well, you do all the time anyway."

"He knows that," said Boris, scraping the hair out of his eyes. "That's why he thanked you. But—I hope you don't mind—I gave him your wrong address."

"Why?"

"Because—" he moved his legs to make room for me to sit by him, without my having to ask — "I think maybe you don't want him rolling up drunk at your house in the middle of the night. Waking your father and Xandra up out of bed. Also—if he ever asks—he thinks your last name is Potter."

"Why?"

"Is better this way," said Boris calmly. "Trust me."

XX.

BORIS AND I LAY on the floor in front of the television at my house, eating potato chips and drinking vodka, watching the Macy's Thanksgiving Day parade. It was snowing in New York. A number of balloons had just passed—Snoopy, Ronald McDonald, SpongeBob, Mr. Peanut—and a troupe of Hawaiian dancers in loincloths and grass skirts was performing a number in Herald Square.

"Glad that's not me," said Boris. "Bet they're freezing their arses off."

"Yeah," I said, though I had no eyes for the balloons or the dancers or any of it. To see Herald Square on television made me feel as if I were stranded millions of light-years from Earth and picking up signals from the early days of radio, announcer voices and audience applause from a vanished civilization.

"Idiots. Can't believe they dress like that. They'll end up in hospital, those girls." As fiercely as Boris complained about the heat in Las Vegas, he also had an unshakable belief that anything "cold" made people ill: unheated swimming pools, the air-conditioning at my house, and even ice in drinks.

He rolled over on his back and passed me the bottle. "You and your mother, you went to this parade?"

"Nah."

"Why not?" said Boris, feeding Popper a potato chip.

"*Nekulturny,*" I said, a word I'd picked up from him. "And too many tourists."

He lit a cigarette, and offered me one. "Are you sad?"

"A little," I said, leaning in to light it from his match. I couldn't stop thinking about the Thanksgiving before; it kept playing and re-playing like a movie I couldn't stop: my mother padding around barefoot in old jeans with the knees sprung out, opening a bottle of wine, pouring me some ginger ale in a champagne glass, setting out some olives, turning up the stereo, putting on her holiday joke apron, and unwrapping the turkey breast she'd bought us in Chinatown, only to wrinkle her nose and start back at the smell—"Oh God, Theo, this thing's gone off, open the door for me"—eyewatering ammonia reek, holding it out before her like an undetonated grenade as she ran with it down the fire stairs and out to the garbage can on the street while I — leaning out from the window — made gleeful retching noises from on high. We'd eaten an austere meal of canned green beans, canned cranberries, and brown rice with toasted almonds: "Our Vegetarian Socialist Thanksgiving," she'd called it. We'd planned carelessly because she had a project due at work; next year, she promised (both of us tired from laughing; the spoiled turkey had for some reason put us in an hilarious mood), we were renting a car and driving to her friend Jed's in Vermont, or else making reservations someplace great like Gramercy Tavern. Only that future had not happened; and I was celebrating my alcoholic potato-chip Thanksgiving with Boris in front of the television.

"What are we going to eat, Potter?" said Boris, scratching his stomach.

"What? Are you hungry?"

He waggled his hand sideways: *comme ci, comme ça.* "You?"

"Not especially." The roof of my mouth was scraped raw from eating so many chips, and the cigarettes had begun to make me feel ill.

Suddenly Boris howled with laughter; he sat up. "Listen," he said — kicking me, pointing to the television. "Did you hear that?"

"What?"

"The news man. He just wished happy holiday to his kids. 'Bastard and Casey.'"

"Oh, come on." Boris was always mis-hearing English words like this, aural malaprops, sometimes amusing but often just irritating.

"'Bastard and Casey!' That's hard, eh? Casey, all right, but call his own kid 'Bastard' on holiday television?"

"That's not what he said."

"Fine, then, you know everything, what did he say?"

"How should I know what the fuck?"

"Then why do you argue with me? Why do you think you always know better? What is the problem with this country? How did so stupid nation get to be so arrogant and rich? Americans...movie stars...TV people...they name their kids like Apple and Blanket and Blue and Bastard and all kind of crazy things."

"And your point is —?"

"My point is like, democracy is excuse for any fucking thing. Violence...greed...stupidity...anything is ok if Americans do it. Right? Am I right?"

"You really can't shut up, can you?"

"I know what I heard, ha! Bastard! Tell you what. If I thought my kid was a bastard I would sure the fuck name him something else."

In the fridge, there were wings and taquitos and cocktail sausages that Xandra had brought home, as well as dumplings from the strip-mall Chinese where my father liked to eat, but by the time we actually got around to eating, the bottle of vodka (Boris's contribution to Thanksgiving) was already half gone and we were well on our way to being sick. Boris—who sometimes had a serious streak when he was drunk, a Russianate bent for heavy topics and unanswerable questions—was sitting on the marble countertop waving around a fork with a cocktail sausage speared on it and talking a bit wildly about poverty and capitalism and climate change and how fucked up the world was.

At some disoriented point, I said: "Boris, shut up. I don't want to hear this." He'd gone back to my room for my school copy of *Walden* and was reading aloud a lengthy passage that bolstered some point he was trying to make.

The thrown book—luckily a paperback—clipped me in the cheekbone. "*Ischézni!* Get out!"

"This is my house, you ignorant fuck."

The cocktail sausage—still impaled on the fork—sailed past my head, missing me narrowly. But we were laughing. By mid-afternoon we were completely wrecked: rolling around on the carpet, tripping each other, laughing and swearing, crawling on hands and knees. A football game was on, and though it was an annoyance to both of us it was too much trouble to find the remote and change the channel. Boris was so hammered he kept trying to talk to me in Russian.

"Speak English or shut up," I said, trying to catch myself on the banister, and ducking his swing so clumsily I crashed and fell into the coffee table.

"*Ty menjá dostáll! Poshël ty!*"

"Gobble gobble gobble," I replied in a whiny girl voice, face down in the carpet. The floor was rocking and bucking like the deck of a ship. "Balalaika pattycake."

"Fucking *télik*," said Boris, collapsing on the floor beside me, kicking out ridiculously at the television. "Don't want to watch this shite."

"Well I mean, fuck"—rolling over, clutching my stomach—"I don't either." My eyes weren't tracking right, objects had halos that shimmered out beyond their normal boundaries.

"Let's watch weathers," said Boris, wading on his knees across the living room. "Want to see the weathers in New Guinea."

"You'll have to find it, I don't know what channel."

"Dubai!" exclaimed Boris, collapsing forward on all fours — and then, a mushy flow of Russian in which I caught a swear word or two.

"*Angliyski!* Speak English."

"Is snowing there?" Shaking my shoulder. "Man says is snowing, crazy man, *ty videsh?*! Snowing in Dubai! A miracle, Potter! Look!"

"That's *Dublin* you ass. Not Dubai."

"*Valí otsyúda!* Fuck off!"

Then I must have blacked out (an all-too-typical occurrence when Boris brought a bottle over) because the next I knew, the light was completely different and I was kneeling by the sliding doors with a puddle of puke on the carpet beside me and my forehead pressed to the glass. Boris was fast asleep, face down and snoring happily, one arm dangling off the sofa. Popchik was sleeping too, chin resting contentedly on the back of Boris's head. I felt rotten. Dead butterfly floating on the surface of the pool. Audible machine hum. Drowned crickets and beetles swirling in the plastic filter baskets. Above, the setting sun flared gaudy and inhuman, blood-red shelves of cloud that suggested end-times footage of catastrophe and ruin: detonations on Pacific atolls, wildlife running before sheets of flame.

I might have cried, if Boris wasn't there. Instead, I went in the bathroom and vomited again and then after drinking some water from the tap came back with paper towels and cleaned up the mess I'd made even though my head hurt so much I could barely see. The vomit was an awful orange color from the barbecue chicken wings and hard to get up, it had left a stain, and while I scrubbed at it with dish detergent I tried hard to fasten on comforting thoughts of New York — the Barbours' apartment with its Chinese porcelains and its friendly doormen, and also the timeless backwater of Hobie's house, old books and loudly-ticking clocks, old furniture, velvet curtains, everywhere the sediment of the past, quiet rooms where things were calm and made sense. Often at night, when I was overwhelmed with the strangeness of where I was, I lulled myself to sleep by thinking of his workshop, rich smells of beeswax and rosewood shavings, and then the narrow stairs up to the parlor, where dusty sunbeams shone on oriental carpets.

I'll call, I thought. Why not? I was still just drunk enough to think it was a good idea. But the telephone rang and rang. Finally — after two or three tries, and then a bleak half hour or so in front of the television — sick and sweating, my stomach killing me, staring at the Weather Channel, icy road conditions, cold fronts sweeping in over Montana — I decided to call Andy, going into the kitchen so I wouldn't wake Boris. It was Kitsey who picked up the phone.

"We can't talk," she said in a rush when she realized it was me. "We're late. We're on the way out to dinner."

"Where?" I said, blinking. My head still hurt so much I could hardly stand up.

"With the Van Nesses over on Fifth. Friends of Mum's."

In the background, I heard indistinct wails from Toddy, Platt roaring: "Get *off* me!"

"Can I say hi to Andy?" I said, staring fixedly at the kitchen floor.

"No, really, we're — Mum, I'm coming!" I heard her yell. To me, she said, "Happy Thanksgiving."

"You too," I said, "tell everybody I said hi," but she'd already hung up.

xxi.

MY APPREHENSIONS ABOUT BORIS's father had been eased somewhat since he'd taken my hands and thanked me for looking after Boris. Though Mr. Pavlikovsky ("Mister!" cackled Boris) was a scary-looking guy, all right, I'd come to think he wasn't quite as awful as he'd seemed. Twice the week after Thanksgiving, we came in after school to find him in the kitchen — mumbled pleasantries, nothing more, as he sat at the table throwing back vodka and blotting his damp forehead with a paper napkin, his fairish hair darkened with some sort of oily hair cream, listening to loud Russian news on his beat-up radio. But then one night we were downstairs with Popper (who I'd walked over from my house) and watching an old Peter Lorre movie called *The Beast with Five Fingers* when the front door slammed, hard.

Boris slapped his forehead. "Fuck." Before I realized what he was doing he'd shoved Popper in my arms, seized me by the collar of the shirt, hauled me up, and pushed me in the back.

"What—?"

He flung out a hand—*just go.* "Dog," he hissed. "My dad will kill him. Hurry."

I ran through the kitchen, and—as quietly as I could—slipped out the back door. It was very dark outside. For once in his life, Popper didn't make a sound. I put him down, knowing he would stick close, and circled around to the living room windows, which were uncurtained.

His dad was walking with a cane, something I hadn't seen. Leaning on it heavily, he limped into the bright room like a character in a stage play. Boris stood, arms crossed over his scrawny chest, hugging himself.

He and his father were arguing—or, rather, his father was talking to him angrily. Boris stared at the floor. His hair hung in his face, so all I could see of him was the tip of his nose.

Abruptly, tossing his head, Boris said something sharp and turned to leave. Then—so viciously I almost didn't have time to register it—Boris's dad snapped out like a snake with the cane and whacked Boris across the back of the shoulders and knocked him to the ground. Before he could get up—he was on his hands and knees—Mr. Pavlikovsky kicked him down, then caught him by the back of the shirt and pulled him, stumbling, to his feet. Ranting and screaming in Russian, he slapped him across the face with his red, beringed hand, backwards and forwards. Then—throwing him staggering out into the middle of the room—he brought up the hooked end of the cane and cracked him square across the face.

Half in shock, I backed away from the window, so disoriented that I tripped and fell over a sack of garbage. Popper—alarmed at the noise—was running back and forth and crying in a high, keening tone. Just as I was clambering up again—panic-stricken, in a crash of cans and beer bottles—the door flew open and a square of yellow light spilled on the concrete. As quickly as I could I scrambled to my feet, snatched up Popper, and ran.

But it was only Boris. He caught up with me, grabbed me by the arm and dragged me down the street.

"Jesus," I said—lagging a little, trying to look back. "What was that?"

Behind us, the front door of Boris's house flew open. Mr. Pavlikovsky stood silhouetted in the light from the doorway and bracing himself with one hand, shaking his fist and shouting in Russian.

Boris pulled me along. "Come *on*." Down the dark street we ran, shoes slapping the asphalt, until at last his father's voice died away.

"Fuck," I said, slowing to a walk as we rounded the corner. My heart was pounding and my head swam; Popper was whining and struggling to get down, and I set him on the asphalt to dash in circles around us. "What happened?"

"Ah, nothing," said Boris, sounding unaccountably cheerful, wiping his nose with a wet snuffling noise. "'Storm in a glass of water' is how we say it in Polish. He was just pissed."

I bent over, hands on knees, to catch my breath. "Pissed angry or pissed drunk?"

"Both. Lucky he didn't see Popchyk, though, or—don't know what. He thinks animals are for outside. Here," he said, holding up the vodka bottle, "look what I got! Nicked it on the way out."

I smelled the blood on him before I saw it. There was a crescent moon—not much, but enough to see by—and when I stood and looked at him head-on, I realized that his nose was pouring and his shirt was dark with it.

"Gosh," I said, still breathing hard, "are you all right?"

"Let's go to the playground, catch our breath," said Boris. His face, I saw, was a mess: swollen eye, and an ugly hook-shaped cut on his forehead that was also pouring blood.

"Boris! We should go home."

He raised an eyebrow. "Home?"

"*My* house. Whatever. You look bad."

He grinned—exposing bloody teeth—and elbowed me in the ribs. "Nyah, I need a drink before I face Xandra. Come on, Potter. Couldn't you use a wind-me-down? After all that?"

xxii.

AT THE ABANDONED COMMUNITY center, the playground slides gleamed silver in the moonlight. We sat on the side of the empty fountain, our feet dangling in the dry basin, and passed the bottle back and forth until we began to lose track of time.

"That was the weirdest thing I've ever seen," I said, wiping my mouth with the back of my hand. The stars were spinning a bit.

Boris—leaning back on his hands, face turned to the sky—was singing to himself in Polish.

Wszystkie dzieci, nawet źle,
pogrążone są we śnie,
a Ty jedna tylko nie.
A-a-a, a-a-a . . .

"He's fucking scary," I said. "Your dad."

"Yah," said Boris cheerfully, wiping his mouth on the shoulder of his blood-stained shirt. "He's killed people. He beat a man to death down the mine once."

"Bullshit."

"No, it's true. In New Guinea it happened. He tried to make it look like loose rocks had fell and killed the man but still we had to leave right after."

I thought about this. "Your dad's not, um, very sturdy," I said. "I mean, I can't really see—"

"Nyah, not with his fists. With a, what do you call it"—he mimed hitting a surface—"pipe wrench."

I was silent. There was something in the gesture of Boris bringing down the imaginary wrench that had the ring of truth about it.

Boris—who'd been fumbling to get a cigarette lit—let out a smoky sigh. "Want one?" He passed it to me and lit another for himself, then brushed his jaw with his knuckles. "Ah," he said, working it back and forth.

"Does it hurt?"

Sleepily he laughed, and punched me in the shoulder. "What do you think, idiot?"

Before long, we were staggering with laughter, blundering around on the gravel on hands and knees. Drunk as I was, my mind felt high and cold and strangely clear. Then at some point—dusty from rolling and scuffling on the ground—we were reeling home in almost total blackness, rows of abandoned houses and the desert night gigantic all around us, bright crackle of stars high above and Popchik trotting along behind us as we weaved side to side, laughing so hard we were gagging and heaving and nearly sick by the side of the road.

He was singing at the top of his lungs, the same tune as before:

A-a-a, a-a-a,
byly sobie kotki dwa.
A-a-a, kotki dwa,
szarobure—

I kicked him. "English!"

"Here, I'll teach you. *A-a-a, a-a-a—*"

"Tell me what it means."

"All right, I will. 'There once were two small kittens,'" sang Boris:

they both were grayish brown.
A-a-a—

"*Two small kittens?*"

He tried to hit me, and almost fell. "Fuck off! I haven't got to the good part." Wiping his mouth with his hand, he threw his head back, and sang:

Oh, sleep, my darling,
And I'll give you a star from the sky,
All the children are fast asleep
All others, even the bad ones,
All children are sleeping but you.
A-a-a, a-a-a—
There once were two small kittens—

When we got to my house—making way too much noise, shushing each other—the garage was empty: no one home. "Thank *God*," said Boris fervently, falling to the concrete to prostrate himself before the Lord.

I caught him by the collar of his shirt. "Get up!"

Inside—under the lights—he was a mess: blood everywhere, eye swollen to a glossy slit. "Hang on," I said, dropping him in the center of the living room carpet, and wobbled to the bathroom to get something for his cut. But there wasn't anything except shampoo and a bottle of green perfume that Xandra had won at some giveaway at the Wynn. Drunkenly remembering something my mother had said, that perfume was antiseptic in a pinch, I went back to the living room where Boris was sprawled on the carpet with Popper sniffing anxiously at his bloodstained shirt.

"Here," I said, pushing the dog aside, dabbing the bloody place on his forehead with a damp cloth. "Hold still."

Boris twitched away, and growled. "The fuck are you doing?"

"Shut up," I said, holding the hair back from his eyes.

He muttered something in Russian. I was trying to be careful but I was as drunk as he was, and when I sprayed perfume on the cut, he shrieked and socked me on the mouth.

"What the fuck?" I said, touching my lip, my fingers coming away bloody. "Look what you did to me."

"*Blyad,*" he said, coughing and batting the air, "it stinks. What'd you put on me, you whore?"

I started laughing; I couldn't help it.

"*Bastard,*" he roared, shoving me so hard I fell. But he was laughing too. He held out a hand to help me up but I kicked it away.

"Fuck off!" I was laughing so hard I could barely get the words out. "You smell like Xandra."

"Christ, I'm choking. I've got to get this off me."

We stumbled outside — shedding our clothes, hopping one-legged out of our pants as we went — and jumped in the pool: bad idea, I realized in the too-late, toppling-over moment before I hit the water, blind drunk and too wrecked to walk. The cold water slammed into me so hard it almost knocked my breath out.

I clawed to the surface: eyes stinging, chlorine burning my nose. A spray of water hit me in the eyes and I spit it back at him. He was a white blur in the dark, cheeks hollow and black hair plastered on either side of his head. Laughing, we grappled and ducked each other, even though my teeth were chattering and I felt way too drunk and sick to be horsing around in eight feet of water.

Boris dove. A hand clamped my ankle and yanked me under, and I found myself staring into a dark wall of bubbles.

I wrenched; I struggled. It was like in the museum again, trapped in the dark space, no way up or out. I thrashed and twisted, as glubs of panicked breath floated before my eyes: underwater bells, darkness. At last —

just as I was about to gulp in a lungful of water—I twisted free and broke to the surface.

Choking for breath, I clung to the edge of the pool and gasped. When my vision cleared, I saw Boris—coughing, cursing—plunging towards the steps. Breathless with anger, I half-swam, half hopped up behind him and hooked a foot around his ankle so that he fell face-forward with a smack.

"Asshole," I sputtered, when he floundered to the surface. He was trying to talk but I struck a sheet of water in his face, and then another, and wound my fingers in his hair and pushed him under. "You miserable shit," I screamed when he surfaced, heaving, water streaming down his face. "Don't *ever* do that to me again." I had both hands on his shoulders and was about to dive on top of him—push him down, hold him for a good long time—when he reached around and clasped my arm, and I saw that he was white and trembling.

"Stop," he said, gasping—and then I realized how unfocused and strange his eyes were.

"Hey," I said, "are you okay?" But he was coughing too hard to answer. His nose was bleeding again, blood gushing dark between his fingers. I helped him up, and together we collapsed on the pool steps—half in, half out of the water, too exhausted even to climb all the way out.

xxiii.

BRIGHT SUN WOKE ME. We were in my bed: wet hair, half-dressed and shivering in the air-conditioned cold, with Popper snoring between us. The sheets were damp and reeking of chlorine; I had a shattering headache and an ugly metallic taste in my mouth like I'd been sucking on a handful of pocket change.

I lay very still, feeling I might vomit if I moved my head even a quarter of an inch, then—very carefully—sat up.

"Boris?" I said, rubbing my cheek with the flat of my hand. Brown streaks of dried blood were smeared on the pillowcase. "You awake?"

"Oh God," groaned Boris, dead-pale and sticky with sweat, rolling on his stomach to clutch at the mattress. He was naked except for his Sid Vicious bracelets and what looked like a pair of my underwear. "I'm gonna be sick."

"Not here." I kicked him. "Up."

Muttering, he stumbled off. I could hear him puking in my bathroom. The sound made me sick, but also a bit hysterical. I rolled over and laughed into my pillow. When he stumbled back in, clasping his head, I was shocked at his black eye, the blood caked at his nostrils and the scabbed cut on his forehead.

"Christ," I said, "that looks bad. You need stitches."

"You know what?" said Boris, throwing himself stomach-down on the mattress.

"What?"

"We're late for fucking school!"

We rolled on our backs and roared with laughter. As weak and nauseated as I felt, I thought I would never be able to stop.

Boris flopped over, groping with one arm for something on the floor. In an instant his head popped back up. "Ah! What's this?"

I sat up and reached eagerly for the glass of water, or what I thought was water, and—when he shoved it under my nose—gagged on the smell.

Boris howled. Quick as a flash he was on top of me: all sharp bones and clammy flesh, reeking of sweat and sick and something else, raw and dirty, like stagnant pond water. Sharply he pinched my cheek, tipping the glass of vodka over my face. "Time for your medicine! Now, now," he said, as I knocked the glass flying and hit him in the mouth, a glancing blow that didn't quite connect. Popper was barking with excitement. Boris got me in a chokehold, grabbed my dirty shirt from the day before, and tried to stuff it in my mouth, but I was too quick for him and flipped him off the bed so that his head knocked against the wall. "Ow, fuck," he said, rubbing his face sleepily with his open palm and chuckling.

Uncertainly I stood, in a prickle of cold sweat, and made my way into the bathroom, where in a violent rush or two—hand braced against the wall—I emptied my stomach into the toilet bowl. From the next room I could hear him laughing.

"Two fingers down the pipe," he called in to me, and then something I missed, in a fresh shudder of nausea.

When it was over, I spat once or twice, then wiped my mouth with the back of my hand. The bathroom was a wreck: shower dripping, door hanging open, sopping towels and blood-stained wash cloths wadded on the floor. Still shivering with sick, I drank from my hands at the sink and splashed some water on my face. My bare-chested reflection was hunched and pale, and I had a fat lip from where Boris had socked me the night before.

Boris was still on the floor, lying bonelessly with his head propped against the wall. When I came back in, he cracked his good eye open and chortled at the sight of me. "All better?"

"Fuck you! Don't fucking talk to me."

"Serves you right. Didn't I tell you not to faff around with that glass?"

"Me?"

"You don't remember, do you?" He touched his tongue to his upper lip to see if his mouth had started bleeding again. When his shirt was off you could see all the spaces between his ribs, marks from old beatings and the heat flush high on his chest. "That glass on the floor, *very* bad idea. Unlucky! I told you not to leave it there! Huge jinx on us!"

"You didn't have to pour it on my head," I said, fumbling for my specs and reaching for the first pair of pants I saw from the communal heap of dirty laundry on the floor.

Boris pinched the bridge of his nose, and laughed. "Was just trying to help you. A little booze will make you feel better."

"Yeah, thanks a lot."

"It's true. If you can keep it down. Will make your headache go like magic. My dad is not helpful person but this is one very helpful thing he has told me. Nice cold beer is the best, if you have it."

"Say, c'mere," I said. I was standing by the window, looking down at the pool.

"Eh?"

"Come look. I want you to see this."

"Just tell me," muttered Boris, from the floor. "I don't want to get up."

"You'd better." Downstairs it looked like a murder scene. A line of blood drips wound across the paving stones to the pool. Shoes, jeans, bloodsoaked shirt, were riotously flung and tossed. One of Boris's busted-up boots lay at the bottom of the deep end. Worse: a greasy scum of vomit floated in the shallow water by the steps.

xxiv.

Later, after a few half-hearted passes with the pool vacuum, we were sitting on the kitchen counter smoking my dad's Viceroys and talking. It was almost noon—too late to even think about going to school. Boris— ragged and unhinged-looking, his shirt hanging off the shoulder on one side, slamming the cabinets, complaining bitterly because there was no tea—had made some hideous coffee in the Russian way, by boiling grounds in a pan on the stove.

"No, no," he said, when he saw I'd poured myself a normal sized cup. "Very strong, very small amount."

I tasted it, made a face.

He dipped a finger in it, and licked it off. "Biscuit would be nice."

"You've got to be kidding."

"Bread and butter?" he said hopefully.

I eased down from the counter—as gently as I could, because my head hurt—and searched around until I found a drawer with sugar enve- lopes and packaged tortilla chips that Xandra had brought home from the buffet at the bar.

"Crazy," I said, looking at his face.

"What?"

"That your dad did that."

"Is nothing," mumbled Boris, turning his head sideways so he could wedge the whole corn chip in. "He broke one of my ribs once."

After a long pause, and because I couldn't think of anything else to say, I said: "A broken rib's not that serious."

"No, but it hurt. This one," he said, pulling up his shirt and pointing it out to me.

"I thought he was going to kill you."

He bumped his shoulder against mine. "Ah, I provoked him on pur- pose. Answered back. So you could get Popchik out of there. Look, is fine," he said, condescendingly, when I kept on looking at him. "Last night he was frothing at mouth but he'll be sorry when he sees me."

"Maybe you ought to stay here for a while."

Boris leaned back on his hands and gave me a dismissive smile. "Is nothing to be fussed about. He gets depressed sometimes, is all."

"Hah." In the old Johnnie Walker Black days—vomit on his dress shirts, angry co-workers calling our house—my dad (in tears sometimes) had blamed his rages on "depression."

Boris laughed, with what seemed like genuine amusement. "And what? You don't get sad yourself sometimes?"

"He should be in jail for doing that."

"Oh, please." Boris had gotten bored with his bad coffee and had ventured to the fridge for a beer. "My father—bad temper, sure, but he loves me. He could have left me with a neighbor when he left Ukraine. That's what happened to my friends Maks and Seryozha—Maks ended up on the street. Besides, I should be in jail myself, if you want to think that way."

"Sorry?"

"I tried to kill him one time. Serious!" he said, when he saw the way I was looking at him. "I did."

"I don't believe you."

"No, is true," he said resignedly. "I feel bad about it. Our last winter in Ukraine, I tricked him to walk outside—he was so drunk, he did it. Then I locked the door. Thought sure he would die in the snow. Glad he didn't, eh?" he said, with a shout of laughter. "Then I'd be stuck in Ukraine, my God. Eating from garbage cans. Sleeping in railway station."

"What happened?"

"Dunno. It wasn't late at night enough. Someone saw him and picked him up in a car—some woman, I'd guess, who knows? Anyway he went out drinking more, made it home a few days later—lucky for me, didn't remember what happened! Instead he brought me a soccer ball and said he was drinking only beer from then on. That lasted one month maybe."

I rubbed my eye behind my glasses. "What are you going to tell them at school?"

He cracked the beer open. "Eh?"

"Well, I mean." The bruise on his face was the color of raw meat. "People are going to ask."

He grinned and elbowed me. "I'll tell 'em *you* did it," he said.

"No, seriously."

"I am serious."

"Boris, it's not funny."

"Oh, come on. Football, skateboard." His black hair fell in his face like a shadow and he tossed it back. "You don't want them to take me away, do you?"

"Right," I said, after an uncomfortable pause.

"Because Poland." He passed me the beer. "I think is what it would be. For deportation. Although Poland—" he laughed, a startling bark — "better than Ukraine, my God!"

"They can't send you back there, can they?"

He frowned at his hands, which were dirty, nails rimmed with dried blood. "No," he said fiercely. "Because I'll kill myself first."

"Oh, boo hoo hoo." Boris was always threatening to kill himself for one reason and another.

"I mean it! I'll die first! I'd rather be dead."

"No you wouldn't."

"Yes I would! The winter—you don't know what it's like. Even the air is bad. All gray concrete, and the wind—"

"Well, it must be summer there sometime."

"Ah, God." He reached for my cigarette, took a sharp drag, blew a stream of smoke up at the ceiling. "Mosquitoes. Stinking mud. Everything smells like mould. I was so starving-to-death and lonely—I mean, sometimes I was so hungry, serious, I would walk on the river bank and think of drowning myself."

My head hurt. Boris's clothes (my clothes, actually) tumbled in the dryer. Outside, the sun shone bright and mean.

"I don't know about you," I said, taking the cigarette back, "but I could use some real food."

"What shall we do then?"

"We should have gone to school."

"Hmpf." Boris made it plain that he only went to school because I went, and because there was nothing else to do.

"No—I mean it. We should have gone. There's pizza today."

Boris winced, with genuine regret. "Fuck it." That was the other thing about school; at least they fed us. "Too late now."

XXV.

Sometimes, in the night, I woke up wailing. The worst thing about the explosion was how I carried it in my body—the heat, the bone-jar and slam of it. In my dreams, there was always a light way out and a dark way out. I had to go the dark way, because the bright way was hot and flickering with fire. But the dark way was where the bodies were.

Happily, Boris never seemed annoyed or even very startled when I woke him, as if he came from a world where there was nothing so unusual in a nocturnal howl of pain. Sometimes he'd gather up Popchik — snoring at the foot of our bed — and deposit him in a limp sleepy heap on my chest. And weighed down like that — the warmth of both of them around me — I lay counting to myself in Spanish or trying to remember all the words I knew in Russian (swear words, mostly) until I went back to sleep.

When I'd first come to Vegas, I'd tried to make myself feel better by imagining that my mother was still alive and going about her routine back in New York — chatting with the doormen, picking up coffee and a muffin at the diner, waiting on the platform by the news stand for the 6 train. But that hadn't worked for long. Now, when I buried my face in a strange pillow that didn't smell at all like her, or home, I thought of the Barbours' apartment on Park Avenue, or, sometimes, Hobie's townhouse in the Village.

I'm sorry your father sold your mother's things. If you had told me, I might have bought some of them and kept them for you. When we are sad — at least I am like this — it can be comforting to cling to familiar objects, to the things that don't change.

Your descriptions of the desert — that oceanic, endless glare — are terrible but also very beautiful. Maybe there's something to be said for the rawness and emptiness of it all. The light of long ago is different from the light of today and yet here, in this house, I'm reminded of the past at every turn. But when I think of you, it's as if you've gone away to sea on a ship — out in a foreign brightness where there are no paths, only stars and sky.

This letter arrived tucked in an old hardcover edition of *Wind, Sand and Stars* by Saint-Exupéry, which I read and re-read. I kept the letter in the book, where it became creased and dirty from repeated re-reading.

Boris was the only person I'd told, in Vegas, how my mother had died — information that to his credit he'd accepted with aplomb; his own life had been so erratic and violent that he didn't seem all that shocked by the story. He'd seen big explosions, out in his father's mines around Batu

Hijau and other places I'd never heard of, and—without knowing the particulars—was able to venture a fairly accurate guess as to the type of explosives employed. As talkative as he was, he also had a secretive streak and I trusted him not to tell anyone without having to ask. Maybe because he himself was motherless and had formed close bonds to people like Bami, his father's "lieutenant" Evgeny, and Judy the barkeep's wife in Karmeywallag—he didn't seem to think my attachment to Hobie was peculiar at all. "People promise to write, and they don't," he said, when we were in the kitchen looking at Hobie's latest letter. "But this fellow writes you all the time."

"Yeah, he's nice." I'd given up trying to explain Hobie to Boris: the house, the workshop, his thoughtful way of listening so different from my father's, but more than anything a sort of pleasing atmosphere of mind: foggy, autumnal, a mild and welcoming micro-climate that made me feel safe and comfortable in his company.

Boris stuck his finger in the open jar of peanut butter on the table between us, and licked it off. He had grown to love peanut butter, which (like marshmallow fluff, another favorite) was unavailable in Russia. "Old poofter?" he asked.

I was taken aback. "No," I said swiftly; and then: "I don't know."

"Doesn't matter," said Boris, offering me the jar. "I've known some sweet old poofters."

"I don't think he is," I said, uncertainly.

Boris shrugged. "Who cares? If he is good to you? None of us ever find enough kindness in the world, do we?"

XXVI.

BORIS HAD GROWN TO like my father, and vice versa. He understood, better than I did, how my father made his living; and although he knew, without being told, to stay away from my dad when he was losing, he also understood that my father was in need of something I was unwilling to give: namely, an audience in the flush of winning, when he was pacing around jacked up and punchy in the kitchen and wanting someone to listen to his stories and praise him about how well he'd done. When we heard him down there jumped-up and high on the downdraft of a win—

bumping around jubilantly, making lots of noise — Boris would put down his book and head downstairs, where patiently he stood listening to my dad's boring, card-by-card replay of his evening at the baccarat table, which often segued into excruciating (to me) stories of related triumphs, all the way back to my dad's college days and blighted acting career.

"You didn't tell me that your dad had been in movies!" said Boris, returning upstairs with a cup of now-cold tea.

"He wasn't in many. Like, two."

"But I mean. That one — that was a really *big* movie — that police movie, you know, the one about policemen taking bribes. What was the name of it?"

"He didn't have a very big part. He was in it for like one second. He played a lawyer who got shot on the street."

Boris shrugged. "Who cares? Still is interesting. If he ever went to Ukraine people would treat him like a star."

"He can go then, and take Xandra with him."

Boris's enthusiasm for what he called "intellectual talks" found an appreciative outlet in my father, as well. Uninterested in politics myself, and even less interested in my father's views on them, I was unwilling to engage in the kind of pointless argument on world events that I knew my father enjoyed. But Boris — drunk or sober — was glad to oblige. Often, in these talks, my father would wave his arms around and mimic Boris's accent for entire conversations, in a way that set my teeth on edge. But Boris himself didn't appear to notice or mind. Sometimes, when he went down to put the kettle on, and didn't return, I found them arguing happily in the kitchen like a pair of actors in a stage production, about the dissolution of the Soviet Union or whatever.

"Ah, Potter!" he said, coming upstairs. "Your dad. Such a nice guy!"

I removed the earbuds of my iPod. "If you say so."

"I mean it," said Boris, flopping down on the floor. "He's so talkative and intelligent! And he loves you."

"I don't see where you get that."

"Come on! He wants to make things right with you, but doesn't know how. He wishes it was you down there having discussions with him and not me."

"He said that to you?"

"No. Is true, though! I know it."

"Could have fooled me."

Boris looked at me shrewdly. "Why do you hate him so much?"

"I don't *hate* him."

"He broke your mother's heart," said Boris decisively. "When he left her. But you need to forgive him. All that's in the past now."

I stared. Was this what my dad went around telling people?

"That's bullshit," I said, sitting up, throwing my comic book aside. "My mother—" how could I explain it?—"you don't understand, he was an asshole to us, we were *glad* when he left. I mean, I know you think he's such a great guy and everything—"

"And why is he so terrible? Because he saw other women?" said Boris—holding out his hands, palms up. "It happens. He has his life. What is that to do with you?"

I shook my head in disbelief. "Man," I said, "he's got you snowed." It never failed to amaze me how my dad could charm strangers and reel them in. They lent him money, recommended him for promotions, introduced him to important people, invited him to use their vacation homes, fell completely under his spell—and then it would all go to pieces somehow and he would move on to someone else.

Boris looped his arms around his knees and leaned his head back against the wall. "All right, Potter," he said agreeably. "Your enemy—my enemy. If you hate him, I hate him too. But—" he put his head to the side—"here I am. Staying in his house. What should I do? Should I talk, be friendly and nice? Or disrespect him?"

"I'm not saying *that*. I'm just saying, don't believe everything he tells you."

Boris chuckled. "I don't believe everything that *any*body tells me," he said, kicking my foot companionably. "Not even you."

xxvii.

As fond as my dad was of Boris, I was constantly trying to divert his attention from the fact that Boris had basically moved into the house with us—which wasn't that difficult, as between the gambling and the drugs my dad was so distracted that he might not have noticed if I'd brought a bobcat to live in the upstairs bedroom. Xandra was a bit tougher to negotiate, more prone to complain about the expense, despite the supply of stolen snack food Boris contributed to the household. When she was at home he stayed upstairs and out of the way, frowning over *The Idiot* in Russian and listening to music on my portable speakers. I brought him beers and food from downstairs and learned to make his tea the way he liked it: boiling hot, with three sugars.

By then it was almost Christmas though you wouldn't have known it from the weather: cool at night, but bright and warm during the day. When the wind blew, the umbrella by the pool snapped with a gunshot sound. There were lightning flashes at night, but no rain; and sometimes the sand picked up and flew in little whirlwinds which spun this way and that in the street.

I was depressed about the holidays, although Boris took them in stride. "It's for little children, all that," he said scornfully, leaning back on his elbows on my bed. "Tree, toys. We'll have our own *praznyky* on Christmas Eve. What do you think?"

"*Praznyky?*"

"You know. A sort of holiday party. Not a proper Holy Supper, just a nice dinner. Cook something special — maybe invite your father and Xandra. You think they might want to eat something with us?"

Much to my surprise, my father — and even Xandra — seemed delighted by the idea (my father, I think, mainly because he enjoyed the word *praznyky,* and enjoyed making Boris say it aloud). On the twenty-third, Boris and I went shopping, with actual money my father had given us (which was fortunate, since our usual supermarket was too crowded with holiday shoppers for carefree shoplifting) and came home with potatoes; a chicken; a series of unappetizing ingredients (sauerkraut, mushrooms, peas, sour cream) for some Polish holiday dish that Boris claimed he knew how to make; pumpernickel rolls (Boris insisted on black bread; white was all wrong for the meal, he said); a pound of butter; pickles; and some Christmas candy.

Boris had said that we would eat with the appearance of the first star in the sky — the Bethlehem star. But we were not used to cooking for anybody but ourselves and as a consequence were running late. On Christmas Eve, at about eight p.m., the sauerkraut dish was made and the chicken (which we'd figured how to cook from the package instructions) had about ten minutes before it came out of the oven when my dad — whistling

"Deck the Halls"—came up and rapped jauntily on a kitchen cabinet to get our attention.

"Come on, boys!" he said. His face was flushed and shiny and his voice very quick, with a strained, staccato quality I knew all too well. He had on one of his sharp old Dolce and Gabbana suits from New York but without a tie, the shirt loose and unbuttoned at the neck. "Go comb your hair and spruce up a bit. I'm taking us all out. Do you have anything better to wear, Theo? Surely you must."

"But—" I stared at him in frustration. This was just like my dad, breezing in and changing the plan at the last moment.

"Oh, come on. The chicken can wait. Can't it? Sure it can." He was talking a mile a minute. "You can put the other thing back in the fridge too. We'll have it tomorrow for Christmas lunch—will it still be *praznyky*? Is *praznyky* only on Christmas Eve? Am I confused about that? Well, okay, that's when we'll have ours—Christmas Day. New tradition. Leftovers are better anyway. Listen, this'll be *fantastic*. Boris—" he was already shepherding Boris out of the kitchen—"what size shirt do you wear, comrade? You don't know? Some of these old Brooks Brothers shirts of mine, I really ought to give the whole lot to you, great shirts, don't get me wrong, they'll probably come down to your knees but they're a little too tight in the collar for me and if you roll up the sleeves they'll look just fine...."

xxviii.

THOUGH I'D BEEN IN Las Vegas almost half a year it was only my fourth or fifth time on the Strip—and Boris (who was content enough in our little orbit between school, shopping plaza, and home) had scarcely been into Vegas proper at all. We stared in amazement at the waterfalls of neon, electricity blazing and pulsing and cascading down in bubbles all around us, Boris's upturned face glowing red and then gold in the crazy drench of lights.

Inside the Venetian, gondoliers propelled themselves down a real canal, with real, chemical-smelling water, as costumed opera singers sang *Stille Nacht* and *Ave Maria* under artificial skies. Boris and I trailed along uneasily, feeling shabby, scuffing our shoes, too stunned to take it all in.

My dad had made reservations for us at a fancy, oak-panelled Italian restaurant — the outpost of its more famous sister restaurant in New York. "Order what you like, everyone," he said, pulling out Xandra's chair for her. "My treat. Go wild."

We took him at his word. We ate asparagus flan with shallot vinaigrette; smoked salmon; smoked sable carpaccio; perciatelli with cardoons and black truffles; crispy black bass with saffron and fava beans; barbecued skirt steak; braised short ribs; and panna cotta, pumpkin cake, and fig ice cream for dessert. It was by leaps and fathoms the best meal I'd eaten in months, or maybe ever; and Boris — who'd eaten two orders of the sable all by himself — was ecstatic. "Ah, *marvelous,*" he said, for the fifteenth time, practically purring, as the pretty young waitress brought out an extra plate of candies and biscotti with the coffee. "Thank you! Thank you Mr. Potter, Xandra," he said again. "Is delicious."

My dad — who hadn't eaten all that much compared to us (Xandra hadn't either) — pushed his plate aside. The hair at his temples was damp and his face was so bright and red he was practically glowing. "Thank the little Chinese guy in the Cubs cap who kept betting the bank in the salon this afternoon," he said. "My God. It was like we *couldn't* lose." In the car, he'd already shown us his windfall: the fat roll of hundreds, wrapped up with a rubber band. "The cards just kept coming and kept coming. Mercury in retrograde and the moon was high! I mean — it was magic. You know, sometimes there's a light at the table, like a visible halo, and you're *it,* you know? *You're* the light? There's this fantastic dealer here, Diego, I *love* Diego — I mean, it's crazy, he looks just like Diego Rivera the painter only in a sharp-ass fucking tuxedo. Did I tell you about Diego already? Been out here forty years, ever since the old Flamingo days. Big, stout, grand-looking guy. Mexican, you know. Fast slippery hands and big rings —" he waggled his fingers — "ba-ca-RRRAT! God, I love these old-school Mexicans in the baccarat room, they're so fucking stylish. Musty old elegant fellows, carry their weight well, you know? Anyway, we were at Diego's table, me and the little Chinese guy, he was a trip too, horn-rimmed glasses and not a word of English, you know, just 'San Bin! San Bin!' drinking this crazy ginseng tea they all drink, tastes like dust but I love the smell, like the smell of luck, and it was incredible, we were on *such* a run, good God, all these Chinese women lined up behind us, we were hitting every hand — Do you think," he said to Xandra, "it would be okay if I took them back into the baccarat salon to meet Diego? I'm sure they'd get a huge kick out of Diego. I wonder if he's still on shift. What do you think?"

"He won't be there." Xandra looked good — bright-eyed and sparkly — in a velvet minidress and jewelled sandals, and redder lipstick than she usually wore. "Not now."

"Sometimes, holidays, he works a double shift."

"Oh, they don't want to go back there. It's a hike. It'll take half an hour to get there through the casino floor and back."

"Yeah, but I know he'd like to meet my kids."

"Yeah, probably so," Xandra said agreeably, running a finger around the rim of her wine glass. The tiny gold dove on her necklace glistened at the base of her throat. "He's a nice guy. But Larry, I mean it, I know you don't take me seriously but if you start getting too chummy with the dealers some day you're going to go down there and have security on your ass."

My father laughed. "God!" he said jubilantly, slapping the table, so loudly that I flinched. "If I hadn't known better, I would have thought Diego really *was* helping at the table today. I mean, maybe he was. Telepathic baccarat! Get your Soviet researchers working on *that*," he said to Boris. "That'll straighten out your economic system over there."

Boris — mildly — cleared his throat and lifted his water glass. "Sorry, may I say something?"

"Is it speechmaking time? Were we meant to prepare toasts?"

"I thank you all for your company. And I wish us all health, and happiness, and that we all shall live until the next Christmas."

In the surprised silence that followed, a champagne cork popped in the kitchen, a burst of laughter. It was just past midnight: two minutes into Christmas Day. Then my father leaned back in his chair, and laughed. "Merry Christmas!" he roared, producing from his pocket a jewelry box which he slid over to Xandra, and two stacks of twenties (Five hundred dollars! Each!) which he tossed across the table to Boris and me. And though in the clockless, temperature-controlled casino night, words like *day* and *Christmas* were fairly meaningless constructs, *happiness,* amidst the loudly clinked glasses, didn't seem quite such a doomed or fatal idea.

Chapter 6.

Wind, Sand and Stars

OVER THE NEXT YEAR, I was so preoccupied in trying to block New York and my old life out of my mind that I hardly noticed the time pass. Days ran changelessly in the seasonless glare: hungover mornings on the school bus and our backs raw and pink from falling asleep by the pool, the gasoline reek of vodka and Popper's constant smell of wet dog and chlorine, Boris teaching me to count, ask directions, offer a drink in Russian, just as patiently as he'd taught me to swear. Yes, please, I'd like that. Thank you, you are very kind. *Govorite li vy po angliyskiy?* Do you speak English? *Ya nemnogo govoryu po-russki.* I do speak Russian, a little.

Winter or summer, the days were dazzling; the desert air burned our nostrils and scraped our throats dry. Everything was funny; everything made us laugh. Sometimes, just before sundown, just as the blue of the sky began darkening to violet, we had these wild, electric-lined, Maxfield Parrish clouds rolling out gold and white into the desert like Divine Revelation leading the Mormons west. *Govorite medlenno,* I said, speak slowly, and *Povtorite, pozhaluysta.* Repeat, please. But we were so attuned to each other that we didn't need to talk at all if we didn't want to; we knew how to tip each other over in hysterics with an arch of the eyebrow or quirk of the mouth. Nights, we ate crosslegged on the floor, leaving greasy fingerprints on our schoolbooks. Our diet had made us malnourished, with soft brown bruises on our arms and legs — vitamin deficiency, said the nurse at school, who gave us each a painful shot in the ass and a colorful jar of children's chewables. ("My bottom hurts," said Boris, rubbing his rear end and cursing the metal seats on the school bus.) I was freckled head to toe from all the swimming we did; my hair (longer then than it's ever been again) got light streaks from the pool chemicals and basically I felt good, though I still had a heaviness in my chest that never went away and my teeth were rotting out in the back from all the candy we ate. Apart from that, I was fine. And so the time passed happily enough; but then — shortly after my fifteenth birthday — Boris met a girl named Kotku; and everything changed.

The name Kotku (Ukrainian variant: *Kotyku*) makes her sound more interesting than she was; but it wasn't her real name, only a pet name ("Kitty cat," in Polish) that Boris had given her. Her last name was Hutchins; her given name was actually something like Kylie or Keiley or Kaylee; and she'd lived in Clark County, Nevada her whole life. Though she went to our school and was only a grade ahead of us, she was a lot older — older than me by three whole years. Boris, apparently, had had his eye on her for a while, but I hadn't been aware of her until the afternoon he threw himself on the foot of my bed and said: "I'm in love."

"Oh yeah? With who?"

"This chick from Civics. That I bought some weed from. I mean, she's eighteen, too, can you believe it? God, she's *beautiful*."

"You have weed?"

Playfully, he lunged and caught me by the shoulder; he knew just where I was weakest, the spot under the blade where he could dig his fingers and make me yelp. But I was in no mood and hit him, hard.

"Ow! Fuck!" said Boris, rolling away, rubbing his jaw with his fingertips. "Why'd you do that?"

"Hope it hurts," I said. "Where's that weed?"

We didn't talk any more about Boris's love interest, at least not that day, but then a few days later when I came out of math I saw him looming over this girl by the lockers. While Boris wasn't especially tall for his age, the girl was tiny, despite how much older than us she seemed: flat-chested, scrawny-hipped, with high cheekbones and a shiny forehead and a sharp, shiny, triangle-shaped face. Pierced nose. Black tank top. Chipped black fingernail polish; streaked orange-and-black hair; flat, bright, chlorine-blue eyes, outlined hard, in black pencil. Definitely she was cute — hot, even; but the glance she slid over me was anxiety-provoking, something about her of a bitchy fast-food clerk or maybe a mean babysitter.

"So what do you think?" said Boris eagerly when he caught up with me after school.

I shrugged. "She's cute. I guess."

"You guess?"

"Well Boris, I mean, she looks like she's, like, twenty-five."

"I know! It's great!" he said, looking dazed. "Eighteen years! Legal adult! She can buy booze no problem! Also she's lived here her whole life, so she knows what places don't check age."

ii.

HADLEY, THE TALKATIVE LETTER-JACKET girl who sat by me in American history, wrinkled her nose when I asked about Boris's older woman. "*Her?*" she said. "*Total* slut." Hadley's big sister, Jan, was in the same grade with Kyla or Kayleigh or whatever her name was. "And her mother, I heard, is a straight-up hooker. Your friend better be careful he doesn't get some disease."

"Well," I said, surprised at her vehemence, though maybe I shouldn't have been. Hadley, an army brat, was on the swim team and sang in the school choir; she had a normal family with three siblings, a Weimaraner named Gretchen that she'd brought over from Germany, and a dad who yelled if she was out past her curfew.

"I'm not kidding," said Hadley. "She'll make out with other girls' boyfriends — she'll make out with other girls — she'll make out with *any-body*. Also I think she does pot."

"Oh," I said. None of these factors, in my view, were necessarily reasons to dislike Kylie or whatever, especially since Boris and I had wholeheartedly taken to smoking pot ourselves in the past months. But what did bother me — a lot — was how Kotku (I'll continue to call her by the name Boris gave her, since I can't now remember her real name) had stepped in overnight and virtually assumed ownership of Boris.

First he was busy on Friday night. Then it was the whole weekend — not just the night, but the day too. Pretty soon, it was Kotku this and Kotku that, and the next thing I knew, Popper and I were eating dinner and watching movies by ourselves.

"Isn't she amazing?" Boris asked me again, after the first time he brought her over to my house — a highly unsuccessful evening, which had consisted of the three of us getting so stoned we could barely move, and then the two of them rolling around on the sofa downstairs while I sat on the floor with my back to them and tried to concentrate on a rerun of *The Outer Limits.* "What do you think?"

"Well, I mean—" What did he want me to say? "She likes you. Sure."

He shifted, restlessly. We were outside by the pool, though it was too windy and cool to swim. "No, really! What do *you* think about *her?* Tell the truth, Potter," he said, when I hesitated.

"I don't know," I said doubtfully, and then—when he still sat looking at me: "Honestly? I don't know, Boris. She seems kind of desperate."

"Yes? Is that bad?"

His tone was genuinely curious—not angry, not sarcastic. "Well," I said, taken aback. "Maybe not."

Boris—cheeks pink with vodka—put his hand on his heart. "I love her, Potter. I mean it. This is the truest thing that has ever happened to me in my life."

I was so embarrassed I had to look away.

"Little skinny witch!" He sighed, happily. "In my arms, she's so bony and light! Like air." Boris, mysteriously, seemed to adore Kotku for many of the reasons I found her disturbing: her slinky alley-cat body, her scrawny, needy adultness. "And so brave and wise, such a big heart! All I want is to look out for her and keep her safe from that Mike guy. You know?"

Quietly, I poured myself another vodka, though I really didn't need one. The Kotku business was all doubly perplexing because—as Boris himself had informed me, with an unmistakable note of pride—Kotku already had a boyfriend: a twenty-six-year-old guy named Mike McNatt who owned a motorcycle and worked for a pool cleaning service. "Excellent," I said, when Boris had broken this news earlier. "We ought to get him out here to help with the vacuuming." I was sick and tired of looking after the swimming pool (a job that had fallen largely to me), especially since Xandra never brought home enough chemicals or the right kind.

Boris wiped his eyes with the heels of his hands. "It's serious, Potter. I think she's scared of him. She wants to break up with him but she's afraid. She's trying to talk him into going to a military recruiter."

"You'd better be careful that guy doesn't come after you."

"Me!" He snorted. "It's her I'm worried about! She's so tiny! Eighty-one pounds!"

"Yeah, yeah." Kotku claimed to be a "borderline anorexic" and could always get Boris worked up by saying she hadn't eaten anything all day.

Boris cuffed me on the side of the head. "You sit too much around here on your own," he said, sitting down beside me and putting his feet in the pool. "Come to Kotku's tonight. Bring someone."

"Such as —?"

Boris shrugged. "What about hot little blondie with the boy's haircut, from your history class? The swimmer?"

"Hadley?" I shook my head. "No way."

"Yes! You should! Because she is hot! And she would totally go!"

"Believe me, not a good idea."

"I'll ask her for you! Come on. She's friendly to you, and always talks. Shall we call her?"

"No! It's not that — stop," I said, grabbing his sleeve as he started to get up.

"No guts!"

"Boris." He was heading indoors to the phone. "Don't. I mean it. She won't come."

"And why?"

The taunting edge in his voice annoyed me. "Honestly? Because —" I started to say *Because Kotku is a ho* which was only the obvious truth but instead I said: "Look, Hadley's on Honor Roll and stuff. She's not going to want to go hang out at Kotku's."

"What?" said Boris — spinning back, outraged. "That whore. What'd she say?"

"Nothing. It's just —"

"Yes she did!" He was charging back to the pool now. "You'd better tell me."

"Come on. It's nothing. Chill out, Boris," I said, when I saw how angry he was. "Kotku's tons older. They're not even in the same grade."

"That snub-nosed bitch. What did Kotku ever do to her?"

"Chill *out*." My eye landed on the vodka bottle, illumined by a clean white sunbeam like a light saber. He'd had way too much to drink, and the last thing I wanted was a fight. But I was too drunk myself to think of any funny or easy way to get him off the subject.

···
iii.

LOTS OF OTHER, BETTER girls our own age liked Boris—most notably Saffi Caspersen, who was Danish, spoke English with a high-toned British accent, had a minor role in a Cirque du Soleil production, and was by leaps and bounds the most beautiful girl in our year. Saffi was in Honors English with us (where she'd had some interesting things to say about *The Heart Is a Lonely Hunter*) and though she had a reputation for being standoffish, she liked Boris. Anyone could see it. She laughed when he made jokes, acted goofy in his study group, and I'd seen her talking enthusiastically to him in the hall—Boris talking back just as enthusiastically, in his gesticulating Russian mode. Yet—mysteriously—he didn't seem attracted to her at all.

"But why not?" I asked him. "She's the best-looking girl in our class." I'd always thought that Danes were large and blonde, but Saffi was small-ish and brunette, with a fairy-tale quality that was accentuated by her glit-tery stage makeup in the professional photo I'd seen.

"Good looking yes. But she is not very hot."

"Boris, she is *smoking* hot. Are you crazy?"

"Ah, she works too hard," said Boris, dropping down beside me with a beer in one hand, reaching for my cigarette with the other. "Too straight. All the time studying or rehearsing or something. Kotku—" he blew out a cloud of smoke, handed the cigarette back to me—"she's like us."

I was silent. How had I gone from AP everything to being lumped in with a derelict like Kotku?

Boris nudged me. "I think you like her yourself. Saffi."

"No, not really."

"You do. Ask her out."

"Yeah, maybe," I said, although I knew I didn't have the nerve. At my old school, where foreigners and exchange students tended to stand politely at the margins, someone like Saffi might have been more accessi-ble but in Vegas she was much too popular, too surrounded by people—and there was also the biggish problem of what to ask her to do. In New York it would have been easy enough; I could have taken her ice skating, asked her to a movie or the planetarium. But I could scarcely see Saffi Caspersen sniffing glue or drinking beer from paper bags at the play-ground or doing any of the things that Boris and I did together.

iv.

I STILL SAW HIM — just not as much. More and more he spent nights with Kotku and her mother at the Double R Apartments — a transient hotel really, a broken down motor court from the 1950s, on the highway between the airport and the Strip, where guys who looked like illegal immigrants stood around the courtyard by the empty swimming pool and argued over motorcycle parts. ("Double R?" said Hadley. "You know what that stands for, right? 'Rats and Roaches.'") Kotku, mercifully, didn't accompany Boris to my house all that much, but even when she wasn't around he talked about her constantly. Kotku had cool taste in music and had made him a mix CD with a bunch of smoking hot hip-hop that I really had to listen to. Kotku liked her pizza with green peppers and olives only. Kotku really *really* wanted an electronic keyboard — also a Siamese kitten, or maybe a ferret, but wasn't allowed to have pets at the Double R. "Serious, you need to spend more time with her, Potter," he said, bumping my shoulder with his. "You'll like her."

"Oh come on," I said, thinking of the smirky way she behaved around me — laughing at the wrong time, in a nasty way, always commanding me to go to the fridge to fetch her beers.

"No! She likes you! She does! I mean, she thinks of you more as a little brother. That's what she said."

"She never says a word to me."

"That's because you don't talk to her."

"Are you guys screwing?"

Boris made an impatient noise, the sound he made when things didn't go his way.

"Dirty mind," he said, tossing the hair out of his eyes, and then: "What? What do you think? Do you want me to make you a map?"

"*Draw* you a map."

"Eh?"

"That's the phrase. 'Do you want me to draw you a map.'"

Boris rolled his eyes. Waving his hands around, he started in again about how intelligent Kotku was, how "crazy smart," how wise she was and how much life she had lived and how unfair I was to judge her and look down on her without bothering to get to know her; but while I sat half listening to him talk, and half watching an old noir movie on television (*Fallen Angel,* Dana Andrews), I couldn't help thinking about how he'd met Kotku in what was essentially Remedial Civics, the section for students who weren't smart enough (even in our extremely non-demanding school) to pass without extra help. Boris—good at mathematics without trying and better in languages than anyone I'd ever met—had been forced into Civics for Dummies because he was a foreigner: a school requirement which he greatly resented. ("Because why? Am I likely to be someday voting for Congress?") But Kotku—eighteen! born and raised in Clark County! American citizen, straight off of *Cops!*—had no such excuse.

Over and over, I caught myself in mean-spirited thoughts like this, which I did my best to shake. What did I care? Yes, Kotku was a bitch; yes, she was too dumb to pass regular Civics and wore cheap hoop earrings from the drugstore that were always getting caught in things, and yes, even though she was only eighty-one pounds or whatever she still scared the hell out of me, like she might kick me to death with her pointy-toed boots if she got mad enough. ("She a little fighta nigga," Boris himself had said boastfully at one point as he hopped around throwing out gang signs, or what he thought were gang signs, and regaling me with a story of how Kotku had pulled out a bloody chunk of some girl's hair—this was another thing about Kotku, she was always getting in scary girl fights, mostly with other white trash girls like herself but occasionally with the real gangsta girls, who were Latina and black.) But who cared what crappy girl Boris liked? Weren't we still friends? Best friends? Brothers practically?

Then again: there was not exactly a word for Boris and me. Until Kotku came along, I had never thought too much about it. It was just about drowsy air-conditioned afternoons, lazy and drunk, blinds closed against the glare, empty sugar packets and dried-up orange peels strewn on the carpet, "Dear Prudence" from the White Album (which Boris adored) or else the same mournful old Radiohead over and over:

For a minute
I lost myself, I lost myself…

The glue we sniffed came on with a dark, mechanical roar, like the windy rush of propellers: *engines on!* We fell back on the bed into darkness, like sky divers tumbling backwards out of a plane, although—that high, that far gone — you had to be careful with the bag over your face or else you were picking dried blobs of glue out of your hair and off the end of your nose when you came to. Exhausted sleep, spine to spine, in dirty sheets that smelled of cigarette ash and dog, Popchik belly-up and snoring, subliminal whispers in the air blowing from the wall vents if you listened hard enough. Whole months passed where the wind never stopped, blown sand rattling against the windows, the surface of the swimming pool wrinkled and sinister-looking. Strong tea in the mornings, stolen chocolate. Boris yanking my hair by the handful and kicking me in the ribs. *Wake up, Potter. Rise and shine.*

I told myself I didn't miss him, but I did. I got stoned alone, watched Adult Access and the Playboy channel, read *Grapes of Wrath* and *The House of the Seven Gables* which seemed as if they had to be tied for the most boring book ever written, and for what felt like thousands of hours — time enough to learn Danish or play the guitar if I'd been trying — fooled around in the street with a fucked-up skateboard Boris and I had found in one of the foreclosed houses down the block. I went to swim-team parties with Hadley — no-drinking parties, with parents present — and, on the weekends, attended parents-away parties of kids I barely knew, Xanax bars and Jägermeister shots, riding home on the hissing CAT bus at two a.m. so fucked up that I had to hold the seat in front of me to keep from falling out in the aisle. After school, if I was bored, it was easy enough to go hang out with one of the big lackadaisical stoner crowds who floated around between Del Taco and the kiddie arcades on the Strip.

But still I was lonely. It was Boris I missed, the whole impulsive mess of him: gloomy, reckless, hot-tempered, appallingly thoughtless. Boris pale and pasty, with his shoplifted apples and his Russian-language novels, gnawed-down fingernails and shoelaces dragging in the dust. Boris — budding alcoholic, fluent curser in four languages — who snatched food from my plate when he felt like it and nodded off drunk on the floor, face red like he'd been slapped. Even when he took things without asking, as he all too frequently did — little things were always disappearing, DVDs and school supplies from my locker, more than once I'd caught him going through my pockets for money — his own possessions meant so little to him that somehow it wasn't stealing; whenever he came into cash himself, he split it with me down the middle and anything that belonged to him, he gave me gladly if I asked for it (and sometimes when I didn't, as when

Mr. Pavlikovsky's gold lighter, which I'd admired in passing, turned up in the outside pocket of my backpack).

The funny thing: I'd worried, if anything, that Boris was the one who was a little too affectionate, if *affectionate* is the right word. The first time he'd turned in bed and draped an arm over my waist, I lay there half-asleep for a moment, not knowing what to do: staring at my old socks on the floor, empty beer bottles, my paperbacked copy of *The Red Badge of Courage.* At last—embarrassed—I faked a yawn and tried to roll away, but instead he sighed and pulled me closer, with a sleepy, snuggling motion.

Ssh, Potter, he whispered, into the back of my neck. *Is only me.*

It was weird. Was it weird? It was; and it wasn't. I'd fallen back to sleep shortly after, lulled by his bitter, beery unwashed smell and his breath easy in my ear. I was aware I couldn't explain it without making it sound like more than it was. On nights when I woke strangled with fear there he was, catching me when I started up terrified from the bed, pulling me back down in the covers beside him, muttering in nonsense Polish, his voice throaty and strange with sleep. We'd drowse off in each other's arms, listening to music from my iPod (Thelonious Monk, the Velvet Underground, music my mother had liked) and sometimes wake clutching each other like castaways or much younger children.

And yet (this was the murky part, this was what bothered me) there had also been other, way more confusing and fucked-up nights, grappling around half-dressed, weak light sliding in from the bathroom and everything haloed and unstable without my glasses: hands on each other, rough and fast, kicked-over beers foaming on the carpet—fun and not that big of a deal when it was actually happening, more than worth it for the sharp gasp when my eyes rolled back and I forgot about everything; but when we woke the next morning stomach-down and groaning on opposite sides of the bed it receded into an incoherence of backlit flickers, choppy and poorly lit like some experimental film, the unfamiliar twist of Boris's features fading from memory already and none of it with any more bearing on our actual lives than a dream. We never spoke of it; it wasn't quite real; getting ready for school we threw shoes, splashed water at each other, chewed aspirin for our hangovers, laughed and joked around all the way to the bus stop. I knew people would think the wrong thing if they knew, I didn't want anyone to find out and I knew Boris didn't either, but all the same he seemed so completely untroubled by it that I was fairly sure it was just a laugh, nothing to take too seriously or get worked up about. And yet, more than once, I had wondered if I should step up my nerve and say something: draw some kind of line, make things clear, just to make absolutely sure he didn't have the wrong idea. But the moment had never come. Now there was no point in speaking up and being awkward about the whole thing, though I scarcely took comfort in the fact.

I hated how much I missed him. There was a lot of drinking going on at my house, on Xandra's end anyway, a lot of slammed doors ("Well, if it wasn't me, it *had* to be you," I heard her yelling); and without Boris there (they were both more constrained with Boris in the house) it was harder. Part of the problem was that Xandra's hours at the bar had changed — schedules at her work had been moved; she was under a lot of stress, people she'd worked with were gone, or on different shifts; on Wednesdays and Mondays when I got up for school, I often found her just in from work, sitting alone in front of her favorite morning show too wired to sleep and swigging Pepto-Bismol straight from the bottle.

"Big old exhausted me," she said, with an attempt at a smile, when she saw me on the stairs.

"You should go for a swim. That'll make you sleepy."

"No thanks, I think I'll just hang out here with my Pepto. What a product. This is definitely some bubble-gum flavored awesomeness."

As for my dad: he was spending a lot more time at home — hanging out with me, which I enjoyed, though his mood swings wore me out. It was football season; he had a bounce in his step. After checking his BlackBerry he high-fived me and danced around the living room: "Am I a genius or what? What?" He consulted spread breakdowns, matchup reports, and — occasionally — a paperbacked book called *Scorpio: Your Sports Year in Forecast.* "Always looking for an edge," he said, when I found him running down the tables and punching out numbers on the calculator like he was figuring out his income tax. "You only have to hit fifty-three, fifty-four percent to grind out a good living on this stuff — see, baccarat is strictly for entertainment, there's no skill to it, I set myself limits and never go over, but you can really make money at the sports book if you're disciplined about it. You have to approach it like an investor. Not like a fan, not even like a gambler because the secret is, the better team usually wins the game and the linemaker is good at setting the number. Your linemaker has got limitations, though, as to public opinion. What he's predicting is not who's going to win but who the general public thinks is going to win. So that margin, between sentimental favorite and actual fact—*fuck,* see that receiver in the end zone, another big one for Pittsburgh right there, we need them to score now like we need a hole in the head—anyway, like I was saying, if I really sit down and do my homework as opposed to Joe Beefburger who picks his team by looking five minutes at the sports page? Who's got the advantage? See, I'm not one of these saps that gets all starry-eyed about the Giants rain or shine—shit, your mother could have told you that. Scorpio is about control—that's me. I'm competitive. Want to win at any price. That's where my acting came from, back when I acted. Sun in Scorpio, Leo rising. All in my chart. Now you're a Cancer, hermit crab, all secretive and up in your shell, completely different MO. It's not bad, it's not good, it's just how it is. Anyway, whatever, I always take my lead from my defensive-offensive lines, but all the same it never hurts to pay attention to these transits and solar-arc progressions on game day—"

"Did Xandra get you interested in all this?"

"Xandra? Half the sports book in Vegas has an astrologer on speed dial. Anyway, like I was saying, all other things equal, do the planets make a difference? Yes. I would definitely have to say yes. It's like, is a player having a good day, is he having a bad day, is he out of sorts, whatever. Honestly it helps to have that edge when you're getting a little, how do I put it, ha ha, *stretched,* although—" he showed me the fat wad of what looked like hundreds, wrapped with a rubber band—"this has been a really amazing year for me. Fifty-three percent, a thousand plays a year. That's the magic spot."

Sundays were what he called major-ticket days. When I got up, I found him downstairs in a crackle of strewn newspapers, zinging around bright and restless like it was Christmas morning, opening and shutting cabinets, talking to the sports ticker on his BlackBerry and crunching on corn chips straight from the bag. If I came down and watched with him for even a little while when the big games were on sometimes he'd give me what he called "a piece—" twenty bucks, fifty, if he won. "To get you interested," he explained, leaning forward on the sofa, rubbing his hands anxiously. "See—what we need is for the Colts to get wiped off the map during this first half of the game. Devastated. And with the Cowboys and the Niners we need the score to go over thirty in the second half—yes!" he shouted, jumping up exhilarated with raised fist. "Fumble! Redskins got the ball. We're in business!"

But it was confusing, because it was the Cowboys who had fumbled.

I'd thought the Cowboys were supposed to win by at least fifteen. His mid-game switches in loyalty were too abrupt for me to follow and I often embarrassed myself by cheering for the wrong team; yet as we surged randomly between games, between spreads, I enjoyed his delirium and the daylong binge of greasy food, accepted the twenties and fifties he tossed at me as if they'd fallen from the sky. Other times—cresting and then tanking on some hoarse wave of enthusiasm—a vague unease took hold of him which as far as I could tell had nothing very much to do with how his games were going and he paced back and forth for no reason I could discern, hands folded atop his head, staring at the set with the air of a man unhinged by business failure: talking to the coaches, the players, asking what the hell was wrong with them, what the hell was happening. Sometimes he followed me into the kitchen, with an oddly supplicant demeanor. "I'm getting killed in there," he said, humorously, leaning on the counter, his bearing comical, something in his hunched posture suggesting a bank robber doubled over from a gunshot wound.

Lines x. Lines y. Yards run, cover the spread. On game day, until five o'clock or so, the white desert light held off the essential Sunday gloom— autumn sinking into winter, loneliness of October dusk with school the next day—but there was always a long still moment toward the end of those football afternoons where the mood of the crowd turned and everything grew desolate and uncertain, onscreen and off, the sheet-metal glare off the patio glass fading to gold and then gray, long shadows and night falling into desert stillness, a sadness I couldn't shake off, a sense of silent people filing toward the stadium exits and cold rain falling in college towns back east.

The panic that overtook me then was hard to explain. Those game days broke up with a swiftness, a sense of losing blood almost, that reminded me of watching the apartment in New York being boxed up and carted away: groundlessness and flux, nothing to hang on to. Upstairs, with the door of my room shut, I turned all the lights on, smoked weed if I had it, listened to music on my portable speakers—previously unlistened-to music like Shostakovich, and Erik Satie, that I'd put on my iPod for my mother and then never got around to taking off—and I looked at library books: art books, mostly, because they reminded me of her.

The Masterworks of Dutch Painting. Delft: The Golden Age. Drawings by Rembrandt, His Anonymous Pupils and Followers. From looking on the computer at school, I'd seen that there was a book about Carel Fabritius (a tiny book, only a hundred pages) but they didn't have it at the school library and our computer time at school was so closely monitored that I was too paranoid to do any research on line—especially after a thoughtlessly clicked link (*Het Puttertje, The Goldfinch,* 1654) had taken me to a scarily official-looking site called Missing Art Database that required me to sign in with my name and address. I'd been so freaked out at the unexpected sight of the words *Interpol* and *Missing* that I'd panicked and shut down the computer entirely, something we weren't supposed to do. "What have you just done?" demanded Mr. Ostrow the librarian before I was able to get it back up again. He reached over my shoulder and began typing in the password.

"I—" In spite of myself, I was relieved that I hadn't been looking at porn once he began surfing back through the history. I'd meant to buy myself a cheap laptop with the five hundred bucks my dad had given me for Christmas, but somehow that money had gotten away from me—Missing Art, I told myself; no reason to panic over that word *missing,* destroyed art was missing art, wasn't it? Even though I hadn't put down a name, it worried me that I'd tried to check out the database from my school's IP address. For all I knew, the investigators who'd been to see me had kept track, and knew that I was in Vegas; the connection, though small, was real.

The painting was hidden, quite cleverly as I thought, in a clean cotton pillowcase duct-taped to the back of my headboard. I'd learned, from Hobie, how carefully old things had to be handled (sometimes he used white cotton gloves for particularly delicate objects) and I never touched it with my bare hands, only by the edges. I never took it out except when Dad and Xandra weren't there and I knew they wouldn't be back for a while—though even when I couldn't see it I liked knowing it was there for the depth and solidity it gave things, the reinforcement to infrastructure, an invisible, bedrock rightness that reassured me just as it was reassuring to know that far away, whales swam untroubled in Baltic waters and monks in arcane time zones chanted ceaselessly for the salvation of the world.

Taking it out, handling it, looking at it, was nothing to be done lightly. Even in the act of reaching for it there was a sense of expansion, a waft and a lifting; and at some strange point, when I'd looked at it long enough, eyes dry from the refrigerated desert air, all space appeared to vanish between me and it so that when I looked up it was the painting and not me that was real.

1622–1654. Son of a schoolteacher. Fewer than a dozen works accurately attributed to him. According to van Bleyswijck, the city historian of Delft, Fabritius was in his studio painting the sexton of Delft's Oude Kerk when, at half past ten in the morning, the explosion of the powder magazine took place. The body of the painter Fabritius had been pulled from the wreckage of his studio by neighboring burghers, "with great sorrow," the books said, "and no little effort." What held me fast in these brief library-book accounts was the element of chance: random disasters, mine and his, converging on the same unseen point, *the big bang* as my father called it, not with any kind of sarcasm or dismissiveness but instead a respectful acknowledgment for the powers of fortune that governed his own life. You could study the connections for years and never work it out—it was all about things coming together, things falling apart, *time warp,* my mother standing out in front of the museum when time flickered and the light went funny, uncertainties hovering on the edge of a vast brightness. The stray chance that might, or might not, change everything.

Upstairs, the tap water from the bathroom sink was too chlorinated to drink. Nights, a dry wind blew trash and beer cans down the street. Moisture and humidity, Hobie had told me, were the worst things in the world for antiques; on the tall-case clock he'd been repairing when I left, he'd showed me how the wood had been rotted out underneath from the damp ("someone sluicing stone floors with a bucket, you see how soft this wood is, how worn away?")

Time warp: a way of seeing things twice, or more than twice. Just as my dad's rituals, his betting systems, all his oracles and magic were predicated on a field awareness of unseen patterns, so too the explosion in Delft was part of a complex of events that ricocheted into the present. The multiple outcomes could make you dizzy. "The money's not important," said my dad. "All money represents is the energy of the thing, you know? It's how you track it. The flow of chance." Steadily the goldfinch gazed at me, with shiny, changeless eyes. The wooden panel was tiny, "only slightly larger than an A-4 sheet of paper" as one of my art books had pointed out, although all that dates-and-dimensions stuff, the dead textbook info, was as irrelevant in its way as the sports-page stats when the Packers were up by two in the fourth quarter and a thin icy snow had begun to fall on the field. The painting, the magic and aliveness of it, was like that odd airy moment of the snow falling, greenish light and flakes whirling in the cameras, where you no longer cared about the game, who won or lost, but just wanted to drink in that speechless windswept moment. When I looked at the painting I felt the same convergence on a single point: a flickering sun-struck instant that existed now and forever. Only occasionally did I notice the chain on the finch's ankle, or think what a cruel life for a little living creature — fluttering briefly, forced always to land in the same hopeless place.

v.

THE GOOD THING: I was pleased at how nice my dad was being. He'd been taking me out to dinners — nice dinners, at white-tablecloth restaurants, just the two of us — at least once a week. Sometimes he invited Boris to come, invitations Boris always jumped to accept — the lure of a good meal was powerful enough to override even the gravitational tug of Kotku — but strangely, I found myself enjoying it more when it was just my dad and me.

"You know," he said, at one of these dinners when we were lingering late over dessert — talking about school, about all sorts of things (this new, involved dad! where had he come from?) — "you know, I really have enjoyed getting to know you since you've been out here, Theo."

"Well, uh, yeah, me too," I said, embarrassed but also meaning it.

"I mean —" my dad ran a hand through his hair — "thanks for giving me a second chance, kiddo. Because I made a huge mistake. I never should have let my relationship with your mother get in the way of my relationship with you. No, no," he said, raising his hand, "I'm not blaming anything on your mom, I'm way past that. It's just that she loved you *so* much, I always felt like kind of an interloper with you guys. Stranger-in-my-own-house kind of thing. You two were so close —" he laughed, sadly — "there wasn't much room for three."

"Well —" My mother and I tiptoeing around the apartment, whispering, trying to avoid him. Secrets, laughter. "I mean, I just —"

"No, no, I'm not asking you to apologize. I'm the dad, I'm the one who should have known better. It's just that it got to be a kind of vicious circle if you know what I mean. Me feeling alienated, bummed-out, drinking a lot. And I never should have let that happen. I missed, like, some really important years in your life. I'm the one that has to live with that."

"Um—" I felt so bad I didn't know what to say.

"Not trying to put you on the spot, pal. Just saying I'm glad that we're friends now."

"Well yeah," I said, staring into my scraped-clean crème brûlée plate, "me too."

"And, I mean—I want to make it up to you. See, I'm doing so well on the sports book this year—" my dad took a sip of his coffee—"I want to open you a savings account. You know, just put a little something aside. Because, you know, I really didn't do right by you as far as your mom, you know, and all those months that I was gone."

"Dad," I said, disconcerted. "You don't have to do that."

"Oh, but I want to! You have a Social Security number, don't you?"

"Sure."

"Well, I've already got ten thousand set aside. That's a good start. If you think about it when we get home, give me your Social and next time I drop by the bank, I'll open an account in your name, okay?"

vi.

APART FROM SCHOOL, I'D hardly seen Boris, except for a Saturday afternoon trip when my dad had taken us in to the Carnegie Deli at the Mirage for sable and bialys. But then, a few weeks before Thanksgiving, he came thumping upstairs when I wasn't expecting him and said: "Your dad has been having a bad run, did you know that?"

I put down *Silas Marner,* which we were reading for school. "What?"

"Well, he's been playing at two hundred dollar tables—two hundred dollars a pop," he said. "You can lose a thousand in five minutes, easy."

"A thousand dollars is nothing for him," I said; and then, when Boris did not reply: "How much did he say he lost?"

"Didn't say," said Boris. "But a lot."

"Are you sure he wasn't just bullshitting you?"

Boris laughed. "Could be," he said, sitting on the bed and leaning back on his elbows. "You don't know anything about it?"

"Well—" As far as I knew, my father had cleaned up when the Bills had won the week before. "I don't see how he can be doing *too* bad. He's been taking me to Bouchon and places like that."

"Yes, but maybe is good reason for that," said Boris sagely.

"Reason? What reason?"

Boris seemed about to say something, then changed his mind.

"Well, who knows," he said, lighting a cigarette and taking a sharp drag. "Your dad — he's part Russian."

"Right," I said, reaching for the cigarette myself. I'd often heard Boris and my father, in their arm-waving "intellectual talks," discussing the many celebrated gamblers in Russian history: Pushkin, Dostoyevsky, other names I didn't know.

"Well — very Russian, you know, to complain how bad things are all the time! Even if life is great — keep it to yourself. You don't want to tempt the devil." He was wearing a discarded dress shirt of my father's, washed nearly transparent and so big that it billowed on him like some item of Arab or Hindu costume. "Only, your dad, sometimes is hard to tell between joking and serious." Then, watching me carefully: "What are you thinking?"

"Nothing."

"He knows we talk. That's why he told me. He wouldn't tell me if he didn't want *you* to know."

"Yeah." I was fairly sure this wasn't the case. My dad was the kind of guy who in the right mood would happily discuss his personal life with his boss's wife or some other inappropriate person.

"He'd tell you himself," said Boris, "if he thought you wanted to know."

"Look. Like you said —" My dad had a taste for masochism, the overblown gesture; on our Sundays together, he loved to exaggerate his misfortunes, groaning and staggering, complaining loudly of being 'wiped out' or 'destroyed' after a lost game even as he'd won half a dozen others and was totting up the profits on the calculator. "Sometimes he lays it on a bit thick."

"Well, yes, is true," said Boris sensibly. He took the cigarette back, inhaled, and then, companionably, passed it to me. "You can have the rest."

"No, thanks."

There was a bit of a silence, during which we could hear the television crowd roar of my dad's football game. Then Boris leaned back on his elbows again and said: "What is there to eat downstairs?"

"Not a motherfucking thing."

"There was leftover Chinese, I thought."

"Not any more. Somebody ate it."

"Shit. Maybe I'll go to Kotku's, her mom has frozen pizzas. You want to come?"

"No, thanks."

Boris laughed, and threw out some fake-looking gang sign. "Suit yourself, yo," he said, in his "gangsta" voice (discernible from his regular voice only by the hand gesture and the "yo") as he got up and roll-walked out. "Nigga gotz to eat."

vii.

THE PECULIAR THING ABOUT Boris and Kotku was how rapidly their relationship had taken on a punchy, irritable quality. They still made out constantly, and could hardly keep their hands off each other, but the minute they opened their mouths it was like listening to people who had been married fifteen years. They bickered over small sums of money, like who had paid for their food-court lunches last; and their conversations, when I could overhear them, went something like this:

Boris: "What! I was trying to be nice!"

Kotku: "Well, it wasn't very nice."

Boris, running to catch up with her: "I mean it, Kotyku! Honest! Was only trying to be nice!"

Kotku: [pouting]

Boris, trying unsuccessfully to kiss her: "What did I do? What's the matter? Why do you think I'm not nice any more?"

Kotku: [silence]

The problem of Mike the pool man—Boris's romantic rival—had been solved by Mike's extremely convenient decision to join the Coast Guard. Kotku, apparently, still spent hours on the phone with him every week, which for whatever reason didn't trouble Boris ("She's only trying to support him, see"). But it was disturbing how jealous he was of her at school. He knew her schedule by heart and the second our classes were over he raced to find her, as if he suspected her of two-timing him during Spanish for the Workplace or whatever. One day after school, when Popper and I were by ourselves at home, he telephoned me to ask: "Do you know some guy named Tyler Olowska?"

"No."

"He's in your American History class."

"Sorry. It's a big class."

"Well, look. Can you find out about him? Where he lives maybe?"

"Where he *lives*? Is this about Kotku?"

All of a sudden — surprising me greatly — the doorbell rang: four stately chimes. In all my time in Las Vegas no one had ever rung the doorbell of our house, not even once. Boris, on the other end, had heard it too. "What is that?" he said. The dog was running in circles and barking his head off.

"Someone at the door."

"The *door*?" On our deserted street — no neighbors, no garbage pickup, no streetlights even — this was a major event. "Who do you think it is?"

"I don't know. Let me call you back."

I grabbed up Popchyk — who was practically hysterical — and (as he wriggled and shrieked in my arms, struggling to get down) managed to get the door open with one hand.

"Wouldja look at that," a pleasant, Jersey-accented voice said. "What a cute little fella."

I found myself blinking up in the late afternoon glare at a very tall, very very tanned, very thin man, of indeterminate age. He looked partly like a rodeo guy and partly like a fucked-up lounge entertainer. His gold-rimmed aviators were tinted purple at the top; he was wearing a white sports jacket over a red cowboy shirt with pearl snaps, and black jeans, but the main thing I noticed was his hair: part toupee, part transplanted or sprayed-on, with a texture like fiberglass insulation and a dark brown color like shoe polish in the tin.

"Go on, put him down!" he said, nodding at Popper, who was still struggling to get away. His voice was deep, and his manner calm and friendly; except for the accent he was the perfect Texan, boots and all. "Let him run around! I don't mind. I love dogs."

When I let Popchyk loose, he stooped to pat his head, in a posture reminiscent of a lanky cowboy by the campfire. As odd as the stranger looked, with the hair and all, I couldn't help but admire how easy and comfortable he seemed in his skin.

"Yeah, yeah," he said. "Cute little fella. Yes you are!" His tanned cheeks had a wrinkled, dried-apple quality, creased with tiny lines. "Have three of my own at home. Mini pennys."

"Excuse me?"

He stood; when he smiled at me, he displayed even, dazzlingly white teeth.

"Miniature pinschers," he said. "Neurotic little bastards, chew the house to pieces when I'm gone, but I love them. What's your name, kid?"

"Theodore Decker," I said, wondering who he was.

Again he smiled; his eyes behind the semi-dark aviators were small and twinkly. "Hey! Another New Yorker! I can hear it in your voice, am I right?"

"That's right."

"A Manhattan boy, that would be my guess. Correct?"

"Right," I said, wondering exactly what it was in my voice that he'd heard. No one had ever guessed I was from Manhattan just from hearing me talk.

"Well, hey — I'm from Canarsie. Born and bred. Always nice to meet another guy from back East. I'm Naaman Silver." He held out his hand.

"Nice to meet you, Mr. Silver."

"Mister!" He laughed fondly. "I love a polite kid. They don't make many like you any more. You Jewish, Theodore?"

"No, sir," I said, and then wished I'd said yes.

"Well, tell you what. Anybody from New York, in my book they're an honorary Jew. That's how I look at it. You ever been to Canarsie?"

"No, sir."

"Well, it used to be a fantastic community back in the day, though now —" He shrugged. "My family, they were there for four generations. My grandfather Saul ran one of the first kosher restaurants in America, see. Big, famous place. Closed when I was a kid, though. And then my mother moved us over to Jersey after my father died so we could be closer to my uncle Harry and his family." He put his hand on his thin hip and looked at me. "Your dad here, Theo?"

"No."

"No?" He looked past me, into the house. "That's a shame. Know when he'll be back?"

"No, sir," I said.

"*Sir*. I like that. You're a good kid. Tell you what, you remind me of myself at your age. Fresh from yeshiva —" he held up his hands, gold bracelets on the tanned, hairy wrists — "and these hands? White, like milk. Like yours."

"Um" — I was still standing awkwardly in the door — "would you like to come in?" I wasn't sure if I should invite a stranger in the house, except I was lonely and bored. "You can wait if you want. But I'm not sure when he'll be home."

Again, he smiled. "No thanks. I have a bunch of other stops to make. But I'll tell you what, I'm gonna be straight with you, because you're a nice kid. I got five points on your dad. You know what that means?"

"No, sir."

"Well, bless you. You don't need to know, and I hope you never do know. But let me just say it aint a good business policy." He put a friendly hand on my shoulder. "Believe it or not, Theodore, I got people skills. I don't like to come to a man's home and deal with his child, like I'm doing with you now. That's not right. Normally I would go to your dad's place of work and we would have our little sit-down there. Except he's kind of a hard man to run down, as maybe you already know."

In the house I could hear the telephone ringing: Boris, I was fairly sure. "Maybe you better go answer that," said Mr. Silver pleasantly.

"No, that's okay."

"Go ahead. I think maybe you should. I'll be waiting right here."

Feeling increasingly disturbed I went back in and answered the telephone. As predicted, it was Boris. "Who was that?" he said. "Not Kotku, was it?"

"No. Look —"

"I think she went home with that Tyler Olowska guy. I got this funny feeling. Well, maybe she didn't go *home* home with him. But they left school together — she was talking to him in the parking lot. See, she has her last class with him, woodwork skills or whatever —"

"Boris, I'm sorry, I *really* can't talk now, I'll call you back, okay?"

"I'm taking your word for it that wasn't your dad in there on the horn," said Mr. Silver when I returned to the door. I looked past him, to the white Cadillac parked by the curb. There were two men in the car — a driver, and another man in the front seat. "That wasn't your dad, right?"

"No sir."

"You would tell me if it was, wouldn't you?"

"Yes sir."

"Why don't I believe you?"

I was silent, not knowing what to say.

"Doesn't matter, Theodore." Again, he stooped to scratch Popper behind the ears. "I'll run him down sooner or later. You'll be sure to remember what I told him? And that I stopped by?"

"Yes sir."

He pointed a long finger at me. "What's my name again?"

"Mr. Silver."

"Mr. Silver. That's right. Just checking."

"What do you want me to tell him?"

"Tell him I said gambling's for tourists," he said. "Not locals." Lightly, lightly, with his thin brown hand, he touched me on the top of the head. "God bless."

viii.

WHEN BORIS SHOWED UP at the door around half an hour later, I tried to tell him about the visit from Mr. Silver, but though he listened, a little, mainly he was furious at Kotku for flirting with some other boy, this Tyler Olowska or whatever, a rich stoner kid a year older than us who was on the golf team. "Fuck her," he said throatily while we were sitting on the floor downstairs at my house smoking Kotku's pot. "She's not answering her phone. I know she's with him now, I *know* it."

"Come on." As worried as I was about Mr. Silver, I was even more sick of talking about Kotku. "He was probably just buying some weed."

"Yah, but is more to it, I *know*. She never wants me to stay over with her any more, have you noticed that? Always has *stuff to do* now. She's not even wearing the necklace I bought her."

My glasses were lopsided and I pushed them back up on the bridge of my nose. Boris hadn't even bought the stupid necklace but shoplifted it at the mall, snatching it and running out while I (upstanding citizen, in school blazer) occupied the salesgirl's attention with dumb but polite questions about what Dad and I ought to get Mom for her birthday. "Huh," I said, trying to sound sympathetic.

Boris scowled, his brow like a thundercloud. "She's a whore. Other day? Was pretending to cry in class—trying to make this Olowska bastard feel *sorry* for her. What a cunt."

I shrugged—no argument from me on that point—and passed him the reefer.

"She only likes him because he has money. His family has two Mercedes. E class."

"That's an old lady car."

"Nonsense. In Russia, is what mobsters drive. And—" he took a deep hit, holding it in, waving his hands, eyes watering, *wait, wait, this is the best part, hold on, get this, would you?* — "you know what he calls her?"

"Kotku?" Boris was so insistent about calling her Kotku that people at school—teachers, even—had begun calling her Kotku as well.

"That's right!" said Boris, outraged, smoke erupting from his mouth. "*My* name! The kliytchka *I* gave her. And, other day in the hallway? I saw him ruffle her on the head."

There were a couple of half-melted peppermints from my dad's pocket on the coffee table, along with some receipts and change, and I unwrapped one and put it in my mouth. I was as high as a paratrooper and the sweetness tingled all through me, like fire. "Ruffled her?" I said, the candy clicking loudly against my teeth. "Come again?"

"Like this," he said, making a tousling motion with his hand as he took one last hit off the joint and stubbed it out. "Don't know the word."

"I wouldn't worry about it," I said, rolling my head back against the couch. "Say, you ought to try one of these peppermints. They taste really great."

Boris scrubbed a hand down his face, then shook his head like a dog throwing off water. "Wow," he said, running both hands through his tangled-up hair.

"Yeah. Me too," I said, after a vibrating pause. My thoughts were stretched-out and viscid, slow to wade to the surface.

"What?"

"I'm fucked up."

"Oh yeah?" He laughed. "How fucked up?"

"Pretty far up there, pal." The peppermint on my tongue felt intense and huge, the size of a boulder, like I could hardly talk with it in my mouth.

A peaceful silence followed. It was about five thirty in the afternoon but the light was still pure and stark. Some white shirts of mine were hanging outside by the pool and they were dazzling, billowing and flapping like sails. I closed my eyes, red burning through my eyelids, sinking back into the (suddenly very comfortable) couch as if it were a rocking boat, and thought about the Hart Crane we'd been reading in English. Brooklyn Bridge. How had I never read that poem back in New York? And how had I never paid attention to the bridge when I saw it practically every day? Seagulls and dizzying drops. *I think of cinemas, panoramic sleights...*

"I could strangle her," Boris said abruptly.

"What?" I said, startled, having heard only the word *strangle* and Boris's unmistakably ugly tone.

"Scrawny fucking bint. She makes me so mad." Boris nudged me with his shoulder. "Come on, Potter. Wouldn't you like to wipe that smirk off her face?"

"Well..." I said, after a dazed pause; clearly this was a trick question. "What's a bint?"

"Same as a cunt, basically."

"Oh."

"I mean, who does she."

"Right."

There followed a long and weird enough silence that I thought about getting up and putting some music on, although I couldn't decide what. Anything upbeat seemed wrong and the last thing I wanted to do was put on something dark or angsty that would get him stirred up.

"Um," I said, after what I hoped was a decently long pause, "*The War of the Worlds* comes on in fifteen minutes."

"I'll give her War of the Worlds," said Boris darkly. He stood up.

"Where are you going?" I said. "To the Double R?"

Boris scowled. "Go ahead, laugh," he said bitterly, elbowing on his gray *sovietskoye* raincoat. "It's going to be the Three Rs for your dad if he doesn't pay the money he owes that guy."

"Three Rs?"

"Revolver, roadside, or roof," said Boris, with a black, Slavic-sounding chuckle.

ix.

WAS THAT A MOVIE or something? I wondered. Three Rs? Where had he come up with that? Though I'd done a fairly good job of putting the afternoon's events out of my mind, Boris had thoroughly freaked me out with his parting comment and I sat downstairs rigidly for an hour or so with *War of the Worlds* on but the sound off, listening to the crash of the icemaker and the rattle of wind in the patio umbrella. Popper, who had picked up on my mood, was just as keyed-up as I was and kept barking sharply and hopping off the sofa to check out noises around the house — so that when, not long after dark, a car did actually turn into the driveway, he dashed to the door and set up a racket that scared me half to death.

But it was only my father. He looked rumpled and glazed, and not in a very good mood.

"Dad?" I was still high enough that my voice came out sounding way too blown and odd.

He stopped at the foot of the stairs and looked at me.

"There was a guy here. A Mr. Silver."

"Oh, yeah?" said my dad, casually enough. But he was standing very still with his hand on the banister.

"He said he was trying to get in touch with you."

"When was this?" he said, coming into the room.

"About four this afternoon, I guess."

"Was Xandra here?"

"I haven't seen her."

He lay a hand on my shoulder, and seemed to think for a minute. "Well," he said, "I'd appreciate if you didn't say anything about it."

The end of Boris's joint was, I realized, still in the ashtray. He saw me looking at it, and picked it up and sniffed it.

"Thought I smelled something," he said, dropping it in his jacket pocket. "You reek a bit, Theo. Where have you boys been getting this?"

"Is everything okay?"

My dad's eyes looked a bit red and unfocused. "Sure it is," he said. "I'm just going to go upstairs and make a few calls." He gave off a strong odor of stale tobacco smoke and the ginseng tea he always drank, a habit he'd picked up from the Chinese businessmen in the baccarat salon: it gave his sweat a sharp, foreign smell. As I watched him walk up the steps to the landing, I saw him retrieve the joint-end from his jacket pocket and run it under his nose again, ruminatively.

X.

ONCE I WAS UPSTAIRS in my room, with the door locked, and Popper still edgy and pacing stiffly around — my thoughts went to the painting. I had been proud of myself for the pillowcase-behind-the-headboard idea, but now I realized how stupid it was to have the painting in the house at all — not that I had any options unless I wanted to hide it in the dumpster a few houses down (which had never been emptied the whole time I'd lived in Vegas) or over in one of the abandoned houses across the street. Boris's house was no safer than mine, and there was no one else I knew well enough or trusted. The only other place was school, also a bad idea, but though I knew there had to be a better choice I couldn't think of it. Every so often they had random locker inspections at school and now — connected as I was, through Boris, to Kotku — I was possibly the sort of dirtbag they might randomly inspect. Still, even if someone found it in my locker — whether the principal, or Mr. Detmars the scary basketball coach, or even the Rent-a-Cops from the security firm whom they brought in to scare the students from time to time — still, it would be better than having it found by Dad or Mr. Silver.

The painting, inside the pillowcase, was wrapped in several layers of taped drawing paper — good paper, archival paper, that I'd taken from the art room at school — with an inner, double layer of clean white cotton dishcloth to protect the surface from the acids in the paper (not that there were any). But I'd taken the painting out so often to look at it — opening the top flap of the taped edge to slide it out — that the paper was torn and the tape wasn't even sticky any more. After lying in bed for a few minutes staring at the ceiling, I got up and retrieved the extra-large roll of heavy-duty packing tape left over from our move, and then untaped the pillowcase from behind the headboard.

Too much — too tempting — to have my hands on it and not look at it. Quickly I slid it out, and almost immediately its glow enveloped me, something almost musical, an internal sweetness that was inexplicable beyond a deep, blood-rocking harmony of rightness, the way your heart beat slow and sure when you were with a person you felt safe with and loved. A power, a shine, came off it, a freshness like the morning light in my old bedroom in New York which was serene yet exhilarating, a light that rendered everything sharp-edged and yet more tender and lovely than it actually was, and lovelier still because it was part of the past, and irretrievable: wallpaper glowing, the old Rand McNally globe in half-shadow.

Little bird; yellow bird. Shaking free of my daze I slid it back in the paper-wrapped dishtowel and wrapped it again with two or three (four? five?) of my dad's old sports pages, then — impulsively, really getting into it in my own stoned, determined way — wound it around and around with tape until not a shred of newsprint was visible and the entire X-tra large roll of tape was gone. Nobody was going to be opening that package on a whim. Even if with a knife, a good one, not just scissors, it would take a good long time to get into it. At last, when I was done — the bundle looked like some weird science-fiction cocoon — I slipped the mummified painting, pillowcase and all, in my book bag, and put it under the covers by my feet. Irritably, with a groan, Popper shifted over to make room. Tiny as he was, and ridiculous-looking, still he was a fierce barker and territorial about his place next to me; and I knew if anyone opened the bedroom door while I was sleeping — even Xandra or my dad, neither of whom he liked much — he would jump up and raise the alarm.

What had started as a reassuring thought was once again morphing into thoughts of strangers and break-ins. The air conditioner was so cold I was shaking; and when I closed my eyes I felt myself lifting up out of my body — floating up fast like an escaped balloon — only to startle with a sharp full-body jerk when I opened my eyes. So I kept my eyes shut and tried to remember what I could of the Hart Crane poem, which wasn't much, although even isolated words like *seagull* and *traffic* and *tumult* and *dawn* carried something of its airborne distances, its sweeps from high to low; and just as I was nodding off, I fell into sort of an overpowering sense-memory of the narrow, windy, exhaust-smelling park near our old apartment, by the East River, roar of traffic washing abstractly above as the river swirled with fast, confusing currents and sometimes appeared to flow in two different directions.

xi.

I DIDN'T SLEEP MUCH that night and was so exhausted by the time I got to school and stowed the painting in my locker that I didn't even notice that

Kotku (hanging all over Boris, like nothing had happened) was sporting a fat lip. Only when I heard this tough senior guy Eddie Riso say, "Mack truck?" did I see that somebody had smacked her pretty good in the face. She was going around laughing a bit nervously and telling people that she got hit in the mouth by a car door, but in a sort of embarrassed way that (to me, at least) didn't ring true.

"Did you do that?" I said to Boris, when next I saw him alone (or relatively alone) in English class.

Boris shrugged. "I didn't want to."

"What do you mean, you 'didn't want to'?"

Boris looked shocked. "She made me!"

"She made you," I repeated.

"Look, just because you're jealous of her—"

"Fuck you," I said. "I don't give a shit about you and Kotku—I have things of my own to worry about. You can beat her head in for all I care."

"Oh, God, Potter," said Boris, suddenly sobered. "Did he come back? That guy?"

"No," I said, after a brief pause. "Not yet. Well, I mean, fuck it," I said, when Boris kept on staring at me. "It's *his* problem, not mine. He'll just have to figure something out."

"How much is he in for?"

"No clue."

"Can't you get the money for him?"

"*Me?*"

Boris looked away. I poked him in the arm. "No, what do you mean, Boris? Can't *I* get it for him? What are you talking about?" I said, when he didn't answer.

"Never mind," he said quickly, settling back in his chair, and I didn't have a chance to pursue the conversation because then Spirsetskaya walked into the room, all primed to talk about boring *Silas Marner,* and that was it.

xii.

THAT NIGHT, MY DAD came home early with bags of carry-out from his favorite Chinese, including an extra order of the spicy dumplings I liked — and he was in such a good mood that it was as if I'd dreamed Mr. Silver and the stuff from the night before.

"So —" I said, and stopped. Xandra, having finished her spring rolls, was rinsing glasses at the sink but there was only so much I felt comfortable saying in front of her.

He smiled his big Dad smile at me, the smile that sometimes made stewardesses bump him up to first class.

"So what?" he said, pushing aside his carton of Szechuan shrimp to reach for a fortune cookie.

"Uh —" Xandra had the water up loud — "Did you get everything straightened out?"

"What," he said lightly, "you mean with Bobo Silver?"

"Bobo?"

"Listen, I hope you weren't worried about that. You weren't, were you?"

"Well —"

"Bobo —" he laughed — "they call him 'The Mensch.' He's actually a nice guy — well, you talked to him yourself — we just had some crossed wires, is all."

"What does five points mean?"

"Look, it was just a mix-up. I mean," he said, "these people are characters. They have their own language, their own ways of doing things. But, hey —" he laughed — "this is great — when I met with him over at Caesars, that's what Bobo calls his 'office,' you know, the pool at Caesars — anyway, when I met with him, you know what he kept saying? 'That's a good kid you've got there, Larry.' 'Real little gentleman.' I mean, I don't know what you said to him, but I do actually owe you one."

"Huh," I said in a neutral voice, helping myself to more rice. But inwardly I was almost drunk at the lift in his mood — the same flood of elation I'd felt as a small child when the silences broke, when his footsteps grew light again and you heard him laughing at something, humming at the shaving mirror.

My dad cracked open his fortune cookie, and laughed. "See here," he said, balling it up and tossing it over to me. "I wonder who sits around in Chinatown and thinks up these things?"

Aloud, I read it: "'You have an unusual equipment for fate, exercise with care!'"

"Unusual equipment?" said Xandra, coming up behind to put her arms around his neck. "That sounds kind of dirty."

"Ah —" my dad turned to kiss her. "A dirty mind. The fountain of youth."

"Apparently."

···

xiii.

"I GAVE *you* a fat lip that time," said Boris, who clearly felt guilty about the Kotku business since he'd brought it up out of nowhere in our companionable morning silence on the school bus.

"Yeah, and I knocked your head against the fucking wall."

"I didn't mean to!"

"Didn't mean what?"

"To hit you in the mouth!"

"You meant it with her?"

"In a way, yeah," he said evasively.

"In a way."

Boris made an exasperated sound. "I told her I was sorry! Everything is fine with us now, no problem! And besides, what business is it of yours?"

"*You* brought it up, not me."

He looked at me for an odd, off-centered moment, then laughed. "Can I tell you something?"

"What?"

He put his head close to mine. "Kotku and me tripped last night," he said quietly. "Dropped acid together. It was great."

"Really? Where did you get it?" E was easy enough to find at our school — Boris and I had taken it at least a dozen times, magical speechless nights where we had walked into the desert half-delirious at the stars — but nobody ever had acid.

Boris rubbed his nose. "Ah. Well. Her mom knows this scary old guy named Jimmy that works at a gun shop. He hooked us up with five hits — I don't know why I bought five, I wish I'd bought six. Anyway I still have some. God it was fantastic."

"Oh, yeah?" Now that I looked at him more closely, I realized that his pupils were dilated and strange. "Are you still on it?"

"Maybe a little. I only slept like two hours. Anyway we totally made up. It was like—even the flowers on her mom's bedspread were friendly. And we were made out of the same stuff as the flowers, and we realized how much we loved each other, and needed each other no matter what, and how everything hateful that had happened between us was only out of love."

"Wow," I said, in a voice that I guess must have sounded sadder than I'd intended, from the way that Boris brought his eyebrows together and looked at me.

"Well?" I said, when he kept on staring at me. "What is it?"

He blinked and shook his head. "No, I can just *see* it. This mist of sadness, sort of, around your head. It's like you're a soldier or something, a person from *history,* walking on a battlefield maybe with all these deep feelings…"

"Boris, you're still completely fried."

"Not really," he said dreamily. "I sort of snap in and out of it. But I still see colored sparks coming off things if I look from the corner of my eye just right."

xiv.

A WEEK OR SO passed, without incident, either with my dad or on the Boris-Kotku front—enough time that I felt safe bringing the pillowcase home. I had noticed, when taking it out of my locker, how unusually bulky (and heavy) it seemed, and when I got it upstairs and out of the pillowcase, I saw why. Clearly I'd been blasted out of my mind when I wrapped and taped it: all those layers of newspaper, wound with a whole extra-large roll of heavy-duty, fiber-reinforced packing tape, had seemed like a prudent caution when I was freaked out and high, but back in my room, in the sober light of afternoon, it looked like it had been bound and wrapped by an insane and/or homeless person—mummified, practically: so much tape on it that it wasn't even quite square any more; even the corners were round. I got the sharpest kitchen knife I could find and sawed at a corner—cautiously at first, worried that the knife would slip in and damage the painting—and then more energetically. But I'd gotten only partway through a three-inch section and my hands were starting to get tired when I heard Xandra coming in downstairs, and I put it back in the pillowcase and taped it to the back of my headboard again until I knew they were going to be gone for a while.

Boris had promised me that we would do two of the leftover hits of acid as soon as his mind got back to usual, which was how he put it; he still felt a bit spaced-out, he confided, saw moving patterns in the fake wood-grain of his desk at school, and the first few times he'd smoked weed he'd started out-and-out tripping again.

"That sounds kind of intense," I said.

"No, it's cool. I can make it stop when I want to. I think we should take it at the playground," he added. "On Thanksgiving holiday maybe." The abandoned playground was where we'd gone to take E every time but the first, when Xandra came beating on my bedroom door asking us to help her fix the washing machine, which of course we weren't able to do, but forty-five minutes of standing around with her in the laundry room during the best part of the roll had been a tremendous bringdown.

"Is it going to be a lot stronger than E?"

"No—well, yes, but is wonderful, trust me. I kept wanting Kotku and me to be outside in the air except was *too much* that close to the high-way, lights, cars—maybe this weekend?"

So that was something to look forward to. But just as I was starting to feel good and even hopeful about things again—ESPN hadn't been on for a week, which was definitely some kind of record—I found my father waiting for me when I got home from school.

"I need to talk to you, Theo," he said, the moment I walked in. "Do you have a minute?"

I paused. "Well, okay, sure." The living room looked almost as if it had been burgled—papers scattered everywhere, even the cushions on the sofa slightly out of place.

He stopped pacing—he was moving a bit stiffly, as if his knee hurt him. "Come over here," he said, in a friendly voice. "Sit down."

I sat. My dad exhaled; he sat down across from me and ran a hand through his hair.

"The lawyer," he said, leaning forward with his clasped hands between his knees and meeting my eye frankly.

I waited.

"Your mom's lawyer. I mean—I know this is short notice, but I really need you to get on the phone with him for me."

It was windy; outside, blown sand rattled against the glass doors and the patio awning flapped with a sound like a flag snapping. "What?" I said, after a cautious pause. She'd spoken of seeing a lawyer after he left — about a divorce, I figured — but what had come of it, I didn't know.

"Well —" My dad took a deep breath; he looked at the ceiling. "Here's the thing. I guess you've noticed I haven't been betting my sports anymore, right? Well," he said, "I want to quit. While I'm ahead, so to speak. It's not —" he paused, and seemed to think — "I mean, quite honestly, I've gotten pretty good at this stuff by doing my homework and being disciplined about it. I crunch my numbers. I don't bet impulsively. And, I mean, like I say, I've been doing pretty good. I've socked away a lot of money these past months. It's just —"

"Right," I said uncertainly, in the silence that followed, wondering what he was getting at.

"I mean, why tempt fate? Because —" hand on heart — "I *am* an alcoholic. I'm the first to admit that. I can't drink *at all*. One drink is too many and a thousand's not enough. Giving up booze was the best thing I ever did. And I mean, with gambling, even with my addictive tendencies and all, it's always been kind of different, sure I've had some scrapes but I've never been like some of these guys that, I don't know, that get so far in that they embezzle money and wreck the family business or whatever. But —" he laughed — "if you don't want a haircut sooner or later, better stop hanging out at the barber shop right?"

"So?" I said cautiously, after waiting for him to continue.

"So — whew." My dad ran both hands through his hair; he looked boyish, dazed, incredulous. "Here's the thing. I'm really wanting to make some big changes right now. Because I have the opportunity to get in on the ground floor of this great business. Buddy of mine has a restaurant. And, I mean, I think it's going to be a *really* great thing for all of us — once in a lifetime thing, actually. You know? Xandra's having such a hard time at work right now with her boss being such a shit and, I don't know, I just think this is going to be a lot more sane."

My dad? A restaurant? "Wow — that's great," I said. "Wow."

"Yeah." My dad nodded. "It's *really* great. The thing is, though, to open a place like this —"

"What kind of restaurant?"

My dad yawned, wiped red eyes. "Oh, you know — just simple American food. Steaks and hamburgers and stuff. Just really simple and well prepared. The thing is, though, for my buddy to get the place open and pay his restaurant taxes—"

"Restaurant taxes?"

"Oh God, yes, you wouldn't believe the kind of fees they've got out here. You've got to pay your restaurant taxes, your liquor-license taxes, liability insurance—it's a huge cash outlay to get a place like this up and running."

"Well." I could see where he was going with this. "If you need the money in my savings account—"

My dad looked startled. "What?"

"You know. That account you started for me. If you need the money, that's fine."

"Oh yeah." My dad was silent for a moment. "Thanks. I really appreciate that, pal. But actually—" he had stood up, and was walking around—"the thing is, I actually see a really smart way we can do this. Just a short term solution, in order to get the place up and running, you know. We'll make it back in a few weeks—I mean, a place like this, the location and all, it's like having a license to print money. It's just the initial expense. This town is crazy with the taxes and the fees and so forth. I mean—" he laughed, half-apologetically, "you know I wouldn't ask if it wasn't an emergency—"

"Sorry?" I said, after a confused pause.

"I mean, like I was saying, I really need you to make this call for me. Here's the number." He had it all written out for me on a sheet of paper— a 212 number, I noticed. "You need to telephone this guy and speak to him yourself. His name is Bracegirdle."

I looked at the paper, and then at my dad. "I don't understand."

"You don't have to understand. All you have to do is say what I tell you."

"What does it have to do with me?"

"Look, just do it. Tell him who you are, need to have a word, business matter, blah blah blah—"

"But—" Who was this person? "What do you want me to say?"

My father took a long breath; he was taking care to control his expression, something he was fairly good at.

"He's a lawyer," he said, on an out breath. "Your mother's lawyer. He needs to make arrangements to wire *this* amount of money—" my eyes popped at the sum he was pointing to, *$65,000*—"into *this* account" (dragging his finger to the string of numbers beneath it). "Tell him I've decided to send you to a private school. He'll need your name and Social Security number. That's it."

"Private school?" I said, after a disoriented pause.

"Well, you see, it's for tax reasons."

"I don't want to go to private school."

"Wait—wait—just hear me out. As long as these funds are used for your benefit, in the official sense, we've got no problem. And the restaurant is for *all* our benefit, see. Maybe, in the end, yours most of all. And I mean, I could make the call myself, it's just that if we angle this the right way we'd be saving like thirty thousand dollars that would go to the government otherwise. Hell, I *will* send you to a private school if you want. Boarding school. I could send you to Andover with all that extra money. I just don't want half of it to end up with the IRS, know what I'm saying? Also—I mean, the way this thing is set up, by the time you end up going to college, it's going to end up costing *you* money, because with that amount of money in there it means you won't be eligible for a scholarship. The college financial aid people are going to look right at that account and put you in a different income bracket and take 75 percent of it the first year, poof. This way, at least, you'll get the full use of it, you see? Right now. When it could actually do some good."

"But—"

"*But—*" falsetto voice, lolled tongue, goofy stare. "Oh, come on, Theo," he said, in his normal voice, when I kept on looking at him. "Swear to God, I don't have time for this. I need you to make this call ASAP, before the offices close back East. If you need to sign something, tell him to FedEx the papers. Or fax them. We just need to get this done as soon as possible, okay?"

"But why do *I* need to do it?"

My dad sighed; he rolled his eyes. "Look, don't give me that, Theo," he said. "I know you know the score because I've seen you checking the mail—yes," he said over my objections, "yes you do, every day you're out at that mailbox like a fucking shot."

I was so baffled by this that I didn't even know how to reply. "But—" I glanced down at the paper and the figure leaped out again: *$65,000*.

Without warning, my dad snapped out and whacked me across the face, so hard and fast that for a second I didn't know what had happened. Then almost before I could blink he hit me again with his fist, cartoon *wham,* bright crack like a camera flash, this time with his fist. As I wobbled — my knees had gone loose, everything white — he caught me by the throat with a sharp upward thrust and forced me up on tiptoe so I was gasping for breath.

"Look here." He was shouting in my face — his nose two inches from mine — but Popper was jumping and barking like crazy and the ringing in my ears had climbed to such a pitch it was like he was screaming at me though radio fuzz. "You're going to call this guy —" rattling the paper in my face — "and say what I fucking tell you. Don't make this any harder than it has to be because I will *make* you do this, Theo, no lie, I will break your arm, I will beat the everloving *shit* out of you if you don't get on the phone right now. Okay? Okay?" he repeated in the dizzy, ear-buzzing silence. His cigarette breath was sour in my face. He let go my throat; he stepped back. "Do you hear me? Say something."

I swiped an arm over my face. Tears were streaming down my cheeks but they were automatic, like tap water, no emotion attached to them.

My dad squeezed his eyes shut, then re-opened them; he shook his head. "Look," he said, in a crisp voice, still breathing hard. "I'm sorry." He didn't *sound* sorry, I noted, in a clear hard remove of my mind; he sounded like he still wanted to beat the shit out of me. "But, I swear, Theo. Just trust me on this. You have to do this for me."

Everything was blurred, and I reached up with both hands to straighten my glasses. My breaths were so loud that they were the noisiest things in the room.

My dad, hand on hips, turned his eyes to the ceiling. "Oh, come on," he said. "Just stop it."

I said nothing. We stood there for another long moment or two. Popper had stopped barking and was looking between us apprehensively like he was trying to figure out what was going on.

"It's just... well you know?" Now he was all reasonable again. "I'm sorry, Theo, I swear I am, but I'm really in a bind here, we need this money right now, this minute, we really do."

He was trying to meet my eyes: his gaze was frank, sensible. "Who is this guy?" I said, looking not at him but at the wall behind his head, my voice for whatever reason coming out scorched-sounding and strange.

"Your mother's lawyer. How many times do I have to tell you?" He was massaging his knuckles like he'd hurt his hand hitting me. "See, the thing is, Theo—" another sigh—"I mean, I'm sorry, but, I swear, I wouldn't be so upset if this wasn't so important. Because I am really, really behind the eight ball here. This is just a temporary thing, you understand— just until the business gets off the ground. Because the whole thing could collapse, just like that—" snapped fingers—"unless I start getting some of these creditors paid off. And the rest of it—I *will* use to send you to a better school. Private school maybe. You'd like that, wouldn't you?"

Already, carried away by his own rap, he was dialing the number. He handed me the telephone and—before anyone answered—dashed over and picked up the extension across the room.

"Hello," I said, to the woman who answered the phone, "um, excuse me," my voice scratchy and uneven, I still couldn't quite believe what was happening. "May I speak to Mr., uh..."

My dad stabbed his finger at the paper: *Bracegirdle.*

"Mr., uh, Bracegirdle," I said, aloud.

"And who may I say is calling?" Both my voice, and hers, were way too loud due to the fact that my dad was listening on the extension.

"Theodore Decker."

"Oh, yes," said the man's voice when he came on the other end. "Hello! Theodore! How are you?"

"Fine."

"You sound like you have a cold. Tell me. Do you have a bit of a cold?"

"Er, yes," I said uncertainly. My dad, across the room, was mouthing the word *Laryngitis.*

"That's a shame," said the echoing voice—so loud that I had to hold the phone slightly away from my ear. "I never think of people catching colds in the sunshine, where you are. At any rate, I'm glad you phoned me—I didn't have a good way to get in touch with you directly. I know things are probably still very hard. But I hope things are better than they were the last time I saw you."

I was silent. I'd met this person?

"It was a bad time," said Mr. Bracegirdle, correctly interpreting my silence.

The velvety, fluent voice struck a chord. "Okay, wow," I said.

"Snowstorm, remember?"

"Right." He'd appeared maybe a week after my mother died: oldish man with a full head of white hair—snappily dressed, striped shirt, bow tie. He and Mrs. Barbour had seemed to know each other, or at any rate he had seemed to know her. He'd sat across from me in the armchair nearest the sofa and talked a lot, confusing stuff, although all that really stuck in my mind was the story he'd told of how he met my mother: massive snowstorm, no taxis in sight—when—preceded by a fan of wet snow—an occupied cab had plowed to the corner of Eighty-Fourth and Park. Window rolled down—my mother ("a vision of loveliness!") going as far as East Fifty-Seventh, was he headed that way?

"She always talked about that storm," I said. My father—phone to his ear—glanced at me sharply. "When the city was shut down that time."

He laughed. "What a lovely young lady! I'd come out of a late meeting—elderly trustee up on Park and Ninety-Second, shipping heiress, now dead alas. Anyway, down I came, from the penthouse to the street—lugging my litigation bag, of course—and a foot had fallen. Perfect silence. Kids were pulling sleds down Park Avenue. Anyway, the trains weren't running above Seventy-Second and there I was, knee deep and trudging, when, whoops! here came a yellow cab with your mother in it! Crunching to a stop. As if she'd been sent by a search party. 'Hop in, I'll give you a ride.' Midtown absolutely deserted...snowflakes whirling down and every light in the city on. And there we were, rolling along at about two miles per hour—we might as well have been in a sleigh—sailing right through the red lights, no point stopping. I remember we talked about Fairfield Porter—there'd just been a show in New York—and then on to Frank O'Hara and Lana Turner and what year they'd finally closed the old Horn and Hardart, the Automat. And then, we discovered that we worked across the street from each other! It was the beginning of a beautiful friendship, as they say."

I glanced over at my dad. He had a funny look on his face, lips pressed tight as if he was about to be sick on the carpet.

"We talked a bit about your mother's estate, if you remember," said the voice on the other end of the phone. "Not much. It wasn't the time. But I had hoped you would come to see me when you were ready to talk. I would have telephoned before you left town if I'd known you were going."

I looked at my dad; I looked at the paper in my hand. "I want to go to private school," I blurted.

"Really?" said Mr. Bracegirdle. "I think that may be an excellent idea. Where were you thinking about going? Back east? Or somewhere out there?"

We hadn't thought this out. I looked at my dad.

"Uh," I said, "uh," while my father grimaced at me and waved his hand frantically.

"There may be good boarding schools out west, though I don't know about them," Mr. Bracegirdle was saying. "I went to Milton, which was a wonderful experience for me. And my oldest son went there too, for a year anyway, though it wasn't at all the right place for him—"

As he talked on—from Milton, to Kent, to various boarding schools attended by children of friends and acquaintances—my dad scribbled a note; he threw it at me. *Wire me the money,* it said. *Down payment.*

"Um," I said, not knowing how else to introduce the subject, "did my mother leave me some money?"

"Well, not exactly," said Mr. Bracegirdle, seeming to cool slightly at the question, or maybe it was just the awkwardness of the interruption. "She was having some financial troubles toward the end, as I'm sure you're well aware. But you do have a 529. And she also set up a little UTMA for you right before she died."

"What is that?" My dad—his eyes on me—was listening very closely.

"Uniform Transfer to Minors. It's to be used for your education. But it can't be used for anything else—not while you're still a minor, anyway."

"Why can't it?" I said, after a brief pause, as he had seemed to stress the final point so much.

"Because it's the law," he said curtly. "But certainly something can be worked out if you want to go away to school. I know of a client who used part of her eldest son's 529 for a fancy kindergarten for her youngest. Not that I think twenty thousand dollars a year is a prudent expenditure at that level—the most expensive crayons in Manhattan, surely—! But yes, so you understand, that's how it works."

I looked at my dad. "So there's no way you could, say, wire me sixty-five thousand dollars," I said. "If I needed it right this minute."

"No! Absolutely not! So just put that out of your mind." His manner had changed—clearly he'd revised his opinion of me, no longer my mother's son and A Good Kid but a grasping little creep. "By the way, may I ask how you happened to arrive at that particular figure?"

"Er—" I glanced at my dad, who had a hand over his eyes. *Shit,* I thought, and then realized I'd said it out loud.

"Well, no matter," said Mr. Bracegirdle silkily. "It's simply not possible."

"No way?"

"No way, no how."

"Okay, fine—" I tried hard to think, but my mind was running in two directions at once. "Could you send me part of it, then? Like half?"

"No. It would all have to be arranged directly with the college or school of your choice. In other words, I'm going to need to see bills, and pay bills. There's a lot of paperwork, as well. And in the unlikely event you decide *not* to attend college..."

As he talked on, confusingly, about various ins and outs of the funds my mother had set up for me (all of which were fairly restrictive, as far as either my father or me getting our hands immediately on actual, spend-able cash) my dad, holding the phone out from his ear, had something very like an expression of horror on his face.

"Well, uh, that's good to know, thank you sir," I said, trying hard to wrap up the conversation.

"There are tax advantages of course. Setting it up like this. But what she really wanted was to make sure your father would never be able to touch it."

"Oh?" I said, uncertainly, in the overly long silence that followed. Something in his tone had made me suspect that he knew my father might be the Lord Vader-ish presence breathing audibly (audibly to me— whether audibly to him I don't know) on the other line.

"There are other considerations, as well. I mean—" decorous silence—"I don't know if I ought to tell you this, but an unauthorized party has twice tried to make a large withdrawal on the account."

"What?" I said, after a sick pause.

"You see," said Mr. Bracegirdle, his voice as distant as if it were coming from the bottom of the sea, "I'm the custodian on the account. And about two months after your mother died, someone walked in the bank in Man-hattan during business hours and tried to forge my signature on the papers. Well, they know me at the main branch, and they called me right away, but while they were still on the phone with me the man slipped out the door, before the security guard was able to approach and ask for ID.

That was, my goodness, nearly two years ago. But then—only last week—did you get the letter I wrote you about this?"

"No," I said, when at last I realized I needed to say something.

"Well, without going into it too much, there was a peculiar phone call. From someone purporting to be your attorney out there, requesting a transfer of funds. And then—checking into it—we found out that some party with access to your Social Security number had applied for, and received, a rather large line of credit in your name. Do you happen to know anything about that?

"Well, not to worry," he continued, when I didn't say anything. "I have a copy of your birth certificate here, and I faxed it to the issuing bank and had the line shut down immediately. And I've alerted Equifax and all the credit agencies. Even though you're a minor, and legally unable to enter into such a contract, you could be responsible for any such debts incurred in your name once you come of age. At any rate, I urge you to be very careful with your Social Security number in future. It's possible to have a new Social issued, in theory, although the red tape is such a headache that I don't suggest it..."

I was in a cold sweat when I hung up the telephone—and completely unprepared for the howl that my father let out. I thought he was angry—angry at me—but when he just stood there with the phone still in his hand, I looked at him a little closer and realized he was crying.

It was horrible. I had no idea what to do. He sounded like he'd had boiling water poured over him—like he was turning into a werewolf—like he was being tortured. I left him there and—Popchik hurrying up the stairs ahead of me; clearly he didn't want any part of this howling, either—went in my room and locked the door and sat on the side of my bed with my head in my hands, wanting aspirin but not wanting to go down to the bathroom to get it, wishing Xandra would hurry up and come home. The screams from downstairs were ungodly, like he was being burned with a blow torch. I got my iPod, tried to find some loud-ish music that wasn't upsetting (Shostakovich's Fourth, which though classical actually *was* a bit upsetting) and lay on my bed with the earbuds in and stared at the ceiling, while Popper stood with his ears up and stared at the closed door, the hairs on his neck erect and bristling.

XV.

"He told me you had a fortune," said Boris, later that night at the playground, while we were sitting around waiting for the drugs to work. I slightly wished we had picked another night to take them, but Boris had insisted it would make me feel better.

"You believed I had a fortune, and wouldn't tell you?" We'd been sitting on the swings for what seemed like forever, waiting for just what I didn't know.

Boris shrugged. "I don't know. There are a lot of things you don't tell me. I would have told *you*. It's all right, though."

"I don't know what to do." Though it was very subtle, I'd begun to notice glittering gray kaleidoscope patterns turning sluggishly in the gravel by my foot — dirty ice, diamonds, sparkles of broken glass. "Things are getting scary."

Boris nudged me. "There's something I didn't tell you either, Potter."

"What?"

"My dad has to leave. For his job. He's going back to Australia in a few months. Then on, I think, to Russia."

There was a silence that maybe lasted five seconds, but felt like it lasted an hour. Boris? Gone? Everything seemed frozen, like the planet had stopped.

"Well, *I'm* not going," said Boris serenely. His face in the moonlight had taken on an unnerving electrified flicker, like a black-and-white film from the silent era. "Fuck that. I'm running away."

"Where?"

"Dunno. Do you want to come?"

"Yes," I said, without thinking, and then: "Is Kotku going?"

He grimaced. "I don't know." The filmic quality had become so stage-lit and stark that all semblance of real life had vanished; we'd been neutralized, fictionalized, flattened; my field of vision was bordered by a black rectangle; I could see the subtitles running at the bottom of what he was saying. Then, at almost exactly the same time, the bottom dropped out of my stomach. *Oh, God,* I thought, running both hands through my hair and feeling way too overwhelmed to explain what I was feeling.

Boris was still talking, and I realized if I didn't want to be lost forever in this grainy Nosferatu world, sharp shadows and achromatism, it was important to listen to him and not get so hung up on the artificial texture of things.

"...I mean, I guess I understand," he was saying mournfully, as speckles and raindrops of decay danced all around him. "With her it's not even running away, she's of age, you know? But she lived on the street once and didn't like it."

"Kotku lived on the street?" I felt an unexpected surge of compassion for her — orchestrated somehow, with a cinematic music swell almost, although the sadness itself was perfectly real.

"Well, I have too, in Ukraine. But I would be with my friends Maks and Seryozha — never more than few days at a time. Sometimes it was good fun. We'd kip in basement of abandoned buildings — drink, take butorphanol, build campfires even. But I always went home when my dad sobered up. With Kotku though, it was different. This one boyfriend of her mother's — he was doing stuff to her. So she left. Slept in doorways. Begged for change — blew guys for money. Was out of school for a while — she was brave to come back, to try and finish, after what happened. Because, I mean, people say stuff. You know."

We were silent, contemplating the awfulness of this, me feeling as if I had experienced in these few words the entire weight and sweep of Kotku's life, and Boris's.

"I'm sorry I don't like Kotku!" I said, really meaning it.

"Well, I'm sorry too," said Boris reasonably. His voice seemed to be going straight to my brain without passing my ears. "But she doesn't like you either. She thinks you're spoiled. That you haven't been through nearly the kind of stuff that she and I have."

This seemed like a fair criticism. "That seems fair," I said.

Some weighty and flickering interlude of time seemed to pass: trembling shadows, static, hiss of unseen projector. When I held out my hand and looked at it, it was dust-speckled and bright like a decaying piece of film.

"Wow, I'm seeing it too now," said Boris, turning to me — a sort of slowed-down, hand-cranked movement, fourteen frames per second. His face was chalk pale and his pupils were dark and huge.

"Seeing—?" I said carefully.

"You know." He waved his floodlit, black-and-white hand in the air. "How it's all flat, like a movie."

"But you—" It wasn't just me? He saw it, too?

"Of course," said Boris, looking less and less like a person every moment, and more like some degraded piece of silver nitrate stock from the 1920s, light shining behind him from some hidden source. "I wish we'd got something color though. Like maybe 'Mary Poppins.'"

When he said this, I began to laugh uncontrollably, so hard I nearly fell off the swing, because I knew then for sure he saw the same thing I did. More than that: we were *creating* it. Whatever the drug was making us see, we were constructing it together. And, with that realization, the virtual-reality simulator flipped into color. It happened for both of us at the same time, pop! We looked at each other and just laughed; everything was hysterically funny, even the playground slide was smiling at us, and at some point, deep in the night, when we were swinging on the jungle gym and showers of sparks were flying out of our mouths, I had the epiphany that laughter was light, and light was laughter, and that this was the secret of the universe. For hours, we watched the clouds rearranging themselves into intelligent patterns; rolled in the dirt, believing it was seaweed (!); lay on our backs and sang "Dear Prudence" to the welcoming and appreciative stars. It was a fantastic night—one of the great nights of my life, actually, despite what happened later.

xvi.

BORIS STAYED OVER AT my house, since I lived closer to the playground and he was (in his own favorite term for loadedness) *v gavno,* which meant "shit-faced" or "in shit" or something of the sort—at any rate, too wrecked to get home on his own in the dark. And this was fortunate, as it meant I wasn't alone in the house at three thirty the next afternoon when Mr. Silver stopped by.

Though we'd barely slept, and were a little shaky, everything still felt the tiniest bit magical and full of light. We were drinking orange juice and watching cartoons (good idea, as it seemed to extend the hilarious Technicolor mood of the evening) and—bad idea—had just shared our second joint of the afternoon when the doorbell rang. Popchyk—who'd been extremely on edge; he sensed that we were off-key somehow and had been barking at us like we were possessed—went off immediately almost as if he'd expected something of the sort.

In an instant, it all came crashing back. "Holy shit," I said.

"*I'll* go," said Boris immediately, tucking Popchyk under his arm. Off he bopped, barefoot and shirtless, with an air of complete unconcern. But in what seemed like one second he was back again, looking ashen.

He didn't say anything; he didn't have to. I got up, put on my sneakers and tied them tight (as I'd gotten in the habit of doing before our shoplifting expeditions, in the event I had to flee), and went to the door. There was Mr. Silver again — white sports coat, shoe-polish hair, and all — only this time standing beside him was a large guy with blurred blue tattoos snaked all over his forearms, holding an aluminum baseball bat.

"Well, Theodore!" said Mr. Silver. He seemed genuinely pleased to see me. "Hiya doing?"

"Fine," I said, marvelling at how un-stoned I suddenly felt. "And you?"

"Can't complain. Quite a bruise you got going on there, pal."

Reflexively, I reached up and touched my cheek. "Uh —"

"Better look after that. Your buddy tells me your Dad's not home."

"Um, that's right."

"Everything okay with you two? You guys having any problems out here this afternoon?"

"Um, no, not really," I said. The guy wasn't brandishing the bat, or being threatening in any way, but still I couldn't help being fairly aware that he had it.

"Because if you ever do?" said Mr. Silver. "Have problems of any nature? I can take care of them for you like *that*."

What was he talking about? I looked past him, out to the street, to his car. Even though the windows were tinted, I could see the other men waiting there.

Mr. Silver sighed. "I'm glad to hear that you don't have any problems, Theodore. I only wish that I could say the same."

"Excuse me?"

"Because here's the thing," he continued, as if I hadn't spoken. "*I* have a problem. A really big one. With your father."

Not knowing what to say, I stared at his cowboy boots. They were black crocodile, with a stacked heel, very pointed at the toe and polished to such a high shine that they reminded me of the girly-girl cowboy boots that Lucie Lobo, a way-out stylist in my mother's office, had always worn.

"You see, here's the thing," said Mr. Silver. "I'm holding fifty grand of your dad's paper. And that is causing some very big problems for me."

"He's getting the money together," I said, awkwardly. "Maybe, I don't know, if you could just give him a little more time..."

Mr. Silver looked at me. He adjusted his glasses.

"Listen," he said reasonably. "Your dad wants to risk his shirt on how some morons handle a fucking ball—I mean, pardon my language. But it's hard for me to have sympathy for a guy like him. Doesn't honor his obligations, three weeks late on the vig, doesn't return my phone calls—" he was ticking off the offenses on his fingers—"makes plans to meet me at noon today and then doesn't show. You know how long I sat and waited for that deadbeat? *An hour and a half.* Like I don't got other, better things to do." He put his head to the side. "It's guys like your dad keep guys like me and Yurko here in business. Do you think I like coming to your house? Driving all the way out here?"

I had thought this was a rhetorical question—clearly no one in their right mind would like driving all the way out where we lived—but since an outrageous amount of time passed, and still he was staring at me like he actually expected an answer, I finally blinked in discomfort and said: "No."

"*No.* That's right, Theodore. I most certainly do not. We got better things to do, me and Yurko, believe me, than spend all afternoon chasing after a deadbeat like your dad. So do me a favor, please, and tell your father we can settle this like gentlemen the second he sits down and works things out with me."

"Work things out?"

"He needs to bring me what he owes me." He was smiling but the gray tint at the top of his aviators gave his eyes a disturbingly hooded look. "And I want you to tell him to do that for me, Theodore. Because next time I have to come out here, believe me, I'm not going to be so nice."

xvii.

WHEN I CAME BACK into the living room Boris was sitting quietly and staring at cartoons with the sound off, stroking Popper—who, despite his earlier upset, was now fast asleep in his lap.

"Ridiculous," he said shortly.

He pronounced the word in such a way that it took me a moment to realize what he'd said. "Right," I said, "I told you he was a freak."

Boris shook his head and leaned back against the couch. "I don't mean the old Leonard Cohen-looking guy with the wig."

"You think that's a wig?"

He made a face like who cares. "Him too, but I mean the big Russian with the, metal, what do you call it?"

"Baseball bat."

"That was just for show," he said disdainfully. "He was just trying to scare you, the prick."

"How do you know he was Russian?"

He shrugged. "Because I know. No one has tattoos like that in U.S. Russian national, no question. He knew I was Russian too, minute I opened my mouth."

Some period of time passed before I realized I was sitting there staring into space. Boris lifted Popchyk and put him down on the sofa, so gently he didn't wake. "You want to get out of here for a while?"

"God," I said, shaking my head suddenly — the impact of the visit had for whatever reason just hit me, a delayed reaction — "fuck, I *wish* my dad had been home. You know? I wish that guy would beat his ass. I really do. He deserves it."

Boris kicked my ankle. His feet were black with dirt and he also had black polish on his toenails, courtesy of Kotku.

"You know what I had to eat yesterday?" he said sociably. "Two Nestlé bars and a Pepsi." All candy bars, for Boris, were 'Nestlé bars,' just as all sodas were 'Pepsi.' "And you know what I had to eat today?" He made a zero with thumb and forefinger. *"Nul."*

"Me neither. This stuff makes you not hungry."

"Yah, but I need to eat something. My stomach—" he made a face.

"Do you want to go get pancakes?"

"Yes — something — I don't care. Do you have money?"

"I'll look around."

"Good. I think I have five dollars maybe."

While Boris was rummaging for shoes and a shirt, I splashed some water on my face, checked out my pupils and the bruise on my jaw, rebuttoned my shirt when I saw it was done up the wrong way, and then went to let Popchik out, throwing his tennis ball to him for a bit, since he hadn't had a proper walk on the leash and I knew he felt cooped-up. When we came back in, Boris—dressed now—was downstairs; we'd done a quick search of the living room and were laughing and joking around, pooling our quarters and dimes and trying to figure out where we wanted to go and the quickest way to get there when all of a sudden we noticed that Xandra had come in the front door and was standing there with a funny look on her face.

Both of us stopped talking immediately and went about our change-sorting in silence. It wasn't a time when Xandra normally came home, but her schedule was erratic sometimes and she'd surprised us before. But then, in an uncertain-sounding voice, she said my name.

We stopped with the change. Generally Xandra called me *kiddo* or *hey you* or anything but Theo. She was, I noticed, still wearing her uniform from work.

"Your dad's had a car accident," she said. It was like she was saying it to Boris instead of me.

"Where?" I said.

"It happened like two hours ago. The hospital called me at work."

Boris and I looked at each other. "Wow," I said. "What happened? Did he total the car?"

"His blood alcohol was .39."

The figure was meaningless to me, though the fact he'd been drinking wasn't. "Wow," I said, pocketing my change, and: "When's he coming home, then?"

She met my eye blankly. "Home?"

"From the hospital."

Rapidly, she shook her head; looked around for a chair to sit in; and then sat in it. "You don't understand." Her face was empty and strange. "He died. He's dead."

xviii.

THE NEXT SIX OR seven hours were a daze. Several of Xandra's friends showed up: her best friend Courtney; Janet from her work; and a couple named Stewart and Lisa who were nicer and way more normal than the usual people Xandra had over to the house. Boris, generously, produced what was left of Kotku's weed, which was appreciated by all parties present; and someone, thankfully (maybe it was Courtney), ordered out for pizza—how she got Domino's to deliver all the way out to us, I don't know, since for over a year Boris and I had wheedled and pleaded and tried every cajolement and excuse we could think of.

While Janet sat with her arm around Xandra, and Lisa patted her head, and Stewart made coffee in the kitchen, and Courtney rolled a joint on the coffee table that was almost as expert as one of Kotku's, Boris and I hung in the background, stunned. It was hard to believe that my dad could be dead when his cigarettes were still on the kitchen counter and his old white tennis shoes were still by the back door. Apparently—it all came out in the wrong order, I had to piece it together in my mind—my dad had crashed the Lexus on the highway, a little before two in the afternoon, veering off on the wrong side of the road and plowing headlong into a tractor-trailer which had immediately killed him (not the driver of the truck, fortunately, or the passengers in the car that had rear-ended the truck, although the driver of the car had a broken leg). The blood-alcohol news was both surprising, and not—I'd suspected my father might be drinking again, though I hadn't seen him doing it—but what seemed to baffle Xandra most was not his extreme drunkenness (he'd been virtually unconscious at the wheel) but the location of the accident—outside Vegas, heading west, into the desert. "He would have told me, he would have told me," she was saying sorrowfully in response to some question or other of Courtney's, only why, I thought bleakly, sitting on the floor with my hands over my eyes, did she think it was in my father's nature to tell the truth about anything?

Boris had his arm over my shoulder. "She doesn't know, does she?"

I knew he was talking about Mr. Silver. "Should I—"

"Where was he going?" Xandra was asking Courtney and Janet, almost aggressively, as if she suspected them of withholding information. "What was he doing all the way over there?" It was strange to see her still in her work uniform, as she usually changed out of it the second she walked in the door.

"He didn't go meet that guy like he was supposed to," whispered Boris.

"I know." Possibly he *had* intended to go to the sit-down with Mr. Silver. But—as my mother and I had so often, so fatally, known him to do — he had probably stopped in a bar somewhere for a quick belt or two, to steady his nerves as he always said. At that point — who knew what might have been going through his mind? nothing helpful to point out to Xandra under the circumstances, but he'd certainly been known to skip town on his obligations before.

I didn't cry. Though cold waves of disbelief and panic kept hitting me, it all seemed highly unreal and I kept glancing around for him, struck again and again by the absence of his voice among the others, that easy, well-reasoned, aspirin-commercial voice (*four out of five doctors...*) that made itself known above all others in a room. Xandra went in and out of being fairly matter-of-fact — wiping her eyes, getting plates for pizza, pouring everybody glasses of the red wine that had appeared from somewhere — and then collapsing in tears again. Popchik alone was happy; it was rare we had so much company in the house and he ran from person to person, undiscouraged by repeated rebuffs. At some bleary point, deep in the evening — Xandra weeping in Courtney's arms for the twentieth time, *oh my God, he's gone, I can't believe it* — Boris pulled me aside and said: "Potter, I have to go."

"No, don't, please."

"Kotku's going to be freaked out. Am supposed to be at her mom's now! She hasn't seen me for like forty-eight hours."

"Look, tell her to come over if she wants — tell her what's happened. It's going to completely suck if you have to leave right now."

Xandra had grown sufficiently distracted with guests and grief that Boris was able to go upstairs to make the call in her bedroom — a room usually kept locked, that Boris and I never saw. In about ten minutes he came skimming rapidly down the steps.

"Kotku said to stay," he said, ducking in to sit beside me. "She told me to say she's sorry."

"Wow," I said, coming close to tears, scrubbing my hand over my face so he wouldn't see how startled and touched I was.

"Well, I mean, she knows how it is. Her dad died too."

"Oh yeah?"

"Yes, a few years ago. In a motor accident, as well. They weren't that close —"

"Who died?" said Janet, swaying over us, a frizzy, silk-bloused presence redolent of weed and beauty products. "Somebody else died?"

"No," I said curtly. I didn't like Janet—she was the ditz who'd volunteered to take care of Popper and then left him locked up alone with his food dispenser.

"Not you, him," she said, stepping backwards and focusing her foggy attention on Boris. "Somebody died? That you were close to?"

"Several people, yeah."

She blinked. "Where are you from?"

"Why?"

"Your voice is so funny. Like British or something—well no. Like a mix of British and Transylvania."

Boris hooted. "Transylvania?" he said, showing her his fangs. "Do you want me to bite you?"

"Oh, funny boys," she said vaguely, before bopping Boris on the top of the head with the bottom of her wine glass and wandering off to say goodbye to Stewart and Lisa, who were just leaving.

Xandra, it seemed, had taken a pill. ("Maybe more than one," said Boris, in my ear.) She appeared on the verge of passing out. Boris—it was shitty of me, but I just wasn't willing to do it—took her cigarette away from her and stubbed it out, then helped Courtney get her up the stairs and into her room, where she lay face down on the bedspread with the door open.

I stood in the doorway while Boris and Courtney got her shoes off—interested to see, for once, the room that she and my dad always kept locked up. Dirty cups and ashtrays, stacks of *Glamour* magazine, puffy green bedspread, laptop I never got to use, exercise bike—who knew they had an exercise bike in there?

Xandra's shoes were off but they'd decided to leave her dressed. "Do you want me to spend the night?" Courtney was asking Boris in a low voice.

Boris, shamelessly, stretched and yawned. His shirt was riding up and his jeans hung so low you could see he wasn't wearing any underwear. "Nice of you," he said. "But she is out cold, I think."

"I don't mind." Maybe I was high—I *was* high—but she was leaning so close to him it looked like she was trying to make out with him or something, which was hilarious.

I must have made some sort of semi-choking or laughter-like noise—

since Courtney turned just in time to see my comical gesture to Boris, a thumb jerked at the door—*get her out of here!*

"Are you okay?" she said coldly, eyeing me up and down. Boris was laughing too but he'd straightened up by the time she turned back to him, his expression all soulful and concerned, which only made me laugh harder.

xix.

XANDRA WAS OUT COLD by the time they all left—asleep so deeply that Boris got a pocket mirror from her purse (which we had rifled, for pills and cash) and held it under her nose to see if she was breathing. There was two hundred and twenty-nine dollars in her wallet, which I didn't feel all that bad about taking since she still had her credit cards and an uncashed check for two thousand and twenty-five.

"I knew Xandra wasn't her real name," I said, tossing him her driver's license: orange-tinged face, different fluffed-up hair, name Sandra Jaye Terrell, no restrictions. "Wonder what these keys go to?"

Boris—like an old-fashioned movie doctor, fingers on her pulse, sitting by her on the side of the bed—held the mirror up to the light. "*Da, da,*" he muttered, then something else I didn't understand.

"Eh?"

"She's out." With one finger, he prodded her shoulder, and then leaned over and peered into the nightstand drawer where I was rapidly sorting through a bewilderment of junk: change, chips, lip gloss, coasters, false eyelashes, nail polish remover, tattered paperbacks (*Your Erroneous Zones*), perfume samples, old cassette tapes, ten years' expired insurance cards, and a bunch of giveaway matchbooks from a Reno legal office that said REPRESENTING DWI AND ALL DRUG OFFENSES.

"Hey, let me have those," said Boris, reaching over and pocketing a strip of condoms. "What's this?" He picked up something that at first glance looked like a Coke can—but, when he shook it, it rattled. He put his ear to it. "Ha!" he said, tossing it to me.

"Good job." I screwed off the top—it was obviously fake—and dumped the contents out on the top of the nightstand.

"Wow," I said, after a few moments. Clearly this was where Xandra kept her tip money—partly cash, partly chips. There was a lot of other stuff, too—so much I had a hard time taking it all in—but my eyes had gone straight to the diamond-and-emerald earrings that my mother had found missing, right before my father took off.

"Wow," I said again, picking one of them up between thumb and forefinger. My mother had worn these earrings for almost every cocktail party or dress-up occasion—the blue-green transparency of the stones, their wicked three a.m. gleam, were as much a part of her as the color of her eyes or the spicy dark smell of her hair.

Boris was cackling. Amidst the cash he'd immediately spotted, and snatched up, a film canister, which he opened with trembling hands. He dipped the end of his little finger in, tasted it. "Bingo," he said, running the finger along his gums. "Kotku's going to be pissed she didn't come over now."

I held out the earrings to him on my open hands. "Yah, nice," he said, hardly looking at them. He was tapping out a pile of powder on the nightstand. "You'll get a couple of thousand dollars for those."

"These were my mother's." My dad had sold most of her jewelry back in New York, including her wedding ring. But now—I saw—Xandra had skimmed some of it for herself, and it made me weirdly sad to see what she'd chosen—not the pearls or the ruby brooch, but inexpensive things from my mother's teenage days, including her junior-high charm bracelet, ajingle with horseshoes and ballet slippers and four leaf clovers.

Boris straightened up, pinched his nostrils, handed me the rolled-up bill. "You want some?"

"No."

"Come on. It'll make you feel better."

"No, thanks."

"There must be four or five eight balls here. Maybe more! We can keep one and sell the others."

"You did that stuff before?" I said doubtfully, eyeing Xandra's prone body. Even though she was clearly down for the count, I didn't like having these conversations over her back.

"Yah. Kotku likes it. Expensive, though." He seemed to blank out for a minute, then blinked his eyes rapidly. "Wow. Come on," he said, laughing. "Here. Don't know what you're missing."

"I'm too fucked-up as it is," I said, shuffling through the money.

"Yah, but this will sober you up."

"Boris, I can't goof around," I said, pocketing the earrings and the charm bracelet. "If we're going, we need to leave now. Before people start showing up."

"What people?" said Boris skeptically, running his finger back and forth under his nose.

"Believe me, it happens fast. Child services coming in, and like that." I'd counted the cash—thirteen hundred and twenty-one dollars, plus change; there was much more in chips, close to five thousand dollars' worth, but might as well leave her those. "Half for you and half for me," I said, as I began to count the cash into two even piles. "There's enough here for two tickets. Probably we're too late to catch the last flight but we should go ahead and take a car to the airport."

"Now? Tonight?"

I stopped counting and looked at him. "I don't have anyone out here. Nobody. *Nada.* They'll stick me in a home so fast I won't know what hit me."

Boris nodded at Xandra's body—which was very unnerving, as in her face-down mattress splay she looked way too much like a dead person. "What about her?"

"What the fuck?" I said after a brief pause. "What should we do? Wait around until she wakes up and finds out we ripped her off?"

"Dunno," said Boris, eyeing her doubtfully. "I just feel bad for her."

"Well, don't. *She* doesn't want me. She'll call them herself as soon as she realizes she's stuck with me."

"Them? I don't understand who is this *them.*"

"Boris, I'm a minor." I could feel my panic rising in an all-too-familiar way—maybe the situation wasn't literally life or death but it sure felt like it, house filling with smoke, exits closing off. "I don't know how it works in your country but I don't have *any* family, no friends out here—"

"Me! You have me!"

"What are you going to do? Adopt me?" I stood up. "Look, if you're coming, we need to hurry. Do you have your passport? You'll need it for the plane."

Boris put his hands up in his Russianate *enough already* gesture. "Wait! This is happening way too fast."

I stopped, halfway out the door. "What the fuck is your problem, Boris?"

"*My* problem?"

"*You* wanted to run away! It was you who asked me to go with you! Last night."

"Where are you going? New York?"

"Where else?"

"I want to go someplace warm," he said instantly. "California."

"That's crazy. Who do we know—"

"California!" he crowed.

"Well—" Though I knew almost nothing about California, it was safe to assume that (apart from the bar of "California Über Alles" he was humming) Boris knew even less. "Where in California? What town?"

"Who cares?"

"It's a big state."

"Fantastic! It'll be fun. We'll stay high all the time—read books—build camp fires. Sleep on the beach."

I looked at him for a long unbearable moment. His face was on fire and his mouth was stained blackish from the red wine.

"All right," I said—knowing full well I was stepping off the edge and into the major mistake of my life, petty theft, the change cup, sidewalk nods and homelessness, the fuck-up from which I would never recover.

He was gleeful. "The beach, then? Yes?"

This was how you went wrong: this fast. "Wherever you want," I said, pushing the hair out of my eyes. I was dead exhausted. "But we need to go now. Please."

"What, this minute?"

"Yes. Do you need to go home and get anything?"

"*Tonight?*"

"I'm not kidding, Boris." Arguing with him was making the panic rise again. "I can't just sit around and wait—" The painting was a problem, I wasn't sure how that was going to work, but once I got Boris out of the house I could figure something out. "Please, come on."

"Is State Care that bad in America?" said Boris doubtfully. "You make it seem like the cops."

"Are you coming with me? Yes or no?"

"I need some time. I mean," he said, following after me, "we can't leave now! Really—I swear. Wait a little while. Give me a day! One day!"

"Why?"

He seemed nonplussed. "Well, I mean, because—"

"Because—?"

"Because—because I have to see Kotku! And—all kinds of things! Honest, you can't leave *tonight*," he repeated, when I said nothing. "Trust me. You'll be sorry, I mean it. Come to my house! Wait till the morning to go!"

"I can't wait," I said curtly, taking my half of the cash and heading back to my room.

"Potter—" he followed after me.

"Yes?"

"There is something important I have to tell you."

"Boris," I said, turning, "what the mother fuck. What is it?" I said, as we stood and stared at each other. "If you have something to say, go on and say it."

"Am afraid it will make you mad."

"What is it? What have you done?"

Boris was silent, gnawing the side of his thumb.

"Well, what?"

He looked away. "You need to stay," he said vaguely. "You're making a mistake."

"Forget it," I snapped, turning away again. "If you don't want to come with me, don't come, okay? But I can't stand around here all night."

Boris—I thought—might ask what was in the pillowcase, particularly since it was so fat and weirdly shaped after my over-enthusiastic wrapping job. But when I un-taped it from the back of the headboard and put it in my overnight bag (along with my iPod, notebook, charger, *Wind, Sand and Stars,* some pictures of my mom, my toothbrush, and a change of clothes) he only scowled and said nothing. When I retrieved, from the back of my closet, my school blazer (too small for me, though it had been too big when my mother bought it) he nodded and said: "Good idea, that."

"What?"

"Makes you look less homeless."

"It's November," I said. I'd only brought one warm sweater from New York; I put it in the bag and zipped it up. "It's going to be cold."

Boris leaned insolently against the wall. "What will you do, then? Live on the street, railway station, where?"

"I'll call my friend I stayed with before."

"If they wanted you, those people, they'd have adopted you already."

"They couldn't! How could they?"

Boris folded his arms. "They didn't want you, that family. You told me so yourself—lots of times. Also, you never hear from them."

"That's not true," I said, after a brief, confused pause. Only a few months before, Andy had sent me a long-ish (for him) email telling me about some stuff going on at school, a scandal with the tennis coach feeling up girls in our class, though that life was so far away that it was like reading about people I didn't know.

"Too many children?" said Boris, a bit smugly as it seemed. "Not enough room? Remember that bit? You said the mother and father were glad to see you go."

"Fuck off." I was already getting a huge headache. What would I do if Social Services showed up and put me in the back of a car? Who—in Nevada—could I call? Mrs. Spear? The Playa? The fat model-store clerk who sold us model glue without the models?

Boris followed me downstairs, where we were stopped in the middle of the living room by a tortured-looking Popper—who ran directly into our path, then sat and stared at us like he knew exactly what was going on.

"Oh, fuck," I said, putting down my bag. There was a silence.

"Boris," I said, "can't you—"

"No."

"Can't Kotku—"

"No."

"Well, fuck it," I said, picking him up and tucking him under my arm. "I'm not leaving him here for her to lock up and starve."

"And where are you going?" said Boris, as I started for the front door. "Eh?"

"Walking? To the airport?"

"Wait," I said, putting Popchik down. All at once I felt sick and like I might vomit red wine all over the carpet. "Will they take a dog on the plane?"

"No," said Boris ruthlessly, spitting out a chewed thumbnail.

He was being an asshole; I wanted to punch him. "Okay then," I said.

"Maybe somebody at the airport will want him. Or, fuck it, I'll take the train."

He was about to say something sarcastic, lips pursed in a way I knew well, but then — quite suddenly — his expression faltered; and I turned to see Xandra, wild-eyed, mascara-smeared, swaying on the landing at the top of the stairs.

We looked at her, frozen. After what seemed like a centuries-long pause, she opened her mouth, closed it again, caught the railing to balance herself, and then said, in a rusty voice: "Did Larry leave his keys in the bank vault?"

We gazed horrified for several more moments before we realized she was waiting for a reply. Her hair was like a haystack; she appeared completely disoriented and so unsteady it seemed she might topple down the steps.

"Er, yes," said Boris loudly. "I mean no." And then, when she still stood there: "It's all right. Go back to bed."

She mumbled something and — uncertain on her feet — staggered off. The two of us stood motionless for some moments. Then — quietly, the back of my neck prickling — I got my bag and slipped out the front door (my last sight of that house, and her, though I didn't even take a last look round) and Boris and Popchik came out after me. Together, all three of us walked rapidly away from the house and down to the end of the street, Popchik's toenails clicking on the pavement.

"All right," said Boris, in the humorous undertone he used when we had a close call at the supermarket. "Okay. Maybe not *quite* so much out-cold as I thought."

I was in a cold sweat, and the night air — though chilly — felt good. Off in the west, silent Frankenstein flashes of lightning twisted in the darkness.

"Well, at least she's not dead, eh?" He chuckled. "I was worried about her. Christ."

"Let me use your phone," I said, elbowing on my jacket. "I need to call a car."

He fished in his pocket, and handed it to me. It was a disposable phone, the one he'd bought to keep tabs on Kotku.

"No, keep it," he said, holding his hands up when I tried to give it back to him after I'd made my call: Lucky Cab, 777-7777, the number plastered on every shifty-looking bus-stop bench in Vegas. Then he dug out the wad of money—his half of the take from Xandra—and tried to press it on me.

"Forget it," I said, glancing back anxiously at the house. I was afraid she might wake up again and come out in the street looking for us. "It's yours."

"No! You might need it!"

"I don't want it," I said, sticking my hands in my pockets to keep him from foisting it on me. "Anyway, you might need it yourself."

"Come on, Potter! I wish you wouldn't go this *moment*." He gestured down the street, at the rows of empty houses. "If you won't come to my house—kip over there for a day or two! That brick house has furniture in it, even. I'll bring you food if you want."

"Or, hey, I can call Domino's," I said, sticking the phone in my jacket pocket. "Since they deliver out here now and everything."

He winced. "Don't be angry."

"I'm not." And, in truth, I wasn't—only so disoriented I felt I might wake up and find I'd been sleeping with a book over my face.

Boris, I realized, was looking up at the sky and humming to himself, a line from one of my mother's Velvet Underground songs: *But if you close the door...the night could last forever...*

"What about you?" I said, rubbing my eyes.

"Eh?" he said, looking at me with a smile.

"What's up? Will I see you again?"

"Maybe," he said, in the same cheerful tone I imagined him using with Bami and Judy the barkeep's wife in Karmeywallag and everyone else in his life he'd ever said goodbye to. "Who knows?"

"Will you meet me in a day or two?"

"Well—"

"Join me later. Take a plane—you have the money. I'll call you and tell you where I am. Don't say no."

"Okay then," said Boris, in the same cheerful voice. "I won't say no." But clearly, from his tone, he *was* saying no.

I closed my eyes. "Oh God." I was so tired I was reeling; I had to fight the urge to lie down on the ground, a physical undertow pulling me to the curb. When I opened my eyes, I saw Boris looking at me with concern.

"Look at you," he said. "Falling over, almost." He reached in his pocket.

"No, no, no," I said, stepping back, when I saw what he had in his hand. "No way. Forget it."

"It'll make you feel better!"

"That's what you said about the other stuff." I wasn't up for any more seaweed or singing stars. "Really, I don't want any."

"But this is different. Completely different. It will *sober you up*. Clear your head — promise."

"Right." A drug that sobered you up and cleared your head didn't sound like Boris's style at all, although he did seem a good bit more with-it than me.

"Look at me," he said reasonably. "Yes." He knew he had me. "Am I raving? Frothing at mouth? No — only being helpful! Here," he said, tapping some out on the back of his hand, "come on. Let me feed it to you."

I half expected it was a trick — that I would pass out on the spot and wake up who knew where, maybe in one of the empty houses across the street. But I was too tired to care, and maybe that would have been okay anyway. I leaned forward and allowed him to press one nostril closed with a fingertip. "There!" he said encouragingly. "Like this. Now, sniff."

Almost instantly, I *did* feel better. It was like a miracle. "Wow," I said, pinching my nose against the sharp, pleasant sting.

"Didn't I tell you?" He was already tapping out some more. "Here, other nose. Don't breathe out. Okay, *now*."

Everything seemed brighter and clearer, including Boris himself.

"What did I tell you?" He was taking more for himself now. "Aren't you sorry you don't listen?"

"You're going to sell this stuff, *god*," I said, looking up at the sky. "Why?"

"It's worth a lot, actually. Few thousand of dollars."

"That little bit?"

"Not that little! This is a lot of grams — twenty, maybe more. Could make a fortune if I divide up small and sell to girls like K. T. Bearman."

"You know K. T. Bearman?" Katie Bearman, who was a year ahead of us, had her own car — a black convertible — and was so far removed from our social scale she might as well have been a movie star.

"Sure. Skye, KT, Jessica, all those girls. Anyway—" he offered me the vial again—"I can buy Kotku that keyboard she wants now. No more money worries."

We went back and forth a few times until I began to feel much more optimistic about the future and things in general. And as we stood rubbing our noses and jabbering in the street, Popper looking up at us curiously, the wonderfulness of New York seemed right on the tip of my tongue, an evanescence possible to convey. "I mean, it's great," I said. The words were spiraling and tumbling out of me. "Really, you *have* to come. We can go to Brighton Beach—that's where all the Russians hang out. Well, I've never been there. But the train goes there—it's the last stop on the line. There's a big Russian community, restaurants with smoked fish and sturgeon roe. My mother and I always talked about going out there to eat one day, this jeweler she worked with told her the good places to go, but we never did. It's supposed to be great. Also, I mean—I have money for school—you can go to *my* school. No—you totally can. I have a scholarship. Well, I did. But the guy said as long as the money in my fund was used for education—it could be *any*body's education. Not just mine. There's more than enough for both of us. Though, I mean, public school, the public schools are good in New York, I know people there, public school's fine with me."

I was still babbling when Boris said: "Potter." Before I could answer him he put both hands on my face and kissed me on the mouth. And while I stood blinking—it was over almost before I knew what had happened— he picked up Popper under the forelegs and kissed him too, in midair, smack on the tip of his nose.

Then he handed him to me. "Your car's over there," he said, giving him one last ruffle on the head. And—sure enough—when I turned, a town car was creeping up the other side of the street, surveying the addresses.

We stood looking at each other—me breathing hard, completely stunned.

"Good luck," said Boris. "I won't forget you." Then he patted Popper on the head. "Bye, Popchyk. Look after him, will you?" he said to me.

Later—in the cab, and afterward—I would replay that moment, and marvel that I'd waved and walked away quite so casually. Why hadn't I grabbed his arm and begged him one last time to get in the car, come on, *fuck it Boris,* just like skipping school, we'll be eating breakfast over cornfields when the sun comes up? I knew him well enough to know that if you asked him the right way, at the right moment, he would do almost anything; and in the very act of turning away I knew he would have run after me and hopped in the car laughing if I'd asked one last time.

But I didn't. And, in truth, it was maybe better that I didn't—I say that now, though it was something I regretted bitterly for a while. More than anything I was relieved that in my unfamiliar babbling-and-wanting-to-talk state I'd stopped myself from blurting the thing on the edge of my tongue, the thing I'd never said, even though it was something we both knew well enough without me saying it out loud to him in the street—which was, of course, *I love you.*

XX.

I WAS SO TIRED that the drugs didn't last long, at least not the feel-good part. The cab driver—a transplanted New Yorker from the sound of him—immediately sussed out something was wrong and tried to give me a card for the National Runaway switchboard, which I refused to take. When I asked him to drive me to the train station (not even knowing if there was a train in Vegas—surely there had to be), he shook his head and said: "You know, don't you, Specs, they don't take dogs on Amtrak?"

"They don't?" I said, my heart sinking.

"The plane—maybe, I don't know." He was a young-ish guy, a fast talker, baby-faced, slightly overweight, in a T-shirt that said PENN AND TELLER: LIVE AT THE RIO. "You'll have to have a crate, or something. Maybe the bus is your best bet. But they don't let kids under a certain age ride without parental permission."

"I told you! My dad died! His girlfriend is sending me to my family back east."

"Well, hey, you don't have anything to worry about then, do you?"

I kept my mouth shut for the rest of the ride. The fact of my father's death had not yet sunk in, and every now and then, the lights zipping past on the highway brought it back in a sick rush. An accident. At least in New York we hadn't had to worry about drunk driving—the great fear was that he would fall in front of a car or be stabbed for his wallet, lurching out of some dive bar at three a.m. What would happen to his

body? I'd scattered my mother's ashes in Central Park, though apparently
there was a regulation against it; one evening while it was getting dark, I'd
walked with Andy to a deserted area on the west side of the Pond and—
while Andy kept a lookout—dumped the urn. What had disturbed me
far more than the actual scattering of the remains was that the urn had
been packed in shredded pieces of porno classifieds: SOAPY ASIAN BABES and
WET HOT ORGASMS were two random phrases that had caught my eye as
the gray powder, the color of moon rock, caught and spun in the May
twilight.

Then there were lights, and the car stopped. "Okay, Specs," said my
driver, turning with his arm along the back seat. We were in the parking
lot of the Greyhound station. "What did you say your name was?"

"Theo," I said, without thinking, and immediately was sorry.

"All right, Theo. J.P." He reached across the back seat to shake my
hand. "You want to take my advice about something?"

"Sure," I said, quailing a bit. Even with everything else that was going
on, and there was quite a lot, I felt incredibly uncomfortable that this guy
had probably seen Boris kissing me in the street.

"None of my business, but you're going to need something to put
Fluffy there in."

"Sorry?"

He nodded at my bag. "Will he fit in that?"

"Umm—"

"You're probably going to have to check that bag, anyway. It might be
too big for you to carry aboard—they'll stow it underneath. It's not like
the plane."

"I—" This was too much to think about. "I don't have anything."

"Hang on. Let me check in my office back here." He got up, went
around to the trunk, and returned with a large canvas shopping bag from
a health food store that said *The Greening of America*.

"If I were you," he said, "I'd go in and buy the ticket without Fluffy
Boy. Leave him out here with me, just in case, okay?"

My new pal had been right about not riding Greyhound without an
Unaccompanied Child form signed by a parent—and there were other
restrictions for kids as well. The clerk at the window—a wan Chicana
with scraped-back hair—began in a monotone to go down the long baleful list of them. No Transfers. No Journeys of Longer than Five Hours in

Duration. Unless the person named on the Unaccompanied Child Form showed up to meet me, with positive identification, I would be released into the custody of Child Protective Services or to local law enforcement officials in the city of my destination.

"But—"

"All children under fifteen. No exceptions."

"But I'm not *under* fifteen," I said, floundering to produce my official-looking state-issued New York ID. "I *am* fifteen. Look." Enrique—envisioning perhaps the likelihood of my having to go into what he called The System—had taken me to be photographed for it shortly after my mother died; and though I'd resented it at the time, Big Brother's far-reaching claw ("Wow, your very own bar code," Andy had said, looking at it curiously), now I was thankful he'd had the foresight to carry me downtown and register me like a second-hand motor vehicle. Numbly, like a refugee, I waited under the sleazy fluorescents as the clerk looked at the card at a number of different angles and in different lights, at length finding it genuine.

"Fifteen," she said suspiciously, handing it back to me.

"Right." I knew I didn't look my age. There was, I realized, no question of being up-front about Popper since a big sign by the desk said in red letters NO DOGS, CATS, BIRDS, RODENTS, REPTILES, OR OTHER ANIMALS WILL BE TRANSPORTED.

As for the bus itself, I was in luck: there was a 1:45 a.m. with connections to New York departing the station in fifteen minutes. As the machine spat out my ticket with a mechanical smack, I stood in a daze wondering what the hell to do about Popper. Walking outside, I was half-hoping my cab driver had driven off—perhaps having whisked Popper away to some more loving and secure home—but instead I found him drinking a can of Red Bull and talking on his cell phone, Popper nowhere in sight. He got off his call when he saw me standing there. "What do you think?"

"Where is he?" Groggily, I looked in the back seat. "What'd you do with him?"

He laughed. "Now you don't and…now you do!" With a flourish, he removed the messily-folded copy of *USA Today* from the canvas bag on the front seat beside him; and there, settled contentedly in a cardboard box at the bottom of the bag, crunching on some potato chips, was Popper.

"Misdirection," he said. "The box fills out the bag so it doesn't look dog-shaped and gives him a little more room to move around. And the newspaper—perfect prop. Covers him up, makes the bag look full, doesn't add any weight."

"Do you think it'll be all right?"

"Well, I mean, he's such a little guy—what, five pounds, six? Is he quiet?"

I looked at him doubtfully, curled at the bottom of the box. "Not always."

J.P. wiped his mouth with the back of his hand, and gave me the package of potato chips. "Give him a couple of these suckers if he gets antsy. You'll be stopping every few hours. Just sit as far in the back of the bus as you can, and make sure you take him away from the station a ways before you let him out to do his business."

I put the bag over my shoulder and tucked my arm around it. "Can you tell?" I asked him.

"No. Not if I didn't know. But can I give you a tip? Magician's secret?"

"Sure."

"*Don't* keep looking down at the bag like that. Anywhere but the bag. The scenery, your shoelace—okay, there we go—that's right. Confident and natural, that's the kitty. Although klutzy and looking for a dropped contact lens will work too, if you think people are giving you the fish eye. Spill your chips—stub your toe—cough on your drink—anything."

Wow, I thought. Clearly they didn't call it Lucky Cab for nothing.

Again, he laughed, as if I'd spoken the thought aloud. "Hey, it's a stupid rule, no dogs on the bus," he said, taking another big slug of the Red Bull. "I mean, what are you supposed to do? Dump him by the side of the road?"

"Are you a magician or something?"

He laughed. "How'd ya guess? I got a gig doing card tricks in a bar over at the Orleans—if you were old enough to get in, I'd tell you to come down and check out my act sometime. Anyways, the secret is, always fix their attention *away* from where the slippery stuff's going on. That's the first law of magic, Specs. Misdirection. Never forget it."

xxi.

UTAH. THE SAN RAFAEL SWELL, as the sun came up, unrolled in inhuman vistas like Mars: sandstone and shale, gorges and desolate rust-red mesas. I'd had a hard time sleeping, partly because of the drugs, partly for fear that Popper might fidget or whine, but he was perfectly quiet as we drove the twisted mountain roads, sitting silently inside his bag on the seat beside me, on the side closest to the window. As it happened my suitcase *had* been small enough to bring aboard, which I was happy about for any number of reasons: my sweater, *Wind, Sand and Stars,* but most of all my painting, which felt like an article of protection even wrapped up and out of view, like a holy icon carried by a crusader into battle. There were no other passengers in the back except a shy-looking Hispanic couple with a bunch of plastic food containers on their laps, and an old drunk talking to himself, and we made it fine on the winding roads all the way through Utah and into Grand Junction, Colorado, where we had a fifty-minute rest stop. After locking my suitcase in a coin-op locker, I walked Popper out behind the bus station, well out of the driver's sight, bought us a couple of hamburgers from Burger King and gave him water from the plastic top of an old carry-out container I found in the trash. From Grand Junction, I slept, until our layover in Denver, an hour and sixteen minutes, just as the sun was going down — where Popper and I ran and ran, for sheer relief of being off the bus, ran so far down shadowy unknown streets that I was almost afraid of getting lost, although I was pleased to find a hippie coffee shop where the clerks were young and friendly ("Bring him in!" said the purple-haired girl at the counter when she saw Popper tied out front, "we love dogs!") and where I bought not only two turkey sandwiches (one for me, one for him) but a vegan brownie and a greasy paper bag of home-made vegetarian dog biscuits.

I read late, creamy paper yellowed in a circle of weak lights, as the unknown darkness sped past, over the Continental Divide and out of the Rockies, Popper content after his romp around Denver and snoozing happily in his bag.

At some point, I slept, then woke and read some more. At two a.m., just as Saint-Exupéry was telling the story of his plane crash in the desert, we came into Salina, Kansas ("Crossroads of America") — twenty minute rest stop, under a moth-beaten sodium lamp, where Popper and I ran around a deserted gas station parking lot in the dark, my head still full of the book while also exulting in the strangeness of being in my mother's state for the first time in my life — had she, on her rounds with her father, ever driven through this town, cars rushing past on the Ninth Street Inter-state Exit, lighted grain silos like starships looming in the emptiness for miles away? Back on the bus—sleepy, dirty, tired-out, cold—Popchik and I slept from Salina to Topeka, and from Topeka to Kansas City, Missouri, where we pulled in just at sunrise.

My mother had often told me how flat it was where she'd grown up—so flat you could see cyclones spinning across the prairies for miles—but still I couldn't quite believe the vastness of it, the unrelieved sky, so huge that you felt crushed and oppressed by the infinite. In St. Louis, around noon, we had an hour and a half layover (plenty of time for Popper's walk, and an awful roast beef sandwich for lunch, although the neighborhood was too dicey to venture far) and—back at the station—a transfer to an entirely different bus. Then—only an hour or two along—I woke, with the bus stopped, to find Popper sitting quietly with the tip of his nose poking out of the bag and a middle aged black lady with bright pink lipstick standing over me, thundering: "You can't have that dog on the bus."

I stared at her, disoriented. Then, much to my horror, I realized she was no random passenger but the driver herself, in cap and uniform.

"Do you hear what I said?" she repeated, with an aggressive side-to-side head tic. She was as wide as a prizefighter; the nametag, atop her impressive bosom, read *Denese.* "You can't *have* that dog on this *bus.*" Then— impatiently—she made a flapping hand gesture as if to say: *get him the hell back in that bag!*

I covered his head up—he didn't seem to mind—and sat with rapidly shrinking insides. We were stopped at a town called Effingham, Illinois: Edward Hopper houses, stage-set courthouse, a hand-lettered banner that said *Crossroads of Opportunity!*

The driver swept her finger around. "Do any of you people back here have objections to this animal?"

The other passengers in back—(unkempt handlebar-moustache guy; grown woman with braces; anxious black mom with elementary-school girl; W. C. Fields–looking oldster with nose tubes and oxygen canister— all seemed too surprised to talk, though the little girl, eyes round, shook her head almost imperceptibly: *no.*

The driver waited. She looked around. Then she turned back to me. "Okay. That's good news for you and the pooch, honey. But if *any*—" she wagged her finger at me—"if *any* these other passengers back here complains about you having an animal on board, at *any* point, I'm going to have to make you get off. Understand?"

She wasn't throwing me off? I blinked at her, afraid to move or speak a word.

"*You understand?*" she repeated, more ominously.

"Thank you—"

A bit belligerently, she shook her head. "*Oh,* no. Don't thank me, honey. Because I am putting you off this bus if there is one single complaint. One."

I sat in a tremble as she strode down the aisle and started the bus. As we swung out of the parking lot I was afraid to even glance at the other passengers, though I could feel them all looking at me.

By my knee, Popper let out a tiny huff and resettled. As much as I liked Popper, and felt sorry for him, I'd never thought that as dogs went he was particularly interesting or intelligent. Instead I'd spent a lot of time wishing he was a cooler dog, a border collie or a Lab or a rescue maybe, some smart and haunted pit mix from the shelter, a scrappy little mutt that chased balls and bit people—in fact almost anything but what he actually was: a girl's dog, a toy, completely gay, a dog I felt embarrassed to walk on the street. Not that Popper wasn't cute; in fact, he was exactly the kind of tiny, prancing fluffball that a lot of people liked—maybe not me but surely some little girl like the one across the aisle would find him by the road and take him home and tie ribbons in his hair?

Rigidly I sat there, re-living the bolt of fear again and again: the driver's face, my shock. What really scared me was that I now knew if she made me put Popper off the bus that I would have to get off with him, too (and do what?) even in the middle of Illinois nowhere. Rain, cornfields: standing by the side of the road. How had I become attached to such a ridiculous animal? A lapdog that Xandra had chosen?

Throughout Illinois and Indiana, I sat swaying and vigilant: too afraid to go to sleep. The trees were bare, rotted-out Halloween pumpkins on the porches. Across the aisle, the mother had her arm around the little girl and was singing, very quietly: *You are my sunshine.* I had nothing to eat but leftover crumbs of the potato chips the cab driver had given me; and— ugly salt taste in my mouth, industrial plains, little nowhere towns rolling past—I felt chilled and forlorn, looking out at the bleak farmland and thinking of songs my mother had sung to me, way back when. *Toot toot tootsie goodbye, toot toot tootsie, don't cry.* At last—in Ohio, when it was dark, and the lights in the sad little far-apart houses were coming on—I felt safe enough to drowse off, nodding back and forth in my sleep, until Cleveland, cold white-lit city where I changed buses at two in the morning. I was afraid to give Popper the long walk I knew he needed, for fear that someone might see us (because what would we do, if we were found out? Stay in Cleveland forever?). But he seemed frightened too; and we stood shivering on a street corner for ten minutes before I gave him some water, put him in the bag, and walked back to the station to board.

It was the middle of the night and everyone seemed half asleep, which made the transfer easier; and we transferred again at noon the next day, in Buffalo, where the bus crunched out through piled-up sleet in the station. The wind was biting, with a sharp wet edge; after two years in the desert I'd forgotten what real winter — aching and raw — was like. Boris had not returned any of my texts, which was perhaps understandable since I was sending them to Kotku's phone, but I sent another one anyway: BFALO NY NYC 2NIT. HPE UR OK HAV U HERD FRM X?

Buffalo is a long way from New York City; but apart from a dream-like, feverish stop in Syracuse, where I walked and watered Popper and bought us a couple of cheese danishes because there wasn't anything else — I managed to sleep almost the whole way, through Batavia and Rochester and Syracuse and Binghamton, with my cheek against the window and cold air coming through at the crack, the vibration taking me back to *Wind, Sand and Stars* and a lonely cockpit high above the desert.

I think I must have been getting quietly sick ever since the stop in Cleveland, but by the time I finally got off the bus, in Port Authority, it was evening and I was burning up with fever. I was chilled, wobbly on my legs and the city — which I'd longed for so fiercely — seemed foreign and noisy and cold, exhaust fumes and garbage and strangers rushing past in every direction.

The terminal was packed with cops. Everywhere I looked there were signs for runaway shelters, runaway hotlines, and one lady cop in particular gave me the fish-eye as I was hurrying outside — after sixty-plus hours on the bus, I was dirty and tired and knew I didn't really pass muster — but nobody stopped me and I didn't look behind me until I was out the door, and well away. Several men of varying age and nationality called out to me on the street, soft voices coming from several directions (*hey, little brother! where you headed? need a ride?*) but though one red-haired guy in particular seemed nice and normal and not much older than me, almost like someone I might be friends with, I was enough of a New Yorker to ignore his cheerful hello and keep walking like I knew where I was going.

I'd thought Popper would be overjoyed to get out and walk, but when I put him down on the sidewalk Eighth Avenue was too much for him and he was too scared to go more than a block or so; he'd never been on a city street before, everything terrified him (cars, car horns, people's legs, empty plastic bags blowing down the sidewalk) and he kept jerking forward, darting toward the crosswalk, jumping this way and that, dashing behind me in terror and winding the leash around my legs so I tripped and nearly fell in front of a van rushing to beat the light.

After I picked him up, paddling, and stuck him back in his bag (where he scrabbled and huffed in exasperation before he got quiet), I stood in the middle of the rush-hour crowd trying to get my bearings. Everything seemed so much dirtier and unfriendlier than I'd remembered—colder too, streets gray like old newspaper. *Que faire?* as my mother had liked to say. I could almost hear her saying it, in her light, careless voice.

I'd often wondered, when my father prowled around banging the kitchen cabinets and complaining that he wanted a drink, what "wanting a drink" felt like—what it felt like to want alcohol and nothing but, not water or Pepsi or anything else. *Now,* I thought bleakly, *I know.* I was dying for a beer but I knew better than to go in a deli and try to buy one without ID. Longingly I thought of Mr. Pavlikovsky's vodka, the daily blast of warmth I'd come to take for granted.

More to the point: I was starving. I was a few doors down from a fancy cupcake place, and I was so hungry I turned right in and bought the first one that caught my eye (green tea flavored, as it turned out, with some kind of vanilla filling, weird but still delicious). Almost at once the sugar made me feel better; and while I ate, licking the custard off my fingers, I stared in amazement at the purposeful mob. Leaving Vegas I'd somehow felt a lot more confident about how all this would play out. Would Mrs. Barbour phone Social Services to tell them I'd turned up? I'd thought not; but now I wondered. There was also the not-so-insignificant question of Popper, since (along with dairy and tree nuts and adhesive tape and sandwich mustard and about twenty-five other commonly-found household items) Andy was violently allergic to dogs—not just dogs, but also cats and horses and circus animals and the class guinea pig ("Pig Newton") that we'd had way back in second grade, which was why there were no pets at the Barbours' house. Somehow this had not seemed such an insurmountable problem back in Vegas, but — standing out on Eighth Avenue when it was cold and getting dark — it did.

Not knowing what else to do, I started walking east toward Park Avenue. The wind hit raw in my face and the smell of rain in the air made me nervous. The skies in New York seemed a lot lower and heavier than out west — dirty clouds, eraser-smudged, like pencil on rough paper. It was as if the desert, its openness, had retrained my distance vision. Everything seemed dank and closed-in.

Walking helped me work out the roll in my legs. I walked east to the library (the lions! I stood still for a moment, like a returning soldier catching my first glimpse of home) and then I turned up Fifth Avenue — streetlamps on, still fairly busy, though it was emptying out for the night — up to Central Park South. As tired as I was, and cold, still my heart stiffened to see the Park, and I ran across Fifty-Seventh (Street of Joy!) to the leafy darkness. The smells, the shadows, even the dappled pale trunks of the plane trees lifted my spirits but yet it was as if I was seeing another Park beneath the tangible one, a map to the past, a ghost Park dark with memory, school outings and zoo visits of long ago. I was walking along the sidewalk on the Fifth Avenue side, looking in, and the paths were tree-shadowed, haloed with streetlamps, mysterious and inviting like the woods from *The Lion, the Witch, and the Wardrobe*. If I turned and walked down one of those lighted paths, would I walk out again into a different year, maybe even a different future, where my mother — just out of work — would be waiting for me slightly wind-blown on the bench (our bench) by the Pond: putting her cell phone away, standing to kiss me, *Hi, Puppy, how was school, what do you want to eat for dinner?*

Then — suddenly — I stopped. A familiar presence in a business suit had shouldered past and was striding down the sidewalk ahead of me. The shock of white hair stood out in the darkness, white hair that looked as if it ought to be worn long and tied back with a ribbon; he was preoccupied, more rumpled than usual, but still I recognized him immediately, the angle of his head with its faint echo of Andy: Mr. Barbour, briefcase and all, on his way home from work.

I ran to catch up with him. "Mr. Barbour?" I called. He was talking to himself, though I couldn't hear what he was saying. "Mr. Barbour, it's Theo," I said loudly, catching him by his sleeve.

With shocking violence, he turned and threw my hand off. It was Mr. Barbour all right; I would have known him anywhere. But his eyes, on mine, were a stranger's — bright and hard and contemptuous.

"No more handouts!" he cried, in a high voice. "Get lost!"

I ought to have known mania when I saw it. It was an amped-up version of the look my dad had sometimes on Game Day — or, for that matter, when he'd hauled off and hit me. I'd never been around Mr. Barbour when he was off his medicine (Andy, typically, had been restrained in describing his father's "enthusiasms," I didn't then know about the episodes where he'd tried to telephone the Secretary of State or wear his pyjamas to work); and his rage was so out of character for the bemused and inattentive Mr. Barbour I knew that all I could do was fall back, in shame. He glared at me for a long moment and then brushed his arm off (as if I were dirty, as if I'd contaminated him by touching him) and stalked away.

"Were you asking that man for money?" said another man who had sidled up out of nowhere as I stood on the sidewalk, astonished. "Were you?" he said, more insistently, when I turned away. His build was pudgy, his suit blandly corporate and married-with-kids-looking; and his sad-sack demeanor gave me the creeps. As I tried to step around him, he stepped in my path and dropped a heavy hand on my shoulder, and in a panic I dodged him and ran off into the park.

I headed down to the Pond, down paths yellow and sodden with fallen leaves, where I went by instinct straight to the Rendezvous Point (as my mother and I called our bench) and sat shivering. It had seemed the most incredible, unbelievable luck, spotting Mr. Barbour on the street; I'd thought, for maybe five seconds, that after the first awkwardness and puzzlement he would greet me happily, ask a few questions, *oh, never mind, never mind, there's time for that later,* and walk with me up to the apartment. *My goodness, what an adventure. Won't Andy be pleased to see you!*

Jesus, I thought — running my hand through my hair, still feeling shaken. In an ideal world, Mr. Barbour would have been the member of the family I would *most* have wanted to meet on the street — more than Andy, certainly more than Andy's siblings, more than even Mrs. Barbour, with her frozen pauses, her social niceties and her codes of behavior unknown to me, her chilling and unreadable gaze.

Out of habit, I checked my phone for texts for what seemed like the ten thousandth time—and was cheered despite myself to find at long last a message—number I didn't recognize, but it had to be Boris. HEY! OPE U2 ROK. NOT 2 MAD. RING XNR OK SHE HZ BEN BUGEN ME

I tried calling him back—I'd texted him about fifty times from the road—but no one picked up at that number and Kotku's phone took me straight to voice mail. Xandra could wait. Walking back to Central Park South, with Popper, I bought three hot dogs from a vendor who was just shutting up for the day (one for Popper, two for me) and while we ate, on an out-of-the-way bench inside the Scholars' Gate, considered my options. In my desert fantasias of New York I'd sometimes entertained perverse images of Boris and me living on the street, around St. Mark's Place or Tompkins Square, quite possibly standing around rattling our change cups with the very skate rats who'd once jeered at Andy and me in our school uniforms. But the real prospect of sleeping on the street was a whole lot less appealing alone and feverish in the November cold.

The hell of it was: I was only about five blocks from Andy's. I thought about phoning him—maybe asking him to meet me—and then decided against it. Certainly I could call him if I got desperate; he would gladly sneak out, bring me a change of clothes and money snitched from his mother's purse and—who knows—maybe a bunch of leftover crabmeat canapés or those cocktail peanuts that the Barbours always ate. But the word *handout* still scalded. As much as I liked Andy, it had been almost two years. And I couldn't forget the way that Mr. Barbour had looked at me. Clearly something had gone wrong, badly, only I wasn't quite sure what—apart from knowing that I was responsible somehow, in the generalized miasma of shame and unworthiness and being-a-burden that never quite left me.

Without meaning to—I'd been staring into space—I'd made accidental eye contact with a man on a bench across from me. Quickly I looked away but it was too late; he was standing up, walking over.

"Cute mutt," he said, stooping to pat Popper, and then, when I didn't answer: "What's your name? Mind if I sit down?" He was a wiry guy, small but strong-looking; and he smelled. I got up, avoiding his eyes, but as I turned to leave he shot his arm out and caught me by the wrist.

"What's the matter," he said, in an ugly voice, "don't you like me?"

I twisted free and ran—Popper running after me, out to the street, too fast, he wasn't used to city traffic, cars were coming—I grabbed him up just in time, and ran across Fifth Avenue, over to the Pierre. My pursuer — trapped on the other side by the changed light — was attracting some glances from pedestrians but when I looked back again, safe in the circle of light pouring from the warm, well-lighted entrance of the hotel — well-dressed couples; doormen hailing cabs — I saw that he had faded back into the park.

The streets were much louder than I remembered — smellier, too. Standing on the corner by A La Vieille Russie I found myself overpowered with the familiar old Midtown stench: carriage horses, bus exhaust, perfume, and urine. For so long I'd thought of Vegas as something temporary — my real life was New York — but was it? *Not any more,* I thought, dismally, surveying the thinned-out trickle of pedestrians hurrying past Bergdorf's.

Though I was aching and chilled with fever again, I walked for ten blocks or so, still trying to work the hum and lightness out of my legs, the pervasive vibration of the bus. But at last the cold was too much for me, and I hailed a cab; it would have been an easy bus ride, half an hour maybe, straight shot down Fifth to the Village, only after three solid days on the bus I couldn't bear the thought of jolting around on another bus for even a minute more.

I wasn't that comfortable at the notion of turning up at Hobie's house cold — not comfortable about it at all, since we hadn't been in touch for a while, my fault, not his; at some point, I'd just stopped writing back. On one level, it was the natural course of things; on another Boris's casual speculation ("old poofter?") had put me off him, subtly, and his last two or three letters had gone unanswered.

I felt bad; I felt awful. Even though it was a short ride I must have nodded off in the back seat because when the cabbie stopped and said: "This all right?" I came to with a jolt, and for a moment sat stunned, fighting to remember where I was.

The shop — I noticed, as the cabbie drove away — was closed-up and dark, as if it had never been opened again in all my time away from New York. The windows were furred with grime and — looking inside — I saw that some of the furniture was draped with sheets. Nothing else had changed at all, except that all the old books and bric-a-brac — the marble cockatoos, the obelisks — were covered with an additional layer of dust.

My heart sank. I stood on the street for a long minute or two before I worked up my nerve to ring the bell. It seemed that I stood for ages listening to the faraway echo, though it was probably no time at all; I'd almost talked myself into believing that no one was at home (and what would I do? Hike back to Times Square, try to find a cheap hotel somewhere or turn myself in to the runaway cops?) when the door opened very suddenly and I found myself looking not at Hobie, but a girl my own age.

It was her—Pippa. Still tiny (I'd grown much taller than her) and thin, though much healthier-looking than the last time I'd seen her, fuller in the face; lots of freckles; different hair too, it seemed to have grown back in with a different color and texture, not red-blonde but a darker, rust color and a bit straggly, like her aunt Margaret's. She was dressed like a boy, in sock feet and old corduroys, a too-big sweater, only with a crazy pink-and-orange striped scarf that a daffy grandmother would wear. Brow furrowed, polite but reticent, she looked at me blankly with the golden-brown eyes: a stranger. "Can I help you?" she said.

She's forgotten me, I thought, dismayed. How could I have expected her to remember? It had been a long time; I knew I looked different too. It was like seeing somebody I'd thought was dead.

And then—thumping down the stairs, coming up behind her, in paint-stained chinos and an out-at-elbows cardigan—was Hobie. *He's cut his hair,* was my first thought; it was close to his head and much whiter than I remembered. His expression was slightly irritated; for a heartsinking moment I thought he didn't recognize me either, and then: "Dear God," he said, stepping back suddenly.

"It's me," I said quickly. I was afraid he was going to shut the door in my face. "Theodore Decker. Remember?"

Quickly, Pippa looked up at him—clearly she recognized my name, even if she didn't recognize *me*—and the friendly surprise on their faces was such an astonishment that I began to cry.

"Theo." His hug was strong and parental, and so fierce that it made me cry even harder. Then his hand was on my shoulder, heavy anchoring hand that was security and authority itself; he was leading me in, into the workshop, dim gilt and rich wood smells I'd dreamed of, up the stairs into the long-lost parlor, with its velvets and urns and bronzes. "It's wonderful to see you," he was saying; and "you look knackered" and "When did you get back?" and "Are you hungry?" and "My goodness, you've grown!" and "that hair! Like Mowgli the Jungle Boy!" and (worried now)—"does it seem close in here to you? should I open a window?"—and, when Popper stuck his head out of the bag: "And ha! who is this?"

Pippa—laughing—lifted him up and cuddled him in her arms. I felt light-headed with fever—glowing red and radiant, like the bars in an electric heater, and so unmoored that I didn't even feel embarrassed for crying. I was conscious of nothing but the relief of being there, and my aching and over-full heart.

Back in the kitchen there was mushroom soup, which I wasn't hungry for, but it was warm, and I was freezing to death—and as I ate (Pippa cross-legged on the floor, playing with Popchik, dangling the pom-pom from her granny scarf in his face, Popper/Pippa, how had I never noticed the kinship in their names?) I told him, a little, in a garbled way, about my father's death and what had happened. Hobie, as he listened, arms folded, had an extremely worried look on his face, his mulish brow furrowing deeper as I talked.

"You need to call her," he said. "Your father's wife."

"But she's not his wife! She's just his girlfriend! She doesn't care anything about me."

Firmly, he shook his head. "Doesn't matter. You have to ring her up and tell her that you're all right. Yes, yes you do," he said, speaking over me as I tried to object. "No buts. Right now. This instant. Pips—" there was an old-fashioned wall phone in the kitchen—"come along and let's clear out of here for a minute."

Though Xandra was just about the last person in the world I wanted to talk to—especially after I'd ransacked her bedroom and stolen her tip money—I was so relieved to be there that I would have done anything he asked. Dialing the number, I tried to tell myself she probably wouldn't pick up (so many solicitors and bill collectors phoned us, all the time, that she seldom took calls from numbers she didn't recognize). Hence I was surprised when she answered on the first ring.

"You left the door open," she said almost immediately, in an accusing voice.

"What?"

"You let the dog out. He's run off—I can't find him anywhere. He probably got hit by a car or something."

"No." I was gazing fixedly at the blackness of the brick courtyard. It was raining, drops pounding hard on the windowpanes, the first real rain I'd seen in almost two years. "He's with me."

"Oh." She sounded relieved. Then, more sharply: "Where are you? With Boris somewhere?"

"No."

"I spoke to him—wired out of his mind, it sounded like. He wouldn't tell me where you were. I know he knows." Though it was still early out there, her voice was gravelly like she'd been drinking, or crying. "I ought to call the cops on you, Theo. I know it was you two who stole that money and stuff."

"Yeah, just like you stole my mom's earrings."

"What—"

"Those emerald ones. They belonged to my grandmother."

"I *didn't* steal them." She was angry now. "How dare you. Larry *gave* those to me, he gave them to me after—"

"Yeah. After he stole them from my mother."

"Um, excuse me, but your mom's dead."

"Yes, but she wasn't when he stole them. That was like a year before she died. She contacted the insurance company," I said, raising my voice over hers. "And filed a police report." I didn't know if the police part was true, but it might as well have been.

"Um, I guess you've never heard of a little something called marital property."

"Right. And I guess you never heard of something called a family heirloom. You and my dad weren't even married. He had no right to give those to you."

Silence. I could hear the click of her cigarette lighter on the other end, a weary inhale. "Look, kid. Can I say something? Not about the money, honest. Or the blow. Although, I can tell you for damn sure, I wasn't doing anything like that when I was your age. You think you're pretty smart and all, and I guess you are, but you're headed down a bad road, you and whats-his-name too. Yeah, yeah," she said, raising her voice over mine, "I like him too, but he's bad news, that kid."

"You should know."

She laughed, bleakly. "Well, kid, guess what? I've been around the track a few times—I *do* know. He's going to end up in jail by the time he's eighteen, that one, and dollars to doughnuts you'll be right there with him. I mean, I can't blame you," she said, raising her voice again, "I loved your dad, but he sure wasn't worth much, and from what he told me, your mother wasn't worth much either."

"Okay. That's it. Fuck you." I was so mad I was trembling. "I'm hanging up now."

"No—wait. Wait. I'm sorry. I shouldn't have said that about your mother. That's not why I wanted to talk to you. Please. Will you wait a second?"

"I'm waiting."

"First off—assuming you care—I'm having your dad cremated. That all right with you?"

"Do what you want."

"You never did have much use for him, did you?"

"Is that it?"

"One more thing. I don't care where you are, quite frankly. But I need an address where I can get in touch with you."

"And why is that?"

"Don't be a wise ass. At some point somebody's going to call from your school or something—"

"I wouldn't count on it."

"—and I'm going to need, I don't know, some kind of explanation of where you are. Unless you want the cops to put you on the side of a milk carton or something."

"I think that's fairly unlikely."

"*Fairly unlikely,*" she repeated, in a cruel, drawling imitation of my voice. "Well, may be. But give it to me, all the same, and we'll call it even. I mean," she said, when I didn't answer, "let me make it plain, it makes no difference to me where you are. I just don't want to be left holding the bag out here in case there's some problem and I need to get in touch with you."

"There's a lawyer in New York. His name's Bracegirdle. George Bracegirdle."

"Do you have a number?"

"Look it up," I said. Pippa had come into the room to get the dog a bowl of water, and, awkwardly, so I wouldn't have to look at her, I turned to face the wall.

"Brace *Girdle?*" Xandra was saying. "Is that the way it sounds? What the hell kind of name is that?"

"Look, I'm sure you'll be able to find him."

There was a silence. Then Xandra said: "You know what?"

"What?"

"That was your father that died. Your own father. And you act like it was, I don't know, I'd say the dog, but not *even* the dog. Because I know you'd care if it was the dog got hit by a car, at least I think you would."

"Let's say I cared about him exactly as much as he did about me."

"Well, let me tell *you* something. You and your dad are a whole lot more alike than you might think. You're his kid, all right, through and through."

"Well, you're full of shit," I said, after a brief, contemptuous pause — a retort that seemed, to me, to sum up the situation pretty nicely. But — long after I'd hung up the phone, when I sat sneezing and shivering in a hot bath, and in the bright fog after (swallowing the aspirins Hobie gave me, following him down the hall to the musty spare room, *you look packed in, extra blankets in the trunk, no, no more talking, I'll leave you to it now*) her parting shot rang again and again in my mind, as I turned my face into the heavy, foreign-smelling pillow. It wasn't true — no more than what she'd said about my mother was true. Even her raspy dry voice coming through the line, the memory of it, made me feel dirty. *Fuck her,* I thought sleepily. Forget about it. She was a million miles away. But though I was dead tired — more than dead tired — and the rickety brass bed was the softest bed I'd ever slept in, her words were an ugly thread running all night long through my dreams.

III.

We are so accustomed to disguise ourselves to others,
that in the end, we become disguised to ourselves.
— François de La Rochefoucauld

Chapter 7.

The Shop-Behind-the-Shop

i.

WHEN I WOKE TO the clatter of garbage trucks, it was as if I'd parachuted into a different universe. My throat hurt. Lying very still under the eider-down, I breathed the dark air of dried-out potpourri and burnt fireplace wood and—very faint—the evergreen tang of turpentine, resin, and varnish.

For some time I lay there. Popper—who'd been curled by my feet—was nowhere in evidence. I'd slept in my clothes, which were filthy. At last—propelled by a sneezing fit—I sat up, pulled my sweater over my shirt and grappled under the bed to make sure the pillowcase was still there, then trudged on cold floors to the bathroom. My hair had dried in knots too tangled to yank the comb through, and even after I doused it in water and started over, one chunk was so matted I finally gave up and sawed it out, laboriously, with a pair of rusted nail scissors from the drawer.

Christ, I thought, turning from the mirror to sneeze. I hadn't been around a mirror in a while and I barely recognized myself: bruised jaw, spattering of chin acne, face blotched and swollen from my cold—eyes swollen too, lidded and sleepy, giving me a sort of dumb, shifty, home-schooled look. I looked like some cult-raised kid just rescued by local law enforcement, brought blinking from some basement stocked with fire-arms and powdered milk.

It was late: nine. Stepping out of my room, I could hear the morning classical program on WNYC, a dream familiarity in the announcer's voice, Köchel numbers, a drugged calm, the same warm public-radio purr I'd woken up to so many mornings back at Sutton Place. In the kitchen, I found Hobie at the table with a book.

But he wasn't reading; he was staring across the room. When he saw me he started.

"Well, there you are," he said as he rose to messily sweep aside a pile of mail and bills so I could sit. He was dressed for the workshop, knee-sprung corduroys and an old peat-brown sweater, ragged and eaten with moth holes, and his receding hairline and new short-cropped hair gave him the ponderous, bald-templed look of the marble senator on the cover of Hadley's Latin book. "How's the form?"

"Fine, thanks." Voice gravelled and croaking.

Down came the brows again and he looked at me hard. "Good heavens!" he said. "You sound like a raven this morning."

What did that mean? Ablaze with shame, I slid into the chair he scraped out for me and — too embarrassed to meet his eye — stared at his book: cracked leather, *Life and Letters* of Lord Somebody, an old volume that had probably come from one of his estate sales, old Mrs. So-and-So up in Poughkeepsie, broken hip, no children, all very sad.

He was pouring me tea, pushing a plate my way. In an attempt to hide my discomfort I put my head down and plowed into the toast — and nearly choked, since my throat was too raw for me to swallow. Too quickly I reached for the tea, so I sloshed it on the tablecloth and had to scramble to blot it up.

"No — no, it doesn't matter — here —"

My napkin was sopping wet; I didn't know what to do with it; in my confusion I dropped it on top of my toast and reached under my glasses to rub my eyes. "I'm sorry," I blurted.

"Sorry?" He was looking at me as if I'd asked him for directions to a place he wasn't sure how to get to. "Oh, come now —"

"Please don't make me go."

"What's that? Make you *go*? Go where?" He pulled his half-moon glasses low and looked at me over the tops of them. "Don't be ridiculous," he said, in a playful, half-irritated voice. "Tell you where I ought to make you go is straight back to bed. You sound like you're down with the Black Death."

But his manner failed to reassure me. Paralyzed with embarrassment, determined not to start crying, I found myself staring hard at the forlorn spot by the stove where once upon a time Cosmo's basket had stood.

"Ah," said Hobie, when he saw me looking at the empty corner. "Yes.

There you go. Deaf as a haddock, having three and four seizures a week but still we wanted him to live forever. I blubbed like a baby. If you'd told me Welty was going to go before Cosmo — he spent half his life carrying that dog back and forth to the vet — Look here," he said in an altered voice, leaning forward and trying to catch my eye when still I sat speechless and miserable. "Come on. I know you've been through a lot but there's no need in the world to fuss about it now. You look very shook — now, now, yes you do," he said crisply. "Very shook indeed and — bless you!" — flinching a bit — "bad dose of something, for sure. Don't fret — everything's all right. Go back to bed, why don't you, and we'll hash it out later."

"I know but —" I turned my head away to stifle a wet, burbling sneeze. "I don't have any place to go."

He leaned back in his chair: courteous, careful, something a little dusty about him. "Theo —" tapping at his lower lip — "how old are you?"

"Fifteen. Fifteen and a half."

"And —" he seemed to be working out how to ask it — "what about your grandfather?"

"Oh," I said, helplessly, after a pause.

"You've spoken to him? He knows that you've nowhere to go?"

"Well, shit —" it had just slipped out; Hobie put up a hand to reassure me — "you don't understand. I mean — I don't know if he has Alzheimer's or what, but when they called him he didn't even ask to speak to me."

"So —" Hobie leaned his chin heavily in his hand and eyed me like a skeptical schoolteacher — "you didn't speak to him."

"No — I mean not personally — this lady was there, helping out —" Xandra's friend Lisa (solicitous, following me around, voicing gentle but increasingly urgent concerns that "the family" be notified) had retreated to a corner at some point to dial the number I gave her — and got off the phone with such a look that it had elicited, from Xandra, the only laugh of the evening.

"This lady?" said Hobie, in the silence that had fallen, in a voice you might employ with a mental patient.

"Right. I mean —" I scrubbed a hand over my face; the colors in the kitchen were too intense; I felt lightheaded, out of control — "I guess Dorothy answered the phone and Lisa said she was like 'okay, wait,' — not even 'Oh no!' or 'what happened?' or 'how terrible!' — just 'hang on, let me get him,' and then my granddad came on and Lisa told him about the wreck and he listened, and then he said well, he was sorry to hear it, but in this sort of *tone,* Lisa said. Not 'what can I do' or 'when is the funeral' or anything. Just, like, thank you for calling, we appreciate it, bye. I mean — I could have told her," I added nervously when Hobie didn't answer. "Because, I mean, they really didn't like my dad — *really* didn't like him — Dorothy is his stepmother and they hated each other from Day One but he never got along with Grandpa Decker either —"

"All right, all right. Steady on —"

"— and, I mean, my dad was in some trouble when he was a kid, that might have had something to do with it — he was arrested but I don't know what for — honestly I don't know why, but they never wanted anything to do with him for as long as I remember and they never wanted anything to do with me either —"

"Calm down! I'm not trying to —"

"— because, I swear, I hardly ever met them, I really don't know them at all but there's no reason for them to hate me — not that my grandpa is such a great guy, he was pretty abusive to my dad actually —"

"Ssh — no carrying on! I'm not trying to put the screws on you, I just want to know — no now, listen," he said as I tried to talk over him, batting away my words as if he were shooing a fly from the table.

"My mother's lawyer is here. In the city. Will you come with me to see him? No," I said in confusion as his eyebrows came together, "not a lawyer lawyer, but that handles money? I talked to him on the phone? Before I left?"

"Okay," said Pippa — laughing, pink-cheeked from the cold — "what's wrong with this dog? Has he never seen a car?"

Bright red hair; green wool hat; the shock of seeing her in broad daylight was a dash of cold water. She had a hitch in her walk, probably from the accident but there was a grasshopper lightness to it like the odd, graceful preliminary to a dance step; and she was wrapped in so many layers against the cold that she looked like a colorful little cocoon, with feet.

"He was yowling like a cat," she said, unwinding one of her many patterned scarves as Popchyk danced at her feet with the end of his leash in his mouth. "Does he always make that weird noise? I mean, a cab would go by and — whoo! in the air! I was flying him like a kite! People were laughing their heads off. Yes —" stooping to speak to the dog, rubbing the top of his head with her knuckles — "you, you need a bath, don't you? Is he a Maltese?" she said, glancing up.

Furiously I nodded, back of my hand to my mouth, trying to choke back a sneeze.

"I love dogs." I could hardly hear what she was saying, so dazzled was I by her eyes on mine. "I have a dog book and I memorized every breed there is. If I had a big dog I'd have a Newfoundland like Nana in Peter Pan, and if I had a small dog — well, I change my mind all the time. I like all the little terriers — Jack Russells especially, they're always so funny and friendly on the street. But I know a wonderful Basenji too. And I met a really great Pekingese the other day. Really really tiny and really intelligent. Only royalty could have them in China. They're a very ancient breed."

"Maltese are ancient, too," I croaked, glad to have an interesting fact to contribute. "They date back to ancient Greece."

"That's why you picked a Maltese? Because it was ancient?"

"Um —" Stifling a cough.

She was saying something else — to the dog, not me — but I'd fallen into another fit of sneezing. Quickly, Hobie scrabbled for the closest thing at hand — a table napkin — and passed it over to me.

"All right, enough," he said. "Back to bed. No, no," he said as I tried to hand the napkin back to him, "you keep it. Now tell me —" eyeing my wrecked plate, spilled tea and soggy toast — "what can I bring you for breakfast?"

Caught between sneezes, I gave a bright, Russian-accented shrug I'd picked up from Boris: *anything.*

"All right then, if you don't mind it, I'll make you some oatmeal. Easy on the throat. Don't you have any socks?"

"Um —" She was busy with the dog, mustard-yellow sweater and hair like an autumn leaf, and her colors were mixed up and confused with the bright colors of the kitchen: striped apples glowing in a yellow bowl, the sharp ding of silver glinting from the coffee can where Hobie kept his paintbrushes.

"Pyjamas?" Hobie was saying. "No? I'll see what I can find of Welty's. And when you get out of those things I'll throw them in the wash. Now, off with you," he said, clapping his hand on my shoulder so suddenly I jumped.

"I —"

"You can stay. As long as however you like. And don't worry, I'll go with you to see your solicitor, it'll all be fine."

ii.

GROGGY, SHIVERING, I MADE my way down the dark hall and eased between the covers, which were heavy and ice-cold. The room smelled damp, and though there were many interesting things to look at — a pair of terra-cotta griffins, Victorian beadwork pictures, even a crystal ball — the dark brown walls, their deep dry texture like cocoa powder, soaked me through and through with a sense of Hobie's voice and also of Welty's, a friendly brown that saturated me to the core and spoke in warm old-fashioned tones, so that drifting in a lurid stream of fever I felt wrapped and reassured by their presence whereas Pippa had cast a shifting, colored nimbus of her own, I was thinking in a mixed-up way about scarlet leaves and bonfire sparks flying up in darkness and also my painting, how it would look against such a rich, dark, light-absorbing ground. Yellow feathers. Flash of crimson. Bright black eyes.

I woke with a jolt — terrified, flailing, back on the bus again with someone lifting the painting from my knapsack — to find Pippa lifting up the sleepy dog, her hair brighter than everything else in the room.

"Sorry, but he needs to go out," she said. "Don't sneeze on me."

I scrambled up on my elbows. "Sorry, hi," I said idiotically, smearing an arm across my face; and then: "I'm feeling better."

Her unsettling golden-brown eyes went around the room. "Are you bored? Do you want me to bring you some colored pencils?"

"Colored pencils?" I was baffled. "Why?"

"Uh, to draw with —?"

"Well —"

"Not a big deal," she said. "All you had to say was no."

Out she whisked, Popchik trotting after her, leaving behind her a smell of cinnamon gum, and I turned my face into the pillow feeling crushed by my stupidity. Though I would have died rather than told anyone, I was worried that my exuberant drug use had damaged my brain and my nervous system and maybe even my soul in some irreparable and perhaps not readily apparent way.

While I was lying there worrying, my cell phone beeped: GES WR I AM? POOL @ MGM GRAND!!!!!

I blinked. BORIS? I texted in reply.

YES, IS ME!

What was he doing there? RUOK? I texted back.

YES BT U SLEEPY! WE BIN DOIN THOS 8BALS OMG :-)

And then, another ding:

* GREAT * FUN. PARTY PARTY. U? LIVING UNDER UNDRPASS?

NYC, I texted back. SICK IN BED. WHY RU AT MGMGR

HERE W KT AND AMBER & THOSE GUYS!!! ;-)

then, coming in a second later: DO U NO OF DRINK CALLED WITE RUSIAN?
U NICE TASTNG NOT U GOOD NAME 4 DRNK THO

A knock. "Are you all right?" said Hobie, sticking his head in the door.
"Can I bring you anything?"

I put the phone aside. "No, thank you."

"Well, tell me when you're hungry, please. There's loads of food, the
fridge is so stuffed I can hardly get the door closed, we had people in for
Thanksgiving—what is that racket?" he said, looking around.

"Just my phone." Boris had texted: U CANT BELIEUE THE LAST FEW
DAZE!!!

"Well, I'll leave you to it. Let me know if you need something."

Once he was gone, I rolled to face the wall and texted back: MGMGR?
W/ KT BEARMAN?!

The answer came almost immediately: YES! ALSO AMBER & MIMI &
JESICA & KT'S SISTR JORDAN WHO IS IN *COLEGE* :-D

WTF???

U LEFT AT A BAD TIME!!! :-D

then, almost immediately, before I could reply: G2GO, AMBR NEEDS HER
PHONE

CALL ME L8R, I texted back. But there was no reply—and it would be a
long, long time before I heard anything from Boris again.

iii.

THAT DAY, AND THE next day or two, flopping around in a bewilderingly
soft pair of Welty's old pyjamas, were so topsy-turvy and deranged with
fever that repeatedly I found myself back at Port Authority running away
from people, dodging through crowds and ducking into tunnels with oily

water dripping on me or else in Las Vegas again on the CAT bus, riding through windwhipped industrial plazas with blown sand hitting the windows and no money to pay my fare. Time slid from under me in drifts like ice skids on the highway, punctuated by sudden sharp flashes where my wheels caught and I was flung into ordinary time: Hobie bringing me aspirins and ginger ale with ice, Popchik—freshly bathed, fluffy and snow-white—hopping up on the foot of the bed to march back and forth across my feet.

"Here," said Pippa, coming over to the bed and poking me in the side so she could sit down. "Move over."

I sat up, fumbling for my glasses. I'd been dreaming about the painting—I'd had it out, looking at it, or had I?—and found myself glancing around anxiously to make sure I'd put it away before I went to sleep.

"What's the matter?"

I forced myself to turn my gaze to her face. "Nothing." I'd crawled under the bed several times just to put my hands on the pillowcase, and I couldn't help wondering if I'd been careless and left it poking from under the bed. *Don't look down there,* I told myself. *Look at her.*

"Here," Pippa was saying. "Made you something. Hold out your hand."

"Wow," I said, staring at the spiked, kelly-green origami in my palm. "Thanks."

"Do you know what it is?"

"Uh—" Deer? Crow? Gazelle? Panicked, I glanced up at her.

"Give up? A frog! Can't you tell? Here, put it on the nightstand. It's supposed to hop when you press on it like this, see?"

As I fooled around with it, awkwardly, I was aware of her eyes on me—eyes that had a light and wildness to them, a careless power like the eyes of a kitten.

"Can I look at this?" She'd snatched up my iPod and was busily scrolling through it. "Hmn," she said. "Nice! Magnetic Fields, Mazzy Star, Nico, Nirvana, Oscar Peterson. No classical?"

"Well, there's some," I said, feeling embarrassed. Everything she'd mentioned except the Nirvana had actually been my mom's, and even some of that was hers.

"I'd make you some CDs. Except I left my computer at school. I guess I could mail you some — I've been listening to a lot of Arvo Pärt lately, don't ask me why, I have to listen on my headphones because it drives my roommates nuts."

Terrified she was going to catch me staring, unable to wrench my eyes away, I watched her studying my iPod with bent head: ears rosy-pink, raised line of scar tissue slightly puckered underneath the scalding-red hair. In profile her downcast eyes were long, heavy-lidded, with a tenderness that reminded me of the angels and page boys in the Northern European Masterworks book I'd checked and re-checked from the library.

"Hey —" Words drying up in my mouth.

"Yes?"

"Um —" Why wasn't it like before? Why couldn't I think of anything to say?

"Oooh —" she'd glanced up at me, and then was laughing again, laughing too hard to talk.

"What is it?"

"Why are you looking at me like that?"

"Like what?" I said, alarmed.

"Like —" I wasn't sure how to interpret the pop-eyed face she made at me. Choking person? Mongoloid? Fish?

"Dont be mad. You're just so serious. It's just —" she glanced down at the iPod, and broke out laughing again. "Ooh," she said, "Shostakovich, *intense.*"

How much did she remember? I wondered, afire with humiliation yet unable to tear my eyes from her. It wasn't the kind of thing you could ask but still I wanted to know. Did she have nightmares too? Crowd fears? Sweats and panics? Did she ever have the sense of observing herself from afar, as I often did, as if the explosion had knocked my body and my soul into two separate entities that remained about six feet apart from one another? Her gust of laughter had a self-propelling recklessness I knew all too well from wild nights with Boris, an edge of giddiness and hysteria that I associated (in myself, anyway) with having narrowly missed death. There had been nights in the desert where I was so sick with laughter, convulsed and doubled over with aching stomach for hours on end, I would happily have thrown myself in front of a car to make it stop.

iv.

ON MONDAY MORNING, THOUGH I was far from well, I roused myself from my fog of aches and dozes and trudged dutifully into the kitchen and telephoned Mr. Bracegirdle's office. But when I asked for him, his secretary (after putting me on hold, and then returning a bit too swiftly) informed me that Mr. Bracegirdle was out of the office and no, she didn't have a number where he could be reached and no, she was afraid she couldn't say when he might be in. Was there anything else?

"Well—" I left Hobie's number with her and was regretting that I'd been too slow on the draw to go ahead and schedule the appointment when the phone rang.

"212, eh?" said the rich, clever voice.

"I left," I said stupidly; the cold in my head made me sound nasal and block-witted. "I'm in the city."

"Yes, I gathered." His tone was friendly but cool. "What can I do for you?"

When I told him about my father, there was a deep breath. "Well," he said carefully. "I'm sorry to hear it. When did this happen?"

"Last week."

He listened without interrupting; in the five minutes or so it took me to fill him in, I heard him turn away at least two other calls. "Crikey," he said, when I'd finished talking. "That's quite a story, Theodore."

Crikey: in a different mood, I might have smiled. This was definitely a person my mother had known and liked.

"It must have been dreadful for you out there," he was saying. "Of course, I'm terribly sorry for your loss. It's all *very* sad. Though quite frankly—and I feel more comfortable saying this to you now—when he turned up, no one knew what to do. Your mother had of course confided some things—even Samantha had expressed concerns—well, as you know, it was a difficult situation. But I don't think anyone expected this. Thugs with baseball bats."

"Well—" *thugs with baseball bats,* I hadn't really meant for him to seize on that detail. "He was just standing there holding it. It's not like he hit me or anything."

"Well—" he laughed, an easy laugh that broke the tension—"sixty-

five thousand dollars did seem like a *very* specific sum. I have to say too—
I went a bit beyond my authority as your counsel when we spoke on the
phone, though under the circumstances I hope you'll forgive me. It was
just that I smelled a bit of a rat."

"Sorry?" I said, after a sick pause.

"Over the phone. The money. You *can* withdraw it, from the 529 anyway. Large tax penalty, but it's possible."

Possible? I could have taken it? An alternate future was flashing
through my mind: Mr. Silver paid, Dad in his bathrobe checking the
sports scores on his BlackBerry, me in Spirsetskaya's class with Boris laz-
ing across the aisle from me.

"Although I do need to tell you that the money in the fund is actually a
bit short of that," Mr. Bracegirdle was saying. "Socked away and growing
all the time, though! Not that we can't arrange for you to use some of it
now, given your circumstances, but your mother was absolutely determined not to dip into it even with her financial troubles. The last thing she
would have wanted was for your dad to get his hands on it. And yes, just
between the two of us, I do think you were very smart to come back to the
city on your own recognizance. Sorry—" muffled conversation—"I've
got an eleven o'clock, I've got to run—you're staying at Samantha's now, I
gather?"

The question threw me for a loop. "No," I said, "with some friends in
the Village."

"Well, splendid. Just so long as you're comfortable. At any rate, I'm
afraid I have to dash now. What do you say we continue this discussion in
my office? I'll put you back through to Patsy so she can schedule an
appointment."

"Great," I said, "thank you," but when I got off the phone, I felt sick—
like someone had just reached a hand in my chest and wrenched loose a
lot of ugly wet stuff around my heart.

"Everything okay?" said Hobie—crossing through the kitchen, stopping suddenly to see the look on my face.

"Sure." But it was a long walk down the hall to my room—and once I
closed the door and climbed back in bed I began to cry, or half-cry, ugly
dry wheezes with my face pressed in the pillow, while Popchik pawed at
my shirt and snuffled anxiously against the back of my neck.

V.
_____

BEFORE THIS, I'D BEEN feeling better, but somehow it was like this news made me ill all over again. As the day wore on and my fever climbed to its former dizzying wobble, I could think of nothing but my dad: *I have to call him,* I thought, starting again and again from bed just as I was drifting off; it was as if his death weren't real but only a rehearsal, a trial run; the real death (the permanent one) was yet to happen and there was time to stop it if only I found him, if only he was answering his cell phone, if Xandra could reach him from work, *I have to get hold of him, I have to let him know.* Then, later—the day was over, it was dark—I had fallen into a troubled half dream where my dad was excoriating me for screwing up some air travel reservations when I became aware of lights in the hallway, a tiny backlit shadow—Pippa, coming suddenly into the room with stumbling step almost like someone had pushed her, looking doubtfully behind her, saying: "Should I wake him?"

"Wait," I said—half to her and half to my dad, who was falling back rapidly into the darkness, some violent stadium crowd on the other side of a tall, arched gate. When I got my glasses on, I saw she had her coat on like she was going out.

"Sorry?" I said, arm over my eyes, confused in the glare from the lamp.

"No, I'm sorry. It's just—I mean—" pushing a strand of hair out of her face—"I'm leaving and I wanted to say goodbye."

"Goodbye?"

"Oh." Her pale brows drew together; she looked in the doorway to Hobie (who had vanished) and back to me. "Right. Well." Her voice seemed slightly panicked. "I'm going back. Tonight. Anyway, it was nice to see you. I hope everything works out for you okay."

"Tonight?"

"Yeah, I'm flying out now. She has me in boarding school?" she said when I continued to goggle at her. "I'm here for Thanksgiving? Here to see the doctor? Remember?"

"Oh. Right." I was staring at her very hard and hoping that I was still asleep. Boarding school rang a vague bell but I thought it was something I'd dreamed.

"Yeah—" she seemed uneasy too—"too bad you didn't get here earlier, it was fun. Hobie cooked—we had tons of people over. Anyway I was lucky I got to come at all—I had to get permission from Dr. Camenzind. We don't have Thanksgiving off at my school."

"What do they do?"

"They don't celebrate it. Well—I think maybe they make turkey or something for the people who do."

"What school is this?"

When she told me the name—with a half-humorous quirk of her mouth—I was shocked. Institut Mont-Haefeli was a school in Switzerland—barely accredited, according to Andy—where only the very dumbest and most disturbed girls went.

"Mont-Haefeli? Really? I thought it was very"—the word *psychiatric* was wrong—"wow."

"Well. Aunt Margaret says I'll get used to it." She was fooling around with the origami frog on the nightstand, trying to make it jump, only it was bent and tipping to one side. "And the view is like the mountain on the Caran d'Ache box. Snowcaps and flower meadow and all that. Otherwise it's like one of those dull Euro horror movies where nothing much happens."

"But—" I felt like I was missing something, or maybe still asleep. The only person I'd ever known who went to Mont-Haefeli was James Villiers's sister, Dorit Villiers, and the story was she'd been sent there because she stabbed her boyfriend in the hand with a knife.

"Yeah, it's a weird place," she said, bored eyes flickering around the room. "A school for loonies. Not many places I could get in with my head injury though. They have a clinic attached," she said, shrugging. "Doctors on staff. Bigger deal than you'd think. I mean, I have problems since I got hit on the head, but it's not like I'm nuts or a shoplifter."

"Yeah, but—" I was still trying to get *horror movie* out of my mind—"Switzerland? That's pretty cool."

"If you say so."

"I knew this girl Lallie Foulkes who went to Le Rosey. She said they had a chocolate break every morning."

"Well, we don't even get jam on our toast." Her hand was speckled and pale against the black of her coat. "Only the eating-disorder girls get it. If you want sugar in your tea you have to steal the packets from the nurses' station."

"Um—" Worse and worse. "Do you know a girl named Dorit Villiers?"

"No. She was there but then they sent her someplace else. I think she tried to scratch somebody in the face. They had her in lock-up for a while."

"What?"

"That's not what they *call* it," she said, rubbing her nose. "It's a farm-looking building they call La Grange—you know, all milkmaid and fake rustic. Nicer than the residence houses. But the doors are alarmed and they have guards and stuff."

"Well, I mean—" I thought of Dorit Villiers—frizzy gold hair; blank blue eyes like a loopy Christmas tree angel—and didn't know what to say.

"That's only where they put the really crazy girls. La Grange. I'm in Bessonet, with a bunch of French-speaking girls. It's supposed to be so I learn French better but all it means is nobody talks to me."

"You should tell her you don't like it! Your aunt."

She grimaced. "I do. But then she starts telling me how much it costs. Or else says I'm hurting her feelings. Anyway," she said, uneasily, in an *I've got to go* voice, looking over her shoulder.

"Huh," I said, at last, after a woozy pause. Day and night, my delirium had been colored with an awareness of her in the house, recurring energy-surges of happiness at the sound of her voice in the hallway, her footsteps: we were going to make a blanket tent, she would be waiting for me at the ice rink, bright hum of excitement at all the things we were going to do when I got better—in fact it seemed we *had* been doing things, such as stringing necklaces of rainbow-colored candy while the radio played Belle and Sebastian and then, later on, wandering through a non-existent casino arcade in Washington Square.

Hobie, I noticed, was standing discreetly in the hall. "Sorry," he said, glancing at his wristwatch. "I really hate to rush you—"

"Sure," she said. To me she said: "Goodbye then. Hope you feel better."

"Wait!"

"What?" she said, half turning.

"You'll be back for Christmas, right?"

"Nope, Aunt Margaret's."

"When are you coming back, then?"

"Well—" one-shouldered shrug. "Dunno. Spring holidays maybe."

"Pips—" said Hobie, though he was really speaking to me instead of her.

"Right," she said, brushing her hair from her eyes.

I waited until I heard the front door shut. Then I got out of bed and pulled aside the curtain. Through the dusty glass, I watched them going together down the front steps, Pippa in her pink scarf and hat hurrying slightly alongside Hobie's large, well-dressed form.

For a while after they turned the corner, I stood at the window looking out at the empty street. Then, feeling light-headed and forlorn, I trudged to her bedroom and — unable to resist — cracked the door a sliver.

It was the same as two years before, except emptier. Wizard of Oz and Save Tibet posters. No wheelchair. Window piled with white pebbles of sleet on the sill. But it smelled like her, it was still warm and alive with her presence, and as I stood breathing in her atmosphere I felt a huge happy smile on my face just to be standing there with her fairy tale books, her perfume bottles, her sparkly tray of barrettes and her valentine collection: paper lace, cupids and columbines, Edwardian suitors with rose bouquets pressed to their hearts. Quietly, tiptoeing even though I was barefoot, I walked over to the silver-framed photographs on the dresser — Welty and Cosmo, Welty and Pippa, Pippa and her mother (same hair, same eyes) with a younger and thinner Hobie —

Low buzzing noise, inside the room. Guiltily I turned — someone coming? No: only Popchik, cotton white after his bath, nestled amongst the pillows of her unmade bed and snoring with a drooling, blissful, half-purring sound. And though there was something pathetic about it — taking comfort in her left-behind things like a puppy snuggled in an old coat — I crawled in under the sheets and nestled down beside him, smiling foolishly at the smell of her comforter and the silky feel of it on my cheek.

vi.

"WELL WELL," SAID Mr. Bracegirdle as he shook Hobie's hand and then mine. "Theodore — I do have to say — you're growing up to look a great deal like your mother. I wish she could see you now."

I tried to meet his eye and not seem embarrassed. The truth was: though I had my mother's straight hair, and something of her light-and-dark coloring, I looked a whole lot more like my father, a likeness so strong that no chatty bystander, no waitress in any coffee shop had allowed it to pass unremarked — not that I'd ever been happy about it, resembling the parent I couldn't stand, but to see a younger version of his sulky, drunk-driving face in the mirror was particularly upsetting now that he was dead.

Hobie and Mr. Bracegirdle were chatting in a subdued way — Mr. Bracegirdle was telling Hobie how he'd met my mother, dawning remembrance from Hobie: "Yes! I remember — a foot in less than an hour! My God, I came out of my auction and nothing was moving, I was uptown at the old Parke-Bernet —"

"On Madison across from the Carlyle?"

"Yes — quite a long hoof home."

"You deal antiques? Down in the Village, Theo says?"

Politely, I sat and listened to their conversation: friends in common, gallery owners and art collectors, the Rakers and the Rehnbergs, the Fawcetts and the Vogels and the Mildebergers and Depews, on to vanished New York landmarks, the closing of Lutèce, La Caravelle, Café des Artistes, what would your mother have thought, Theodore, she loved Café des Artistes. (How did he know that? I wondered.) While I didn't for an instant believe some of the things my dad, in moments of meanness, had insinuated about my mother, it *did* appear that Mr. Bracegirdle had known my mother a good deal better than I would have thought. Even the non-legal books on his shelf seemed to suggest a correspondence, an echo of interests between them. Art books: Agnes Martin, Edwin Dickinson. Poetry too, first editions: Ted Berrigan. Frank O'Hara, *Meditations in an Emergency.* I remembered the day she'd turned up flushed and happy with the exact same edition of Frank O'Hara — which I assumed she'd found at the Strand, since we didn't have the money for something like that. But when I thought about it, I realized she hadn't told me where she'd got it.

"Well, Theodore," said Mr. Bracegirdle, calling me back to myself. Though elderly, he had the calm, well-tanned look of someone who spent a lot of his spare time on the tennis court; the dark pouches under his eyes gave him a genial panda-bear aspect. "You're old enough that a judge would consider your wishes above all in this matter," he was saying. "Especially since your guardianship would be uncontested — of course," he said to Hobie, "we could seek a temporary guardianship for the upcoming interlude, but I don't think that will be necessary. Clearly this arrangement is in the minor's best interests, as long as it's all right with you?"

"That and more," said Hobie. "I'm happy if he's happy."

"You're fully prepared to act in an informal capacity as Theodore's adult custodian for the time being?"

"Informal, black tie, whatever's called for."

"There's your schooling to look after as well. We'd spoken of boarding school, as I recall. But that seems a lot to think of now, doesn't it?" he said, noting the stricken look on my face. "Shipping out as you've just arrived, and with the holidays coming up? No need to make any decisions at all at the moment, I shouldn't think," he said, with a glance at Hobie. "I should think it would be fine if you just sat out the rest of this term and we can sort it out later. And you know that you can of course call upon me at *any* time. Day or night." He was writing a phone number on a business card. "This is my home number, and this is my cell — my, my, that's a nasty cough you have there!" he said, glancing up — "quite a cough, are you having that looked after, yes? and this is my number out in Bridgehampton. I hope you won't hesitate to call me for any reason, if you need anything."

Trying hard, doing my best, to swallow another cough. "Thank you —"

"This is definitely what you want?" He was looking at me keenly with an expression that made me feel like I was on the witness stand. "To be at Mr. Hobart's for the next few weeks?"

I didn't like the sound of *the next few weeks*. "Yes," I said into my fist, "but —"

"Because — boarding school." He folded his hands and leaned back in his chair and regarded me. "Almost certainly the best thing for you in the long term but quite frankly, given the situation, I believe I could telephone my friend Sam Ungerer at Buckfield and we could get you up there right now. Something could be arranged. It's an excellent school. And I think it would be possible to arrange for you to stay in the home of the headmaster or one of the teachers rather than the dormitory, so you could be in more of a family setting, if you thought that would be something you'd like."

He and Hobie were both looking at me, encouragingly as I thought. I stared at my shoes, not wanting to seem ungrateful but wishing that this line of suggestion would go away.

"Well." Mr. Bracegirdle and Hobie exchanged a glance—was I wrong to see a hint of resignation and/or disappointment in Hobie's expression? "As long as this is what you want, and Mr. Hobart's amenable, I see nothing wrong with this arrangement for the time being. But I do urge you to think about where you'd like to be, Theodore, so we can go ahead and work out something for the next school term or maybe even summer school, if you'd like."

vii.

TEMPORARY GUARDIANSHIP. IN THE next weeks, I did my best to buckle down and not think too much about what *temporary* might mean. I'd applied to an early-college program in the city—my reasoning being that it would keep me from being shipped out to the sticks if for some reason things at Hobie's didn't work. All day in my room, under a weak lamp, as Popchik snoozed on the carpet by my feet, I spent hunched over test preparation booklets, memorizing dates, proofs, theorems, Latin vocabulary words, so many irregular verbs in Spanish that even in my dreams I looked down the lines of long tables and despaired of keeping them straight.

It was as if I was trying to punish myself—maybe even make things up to my mother—by setting my sights so high. I'd fallen out of the habit of doing schoolwork; it wasn't exactly as if I'd kept up my studies in Vegas and the sheer amount of material to memorize gave me a feeling of torture, lights turned in the face, not knowing the correct answer, catastrophe if I failed. Rubbing my eyes, trying to keep myself awake with cold showers and iced coffee, I goaded myself on by reminding myself what a good thing I was doing, though my endless cramming felt a lot more like self destruction than any glue-sniffing I'd ever done; and at some bleary point, the work itself became a kind of drug that left me so drained that I could hardly take in my surroundings.

And yet I was grateful for the work because it kept me too mentally bludgeoned to think. The shame that tormented me was all the more corrosive for having no very clear origin: I didn't know why I felt so tainted, and worthless, and wrong—only that I did, and whenever I looked up from my books I was swamped by slimy waters rushing in from all sides.

Part of it had to do with the painting. I knew nothing good would come of keeping it, and yet I also knew I'd kept it too long to speak up. Confiding in Mr. Bracegirdle was foolhardy. My position was too precarious; he was already champing at the bit to send me to boarding school. And when I thought, as I often did, of confiding in Hobie, I found myself drifting into various theoretical scenarios none of which seemed any more or less probable than the others.

I would give the painting to Hobie and he would say, 'oh, no big deal' and somehow (I had problems with this part, the logistics of it) he would take care of it, or phone some people he knew, or have a great idea about what to do, or something, and not care, or be mad, and somehow it would all be fine?

Or: I would give the painting to Hobie and he would call the police.

Or: I would give the painting to Hobie and he would take the painting for himself and then say, 'what, are you crazy? Painting? I don't know what you're talking about.'

Or: I would give the painting to Hobie and he would nod and look sympathetic and tell me I'd done the right thing but then as soon as I was out of the room he would phone his own lawyer and I would be dispatched to boarding school or a juvenile home (which, painting or not, was where most of my scenarios ended up anyway).

But by far the greater part of unease had to do with my father. I knew that his death wasn't my fault, and yet on a bone-deep, irrational, completely unshakable level I also knew that it was. Given how coldly I'd walked away from him in his final despair, the fact that he'd lied was beside the point. Maybe he'd known that it was in my power to pay his debt—a fact which had haunted me since Mr. Bracegirdle had so lightly let it slip. In the shadows beyond the desk lamp, Hobie's terra-cotta griffins stared at me with beady glass eyes. Did he think I'd stiffed him on purpose? That I wanted him to die? At night, I dreamed of him beaten and chased through casino parking lots, and more than once awoke with a jolt to him sitting in the chair by my bed and observing me quietly, the coal of his cigarette glowing in the dark. But they told me you died, I said aloud, before realizing he wasn't there.

Without Pippa, the house was deathly quiet. The closed-off formal rooms smelled faint and damp, like dead leaves. I mooned about looking at her things, wondering where she was and what she was doing and trying hard to feel connected to her by such tenuous threads as a red hair in the bathtub drain or a balled-up sock under the sofa. But as much as I missed the nervous tingle of her presence, I was soothed by the house, its sense of safety and enclosure: old portraits and poorly lit hallways, loudly ticking clocks. It was as if I'd signed on as a cabin boy on the *Marie Céleste*. As I moved about through the stagnant silences, the pools of shadow and deep sun, the old floors creaked underfoot like the deck of a ship, the wash of traffic out on Sixth Avenue breaking just audibly against the ear. Upstairs, puzzling light-headed over differential equations, Newton's Law of Cooling, independent variables, *we have used the fact that tau is constant to eliminate its derivative,* Hobie's presence below stairs was an anchor, a friendly weight: I was comforted to hear the tap of his mallet floating up from below and to know that he was down there pottering quietly with his tools and his spirit gums and varicolored woods.

With the Barbours, my lack of pocket money had been a continual worry; having always to hit Mrs. Barbour up for lunch money, lab fees at school, and other small expenses had occasioned dread and anxiety quite out of proportion to the sums she carelessly disbursed. But my living stipend from Mr. Bracegirdle made me feel a lot less awkward about throwing myself down in Hobie's household, unannounced. I was able to pay Popchik's vet bills, a small fortune, since he had bad teeth and a mild case of heartworm—Xandra to my knowledge never having given him a pill or taken him for shots my whole time in Vegas. I was also able to pay my own dentist bills, which were considerable (six fillings, ten hellish hours in the dentist's chair) and buy myself a laptop and an iPhone, as well as the shoes and winter clothes I needed. And—though Hobie wouldn't accept grocery money—still I went out and got groceries for him all the same, groceries I paid for: milk and sugar and washing powder from Grand Union, but more often fresh produce from the farmers' market at Union Square, wild mushrooms and winesap apples, raisin bread, small luxuries which seemed to please him, unlike the large containers of Tide which he looked at sadly and took to the pantry without a word.

It was all very different from the crowded, complicated, and overly formal atmosphere of the Barbours', where everything was rehearsed and scheduled like a Broadway production, an airless perfection from which Andy had been in constant retreat, scuttling to his bedroom like a frightened squid. By contrast Hobie lived and wafted like some great sea mammal in his own mild atmosphere, the dark brown of tea stains and tobacco, where every clock in the house said something different and time didn't actually correspond to the standard measure but instead meandered along at its own sedate tick-tock, obeying the pace of his antique-crowded backwater, far from the factory-built, epoxy-glued version of the world. Though he enjoyed going out to the movies, there was no television; he read old novels with marbled end papers; he didn't own a cell phone; his computer, a prehistoric IBM, was the size of a suitcase and useless. In blameless quiet, he buried himself in his work, steam-bending veneers or hand-threading table legs with a chisel, and his happy absorption floated up from the workshop and diffused through the house with the warmth of a wood-burning stove in winter. He was absent-minded and kind; he was neglectful and muddle-headed and self-deprecating and gentle; often he didn't hear the first time you spoke to him, or even the second time; he lost his glasses, mislaid his wallet, his keys, his dry-cleaning tickets, and was always calling me downstairs to get on my hands and knees with him to help him search for some minuscule fitting or piece of hardware he'd dropped on the floor. Occasionally he opened the store by appointment, for an hour or two at a time, but—as far as I could tell—this was little more than an excuse to bring out the bottle of sherry and visit with friends and acquaintances; and if he showed a piece of furniture, opening and shutting drawers to oohs and aahs, it seemed to be mostly in the spirit in which Andy and I, once upon a time, had dragged out our toys for show and tell.

If he ever actually sold a piece, I never saw him do it. His bailiwick (as he called it) was the workshop, or the 'hospital' rather, where the crippled chairs and tables stood stacked awaiting his care. Like a gardener occupied with greenhouse specimens, brushing aphids from individual plant leaves, he absorbed himself in the texture and grain of individual pieces, the hidden drawers, the scars and marvels. Though he owned a few items of modern woodworking equipment—a router, a cordless drill and a circular saw—he seldom used them. ("If it requires earplugs, I haven't much call for it.") He went down there early and sometimes, if he had a project, stayed down there after dark, but generally when the light started to go he came upstairs and—before washing up for dinner—poured himself the same inch of whiskey, neat, in a small tumbler: tired, congenial, lamp-black on his hands, something rough and soldierly in his fatigue. Has he takn u out to dinner, Pippa texted me.

Yes like 3 or 4x

He only likes 2go 2 3mpty rstrnts where nobody goes.

Thats right the place he took me last week was like king tuts tomb

Yes he only goes places where he feels sorry for the owners! because he is scared they will go out of business and then he will feel guilty

I like it better when he cooks

Ask him to make gingerbread for u I wish i had some now

Dinner was the time of day I looked forward to most. In Vegas—especially after Boris had taken up with Kotku—I'd never gotten used to the sadness of having to scrabble around to feed myself at night, sitting on the side of my bed with a bag of potato chips or maybe a dried-up container of rice left over from my dad's carry out. By happy contrast, Hobie's whole day revolved around dinner. Where shall we eat? Who's coming over? What shall I cook? Do you like pot-au-feu? No? Never had it? Lemon rice or saffron? Fig preserves or apricot? Do you want to walk over to Jefferson Market with me? Sometimes on Sundays there were guests, who among New School and Columbia professors, opera-orchestra and preservation-society ladies, and various old dears from up and down the street also included a great many dealers and collectors of all stripes, from batty old ladies in fingerless gloves who sold Georgian jewelry at the flea market to rich people who wouldn't have been out of place at the Barbours (Welty, I learned, had helped many of these people build their collections, by advising them what pieces to buy). Most of the conversation left me wholly at sea (St-Simon? Munich Opera Festival? Coomaraswamy? The villa at Pau?). But even when the rooms were formal and the company was "smart" his lunches were the sort where people didn't seem to mind serving themselves or eating from plates in their laps, as opposed to the rigidly catered parties always tinkling frostily away at the Barbours' house.

In fact, at these dinners, as agreeable and interesting as Hobie's guests were, I constantly worried that somebody who knew me from the Barbours was going to turn up. I felt guilty for not calling Andy; and yet, after what had happened with his dad on the street, I felt even more ashamed for him to know that I'd washed up in the city again with no place of my own to live.

And—though it was a small matter enough—I was still bothered by how I'd turned up at Hobie's in the first place. Though he never told the story in front of me, how I'd showed up on the doorstep, mainly because he could see how uncomfortable it made me, still he'd told people—not that I blamed him; it was too good a story not to tell. "It's so fitting if you knew Welty," said Hobie's great friend Mrs. DeFrees, a dealer in nineteenth-century watercolors who for all her stiff clothes and strong perfumes was a hugger and a cuddler, with the old-ladyish habit of liking to hold your arm or pat your hand as she talked. "Because, my dear, Welty was an agora*maniac.* Loved people, you know, loved the marketplace. The to and the fro of it. Deals, goods, conversation, exchange. It was that eeny bit of Cairo from his boyhood, I always said he would have been perfectly happy padding around in slippers and showing carpets in the souk. He had the antiquaire's gift, you know—he knew what belonged with whom. Someone would come in the shop never intending to buy a thing, ducking in out of the rain maybe, and he'd offer them a cup of tea and they'd end up having a dining room table shipped to Des Moines. Or a student would wander in to admire, and he'd bring out just the little inexpensive print. Everyone was happy, do you know. He knew everybody wasn't in the position to come in and buy some big important piece—it was all about matchmaking, finding the right home."

"Well, and people trusted him," said Hobie, coming in with Mrs. DeFrees's thimble of sherry and a glass of whiskey for himself. "He always said his handicap was what made him a good salesman and I think there's something to that. 'The sympathetic cripple.' No axe to grind. Always on the outside, looking in."

"Ah, Welty was never on the outside of anything," said Mrs. DeFrees, accepting her glass of sherry and patting Hobie affectionately on the sleeve, her little paper-skinned hand glittering with rose-cut diamonds. "He was always right in the thick of it, bless him, laughing that laugh, never a word of complaint. Anyway, my dear," she said, turning back to me, "make no mistake about it. Welty knew *exactly* what he was doing by giving you that ring. Because by giving it to you, he brought you straight here to Hobie, you see?"

"Right," I said—and then I'd had to get up and walk in the kitchen, so troubled was I by this detail. Because, of course, it wasn't just the ring he had given me.

... viii.

AT NIGHT, IN WELTY's old room, which was now my room, his old reading glasses and fountain pens still in the desk drawers, I lay awake listening to the street noise and fretting. It had crossed my mind in Vegas that if my dad or Xandra found the painting they might not know what it was, at least not right away. But Hobie would know. Over and over I found myself envisioning scenarios where I came home to discover Hobie waiting for me with the painting in his hands — "what's this?" — for there was no flim-flam, no excuse, no pre-emptive line with which to meet such a catastrophe; and when I got on my knees and reached under the bed to put my hands on the pillowcase (as I did, blindly and at erratic interludes, to make sure it was still there) it was a quick feint and drop like grabbing at a too-hot microwave dinner.

A house fire. An exterminator visit. Big red INTERPOL on the Missing Art Database. If anyone cared to make the connection, Welty's ring was proof positive that I'd been in the gallery with the painting. The door to my room was so old and uneven on its hinges that it didn't even catch properly; I had to prop it shut with an iron doorstop. What if, driven by some unanticipated impulse, he took it in his head to come upstairs and clean? Admittedly this seemed out of character for the absent-minded and not-particularly-tidy Hobie I knew — No he dosn't care if U R messy he never goes in my room except to change sheets & dust Pippa had texted, prompting me to strip my bed immediately and spend forty-five frantic minutes dusting every surface in my room — the griffons, the crystal ball, the headboard of the bed — with a clean T-shirt. Dusting soon became an obsessive habit — enough that I went out and bought my own dust cloths, even though Hobie had a house full of them; I didn't want him to *see* me dusting, my only hope was that the word *dust* would never occur to him if he happened to poke his head in my room.

For this reason, because I was really only comfortable leaving the house in his company, I spent most of my days in my room, at my desk, with scarcely a break for meals. And when he went out, I tagged along with him to galleries, estate sales, showrooms, auctions where I stood with him in the very back ("no, no," he said, when I pointed out the empty chairs in front, "we want to be where we can see the paddles") — exciting at first, just like the movies, though after a couple of hours as tedious as anything in *Calculus: Concepts and Connections.*

But though I tried (with some success) to act blasé, trailing him indifferently around Manhattan as if I didn't care one way or another, in truth I stuck to him in much the same anxious spirit that Popchik—desperately lonely—had followed along constantly behind Boris and me in Vegas. I went with him to snooty lunches. I went with him on appraisals. I went with him to his tailor. I went with him to poorly attended lectures on obscure Philadelphia cabinet-makers of the 1770s. I went with him to the Opera Orchestra, even though the programs were so boring and dragged on so long that I feared I might actually black out and topple into the aisle. I went with him to dinner with the Amstisses (on Park Avenue, uncomfortably close to the Barbours') and the Vogels, and the Krasnows, and the Mildebergers, where the conversation was either a.) so eye-crossingly dull or b.) so far over my head that I could never manage much more than *hmn*. ("Poor boy, we must be hopelessly uninteresting to you," said Mrs. Mildeberger brightly, not appearing to realize how truly she spoke.) Other friends, like Mr. Abernathy—my dad's age, with some ill-articulated scandal or disgrace in his past—were so mercurial and articulate, so utterly dismissive of me ("And *where* did you say you obtained this child, James?") that I sat dumbfounded among the Chinese antiquities and Greek vases, wanting to say something clever while at the same time terrified of attracting attention in any way, feeling tongue-tied and completely at sea. At least once or twice a week we went to Mrs. DeFrees in her antique-packed townhouse (the uptown analogue of Hobie's) on East Sixty-Third, where I sat on the edge of a spindly chair and tried to ignore her frightening Bengal cats digging their claws in my knees. ("He's a socially alert little creature, isn't he?" I heard her remark not so *sotto voce* when they were across the room fussing over some Edward Lear watercolors.) Sometimes she accompanied us to the showings at Christie's and Sotheby's, Hobie poring over every piece, opening and shutting drawers, showing me various points of workmanship, marking up his catalogue with a pencil—and then, after a stop or two at a gallery along the way, she went back to Sixty-Third Street and we went to Sant Ambrœus, where Hobie, in his smart suit, stood at the counter and drank an espresso while I ate a chocolate croissant and looked at the kids with book bags coming in and hoped I didn't see anyone I knew from my old school.

"Would your dad like another espresso?" the counterman asked when Hobie excused himself to go to the gents'.

"No thanks, I think just the check." It thrilled me, deplorably, when people mistook Hobie for my parent. Though he was old enough to be my grandfather, he projected a vigor more in keeping with older European dads you saw on the East Side—polished, portly, self-possessed dads on their second marriages who'd had kids at fifty and sixty. In his gallery-going clothes, sipping his espresso and looking out peacefully at the street, he might have been a Swiss industrial magnate or a restaurateur with a Michelin star or two: substantial, late-married, prosperous. Why, I thought sadly, as he returned with his topcoat over his arm, why hadn't my mother married someone like him—? Or Mr. Bracegirdle? somebody she actually had something in common with—older maybe but personable, someone who enjoyed galleries and string quartets and poking around used book stores, someone attentive, cultivated, kind? Who would have appreciated her, and bought her pretty clothes and taken her to Paris for her birthday, and given her the life she deserved? It wouldn't have been hard for her to find someone like that, if she'd tried. Men had loved her: from the doormen to my schoolteachers to the fathers of my friends right on up to her boss Sergio at work (who had called her, for reasons unknown to me, Dollybird), and even Mr. Barbour had always been quick to jump up and greet her when she came to pick me up from sleepovers, quick with the smiles and quick to touch her elbow as he steered her to the sofa, voice low and companionable, won't you sit down? would you like a drink, a cup of tea, anything? I did not think it was my imagination—not quite— how closely Mr. Bracegirdle had looked at me: almost as if he were looking at her, or looking for some trace of her ghost in me. Yet even in death my dad was ineradicable, no matter how hard I tried to wish him out of the picture— for there he always was, in my hands and my voice and my walk, in my darting sideways glance as I left the restaurant with Hobie, the very set of my head recalling his old, preening habit of checking himself out in any mirror-like surface.

ix.

IN JANUARY, I HAD my tests: the easy one and the hard one. The easy one was in a high school classroom in the Bronx: pregnant moms, assorted cabdrivers, and a raucous gaggle of Grand Concourse homegirls with short fur jackets and sparkle fingernails. But the test was not actually so easy as I thought it would be, with a lot more questions about arcane matters of New York State government than I'd anticipated (how many months of the year was the legislature in Albany in session? How the hell was I supposed to know?), and I came home on the subway preoccupied and depressed. And the hard test (locked classroom, uptight parents pacing the hallways, the strained atmosphere of a chess tournament) seemed to have been designed with some twitching, MIT-bred recluse in mind, with many of the multiple-choice answers so similar that I came away with literally no idea how I'd done.

So what, I told myself, walking up to Canal Street to catch the train with my hands shoved deep in my pockets and my armpits rank with anxious classroom perspiration. Maybe I wouldn't get into the early-college program—and what if I didn't? I had to do well, very well, in the top thirty per cent, if I stood any chance at all.

Hubris: a vocabulary word that had featured prominently on my pretests though it hadn't shown up on the tests proper. I was competing with five thousand applicants for something like three hundred places—if I didn't make the cut, I wasn't sure what would happen; I didn't think I could bear it if I had to go to Massachusetts and stay with these Ungerer people Mr. Bracegirdle kept talking about, this good-guy headmaster and his "crew," as Mr. Bracegirdle called them, mom and three boys, whom I imagined as a slab-like, stair-stepped, whitely smiling line of the same prep-school hoods who with cheerful punctuality in the bad old days had beaten up Andy and me and made us eat dust balls off the floor. But if I failed the test (or, more accurately, didn't do quite well enough to make the early-college program), how would I be able to work things so I could stay in New York? Certainly I should have aimed for a more achievable goal, some decent high school in the city where I would have at least had a chance of getting in. Yet Mr. Bracegirdle had been so adamant about boarding school, about fresh air and autumn color and starry skies and the many joys of country life ("*Stuyvesant.* Why would you stay here and go to Stuyvesant when you could get out of New York? Stretch your legs, breathe a bit easier? Be in a family situation?") that I'd stayed away from high schools altogether, even the very best ones.

"I know what your mother would have wanted for you, Theodore," he'd said repeatedly. "She would have wanted a fresh start for you. Out of the city." He was right. But how could I explain to him, in the chain of disorder and senselessness that had followed her death, exactly how irrelevant those old wishes were?

Still lost in thought as I turned the corner to the station, fishing in my pocket for my MetroCard, I passed a newsstand where I saw a headline reading:

MUSEUM MASTERWORKS RECOVERED IN BRONX
MILLIONS IN STOLEN ART

I stopped on the sidewalk, commuters streaming past me on either side. Then—stiffly, feeling observed, heart pounding—I walked back and bought a copy (certainly buying a newspaper was a less suspicious thing for a kid my age to do than it seemed to be—?) and ran across the street to the benches on Sixth Avenue to read it.

Police, acting on a tip, had recovered three paintings—a George van der Mijn; a Wybrand Hendriks; and a Rembrandt, all missing from the museum since the explosion—from a Bronx home. The paintings had been found in an attic storage area, wrapped in tinfoil and stacked amidst a bunch of spare filters for the building's central air-conditioning unit. The thief, his brother, and the brother's mother-in-law—owner of the premises—were in custody pending bail; if convicted on all charges, they faced combined sentences of up to twenty years.

It was a pages-long article, complete with timelines and diagram. The thief—a paramedic—had lingered after the call to evacuate, removed the paintings from the wall, draped them with a sheet, concealed them beneath a folded-up portable stretcher, and walked with them from the museum unobserved. "Chosen with no eye to value," said the FBI investigator interviewed for the article. "Snatch and grab. The guy didn't know a thing about art. Once he got the paintings home he didn't know what to do with them so he consulted with his brother and together they hid the works at the mother-in-law's, without her knowledge according to her." After a little Internet research, the brothers had apparently realized that the Rembrandt was too famous to sell, and it was their efforts to sell one of the lesser-known works that led investigators to the cache in the attic.

But the final paragraph of the article leaped out as if it had been printed in red.

> As for other art still missing, the hopes of investigators have been revived, and authorities are now looking into several local leads. "The more you shake the trees, the more falls out of them," said Richard Nunnally, city police liaison with the FBI art crimes unit. "Generally, with art theft, the pattern is for pieces to be whisked out of the country very quickly, but this find in the Bronx only goes to confirm that we probably have quite a few amateurs at work, inexperienced parties who stole on impulse and don't have the know-how to sell or conceal these objects." According to Nunnally, a number of people present at the scene are being questioned, contacted, and reinvestigated: "Obviously, now, the thinking is that a lot of these missing pictures may be here in the city right under our noses."

I felt sick. I got up and dumped the paper in the nearest trash can, and — instead of getting on the subway — wandered back down Canal Street and roamed around Chinatown for an hour in the freezing cold, cheap electronics and blood red carpets in the dim sum parlors, staring in fogged windows at mahogany racks of rotisseried Peking duck and thinking: *shit, shit*. Red-cheeked street vendors, bundled like Mongolians, shouting above smoky braziers. District Attorney. FBI. New information. *We are determined to prosecute these cases to the fullest extent of the law. We have full confidence that other missing works will surface soon. Interpol, UNESCO and other federal and international agencies are cooperating with local authorities in the case.*

It was everywhere. All the newspapers had it: even the Mandarin newspapers, the recovered Rembrandt portrait amid streams of Chinese print, peeping out from bins of unidentifiable vegetables and eels on ice.

"*Really* disturbing," said Hobie later that night at dinner with the Amstisses, brow knitted with anxiety. The recovered paintings were all he'd been able to talk about. "Wounded people everywhere, people bleeding to death, and here's this fellow snatching paintings off the walls. Carrying them around outside in the *rain*."

"Well, can't say I'm surprised," said Mr. Amstiss, who was on his fourth scotch on the rocks. "After that second heart attack of Mother's? You can't believe the mess these goons from Beth Israel left. Black footprints *all* over the carpet. We were finding plastic needle caps all over the floor for weeks, the dog almost swallowed one. And they broke something too, Martha, something in the china cabinet, what was it?"

"Listen, you won't catch me complaining about paramedics," said Hobie. "I was really impressed with the ones we had when Juliet was ill. I'm just glad they found the paintings before they were too badly damaged, it could have been a real—Theo?" he said to me, rather suddenly, causing me to glance up quickly from my plate. "Everything all right?"

"Sorry. I'm just tired."

"No wonder," said Mrs. Amstiss kindly. She taught American history at Columbia; she, of the pair, was the one Hobie liked and was friends with, Mr. Amstiss being the unfortunate half of the package. "You've had a tough day. Worried about your test?"

"No, not really, " I said without thinking, and then was sorry.

"Oh, I'm *sure* he'll get in," said Mr. Amstiss. "You'll get in," he said to me, in a tone implying that any idiot could expect to do so, and then, turning back to Hobie: "Most of these early-college programs don't deserve the name, isn't that right, Martha? Glorified high school. Tough pull to get in but then a doddle once you've made it. That's the way it is these days with the kids—participate, show up, and they expect a prize. Everybody wins. Do you know what one of Martha's students said to her the other day? Tell them, Martha. This kid comes up after class, wants to talk. Shouldn't say kid—graduate student. And you know what he says?"

"Harold," said Mrs. Amstiss.

"Says he's worried about his test performance, wants her advice. Because *he has a hard time remembering things.* Does that take the cake, or what? Graduate student in American history? *Hard time remembering things?*"

"Well, God knows, I have a hard time remembering things too," said Hobie affably, and rising with the dishes, steered the conversation into other channels.

But late that night, after the Amstisses had left and Hobie was asleep, I sat up in my room staring out the window at the street, listening to the distant two a.m. grindings of trucks over on Sixth Avenue and doing my best to talk myself down from my panic.

Yet what could I do? I'd spent hours on my laptop, clicking rapidly through what seemed like hundreds of articles—*Le Monde, Daily Telegraph, Times of India, La Repubblica,* languages I couldn't read, every paper in the world was covering it. The fines, in addition to the prison sentences, were ruinous: two hundred thousand, half a million dollars. Worse: the woman who owned the house was being charged because the paintings had been found on her property. And what this meant, very likely, was that Hobie would be in trouble too—much worse trouble than me. The woman, a retired beautician, claimed she'd had no idea the paintings were in her house. But Hobie? An antiques dealer? Never mind that he'd taken me in innocently, out of the goodness of his heart. Who would believe he hadn't known about it?

Up, down and around my thoughts plunged, like a bad carnival ride. *Though these thieves acted impulsively and have no prior criminal records, their inexperience will not deter us from prosecuting this case to the letter of the law.* One commentator, in London, had mentioned my painting in the same breath with the recovered Rembrandt: ...*has drawn attention to more valuable works still missing, most particularly Carel Fabritius's* Goldfinch *of 1654, unique in the annals of art and therefore priceless*...

I reset the computer for the third or fourth time and shut it down, and then, a bit stiffly, climbed in bed and turned out the light. I still had the baggie of pills I'd stolen from Xandra—hundreds of them, all different colors and sizes, all painkillers according to Boris, but though sometimes they knocked my dad out cold I'd also heard him complaining how sometimes they kept him awake at night, so—after lying paralyzed with discomfort and indecision for an hour or more, seasick and tossing, staring at the spokes of car lights wheeling across the ceiling—I snapped on the light again and scrabbled around in the nightstand drawer for the bag and selected two different colored pills, a blue and a yellow, my reasoning being that if one didn't put me to sleep, the other might.

Priceless. I rolled to face the wall. The recovered Rembrandt had been valued at forty million. But forty million was still a price.

Out on the avenue, a fire engine screamed high and hard before trailing into the distance. Cars, trucks, loudly-laughing couples coming out of the bars. As I lay awake trying to think of calming things like snow, and stars in the desert, hoping I hadn't swallowed the wrong mix and accidentally killed myself, I did my best to hold tight to the one helpful or comforting fact I'd gleaned from my online reading: stolen paintings were almost impossible to trace unless people tried to sell them, or move them, which was why only twenty per cent of art thieves were ever caught.

Chapter 8.

The Shop-Behind-the-Shop, continued

i.

SUCH WAS MY TERROR and anxiety about the painting that it overshadowed, somewhat, the arrival of the letter: I'd been accepted for the spring term of my early college program. The news was so shocking that I put the envelope in a desk drawer, where it sat alongside a stack of Welty's monogrammed letter paper for two days, until I worked up the nerve to go to the head of the stairs (brisk scratch of handsaw floating up from the shop) and say: "Hobie?"

The saw stopped.

"I got in."

Hobie's large, pale face appeared at the foot of the stairs. "What's that?" he said, still in his work trance, not quite there, wiping his hands and leaving white handprints on his black apron—and then his expression changed when he saw the envelope. "Is that what I think it is?"

Without a word I handed it to him. He looked at it, then at me—then laughed what I thought of as his Irish laugh, harsh and surprised at itself.

"Well done you!" he said, untying his apron and slinging it across the railing of the stairs. "I'm glad about it, I won't lie to you. I hated to think of packing you up there all on your own. And when were you going to mention it? Your first day of school?"

It made me feel terrible, how pleased he was. At our celebratory dinner—me, Hobie, and Mrs. DeFrees at a struggling little neighborhood Italian—I looked at the couple drinking wine at the only other occupied table besides our own; and—instead of being happy, as I'd hoped—felt only irritated and numb.

"Cheers!" said Hobie. "The tough part is over. You can breathe a little easier now."

"You must be *so* pleased," said Mrs. DeFrees, who all night long had been linking her arm through mine and giving little squeezes and chirrups of delight. ("You look *bien élégante*," Hobie had said to her when he kissed her on the cheek: gray hair piled atop her head, and velvet ribbons threaded through the links of her diamond bracelet.)

"Model of dedication!" said Hobie to her. It made me feel even worse about myself, hearing him tell his friends how hard I'd worked and what an excellent student I was.

"Well, it's wonderful. *Aren't* you pleased? And on such short notice, too! Do try to look a bit happier, my dear. When does he start?" she said to Hobie.

ii.

THE PLEASANT SURPRISE WAS that after the trauma of getting in, the early-college program wasn't nearly as rigorous as I'd feared. In certain respects it was the least demanding school I'd ever attended: no AP classes, no hectoring about SATs and Ivy League admissions, no back-breaking math and language requirements—in fact, no requirements at all. With increasing bewilderment, I looked around at the geeky academic paradise I'd tumbled into and realized why so many gifted and talented high school kids in five boroughs had been knocking themselves senseless to get into this place. There were no tests, no exams, no grades. There were classes where you built solar panels and had seminars with Nobel-winning economists, and classes where all you did was listen to Tupac records or watch old episodes of *Twin Peaks*. Students were free to concoct their own Robotics or History of Gaming tutorials if they so chose. I was free to pick and choose among interesting electives with only some take-home essay questions at midterm and a project at the end. But though I knew just how lucky I was, still it was impossible to feel happy or even grateful for my good fortune. It was as if I'd suffered a chemical change of the spirit: as if the acid balance of my psyche had shifted and leached the life out of me in aspects impossible to repair, or reverse, like a frond of living coral hardened to bone.

I could do what I had to. I'd done it before: gone blank, pushed forward. Four mornings a week I rose at eight, showered in the claw-foot tub in the bath off Pippa's bedroom (dandelion shower curtain, the smell of her strawberry shampoo wafting me up into a mocking vapor where her presence smiled all around me). Then—abrupt plunge to earth—I exited the cloud of steam and dressed silently in my room and—after dragging Popchik around the block, where he darted to and fro and screamed in terror—ducked my head into the workshop, said goodbye to Hobie, hoisted my backpack over my shoulder, and took the train two stops downtown.

Most kids were taking five or six courses but I went for the minimum, four: Studio art, French, Intro to European Cinema, Russian literature in translation. I'd wanted to take conversational Russian but Russian 101—the introductory level—wasn't available until the fall. With knee-jerk coldness I showed up for class, spoke when spoken to, completed my assignments, and walked back home. Sometimes after class I ate in cheap Mexican and Italian places around NYU with pinball machines and plastic plants, sports on the wide screen television and dollar beer at Happy Hour (though no beer for me: it was weird readjusting to my life as a minor, like going back to crayons and kindergarten). Afterwards, all sugared-up from unlimited-refill Sprites, I walked back to Hobie's through Washington Square Park with my head down and my iPod turned up loud. Because of anxiety (the recovered Rembrandt was still all over the news) I was having big problems sleeping and whenever the doorbell at Hobie's rang unexpectedly I jumped as if at a five-alarm fire.

"You're missing out, Theo," said Susanna my counselor (first names only: all pals), "extracurricular activities are what anchor our students in an urban campus. Our younger students especially. It can be easy to get lost."

"Well—" She was right: school was lonely. The eighteen and nineteen year olds didn't socialize with the younger kids, and though there were plenty of students my age and younger (even one spindly twelve year old rumored to have an IQ of 260) their lives were so cloistered and their concerns so foolish and foreign-seeming that it was as if they spoke some lost middle-school tongue I'd forgotten. They lived at home with their parents; they worried about things like grade curves and Italian Abroad and summer internships at the UN; they freaked out if you lit a cigarette in front of them; they were earnest, well-meaning, undamaged, clueless. For all I had in common with any of them, I might as well have tried to go down and hang out with the eight year olds at PS 41.

"I see you're taking French. The French Club meets once a week, in a French restaurant on University Place. And on Tuesdays they go up to the

Alliance Française and watch French-language movies. That seems like something you might enjoy."

"Maybe." The head of the French department, an elderly Algerian, had already approached me (shockingly—at his large firm hand on my shoulder, I'd jumped like I was being mugged) and told me without preamble that he was teaching a seminar that I might like to sit in on, the roots of modern terrorism starting with the FLN and the Guerre d'Algérie—I hated how all the teachers in the program seemed to know who I was, addressing me with apparent foreknowledge of "the tragedy," as my cinema teacher, Mrs. Lebowitz ("Call me Ruthie") had termed it. She too—Mrs. Lebowitz—had been after me to join the Cinema club after reading an essay I'd written about *The Bicycle Thief;* she'd suggested as well that I might also enjoy the Philosophy Club, which entailed weekly discussion of what she called The Big Questions. "Um, maybe," I said politely.

"Well, from your essay, it seems as if you are drawn to what I'll call for lack of a better term, the metaphysical territory. Such as why do good people suffer," she said, when I continued to look at her blankly. "And is fate random. What your essay deals with is really not so much the cinematic aspect of De Sica as the fundamental chaos and uncertainty of the world we live in."

"I don't know," I said, in the uneasy pause that fell. Was my essay really about these things? I hadn't even liked *The Bicycle Thief* (or *Kes,* or *La Mouette,* or *Lacombe Lucien,* or any of the other extremely depressing foreign films we had watched in Mrs. Lebowitz's class).

Mrs. Lebowitz looked at me so long I felt uncomfortable. Then she adjusted her bright red eyeglasses and said: "Well, most of what we do in European Cinema is pretty heavy. Which is why I'm thinking maybe you'd like to sit in on one of my seminars for film majors. 'Screwball Comedies of the Thirties' or maybe even 'Silent Cinema.' We do *Dr. Caligari* but also a lot of Buster Keaton, a lot of Charlie Chaplin—chaos, you know, but in a non-threatening framework. Life-affirming stuff."

"Maybe," I said. But I had no intention of burdening myself with even one scrap of extra work, no matter how life-affirming in nature. For—from almost the moment I'd gotten in the door—the deceptive burst of energy by which I had clawed my way into the Early College program had collapsed. Its lavish offerings left me unmoved; I had no desire to exert myself one bit more than I absolutely had to. All I wanted was to scrape by.

Consequently, the enthusiastic welcome of my teachers soon began to wane into resignation and a sort of vague, impersonal regret. I was not seeking out challenges, developing my skills, expanding my horizons, utilizing the many resources available to me. I was not, as Susanna had delicately put it, adjusting to the program. In fact—increasingly as the term wore on, as my teachers slowly distanced themselves and a more resentful note began to surface ("the academic opportunities offered do not seem to spur Theodore to greater efforts, on any front") I grew more and more suspicious that the only reason I'd been allowed into the program at all was because of "the tragedy." Someone had flagged my application in the admissions office, passed it to an administrator, my God, this poor kid, victim of terrorism, blah blah blah, school has a responsibility, how many places do we have left, do you think we can fit him in? Almost certainly I had ruined the life of some deserving brainiac out in the Bronx—some poor clarinet-playing loser in the projects who was still getting beaten up for his algebra homework, who was going to end up punching tickets in a tollbooth instead of teaching fluid mechanics at Cal Tech because I'd taken his or her rightful place.

Clearly a mistake had been made. "Theodore participates very little in class and appears to have no desire to expend any more attention on his studies than absolutely necessary," wrote my French professor, in a scathing midterm report that—in the absence of any closely supervising adult—no one saw but me. "It is to be hoped that his failures will drive him to prove himself so that he may profit from his situation in the second half of the term."

But I had no desire to profit from my situation, even less to prove myself. Like an amnesiac I roamed the streets and (instead of doing my homework, or attending my language lab, or joining any of the clubs to which I had been invited) rode the subway out to purgatorial end-of-the-line neighborhoods where I wandered alone among bodegas and hair-weave emporiums. But soon I lost interest even in my newfound mobility—hundreds of miles of track, riding just for the hell of it—and instead, like a stone sinking soundlessly into deep water, lost myself in idlework down in Hobie's basement, a welcoming drowsiness beneath the sidewalk where I was insulated from the city blare and all the airborne bristle of office towers and skyscrapers, where I was happy to polish tabletops and listen to classical music on WNYC for hours on end.

After all: what did I care about *passé composé* or the works of Turgenev? Was it wrong, wanting to sleep late with the covers over my head and wander around a peaceful house with old seashells in drawers and wicker baskets of folded upholstery fabric stored under the parlor secretary, sunset falling in drastic coral spokes through the fanlight over the front door? Before long, between school and workshop, I had slipped into a sort of forgetful doze, a skewed, dreamlike version of my former life where I walked familiar streets yet lived in unfamiliar circumstances, among different faces; and though often walking to school I thought of my old, lost life with my mother — Canal Street Station, lighted bins of flowers at the Korean market, anything could trigger it — it was as if a black curtain had come down on my life in Vegas.

Only sometimes, in unguarded moments, it struck through in such mutinous bursts that I stopped mid-step on the sidewalk, amazed. Somehow the present had shrunk into a smaller and much less interesting place. Maybe it was just I'd sobered up a bit, no longer the chronic waste and splendor of those blazing adolescent drunks, our own little warrior tribe of two rampaging in the desert; maybe this was just how it was when you got older, although it was impossible to imagine Boris (in Warsaw, Karmeywallag, New Guinea, wherever) living a sedate prelude-to-adulthood life such as the one I'd fallen into. Andy and I — even Tom Cable and I — had always talked obsessively about what we were going to be when we grew up, but with Boris, the future had never appeared to enter his head any further than his next meal. I could not envision him preparing in any way to earn a living or to be a productive member of society. And yet to be with Boris was to know that life was full of great, ridiculous possibilities — far bigger than anything they taught in school. I'd long ago given up trying to text him or call; messages to Kotku's phone went unanswered, his home number in Vegas had been disconnected. I could not imagine — given his wide sphere of movement — that I would ever see him again. And yet I thought of him almost every day. The Russian novels I had to read for school reminded me of him; Russian novels, and *Seven Pillars of Wisdom,* and so too the Lower East Side — tattoo parlors and pierogi shops, pot in the air, old Polish ladies swaying side to side with grocery bags and kids smoking in the doorways of bars along Second Avenue.

And — sometimes, unexpectedly, with a sharpness that was almost pain — I remembered my father. Chinatown made me think of him in its flash and seediness, its slippery unreadable moods: mirrors and fishtanks, shop windows with plastic flowers and pots of lucky bamboo. Sometimes when I walked down to Canal Street for Hobie, to buy rottenstone and Venice turpentine at Pearl Paint, I ended up drifting over to Mulberry Street to a restaurant my dad had liked, not far from the E train, eight stairs down to a basement with stained Formica tables where I bought crispy scallion pancakes, spicy pork, dishes I had to point at because the menu was in Chinese. The first time I'd shown up at Hobie's laden with greasy paper bags his blank expression had stopped me cold, and I stood in the middle of the floor like a sleepwalker awakened mid-dream wondering what exactly I'd been thinking — not of Hobie, certainly; he wasn't the person who craved Chinese food all hours of the day and night.

"Oh, I *do* like it," said Hobie hastily, "only I never think of it." And we ate downstairs in the shop straight from the cartons, Hobie seated atop a stool in his black work apron and sleeves rolled to the elbow, the chopsticks oddly small-looking in his large fingers.

iii.

THE INFORMAL NATURE OF my stay at Hobie's worried me too. Though Hobie himself, in his foggy beneficence, didn't appear to mind me at his house, Mr. Bracegirdle clearly viewed it as a temporary arrangement and both he and my counselor at school had taken great pains to explain that though the dormitories at my college were reserved for older students, something could be worked out in my case. But whenever the topic of living arrangements came up, I fell silent and stared at my shoes. The residence halls were crowded, fly-specked, with a graffiti-scrawled cage lift that clanked like a prison elevator: walls papered with band flyers, floors sticky with spilled beer, zombified mob of blanket-wrapped hulks drowsing on the sofas in the TV room and wasted-looking guys with facial hair — grown men in my view, big scary guys in their twenties — throwing empty forty-ounce cans at each other in the hall. "Well, you're still a bit young," said Mr. Bracegirdle, when — cornered — I expressed my reservations, although the true reason for my reservations was something I couldn't discuss: how — given my circumstances — could I possibly live with a roommate? What about security? Sprinkler systems?

Theft? *The school is not responsible for the personal property of students,* said the handbook I'd been given. *We recommend that students take out a dorm insurance policy on any valuable objects that may be accompanying them to school.*

In a trance of anxiety, I threw myself into the task of being indispensable to Hobie: running errands, cleaning brushes, helping him inventory his restorations and sort through fittings and old pieces of cabinet wood. While he carved splats and turned new chair legs to match old, I melted beeswax and resin on the hot plate for furniture polish: 16 parts beeswax, 4 parts resin, 1 part Venice turpentine, a fragrant butterscotch gloss that was thick like candy and satisfying to stir in the pan. Soon he was teaching me how to lay down the red on white ground for gilding: always a little of the gold rubbed down at the point where the hand would naturally touch, then a little dark wash with lampblack rubbed in interstices and backing. ("Patination is always one of the biggest problems in a piece. With new wood, if you're going for an effect of age, a gilded patina is always easiest to fudge.") And if, post-lampblack, the gilt was still too bright and raw-looking, he taught me to scar it with a pinpoint—light, irregular scratches of different depth—and then to ding it lightly with a ring of old keys before reversing the vacuum cleaner over it to dull it down. "Heavily restored pieces—where there are no worn bits or honorable scars, you have to hand out a few ancients and honorables yourself. The trick of it," he explained, wiping his forehead with the back of his wrist, "is never to be too nice about it." By *nice* he meant 'regular.' Anything too evenly worn was a dead giveaway; real age, as I came to see from the genuine pieces that passed through my hands, was variable, crooked, capricious, singing here and sullen there, warm asymmetrical streaks on a rosewood cabinet from where a slant of sun had struck it while the other side was as dark as the day it was cut. "What ages wood? Anything you like. Heat and cold, fireplace soot, too many cats—or that," he said, stepping back as I ran my finger along the rough, muddied top of a mahogany chest. "What do you suppose wrecked that surface?"

"Gosh—" I squatted on my heels to where the finish—black and sticky, like the burnt-on crust of some Easy-Bake Oven item you didn't want to eat—feathered out to a clear, rich shine.

Hobie laughed. "Hair spray. Decades of. Can you believe it?" he said, scratching at an edge with his thumbnail so that a curl of black peeled away. "The old beauty was using it as a dressing table. Over the years it builds up like lacquer. I don't know what they put in it but it's a nightmare to get off, especially the stuff from the fifties and sixties. It'd be a really interesting piece if she hadn't wrecked the finish. All we can do is clean it up, on top, so you can see the wood again, maybe give it a light wax. It's a beautiful old thing, though, isn't it?" he said, with warmth, trailing a finger down the side. "Look at the turn of the leg and this graining, the figure of it—see that bloom, here and here, how carefully it's matched?"

"Are you going to take it apart?" Though Hobie viewed it as an undesirable step I loved the surgical drama of dismembering a piece and re-assembling it from scratch—working fast before the glue set, like doctors rushing through a shipboard appendectomy.

"No—" knocking it with his knuckles, ear to the wood—"seems pretty sound, but we've got some damage to the rail," he said, pulling a drawer which screeched and stuck. "That's what comes from keeping a drawer crammed too full with junk. We'll refit these—" tugging the drawer out, wincing at the shriek of wood on wood—"plane down the spots where it binds. See, the rounding? Best way to fix this is square out the groove—that'll make it wider, but I don't think we'll have to prize the old runners out of the dovetails—you remember what we did on the oak piece, right? But—" running a fingertip along the edge—"mahogany's a little different. So's walnut. Surprising how often wood is taken from spots that aren't actually causing the trouble. With mahogany in particular, it's so tightly grained, mahogany of this age especially, you really don't want to plane except where you absolutely have to. A little paraffin on the rails and she'll be as good as new."

iv.

AND SO THE TIME slipped by. The days were so much alike I barely noticed the months pass. Spring turned to summer, humidity and garbage smells, the streets full of people and the ailanthus trees leafing out dark and full; and then summer to autumn, forlorn and chilled. Nights, I spent reading *Eugene Onegin* or else poring over one of Welty's many furniture books (my favorite: an ancient two-volume work called *Chippendale Furniture: Genuine and Spurious*) or Janson's fat and satisfying *History of*

Art. Though sometimes I worked down in the basement with Hobie for six or seven hours at a time, barely a word spoken, I never felt lonely in the beam of his attention: that an adult not my mother could be so sympathetic and attuned, so fully there, astonished me. Our large age difference made us shy with each other; there was a formality, a generational reserve; and yet we'd also grown to have sort of a telepathy in the shop so that I would hand him the correct plane or chisel before he even asked for it. "Epoxy-glued" was his short-hand for shoddy work, and cheap things generally; he'd shown me a number of original pieces where the joints had held undisturbed for two hundred years or more, whereas the problem with a lot of modern work was that it held too tight, bonded too hard with the wood and cracked it and didn't let it breathe. "Always remember, the person we're really working for is the person who's restoring the piece a hundred years from now. He's the one we want to impress." Whenever he was gluing up a piece of furniture it was my job to set out all the right cramps, each at the right opening, while he lay out the pieces in precise mortise-to-tenon order — painstaking preparation for the actual gluing-and-cramping when we had to work frantically in the few minutes open to us before the glue set, Hobie's hands sure as a surgeon's, snatching up the right piece when I fumbled, my job mostly to hold the pieces together when he got the cramps on (not just the usual G-cramps and F-cramps but also an eccentric array of items he kept to hand for the purpose, such as mattress springs, clothes pins, old embroidery hoops, bicycle inner tubes, and — for weights — colorful sandbags stitched out of calico and various snatched-up objects such as old leaden door stops and cast-iron piggy banks). When he didn't require an extra pair of hands, I swept saw-dust and replaced tools on the peg, and — when there was nothing else to do — was happy enough to sit and watch him sharpening chisels or steam-bending wood with a bowl of water on the hot plate. OMG it stinks down there texted Pippa. The fumes are awful how can u stand it? But I loved the smell — bracingly toxic — and the feel of old wood under my hands.

V.

DURING ALL THIS TIME, I had carefully followed the news about my fellow art thieves in the Bronx. They had all pleaded guilty — the mother-in-law too — and had received the most severe sentences allowed by law: fines in the hundreds of thousands, and prison sentences ranging from five to fifteen without parole. The general view seemed to be that they would all still be living happily out in Morris Heights and eating big Italian dinners at Mom's house had they not made the dumb move of trying to sell the Wybrand Hendriks to a dealer who phoned the cops.

But this did not assuage my anxiety. There had been the day when I'd returned from school to find the upstairs thick with smoke and firemen trooping around the hall outside my bedroom — "mice," said Hobie, looking wild-eyed and pale, roaming the house in his workman's smock and his safety goggles atop his head like a mad scientist, "I can't abide glue traps, they're cruel, and I've put off having an exterminator in but good Lord, this is outrageous, I can't have them chewing through the electrical wires, if not for the alarm the place could have gone up like *that,* here" — (to the fireman) "is it all right if I bring him over here?" sidestepping equipment, "you have to see this...." standing well back to point out a tangle of charred mouse skeletons smouldering in the baseboard. "Look at that! A whole nest of them!" Though Hobie's house was alarmed to the nines — not just for fire, but burglary — and the fire had done no real damage apart from a section of floorboard in the hall, still the incident had shaken me badly (what if Hobie hadn't been home? what if the fire had started in my room?) and deducing that so many mice in a two-foot section of baseboard only meant more mice (and more chewed wires) elsewhere, I wondered if despite Hobie's aversion to mousetraps I should set out some myself. My suggestion that he get a cat — though welcomed enthusiastically by Hobie and cat-loving Mrs. DeFrees — was discussed with approval but not acted upon and soon sank from view. Then, only a few weeks later, just as I was wondering if I should broach the cat issue again, I'd almost fainted from the cardiac plunge of coming in my room to find him kneeling on the rug near my bed — reaching *under* the bed, as I thought, but in fact reaching for the putty knife on the floor; he was replacing a cracked pane in the bottom of the bedroom window.

"Oh, hi," said Hobie, standing to brush off his trouser leg. "Sorry! Didn't mean to give you a jump! Been intending to get this new pane in ever since you arrived. Of course, I like to use wavy glass in these old windows, the Bendheim, but if you throw in a few clear pieces it really doesn't matter — say, careful there," he said, "are you all right?" as I dropped my school bag and sank in an armchair like some shellshocked first lieutenant stumbling in from the field.

It was crackers, as my mother would have said. I didn't know what to do. Though I was only too aware how strangely Hobie looked at me at times, how crazy I must seem to him, still I existed in a low-grade fog of internal clangor: starting up every time someone came to the door; jumping as if scalded when the phone rang; jolted by electric-shock "premonitions" that—mid class—would compel me to rise from my desk and rush straight home to make sure that the painting was still in the pillowcase, that no one had disturbed the wrapping or tried to scratch up the tape. On my computer, I scoured the Internet for laws dealing with art theft but the fragments I turned up were all over the map, and did not provide any kind of relevant or cohesive view. Then, after I'd been at Hobie's for an otherwise uneventful eight months, an unexpected solution presented itself.

I was on good terms with all Hobie's moving-and-storage guys. Most of them were New York City Irish, lumbering, good-natured guys who hadn't quite made it into the police force or the fire department—Mike, Sean, Patrick, Little Frank (who was not little at all, the size of a refrigerator)—but there were also a couple of Israeli guys named Raviv and Avi, and— my favorite—a Russian Jew named Grisha. ("'Russian Jew' contradiction in terms," he explained, in a lavish plume of menthol smoke. "To Russian mind anyway. Since 'Jew' to antisemite mind is not the same as true Russian—Russia is notorious of this fact.") Grisha had been born in Sevastopol, which he claimed to remember ("black water, salt") though his parents had emigrated when he was two. Fair-haired, brick red in the face with startling robin's-egg eyes, he was paunchy from drinking and so careless about his clothes that sometimes the lower buttons of his shirt gaped open, yet from the easy, arrogant way he carried himself, he clearly believed himself to be good-looking (as who knew, maybe he had been, once). Unlike stone-faced Mr. Pavlikovsky he was quite talkative, full of jokes or *anekdoty* as he called them, which he told in a droll, rapid-fire monotone. "You think you can curse, *mazhor?*" he'd said goodnaturedly, from the chessboard set up in a corner of the workshop where he and Hobie sometimes played in the afternoon. "Go then. Burn my ears off." And I had let rip such an eyewatering torrent of filth that even Hobie—not understanding a word—had leaned back laughing with his hands over his ears.

One gloomy afternoon, not long after my first fall term in school had begun, I happened to be alone in the house when Grisha stopped by to drop off some furniture. "Here, *mazhor,*" he said, flicking the butt of his cigarette away between scarred thumb and forefinger. *Mazhor*—one of his several derisive nicknames for me—meant "Major" in Russian. "Make yourself useful. Come help with this garbage in the truck." All furniture, for Grisha, was "garbage."

I looked past him, to the truck. "What have you got? Is it heavy?"

"If it was heavy, *poprygountchik,* would I ask you?"

We brought in the furniture—gilt-edged mirror, wrapped in padding; a candle stand; a set of dining room chairs—and as soon as it was unwrapped, Grisha leaned against a sideboard Hobie was working on (after first touching it with a fingertip, to make sure it wasn't sticky) and lit himself a Kool. "Want one?"

"No thanks." In fact, I did, but I was afraid Hobie would smell it on me.

Grisha fanned away the cigarette smoke with one dirty-nailed hand. "So what are you doing?" he said. "Want to help me out this afternoon?"

"Help you how?"

"Put down your naked-lady book" (Janson's *History of Art*) "and ride out to Brooklyn with me."

"What for?"

"I have to take some of this garbage out to storage, could use an extra hand. Mike was supposed to help but *sick* today. Ha! Giants played last night, they lost, he had a lot of rocks on the game. Bet he is home in bed up in Inwood with a hangover and a black eye."

vi.

ON THE WAY OUT to Brooklyn with a van full of furniture, Grisha kept up a steady monologue about on the one hand Hobie's fine qualities and on the other how he was running Welty's business into the ground. "Honest man, in dishonest world? Living in reclusion? It hurts me right here, in my heart, to see him throwing his moneys out the window every day. No no," he said, holding up a grimy palm as I tried to speak, "takes time what he does, the restorations, working by hand like the Old Masters—I understand. He is artist—not businessman. But explain for me, please, why he is paying for storage out at Brooklyn Navy Yard instead of moving inventorys and getting bills paid? I mean — just look, the junk in basement! Things Welty bought at auction — more coming in every week. Upstairs, store is packed tight! He is sitting on a fortune — would take hundred years to sell it all! People looking in the window — cash in hand — wanting to buy — sorry, lady! Fuck off! Store is closed! And there he is downstairs with his carpenter tools spending ten hours to carve *this-small*" (thumb and forefinger) "— piece of wood for some piece-of-shit old lady chair."

"Yeah, but he has clients in too. He sold a whole bunch of stuff just last week."

"What?" said Grisha angrily, whipping his head from the road to glare at me. "Sold? To who?"

"The Vogels. He opened the store for them — they bought a bookcase, a games table —"

Grisha scowled. "*Those* people. His *friends,* so called. You know why they buy from him? Because they know they can get low price from him — 'open by appointment,' ha! Better for him if he keeps the place shut from those vultures. I mean —" fist on breastbone — "you know my heart. Hobie is family to me. But —" he rubbed three fingers together, an old gesture of Boris's, *money! money!* — "unwise in business dealing. He gives away his last matchstick, scrap of food, whatever, to any phony and con man. You watch and see — soon, in four-five years, he will be broke on the street unless he finds someone to run the shop for him."

"Such as who?"

"Well —" he shrugged — "some person like maybe my cousin Lidiya. That woman can sell water to drowning man."

"You should tell him. I know he wants to find somebody."

Grisha laughed cynically. "Lidiya? Work in *that* dump? Listen — Lidiya sells gold, Rolex, diamonds from Sierra Leone. Gets picked up from home in Lincoln Town Car. White leather pants…floor length sable…. nails out to *here.* No way is woman like that going to sit in junk shop with a bunch of dust and old garbage all day."

He stopped the van and shut off the engine. We were in front of a blocky, ash-gray building in a desolate waterfront area, empty lots and auto-body shops, the sort of neighborhood where gangsters in the movies always drive the guy they're going to kill.

"Lidiya—Lidiya is sexy woman," he said contemplatively. "Long legs—bazooms—good looking. Big zest for life. But this business—you don't want big flash, like her."

"Then what?"

"Someone like Welty. There was innocent about him, you know? Like scholar. Or priest. He was grandfather to everyone. But very smart businessman all the same. Fine to be nice, kind, good friends with everyone, but once you have your customer trusting and believing lowest price is from you, you've got to take your profit, ha! That's retail, *mazhor.* Way of the fucking world."

Inside, after we were buzzed in, there was a desk with a lone Italian guy reading a newspaper. As Grisha was signed in, I examined a brochure on a rack beside the display of bubble wrap and packing tape:

ARISTON FINE ARTS STORAGE
STATE-OF-THE-ART FACILITY
FIRE SUPPRESSION, CLIMATE CONTROL, 24 HOUR SECURITY
INTEGRITY—QUALITY—SAFETY
FOR ALL YOUR FINE ARTS NEEDS
KEEPING YOUR VALUABLES SAFE SINCE 1968

Apart from the desk clerk, the place was deserted. We loaded the service elevator and—with the aid of a key card and a punched-in code—took the elevator up to the sixth floor. Down corridor after long, faceless corridor we walked, ceiling-mounted cameras and anonymous numbered doors, Aisle D, Aisle E, windowless Death Star walls that seemed to stretch into infinity, a feel of underground military archives or maybe columbarium walls in some futuristic cemetery.

Hobie had one of the larger spaces—double doors, wide enough to drive a truck through. "Here we go," said Grisha, rattling the key in the padlock and throwing the door open with a crash of metal. "Just look at all this shit he has in here." It was jammed so full of furniture and other items (lamps, books, china, little bronzes; old B. Altman bags full of papers and moldy shoes) that at first confused glance I wanted to back off and shut the door, as if we'd stumbled into the apartment of some old hoarder who had just died.

"Two thousand a month he pays for this," he said gloomily as we took the padding off the chairs and stacked them, precariously, atop a cherrywood desk. "Twenty-four thousand dollars a year! He should rather be using those moneys to light his cigarettes than pay rents for this shithole."

"What about these smaller units?" Some of the doors were quite tiny — suitcase-sized.

"People are crazy," said Grisha resignedly. "For space the size of car trunk? Hundreds of dollars a month?"

"I mean—" I didn't know how to ask it—"what keeps people from putting illegal stuff here?"

"Illegal?" Grisha blotted the sweat from his brow with a dirty handkerchief and then reached around and mopped the inside of his collar. "You mean like, what, guns?"

"Right. Or, you know, stolen stuff."

"What keeps them? I will tell you. Nothing is what keeps them. Bury something here and no one will find it, unless you get bumped off or sent to the can and don't pay the fee. Ninety per cent of this stuff — old baby pictures, junk from Bubbe's attic. But—if walls could talk, you know? Probably millions of dollars hidden away if you knew where to look. All kind of secrets. Guns, jewels, murder victim bodies — crazy things. Here—" he'd slammed the door with a crash, was fumbling with the slide bolt—"help me with this fucker. I hate this place, my God. Is like death, you know?" He gestured down the sterile, endless-looking corridor. "Everything shut up, sealed away from life! Whenever I'm coming here, I get a feeling like hard to breathe. Worse than a fucking library."

vii.

THAT NIGHT, I GOT the Yellow Pages from Hobie's kitchen and carried it back to my room and looked under *Storage: Fine Arts*. There were dozens of places in Manhattan and the outer boroughs, many with stately print ads detailing their services: white gloves, from our door to yours! A cartoon butler proffered a business card on a silver tray: BLINGEN AND TARK-WELL, SINCE 1928. *We provide discreet and confidential State-of-the-Art storage solutions for a wide range of businesses and private clients.* ArtTech. Heritage Works. Archival Solutions. *Facilities monitored by hygrothermograph recording equipment. We maintain custom temperature control to AAM (American Association of Museums) requirements of 70 degrees and 50 percent relative humidity.*

But all this was much too elaborate. The last thing I wanted was to draw attention to the fact that I was storing a piece of art. What I needed was something safe and inconspicuous. One of the biggest and most popular chains had twenty locations in Manhattan — including one in the East Sixties by the river, my old neighborhood, only a few streets away from where my mother and I had lived. *Our premises are secured by our custom 24-hour manned security command center and feature the latest technology in smoke and fire detection.*

Hobie was asking me something from the hallway. "What?" I said hoarsely, my voice loud and false, shutting the phone book on my finger.

"Moira's here. Want to run down to the local with us for a hamburger?" The Local was what he called the White Horse.

"Sounds great, be there in a minute." I went back to the ad in the Yellow Pages. *Make Space for Summer Funtime! Easy solutions for your sports and hobby equipment!* How simple they made it sound: no credit card required, cash deposit and off you went.

The next day, instead of going to class, I retrieved the pillowcase from under my bed, taped it shut with duct tape, put it in a brown bag from Bloomingdale's, and took a cab to the sporting goods store in Union Square, where after a bit of dithering I purchased a cheap pup tent and then caught a cab back up to Sixtieth Street.

At the space-age, glassed-in office of the storage facility, I was the only customer; and though I'd prepared a cover story (ardent camper; neat-freak mom) the men at the desk seemed completely uninterested in my large, well-labeled sporting goods bag with the tag of the pup tent dangling artfully outside. Nor did anyone seem to find it at all noteworthy or unusual that I wanted to pay for the locker a year in advance, in cash — or two years maybe? Was that all right? "ATM right out there," said the Puerto Rican at the cash register, pointing without looking away from his bacon and egg sandwich.

That easy? I thought, in the elevator on the way down. "Write your locker number down," the guy at the register said, "and your combination too, and keep it in a safe place," but I'd already memorized both—I'd seen enough James Bond movies that I knew the drill—and the minute I was outside tossed the paper in the trash.

Walking out of the building, its vaultlike hush and the stale breezelet humming evenly from the air vents, I felt giddy, unblinkered, and the blue sky and trumpeting sunlight, familiar morning exhaust haze and the call and cry of car horns all seemed to stretch down the avenue into a larger, better scheme of things: a sunny realm of crowds and luck. It was the first time I'd been anywhere near Sutton Place since returning to New York and it was like falling back in a friendly old dream, crossfade between past and present, pocked texture of the sidewalks and even the same old cracks I'd always jumped over when I was running home, leaning in, imagining myself in an airplane, tilt of an airplane's wings, *I'm coming in,* that final stretch, strafing in fast towards home—lots of the same places still in business, the deli, the Greek diner, the wine shop, all the forgotten neighborhood faces muddling through my mind, Sal the florist and Mrs. Battaglina from the Italian restaurant and Vinnie from the dry cleaner's with his tape measure around his neck, down on his knees pinning up my mother's skirt.

I was only a few blocks from our old building: and looking down towards Fifty-Seventh Street, that bright familiar alley with the sun striking it just right and bouncing gold off the windows I thought: Goldie! Jose!

At the thought, my step quickened. It was morning; one or both of them should be on duty. I'd never sent the postcard from Vegas like I'd promised: they'd be thrilled to see me, clustering round, hugging me and slapping me on the back, interested to hear about everything that had happened, including the death of my dad. They'd invite me back to the package room, maybe call up Henderson the manager, fill me in on all the building gossip. But when I turned the corner, amidst stalled traffic and car horns, I saw from halfway down the block that the building was cicatriced with scaffolding and the windows slapped shut with official notices.

I stopped, dismayed. Then—disbelieving—I walked closer and stood, appalled. The art-deco doors were gone, and—in place of the cool dim lobby, with its polished floors, its sunburst panelling—gaped a cavern of gravel and concrete hunks and workmen in hard hats were coming out with wheelbarrows of rubble.

"What happened here?" I said to a dirt-ingrained guy with a hard hat standing back a bit, hunched and slurping guiltily at his coffee.

"Whaddaya mean, what happened?"

"I—" Standing back, looking up, I saw it wasn't just the lobby; they had gutted the entire building, so you could see straight through to the courtyard in back; glazed mosaic on the façade still intact but the windows dusty and blank, nothing behind them. "I used to live here. What's going on?"

"Owners sold." He was shouting over jackhammers in the lobby. "Got the last tenants out a few months ago."

"But—" I looked up at the empty shell, then peered inside at the dusty, floodlit rubblehouse—men shouting, wires dangling. "What are they doing?"

"Upscale condos. Five mil plus—swimming pool on the roof—can you believe it?"

"Oh my God."

"Yeah, you'd think it'd be protected wouldn't you? Nice old place—yesterday had to jackhammer up the marble stairs in the lobby, remember those stairs? Real shame. Wish we coulda got 'em out whole. You don't see that quality marble so much like you used to, the nice old marble like that. Still—" He shrugged. "That's the city for you."

He was shouting to someone above—a man lowering a bucket of sand on a rope—and I walked along, feeling sick, right under our old living room window or the bombed-out shell of it rather, too disturbed to look up. *Out of the way, baby,* Jose had said, hoisting my suitcase up on the shelf of the package room. Some of the tenants, like old Mr. Leopold, had lived in the building for seventy-plus years. What had happened to him? Or to Goldie, or Jose? Or—for that matter: Cinzia—? Cinzia, who at any given time had a dozen or more part-time cleaning jobs, worked only a few hours a week in the building, not that I'd even been thinking about Cinzia until the moment before, but it had all seemed so solid, so immutable, the whole social system of the building, a nexus where I could always stop in and see people, say hello, find out what was going on. People who had known my mother. People who had known my dad.

And the farther I walked away, the more upset I got, at the loss of one of the few stable and unchanging docking-points in the world that I'd taken for granted: familiar faces, glad greetings: hey manito! For I had thought that this last touchstone of the past, at least, would be where I'd left it. It was weird to think I'd never be able to thank Jose and Goldie for the money they'd given me—or, even weirder, that I'd never be able to tell them my father had died: because who else did I know who had known him? Or would care? Even the sidewalk felt like it might break under my feet and I might drop through Fifty-Seventh Street into some pit where I never stopped falling.

IV.

It is not flesh and blood, but heart which makes us fathers and sons.

— Schiller

Chapter 9.

Everything of Possibility

i.
_____

ONE AFTERNOON EIGHT YEARS later — after I'd left school and gone to work for Hobie — I'd just come out of Bank of New York and was walking up Madison upset and preoccupied when I heard my name.

I turned. The voice was familiar but I didn't recognize the man: thirty-ish, bigger than me, with morose gray eyes and colorless blond hair to his shoulders. His clothes — shaggy tweeds; rough shawl-collared sweater — were more suited for a muddy country lane than a city street; and he had an indefinable look of privilege gone wrong, like someone who'd slept on some friends' couches, done some drugs, wasted a good bit of his parents' money.

"It's Platt," he said. "Platt Barbour."

"Platt," I said, after a stunned pause. "Long time. Good Lord." It was difficult to recognize the lacrosse thug of old in this sobered and attentive-looking pedestrian. The insolence was gone, the old aggressive glint; now he looked worn out and there was an anxious, fatalistic quality in his eyes. He might have been an unhappy husband up from the suburbs, worried about an unfaithful wife, or maybe a disgraced teacher at some second-rate school.

"Well. So. Platt. How are you?" I said after an uncomfortable silence, stepping backwards. "Are you still in the city?"

"Yes," he said, clasping the back of his neck with one hand, seeming highly ill at ease. "Just started a new job, actually." He had not aged well; in the old days he'd been the blondest and best-looking of the brothers, but he'd grown thick in the jaw and around the middle and his face had coarsened away from its perverse old _Jungvolk_ beauty. "I'm working for an academic publisher. Blake-Barrows. They're based in Cambridge but they've got an office here?"

"Great," I said, as if I'd heard of the publisher, though I hadn't — nodding, fiddling with the change in my pocket, already planning my getaway. "Well, fantastic to see you. How's Andy?"

His face seemed to grow very still. "You don't know?"

"Well —" faltering — "I heard he was at MIT. I ran into Win Temple on the street a year or two back — he said Andy had a fellowship — astrophysics? I mean," I said nervously, discomfited by Platt's stare, "I really don't keep in touch with the crowd from school very much...."

Platt ran his hand down the back of his head. "I'm sorry. I'm not sure we knew how to get in touch with you. Things are still very confused. But I certainly thought you would have heard by now."

"Heard what?"

"He's dead."

"Andy?" I said, and then, when he didn't react: "No."

Fleeting grimace — gone almost the moment I saw it. "Yes. It was pretty bad, I'm sorry to say. Andy and Daddy too."

"What?"

"Five months ago. He and Daddy drowned."

"No." I looked at the sidewalk.

"The boat capsized. Off Northeast Harbor. We really weren't out so far, maybe we shouldn't have been out there at all, but Daddy — you know how he was —"

"Oh my God." Standing there, in the uncertain spring afternoon with children just out of school running all around me, I felt pole-axed and confused as if at an un-funny practical joke. Though I had thought of Andy often over the years, and just missed seeing him once or twice, we'd never gotten back in touch after I returned to New York. I'd felt sure I'd run into him at some point — as I had Win, and James Villiers, and Martina Lichtblau, and a few other people from my school. But though I'd often considered picking up the phone to say hello, somehow I never had.

"Are you okay?" said Platt — massaging the back of his neck, looking as uneasy as I felt.

"Um —" I turned to the shop window to compose myself, and my transparent ghost turned to meet me, crowds passing behind me in the glass.

"Gosh," I said. "I can't believe it. I don't know what to say."

"Sorry to blurt it on the street like that," said Platt, rubbing his jaw. "You look a bit green around the gills."

Green around the gills: a phrase of Mr. Barbour's. With a pang, I remembered Mr. Barbour searching through the drawers in Platt's room, offering to build me a fire. *Hell of a thing that's happened, good Lord.*

"Your dad, too?" I said, blinking as if someone had just shaken me awake from a sound sleep. "Is that what you just said?"

He looked around, with a lift of the chin that brought back for a moment the arrogant old Platt I remembered, then glanced at his watch.

"Come on, have you got a minute?" he said.

"Well—"

"Let's get a drink," he said, pounding a hand on my shoulder so heavily I flinched. "I know a quiet place on Third Avenue. What do you say?"

ii.

WE SAT IN THE nearly empty bar—a once-famous oak-panelled joint smelling of hamburger grease, Ivy League pennants on the walls, while Platt talked in a rambling, uneasy monotone so quietly I had to strain to follow.

"Daddy," he said, looking down into his gin and lime: Mrs. Barbour's drink. "We all shrank from talking about it—but. Chemical imbalance is how our grandmother spoke of it. Bipolar disorder. He had his first episode, or attack, or whatever you call it, at Harvard Law—1L, never made it to the second year. All these wild plans and enthusiasms…combative in class, talking out of turn, had set out writing some epic book-length poem about the whaling ship *Essex* which was just a bunch of nonsense and then his roommate, who was apparently more of a stabilizing influence than anyone knew, left for a semester abroad in Germany and—well. My grandfather had to take the train up to Boston to fetch him. He'd been arrested for starting a fire out in front of the statue of Samuel Eliot Morison on Commonwealth Avenue and he resisted arrest when the policeman tried to take him in."

"I knew he'd had problems. I never knew it was like that."

"Well." Platt stared into his drink, and then knocked it back. "That was well before I came along. Things changed after he married Mommy and he'd been on his medicine for a while, although our grandmother never really trusted him after all that."

"All what?"

"Oh, of course *we* got on with her quite well, the grandchildren," he said hastily. "But you can't imagine the trouble Daddy caused when he was younger...tore through worlds of money, terrible rows and rages, some awful problems with underage girls...he'd weep and apologize, and then it would happen all over again....Gaga always blamed him for our grandfather's heart attack, the two of them were quarreling at my grandfather's office and *boom*. Once on the medicine, though, he was a lamb. Wonderful father — well — you know. Wonderful with us children."

"He was lovely. When I knew him."

"Yes." Platt shrugged. "He could be. After he married Mommy, he was on an even keel for a while. Then — I don't know what happened. He made some terribly unsound investments — that was the first sign. Embarrassing late-night phone calls to acquaintances, that sort of thing. Became romantically obsessed with a college girl interning in his office — girl whose family Mommy knew. It was terribly hard."

For some reason, I was incredibly touched by hearing him call Mrs. Barbour 'Mommy.' "I never knew any of this," I said.

Platt frowned: a hopeless, resigned expression that brought out sharply his resemblance to Andy. "We hardly knew it ourselves — we children," he said bitterly, drawing his thumb across the tablecloth. "'Daddy's ill' — that's all we were told. I was off at school, see, when they sent him to the hospital, they never let me talk to him on the phone, they said he was too sick and for weeks and weeks I thought he was dead and they didn't want to tell me."

"I remember all that. It was awful."

"All what?"

"The, uh, nervous trouble."

"Yeah, well —" I was startled by the snap of anger in his eyes — "and how was *I* supposed to know if it was 'nervous trouble' or terminal cancer or what the fuck? 'Andy's so sensitive...Andy's better off in the city...we don't think Andy would thrive with boarding...' well, all I can say is Mommy and Daddy packed *me* off pretty much the second I could tie my shoes, stupid fucking equestrian school called Prince George's, completely third-rate but oh, wow, such a character-building experience, such a great preparation for Groton, and they took really young kids, seven through thirteens. You should have seen the brochure, Virginia hunt country and all that, except it wasn't all green hills and riding habits like the pictures. I got trampled in a stall and broke my shoulder and there I was in the infirmary with this view of the empty driveway and no car coming up it. Not *one* fucking person came to visit me, not even Gaga. Plus the doctor was a drunk and set the shoulder wrong, I still have problems with it. I hate horses to this motherfucking day.

"*Anyhow*—" self-conscious change of tone—"they'd yanked me out of that place and got me into Groton by the time things really came to a head with Daddy and he was sent away. Apparently there was an incident on the subway...conflicting stories there, Daddy said one thing and the cops said another *but*—" he lifted his eyebrows, with a sort of mannered, black-humored whimsy—"off went Daddy to the ding farm! Eight weeks. No belt, no shoelaces, no sharps. But they gave him shock treatments in there, and they really seemed to work because when he came out again he was an all-new person. Well—you remember. Father of the Year, practically."

"So—" I thought of my ugly run-in with Mr. Barbour on the street, decided not to bring it up—"what happened?"

"Well, who knows. He started having problems again a few years ago and had to go back in."

"What kind of problems?"

"Oh—" Platt exhaled noisily—"much the same, embarrassing phone calls, public outbursts, et cetera. Nothing was wrong with him, of course, *he* was perfectly fine, it all started when they were doing some renovations on the building, which he was against, constant hammers and saws and all these corporations destroying the city, nothing that wasn't true to start with, and then it just sort of snowballed, to the point where he thought he was being followed and photographed and spied on all the time. Wrote some pretty crazy letters to people, including some clients at his firm... made a terrible nuisance of himself at the Yacht Club...quite a few of the members complained, even some very old friends of his, and who can blame them?

"Anyway, when Daddy got back from the hospital that second time— he was never quite the same. The swings were less extreme, but he couldn't concentrate and he was very irritable all the time. About six months ago he switched doctors and took a leave of absence from work and went up to Maine—our uncle Harry has a place on a little island up there, no one was there except the caretaker, and Daddy said the sea air did him good.

All of us took turns going up to be with him ... Andy was in Boston then, at MIT, the last thing he wanted was to be saddled with Daddy but unfortunately since he was closer than us, he got stuck with it a bit."

"He didn't go back to the, er—" I didn't want to say *ding farm*— "where he went before?"

"Well, how was anyone to make him? It's not an easy matter to send someone away against their will, especially when they won't admit anything is wrong with them which at that point he wouldn't, and besides we were led to believe it was all a matter of medication, that he would be right as rain as soon as the new dose kicked in. The caretaker checked in with us, made sure he ate well and took his medicine, Daddy spoke on the phone to his shrink every day—I mean, the doctor *said* it was all right," he said defensively. "Fine for Daddy to drive, to swim, to sail if he felt like it. Probably it wasn't a terrific idea to go out *quite* so late in the day but the conditions weren't so bad when we set out and of course you know Daddy. Dauntless seaman and all that. Heroics and derring-do."

"Right." I'd heard many, many stories of Mr. Barbour sailing off into "snappy waters" that turned out to be nor'easters, State of Emergency declared in three states and power knocked out along the Atlantic Coast, Andy seasick and vomiting as he bailed salt water out of the boat. Nights tilted sideways, run aground upon sandbars, in darkness and torrential rain. Mr. Barbour himself—laughing uproariously over his Virgin Mary and his Sunday morning bacon and eggs—had more than once told the story how he and the children were blown out to sea off Long Island Sound during a hurricane, radio knocked out, how Mrs. Barbour had phoned a priest at St. Ignatius Loyola on Park and Eighty-Fourth and sat up all night praying (Mrs. Barbour!) until the ship-to-shore call from the Coast Guard came in. ("First strong wind, and she hightails it to Rome, didn't you, my dear? Ha!")

"Daddy—" Platt shook his head sadly. "Mommy used to say that if Manhattan wasn't an island, he could never have lived here one minute. Inland he was miserable—always pining for the water—had to *see* it, had to *smell* it—I remember driving from Connecticut with him when I was a boy, instead of going straight up 84 to Boston we had to go miles out of the way and up the coast. Always looking to the Atlantic—really really sensitive to it, how the clouds changed the closer you got to the ocean." Platt closed his cement-gray eyes for a moment, then re-opened them.

"You knew Daddy's little sister drowned herself, didn't you," he said, in so flat a voice that for a moment I thought I'd misheard.

I blinked, not knowing what to say. "No. I didn't know that."

"Well, she did," said Platt tonelessly. "Kitsey's named after her. Jumped off a boat in the East River during a party—a lark supposedly, that's what they all said, 'accident,' but I mean anyone knows not to do that, the currents were crazy, pulled her right under. Another kid died too, jumping in trying to save her. And then there was Daddy's uncle Wendell back in the sixties, half-crocked, tried to swim to the mainland one night on a dare— I mean, Daddy, he used to yammer on how the water was the source of life itself for him, fountain of youth and all that and—sure, it was. But it wasn't just life for him. It was death."

I didn't reply. Mr. Barbour's boating stories, never particularly cogent, or focused, or informative about the actual sport, had always vibrated with a majestic urgency all their own, an appealing tingle of disaster.

"And—" Platt's mouth was a tight line—"of course the hell of it was, he thought he was immortal as far as the water was concerned. Son of Poseidon! Unsinkable! And as far as he was concerned, the rougher the water, the better. He used to get very storm-giddy, you know? Lowered barometric pressure for him was like laughing gas. Although that particular day…it was choppy but warm, one of those bright sunny days in fall when all you want is to get out on the water. Andy was annoyed at having to go, he was coming down with a cold and in the middle of doing something complicated on the computer, but neither of us thought there was any actual *danger*. The plan was to take him out, get him calmed down, and hopefully hop over to the restaurant on the pier and try to get some food down him. See—" restlessly he crossed his legs—"it was just the two of us there with him, Andy and me, and to be quite frank Daddy was a bit off his rocker. He had been keyed up since the day before, talking a little wildly, really on the boil—Andy called Mommy because he had work to do and didn't feel able to cope, and Mommy called me. By the time I got up there and took the ferry out, Daddy was in the wild blue yonder. Raving about the flung spray and the blown fume and all that— the wild green Atlantic—absolutely *flying*. Andy was never able to tolerate Daddy in those moods, he was up in his room with the door locked. I suppose he'd had a party-sized dose of Daddy before I arrived.

"In hindsight, I know, it seems poorly considered, but—you see, I *could* have sailed it single-handed. Daddy was going stir-crazy in the house and what was I to do, wrestle him down and lock him up? and then too, you know Andy, he never thought about food, the cupboard was bare, nothing in the fridge but some frozen pizzas...short hop, something to eat on the pier, it seemed like a good plan, you know? 'Feed him,' Mommy always used to say when Daddy started getting a little too exhilarated. 'Get some food down him.' That was always the first line of defense. Sit him down—make him eat a big steak. Often that's all it took to get him back on keel. And I mean—it was in the back of my mind that if his spirits didn't settle once we were on the mainland we could forget about the steakhouse and take him in to the emergency room if need be. I only made Andy come to be on the safe side. I thought I could use an extra hand— quite frankly I'd been out late the night before, I was feeling a little less than all a-taunto, as Daddy used to say." He paused, rubbing the palms of his hands on the thighs of his tweed trousers. "Well. Andy never liked the water much. As you know."

"I remember."

Platt winced. "I've seen cats that swam better than Andy. I mean, quite frankly, Andy was just about the clumsiest kid I ever saw that wasn't out-and-out spastic or retarded...good God, you ought to have seen him on the tennis court, we used to joke about entering him in the Special Olympics, he would have swept every event. Still he'd put in enough hours on the boat, God knows—it seemed smart to have an extra man aboard, and Daddy less than his best, you know? We could easily have handled the boat—I mean it was *fine*, it would have been perfectly fine except I hadn't been keeping my eye on the sky like I should, the wind blew up, we were trying to reef the mainsail and Daddy was waving his arms around and shouting about the empty spaces between the stars, really just all kinds of nutty stuff, and he lost his balance on a swell and fell overboard. We were trying to haul him back aboard, Andy and me—and then we got broadsided at just the wrong angle, huge wave, just one of these steep cresting things that pops up and slaps you out of nowhere, and boom, we capsized. Not even that it was so cold out but fifty-three-degree water is enough to send you into hypothermia if you're out there long enough, which unfortunately we were, and I mean to say Daddy, he was *soaring*, off in the stratosphere—"

Our chummy college-girl waitress was approaching behind Platt's back, about to ask if we wanted another round—I caught her eye, shook my head slightly, warning her away.

"It was the hypothermia that got Daddy. He'd gotten so thin, no body fat on him at all, an hour and a half in the water was enough to do it, floundering around at those temperatures. You lose heat faster if you're not perfectly still. Andy—" Platt, seeming to sense that the waitress was there, turned and held up two fingers, *another round*—"Andy's jacket, well, they found it trailing behind the boat still attached to the line."

"Oh God."

"It must have come up over his head when he went over. There's a strap that goes around the crotch—a bit uncomfortable, nobody likes to wear it—anyway, there was Andy's jacket, still shackled to the life-line, but apparently he wasn't buckled in all the way, the little shit. Well, I mean," he said, his voice rising, "*the* most typical thing. You know? Couldn't be bothered to fasten the thing properly? He was always such a goddamned klutz—"

Nervously, I glanced at the waitress, conscious how loud Platt had gotten.

"God." Platt pushed himself back from the table very suddenly. "I was always so hateful to Andy. An absolute bastard."

"Platt." I wanted to say *No you weren't* only it wasn't true.

He glanced up at me, shook his head. "I mean, my God." His eyes were blown-out and empty looking, like the Huey pilots in a computer game (Air Cav II: Cambodian Invasion) that Andy and I had liked to play. "When I think of some of the things I did to him. I'll never forgive myself, never."

"Wow," I said, after an uncomfortable pause, looking at Platt's big-knuckled hands resting palms down on the table—hands that after all these years still had a blunt, brutal look, a residue of old cruelty about them. Although we had both endured our share of bullying at school, Platt's persecution of Andy—inventive, joyous, sadistic—had verged on outright torture: spitting in Andy's food, yes, tearing up his toys, but also leaving dead guppies from the fish tank and autopsy photos from the Internet on his pillow, throwing back the covers and peeing on him while he was asleep (and then crying *Android's wet the bed!*); pushing his head under in the bathtub Abu Ghraib style; forcing his face down in the play-ground sandbox as he cried and fought to breathe. Holding his inhaler over his head as he wheezed and pleaded: *want it? want it?* Some hideous story too about Platt and a belt, an attic room in some country house, bound hands, a makeshift noose: ugliness. *He'd have killed me,* I remembered Andy saying, in his remote, emotionless voice, *if the sitter hadn't heard me kicking on the floor.*

A light spring rain was tapping at the windows of the bar. Platt looked down at his empty glass, then up.

"Come see Mother," he said. "I know she really wants to see you."

"Now?" I said, when I realized he meant that instant.

"Oh, do please come. If not now, later. Don't just promise like we all do on the street. It would mean so much to her."

"Well—" Now it was my turn to look at my watch. I'd had some errands to do, in fact I had a lot on my mind and several very pressing worries of my own but it was getting late, the vodka had made me foggy, the afternoon had slipped away.

"Please," he said. He signalled for the check. "She'll never forgive me if she knows I ran into you and let you get away. Won't you walk over for just a minute?"

...

iii.
———

STEPPING INTO THE FOYER was like stepping into a portal back to childhood: Chinese porcelains, lighted landscape paintings, silk-shaded lamps burning low, everything exactly as when Mr. Barbour had opened the door to me the night my mother died.

"No, no," said Platt, when by habit I walked toward the bull's-eye mirror and through to the living room. "Back here." He was heading to the rear of the apartment. "We're very informal now—Mommy usually sees people back here, if she sees anybody at all...."

Back in the day, I had never been anywhere near Mrs. Barbour's inner sanctum, but as we approached the smell of her perfume—unmistakable, white blossoms with a powdery strangeness at the heart—was like a blown curtain over an open window.

"She doesn't go out the way she once did," Platt was saying quietly. "None of these big dinners and events—maybe once a week she'll have someone over for tea, or go for dinner with a friend. But that's it."

Platt knocked; he listened. "Mommy?" he called, and—at the indistinct reply—opened the door a crack. "I've got a guest for you. You'll never guess who I found on the street...."

It was an enormous room, done up in an old-ladyish, 1980s peach. Directly off the entrance was a seating area with a sofa and slipper chairs—lots of knickknacks, needlepoint cushions, nine or ten Old Master drawings: the flight into Egypt, Jacob and the Angel, circle of Rembrandt mostly though there was a tiny pen-and-brown-ink of Christ washing the feet of St. Peter that was so deftly done (the weary slump and drape of Christ's back; the blank, complicated sadness on St. Peter's face) it might have been from Rembrandt's own hand.

I leaned forward for a closer look; and on the far side of the room, a lamp with a pagoda-shaped shade popped on. "Theo?" I heard her say, and there she was, propped on piles of pillows in an outlandishly large bed.

"You! I can't believe it!" she said, holding out her arms to me. "You're all grown up! Where in the world have you been? Are you in the city now?"

"Yes. I've been back for a while. You look wonderful," I added dutifully, though she didn't.

"And you!" She put both hands over mine. "How handsome you are! I'm quite overcome." She looked both older and younger than I remembered: very pale, no lipstick, lines at the corner of her eyes but her skin still white and smooth. Her silver-blonde hair (had it always been quite that silver, or had she gone gray?) fell loose and uncombed about her shoulders; she was wearing half-moon glasses and a satin bed jacket pinned with a huge diamond brooch in the shape of a snowflake.

"And here you find me, in my bed, with my needlework, like an old sailor's widow," she said, gesturing at the unfinished needlepoint canvas across her knees. A pair of tiny dogs—Yorkshire terriers—were asleep on a pale cashmere throw at her feet, and the smaller of the two, spotting me, sprang up and began to bark furiously.

Uneasily I smiled as she tried to quiet him—the other dog had set up a racket as well—and looked around. The bed was modern—king-sized, with a fabric covered headboard—but she had a lot of interesting old things back there that I wouldn't have known to pay attention to when I was a kid. Clearly, it was the Sargasso Sea of the apartment, where objects banished from the carefully decorated public rooms washed up:

mismatched end tables; Asian bric-a-brac; a knockout collection of silver table bells. A mahogany games table that from where I stood looked like it might be Duncan Phyfe and atop it (amongst cheap cloisonné ashtrays and endless coasters) a taxidermied cardinal: moth-eaten, fragile, feathers faded to rust, its head cocked sharply and its eye a dusty black bead of horror.

"Ting-a-Ling, ssh, please be quiet, I can't bear it. This is Ting-a-Ling," said Mrs. Barbour, catching the struggling dog up in her arms, "he's the naughty one, aren't you darling, never a moment's peace, and the other, with the pink ribbon, is Clementine. Platt," she called, over the barking, "Platt, will you take him in the kitchen? He's really a bit of a nuisance with guests," she said to me, "I ought to have a trainer in..."

While Mrs. Barbour rolled up her needlework and put it in an oval basket with a piece of scrimshaw set in the lid, I sat down in the armchair by her bed. The upholstery was worn, and the subdued stripe was familiar to me — a former living-room chair exiled to the bedroom, the same chair I'd found my mother sitting in when she'd come to the Barbours' many years ago to pick me up after a sleepover. I drew a finger over the cloth. All at once I saw my mother standing to greet me, in the bright green peacoat she'd been wearing that day — fashionable enough that people were always stopping her on the street to ask her where she got it, yet all wrong for the Barbours' house.

"Theo?" said Mrs. Barbour. "Would you like something to drink? A cup of tea? Or something stronger?"

"No, thank you."

She patted the brocade coverlet of the bed. "Come sit next to me. Please. I want to be able to see you."

"I —" At her tone, at once intimate and formal, a terrible sadness came over me, and when we looked at each other it seemed that the whole past was redefined and brought into focus by this moment, clear as glass, a complexity of stillness that was rainy afternoons in spring, a dark chair in the hallway, the light-as-air touch of her hand on the back of my head.

"I'm so glad you came."

"Mrs. Barbour," I said, moving to the bed, sitting down gingerly with one hip, "my God. I can't believe it. I didn't find out till just now. I'm so sorry."

She pressed her lips together like a child trying not to cry. "Yes," she said, "well," and there issued between us an awful and seemingly unbreakable silence.

"I'm so sorry," I repeated, more urgently, aware just how clumsy I sounded, as if by speaking more loudly I might convey my acuity of sorrow.

Unhappily she blinked; and, not knowing what to do, I reached out and put my hand on top of hers and we sat for an uncomfortably long time.

In the end, it was she who spoke first. "At any rate." Resolutely she dashed a tear from her eye while I flailed about for something to say. "He had mentioned you not three days before he died. He was engaged to be married. To a Japanese girl."

"No kidding. Really?" Sad as I was, I couldn't help smiling, a little: Andy had chosen Japanese as his second language precisely because he had such a thing for fanservice *miko* and slutty manga girls in sailor uniform. "Japanese from Japan?"

"Indeed. Tiny little thing with a squeaky voice and a pocketbook shaped like a stuffed animal. Oh yes, I met her," she said with a raised eyebrow. "Andy translating over tea sandwiches at the Pierre. She was at the funeral, of course — the girl — her name was Miyako — well. Different cultures and all that, but it's true what they say about the Japanese being undemonstrative."

The little dog, Clementine, had crawled up to curl around Mrs. Barbour's shoulder like a fur collar. "I have to admit, I'm thinking of getting a third," she said, reaching over to stroke her. "What do you think?"

"I don't know," I said, disconcerted. It was extremely unlike Mrs. Barbour to solicit opinions from anyone at all on any subject, certainly not from me.

"I must say, they've been an enormous comfort, the pair of them. My old friend Maria Mercedes de la Pereyra turned up with them a week after the funeral, quite unexpected, two pups in a basket with ribbons on, and I have to say I wasn't sure at first, but actually I don't think I've ever received a more thoughtful gift. We could never have dogs before because of Andy. He was so terribly allergic. You remember."

"I do."

Platt — still in his tweed gamekeeper's jacket, with big sagged-out pockets for dead birds and shotgun shells — had come back in. He pulled up a chair. "So, Mommy," he said, biting his lower lip.

"So, Platypus." A formal silence. "Good day at work?"

"Great." He nodded, as if trying to reassure himself of the fact. "Yeah. Really really busy."

"I'm so glad to hear it."

"New books. One on the Congress of Vienna."

"Another one?" She turned to me. "And you, Theo?"

"Sorry?" I'd been looking at the scrimshaw (a whaling ship) set in the lid of her sewing basket, and thinking of poor Andy: black water, salt in his throat, nausea and flailing. The horror and cruelty of dying in his most hated element. *The problem essentially is that I despise boats.*

"Tell me. What are you doing with yourself these days?"

"Um, dealing antiques. American furniture, mostly."

"No!" She was rapturous. "But *how* perfect!"

"Yes — down in the Village. I run the shop and manage the sales end. My partner —" it was still so new I wasn't used to saying it — "my partner in the business, James Hobart, he's the craftsman, takes care of restorations. You should come down and visit sometime."

"Oh, delicious. Antiques!" She sighed. "Well — you know how I love old things. I wish my children had shown an interest. I'd always hoped at least one of them would."

"Well, there's always Kitsey," said Platt.

"It's curious," Mrs. Barbour continued, as if she hadn't heard this. "Not one of my children had an artistic bone in their bodies. Isn't that extraordinary? Little philistines, all four of them."

"Oh, please," I said, in as playful a tone as I could manage. "I remember Toddy and Kitsey with all those piano lessons. Andy with his Suzuki violin."

She made a dismissive gesture. "Oh, you know what I mean. None of my children have any *visual* sense. No appreciation whatever for painting or interiors or any of that. Now —" again she took my hand — "when *you* were a child, I used to catch you in the hallway studying my paintings. You'd always go straight to the very best ones. The Frederic Church landscape, my Fitz Henry Lane and my Raphaelle Peale, or the John Singleton Copley — you know, the oval portrait, the tiny one, girl in the bonnet?"

"That was a Copley?"

"Indeed. And I saw you with the little Rembrandt just now."

"So it *is* Rembrandt, then?"

"Yes. Only the one, the washing-of-the-feet. The rest are all school-of. My own children have lived with those drawings their whole lives and never displayed the slightest particle of interest, isn't that right, Platt?"

"I like to think that some of us have excelled at other things."

I cleared my throat. "You know, I really did just stop in to say hello," I said. "It's wonderful to see you — to see you both —" turning to include Platt in this. "I wish it were under happier circumstances."

"Will you stay and have dinner?"

"I'm sorry," I said, feeling cornered. "I can't, not tonight. But I did want to run up for a minute and see you."

"Then will you come back for dinner? Or lunch? Or drinks?" She laughed. "Or whatever you will."

"Dinner, sure."

She held up her cheek for a kiss, as she had never done when I was a child, not even with her own children.

"How lovely to have you here again!" she said, catching my hand and pressing it to her face. "Like old times."

iv.

ON MY WAY OUT the door, Platt threw out some kind of weird handshake — part gang member, part fraternity boy, part International Sign Language — that I wasn't sure how to return. In confusion I withdrew my hand and — not knowing what else to do — bumped fists with him, feeling stupid.

"So, hey. Glad we ran into each other," I said, in the awkward silence. "Give me a call."

"About dinner? Oh, yes. We'll probably eat in if that's all right, Mommy really doesn't like to go out that much." He dug his hands into the pockets of his jacket. Then, shockingly: "I've seen a good bit of your old friend Cable lately. Bit more than I care to, actually. He'll be interested to know I've seen you."

"*Tom* Cable?" I laughed, incredulously, although it wasn't much of a laugh; the bad old memory of how we'd been suspended from school together and how he'd blown me off when my mother died still made me uneasy. "You're in touch with him?" I said, when Platt didn't respond. "I haven't thought of Tom in years."

Platt smirked. "I have to admit, back in the day, I thought it was weird that any friend of that kid's would put up with a drip like Andy," he said quietly, slouching against the door frame. "Not that I minded. God knows Andy needed somebody to take him out and get him stoned or something."

Andrip. Android. One-nut. Pimple Face. Sponge Bob Shit Pants.

"No?" said Platt casually, misreading my blank stare. "I thought you were into that. Cable was certainly quite the little pothead in his day."

"That must have been after I left."

"Well, maybe." Platt looked at me, in a way I wasn't sure I liked. "Mommy certainly thought butter wouldn't melt in your mouth, but I knew you were pals with Cable. And Cable was a little thief." Sharply — in a way that brought the old, unpleasant Platt ringing back — he laughed. "I told Kitsey and Toddy to keep their rooms locked when you were here so you wouldn't steal anything."

"That's what all that was about?" I had not thought of the piggy-bank incident in years.

"Well, I mean, Cable" — he glanced at the ceiling. "See, I used to date Tom's sister Joey, holy Hell, she was a piece of work too."

"Right." I remembered all too well Joey Cable — sixteen, and stacked — brushing by twelve-year-old me in the hallway of the Hamptons house in tiny T-shirt and black thong panties.

"Sloppy Jo! What an ass she had on her. Remember how she used to parade around naked by the hot tub out there? Anyway, Cable. Out in the Hamptons at Daddy's club he got caught rifling lockers in the men's changing rooms, couldn't have been more than twelve or thirteen. That was after you left, eh?"

"Must have been."

"That sort of thing happened at *several* clubs out there. Like during big tournaments and stuff—he'd sneak into the locker room and steal whatever he could get his hands on. Then, maybe college by then — oh, darn, where was it, not Maidstone but—anyway, Cable had a summer job in the clubhouse helping out at the bar, ferrying home old folks too blotto to drive. Personable guy, good talker — well, you know. He'd get the old fellows talking about their war stories or whatever. Light their cigarettes, laugh at their jokes. Except sometimes he'd help the old fellows up to the door and the next day their wallets would be missing."

"Well, I haven't laid eyes on him in years," I said curtly. I didn't like the tone Platt had taken. "What's he doing now, anyway?"

"Well, you know. Up to his old tricks. As a matter of fact, he sees my sister from time to time, though I certainly wish I could put a stop to that. At any rate," he said, on a slightly altered note, "here I am, keeping you. I can't wait to tell Kitsey and Toddy I've seen you — Todd especially. You made quite an impression on him — he speaks of you all the time. He'll be in town next weekend and I know he'll want to see you."

V.

INSTEAD OF TAKING A cab I walked, to clear my head. It was a clean damp spring day, storm clouds pierced with bars of light and office workers milling in the crosswalks, but spring in New York was always a poisoned time for me, a seasonal echo of my mother's death blowing in with the daffodils, budding trees and blood splashes, a thin spray of hallucination and horror (*Neat! Fun!* as Xandra might have said). With the news about Andy, it was like someone had thrown an x-ray switch and reversed everything into photographic negative, so that even with the daffodils and the dogwalkers and the traffic cops whistling on the corners, death was all I saw: sidewalks teeming with dead, cadavers pouring off the buses and hurrying home from work, nothing left of any of them in a hundred years except tooth fillings and pacemakers and maybe a few scraps of cloth and bone.

It was unthinkable. I'd thought of calling Andy a million times and it was only embarrassment that had kept me from it; it was true that I didn't keep up with anyone from the old days but I did bump into someone from our school every now and again and our old schoolmate Martina Lichtblau (with whom, the year before, I had had a brief and unsatisfying affair, a total of three stealthy fucks on a fold-out sofa) — Martina Lichtblau had spoken of him, Andy's in Massachusetts now, are you still in touch with Andy, oh yeah, just as humongous a geek as ever except he plays it up so much now it's almost, like, kind of retro and cool? Coke bottle glasses? Orange corduroys and a haircut like Darth Vader's helmet?

Wow, Andy, I'd thought, shaking my head fondly, reaching over Martina's bare shoulder for one of her cigarettes. I had thought then how good it would be to see him — too bad he wasn't in New York — maybe I'd call him some time over the holidays when he was home.

Only I hadn't. I wasn't on Facebook for reasons of paranoia and seldom looked at the news but still I couldn't imagine how I hadn't heard—except that, in recent weeks, I'd been worried about the shop to the point I thought of little else. Not that we had worries financially— we'd been pulling in money almost literally hand over fist, so much money that Hobie, crediting me with his salvation (he'd been on the verge of bankruptcy) had insisted on making me partner, which I hadn't been all that keen on given the circumstances. But my efforts to put him off had only made him more determined that I should share in the profits; the more I tried to brush off his offer, the more persistent he grew; with typi- cal generosity, he attributed my reticence to "modesty" although my real fear was that a partnership would shed a certain official light on unofficial goings-on in the shop—goings-on that would shock poor Hobie to the soles of his John Lobb shoes, if he knew. Which he didn't. For I'd inten- tionally sold a fake to a client, and the client had figured it out and was kicking up a fuss.

I didn't mind giving the money back—in fact, the only thing to do was buy the piece back at a loss. In the past, this had worked for me well. I sold heavily altered or outright reconstructed pieces as original; if—out of the dim light of Hobart and Blackwell—the collector got the piece home and noticed something amiss ("always carry a pocket light with you," Hobie had counselled me, early in the game; "there's a reason so many antique shops are dark") then I—grieved at the mix-up, while stalwart in my conviction that the piece was genuine—gallantly offered to buy it back at ten percent more than the collector had paid, under the conditions and terms of an ordinary sale. This made me look like a good guy, confi- dent in the integrity of my product and willing to go to absurd lengths to ensure my client's happiness, and more often than not the client was molli- fied and decided to keep the piece. But on the three or four occasions when distrustful collectors had taken me up on my offer: what the collector didn't realize was that the fake—passing from his possession to mine, at a price indicative of its apparent worth—had overnight acquired a prove- nance. Once it was back in my hands, I had a paper trail to show it had been part of the illustrious So-and-So collection. Despite the mark-up I'd paid in repurchasing the fake from Mr. So-and-So (ideally an actor or a clothing designer who collected as a hobby, if not illustrious as a collector per se) I could then turn around and sell it again for sometimes twice what I'd bought it back for, to some Wall Street cheese fry who didn't know

Chippendale from Ethan Allen but was more than thrilled with "official documents" proving that his Duncan Phyfe secretary or whatever came from the collection of Mr. So-and-So, noted philanthropist/interior decorator/leading light of Broadway/fill-in-the-blank.

And so far it had worked. Only this time, Mr. So-and-So—in this case, a prize Upper East Side swish named Lucius Reeve—was not biting. What troubled me was that he seemed to think that, A: he'd been taken on purpose, which was true, and, B: that Hobie was in on it, was in fact the mastermind of the whole scam which could not have been farther from the truth. When I had tried to salvage the situation by insisting that the mistake was wholly mine—cough cough, honestly sir, misunderstanding with Hobie, I'm really quite new at this and hope you won't hold it against me, the work he does is of such a high quality you can see how sometimes these mix-ups happen, don't you?—Mr. Reeve ("Call me Lucius") a well-dressed figure of uncertain age and occupation, was implacable. "You don't deny that the work is from James Hobart's hand then?" he'd said at our nervewracking lunch at the Harvard Club, leaning back slyly in his chair and running his finger around the rim of his club soda glass.

"Listen—" It had been a tactical mistake, I realized, to meet him on his own territory, where he knew the waiters, where he did the ordering with pad and pencil, where I could not be magnanimous and suggest that he try this or that.

"Or that he deliberately took this carved phoenix ornament from a Thomas Affleck, from a—yes yes, I believe it *is* Affleck, Philadelphia at any rate—and affixed it to the top of this genuinely antique but otherwise undistinguished chest-on-chest of the same period? Are we not speaking of the same piece?"

"Please, if you'd only let me—" We'd been seated at a table by the window, the sun was in my eyes, I was sweating and uncomfortable—

"How then can you maintain that the deception was not deliberate? On his part and yours?"

"Look—" the waiter was hovering, I wanted him to leave—"the mistake was mine. As I've said. And I've offered to buy the piece back at a premium so I'm not sure what else you want me to do."

But despite my cool tone, I had been in a froth of anxiety, anxiety that had not been relieved by the fact that it was twelve days later and Lucius

Reeve still had not deposited the money that I'd given him—I'd been checking at the bank right before I ran into Platt.

What Lucius Reeve wanted I didn't know. Hobie had been making these cannibalized and heavily altered pieces ("changelings" as he called them) for virtually his whole working life; the storage space at Brooklyn Navy Yard had been crammed full of pieces with tags going back thirty years or more. The first time I'd gone out by myself and really poked around, I'd been thunderstruck to discover what looked like real Hepplewhite, real Sheraton, Ali Baba's cave spilling with treasure—"Oh Lord, no," said Hobie, his voice crackly on the cell phone—the facility was like a bunker, no phone reception, I'd gone straight outside to call him, standing on the windy loading dock with one finger in my ear—"believe me, if it was real, I'd have been on the phone to the American Furniture department at Christie's a long time ago—"

I had admired Hobie's changelings for years and had even helped work on some of them, but it was the shock of being fooled by these previously-unseen pieces that (to employ a favored phrase of Hobie's) filled me with a wild surmise. Every so often there passed through the shop a piece of museum quality too damaged or broken to save; for Hobie, who sorrowed over these elegant old remnants as if they were unfed children or mistreated cats, it was a point of duty to rescue what he could (a pair of finials here, a set of finely turned legs there) and then with his gifts as carpenter and joiner to recombine them into beautiful young Frankensteins that were in some cases plainly fanciful but in others such faithful models of the period that they were all but indistinguishable from the real thing.

Acids, paint, gold size and lampblack, wax and dirt and dust. Old nails rusted with salt water. Nitric acid on new walnut. Drawer runners worn with sandpaper, a few weeks under the sun lamp to age new wood a hundred years. From five destroyed Hepplewhite dining chairs he was capable of fashioning a solid and completely authentic-looking set of eight by taking the originals apart, copying the pieces (using wood salvaged from other damaged furniture of the period) and re-assembling them with half original and half new parts. ("A chair leg—" running a finger down it—"typically, they're scuffed and dented at the bottom—even if you use old wood, you need to take a chain to the bottom of the new-cut legs if you want them all to match... very very light, I'm not saying whale the hell out of it... very distinctive patterning too, front legs usually a bit more dented than the back, see?") I had seen him reconfigure original wood from a practically-in-splinters eighteenth-century sideboard into a table that might have been from the hand of Duncan Phyfe himself. ("Will it do?" said Hobie, stepping back anxiously, not appearing to understand the marvel he had wrought.) Or — as with Lucius Reeve's "Chippendale" chest-on-chest — a plain piece could in his hands become by the addition of ornament salvaged from a grand old ruin of the same period something almost indistinguishable from a masterwork.

A more practical or less scrupulous man would have worked this skill to calculated ends and made a fortune with it (or, in Grisha's cogent phrase, "fucked it harder than a five-grand prostitute"). But as far as I knew, the thought of selling the changelings for originals or indeed of selling them at all had never crossed Hobie's mind; and his complete lack of interest in goings-on in the store gave me considerable freedom to set about the business of raising cash and taking care of bills. With a single "Sheraton" sofa and a set of riband-back chairs I'd sold at Israel Sack prices to the trusting young California wife of an investment banker, I'd managed to pay off hundreds of thousands in back taxes on the townhouse. With another dining room set and a "Sheraton" settee — sold to an out-of-town client who ought to have known better, but who was blinkered by Hobie and Welty's unimpeachable reputations as dealers — I'd gotten the shop out of debt.

"It's very convenient," said Lucius Reeve pleasantly, "that he leaves all the business end of the shop to you? That he has a workshop turning out these frauds but washes his hands of how you dispose of them?"

"You have my offer. I'm not going to sit here and listen to this."

"Why then do you continue to sit?"

I did not for one instant doubt Hobie's astonishment if he learned I was selling his changelings for real. For one thing, a lot of his more creative efforts were rife with small inaccuracies, in-jokes almost, and he was not always so fastidious about his materials as someone turning out deliberate forgeries would have been. But I had found it very easy to fool even relatively experienced buyers if I sold about twenty per cent cheaper than the real thing. People loved to think they were getting a deal. Four times out of five they would look right past what they didn't want to see. I knew how to draw people's attention to the extraordinary points of a piece, the hand-cut veneer, the fine patination, the honorable scars, drawing a finger down an exquisite cyma curve (which Hogarth himself had called "the line of beauty") in order to lead the eye away from reworked bits in back, where in a strong light they might find the grain didn't precisely match. I declined to suggest that clients examine the underside of the piece, as Hobie himself—eager to educate, at the price of fatally undermining his own interests—was only too quick to do. But just in case someone did want to have a look, I made sure that the floor around the piece was very, very dirty, and that the pocket light I happened to have on hand was very, very weak. There were a lot of people in New York with a lot of money and plenty of time-pressed decorators who, if you showed them a photo of a similar-looking item in an auction catalogue, were happy to plump for what they saw as a discount, particularly if they were spending someone else's money. Another trick—calculated to lure a different, more sophisticated customer—was to bury a piece in the back of the store, reverse the vacuum cleaner over it (instant antiquity!) and allow the nosy customer to ferret it out on his or her own—look, under all this dusty junk, a Sheraton settee! With this species of cheat—whom I took great pleasure in rooking—the trick was to play dumb, look bored, stay engrossed in my book, act as if I didn't know what I had, and let them think they were rooking *me:* even as their hands were trembling with excitement, even as they tried to appear unhurried while rushing out to the bank for a massive cash withdrawal. If the customer was someone important, or too connected to Hobie, I could always claim the piece wasn't for sale. A curt "not for sale" was quite often the correct starting position with strangers as well, as it not only made the kind of buyer I was looking for more eager to strike a quick bargain, in cash, but also set the stage for me to abort mid-deal if something went wrong. Hobie wandering upstairs at a bad moment was the main thing that might go wrong. Mrs. DeFrees popping in the shop at a bad moment was another thing that could, and had, gone wrong—I'd had to break off just at the point of closing the sale, much to the annoyance of the movie-director's wife who got tired of waiting and walked out, never to return. Short of black light or lab analysis, much of Hobie's fudging wasn't visible to the naked eye; and though he had a lot of serious collectors coming in, he also had plenty of people who would never know, for instance, that no such thing as a Queen Anne cheval glass was ever made. But even if someone was clever enough to detect an inaccuracy— say a style of carving or a type of wood anachronistic for the maker or period — I had once or twice been bold enough to talk past even this: by claiming the piece was made to order for a special customer and hence, strictly speaking, more valuable than the usual article.

In my shaky and agitated state, I'd turned almost unconsciously into the park and down the path to the Pond, where Andy and I had sat in our parkas on many winter afternoons in elementary school waiting for my mother to pick us up from the zoo or take us to the movies — *rendezvous point, seventeen hundred hours!* But at that point, unfortunately, I found myself sitting there more often than not waiting for Jerome, the bike messenger I bought my drugs from. The pills I'd stolen from Xandra all those years before had started me on a bad road: oxys, roxys, morphine and Dilaudid when I could get it, I'd been buying them off the street for years; for the past months, I'd been keeping myself (for the most part) to a one-day-on, one-day-off schedule (although what constituted an "off" day was a dose just small enough to keep from getting sick) but even though it was officially an "off" day I was feeling increasingly grim and the vodkas I'd had with Platt were wearing off and though I knew very well that I didn't have anything on me still I kept patting myself down, my hands stealing again and again to my overcoat and the pockets of my suit jacket.

At college I had achieved nothing commendable or remarkable. My years in Vegas had rendered me unfit for any manner of hard work; and when at last I graduated, at twenty-one (it had taken me six years to finish, instead of the expected four), I did so without distinctions of any type. "Quite honestly, I'm not seeing a lot here that's going to make a master's program take a chance on you," my counselor had said. "Particularly since you would be relying so heavily on financial aid."

But that was all right; I knew what I wanted to do. My career as a dealer had started at about seventeen when I happened upstairs on one of the rare afternoons Hobie had decided to open the shop. By that time, I had begun to be aware of Hobie's financial problems; Grisha had spoken only too truly about the dire consequences if Hobie continued to accumulate inventory without selling it. ("Will still be downstairs, painting, carving, the day they come and put evacuation notice on front door.") But despite the envelopes from the IRS that had begun to accumulate among the Christie's catalogues and old concert programs on the hall table (Notice of Unpaid Balance, Reminder Notice Balance Due, Second Notice Balance Due) Hobie couldn't be bothered to keep the store open more than half an hour at a time unless friends happened to stop in; and when it was time for his friends to go, he often shooed out the actual customers and locked up shop. Almost invariably I came home from school to find the "Closed" sign on the door and people peering in at the windows. Worst of all, when he did manage to stay open for a few hours, was his habit of wandering trustfully away to make a cup of tea while leaving the door open and the register untended; though Mike his moving man had had the foresight to lock the silver and jewelry cases, a number of majolica and crystal items had walked away and I myself had come upstairs unexpectedly on the day in question to find a gym-toned, casually dressed mom who looked like she'd just come from a Pilates class slipping a paperweight in her bag.

"That's eight hundred and fifty dollars," I said, and at my voice she froze and looked up in horror. Actually it was only two fifty, but she handed me her credit card without a word and let me ring up the sale—probably the first profitable transaction that had taken place since Welty's death; for Hobie's friends (his main customers) were only too aware that they could talk Hobie down to criminal levels on his already too-low prices. Mike, who also helped in the shop on occasion, hiked up the prices indiscriminately and refused to negotiate and in consequence sold very little at all.

"Well done!" Hobie had said, blinking delightedly in the glare of his work lamp, when I went downstairs and informed him of my big sale (a silver teapot, in my version; I didn't want to make it seem like I'd outright robbed the woman, and besides I knew he was uninterested in what he called the smalls, which I'd come to realize through my perusal of antiques books formed a huge part of the inventory of the store). "Sharp-eyed little customer. Welty would have taken to you like a baby on the doorstep, ha! Taking an interest in his silver!"

From then on, I'd made it a habit to sit upstairs with my schoolbooks in the afternoons while Hobie busied himself downstairs. At first it was simply for fun—fun that was sorely missing from my dreary student life, coffees in the lounge and lectures on Walter Benjamin. In the years since Welty's death, Hobart and Blackwell had evidently acquired a reputation as an easy mark for thieves; and the thrill of pouncing on these well-dressed filchers and pilferers and extorting large sums from them was almost like shoplifting in reverse.

But I also learned a lesson: a lesson which sifted down to me only by degrees but which was in fact the truest thing at the heart of the business.

It was the secret no one told you, the thing you had to learn for yourself: viz. that in the antiques trade there was really no such thing as a "correct" price. Objective value—list value—was meaningless. If a customer came in clueless with money in hand (as most of them did) it didn't matter what the books said, what the experts said, what similar items at Christie's had recently gone for. An object—*any* object—was worth whatever you could get somebody to pay for it.

In consequence, I'd started going through the store, removing some tags (so the customer would have to come to me for the price) and changing others—not all, but some. The trick, as I discovered through trial and error, was to keep at least a quarter of the prices low and jack up the rest, sometimes by as much as four and five hundred percent. Years of abnormally low prices had built up a base of devoted customers; leaving a quarter of the prices low kept them devoted, and ensured that people hunting for a bargain could still find one, if they looked. Leaving a quarter of the prices low also meant that, by some perverse alchemy, the marked-up prices seemed legitimate in comparison: for whatever reason, some people were more apt to put out fifteen hundred bucks for a Meissen teapot if it was placed next to a plainer but comparable piece selling (correctly, but cheaply) for a few hundred.

That was how it had started; that was how Hobart and Blackwell, after languishing for years, had begun under my beady auspices to turn a profit. But it wasn't just about money. I liked the game of it. Unlike Hobie—who assumed, incorrectly, that anyone who walked into his store was as fascinated by furniture as he was, who was extremely matter-of-fact in pointing out the flaws and virtues of a piece—I had discovered I possessed the opposite knack: of obfuscation and mystery, the ability to talk about inferior articles in ways that made people want them. When selling a piece, talking it up (as opposed to sitting back and permitting the unwary to wander into my trap) it was a game to size up a customer and figure out the image they wanted to project—not so much the people they were (know-it-all decorator? New Jersey housewife? self-conscious gay man?) as the people they wanted to be. Even on the highest levels it was smoke and mirrors; everyone was furnishing a stage set. The trick was to address yourself to the projection, the fantasy self—the connoisseur, the discerning bon vivant—as opposed to the insecure person actually standing in front of you. It was better if you hung back a bit and weren't too direct. I soon learned how to dress

(on the edge between conservative and flash) and how to deal with sophisticated and unsophisticated customers, with differing calibrations of courtesy
and indolence: presuming knowledge in both, quick to flatter, quick to lose
interest or step away at exactly the right moment.

And yet, with this Lucius Reeve, I had screwed up badly. What he
wanted I didn't know. In fact he was so relentless in sidestepping my apologies and directing his anger full-bore on Hobie that I was starting to think
that I had stumbled into some preexisting grudge or hatred. I didn't want to
tip my hand with Hobie by bringing up Reeve's name, though who could
bear such a fierce grudge against Hobie, most well-intentioned and
unworldly of persons? My Internet research had turned up nothing on
Lucius Reeve apart from a few innocuous mentions in the society pages, not
even a Harvard or Harvard Club affiliation, nothing but a respectable Fifth
Avenue address. He had no family that I could tell, no job or visible means
of support. It had been stupid of me to write him a check — greediness on
my part; I'd been thinking about establishing a lineage for the piece, though
at this point even an envelope of cash placed under a napkin and slid across
the table was no assurance he was going to let the matter drop.

I was standing with my fists in the pockets of my overcoat, glasses
fogged from the spring damp, staring unhappily into the muddy waters of
the Pond: a few sad brown ducks, plastic bags washing in the reeds. Most
of the benches bore the names of benefactors — in memory of Mrs. Ruth
Klein or whatever — but my mother's bench, the Rendezvous Point, alone
of all the benches in that part of the park had been given by its anonymous
donor a more mysterious and welcoming message: EVERYTHING OF POSSI-
BILITY. It had been Her Bench since before I was born; in her early days in
the city, she had sat there with her library book on her afternoons off,
going without lunch when she needed the price of a museum pass at
MoMA or a movie ticket at the Paris Theatre. Further along, past the
Pond, where the path turned empty and dark, was the unkempt and desolate patch of ground where Andy and I had scattered her ashes. It was
Andy who had talked me into sneaking over and scattering them in defi-
ance of the city rule, scattering them moreover in that particular spot:
well, I mean, it's where she used to meet us.

Yeah, but rat poison, look, these signs.

Go on. You can do it now. No one's coming.

She loved the sea lions, too. We always had to walk over and look at them.

Yeah but you definitely don't want to dump her over there, it smells like fish. Besides it creeps me out having that jar or whatever in my room.

vi.

"MY GOD," SAID HOBIE when he got a good look at me under the lights. "You're white as a sheet. You're not coming down with something?"

"Um—" He was just going out, coat over his arm; behind him stood Mr. and Mrs. Vogel, buttoned-up and smiling poisonously. My relations with the Vogels (or "the Vultures," as Grisha called them) had cooled, significantly, since I'd taken over the shop; mindful of the many, many pieces they'd in my view as good as stolen from Hobie, I now tacked on a premium to anything I even vaguely suspected they were interested in; and though Mrs. Vogel—no fool—had taken to telephoning Hobie directly, I usually managed to thwart her by (among other means) claiming to Hobie that I'd already sold the piece in question and forgotten to tag it.

"Have you eaten?" Hobie, in his gentle woolly-mindedness and unwisdom, remained completely unaware that the Vogels and I no longer held each other in anything but the very highest regard. "We're just running down the street for dinner. Come with us, why don't you."

"No thanks," I said, conscious of Mrs. Vogel's gaze boring into me, cold fraudulent smile, eyes like agate chips in her smooth, aging-milkmaid face. As a rule I took pleasure in stepping up and smiling back in her teeth—but in the stern hall lights I felt clammy and used-up, demoted somehow. "I think, um, I'll eat in tonight, thanks."

"Not feeling well?" said Mr. Vogel blandly—balding midwesterner in rimless glasses, prim in his reefer coat, tough luck to you if he was the banker and you were late with the mortgage. "What a shame."

"Lovely to see you," Mrs. Vogel said, stepping forward and putting her plump hand on my sleeve. "Did you enjoy Pippa's visit? I wish I'd got to see her but she was so busy with the boyfriend. What did you think of him—what was his name—?" turning back to Hobie. "Elliot?"

"Everett," said Hobie neutrally. "Nice boy."

"Yeah," I said, turning to shoulder my coat off. The appearance of Pippa fresh off the plane from London with this "Everett" had been one of the uglier shocks of my life. Counting the days, the hours, shaky from sleeplessness and excitement, unable to stop myself looking at my watch every five minutes, leaping at the doorbell and literally running to throw open the door—and there she stood, hand-in-hand with this shoddy Englishman?

"And what does he do? A musician too?"

"Music librarian actually," said Hobie. "Don't know what that entails nowadays with computers and all."

"Oh, I'm sure Theo knows all about it," said Mrs. Vogel.

"No, not really."

"*Cybrarian?*" said Mr. Vogel, with an uncharacteristically loud and merry chuckle. Addressing me: "Is it true what they say, that young people today can make it through school without once setting foot in a library?"

"I wouldn't know." A music librarian! It had taken every ounce of possession I had to keep my face empty (guts crumbling, end of everything) to accept his moist English hand, *Hullo, Everett, you must be Theo, heard so much about you,* blah blah blah, while I stood frozen in the doorway like a bayoneted Yank staring at the stranger who'd run me through to death. He was a slight, wide-eyed bounce of a guy, innocent, bland, infuriatingly cheerful, dressed in jeans and hoodie like a teenager; and his quick, apologetic smile when we were alone in the living room had sent me blank with rage.

Every moment of their visit had been torture. Somehow I'd stumbled through it. Though I'd tried to stay away from them as much as I could (as skilled a dissembler as I was, I could barely be civil to him; everything about him, his pinkish skin, his nervous laugh, the hair sprouting out the cuffs of his shirt sleeves, made me want to jump on him and knock his horsey English teeth out; and wouldn't that be a surprise, I thought grimly, glaring at him across the table, if old antique-dealing Specs hauled off and busted his eggs for him?) still, as hard as I'd tried, I hadn't been able to stay away from Pippa, I'd hovered obtrusively and hated myself for it, so painfully excited had I been by her nearness: her bare feet at breakfast, bare legs, her voice. Unexpected glimpse of her white armpits when she pulled her sweater over her head. The agony of her hand on my sleeve. "Hi, lovey. Hi, darling." Coming up behind me, cupping my eyes with her hands: surprise! She wanted to know everything about me, everything I was doing. Wedging in beside me on the Queen Anne loveseat so that our legs touched: oh God. What was I reading? Could she look at my iPod? Where did I get that fantastic wristwatch? Whenever she smiled at me Heaven blew in.

And yet every time I devised some pretext to get her on her own, here he came, thump thump thump, sheepish grin, arm around her shoulder, wrecking everything. Conversation in the next room, a burst of laughter: were the two of them talking about me? Putting his hands on her waist! Calling her "Pips!" The only even vaguely tolerable or amusing moment of his visit was when Popchik — territorial in his old age — had jumped up unprovoked and bitten him on the thumb — "oh, God!" Hobie rushing for the alcohol, Pippa fretting, Everett trying to be cool but visibly put out: sure, dogs are great! I love them! we just never had them because my mom's allergic. He was the "poor relation" (his phrase) of an old schoolmate of hers; American mother, numerous siblings, father who taught some incomprehensible mathematical/philosophical something-or-other at Cambridge; like her, he was a vegetarian "verging on vegan;" to my dismay, it had emerged that the two of them were sharing a flat (!) — he had of course slept in her room during the visit; and for five nights, the whole time he was there, I'd lain awake bilious with fury and sorrow, ears attuned to every rustle of bedclothes, every sigh and whisper from next door.

And yet — waving goodbye to Hobie and the Vogels, *have a great time!* then turning grimly away — what could I have expected? It had enraged me, cut me to the bone, the careful, kindly tone she had taken with me around this "Everett" — "no," I said politely, when she asked me whether I was seeing someone, "not really," although (I was proud of it in a lucid, gloomy way) I was in fact sleeping with two different girls, neither of whom knew about the other. One of them had a boyfriend in another town and the other had a fiancé whom she was tired of, whose calls she screened when we were in bed together. Both of them were pretty and the girl with the cuckolded fiancé was downright beautiful — a baby Carole Lombard — but neither of them was real for me; they were only stand-ins for her.

I was irritated at how I felt. To sit around "heartbroken" (the first word, unfortunately, that came to mind) was foolish, it was maudlin and contemptible and weak — oh boo hoo, she's in London, she's with someone else, go pick up some wine and fuck Carole Lombard, get over it. But the thought of her gave me such continual anguish that I could no more forget her than an aching tooth. It was involuntary, hopeless, compulsive. For years she had been the first thing I remembered when I woke up, the last thing that drifted through my mind as I went to sleep, and during the day she came to me obtrusively, obsessively, always with a painful shock:

what time was it in London? always adding and subtracting, totting up the time difference, compulsively checking the London weather on my phone, 53 degrees Fahrenheit, 10:12 p.m. and light precipitation, standing on the corner of Greenwich and Seventh Avenue by boarded-up St. Vincent's heading downtown to meet my dealer, and what about Pippa, where was she? in the back of a taxicab, out at dinner, drinking with people I didn't know, asleep in a bed I'd never seen? I desperately wanted to see photos of her flat, in order to add some much-needed detail to my fantasies, but was too embarrassed to ask. With a pang I thought of her bedsheets, what they must be like, a dark dorm-room color as I imagined them, tumbled, unwashed, a student's dark nest, her freckled cheek pale against a maroon or purple pillowcase, English rain tapping against her window. Her photographs, lining the hall outside my bedroom—many different Pippas, at many different ages—were a daily torment, always unexpected, always new; but though I tried to keep my eyes away always it seemed I was glancing up by mistake and there she was, laughing at somebody else's joke or smiling at someone who wasn't me, always a fresh pain, a blow straight to the heart.

And the strange thing was: I knew that most people didn't see her as I did—if anything, found her a bit odd-looking with her off-kilter walk and her spooky redhead pallor. For whatever dumb reason I had always flattered myself that I was the only person in the world who really appreciated her—that she would be shocked and touched and maybe even come to view herself in a whole new light if she knew just how beautiful I found her. But this had never happened. Angrily, I concentrated on her flaws, willfully studying the photographs that caught her at awkward ages and less flattering angles—long nose, thin cheeks, her eyes (despite their heartbreaking color) naked-looking with their pale lashes—Huck-Finn plain. Yet all these aspects were—to me—so tender and particular they moved me to despair. With a beautiful girl I could have consoled myself that she was out of my league; that I was so haunted and stirred even by her plainness suggested—ominously—a love more binding than physical affection, some tar-pit of the soul where I might flop around and malinger for years.

For in the deepest, most unshakable part of myself reason was useless. She was the missing kingdom, the unbruised part of myself I'd lost with my mother. Everything about her was a snowstorm of fascination, from the antique valentines and embroidered Chinese coats she collected to her tiny scented bottles from Neal's Yard Remedies; there had always been something bright and magical about her unknown faraway life: Vaud Suisse, 23 rue de Tombouctou, Blenheim Crescent W11 2EE, furnished rooms in countries I had never seen. Clearly this Everett ("poor as a churchmouse"—his phrase) was living off her money, Uncle Welty's money rather, old Europe preying off young America, to use a phrase I'd employed in my Henry James paper in my last semester of school.

Could I write him a check to make him leave her alone? Alone in the shop, in the slow cool afternoons, the thought had crossed my mind: *fifty thousand if you walk out tonight, a hundred if you never see her again.* Money was a concern with him, clearly; during his visit he'd always been digging anxiously in his pockets, constant stops at the cash machine, taking out twenty bucks at a time, good God.

It was hopeless. There was simply no way in hell she could matter half as much to Mr. Music Library as she did to me. We belonged together; there was a dream rightness and magic to it, inarguable; the thought of her flooded every corner of my mind with light and poured brightness into miraculous lofts I hadn't even known were there, vistas that seemed to exist not at all except in relationship to her. Over and over I played her favorite Arvo Pärt, as a way of being with her; and she had only to mention a recently read novel for me to grab it up hungrily, to be inside her thoughts, a sort of telepathy. Certain objects that passed through the shop—a Pleyel piano; a strange little scratched-up Russian cameo— seemed to be tangible artifacts of the life that she and I, by rights, ought to be living together. I wrote thirty-page emails to her that I erased without sending, opting instead for the mathematical formula I'd devised to keep from making too big a fool of myself: always three lines shorter than the email she'd sent, always one day longer than I'd waited for her reply. Sometimes in bed—adrift in my sighing, opiated, erotic reveries—I carried on long candid conversations with her: *we are inseparable,* I imagined us saying (cornily) to each other, each with a hand on the other's cheek, *we can never be apart.* Like a stalker, I hoarded a snippet of autumn-leaf hair I'd retrieved from the trash after she'd trimmed her bangs in the bathroom—and, even more creepily, an unwashed shirt, still intoxicating with her hay-smelling, vegetarian sweat.

It was hopeless. More than hopeless: humiliating. Always leaving the door of my room partially open when she came to visit, a not-so-subtle invitation. Even the adorable drag in her step (like the little mermaid, too fragile to walk on land) drove me crazy. She was the golden thread running through everything, a lens that magnified beauty so that the whole world stood transfigured in relation to her, and her alone. Twice I'd tried to kiss her: once drunk in a taxicab; once at the airport, desperate at the thought that I would not be seeing her again for months (or, who knew, years) — "I'm sorry," I said, a beat too late —

"It's okay."

"No, really, I —"

"Listen —" sweet unfocused smile — "it's fine. But they're boarding my flight soon" (they weren't, in fact). "I have to go. Take care of yourself, okay?"

Take care. What on earth did she see in this "Everett"? I could only think how boring she must find me if she preferred such a lukewarm gloop of a guy to me. *Someday, when we have kids...* though he'd said it half jokingly, my blood had gone cold. He was just the kind of loser you could see hauling around a diaper bag and loads of padded baby equipment....I berated myself for not being more forceful with her, though in truth there was no way I could have pursued her any harder without at least a tiny bit of encouragement on her end. Already it was embarrassing enough: Hobie's tact whenever her name came up, the careful flatness in his voice. Yet my longing for her was like a bad cold that had hung on for years despite my conviction that I was sure to get over it at any moment. Even a cow like Mrs. Vogel could see it. It wasn't as if Pippa had led me on — quite the contrary; if she cared anything about me she would have come back to New York instead of staying in Europe after school; and still for whatever dumb reason I couldn't let go of the way she'd looked at me the day when I first came to visit, sitting on the side of her bed. The memory of that childhood afternoon had sustained me for years; it was as if — sick with loneliness for my mother — I'd imprinted on her like some orphaned animal; when in fact, joke on me, she'd been doped up and knocked lamb-daffy from a head injury, ready to throw her arms around the first stranger who'd walked in.

My "opes" as Jerome called them were in an old tobacco tin. On the marble top of the dresser I crushed one of my hoarded old-style Oxycontins, cut it and drew it into lines with my Christie's card and — rolling the crispest bill in my wallet—leaned to the table, eyes damp with anticipation: ground zero, bam, bitter taste in the back of the throat and then the gust of relief, falling backward on the bed as the sweet old punch hit me square in the heart: pure pleasure, aching and bright, far from the tin-can clatter of misery.

vii.

THE NIGHT OF MY dinner at the Barbours was rainwhipped and stormy, with blasting winds so strong I could scarcely get my umbrella up. On Sixth Avenue there were no cabs to be had, pedestrians head-down and shouldering into sideways rain; in the humid, bunker-like damp of the subway platform, drips plinked monotonously from the concrete ceiling.

When I emerged, Lexington Avenue was deserted, raindrops dancing and prickling on the sidewalks, a smashing rain that seemed to amplify all the noise on the streets. Taxis lashed by in loud sprays of water. A few doors from the station I ducked into a market to buy flowers—lilies, three bunches since one was too puny; in the tiny, overheated shop their fragrance hit me exactly the wrong way and only at the cash register did I realize why: their scent was the same sick, unwholesome sweetness of my mother's memorial service. As I ducked out again and ran the flooded sidewalk to Park Avenue—socks squelching, cold rain pelting in my face—I regretted I'd bought them at all and came close to tossing them in a trash can, only the squalls of rain were so fierce I couldn't bring myself to slow down, for even a moment, and ran on.

As I stood in the vestibule—my hair plastered to my head, my supposedly waterproof raincoat sopping like I'd soaked it in the bathtub—the door opened quite suddenly to a large, open-faced college kid that it took me a pulse or two to recognize as Toddy. Before I could apologize for the water streaming off me, he embraced me solidly with a clap on the back.

"Oh my God," he was saying as he led me into the living room. "Let me take your coat—and these, Mum will love them. Awesome to see you! How long has it been?" He was larger and more robust than Platt, with un-Barbour like hair of a darker, cardboard-colored blond and a very un-Barbour like smile on him as well—eager and bright with no irony about it.

"Well—" His warmth, which seemed to presume upon some happy old intimacy we did not share, had thrown me into awkwardness. "It's been a long time. You must be in college now, right?"

"Yes—Georgetown—up for the weekend. I'm studying political science but really I'm hoping to go into nonprofit management maybe, something to do with young people?" With his ready, student-government smile, he had clearly grown up to be the high achiever that, at one time, Platt had promised to be. "And, I mean, I hope it's not too weird of me to say but I have you in part to thank for it."

"Sorry?"

"Well, I mean. Wanting to work with disadvantaged young people. You made quite an impression on me, you know, back when you were staying with us all those years ago. It was a real eye-opener, your situation. Because, even back in third grade or whatever, you made me think—that this was what I wanted to do someday, you know, something to do with helping kids."

"Wow," I said, still stuck on the *disadvantaged* part. "Huh. That's great."

"And, I mean, it's really exciting, because there are so many ways to give back to youth out there in need. I mean, I don't know how familiar you are with DC, but there are lots of under-served neighborhoods, I'm involved in a service project tutoring at-risk kids in reading and math, and this summer, I'm going to Haiti with Habitat for Humanity—"

"Is that him?" Decorous click of shoes on the parquet, light fingertips on my sleeve, and the next thing I knew Kitsey had her arms around me and I was smiling down into her white-blonde hair.

"Oh, you're completely soaked," she was saying, holding me out at arm's length. "Look at you. How on earth did you get here? Did you swim?" She had Mr. Barbour's long fine nose and his bright, almost goofy clarity of gaze—much the same as when she was a straggle-haired nine year old in school uniform, flushed and struggling with her backpack—only now, when she looked at me, I went blank to see how coldly, impersonally beautiful she'd grown.

"I—" To hide my confusion, I looked back at Toddy, busy with raincoat and flowers. "Sorry, this is just so weird. I mean—you especially" (to Toddy). "How old were you the last time I saw you? Seven? Eight?"

"I know," said Kitsey, "the little rat, he's so *exactly* like a person now, isn't he? Platt—" Platt had ambled into the living room, poorly shaven, in tweeds and rough Donegal sweater, like some gloomy fisherman in a Synge play — "where does she want us?"

"Mm —" he seemed embarrassed, rubbing his stubbled cheek — "in her quarters, actually. You don't mind, do you?" he said to me. "Etta's set up a table back there."

Kitsey wrinkled her brow. "Oh, rats. Well, it's okay, I guess. Why don't you put the dogs in the kitchen? Come on —" seizing me by the hand and dragging me down the hall with a sort of madcap, fluttery, forward-leaning quality — "we have to get you a drink, you'll need one." There was something of Andy in her fixity of gaze, also her breathlessness — his asthmatic gape reconfigured, delightfully, into parted lips and a sort of whispery starlet quality. "I was hoping she'd have us in the dining room or at least the kitchen, it's so gruesome back in her lair — what are you drinking?" she said, turning into the bar off the pantry where glasses and a bucket of ice were set out.

"Some of that Stolichnaya would be great. On the rocks please."

"Really? Are you sure it's all right? We none of us drink it — Daddy always ordered *this* kind" — hoisting Stoli bottle — "because he liked the label ... very Cold War ... how do you say it again...."

"Stolichnaya."

"*Very* authentic-sounding. Won't even try. You know," she said, turning the gooseberry-gray eyes to me, "I was afraid you wouldn't come."

"It's not that bad out."

"Yes but —" blink blink — "I thought you hated us."

"Hated you? No."

"No?" When she laughed, it was fascinating to see Andy's leukemic wanness — in her — remodeled and prettified, the candyfloss twinkle of a Disney princess. "But I was so awful!"

"I didn't care."

"Good." After a too-long pause, she turned back to the drinks. "We were horrible to you," she said flatly. "Todd and me."

"Come on. You two were just little."

"Yes but —" she bit her lower lip — "we knew better. Especially after what had happened to you. And now ... I mean with Daddy and Andy..."

I waited, as it seemed she was trying to formulate a thought, but instead she only took a sip of her wine (white; Pippa drank red) then touched me on the back of the wrist. "Mum's waiting to see you," she said. "She's been so excited all day. Shall we go in?"

"Certainly." Lightly, lightly, I put my hand at her elbow, as I had seen Mr. Barbour do with guests "of the female persuasion," and steered her into the hall.

···

viii.

THE NIGHT WAS A dreamlike mangle of past and present: a childhood world miraculously intact in some respects, grievously altered in others, as if the Ghost of Christmas Past and the Ghost of Christmas Yet to Come had joined to host the evening. But despite the continual, ugly scrape of Andy's absence (*Andy and I...? remember when Andy...?*) and everything else so strange and shrunken (pot pies at a folding table in Mrs. Barbour's room?) the oddest part of the evening was my blood-deep, unreasoning sense of returning home. Even Etta, when I'd gone back to the kitchen to say hi, had untied her apron and rushed to hug me: *I had the night off but I wanted to stay, I wanted to see you.*

Toddy ("It's Todd now, please") had risen to his father's position as Captain of the Table, guiding the conversation with a slightly automatic-seeming but evidently sincere charm, although Mrs. Barbour hadn't really been interested in talking to anyone but me — about Andy, a little, but mostly about her family's furniture, a few pieces of which had been purchased from Israel Sack in the 1940s but most of which had come down through her family from colonial times — rising from the table at one point mid-meal and leading me off by the hand to show me a set of chairs and a mahogany lowboy — Queen Anne, Salem Massachusetts — that had been in her mother's family since the 1760s. (Salem? I thought. Were these Phipps ancestors of hers witch-burners? Or witches themselves? Apart from Andy — cryptic, isolated, self-sufficient, incapable of dishonesty and completely lacking in both malice and charisma — the other Barbours, even Todd, all had something slightly uncanny about them, a watchful, sly amalgam of decorum and mischief that made it all too easy to imagine their forebears gathering in the forest by night, casting off their Puritan garb to frolic by the pagan bonfire.) Kitsey and I hadn't talked much — we hadn't been able to, thanks to Mrs. Barbour; but almost every time I'd glanced in her direction I'd been aware of her eyes on me. Platt—voice thick after five (six?) large gin and limes, pulled me aside at the bar after dinner and said: "She's on antidepressants."

"Oh?" I said, taken aback.

"Kitsey, I mean. Mommy won't touch them."

"Well—" His lowered voice made me uncomfortable, as if he were seeking my opinion or wanting me to weigh in somehow. "I hope they work better for her than they did for me."

Platt opened his mouth and then seemed to reconsider. "Oh—" reeling back slightly—"I suppose she's bearing up. But it's been rough for her. Kits was very close to both of them—closer to Andy I would say than any of us."

"Oh really?" 'Close' would not have been my description of their relationship in childhood, though she more than Andy's brothers had always been in the background, if only to whine or tease.

Platt sighed—a gin-crocked blast that almost knocked me over. "Yeah. She's on a leave of absence from Wellesley—not sure if she'll go back, maybe she'll take some classes at the New School, maybe she'll get a job—too hard for her being in Massachusetts, after, you know. They saw an awful lot of each other in Cambridge—she feels rotten, of course, that *she* didn't go up to see after Daddy. She was better with Daddy than anyone else but there was a party, she phoned Andy and begged him to go up instead... well."

"Shit." I stood appalled at the bar, ice tongs in hand, feeling sick to think of another person ruined by the same poison of *why did I* and *if only* that had wrecked my own life.

"Yep," said Platt, pouring himself another hefty slug of gin. "Rough stuff."

"Well, she shouldn't blame herself. She can't. That's crazy. I mean," I said, unnerved by the watery, dead-eye look Platt was giving me over the top of his drink, "if she'd been on that boat *she'd* be the one dead now, not him."

"No she wouldn't," Platt said flatly. "Kits is a crackerjack sailor. Good reflexes, good head on her shoulders ever since she was tiny. Andy—Andy was thinking about his orbit-orbit resonances or whatever computational shite he was doing back at home on his laptop and he spazzed out in the pinch. Completely fucking typical. Anyway," he continued calmly—not appearing to notice my astonishment at this remark—"she's a bit at loose ends right now, as I'm sure you'll understand. You should ask her to dinner or something, it would thrill Mommy senseless."

ix.

By the time I left, after eleven, the rain had stopped and the streets were glassy with water and Kenneth the night man (same heavy eyes and malt-liquor smell, bigger in the stomach but otherwise unchanged) was on the door. "Don't be a stranger, eh?" he said, which was the same thing he'd always said when I was a little kid and my mother came to pick me up after sleepovers—same torpid voice, just a half beat too slow. Even in some smoky post-catastrophe Manhattan you could imagine him swaying genially at the door in the rags of his former uniform, the Barbours up in the apartment burning old *National Geographic*s for warmth, living off gin and tinned crabmeat.

Though it had pervaded every aspect of the evening like a simmering toxin, Andy's death was still too huge to grasp—though the strange thing too was how inevitable it seemed in hindsight, how weirdly predictable, almost as if he'd suffered from some fatal inborn defect. Even as a six year old—dreamy, stumbling, asthmatic, hopeless—the slur of misfortune and early demise had been perfectly visible about his rickety little person, marking him off like a cosmic *kick me* sign pinned to his back.

And yet it was remarkable too how his world limped on without him. Strange, I thought, as I jumped a sheet of water at the curb, how a few hours could change everything—or rather, how strange to find that the present contained such a bright shard of the living past, damaged and eroded but not destroyed. Andy had been good to me when I had no one else. The least I could do was be kind to his mother and sister. It didn't occur to me then, though it certainly does now, that it was years since I'd roused myself from my stupor of misery and self-absorption; between anomie and trance, inertia and parenthesis and gnawing my own heart out, there were a lot of small, easy, everyday kindnesses I'd missed out on; and even the word *kindness* was like rising from unconsciousness into some hospital awareness of voices, and people, from a stream of digitized machines.

X.

AN EVERY-OTHER-DAY HABIT WAS still a habit, as Jerome had often reminded me, particularly when I didn't stick too faithfully to the every-other-day part. New York was full of all kinds of daily subway-and-crowd horror; the suddenness of the explosion had never left me, I was always looking for something to happen, always expecting it just out of the corner of my eye, certain configurations of people in public places could trigger it, a wartime urgency, someone cutting in front of me the wrong way or walking too fast at a particular angle was enough to throw me into tachy-cardia and trip-hammer panic, the kind that made me stumble for the nearest park bench; and my dad's painkillers, which had started as relief for my nigh-on uncontrollable anxiety, provided such a rapturous escape that soon I'd started taking them as a treat: first an only-on-weekends treat, then an after-school treat, then the purring aetherous bliss that wel-comed me whenever I was unhappy or bored (which was, unfortunately, quite a lot); at which time I made the earth-shaking discovery that the tiny pills I'd ignored because they were so insignificant and weak-looking were literally ten times as strong as the Vicodins and Percocets I'd been downing by the handful—Oxycontins, 80s, strong enough to kill some-one without a tolerance, which person by that point was definitely not me; and when at last my endless-seeming trove of oral narcotics ran out, shortly before my eighteenth birthday, I'd been forced to start buying on the street. Even dealers were censorious of the sums I spent, thousands of dollars every few weeks; Jack (Jerome's predecessor) had scolded me about it repeatedly even as he sat in the filthy beanbag chair from which he con-ducted his business, counting my hundreds fresh from the teller's window. "Might as well light it on fire, brah." Heroin was cheaper—fifteen bucks a bag. Even if I didn't bang it—Jack, laboriously, had done the math for me on the inside of a Quarter Pounder wrapper—I would be looking at a much more reasonable expenditure, something in the neighborhood of four hundred and fifty dollars a month.

But heroin I only did on offer—a bump here, a bump there. As much as I loved it, and craved it constantly, I never bought it. There would never be a reason to stop. With pharmaceuticals on the other hand, the expense was a helpful factor since it not only kept my habit in control but provided an excellent reason for me to go downstairs and sell furniture every day. It was a myth you couldn't function on opiates: shooting up was one thing but for someone like me — jumping at pigeons beating from the sidewalk, afflicted with Post Traumatic Stress Disorder practically to the point of spasticity and cerebral palsy — pills were the key to being not only competent, but high-functioning. Booze made people sloppy and unfocused: all you had to do was look at Platt Barbour sitting around at J. G. Melon at three o'clock in the afternoon feeling sorry for himself. As for my dad: even after he'd sobered up he'd retained the faint clumsiness of a punch-drunk boxer, butterfingered with a phone or a kitchen timer, wet brain people called it, the mental damage from hard-core drinking, neurological stuff that never went away. He'd been seriously screwy in his reasoning, never able to hold down any kind of a long-term job. Me — well, maybe I didn't have a girlfriend or even any non-drug friends to speak of but I worked twelve hours a day, nothing stressed me out, I wore Thom Browne suits, socialized smilingly with people I couldn't stand, swam twice a week and played tennis on occasion, stayed away from sugar and processed foods. I was relaxed and personable, I was as thin as a rail, I did not indulge in self pity or negative thinking of any kind, I was an excellent salesman — everyone said so — and business was so good that what I spent on drugs, I scarcely missed.

Not that I hadn't had a few lapses — unpredictable glides where things flashed out of control for a few eerie blinks like an ice-skid on a bridge and I saw just how badly things could go, how quick. It wasn't a matter of money — more a matter of escalating doses, forgetting I'd sold pieces or forgetting to send bills, Hobie looking at me funny when I'd overdone things and come downstairs a bit too glassy and out-of-it. Dinner parties, clients... sorry, were you talking to me, did you just say something? no, just a little tired, coming down with something, maybe I'll go to bed a little early, folks. I'd inherited my mother's light-colored eyes, which short of sunglasses at gallery openings made it pretty much impossible to hide pinned pupils — not that anybody in Hobie's crowd seemed to notice, except (sometimes) a few of the younger, more with-it gay guys — "You're a bad boy," the bodybuilder boyfriend of a client had whispered into my ear at a formal dinner, freaking me out thoroughly. And I dreaded going up to the Accounts department at one of the auction houses because one of the guys there — older, British, an addict himself — was always hitting on

me. Of course it happened with women too: one of the girls I slept with—
the fashion intern—I'd met in the small-dog run in Washington Square
with Popchik, it being rapidly apparent to both of us after thirty seconds
on the park bench that we shared the same condition. Whenever things
started getting out of hand I'd dialed it back and I'd even quit altogether a
number of times—the longest, for a six-week stretch. Not everyone was
able to do that, I told myself. It was simply a matter of discipline. But at
this point, in the spring of my twenty-sixth year, I had not been more than
three days clean in a row in over three years.

I'd worked out how to quit for good, if I wanted to: steep taper, seven
day timetable, plenty of loperamide; magnesium supplements and free
form amino acids to replenish my burnt-out neurotransmitters; protein
powder, electrolyte powder, melatonin (and weed) for sleep as well as various herbal tinctures and potions my fashion intern swore by, licorice root
and milk thistle, nettles and hops and black cumin seed oil, valerian root
and skullcap extract. I had a shopping bag from the health food store with
all the stuff I needed, which had been sitting on the floor at the back of my
closet for a year and a half. All of it was mostly untouched except the
weed, which was long gone. The problem (as I'd learned, repeatedly) was
that thirty-six hours in, with your body in full revolt, and the remainder
of your un-opiated life stretching out bleakly ahead of you like a prison
corridor, you needed some fairly compelling reason to keep moving forward into darkness, rather than falling straight back into the gorgeous
feather mattress you'd so foolishly abandoned.

That night when I got back from the Barbours' I swallowed a long-acting
morphine tablet, as was my habit whenever I happened to come home in a
remorseful mood and feeling I needed to straighten up: low dose, less than
half of what I needed to feel anything, just enough on top of the booze to
keep me from being too agitated to sleep. The next morning, losing heart (for,
usually, waking up sick at this phase of the kick plan, I very quickly lost my
nerve), I crushed thirty and then sixty milligrams of Roxicodone on the marble top of the nightstand, inhaled it through a cut straw, then unwilling to
flush the rest of the pills (well over two thousand dollars' worth) got up,
dressed, flushed my nose with saline spray, and, after squirrelling away a few
more of the long-acting morphs in case the "withdraws" as Jerome called
them got too uncomfortable, slipped the Redbreast Flake tin in my pocket
and—at six a.m., before Hobie awoke—took a cab up to the storage facility.

The storage facility—open twenty-four hours—was like a Mayan burial complex, save for an empty-eyed clerk watching TV at the front desk. Nervously I walked to the elevators. I had set foot on the premises only three times in seven years—always with dread, and then never venturing upstairs to the locker itself but only executing a quick duck in the lobby to pay the rent, in cash: two years' rent at a time, the maximum allowed by state law.

The freight elevator required a key card, which fortunately I'd remembered to bring. Unfortunately, it failed to engage properly; and—for several minutes, hoping that the desk clerk was too out-of-it to notice—I stood in the open elevator trying to finesse the card-slide until the steel doors hissed and slid shut. Feeling jittery and observed, doing my best to avert my face from my fuzzed-out shadow on the monitor, I rode to the eighth floor, 8D 8E 8F 8G, cinderblock walls and rows of faceless doors like some pre-fab Eternity where there was no color but beige and no dust would settle for the rest of time.

8R, two keys and a combination padlock, 7522, the last four digits of Boris's home phone in Vegas. The locker creaked with a metallic squeal. There was the shopping bag from Paragon Sporting Goods—tag of the pup tent dangling, King Kanopy, $43.99, just as crisp and new-looking as the day I'd bought it eight years before. And though the texture of the pillowcase peeking out of the bag threw me an ugly short-circuit, like an electric pop in the temple, more than anything I was struck by the smell—for the plastic, pool-liner odor of masking tape had grown overwhelming from being shut up in such a small space, an emotionally evocative odor I hadn't remembered or thought of in years, a distinct polyvinyl reek that threw me straight back to childhood and my bedroom back in Vegas: chemicals and new carpet, falling asleep and waking up every morning with the painting taped behind my headboard and the same adhesive smell in my nostrils. I had not properly unwrapped it in years; just to get it open would take ten or fifteen minutes with an X-Acto knife but as I stood there overwhelmed (slippage and confusion, almost like the time I'd waked, sleepwalking, in the door of Pippa's bedroom, I didn't know what I'd been thinking or what I ought to do) I was transfixed with an urge amounting almost to delirium: for to have it only a handbreadth away again, after so long, was to find myself suddenly on some kind of dangerous, yearning edge I hadn't even known was there. In the shadows the mummified bundle—what little was visible—had a ragged, poignant, oddly personal look, less like an inanimate object than some poor creature bound and helpless in the dark, unable to cry out and dreaming of rescue. I hadn't been so close to the painting since I was fifteen years old, and for a moment it was all I could do to keep from snatching it up and tucking it under my arm and walking out with it. But I could feel the security cameras hissing at my back; and—quick spasmodic movement—I dropped my Redbreast Flake tin in the Bloomingdale's bag and shut the door and turned the key. "Just flush them if you ever really want to kick," Jerome's extremely hot girlfriend Mya had advised me, "else your ass is going to be up at that storage unit at two in the morning," but as I walked out the door, lightheaded and buzzed, the drugs were the last thing on my mind. Just the sight of the bundled painting, lonely and pathetic, had scrambled me top to bottom, as if a satellite signal from the past had burst in and jammed all other transmissions.

xi.

THOUGH MY (SOMETIME) DAYS off had kept my dose from escalating too much, the withdrawals got uncomfortable sooner than I'd expected and even with the pills I'd saved to taper I spent the next days feeling pretty low: too sick to eat, unable to stop sneezing. "Just a cold," I told Hobie. "I'm fine."

"Nope, if you've got a bad stomach, it's the flu," said Hobie, grimly, just back from Bigelow with more Benadryl and Imodium, plus crackers and ginger ale from Jefferson Market. "There's not a reason on the earth—bless you! If I were you, I'd get myself to the doctor and no fuss about it."

"Look, it's just a bug." Hobie had an iron constitution; whenever he came down with anything himself, he drank a Fernet-Branca and kept going.

"Maybe, but you've eaten hardly a bite in days. There's no point scraping away down here and making yourself miserable."

But working took my mind off my discomfort. The chills came in ten minute spasms and then I was sweating. Runny nose, runny eyes, startling electrical twitches. The weather had turned, the shop was full of people, murmur and drift; the trees flowering on the streets outside were white pops of delirium. My hands were steady at the register, for the most part, but inside I was squirming. "Your first rodeo isn't the bad one," Mya had told me. "It's around the third or fourth you'll start wishing you were dead." My stomach flopped and seethed like a fish on the hook; aches, jumpy muscles, I couldn't lie still or get comfortable in bed and nights, after I closed the shop, I sat red-faced and sneezing in a tub that was hot almost beyond endurance, a glass of ginger ale and mostly melted ice pressed to my temple, while Popchik — too stiff and creaky to stand with his paws on the edge of the tub, as he had once liked to do — sat on the bath mat and watched me anxiously.

None of this was as bad as I'd feared. But what I hadn't expected to hit even a quarter so hard was what Mya called "the mental stuff," which was unendurable, a sopping black curtain of horror. Mya, Jerome, my fashion intern — most of my drug friends had been at it longer than I had; and when they sat around high and talking about what it was like to quit (which was apparently the only time they could stand to talk about quitting), everyone had warned me repeatedly that the physical symptoms weren't the rough part, that even with a baby habit like mine the depression would be like "nothing I'd ever dreamed" and I'd smiled politely as I leaned to the mirror and thought: *wanna bet?*

But *depression* wasn't the word. This was a plunge encompassing sorrow and revulsion far beyond the personal: a sick, drenching nausea at all humanity and human endeavor from the dawn of time. The writhing loathsomeness of the biological order. Old age, sickness, death. No escape for anyone. Even the beautiful ones were like soft fruit about to spoil. And yet somehow people still kept fucking and breeding and popping out new fodder for the grave, producing more and more new beings to suffer like this was some kind of redemptive, or good, or even somehow morally admirable thing: dragging more innocent creatures into the lose-lose game. Squirming babies and plodding, complacent, hormone-drugged moms. *Oh, isn't he cute? Awww.* Kids shouting and skidding in the playground with no idea what future Hells awaited them: boring jobs and ruinous mortgages and bad marriages and hair loss and hip replacements and lonely cups of coffee in an empty house and a colostomy bag at the hospital. Most people seemed satisfied with the thin decorative glaze and the artful stage lighting that, sometimes, made the bedrock atrocity of the human predicament look somewhat more mysterious or less abhorrent. People gambled and golfed and planted gardens and traded stocks and had sex and bought new cars and practiced yoga and worked and prayed and redecorated their homes and got worked up over the news and fussed over their children and gossiped about their neighbors and pored over restaurant reviews and founded charitable organizations and supported political candidates and attended the U.S. Open and dined and travelled and distracted themselves with all kinds of gadgets and devices, flooding themselves incessantly with information and texts and communication and entertainment from every direction to try to make themselves forget it: where we were, what we were. But in a strong light there was no good spin you could put on it. It was rotten top to bottom. Putting your time in at the office; dutifully spawning your two point five; smiling politely at your retirement party; then chewing on your bedsheet and choking on your canned peaches at the nursing home. It was better never to have been born—never to have wanted anything, never to have hoped for anything. And all this mental thrashing and tossing was mixed up with recurring images, or half-dreams, of Popchik lying weak and thin on one side with his ribs going up and down—I'd forgotten him somewhere, left him alone and forgotten to feed him, he was dying—over and over, even when he was in the room with me, head-snaps where I started up guiltily, where is Popchik; and this in turn was mixed up with head-snapping flashes of the bundled pillowcase, locked away in its steel coffin. Whatever reason I'd had for storing the painting all those years ago—for keeping it in the first place—for taking it out of the museum even—I now couldn't remember. Time had blurred it. It was part of a world that didn't exist— or, rather, it was as if I lived in two worlds, and the storage locker was part of the imaginary world rather than the real one. It was easy to forget about the storage locker, to pretend it wasn't there; I'd half expected to open it to find the painting gone, although I knew it wouldn't be, it would still be shut away in the dark and waiting for me forever as long as I left it there, like the body of a person I'd murdered and stuck in a cellar somewhere.

On the eighth morning I woke sweat-drenched after four hours' bad sleep, hollowed to the core and as despairing as I'd ever felt in my life, but steady enough to walk Popchik around the block and come up to the kitchen and eat the convalescent's breakfast—poached eggs and English muffin—that Hobie pressed on me.

"And about time too." He'd finished his own breakfast and was unhurriedly clearing the dishes. "White as a lily—I'd be too, a week of soda crackers and nothing but. A bit of sunshine is what you are in need of, a bit of air. You and the pup should take yourselves out for a good long stroll."

"Right." But I had no intention of going anywhere except straight down to the shop, where it was quiet and dark.

"I haven't bothered you, you've been so low—" his back-to-business voice, along with the friendly tilt of his head, made me look away uncomfortably and stare into my plate—"but when you were out of commission you had some calls on the home line. "

"Oh yeah?" I'd switched my cell phone off and left it in a drawer; I hadn't even looked at it for fear of finding messages from Jerome.

"Awfully nice girl—" he consulted the notepad, peering over the top of his glasses—"Daisy Horsley?" (Daisy Horsley was Carole Lombard's real name.) "Said she was busy with work" (code for *Fiancé around, Stay away*) "and to text-message her if you wanted to get in touch."

"Okay, great, thanks." Daisy's big important National Cathedral wedding, if it actually went off, would be happening in June, after which she would be moving to DC with the BF, as she called him.

"Mrs. Hildesley called too, about the cherrywood high-chest—not the bonnet top, the other. Countered with a good offer—eight thousand—I accepted, hope you don't mind, that chest isn't worth three thousand if you ask me. Also—this fellow called twice—a Lucius Reeve?"

I nearly choked on my coffee—the first I'd been able to stomach in days—but Hobie didn't seem to notice.

"Left a number. Said you would know what it was about. Oh—" he sat down, suddenly, drummed the table with his palm—"and one of the Barbour children phoned!"

"Kitsey?"

"No—" he took a gulp of his tea—"Platt? Does that sound right?"

̈xii.

THE THOUGHT OF DEALING with Lucius Reeve, unmedicated, was just about enough to send me back to the storage unit. As for the Barbours: I wasn't all that anxious to speak to Platt either, but to my relief it was Kitsey who answered.

"We're going to have a dinner for you," she said immediately.

"Excuse me?"

"Didn't we tell you? Oh—maybe I should have phoned! Anyway, Mum loved seeing you *so* much. She wants to know when you're coming back."

"Well—"

"Do you need an invitation?"

"Well, sort of."

"You sound weird."

"Sorry, I've had the, uh, flu."

"Really? Oh my goodness. We've all been perfectly fine, I don't think you can have caught it from us—sorry?" she said to an indistinct voice in the background. "Here...Platt's trying to take the phone away. Talk to you soon."

"Hi, brother," said Platt when he got on the line.

"Hi," I said, rubbing my temple, trying not to think how weird it was for Platt to be calling me *brother.*

"I—" Footsteps; a door shutting. "I want to cut right to the chase."

"Yes?"

"Matter of some furniture," he said cordially. "Any chance you could sell some of it for us?"

"Sure." I sat down. "Which pieces is she thinking of selling?"

"Well," said Platt, "the thing is, I would really not like to bother Mommy with this, if possible. Not sure she's up for it, if you know what I mean."

"Oh?"

"Well, I mean, she's just got so much stuff...things up in Maine and out in storage that she'll never look at again, you know? Not just furniture. Silver, a coin collection...some ceramics that I think are supposed to be a big deal but, I'll be frank, look like shit. I don't mean figuratively. I mean like literal clods of cow shit."

"I guess my question would be, why would you want to sell it."

"Well, there's no *need* to sell it," he said hastily. "But the thing is, she gets so tenacious about some of this old nonsense."

I rubbed my eye. "Platt—"

"I mean, it's just sitting there. All this junk. Much of which is mine, the coins and some old guns and things, because Gaga left them to me. I mean—" crisply—"I'll be frank with you. I have another guy I've been dealing with, but honestly I'd rather work with you. You know us, you know Mommy, and I know you'll give me a fair price."

"Right," I said uncertainly. There followed an expectant, endless-seeming pause — as if we were reading from a script and he was waiting with confidence for me to deliver the rest of my line — and I was wondering how to put him off when my eye fell on Lucius Reeve's name and number dashed out in Hobie's open, expressive hand.

"Well, um, it's very complicated," I said. "I mean, I would have to see the things in person before I could really say anything. Right, right —" he was trying to put in something about photos — "but photographs aren't good enough. Also I don't deal with coins, or the kind of ceramics you're talking about either. With coins especially, you really need to go to a dealer who does nothing but. But in the meantime," I said — he was still trying to talk over me — "if it's a question of raising a few thousand bucks? I think I can help you out."

That shut him up all right. "Yes?"

I reached under my glasses to pinch the bridge of my nose. "Here's the thing. I'm trying to establish a provenance on a piece — it's a real nightmare, guy won't leave me alone, I've tried to buy the piece back from him, he seems intent on raising a stink. For what reason I don't know. Anyway it would help me out, I think, if I could produce a bill of sale proving I'd bought this piece from another collector."

"Well, Mommy thinks you hung the moon," he said sourly. "I'm sure she'll do whatever you want."

"Well, the thing is —" Hobie was downstairs with the router going, but I lowered my voice just the same — "we're speaking in complete confidence, of course?"

"Of course."

"I don't actually see any reason to involve your mother at all. I can write out a bill of sale, and back-date it. But if the guy has any questions, and he may, what I'd like to do is refer him to you — give him your number, eldest son, mother recently bereaved, blah blah blah —"

"Who is this guy?"

"His name is Lucius Reeve. Ever heard of him?"

"Nope."

"Well — just so you know, it's not out of the realm of possibility that he knows your mother, or has met her at some point."

"That shouldn't be a problem. Mommy hardly sees anyone these days." A pause; I could hear him lighting a cigarette. "So—this guy phones."

I described the chest-on-chest. "Happy to email a photo. The distinctive feature is the phoenix carving on the top. All *you* need to tell him, if he calls, is that the piece was up at your place in Maine until your mother sold it to me a couple of years back. She will have bought it from a dealer out of business you see, some old guy who passed away a few years back, can't remember the name, darn, you'll have to check. Though if he presses—" it was astonishing, I'd learned, how a few tea stains and a few minutes of crisping in the oven, at low temperatures, could further age the blank receipts in the 1960s receipt book I'd bought at the flea market—"it'll be easy enough for me to provide that bill of sale for you too."

"I got it."

"Right. Anyway—" I was groping around for a cigarette which I didn't have—"if you take care of things on your end—you know, if you commit to backing me up if the guy *does* call—I'll give you ten percent on the price of the piece."

"Which is how much?"

"Seven thousand dollars."

Platt laughed—an oddly happy and carefree-sounding laugh. "Daddy always did say that all you antiques fellows were crooked."

xiii.

I HUNG UP THE phone, feeling goofy with relief. Mrs. Barbour had her share of second and third rate antiques, but she also owned so many important pieces that it disturbed me to think of Platt selling things out from under her with no clue what he was doing. As for being "over a barrel"—if anyone gave off the aroma of being embroiled in some sort of ongoing and ill-defined trouble, it was Platt. Though I had not thought of his expulsion in years, the circumstances had been so diligently hushed up that it seemed likely he'd done something fairly serious, something that in less controlled circumstances might have involved the police: which in a weird way reassured me, in terms of trusting him to collect his cash and keep his mouth shut. Besides—it gladdened my heart to think of it—if anyone alive could high-hand or intimidate Lucius Reeve it was Platt: a world-class snob and bully in his own right.

"Mr. Reeve?" I said courteously when he picked up the phone.

"Lucius, please."

"Well then, Lucius." His voice had made me go cold with anger; but knowing I had Platt in my corner made me more cocky than I had reason to be. "Returning your call. What's on your mind?"

"Probably not what you think," came the swift reply.

"No?" I said, easily enough, though his tone took me aback. "Well then. Fill me in."

"I think you'd probably rather I do that in person."

"Fine. How about downtown," I said quickly, "since you were good enough to take me to your club last time?"

xiv.

THE RESTAURANT I CHOSE was in Tribeca — far enough downtown that I didn't have to worry too much about running into Hobie or any of his friends, and with a young enough crowd (I hoped) to throw Reeve off-balance. Noise, lights, conversation, relentless press of bodies: with my fresh, un-blunted senses the smells were overwhelming, wine and garlic and perfume and sweat, sizzling platters of lemongrass chicken hurried out of the kitchen, and the turquoise banquettes, the bright orange dress of the girl next to me, were like industrial chemicals squirted directly into my eyes. My stomach boiled with nerves, and I was chewing an antacid from the roll in my pocket when I looked up and saw the beautiful tattooed giraffe of a hostess — blank and indolent — pointing Lucius Reeve indifferently to my table.

"Well, hello," I said, not standing to greet him. "How nice to see you."

He was casting his glance round in distaste. "Do we really have to sit here?"

"Why not?" I said blandly. I'd deliberately chosen a table in the middle of traffic — not so loud we had to shout, but loud enough to be off-putting; moreover, had left him the chair that would put the sun in *his* eyes.

"This is completely ridiculous."

"Oh. I'm sorry. If you're not happy here..." I nodded at the self-absorbed young giraffe, back at her post and swaying absently.

Conceding the point—the restaurant was packed—he sat down. Though he was tight and elegant in his speech and gestures, and his suit was modishly cut for a man his age, his demeanor made me think of a puffer fish—or, alternately, a cartoon strongman or Mountie blown up by a bicycle pump: cleft chin, doughball nose, tense slit of a mouth, all bunched tight in the center of a face which glowed a plump, inflamed, blood-pressure pink.

After the food arrived—Asian fusion, with lots of crispy flying buttresses of wonton and frizzled scallion, from his expression not much to his liking—I waited for him to work around to whatever he wanted to tell me. The carbon of the fake bill of sale, which I'd written out on a blank page in one of Welty's old receipt books and backdated five years, was in my breast pocket, but I didn't intend to produce it until I had to.

He had asked for a fork; from his slightly alarming plate of "scorpion prawn" he pulled out several architectural filaments of vegetable matter and laid them to the side. Then he looked at me. His small sharp eyes were bright blue in his ham-pink face. "I know about the museum," he said.

"Know what?" I said, after a waver of surprise.

"Oh, please. You know very well what I'm talking about."

I felt a jab of fear at the base of my spine, though I took care to keep my eyes on my plate: white rice and stir-fried vegetables, the blandest thing on the menu. "Well, if you don't mind. I'd rather not talk about it. It's a painful subject."

"Yes, I can imagine."

He said this in such a taunting and provocative tone I glanced up sharply. "My mother died, if that's what you mean."

"Yes, she did." Long pause. "Welton Blackwell did too."

"That's correct."

"Well, I mean. Written about in the papers, for heaven's sake. Matter of public record. But—" he darted the tip of his tongue across his upper lip—"here's what I wonder. Why did James Hobart go about repeating that tale to everyone in town? You turning up on his doorstep with his partner's ring? Because if he'd just kept his mouth shut, no one would have ever made the connection."

"I don't understand what you mean."

"You know very well what I mean. You have something that I want. That a lot of people want, actually."

I stopped eating, chopsticks halfway to my mouth. My immediate, unthinking impulse was to get up and walk out of the restaurant but almost as quickly I realized how stupid that would be.

Reeve leaned back in his chair. "You're not saying anything."

"That's because you're not making any sense," I rejoined sharply, putting down the chopsticks, and for a flash — something in the quickness of the gesture — my thoughts went to my father. How would he handle this?

"You seem very perturbed. I wonder why."

"I guess I don't see what this has to do with the chest-on-chest. Because I was under the impression that was why we were here."

"You know very well what I'm talking about."

"No —" incredulous laugh, authentic-sounding — "I'm afraid I don't."

"Do you want me to spell it out? Right here? All right, I will. You were with Welton Blackwell and his niece, you were all three of you in Gallery 32 and *you* —" slow, teasing smile — "were the only person to walk out of there. And we know what else walked out of Gallery 32, don't we?"

It was as if all the blood had drained to my feet. Around us, everywhere, clatter of silverware, laughter, echo of voices bouncing off the tiled walls.

"You see?" said Reeve smugly. He had resumed eating. "Very simple. I mean surely," he said, in a chiding tone, putting down his fork, "surely you didn't think no one would put it together? You took the painting, and when you brought the ring to Blackwell's partner you gave him the painting too, for what reason I don't know — yes, yes," he said, as I tried to talk over him, shifting his chair slightly, bringing up his hand to shade his eyes from the sun — "you end up James Hobart's *ward* for Christ's sake, you end up his ward, and he's been farming that little souvenir of yours out hither and yon and using it to raise money ever since."

Raise money? Hobie? "Farming it *out*?" I said; and then, remembering myself: "Farming out what?"

"Look, this 'what's going on?' act of yours is beginning to get a bit tiresome."

"No, I mean it. What the hell are you talking about?"

Reeve pursed his lips, looking very pleased with himself.

"It's an exquisite painting," he said. "A beautiful little anomaly —

absolutely unique. I'll never forget the first time I saw it in the Maurits-huis . . . really quite different from any work there, or any other work of its day if you ask me. Difficult to believe it was painted in the 1600s. One of the greatest small paintings of all time, wouldn't you agree? What was it"—he paused, mockingly—"what was it that the collector said—you know, the art critic, the Frenchman, who rediscovered it? Found it buried in some nobleman's store room back in the 1890s, and from then on made 'desperate efforts' "—inserting quotations with his fingers—"to acquire it. 'Don't forget, I must have this little goldfinch at any price.' But of course that's not the quote I mean. I mean the famous one. Surely you must know it yourself. After all this time, you must be very familiar with the painting and its history."

I put down my napkin. "I don't know what you're talking about." There was nothing I could do but hold my ground and keep saying it. *Deny, deny, deny,* as my dad—in his one big movie turn as the mob lawyer—had advised his client in the scene right before he got shot.

But they saw me.
Musta been somebody else.
There are three eyewitnesses.
Don't care. They're all mistaken. "It wasn't me."
They'll be bringing up people to testify against me all day long.
Fine then. Let them.

Someone had pulled a window blind, throwing our table into tiger-striped shadow. Reeve, eyeing me smugly, speared a bright orange prawn and ate it.

"I mean, I've been trying to think," he said. "Maybe you can help me. What other painting of its size would be anywhere near its class? Maybe that lovely little Velázquez, you know, the garden of the Villa Medici. Of course rarity doesn't even enter into it."

"Tell me again, what are we talking about? Because I'm really not sure what you're getting at."

"Well, keep it up if you want," he said affably, wiping his mouth with his napkin. "You're not fooling anybody. Although I have to say it's pretty bloody irresponsible to entrust it to these goons to handle and pawn around."

At my astonishment, which was perfectly genuine, I saw a blink of what might have been surprise cross his face. But just as quickly it was gone.

"People like that can't be entrusted with something so valuable," he said, chewing busily. "Street thugs—ignoramuses."

"You are making absolutely no sense," I snapped.

"No?" He put down the fork. "Well. What I'm offering—if you ever care to understand what I'm talking about—is to buy the thing off you."

My tinnitus—old echo of the explosion—had kicked in, as it often did in moments of stress, a high-pitched drone like incoming aircraft.

"Shall I name a figure? Well. I think half a million should do nicely, considering that I'm in a position to make a phone call this moment—" he removed his cell phone from his pocket and put it on the table beside his water glass—"and put this enterprise of yours to a stop."

I closed my eyes, then opened them. "Look. How many times can I say it? I really don't know what you're thinking but—"

"I'll tell you exactly what I'm thinking, Theodore. I'm thinking conservation, preservation. Concerns which clearly haven't been paramount for you or the people you're working with. Surely you'll realize it's the wisest thing to do—for you, and for the painting as well. Obviously you've made a fortune but it's irresponsible, wouldn't you agree, to keep it bouncing around in such precarious conditions?"

But my unfeigned confusion at this seemed to serve me well. After a weird, off-beat lag, he reached into the breast pocket of his suit—

"Is everything okay?" said our male-model waiter, appearing suddenly.

"Yes yes, fine."

The waiter disappeared, sliding across the room to talk to the beautiful hostess. Reeve, from his pocket, took out several sheets of folded paper, which he pushed across the tablecloth to me.

It was a print-out of a Web page. Quickly I scanned it: FBI...international agencies...botched raid...investigation...

"What the fuck is this?" I said, so loudly that a woman at the next table jumped. Reeve—involved in his lunch—said nothing.

"No, I mean it. What does this have to do with me?" Scanning the page irritably—wrongful death suit...Carmen Huidobro, housekeeper from Miami temp agency, shot dead by agents who stormed the home—I was about to ask again what anything in this article had to do with me when I stopped cold.

An Old Master painting once believed destroyed (*The Goldfinch,* Carel Fabritius, 1654) was employed as rumored collateral in the deal with Contreras, but unfortunately was not recovered in the raid on the South Florida compound. Though stolen artworks are often used as negotiable instruments to supply venture capital for drug trafficking and arms deals, the DEA has defended itself against criticism in what the art-crimes division of the FBI has called a "bungled" and "amateurish" handling of the matter, issuing a public statement apologizing for the accidental death of Mrs. Huidobro while also explaining that their agents are not trained to identify or recover stolen artwork. "In pressured situations such as this," said Turner Stark, spokesman for the DEA press office, "our top priority will always be the safety of agents and civilians as we secure the prosecution of major violations of America's controlled substance laws." The ensuing furor, especially in the wake of the suit over Mrs. Huidobro's wrongful death, has resulted in a call for greater cooperation between federal agencies. "All it would have taken was one phone call," said Hofstede Von Moltke, spokesman for the art-crimes division of Interpol in a press conference yesterday in Zurich. "But these people weren't thinking about anything but making their arrest and getting their conviction, and that's unfortunate because now this painting has gone underground, it may be decades until it's seen again."

The trafficking of looted paintings and sculptures is estimated to be a six-billion-dollar industry worldwide. Though the sighting of the painting was unconfirmed, detectives believe that the rare Dutch masterwork has already been whisked out of the country, possibly to Hamburg, where it has likely passed hands at a fraction of the many millions it would raise at auction....

I put down the paper. Reeve, who had stopped eating, was regarding me with a tight feline smile. Maybe it was the primness of that tiny smile in his pear-shaped face but unexpectedly I burst out laughing: the pent-up laughter of terror and relief, just as Boris and I had laughed when the fat mall cop chasing us (and about to catch us) slipped on wet tile in the food court and fell smack on his ass.

"Yes?" said Reeve. He had an orange stain on his mouth from the prawns, the old jabberwock. "Found something that amuses you?"

But all I could do was shake my head and look out across the restaurant. "Man," I said, wiping my eyes, "I don't know what to say. Clearly you are delusional or — I don't know."

Reeve, to his credit, did not look perturbed, though clearly he wasn't pleased.

"No, really," I said, shaking my head. "I'm sorry. I shouldn't laugh. But this is the most absurd fucking thing I have ever seen."

Reeve folded his napkin and put it down. "You're a liar," he said pleasantly. "You may think you can bluff your way out of this, but you can't."

"Wrongful-death suit? Florida compound? What? You actually think this has something to do with me?"

Reeve regarded me fiercely with his tiny, bright blue eyes. "Be reasonable. I'm giving you a way out."

"Way *out?*" Miami, Hamburg, even the place names made me burst into an incredulous huff of laughter. "Way out of what?"

Reeve blotted his lips with his napkin. "I'm delighted you find it so amusing," he said smoothly. "Since I'm fully prepared to phone this gentleman at the art-crimes division they mention and tell him exactly what I know about you and James Hobart and this scheme you're running together. What would you say to that?"

I threw down the paper, pushed back my chair. "I would say, go right ahead and phone him. Be my guest. Whenever you want to talk about the other matter, call me."

XV.

MOMENTUM SPUN ME OUT of the restaurant so fast I hardly noticed where I was going; but as soon as I was three or four blocks away I began to shake so violently that I had to stop in the grimy little park just south of Canal Street and sit on a bench, hyperventilating, head between my knees, the armpits of my Turnbull and Asser suit drenched with sweat, looking (I knew, to the surly Jamaican nannies, the old Italians fanning themselves with newspapers and eyeing me suspiciously) like some coked-out junior trader who'd pressed the wrong button and lost ten million.

There was a mom-and-pop drugstore across the street. Once my breathing had settled I walked over—feeling clammy and isolated in the mild-hearted spring breeze—and bought a Pepsi from the cold case and walked away without taking my change and went back to the leaf shade of the park, the soot-dusted bench. Pigeons aloft and beating. Traffic roaring past to the tunnel, other boroughs, other cities, malls and parkways, vast impersonal streams of interstate commerce. There was a great, seductive loneliness in the hum, a summons almost, like the call of the sea, and for the first time I understood the impulse that had driven my dad to cash out his bank account, pick up his shirts from the cleaners, gas up the car, and leave town without a word. Sunbaked highways, twirled dials on the radio, grain silos and exhaust fumes, vast tracts of land unrolling like a secret vice.

Inevitably my thoughts went to Jerome. He lived way up on Adam Clayton Powell, a few blocks from the last stop on the 3 line, but there was a bar called Brother J's where we sometimes met on 110th: a workingman's dive with Bill Withers on the jukebox and a sticky floor, career alcoholics slumped over their third bourbon at two p.m. But Jerome did not sell pharmaceuticals in increments of less than a thousand dollars and though I knew he would be perfectly glad to let me have a few bags of smack it seemed like a lot less trouble if I just went ahead and took a cab straight down to the Brooklyn Bridge.

Old lady with a Chihuahua; little kids squabbling over a Popsicle. Up above Canal streamed a remote delirium of sirens, a formal offstage note that clashed with the ringing in my ears: something of mechanical warfare about it, sustained drone of incoming missiles.

With my hands pressed over my ears (which didn't help the tinnitus at all—if anything, amplified it) I sat very still and tried to think. My childish machinations about the chest-on-chest now struck me as ridiculous— I would simply have to go to Hobie and admit what I'd done: not much fun, pretty shitty in fact, but better if he heard it from me. How he would react I couldn't imagine; antiques were all I knew, I'd have a hard time getting another job in sales but I was just handy enough to find a place in a workshop if I had to, gilding frames or cutting bobbins; restorations didn't pay well but so few people knew how to repair antiques to any kind of decent standard that someone was sure to take me on. As for the article: I was confused by what I'd read, almost as if I'd walked in on the middle of the wrong movie. On one level it was clear enough: some enterprising crook had faked my goldfinch (in terms of size and technique, not all that difficult a piece to fake) and the phony was floating around somewhere being fronted as collateral in drug deals and mis-identified by various clueless drug lords and federal agents. But no matter how fanciful or off-base the story, how lacking in relevance to the painting or me, the connection Reeve had made was real. Who knew how many people Hobie had told about me showing up at his house? or how many people those people had told? But so far no one, not even Hobie, had made the connection that Welty's ring put me *in* the gallery with the painting. This was the crux of the biscuit, as my father would have said. This was the story that would get me put in jail. The French art thief who'd panicked, who'd *burned* a lot of the paintings he'd stolen (Cranach, Watteau, Corot) had gotten only twenty-six months in prison. But that was France, only shortly after 9/11; and, under the new rubric of federal anti-terrorism laws, the museum thefts carried an additional, more serious charge of "looting of cultural artifacts." Penalties had grown much stiffer, in America particularly. And my personal life didn't stand a lot of scrutiny. Even if I was lucky I would be looking at five to ten years.

Which—if I was honest—I deserved. How had I ever thought I could keep it hidden? I'd meant to deal with the painting for years, get it back where it belonged, and yet somehow I had kept on and on finding reasons not to. To think of it wrapped and sealed uptown made me feel self-erased, blanked-out, as if burying it away had only increased its power and given it a more vital and terrible form. Somehow, even shrouded and entombed in the storage locker, it had worked itself free and into some fraudulent public narrative, a radiance that glowed in the mind of the world.

xvi.

"Hobie," I said, "I'm in a jam."

He glanced up from the Japaned chest he was retouching: roosters and cranes, golden pagodas on black. "Can I help?" He was outlining a crane's wing with water-based acrylic—very different from the shellac-based original, but the first rule of restorations, as he'd taught me early on, was that you never did what you couldn't reverse.

"Actually, the thing is. I've sort of gotten you in a jam. Inadvertently."

"Well —" the line of his brush did not waver — "if you told Barbara Guibbory we'd help with that home she's decorating in Rhinebeck, you're on your own. 'Colors of the Chakras.' I never heard of such a thing."

"No —" I tried to think of something funny or easy to say — Mrs. Guibbory, aptly nicknamed "Trippy," was usually a wellspring of comedy — but my mind had gone completely blank. "Afraid not."

Hobie straightened up, stuck the paintbrush behind one ear, blotted his forehead with a wildly patterned handkerchief, psychedelic purple like an African violet had thrown up on it, something he'd found probably in a crazy old lady's effects at one of his sales upstate. "What's going on, then?" he said reasonably, reaching for one of the saucers he mixed his paint in. Now that I was in my twenties, the generational formality between us had vanished, so that we were collegial in a way it was difficult to imagine being with my dad had he lived — me always on edge, trying to figure out how fucked-up he was and what my percentage point was of trying to get any kind of straight answer.

"I —" I reached to make sure that the chair behind me wasn't sticky before I sat. "Hobie, I've made a stupid mistake. No, a really stupid one," I said, at his good-natured, dismissive gesture.

"Well —" he was dripping raw umber into the saucer with an eyedropper — "I don't know about stupid, but I can tell you it wholly ruined my day last week to see that drill bit coming through Mrs. Wasserman's tabletop. That was a good William and Mary table. I know she won't see where I've patched the hole but believe me it was a bad moment."

His half-attentive manner made it worse. Quickly, with a sort of sick, dreamlike glide, I rushed headlong into the matter of Lucius Reeve and the chest-on-chest, leaving out Platt and the back-dated receipt in my breast pocket. Once I got started it was like I couldn't stop, like the only thing to do was keep talking and talking like some highway killer droning on under a light bulb at a rural police station. At some point Hobie stopped working, stuck the paintbrush behind his ear; he listened steadily, with a sort of heavy-browed, Arctic, ptarmigan-settling-into-itself look that I knew well. Then he plucked the sable brush from behind his ear and dabbled it in some water before he wiped it on a piece of flannel.

"Theo," he said, putting up a hand, closing his eyes — I'd stalled, going on and on about the uncashed check, dead end, bad position — "Stop. I get the picture."

"I'm so sorry." I was babbling. "I should never have done it. *Never.* But it's a real nightmare. He's pissed off and vindictive and he seems to have it in for us for some reason — you know, some other reason, something apart from this."

"Well." Hobie removed his glasses. I could see his confusion in just how gingerly he was feeling around in the pause that followed, trying to shape his response. "What's done is done. No point making it worse. But —" he stopped, and thought. "I don't know who this guy is, but if he thought that chest was an Affleck, he has more money than sense. To pay seventy-five thousand — that's what he gave you for the thing?"

"Yes."

"Well, he needs his head examined, that's all I can say. Pieces of that quality turn up once or twice in a decade, *maybe.* And they don't appear on the scene from nowhere."

"Yes, but —"

"Also, *any* fool knows, a real Affleck would be worth much more. Who buys a piece like that without doing their homework? An idiot, that's who. Also," he said, speaking over me, "you did the correct thing once he called you on it. You tried to refund his money, and he didn't take it, that's what you're saying?"

"I didn't offer to refund it. I tried to buy the piece back."

"At a greater price than he paid! And how's that going to look if he takes it to law? Which I can tell you, he won't do."

In the silence that followed, in the clinical blare of his work lamp, I was aware just how uncertain we both were how to move forward. Popchyk — napping on the folded towel that Hobie had set out for him between the clawed feet of a pier table — twitched and grumbled in his sleep.

"I mean," said Hobie — he'd wiped the black off his hands, was reaching for his brush with a sort of apparitional fixity, like a ghost intent upon his task — "the sales end has never been my bailiwick, you know that, but I've been in this business a long time. And sometimes —" darting flick of the brush — "the edge between puffery and fraud is very cloudy indeed."

I waited, uncertainly, my eyes on the Japanned chest. It was a beauty, a prize for a retired sea-captain's home in backwater Boston: scrimshaw and cowrie shells, Old Testament samplers cross-stitched by unmarried sisters, the smell of whale oil burning in the evenings, the stillness of growing old.

Hobie put down the brush again. "Oh, Theo," he said, half-angrily, scrubbing at his forehead with the back of his hand and leaving a dark smudge. "Do you expect me to stand around and scold you? You lied to the fellow. You've tried to put it right. But the fellow doesn't want to sell. What more can you do?"

"It's not the only piece."

"What?"

"I should never have done it." Unable to meet his eye. "I did it first to pay the bills, to get us out from under, and then I guess — I mean some of those pieces are *amazing,* they fooled me, they were just sitting out in storage —"

I suppose I'd been expecting incredulity, raised voices, outrage of some sort. But it was worse. A blow-up I could have handled. Instead he didn't say a word, only gazed at me with a sort of grieved fubsiness, haloed by his work lamp, tools arrayed on the walls behind him like Masonic icons. He let me tell him what I had to, and listened quietly while I did it, and when at last he spoke his voice was quieter than usual and without heat.

"All right." He looked like a figure from an allegory: black-aproned carpenter-mystic, half in shadow. "Okay. So how do you propose to deal with this?"

"I —" This wasn't the response I'd anticipated. Dreading his anger (for Hobie, though good-natured and slow to wrath, definitely had a temper) I'd had all kinds of justifications and excuses prepared but faced with his eerie composure it was impossible to defend myself. "I'll do whatever you say." I hadn't felt so ashamed or humiliated since I was a kid. "It's my fault — I take full responsibility."

"Well. The pieces are out there." He seemed to be figuring it out as he went along, half-talking to himself. "No one else has contacted you?"

"No."

"How long has it been going on?"

"Oh —" five years, at least — "one year, two?"

He winced. "Jesus. No, no," he said, hastily, "I'm just glad you were honest with me. But you'll just have to get busy, contact the clients, say you have doubts — you needn't go into the whole business, just say a question has arisen, provenance is suspect—and offer to buy the pieces back for what they paid. If they don't take you up on it—fine. You've offered. But if they do—you'll have to bite the bullet, understand?"

"Right." What I didn't—and couldn't—say was that there wasn't enough money to reimburse even a quarter of the clients. We would be bankrupt in a day.

"You say pieces. Which pieces? How many?"

"I don't know."

"You don't *know?*"

"Well, I do, it's just that I—"

"Theo, please." He was angry now; it was a relief. "No more of this. Be straight with me."

"Well—I did the deals off the books. In cash. And, I mean, there's no way you could have known, even if you'd checked the ledgers—"

"Theo. Don't make me keep asking. How many pieces?"

"Oh—" I sighed—"a dozen? Maybe?" I added when I saw the stunned look on Hobie's face. In truth, it was three times as many, but I was pretty sure that most of the people I'd rooked were too clueless to figure it out or too rich to care.

"Good God, Theo," said Hobie, after a dumbstruck silence. "*A dozen pieces?* Not at those prices? Not like the Affleck?"

"No, no," I said hastily (though in fact I'd sold some of the pieces for twice as much). "And none of our regulars." That part, at least, was true.

"Who then?"

"West Coast. Movie people—tech people. Wall Street too but— young guys, you know, hedgies. Dumb money."

"You have a list of the clients?"

"Not an actual list, but I—"

"Can you contact them?"

"Well, you see, it's complicated, because—" I wasn't worried about the people who believed they'd unearthed genuine Sheraton at bargain prices and hurried away with their copies thinking they'd swizzled me. The old Caveat Emptor rule more than applied there. I'd never claimed those pieces were genuine. What worried me was the people I'd deliberately sold—deliberately lied to.

"You didn't keep records."

"No."

"But you have an idea. You can track them down."

"More or less."

" 'More or less.' I don't know what that means."

"There are notes — shipping forms. I can piece it together."

"Can we afford to buy them all back?"

"Well —"

"Can we? Yes or no?"

"Um —" there was no way I could tell him the truth, which was No — "it's a stretch."

Hobie rubbed his eye. "Well, stretch or not, we'll have to do it. No choice. Tighten our belts. Even if it's rough for a while — even if we let the taxes slide. Because," he said, when I kept looking at him, "we can't have even one of these things out there purporting to be real. Good God —" he shook his head disbelievingly — "how the hell did you do it? They're not even good fakes! Some of the materials I used — anything I had to hand — cobbled together any which way —"

"Actually —" truth was, Hobie's work had been good enough to fool some fairly serious collectors, though it probably wasn't a great idea to bring that up —

"— and, you see, thing is, if one of the pieces you've sold as genuine is wrong — they're *all* wrong. *Everything* is called into question — every stick of furniture that's ever gone out of this shop. I don't know if you've thought about that."

"Er —" I had thought about it, plenty. I had thought about it pretty much without stopping ever since the lunch with Lucius Reeve.

He was so quiet, for so long, that I started getting nervous. But he only sighed and rubbed his eyes and then turned partly away, leaning back to his work again.

I was silent, watching the glossy black line of his brush trace out a cherry bough. Everything was new now. Hobie and I had a corporation together, filed our taxes together. I was the executor of his will. Instead of moving out and getting my own apartment, I'd chosen to stay upstairs and pay him a scarcely-token rent, a few hundred dollars a month. Insofar as I had a home, or a family, he was it. When I came downstairs and helped him with the gluing up, it wasn't so much because he actually needed me as for the pleasure of scrabbling for clamps and shouting at each other over the Mahler turned up loud; and sometimes, when we wandered over to the White Horse in the evenings for a drink and a club sandwich at the bar, it was very often for me the best time of the day.

"Yes?" said Hobie, without turning from his work, aware that I was still standing at his back.

"I'm sorry. I didn't mean for it to go this far."

"Theo." The brush stopped. "You know it very well — a lot of people would be clapping you on the back right now. And, I'll be straight with you, part of me feels the same way because honest to goodness I don't know how you pulled off such a thing. Even Welty — Welty was like you, the clients loved him, he could sell anything, but even he used to have a devil of a time up there with the finer pieces. Real Hepplewhite, real Chippendale! Couldn't get rid of the stuff! And you up there, unloading this junk for a fortune!"

"It's not junk," I said, glad to be telling the truth for once. "A lot of the work is really good. It fooled me. I think, because you did it yourself, you can't see it. How convincing it is."

"Yes but—" he paused, seemingly at a loss for words — "people who don't know furniture, it's hard to make them spend *money* on furniture."

"I know." We had an important drake-front highboy, Queen Anne, that during the lean days I'd tried despairingly to sell at the correct price, which on the low end was somewhere in the two hundred thousand range. It had been in the shop for years. But though some fair offers had come in recently I'd turned them all down — simply because such an irreproachable piece standing in the well-lighted entrance of the shop shed such a flattering glow on the frauds buried in back.

"Theo, you're a marvel. You're a genius at what you do, no question about it. But—" his tone was uncertain again; I could sense him trying to feel his way forward — "well, I mean, dealers live by their reputations. It's the honor system. Nothing you don't know. Word gets around. So, I mean—" dipping his brush, peering myopically at the chest — "fraud's hard to prove, but if you don't take care of this, it's a pretty sure thing that this will pop back and bite us somewhere down the road." His hand was steady; the line of his brush was sure. "A heavily restored piece…forget about blacklight, you'd be surprised, someone moves it to a brightly lit room…even the camera picks up differences in grain that you'd never spot with the naked eye. As soon as someone has one of these pieces photographed, or God forbid decides to put it up at Christie's or Sotheby's in an Important Americana sale..."

There was a silence, which—as it swelled between us—grew more and more serious, unfillable.

"Theo." The brush stopped, and then started again. "I'm not trying to make excuses for you but—don't think I don't know it, I'm the very person who put you in this position. Turning you loose up there all on your own. Expecting you to perform the Miracle of the Loaves and Fishes. You are very young, yes," he said curtly, turning halfway when I tried to interrupt, "you are, and you are very very gifted at all the aspects of the business I don't care to deal with, and you have been so brilliant at getting us back in the black again that it has suited me very, very well to keep my head in the sand. As regards what goes on upstairs. So I'm as much to blame for this as you."

"Hobie, I swear. I never—"

"Because—" he picked up the open bottle of paint, looked at the label as if he couldn't recall what it was for, put it down again—"well, it was too good to be true, wasn't it? All this money pouring in, wonderful to see? And did I inquire too closely? No. Don't think I don't know it—if you hadn't got busy with your flim-flam up there we'd likely be renting this space right now and hunting for a new place to live. So look here— we'll start fresh—wipe the board down—and take it as it comes. One piece at a time. That's all we can do."

"Look, I want to make it plain—" his calmness harrowed me—"the responsibility is mine. If it comes down to that. I just want you to know."

"Sure." When he flicked his brush, his deftness was practiced and reflexive, weirdly unsettling. "Still and all, let's leave it for now, all right? No," he said, when I tried to say something else, "please. I want you to take care of it and I'll do what I can to help you if there's anything specific but otherwise, I don't want to talk about it any more. All right?"

Outside: rain. It was clammy in the basement, an ugly subterranean chill. I stood watching him, not knowing what to do or say.

"Please. I'm not angry, I just want to be getting on with this. It'll be all right. Now go upstairs, please, would you?" he said, when I still stood there. "This is a tricky patch of work, I really need to concentrate if I don't want to make a hash of it."

xvii.

SILENTLY I WALKED UPSTAIRS, steps creaking loudly, past the gauntlet of Pippa's pictures that I couldn't bear to look at. Going in, I'd thought to break the easy news first and then move along to the showstopper. But as dirty and disloyal as I felt, I couldn't do it. The less Hobie knew about the painting, the safer he would be. It was wrong on every level to drag him into it.

Yet I wished there were someone I could talk to, someone I trusted. Every few years, there seemed to be another news article about the missing masterworks, which along with my Goldfinch and two loaned van der Asts also included some valuable Medieval pieces and a number of Egyptian antiquities; scholars had written papers, there had even been books; it was mentioned as one of the Ten Top Art Crimes on the FBI's website; previously, I'd taken great comfort in the fact that most people assumed that whoever had made off with the van der Asts from Galleries 29 and 30 had stolen my painting, too. Almost all the bodies in Gallery 32 had been concentrated near the collapsed doorway; according to investigators there would have been ten seconds, maybe even thirty, before the lintel fell, just time for a few people to make it out. The wreckage in Gallery 32 had been sifted through with white gloves and whisk brooms, with fanatic care— and while the frame of *The Goldfinch* had been found, intact (and had been hung empty on the wall of the Mauritshuis, in the Hague, "as a reminder of the irreplaceable loss of our cultural patrimony"), no confirmed fragment of the painting itself, no splinter or antique nail fragment or chip of its distinctive lead-tin pigment had been found. But as it was painted on wood, there was a case to be made (and one blowhard celebrity historian, to whom I was grateful, had made it forcefully) that *The Goldfinch* had been knocked from its frame and into the rather large fire burning in the gift shop, the epicenter of the explosion. I had seen him in a PBS documentary, striding back and forth meaningfully in front of the empty frame in the Mauritshuis, fixing the camera with his powerful, media-savvy eye. "That this tiny masterwork survived the powder explosion at Delft only to meet its fate, centuries later, in another man-made explosion is one of those stranger-than-life twists out of O. Henry or Guy de Maupassant."

As for me: the official story—printed in a number of sources, accepted as truth—was that I'd been rooms away from *The Goldfinch* when the bomb went off. Over the years a number of writers had tried to interview me and I'd turned them all away; but numerous people, eyewitnesses, had seen my mother in her last moments in Gallery 24, the beautiful dark-haired woman in the satin trenchcoat, and many of these eyewitnesses placed me at her side. Four adults and three children had died in Gallery 24 — and in the public version of the story, the received version, I'd been just another of the bodies on the ground, knocked cold and overlooked in the hubbub.

But Welty's ring was physical proof of my whereabouts. Luckily for me, Hobie didn't like to talk about Welty's death but every now and then — not often, usually late at night when he'd had a few drinks — he was moved to reminisce. "Can you imagine how I felt —? Isn't it a miracle that —?" Someday, someone had been bound to make the connection. I'd always known it and yet in my drugged-out fog I'd drifted along ignoring the danger for years. Maybe no one was paying attention. Maybe no one would ever know.

I was sitting on the side of my bed, staring out the window onto Tenth Street — people just getting off work, going out to dinner, shrill bursts of laughter. Fine, misty rain slanted in the white circle of street light just outside my window. Everything felt shaky and harsh. I wanted a pill badly, and I was just about to get up and make myself a drink when — just outside of the light, unusual for the coming-and-going traffic of the street — I noticed a figure standing unaccompanied and motionless in the rain.

After half a minute passed and still he stood there, I switched the lamp off and moved to the window. In an answering gesture the silhouette moved well out of the streetlight; and though his features weren't plain in the dark I got the idea of him well enough: high hunched shoulders, shortish legs and thick Irish torso. Jeans and hoodie, heavy boots. For a while he stood motionless, a workmanly silhouette out of place on the street at that hour, photo assistants and well-dressed couples, exhilarated college students heading out for dinner dates. Then he turned. He was walking away with a quick impatience; when he stepped forward into the next pool of light I saw him reaching in his pockets, dialing a cell phone, head down, distracted.

I let the curtain fall. I was pretty sure I was seeing things, in fact I saw things all the time, part of living in a modern city, this half-invisible grain of terror, disaster, jumping at car alarms, always expecting something to happen, the smell of smoke, the splash of broken glass. And yet — I wished I were a hundred percent sure it was my imagination.

Everything was dead quiet. The street light through the lace curtains cast spidery distortions on the walls. All the time, I'd known it was a mistake, keeping the painting, and still I'd kept it. No good could come of keeping it. It wasn't even as if it had done me any good or given me any pleasure. Back in Las Vegas, I'd been able to look at it whenever I wanted, when I was sick or sleepy or sad, early morning and the middle of the night, autumn, summer, changing with weather and sun. It was one thing to see a painting in a museum but to see it in all those lights and moods and seasons was to see it a thousand different ways and to keep it shut in the dark — a thing made of light, that only lived in light — was wrong in more ways than I knew how to explain. More than wrong: it was crazy.

I got a glass of ice from the kitchen, went to the sideboard and poured myself a vodka, came back to my room and got my iPhone from my jacket pocket and — after reflexively dialing the first three digits of Jerome's beeper — hung up and dialed the Barbours' number instead.

Etta answered. "Theo!" she said, sounding pleased, the kitchen television going in the background. "You calling for Katherine?" Only Kitsey's family and very close friends called her Kitsey; she was Katherine to everyone else.

"Is she there?"

"She'll be in after dinner. I know she was looking for you to call."

"Mm —" I couldn't help feeling pleased. "Will you tell her I phoned then?"

"When are you coming back to see us?"

"Soon, I hope. Is Platt around?"

"No — he's out too. I'll be sure to tell him you called. Come back to see us soon, all right?"

I hung up the phone and sat on the side of the bed drinking my vodka. It was reassuring to know that I could call Platt if I needed to — not about the painting, I didn't trust him as far as I could throw him with that, but insofar as dealing with Reeve about the chest. It was ominous that Reeve had said not a word about that.

Yet — what could he do? The more I thought about it, the more it seemed Reeve had overplayed his hand by confronting me so nakedly. What good was it going to do him to come after me for the furniture? What did he have to gain if I was arrested, the painting recovered, whisked out of his reach forever? If he wanted it, there was nothing for him to do but stand back and allow me to lead him to it. The only thing I had going for me — the *only* thing — was that Reeve didn't know where it was. He could hire whomever he wanted to tail me, but as long as I kept clear of the storage unit, there was no way he could track it down.

Chapter 10.

The Idiot

"OH, THEO!" SAID KITSEY one Friday afternoon shortly before Christmas, plucking up one of my mother's emerald earrings and holding it to the light. We'd had a long lunch at Fred's after having spent all morning going around Tiffany's looking at silver and china patterns. "They're beautiful! It's just..." her forehead wrinkled.

"Yes — ?" It was three; the restaurant was still chattering and crowded. When she'd gone to make a telephone call I'd pulled the earrings from my pocket and laid them on the tablecloth.

"Well, it's just — I wonder." She puckered her eyebrows as if at a pair of shoes she wasn't quite sure she wanted to buy. "I mean — they're gorgeous! Thank you! But... will they be quite right? For the actual day?"

"Well, up to you," I said, reaching for my Bloody Mary and taking a large drink to conceal my surprise and annoyance.

"Because, emeralds." She held an earring up to her ear, cutting her eyes thoughtfully to the side as she did it. "I adore them! But —" holding it up again to sparkle, in the diffuse luminance of the overheads — "emeralds aren't really my stone. I think they may just seem a bit hard, you know? With white? And my skin? Eau de Nil! Mum can't wear green either."

"Whatever you think."

"Oh, now you're annoyed."

"No, I'm not."

"Yes you are! I've hurt your feelings!"

"No, I'm just tired."

"You seem in a really dire mood."

"Please Kitsey, I'm tired." We'd been expending heroic effort searching for an apartment, a frustrating process which we'd borne in mostly good

humor although the bare spaces and empty rooms haunted with other people's abandoned lives kicked up (for me) a lot of ugly echoes from childhood, moving boxes and kitchen smells and shadowed bedrooms with the
life gone out of them all but more than this, pulsing throughout, a sort of
ominous mechanical hum audible (apparently) only to me, heavily-
breathing apprehensions which the voices of the brokers, ringing cheerfully
against the polished surfaces as they walked around switching on the lights
and pointing out the stainless-steel appliances, did little to dispel.

And why was this? Not every apartment we saw had been vacated for
reasons of tragedy, as I somehow believed. The fact that I smelled divorce,
bankruptcy, illness and death in almost every space we viewed was clearly
delusional—and, besides, how could the troubles of these previous tenants, real or imagined, harm Kitsey or me?

"Don't lose heart," said Hobie (who, like me, was overly sensitive to the
souls of rooms and objects, the emanations left by time). "Look on it as a
job. Sorting through a box of fiddly bits. You'll turn up just the one as long
as you grit your teeth and keep looking."

And he was right. I'd been a good sport throughout, as had she, pow-
ering through from open house to open house of gloomy pre-wars haunted
by the ghosts of lonely old Jewish ladies, and icy glass monstrosities I knew
I could never live in without feeling I had sniper rifles trained on me from
across the street. No one expected apartment hunting to be fun.

In contrast, the prospect of walking over with Kitsey to set up our
wedding registry at Tiffany's had seemed a pleasing diversion. Meeting
with the Registry Consultant, pointing at what we liked and then wafting
out hand-in-hand for a Christmas lunch? Instead—quite unexpectedly—
I'd been knocked reeling by the stress of navigating one of the most
crowded stores in Manhattan on a Friday close to Christmas: elevators
packed, stairwells packed, flowing with shoals of tourists, holiday shoppers jostling five and six deep at the display cases to buy watches and
scarves and handbags and carriage clocks and etiquette books and all
kinds of extraneous merchandise in Signature Robin's Egg Blue. We'd
slogged round the fifth floor for hours, trailed by a bridal consultant who
was working so hard to provide Flawless Service and assist us in making
our choices with confidence that I couldn't help but feel a bit stalked ("A
china pattern should say to both of you, 'this is who we are, as a couple' …
it's an important statement of your style") while Kitsey flitted from setting

to setting: the gold band! no, the blue! wait...which was the first one? is the octagonal too much? and the consultant chimed in with her helpful exegesis: urban geometrics...romantic florals...timeless elegance... flamboyant flash...and even though I'd kept saying sure, that one's fine, that one too, I'd be happy with either, your decision Kits, the consultant kept showing us more and more settings, clearly hoping to wheedle some firmer show of preference from me, gently explaining to me the fine points of each, the vermeil here, the hand-painted borders there, until I had been forced to bite my tongue to keep from saying what I really thought: that despite the craftsmanship it made absolutely zero difference whether Kitsey chose the x pattern or the y pattern since as far as I was concerned it was basically all the same: new, charmless, dead-in-hand, not to mention the expense: eight hundred dollars for a made-yesterday plate? One plate? There were beautiful eighteenth-century sets to be had for a fraction of the price of this cold, bright, newly-minted stuff.

"But you can't like all of it *exactly* the same! And yes, absolutely, I keep coming back to the Deco," Kitsey said to our patiently-hovering saleswoman, "but as much as I love it, it may not be quite right for us," and then, to me: "What are your thoughts?"

"Whatever you want. Any of them. Really," I said, shoving my hands in my pockets and looking away when still she stood blinking respectfully at me.

"You are looking very fidgety. I wish you'd tell me what you like."

"Yes, but—" I'd unboxed so much china from funeral sales and broken-up households that there was something almost unspeakably sad about the pristine, gleaming displays, with their tacit assurance that shiny new tableware promised an equally shiny and tragedy-free future.

"Chinois? Or Birds of the Nile? Do say, Theo, I know you must prefer one of the two."

"You can't go wrong with either. Both are fun and fancy. And this one is simple, for everyday," said the consultant helpfully, *simple* obviously being in her mind a key word in dealing with overwhelmed and cranky grooms. "Really really simple and neutral." It seemed to be registry protocol that the groom should be allowed to select the casual china (I guess for all those Super Bowl parties I would be hosting with the guys, ha ha) while the "formal ware" should be left to the experts: the ladies.

"It's fine," I said, more curtly than I'd meant to, when I realized they were waiting for me to say something. Plain, white, modern earthenware wasn't something I could work up a lot of enthusiasm for, particularly when it went for four hundred dollars a plate. It made me think of the nice old Marimekko-clad ladies I sometimes went to see in the Ritz Tower: gravel-voiced, turban-wearing, panther-braceleted widows looking to move to Miami, their apartments filled with smoked-glass and chromed-steel furniture that, in the seventies, they'd purchased through their decorators for the price of good Queen Anne — but (I was responsible for telling them, reluctantly) had not held its value and could not be re-sold at even half what they'd bought it for.

"China —" the bridal consultant traced the plate's edge with a neutrally manicured finger. "The way I like for my couples to think of fine silver, fine crystal and china —? It's the end-of-day ritual. It's wine, fun, family, togetherness. A set of fine china is a great way to put some permanent style and romance in your marriage."

"Right," I said again. But the sentiment had appalled me; and the two Bloody Marys I'd had at Fred's had not wholly washed the taste of it away.

Kitsey was looking at the earrings, doubtfully it seemed. "Well look. I *will* wear them for the wedding. They're beautiful. And I know they were your mother's."

"I want you to wear what you want."

"I'll tell you what *I* think." Playfully, she reached across the table and took my hand. "I think you need to have a nap."

"Absolutely," I said, pressing her palm to my face, remembering how lucky I was.

ii.

IT HAD HAPPENED REALLY fast. Within two months of my dinner at the Barbours', Kitsey and I were seeing each other every day practically — long walks and dinner (sometimes Match 65 or Le Bilboquet, sometimes sandwiches in the kitchen) and talking about old times: about Andy, and rainy Sundays with the Monopoly board ("you two were *so* mean… it was like Shirley Temple against Henry Ford and J. P. Morgan…") about the night she'd cried when we made her watch *Hellboy* instead of *Pocahontas,* and our excruciating coat-and-tie nights — excruciating for the little boys anyway, sitting stiffly at the Yacht Club, Coca-Colas with lime, and Mr. Barbour looking restlessly around the dining room for Amadeo, his favorite waiter, with whom he insisted on practicing his ridiculous Xavier Cugat Spanish — school friends, parties, always something to talk about, do you remember this, do you remember that, remember when we…not like Carole Lombard's where it was all booze and bed and not that much to say to each other.

Not that Kitsey and I weren't very different people, as well, but that was all right: after all, as Hobie had pointed out sensibly enough, wasn't marriage supposed to be a union of opposites? Wasn't I supposed to bring new undertakings to her life and she to mine? And besides (I told myself) wasn't it time to Move Forward, Let Go, turn from the garden that was locked to me? Live In The Present, Focus On The Now instead of grieving for what I could never have? For years I'd been wallowing in a hothouse of wasteful sorrow: Pippa Pippa Pippa, exhilaration and despair, it was never-ending, incidents of virtually no significance threw me to the stars or plunged me into speechless depressions, her name on my phone or an e-mail signed "Love" (which was how Pippa signed all her e-mails, to everyone) had me flying for days whereas — if, when phoning Hobie, she didn't ask to speak to me (and why should she?) I was crushed beyond any reasonable prospect. I was deluded, and I knew it. Worse: my love for Pippa was muddied-up below the waterline with my mother, with my mother's death, with losing my mother and not being able to get her back. All that blind, infantile hunger to save and be saved, to repeat the past and make it different, had somehow attached itself, ravenously, to her. There was an instability in it, a sickness. I was seeing things that weren't there. I was only one step away from some trailer park loner stalking a girl he'd spotted in the mall. For the truth of it was: Pippa and I saw each other maybe twice a year; we e-mailed and texted, though with no great regularity; when she was in town we loaned each other books and went to the movies; we were friends; nothing more. My hopes for a relationship with her were wholly unreal, whereas my ongoing misery, and frustration, were an all-too-horrible reality. Was groundless, hopeless, unrequited obsession any way to waste the rest of my life?

It had been a conscious decision to pull free. It had taken everything I had to do it, like an animal gnawing a limb off to escape a trap. And somehow I had done it; and there on the other side was Kitsey, looking at me with the amused, gooseberry-gray eyes.

We had fun together. We got on. It was her first summer in the city, "my whole life, ever" — the house in Maine was closed tight, Uncle Harry and the cousins had gone up to Canada to the Îles de la Madeleine — "and, I'm a bit at loose ends here with Mum, and — oh, *please,* do something with me. Won't you please go out to the beach with me this weekend?" So on the weekends we went out to East Hampton, where we stayed in the house of friends of hers who were summering in France; and during the week we met downtown after I got off work, drinking tepid wine in side-walk cafés, deserted Tribeca evenings with fever-hot sidewalks and hot wind from the subway grates blowing sparks from the end of my cigarette. Movie theaters were always cool, and the King Cole room, and the Oyster Bar at Grand Central. Two afternoons a week — hatted, gloved, in Jack Purcells and tidy skirts, sprayed head to toe with medical-grade sunblock (for she, like Andy, was allergic to the sun) she drove out on her own to Shinnecock or Maidstone in her black Mini Cooper which had been spe-cially fitted in the back to hold a set of golf clubs. Unlike Andy she chat-tered and fluttered, laughed nervously and at her own jokes, with a ghost of her father's scattered energies but without the disengaged quality, the irony. You could have powdered her and drawn a beauty mark on her face and she might have been a lady-in-waiting at Versailles with her white skin and pink cheeks, her stammering gaiety. She wore tiny linen shift dresses, country and city, accessorized by vintage crocodile bags of Gaga's, and kept her name and address taped inside the crucifyingly high Chris-tian Louboutins she teetered around in ("Hurty-hurty shoes!") in case she kicked them off to dance or swim and forgot where she'd left them: silver shoes, embroidered shoes, ribboned and pointy-toed, a thousand dollars a pair. "Meanypants!" she shouted down the stairwell when — three a.m., three sheets to the wind on rum and Coke — I finally staggered down to catch a cab because I had to work the next day.

She was the one who had asked me to marry. On our way to a party. Chanel No. 19, baby blue dress. We'd stepped out on Park Avenue — both a little looped from cocktails upstairs — and the street lights had snapped on the moment we stepped out the door and we'd stopped dead and looked at each other: did *we* do that? The moment was so funny we both began laughing hysterically — it was like the light was pouring off us, like we could power up Park Avenue. And when Kitsey seized my hand and said: "You know what I think we should do, Theo?" I knew exactly what she was going to say.

"Should we?"

"Yes, please! Don't you think? I think it would make Mum so happy."

We hadn't even firmed up the date. It kept getting changed, due to the availability of the church, the availability of certain indispensable members of the party, someone else's cup race or due date or whatever. Hence, how the wedding seemed to be gearing up into quite such a big deal — guest list of many hundreds, cost of many thousands, costumed and choreographed like a Broadway show — how this wedding seemed to be spiraling into quite such a production I wasn't quite sure. Sometimes, I knew, the mother of the bride got blamed for out-of-control weddings but in this case anyway you couldn't pin the rap on Mrs. Barbour, who could scarcely be prised from her room and the embroidery basket, who never took phone calls and never accepted invitations and never even went to the hairdresser any more, she who had once had her hair done every other day without fail, a standing eleven a.m. appointment before lunching out.

"*Won't* Mum be pleased?" Kitsey had whispered, jabbing me in the rib with her sharp little elbow as we were hurrying back to Mrs. Barbour's room. And the memory of Mrs. Barbour's joy at the news (*you tell her,* Kitsey had said, *she'll be extra happy if she hears it from you*) was a moment I played and replayed and never tired of: her startled eyes, then delight blooming unguarded on her cool, tired face. One hand held to me and the other to Kitsey, but that beautiful smile — I would never forget it — had been all for me.

Who knew it was in my power to make anyone so happy? Or that I could ever be so happy myself? My moods were a slingshot; after being locked-down and anesthetized for years my heart was zinging and slamming itself around like a bee under a glass, everything bright, sharp, confusing, wrong — but it was a clean pain as opposed to the dull misery that had plagued me for years under the drugs like a rotten tooth, the sick dirty ache of something spoiled. The clarity was exhilarating; it was as if I'd removed a pair of smudged-up glasses that fuzzed everything I saw. All summer long I had been practically delirious: tingling, daffy, energized, running on gin and shrimp cocktail and the invigorating *whock* of tennis balls. And all I could think was Kitsey, Kitsey, Kitsey!

And four months had passed, and it was December, brisk mornings and a chime of Christmas in the air; and Kitsey and I were engaged to be married and how lucky was I? but though it was all too perfect, hearts and flowers, the end of a musical comedy, I felt sick. For unknown reasons, the gust of energy that had swept me up and fizzed me around all summer had dropped me hard, mid-October, into a drizzle of sadness that stretched endlessly in every direction: with a very few exceptions (Kitsey, Hobie, Mrs. Barbour) I hated being around people, couldn't pay attention to what any-one was saying, couldn't talk to clients, couldn't tag my pieces, couldn't ride the subway, all human activity seemed pointless, incomprehensible, some blackly swarming ant hill in the wilderness, there was not a squeak of light anywhere I looked, the antidepressants I'd been dutifully swallowing for eight weeks hadn't helped a bit, nor had the ones before that (but then, I'd tried them all; apparently I was among the twenty percent of unfortunates who didn't get the daisy fields and the butterflies but the Severe Headaches and the Suicidal Thoughts); and though the darkness sometimes lifted just enough so I could construe my surroundings, familiar shapes solidifying like bedroom furniture at dawn, my relief was never more than temporary because somehow the full morning never came, things always went black before I could orient myself and there I was again with ink poured in my eyes, guttering around in the dark.

Just why I felt so lost I didn't know. I wasn't over Pippa and I knew it, might never be over her, and that was just something I was going to have to live with, the sadness of loving someone I couldn't have; but I also knew my more immediate difficulty was in rising to (what I found, anyway) an uncomfortably escalating social pace. No longer did Kitsey and I enjoy so many of our restorative evenings à deux, the two of us holding hands on the same side of a dark restaurant booth. Instead, almost every night it was dinner parties and busy restaurant tables with her friends, strenuous occasions where (jumpy, un-opiated, wracked to the last synapse), it was hard for me to make the proper show of social ardor, particularly when I was tired after work—and then too the wedding preparations, an ava-lanche of trivia in which I was expected to interest myself as enthusiasti-cally as she, bright tissue-paper flurries of brochures and merchandise. For her, it amounted to a full-time job: visiting stationers and florists, research-ing caterers and vendors, amassing fabric swatches and boxes of petit-four and cake samples, fretting and repeatedly asking me to help her choose between virtually identical shades of ivory and lavender on a color chart, co-ordinating a series of "girly-girl" sleepovers with her bridesmaids and a "boys' weekend" for me (organized by Platt?? at least I could count on staying drunk)—and then the honeymoon plans, stacks of glossy book-lets (Fiji or Nantucket? Mykonos or Capri?) "Fantastic," I kept saying, in my affable new talking-to-Kitsey voice, "it all looks great," although given her family and its history with water, it did seem odd that she wasn't inter-ested in Vienna or Paris or Prague or any destination, actually, that wasn't a literal island in the middle of the freaking ocean.

Still, I'd never felt so sure of the future; and when I reminded myself of the right-ness of my course, as I often had occasion to do, my thoughts went not only to Kitsey but also Mrs. Barbour, whose happiness made me feel reassured and nourished in channels of my heart which had stood scraped dry for years. Our news had visibly brightened and straightened her; she'd begun stirring about the apartment, she'd pinked up with just the tiniest bit of lipstick, and even her most commonplace interactions with me were colored with a steady, stable, peaceful light that enlarged the space around us and beamed calmly into all my darkest corners.

"I never thought I'd be quite so happy ever again," she'd confided qui-etly, one night at dinner, when Kitsey had jumped up very suddenly and run out to get the telephone as she was apt to do, and it was just the two of us at the card table in her room, poking awkwardly at our asparagus spears and our salmon steaks. "Because—you were always so good to Andy—bolstering him, improving his confidence. He was absolutely his best self with you, always. And—I'm so glad you're going to be an official part of the family, that we're going to make it legal now, because—oh, I suppose I shouldn't say this, I hope you don't mind if I speak from the heart for a moment, but I always did think of you as one of my very own, did you know that? Even when you were a little boy."

This remark so shocked and touched me that I reacted clumsily—stammering in discomposure—so that she took pity and turned the con-versation into another channel. Yet every time I remembered it I was suffused with a glow of warmth. An equally gratifying (if ignoble) mem-ory was Pippa's slight, shocked pause when I'd broken the news to her on the phone. Over and over again I had played that pause in my mind, rel-ishing it, her stunned silence: "Oh?" And then, recovering: "Oh, Theo, how wonderful! I can't wait to meet her!"

"Oh, she's *amazing*," I'd said venomously. "I've been in love with her ever since we were kids."

Which—in all sorts of ways I was still coming to realize—was absolutely true. The interplay of past and present was wildly erotic: I drew endless delight from the memory of nine-year-old Kitsey's contempt for geeky thirteen-year-old me (rolling her eyes, pouting when she had to sit by me at dinner). And I relished even more the undisguised shock of people who'd known us as children: You? and Kitsey Barbour? Really? *Her?* I loved the fun and wickedness of it, the sheer improbability: slipping into her room after her mother was asleep—same room she'd kept shut against me when we were kids, same pink toile wallpaper, unchanged since the days of Andy, hand-lettered signs, KEEP OUT, DO NOT DISTURB— me backing her in, Kitsey locking the door behind us, putting her finger to my mouth, tracing it across my lips, that first, delicious tumble to her bed, Mommy's sleeping, ssh!

Every day, I had multiple occasions to remind myself how lucky I was. Kitsey was never tired; Kitsey was never unhappy. She was appealing, enthusiastic, affectionate. She was beautiful, with a luminous, sugar-white quality that turned heads on the street. I admired how gregarious she was, how engaged with the world, how amusing and spontaneous—"little feather-head!" as Hobie called her, with a great deal of tenderness—what a breath of fresh air she was! Everyone loved her. And for all her infectious lightness of heart, I knew it was an extremely petty cavil that Kitsey never seemed very *moved* by anything. Even dear old Carole Lombard had got teary-eyed about ex-boyfriends and abused pets on the news and the closing of certain old-school bars in Chicago, where she was from. But nothing ever seemed to strike Kitsey as particularly urgent or emotional or even surprising. In this, she resembled her mother and brother—and yet Mrs. Barbour's restraint, and Andy's, were somehow very different from Kitsey's way of making a flippant or trivializing comment whenever anyone brought up something serious. ("No fun," I'd heard her say with a half-whimsical sigh, wrinkling her nose, when people inquired about her mother.) Then too—I felt morbid and sick even thinking it—I kept watching for some evidence of sorrow about Andy and her dad, and it was starting to disturb me that I hadn't seen it. Hadn't their deaths affected her at all? Weren't we supposed to at least talk about it at some point? On one level, I admired her bravery: chin up, carrying on in the face of tragedy or whatever. Maybe she was just really really guarded, really locked-down, putting up a masterly front. But those sparkling blue shallows — so enticing at first glance — had not yet graded off into depths, so that sometimes I got the disconcerting sensation of wading around in knee-high waters hoping to step into a drop-off, a place deep enough to swim.

Kitsey was tapping my wrist. "What?"

"*Barneys.* I mean, since we're here? Maybe we should take a spin round the Homes department? I know Mother won't love it if we register here but it might be fun to go for something a little less traditional for everyday."

"No —" reaching for my glass, knocking the rest of it back — "I really need to get downtown, if that's all right. Supposed to meet a client."

"Will you be coming uptown tonight?" Kitsey shared an apartment in the East Seventies with two roommates, not far from the office of the arts organization where she worked.

"Not sure. Might have to go to dinner. I'll get out of it if I can."

"Cocktails? Please? Or an after-dinner drink, at least? Everyone will be so disappointed if you don't put in at least a *tiny* appearance. Charles and Bette —"

"I'll try. Promise. Don't forget those," I said, nodding at the earrings, which were still lying on the tablecloth.

"Oh! No! Of course not!" she said guiltily, grabbing them up and throwing them into her bag like a handful of loose change.

iii.

As we walked outside together, into the Christmas crowds, I felt unsteady and sorrowful; and the ribbon-wrapped buildings, the glitter of windows only deepened the oppressive sadness: dark winter skies, gray canyon of jewels and furs and all the power and melancholy of wealth.

What was wrong with me? I thought, as Kitsey and I crossed Madison Avenue, her pink Prada overcoat bobbing exuberantly in the throng. Why did I hold it against Kitsey that she didn't seem haunted over Andy and her dad, that she was getting on with her life?

But — clasping Kitsey's elbow, rewarded by a radiant smile — I felt momentarily relieved again, and distracted from my worries. It had been eight months since I left Reeve in that Tribeca restaurant; no one had yet

contacted me about any of the bad pieces I'd sold though I was fully prepared to admit my mistake if they did: inexperienced, new to the business,
here's your money back sir, accept my apologies. Nights, lying awake, I
reassured myself that if things got ugly, at least I hadn't left much of a trail:
I'd tried not to document the sales any more than I'd had to, and on the
smaller pieces had offered a discount for cash.

But still. But still. It was only a matter of time. Once one client stepped
forward, there would be an avalanche. And it would be bad enough if I
wrecked Hobie's reputation but the moment there were so many claims
that I stopped being able to refund people's money, there would be lawsuits: lawsuits in which Hobie, co-owner of the business, would be named.
It would be hard to convince a court he hadn't known what I was doing,
especially on some of the sales I'd made at the Important Americana
level—and, if it came down to it, I wasn't even sure that Hobie would
speak up adequately in his own defense if that meant leaving me out to
hang alone. Granted: a lot of the people I'd sold to had so much money
they didn't give a shit. But still. But still. When would someone decide to
look under the seats of those Hepplewhite dining chairs (for instance) and
notice that they weren't all alike? That the grain was wrong, that the legs
didn't match? Or take a table to be independently evaluated and learn that
the veneer was of a type not used, or invented, in the 1770s? Every day, I
wondered when and how the first fraud might surface: a letter from a lawyer, a phone call from the American Furniture department at Sotheby's, a
decorator or a collector charging into the store to confront me, Hobie coming downstairs, listen, we've got a problem, do you have a minute?

If the marriage-wrecking knowledge of my liabilities surfaced before
the wedding, I wasn't sure what would happen. It was more than I could
bear to think of. The wedding might not go off at all. Yet—for Kitsey's
sake, and her mother's—it seemed even more cruel if it surfaced after,
especially since the Barbours were not nearly so well-off as they had been
before Mr. Barbour's death. There were cash flow problems. The money
was tied up in trust. Mommy had had to reduce some of the employees to
part time hours, and let the rest of them go. And Daddy—as Platt had
confided, when attempting to interest me in more antiques from the
apartment—had gone a bit bonkers at the end and invested more than
fifty percent of the portfolio in VistaBank, a commercial-banking monster, for "sentimental reasons" (Mr. Barbour's great-great-grandfather had

been president of one of the historic founding banks, in Massachusetts, long since stripped of its name after merging with Vista). Unfortunately VistaBank had ceased paying dividends, and failed, shortly before Mr. Barbour's death. Hence Mrs. Barbour's drastically reduced support of the charities with which she had once been so generous; hence Kitsey's job. And Platt's editorial position at his tasteful little publishing house, as he'd often reminded me when in his cups, paid less than Mommy in the old days had paid her housekeeper. If things got bad, I was pretty sure Mrs. Barbour would do what she could to help; and Kitsey, as my spouse, would be obligated to help whether she wanted to or not. But it was a dirty trick to play on them, especially since Hobie's lavish praise had convinced them all (Platt especially, concerned with the family's dwindling resources) that I was some kind of financial magician sweeping in to his sister's rescue. "You know how to *make* money," he'd said, bluntly, when he told me how thrilled they all were Kitsey was marrying me instead of some of the lay-abouts she'd been known to go around with. "She doesn't."

But what worried me most of all was Lucius Reeve. Though I had never heard another peep from him about the chest-on-chest, I had begun in the summer to receive a series of troubling letters: handwritten, unsigned, on blue-bordered correspondence cards printed at the top with his name in copperplate: **LUCIUS REEVE**

> *It is getting on for three months since I made what, by any standards, is a fair and sensible proposal. How do you conclude my offer is anything but reasonable?*

And, later:

> *A further eight weeks has passed. You can understand my dilemma. The frustration level rises.*

And then, three weeks after that, a single line:

> *Your silence is not acceptable.*

I agonized over these letters, though I tried to block them from my mind. Whenever I remembered them—which was often and unpredictably, mid-meal, fork halfway to my mouth—it was like being slapped awake from a dream. In vain, I tried to remind myself that Reeve's claims in the restaurant were wildly off-base. To respond to him in any way was foolish. The only thing was to ignore him as if he were an aggressive panhandler on the street.

But then two disturbing things had happened in rapid succession. I had come upstairs to ask Hobie if he wanted to go out for lunch—"Sure, hang on," he said; he was going through his mail at the sideboard, glasses perched on the tip of his nose. "Hmn," he said, flipping an envelope over to look at the front. He opened it and looked at the card—holding it out at arm's length to peer at it over the top of his glasses, then bringing it in closer.

"Look at this," he said. He handed me the card. "What's this about?"

The card, in Reeve's all-too-familiar writing, was only two sentences: no heading, no signature.

At what point is this delay unreasonable? Can we not move forward on what I have proposed to your young partner, since there is no benefit to either of you in continuing this stalemate?

"Oh, God," I said, putting the card down on the table and looking away. "For Pete's sake."

"What?"

"It's him. With the chest-on-chest."

"Oh, him," said Hobie. He adjusted his glasses, regarded me quietly. "Did he ever cash that check?"

I ran a hand through my hair. "No."

"What's this proposal? What's he talking about?"

"Look—" I went to the sink to get a glass of water, an old trick of my father's when he needed a moment to compose himself—"I haven't wanted to bother you but this guy's been a huge nuisance. I've started throwing away the letters without opening them. If you get another one, I suggest you toss it in the trash."

"What does he want?"

"Well—" the faucet was noisy; I ran my glass; "well." I turned, wiped my hand across my forehead. "It's really nuts. I've written him a check for the piece, as I said. For more than he paid."

"So what's the problem?"

"Ah —" I took a swallow of my water — "unfortunately he has something else in mind. He thinks, ah, he thinks we're running an assembly line down here, and he's trying to cut himself in on it. See, instead of cashing my check? he's got some elderly woman lined up, nurses twenty-four hours a day, and what he wants is for us to use her apartment to, uh —"

Hobie's eyebrows went up. "Plant?"

"Right," I said, glad he'd been the one to say it. 'Planting' was a racket whereby fakes or inferior antiques were placed in private homes — often homes belonging to the elderly — to be sold to vultures clustering at the deathbed: bottom feeders so eager to rip off the old lady in the oxygen tent that they didn't realize they were being ripped off themselves. "When I tried to give his money back — this was his counter-proposal. We supply the pieces. Fifty-fifty split. He's been harassing me ever since."

Hobie looked blank. "That's absurd."

"Yes —" closing my eyes, pinching my nose — "but he's very insistent. That's why I advise you to —"

"Who's this woman?"

"Woman, elderly relative, whatever."

"What's her name?"

I held the glass to my temple. "Don't know."

"Here? In the city?"

"I assume so." I didn't care for this avenue of inquiry. "Anyway — just throw that thing in the trash. I'm sorry I didn't tell you earlier but I really didn't want to worry you. He's got to get tired of this if we ignore him."

Hobie looked at the card, then at me. "I'm keeping this. No," he said sharply when I tried to interrupt him, "this is more than enough to go to the police with if we have to. I don't care about the chest — no, no," he said, raising a hand to hush me, "this won't do, you've tried to set it right and he's trying to force you into something criminal. How long has this been going on?"

"Don't know. Couple months?" I said, when he kept on looking at me.

"Reeve." He studied the card with furrowed brow. "I'll ask Moira." Moira was Mrs. DeFrees's first name. "You'll tell me if he writes again."

"Of course."

I could not even think what might happen if Mrs. DeFrees happened to know Lucius Reeve, or know of him, but fortunately there had been no further word on that score. It seemed only the rankest luck that the letter to Hobie had been so ambiguous. But the menace behind it was plain. It was stupid to worry that Reeve would follow through on his threat of calling the law, since — I reminded myself of it, again and again — his only chance of obtaining the painting for himself was to leave me at liberty to retrieve it.

And yet, perversely, this only made me long even more to have the painting close to hand, to look at whenever I wanted. Though I knew it was impossible, still I thought of it. Everywhere I looked, every apartment that Kitsey and I went to see, I saw potential hiding places: high cupboards, fake fireplaces, wide rafters that could only be reached by very tall ladder, floorboards that might easily be prised up. At night I lay staring into the dark, fantasizing about a specially built fireproof cabinet where I could lock it away in safety or — even more absurdly — a secret, climate-controlled Bluebeard closet, combination lock only.

Mine, mine. Fear, idolatry, hoarding. The delight and terror of the fetishist. Fully conscious of my folly, I'd downloaded pictures of it to my computer and my phone so I could gloat upon the image in private, brush-strokes rendered digitally, a scrap of seventeenth-century sunlight compressed into dots and pixels, but the purer the color, the richer the sense of impasto, the more I hungered for the thing itself, the irreplaceable, glorious, light-rinsed object.

Dust-free environment. Twenty-four-hour security. Though I tried not to think of the Austrian man who had kept the woman locked in a basement for twenty years, unfortunately it was the metaphor that came to mind. What if I died? Got hit by a bus? Might the ungainly package be mistaken for garbage and tossed in the incinerator? Three or four times I'd made anonymous phone calls to the facility to reassure myself of what I already knew from obsessively visiting the website: temperature and humidity guaranteed within acceptable conservatorial range for artworks. Sometimes when I woke up the whole thing seemed like a dream, although soon enough I remembered it wasn't.

But it was impossible to even think of going up there with Reeve like a cat waiting for me to scurry across the floor. I had to sit tight. Unfortunately, the rent on the storage unit was due in three months; and what with everything else I saw no point whatsoever in going up to pay it in person. The thing was just to have Grisha or one of the guys go in and pay it for me, in cash, which I was confident they would do no questions asked. But then the second unfortunate thing had happened: because only a few days earlier Grisha had shocked me, thoroughly, by sidling up with a sideways tick of his head when I was alone in the shop and adding up my receipts at the end of the week and saying: "*Mazhor,* I need a sit-down."

"Oh yeah?"

"You on lock?"

"What?" Between Yiddish and gutter Russian, jumbled through a slur of Brooklynese and slang picked up from rap songs, sometimes Grisha's idioms didn't make it into any kind of English I could understand.

Grisha snorted noisily. "I don't think you understanding me right, champ. I am asking is everything square with you. With the laws."

"Hang on," I said—I was in the middle of a column of figures—and then looked up from the calculator: "Wait, what are you talking about?"

"You my brother, not condemning or judging. I just need to know, all right?"

"Why? What happened?"

"Peoples are hanging around the shop, keeping an eye on. You know anything about it?"

"Who?" I glanced out the window. "What? When was this?"

"I wanted to ask you. Scared to drive out to Borough Park to meet with my cousin Genka for some business he got going—afraid of getting these guys on me."

"On you?" I sat down.

Grisha shrugged. "Four, five times now. Yesterday, getting out of my truck, I saw one of them hanging around out front again, but he slipped across the street. Jeans—older—very casual dressed. Genka, he don't know nothing about it but he's freaked, like I say we got some stuff going, he told me to ask you what you knew about it. Never talks, just stands and waits. I am wondering if it is some of your business with the Shvatzah," he said discreetly.

"Nope." The Shvatzah was Jerome; I hadn't seen him in months.

"Well then. I hate to break it to you but I think is maybe poh-lices smelling around. Mike—he has noticed too. He thought it was because of his child supports. But the guy just hangs around and does nothing."

"How long has this been going on?"

"Who knows? But one month, at least. Mike says longer."

"Next time, when you see him, will you point him out to me?"

"He might be private investigator."

"Why do you say that?"

"Because in some ways he looks more like ex-cop. Mike thinks this—Irish, they know from cops, Mike said he looked older, like poh-lice retired from the force maybe?"

"Right," I said, thinking of the heavyset guy I'd seen out my window. I'd spotted him four or five times subsequently, or someone who looked like him, lingering out front during business hours—always when I was with Hobie or a customer, inconvenient to confront him—although he was so innocuous-looking, hoodie and construction-worker boots, I could hardly be sure. Once—it had scared me, badly—I'd seen a guy who looked like him lingering out in front of the Barbours' building but when I got a better look I'd been sure I was wrong.

"He's been around for a while. But this—" Grisha paused—"normally I would not say anything, maybe is nothing, but yesterday..."

"Well, what? Go on," I said, when he massaged his neck and looked guiltily to the side.

"Another guy. Different. I'd seen him hanging about the shop before. Outside. But yesterday he came in the shop to ask for you by your name. And I did not like the looks of him at all."

I sat back abruptly in my chair. I'd been wondering when Reeve would take it in his head to drop by in person.

"I did not talk to him. I was out—" nodding—"so. Loading the truck. But I saw him go in. Kind of guy you notice. Nice dressed, but not like a client. You were at lunch and Mike was in the shop by himself—guy comes in, asks, Theodore Decker? Well, you're not in, Mike says so. 'Where is he.' Lot a lot a questions about you, like do you work here, do you live here, how long, where you are, all sorts."

"Where was Hobie?"

"He didn't want Hobie. He wanted you. Then—" he drew a line on the desk top with his finger—"out he comes. Walks around the shop. Looks here, looks there. Looks all around. This—I see from where I am, across the street. It looks strange. And—Mike did not mention this visit to you because he said maybe is nothing, maybe something personal, 'better keep out of it,' but I saw him too and thought you should know. Because, hey, game recognize game, you get me?"

"What'd he look like?" I asked, and then—when Grisha did not reply—"Older fellow? Heavy? White hair?"

Grisha made an exasperated sound. "No no no." Shaking his head with resolute firmness. "This was nobody's grandpappy."

"What'd he look like, then?"

"He looked like a guy you would not want to get into a fight with, is what he looked like."

In the silence that followed, Grisha lit a Kool and offered me one. "So what should I do, *Mazhor?*"

"Sorry?"

"Do me and Genka need to worry?"

"I don't think so. Right," I said, hitting a little awkwardly the triumphant palm that he held up for me to slap, "okay, but will you do me a favor? Will you come and get me if you see either of them again?"

"Sure thing." He paused, looking at me critically. "You sure me and Genka don't need to worry?"

"Well, I don't know what you're doing, do I?"

Grisha flipped a dirty handkerchief from his pocket and scrubbed his purpled nose with it. "I don't like this answer from you."

"Well, be careful, whatever. Just in case."

"*Mazhor,* I should say the same of you."

iv.

I HAD LIED TO Kitsey; I didn't have a thing to do. Outside Barneys, we kissed goodbye on the corner of Fifth before she walked back to Tiffany to look at the crystal—we hadn't even made it to the crystal—and I went to catch the 6. But instead of joining the stream of shoppers pouring down the stairs to the station I felt so empty and distracted, so lost and tired and unwell, I stopped instead to look in at the dirty window of the Subway Inn, straight across from the loading dock at Bloomingdale's, a time warp straight out of *The Lost Weekend* and unchanged since my father's drinking days. Outside: film-noir neon. Inside: same grimy red walls, sticky tables, broken floor tiles, strong Clorox smell, and a concave bartender with a rag over his shoulder pouring a drink for a bloodshot solitary at the bar. I remembered my mom and me losing my dad at Bloomingdale's once, and how—mysteriously to me, at the time—she'd known to leave the store and walk straight across the street and find him here, throwing back four-dollar shots with a wheezy old Teamster and a bandanna-wearing senior who looked homeless. I'd stood waiting inside the doorway, overpowered by the waft of stale beer and fascinated by the warm secretive dark of the place, the Twilight Zone glow of the jukebox and the Buck Hunter arcade game blinking away in the depths—"Ah, the smell of old men and desperation," my mother had said wryly, wrinkling her nose as she exited the bar with her shopping bags and caught me by the hand.

A shot of Johnnie Walker Black, for my dad. Two shots maybe. Why not? The dark recesses of the bar looked warm, comradely, that sentimental boozy aura that made you forget for a moment who you were and how you'd ended up there. But at the last moment, starting in the doorway so the bartender glanced over at me, I turned away and kept walking.

Lexington Avenue. Wettish wind. The afternoon was haunted and dank. I walked right by the stop on Fifty-First Street, and the Forty-Second stop, and still I kept going to clear my head. Ash-white apartment blocks. Hordes of people on the street, lighted Christmas trees sparkling high on penthouse balconies and complacent Christmas music floating out of shops, and weaving in and out of crowds I had a strange feeling of being already dead, of moving in a vaster sidewalk grayness than the street or even the city could encompass, my soul disconnected from my body and drifting among other souls in a mist somewhere between past and present, Walk Don't Walk, individual pedestrians floating up strangely isolated and lonely before my eyes, blank faces plugged into earbuds and staring straight ahead, lips moving silently, and the city noise dampened and deafened, under crushing, granite-colored skies that muffled the noise from the street, garbage and newsprint, concrete and drizzle, a dirty winter grayness weighing like stone.

I'd thought, having successfully escaped the bar, I might see a movie—that maybe the solitude of a movie theater would set me aright, some near-empty afternoon showing of a film ending its popular run. But when, lightheaded and sniffling with cold, I got to the theater on Second and Thirty-Second, the French cop film I wanted to see had already started and so had the mistaken-identity thriller. All that remained were a host of holiday movies and intolerable romantic comedies: posters of bedraggled brides, battling bridesmaids, a dismayed dad in a Santa hat with two howling babies in his arms.

The cabs were starting to go off duty. High above the street, in the dark afternoon, lights burned in lonely offices and apartment towers. Turning away, I continued to drift downtown, with no very clear idea where I was going or why, and as I walked I had the oddly appealing sensation that I was undoing myself, unwinding myself thread by thread, rags and tatters falling away from me in the very act of crossing Thirty-Second Street and flowing along amongst the rush-hour pedestrians and rolling along from the next moment to the next.

At the next theater, ten or twelve blocks down, it was the same story: the CIA film had started, as had the well-reviewed biopic of a 1940s leading lady; the French cop movie didn't start for another hour and a half; and unless I wanted the psychopath film or the searing family drama, which I didn't, it was more brides and bachelor parties and Santa hats and Pixar.

By the time I made it to the theater at Seventeenth Street I didn't stop at the box office at all but kept walking. Somehow, mysteriously, in the process of crossing Union Square, swept along in a dark eddy that had hit me from nowhere, I'd arrived at the decision to call Jerome. There was a mystic joy in the idea, a saintly mortification. Would he even have pharms on such short notice, would I have to buy regular old street dope? I didn't care. I hadn't done drugs in months but for whatever reason, an evening nodding and unconscious in my bedroom at Hobie's had begun to seem like a perfectly reasonable response to the holiday lights, the holiday crowds, the incessant Christmas bells with their morbid funeral note, Kitsey's candy-pink notebook from Kate's Paperie with tabs reading MY BRIDESMAIDS MY GUESTS MY SEATING MY FLOWERS MY VENDORS MY CHECKLIST MY CATERING.

Stepping back quickly — the light had changed, I'd almost walked in front of a car — I reeled and nearly slipped. There was no point dwelling on my unreasoning horror of a large public wedding — enclosed spaces, claustrophobia, sudden movements, phobic triggers everywhere, for some reason the subway didn't bother me so much it had more to do with crowded buildings, always expecting something to happen, the puff of smoke, the fast-running man at the crowd's margin, I couldn't even bear being in a movie theater if there were more than ten or fifteen people in it,

I would turn around with my fully paid ticket and walk right out. And yet somehow this massive, jam-packed church ceremony was springing up around me like a flash mob. I would swallow a few Xanax and sweat my way through it.

Then too: I hoped that the escalating social roar which I'd been riding like a boat in a hurricane would slow, post-wedding, since all I really wanted was to get back to the halcyon days of summer when I'd had Kitsey all to myself: dinners alone, watching movies in bed. The constant invitations and gatherings were wearing me down: brightly-shifting whirlwinds of her friends, crowded evenings and hectic weekends that I weathered with my eyes squeezed shut and clutching on for dear life: Linsey? no, Lolly? sorry...and this is—? Frieda? Hi, Frieda, and...Trev? Trav? nice to see you! Politely I stood around their antique farm tables, drinking myself into a stupor as they chatted about their country houses, their co-op boards, their school districts, their gym routines—that's right, seamless transition from breast feeding although we've had some big changes in the nap schedule lately, our oldest just starting pre-K and the fall color in Connecticut is stunning, oh yes, of course, we all have our annual trip with the girls but you know these boys' trips we do twice a year, out to Vail, down to the Caribbean, last year we went fly-fishing in Scotland and we hit some really outstanding golf courses—but oh, that's right, Theo, you don't golf, you don't ski, you don't sail, do you.

"Sorry, afraid not." The group mind was such (private jokes and bemusement, everyone clustered round vacation videos on the iPhone) that it was hard to imagine any of them going to a movie by themselves or eating alone at a bar; sometimes, the affable sense of committee among the men particularly gave me the slight feeling of being interviewed for a job. And—all these pregnant women? "Oh, Theo! Isn't he adorable!" Kitsey unexpectedly thrusting a friend's newborn at me—me in all sincere horror leaping back as if from a lighted match.

"Oh, sometimes it takes us guys a while," said Race Goldfarb complacently, observing my discomfort, raising his voice above the infants wailing and tumbling in a nanny-supervised area of the living room. "But let me tell you, Theo, when you hold that little one of your own in your arms for the first time—?" (patting his wife's pregnant tummy)—"your heart just breaks a little. Because when I first saw little Blaine?" (sticky-faced, staggering around unattractively at his feet) "and gazed into those big blue eyes?

Those beautiful baby blues? I was *transformed*. I was in *love*. It was like: hey, little buddy! you are here to teach me everything! And I'm telling you, at that first smile I just melted into goo like we all do, didn't I, Lauren?"

"Right," I said politely, going into the kitchen and pouring myself a huge vodka. My dad too had been wildly squeamish around pregnant women (had in fact been fired from a job for one too many ill-advised remarks; those breeder cracks hadn't gone over too well at the office) and, far from the conventional "melting into goo" wisdom, he'd never been able to stand kids or babies either, much less the whole doting-parent scene, dumbly-smiling women feeling up their own bellies and guys with infants bound to their chests, would go outside to smoke or else skulk darkly at the margins looking like a drug pusher whenever he was forced to attend any sort of school event or kiddie party. Apparently I'd inherited it from him and, who knew, maybe Grandpa Decker as well, this violent procreative disgust buzzing loudly in my bloodstream; it felt inborn, wired-in, genetic.

Nodding the night away. The dark-throated bliss of it. No thanks, Hobie, already ate, think I'll just head up to bed with my book. The things these people talked about, even the men? Just thinking about that night at the Goldfarbs' made me want to be so wrecked I couldn't walk straight.

As I approached Astor Place — African drum players, drunks arguing, clouds of incense from a street vendor — I felt my spirits lifting. My tolerance was sure to be way down: a cheering thought. Only one or two pills a week, to get me through the very worst of the socializing, and only when I really really needed them. In lieu of the pharms I'd been drinking too much and that really wasn't working for me; with opiates I was relaxed, I was tolerant, I was up for anything, I could stand pleasantly for hours in unbearable situations listening to any old tiresome or ridiculous bullshit without wanting to go outside and shoot myself in the head.

But I hadn't phoned Jerome in a long time, and when I ducked in the doorway of a skate shop to make the call, it went straight to voice mail — a mechanical message that didn't sound like his. Has he changed his number? I thought, starting to worry after the second try. People like Jerome — it had happened with Jack, before him — could drop off the map pretty suddenly even if you were in regular contact.

Not knowing what to do, I started walking down St. Mark's toward Tompkins Square. All Day All Night. You Must Be Twenty One To Enter. Downtown, away from the high-rise press, the wind cut more bitterly and yet the sky was more open too, it was easier to breathe. Muscle guys walking paired pit bulls, inked-up Bettie Page girls in wiggle dresses, stumble-bums with drag-hemmed pants and Jack O'Lantern teeth and taped-up shoes. Outside the shops, racks of sunglasses and skull bracelets and multi-colored transvestite wigs. There was a needle exchange somewhere, maybe more than one but I wasn't sure where; Wall Street guys bought off the street all the time if you believed what people said but I wasn't wise enough to know where to go or who to approach, and besides who was going to sell to me, a stranger with horn rimmed glasses and an uptown haircut, dressed for picking out wedding china with Kitsey?

Unsettled heart. The fetishism of secrecy. These people understood— as I did—the back alleys of the soul, whispers and shadows, money slipping from hand to hand, the password, the code, the second self, all the hidden consolations that lifted life above the ordinary and made it worth living.

Jerome—I stopped on the sidewalk outside a cheap sushi bar to get my bearings—Jerome had told me about a bar, red awning, around St. Mark's, Avenue A maybe? He was always coming from there, or stopping off on his way to me. The bartender dealt from behind the counter to patrons who didn't mind paying double for not having to buy on the street. Jerome was always making deliveries to her. Her name—I remembered it, even— Katrina! But every other storefront in the neighborhood seemed to be a bar.

I walked up A and down First; ducked into the first bar I saw with an even vaguely red awning—liverish tan, but it might have been red once—and asked: "Does Katrina work here?"

"Nope," said the scorched redhead at the bar, not even looking at me as she pulled her pint.

Shopping cart ladies asleep with their heads on bundles. Shop window of glitter Madonnas and Day of the Dead figures. Gray flocks of pigeons beating soundlessly.

"You know you thinking about it, you know you thinking about it," said a low voice in my ear—

I turned to find a ripe, heavyset, broadly smiling black man with a gold tooth in front, who pressed a card into my hand: TATTOOS BODY ART PIERCING.

I laughed—him too, a rich full-body laugh, both of us sharing in the joke—and slipped the card in my pocket and walked on. But a moment later I was sorry I hadn't asked him where to find what I wanted. Even if he wouldn't tell me, he'd looked like he would know.

Body Piercing. Acupressure Footrub. We Buy Gold We Buy Silver. Many pallid kids, and then, further down—all on her own—a wan dreadlocked girl with a filthy puppy and a cardboard sign so worn I couldn't read it. I was reaching guiltily into my pockets for some money—the money clip Kitsey had given me was too tight, I was having a hard time getting the bills out, as I fumbled I was aware of everyone looking at me and then—"hey!" I cried, stepping back, as the dog snarled and lunged, snapping and catching the hem of my pants leg in its needlelike teeth.

Everyone was laughing—the kids, a street vendor, a cook in a hair net sitting on a stoop talking on a cell phone. Wrenching my pants leg loose—more laughter—I turned away and, to recover from my consternation, ducked into the next bar I saw—black awning with some red on it—and said to the bartender: "Does Katrina work here?"

He stopped drying his glass. "Katrina?"

"I'm a friend of Jerome's."

"Katrina? Not Katya, you mean?" The guys at the bar—Eastern Europeans—had gone silent.

"Maybe, uh—?"

"What's her last name?"

"Um—" One leather-jacket guy had lowered his chin and turned full on his stool to fix me with a Bela Lugosi stare.

The bartender was eyeballing me steadily. "This girl you want. What is it that you want with her?"

"Well, actually, I—"

"What color hair?"

"Uh—blonde? Or—actually—" clearly, from his expression, I was about to be thrown out, or worse; my eyes lit on the sawed-off Louisville Slugger behind the bar—"my mistake, forget it—"

I was out of the bar and well down the street when I heard a shout behind me: *"Potter!"*

I froze, as I heard him shout it again. Then, in disbelief, I turned. And while I still stood unable to believe it, people streaming round us on either side, he laughed and barged forward to throw his arms around me.

"Boris." Pointed black eyebrows, merry black eyes. He was taller, face hollower, long black coat, same old scar over his eye plus a couple of new ones. "Wow."

"And wow, yourself!" He held me out at arm's length. "Hah! Look at you! Long time, no?"

"I —" I was too stunned to speak. "What are you doing here?"

"And, I should ask —" stepping back to give me the once-over, then gesturing down the street as if it belonged to him — "what are *you* doing? To what do I owe this surprise?"

"What?"

"I stopped by your shop the other day!" Throwing the hair out of his face. "To see you!"

"That was you?"

"Who else? How'd you know where to find me?"

"I —" I shook my head in disbelief.

"You weren't looking for me?" Drawing back in surprise. "No? This is accident? Ships passing? Amazing! And why this white face on you?"

"What?"

"You look terrible!"

"Fuck you."

"Ah," he said, slinging his arm around my neck. "Potter, Potter! Such dark rings!" tracing a fingertip under one eye. "Nice suit though. And hey—" releasing me, flicking me with thumb and forefinger on the temple — "same glasses on the face? You never got them changed?"

"I —" All I could do was shake my head.

"What?" He held out his hands. "You don't blame me, for being happy to see you?"

I laughed. I didn't know where to start. "Why didn't you leave a number?" I said.

"So you're not angry with me? Hate me forever?" Though he wasn't smiling, he was biting his lower lip in amusement. "You don't—" he jerked his head at the street— "you don't want to go fight me or something?"

"Hi there," said a lean steely-eyed woman, slim-hipped in black jeans, sliding forward to Boris's side rather suddenly in a manner that made me think she was his girlfriend or wife.

"The famous Potter," she said, extending a long white hand ringed to the knuckles in silver. "Pleasure. I've heard all about you." She was slightly taller than him, with long limp hair and a long, elegant black-clad body like a python. "I'm Myriam."

"Myriam? Hi! It's Theo, really."

"I know." Her hand, in mine, was cold. I noticed a blue pentagram tattooed on the inside of her wrist. "But Potter's how he speaks of you."

"Speaks of me? Oh yeah? What'd he say?" No one had called me Potter in years but her soft voice had brought to mind a forgotten word from those old books, the language of snakes and dark wizards: Parseltongue.

Boris, who'd had his arm around my shoulder, had unhanded me when she'd approached as if a code had been spoken. A glance was exchanged — the heft of which I recognized instantly from our shoplifting days, when we had been able to say *Let's go* or *here he comes* without uttering a word — and Boris, seeming flustered, ran his hands through his hair and looked at me intently.

"You'll be around?" he inquired, walking backward.

"Around where?"

"Around the neighborhood."

"I can be."

"I want to —" he stopped, brow furrowed, and looked over my head at the street — "I want to talk to you. But now —" he looked worried — "Not a good time. An hour maybe?"

Myriam, glancing at me, said something in Ukrainian. There was a brief exchange. Then Myriam slipped her arm through mine in a curiously intimate manner and started leading me down the street.

"There." She pointed. "Go down that way, four-five blocks. There's a bar, off Second. Old Polack place. He'll meet you."

V.

ALMOST THREE HOURS LATER I was still sitting in a red vinyl booth in the Polack bar, flashing Christmas lights, annoying mix of punk rock and Christmas polka music honking away on the jukebox, fed up from waiting and wondering if he was going to show or not, if maybe I should just go home. I didn't even have his information — it had all happened so fast. In the past I'd Googled Boris for the hell of it — never a whisper — but then I'd never envisioned Boris as having any kind of a life that might be traceable online. He might have been anywhere, doing anything: mopping a hospital floor, carrying a gun in some foreign jungle, picking up cigarette butts off the street.

It was getting toward the end of Happy Hour, a few students and art-ist types trickling in among the pot-bellied old Polish guys and grizzled, fifty-ish punks. I'd just finished my third vodka; they poured them big, it was foolish to order another one; I knew I should get something to eat but I wasn't hungry and my mood was turning bleaker and darker by the moment. To think that he'd blown me off after so many years was incred-ibly depressing. If I had to be philosophical, at least I'd been diverted from my dope mission: hadn't OD'd, wasn't vomiting in some garbage can, hadn't been ripped off or run in for trying to buy from an undercover cop—

"Potter." There he was, sliding in across from me, slinging the hair from his face in a gesture that brought the past ringing back.

"I was just about to leave."

"Sorry." Same dirty, charming smile. "Had something to do. Didn't Myriam explain?"

"No she didn't."

"Well. Is not like I work in accounting office. Look," he said, leaning forward, palms on the table, "don't be mad! Was not expecting to run into you! I came as quick as I could! Ran, practically!" He reached across with cupped hand and slapped me gently on the cheek. "My God! Such a long time it is! Glad to see you! You're not glad to see me too?"

He'd grown up to be good-looking. Even at his gawkiest and most pinched he'd always had a likable shrewdness about him, lively eyes and a quick intelligence, but he'd lost that half-starved rawness and everything else had come together the right way. His skin was weather-beaten but his clothes fell well, his features were sharp and nervy, cavalry hero by way of concert pianist; and his tiny gray snaggleteeth—I saw—had been replaced by a standard-issue row of all-American whites.

He saw me looking, flicked a showy incisor with his thumbnail. "New snaps."

"I noticed."

"Dentist in Sweden did it," said Boris, signalling for a waiter. "Cost a fucking fortune. My wife kept after me—Borya, your mouth, disgrace-ful! I said no way am I doing this, but was the best money I ever spent."

"When'd you get married?"

"Eh?"

"You could have brought her if you wanted."

He looked startled. "What, you mean Myriam? No, no—" reaching into the pocket of his suit jacket, punching around on his telephone, "Myriam's not my wife! This—" he handed me the phone—"*this* is my wife. What are you drinking?" he said, before turning to address the waiter in Polish.

The photo on the iPhone was of a snow-topped chalet and, out in front, a beautiful blonde on skis. At her side, also on skis, were a pair of bundled-up little blond kids of indeterminate sex. It didn't look so much like a snapshot as an ad for some healthful Swiss product like yogurt or Bircher muesli.

I looked up at him stunned. He glanced away, with a Russianate gesture of old: yeah, well, it is what it is.

"Your *wife?* Seriously?"

"Yah," he said, with a lifted eyebrow. "My kids, too. Twins."

"Fuck."

"Yes," he said regretfully. "Born when I was very young—too young. It wasn't a good time—she wanted to keep them—'Borya, how could you'—what could I say? To be truthful I don't know them so well. Actually the little one—he is not in the picture—the little one I have not met at all. I think he is only, what? Six weeks old?"

"What?" Again I looked at the picture, struggling to reconcile this wholesome Nordic family with Boris. "Are you divorced?"

"No no no—" the vodka had arrived, icy carafe and two tiny glasses, he was pouring a shot for each of us—"Astrid and the children are mostly in Stockholm. Sometimes she comes to Aspen to the winter, to ski—she was ski champion, qualified for the Olympics when she was nineteen—"

"Oh yeah?" I said, doing my best not to sound incredulous at this. The kids, as was fairly evident upon closer viewing, looked far too blond and bonny to be even vaguely related to Boris.

"Yes yes," said Boris, very earnestly, with a vigorous nod of the head. "She always has to be where there is skiing and—you know me, I hate the fucking snow, ha! Her father very very right-wing—a Nazi basically. I think—no wonder Astrid has depression problems with father like him! What a hateful old shit! But they are very unhappy and miserable people, all of them, these Swedes. One minute laughing and drinking and the next—darkness, not a word. *Dziękuję,*" he said to the waiter, who had reappeared with a tray of small plates: black bread, potato salad, two kinds of herring, cucumbers in sour cream, stuffed cabbage, and some pickled eggs.

"I didn't know they served food here."

"They don't," said Boris, buttering a slice of black bread and sprinkling it with salt. "But am starving. Asked them to bring something from next door." He clinked his shot glass with mine. *"Sto lat!"* he said—his old toast.

"Sto lat." The vodka was aromatic and flavored with some bitter herb I couldn't identify.

"So," I said, helping myself to some food. "Myriam?"

"Eh?"

I held out open palms in our childhood gesture: *please explain.*

"Ah, Myriam! She works for me! Right-hand man, suppose you'd say. Although, I'll tell you, she's better than any man you'll find. What a woman, my God. Not many like her, I'll tell you. Worth her weight in gold. Here here," he said, refilling my glass and sliding it back to me. *"Za vstrechu!"* lifting his own to me. "To our meeting!"

"Isn't it my turn to toast?"

"Yes, it is—" clinking my glass—"but I am hungry and you are waiting too long."

"To our meeting, then."

"To our meeting! And to fortune! For bringing us together again!"

As soon as we'd drunk, Boris fell immediately on the food. "And what exactly is it that you do?" I asked him.

"This, that." He still ate with the innocent, gobbling hunger of a child. "Many things. Getting by, you know?"

"And where do you live? Stockholm?" I said, when he didn't answer.

He waved an expansive hand. "All over."

"Like—?"

"Oh, you know. Europe, Asia, North and South America…"

"That covers a lot of territory."

"Well," he said, mouth full of herring, wiping a glob of sour cream off his chin, "am also small business owner, if you understand me rightly."

"Sorry?"

He washed down the herring with a big slug of beer. "You know how it is. My official business so called is housecleaning agency. Workers from Poland, mostly. Nice pun in title of business, too. 'Polish Cleaning Service.' Get it?" He bit into a pickled egg. "What's our motto, can you guess? 'We clean you out,' ha!"

I chose to let that one lie. "So you've been in the States this whole time?"

"Oh no!" He had poured us each a new shot of vodka, was lifting his glass to me. "Travel a lot. I am here maybe six, eight weeks of the year. And the rest of the time—"

"Russia?" I said, downing my shot, wiping my mouth with the back of my hand.

"Not so much. Northern Europe. Sweden, Belgium. Germany sometimes."

"I thought you went back."

"Eh?"

"Because—well. I never heard from you."

"Ah." Boris rubbed his nose sheepishly. "It was a messed up time. Remember your house—that last night?"

"Of course."

"Well. I'd never seen so much drugs in my life. Like half an ounce of coka and didn't sell one stitch of it, not even one quarter gram. Gave a lot away, sure—was very popular at school, ha! Everyone loved me! But most of it—right up my nose. Then—the baggies we found—tablets of all assortments—remember? Those little greens? Some very serious cancer-patient-end-of-life pills—your dad must have been crazy addicted if he was taking that stuff."

"Yeah, I wound up with some of those too."

"Well then, you know! They don't even make those good green oxys any more! Now they have the junkie-defeat so you can't shoot them or snort! But your dad? Like—to go from drinking to *that*? Better a drunk in the street, any old day. First one I did—passed out before I hit my second line, if Kotku hadn't been there—" he drew a finger across his throat—"*pfft*."

"Yep," I said, remembering my own stupid bliss, keeling face-down on my desk upstairs at Hobie's.

"Anyway—" Boris downed his vodka in a gulp and poured us both another—"Xandra was selling it. Not *that*. That was your dad's. For his own personal. But the other, she was dealing from where she worked. That couple Stewart and Lisa? Those like super straight real-estate looking people? They were bankrolling her."

I put down my fork. "How do you know that?"

"Because she told me! And I guess they got ugly when she came up short, too. Like Mr. Lawyer Face and Miss Daisy Tote Bag all nice and kind at your house...petting her on the head...'what can we do'...'Poor Xandra...' 'we're so sorry for you'...then their drugs are gone—phew. Different story! I felt really bad when she told me, for what we'd done! Big trouble for her! But, by then—" flicking his nose—"was all up here. Kaput."

"Wait—Xandra told you this?"

"Yes. After you left. When I was living over there with her."

"You need to back up a little bit."

Boris sighed. "Well, okay. Is long story. But we have not seen each other in long while, right?"

"You lived with Xandra?"

"You know—in and out. Four-five months maybe. Before she moved back to Reno. I lost touch with her after that. My dad had gone back to Australia, see, and also Kotku and I were on the rocks—"

"That must have been really weird."

"Well—sort of," he said restlessly. "See—" leaning back, signalling to the waiter again—"I was in pretty bad shape. I'd been up for days. You know how it is when you crash hard off cocaine—terrible. I was alone and really frightened. You know that sickness in your soul—fast breaths, lots of fear, like Death will reach a hand out and take you? Thin— dirty—scared shivering. Like a little half-dead cat! And Christmas too—everyone away! Called a bunch of people, no one picking up— went by this guy Lee's where I stayed in the pool house sometime but he was gone, door locked. Walking and walking—staggering almost. Cold and frightened! Nobody home! So I went by to Xandra's. Kotku was not talking to me by then."

"Man, you had some kind of serious balls. I wouldn't have gone back there for a million dollars."

"I know, it took some onions, but was *so* lonely and ill. Mouth all gittering. Like—where you want to lie still and to look at a clock and count your heartbeats? except no place to lie still? and you don't have a clock? Almost in tears! Didn't know what to do! Didn't even know was she still there. But lights were on—only lights on the street—came around by the glass door and there she was, in her same Dolphins shirt, in the kitchen making margaritas."

"What'd she do?"

"Ha! Wouldn't let me in, at first! Stood in the door and yelled a long while—cursed me, called me every name! But then I started crying. And when I asked could I stay with her?"—he shrugged—"she said yes."

"What?" I said, reaching for the shot he'd poured me. "You mean like stay stay—?"

"I was scared! She let me sleep in her room! With TV turned to Christmas movies!"

"Hmn." I could see he wanted me to press for details, only from his gleeful expression I was not so sure I believed him about the sleeping-in-her-room business, either. "Well, glad that worked out for you, I guess. She say anything about me?"

"Well, yes a little." He chortled. "A lot actually! Because, I mean, don't be mad, but I blamed some things on you."

"Glad I could help."

"Yes, of course!" He clinked my glass jubilantly. "Many thanks! You'd do the same, I wouldn't mind. Honest, though, poor Xandra, I think she was glad to see me. To see *any*one. I mean —" throwing his shot back — "it was crazy…those bad friends…she was all alone out there. Drinking a lot, afraid to go to work. Something could have happened to her, easy — no neighbors, really creepy. Because Bobo Silver—well, Bobo was actually not so bad guy. 'The Mensch'? They don't call him that for nothing! Xandra was scared to death of him but he didn't go after her for your dad's debt, not serious anyway. Not at all. And your dad was in for a lot. Probably he realized she was broke—your dad had fucked *her* over good and proper, too. Might as well be decent about it. Can't get blood out of a turnip. But those other people, those friends of hers so called, were mean like bankers. You know? 'You owe me,' *really* hard, fucking connected, scary. Worse than him! Not so big sum even, but she was still way short and they were being nasty, all—" (mocking head tilt, aggressive finger point) "'*fuck* you, we're not going to wait, you better figure something out,' like that. Anyway—good I went back when I did because then I was able to help."

"Help how?"

"By giving her back the moneys I took."

"You'd kept it?"

"Well, no," he said reasonably. "Had spent it. But—had something else going, see. Because right after the coke ran out? I had taken the money to Jimmy at the gun shop and bought more. See, I was buying it for me and Amber—just the two of us. Very very beautiful girl, very innocent and special. Very young too, like only fourteen! But just that one night at MGM Grand, we had got so close, just sitting on the bathroom floor all night up at KT's dad's suite and talking. Didn't even kiss! Talk talk talk! I all but wept from it. Really opened up our hearts to each other. And—" hand to his breastbone—"I felt so sad when the day came, like why did it have to be over? Because we could have sat there talking forever to each other! and been so perfect and happy! That's how close we got to each other, see, in just that one night. Anyway—this is why I went to Jimmy. He had really shitty coke—not half so good as Stewart and Lisa's. But everyone knew, see—everyone had heard about that weekend at MGM Grand, me with all that blow. So people came to me. Like—dozen people my first day back at school. Throwing their moneys at me. 'Will you get me some…will you get me some…will you get some for my bro…I have ADD, I need it for my homework….' Pretty soon was selling to senior football players and half the basketball team. Lots of girls too… friends of Amber and KT's…Jordan's friends too…college students at UNLV! Lost money on the first few batches I sold—didn't know what to ask, sold fat for low price, wanted everyone to like me, yah yah yah. But once I figured it out—I was rich! Jimmy gave me huge discount, he was making lots of green off it too. I was doing him big favor, see, selling drugs to kids too scared to buy them—scared of people like Jimmy who sold them. KT…Jordan…those girls had a lot of money! *Always* happy to front me. Coke is not like E—I sold that too, but it was up and down, whole bunch then none for days, for coka I had a lot of regulars and they called two and three times a week. I mean, just KT—"

"Wow." Even after so many years, her name struck a chord.

"Yes! To KT!" We raised our glasses and drank.

"What a beauty!" Boris slammed his glass down. "I used to get dizzy around her. Just to breathe her same air."

"Did you sleep with her?"

"No…God I tried…but she gave me a hand job in her little brother's bedroom one night when she was wasted and in a very nice mood."

"Man, I sure left at the wrong time."

"You sure did. I came in my pants before she even got the zip down.

And KT's allowance—" reaching for my empty shot glass. "Two thousand a month! That is what she got for clothes only! Only KT already has so many clothes it is like, why does she need to buy more? Anyway by Christmas for me it was like in the movies where they have the ching-ching and the dollar signs. Phone never stopped ringing. Everybody's best friend! Girls I never saw before, kissing me, giving me gold jewelry off their own necks! I was doing all the drugs I could do, drugs every day, every night, lines as long as my hand, and still money everywhere. I was like the Scarface of our school! One guy gave me a motorcycle—another guy, a used car. I would go to pick my clothes from off the floor—hundreds of dollars falling out from the pockets—no idea where it came from."

"This is a lot of information, really fast."

"Well, tell me about it! This is my usual learning process. They say experience is good teacher, and normally is true, but I am lucky this experience did not kill me. Now and then...when I have some beers sometimes...I'll maybe hit a line or two? But mostly I do not like it any more. Burned myself out good. If you had met me maybe five years ago? I was all like—" sucking in his cheeks—"so. But—" the waiter had reappeared with more herring and beer—"enough about all that. You—" he looked me up and down—"what? Doing very nicely for yourself, I'd say?"

"All right, I guess."

"Ha!" He leaned back with his arm along the back of the booth. "Funny old world, right? Antiques trade? The old poofter? He got you in to it?"

"That's right."

"Big racket, I heard."

"That's right."

He eyed me up and down. "You happy?" he said.

"Not very."

"Listen, then! I have great idea! Come work for me!"

I burst out laughing.

"No, not kidding! No no," he said, shushing me imperiously as I tried to talk over him, pouring me a new shot, sliding the glass across the table to me, "what is he giving you? Serious. I will give you two times."

"No, I like my *job*—" over-pronouncing the words, was I as wrecked as I sounded?—"I like what I *do.*"

"Yes?" He lifted his glass to me. "Then why aren't you happy?"

"I don't want to talk about it."

"And why not?"

I waved my hand dismissively. "Because—" I'd lost track quite how many shots I'd had. "Just because."

"If not job then—which is it?" He had thrown back his own shot, tossing his head grandly, and started in on the new plate of herring. "Money problems? Girl?"

"Neither."

"Girl then," he said triumphantly. "I knew it."

"Listen—" I drained the rest of my vodka, slapped the table—what a genius I was, I couldn't stop smiling, I'd had the best idea in years! —"enough of this. Come on—let's go! I've got a big big surprise for you."

"*Go?*" said Boris, visibly bristling. "Go where?"

"Come with me. You'll see."

"I want to stay here."

"Boris—"

He sat back. "Let it go, Potter," he said, putting his hands up. "Just relax."

"Boris!" I looked at the bar crowd, as if expecting mass outrage, and then back at him. "I'm sick of sitting here! I've *been here for hours.*"

"But—" He was annoyed. "I cleared this whole night for you! I had stuff to do! You're leaving?"

"Yes! And you're coming with me. Because—" I threw my arms out—"you have to see the surprise!"

"Surprise?" He threw down his balled-up napkin. "What surprise?"

"You'll find out." What was the matter with him? Had he forgotten how to have fun? "Now come on, let's get out of here."

"Why? Now?"

"Just because!" The bar room was a dark roar; I'd never felt so sure of myself in my life, so pleased at my own cleverness. "Come on. Drink up!"

"Do we really have to do this?"

"You'll be glad. Promise. Come on!" I said, reaching over and shaking his shoulder amicably as I thought. "I mean, no shit, this is a surprise you can't believe how good."

He leaned back with folded arms and regarded me suspiciously. "I think you are angry with me."

"Boris, what the fuck." I was so drunk I stumbled, standing up, and had to catch myself on the table. "Don't argue. Let's just go."

"I think it is a mistake to go somewhere with you."

"Oh?" I looked at him with one half closed eye. "You coming, or not?"

Boris looked at me coolly. Then he pinched the bridge of his nose and said: "You won't tell me where we're going."

"No."

"You won't mind if my driver takes us then?"

"Your driver?"

"Sure. He is waiting like two-three blocks away."

"Fuck." I looked away and laughed. "You have a *driver?*"

"You don't mind if we go with him, then?"

"Why would I?" I said, after a brief pause. Drunk as I was, his manner had brought me up short: he was looking at me with a peculiar, calculating, uninflected quality I had never seen before.

Boris tossed back the rest of his vodka and then stood up. "Very well," he said, twirling an unlit cigarette loosely in his fingertips. "Let's get this nonsense over with, then."

vi.

BORIS HUNG SO FAR back, when I was unlocking the front door at Hobie's, that it was as if he thought my key in the lock was going to set off a massive townhouse explosion. His driver was double-parked out front in clouds of ostentatious fume. Once in the car, all the conversation between him and the driver had been in Ukrainian: nothing I'd been able to pick up even with my two semesters of Conversational Russian in college.

"Come in," I said, barely able to suppress a smile. What did he think, the idiot, that I was going to jump him or kidnap him or something? But he was still on the street, fists in the pockets of his overcoat, looking back over his shoulder at the driver, whose name was Genka or Gyuri or Gyorgi or I'd forgotten what the fuck.

"What's the matter?" I said. If I'd been less tanked, his paranoia might have made me angry, but I only thought it was hilarious.

"Tell me again, why are we having to come here?" he said, still standing well back.

"You'll see."

"And you live up here?" he said, suspiciously, looking inside the parlor. "This is your place?"

I'd made more noise than I'd meant with the door. "Theo?" called Hobie from the back of the house. "That you?"

"Right." He was dressed for dinner, suit and tie—shit, I thought, are there guests? with a jolt I realized it was barely dinnertime, it felt like three in the morning.

Boris had slid in cautiously behind me, hands in the pockets of his overcoat, leaving the front door wide open behind him, eyes on the big basalt urns, the chandelier.

"Hobie," I said—he had ventured out into the hall, eyebrows lifted, Mrs. DeFrees pattering apprehensively after him—"Hi, Hobie, you remember me talking about—"

"Popchik!"

The little white bundle—toddling dutifully down the hall to the front door—froze. Then a high-pitched scream as he began to run as fast as he could (which was not very fast at all, any more) and Boris—whooping with laughter—dropped to his knees.

"Oh!" snatching him up, as Popchik wriggled and struggled. "You got fat! He got fat!" he said indignantly as Popchik jumped up and kissed him on the face. "You let him get fat! Yes, hello, *poustyshka,* little bit of fluff you, hello! You remember me, don't you?" He had toppled over on his back, stretched out and laughing, as Popchik—still screaming with joy—jumped all over him. "He remembers me!"

Hobie, adjusting his glasses, was standing by amused—Mrs. DeFrees, not quite so amused, standing behind Hobie and frowning slightly at the spectacle of my vodka-smelling guest rolling and tumbling with the dog on the carpet.

"Don't tell me," he said, putting his hands in the pockets of his suit jacket. "This would be—?"

"Exactly."

vii.

WE DIDN'T STAY LONG—Hobie had heard a lot about Boris over the years, let's go have a drink! and Boris was just as interested, and curious, as I might have been if Judy from Karmeywallag or some other mythical person of his past had turned up — but we were drunk and too boisterous and I felt that we might be upsetting Mrs. DeFrees, who though smiling politely was sitting rather still in a hall chair with her tiny beringed hands folded in her lap and not saying much.

So we left — Popchik in tow, paddling along excitedly with us, Boris shouting and delighted, waving at the car to go round the block and pick us up: "Yes, *poustyshka,* yes!" — to Popper — "That's us! We have a car!"

Then all of a sudden it seemed that Boris's driver spoke English as well as Boris did, and we were all three of us pals — four of us, counting Popper, who was standing on his hind legs with his paws propped on the window glass and staring out very seriously at the lights of the West Side Highway as Boris gabbled to him and cuddled him and kissed him on the back of the neck while — simultaneously — explaining to Gyuri (the driver) in both English and Russian how wonderful I was, friend of his youth and blood of his heart! (Gyuri reaching around his body and across the seat with his left hand, to shake my hand solemnly in the rear) and how precious was life that two such friends, in so big world, should find each other again after so great separation?

"Yes," said Gyuri gloomily as he made the turn onto Houston Street so hard and sharp I slid into the door, "it was the same with me and Vadim. Daily I grieve him — I grieve him so hard I wake in the night to grieve. Vadim was my brother —" glancing back at me; pedestrians scattering as he plowed into the crosswalk, startled faces outside tinted windows — "my more-than-brother. Like Borya and me. But Vadim —"

"This was a terrible thing," Boris said quietly to me, and then, to Gyuri: — "yes, yes, terrible —"

"— we have Vadim go too soon in the ground. Is true, the radio song, you know it? Piano Man singer? 'Only the good die young.'"

"He will be waiting for us there," said Boris consolingly, reaching across the seat to pat Gyuri on the shoulder.

"Yes, that just is what I instructed him to do," Gyuri muttered, cutting in front of a car so suddenly that I fell against my seat belt and Popchyk went flying. "These things are deep — they cannot be honored in words. Human tongue cannot express. But at the end — putting him to bed with the shovel — I spoke to him with my soul. 'So long, Vadim. Hold the gates open for me, brother. Save me a seat up there where you at.' Only God —" *please,*

I thought, trying to keep a composed expression while gathering Popchyk in my lap, *for fuck's sake look at the road*—"Fyodor, please help me, I have two big questions about God. You are college professor" (what?) "so perhaps you can answer for me. First question—" eyes meeting mine in the rear view mirror, holding up pointed finger—"does God have sense of humor? Second question: does God have *cruel* sense of humor? Such as: does God toy with us and torture us for His own amusement, like vicious child with garden insect?"

"Uh," I said, alarmed at the intense way he was looking at me and not his upcoming turn, "well, maybe, I don't know, I sure hope not."

"This is not the right man to ask these questions," Boris said, offering me a cigarette and then passing one to Gyuri across the front seat. "God has tortured Theo plenty. If suffering makes noble, then he is a prince. Now Gyuri—" reclining in clouds of smoke—"a favor."

"Anything."

"Will you look after the dog after you drop us off? Drive him around in back seat, wherever he wants to go?"

The club was out in Queens, I couldn't have said where. In the red-carpeted front room, which felt like a room where you'd go to kiss your grandfather on the cheek after being freshly released from prison, large family-style gatherings of drinkers in Louis XVI–style chairs ate and smoked and shouted and pounded each other on the back around tables swagged with metallic gold fabric. Behind, on the deep lacquer-red walls, Christmas garlands and Soviet-era holiday decorations of wired bulbs and colored aluminum—roosters, nesting birds, red stars and rocket ships and hammer-and-sickles with kitschy Cyrillic slogans (*Happy New Year, dear Stalin*)—were slung up in exuberant and makeshift-seeming fashion. Boris (well in the bag himself; he'd been drinking from a bottle in the back seat) had his arm around me and, in Russian, was introducing me to young and old as his brother which I gathered people were understanding literally to judge from all the men and women who embraced me and kissed me and tried to pour me shots from magnums of vodka in crystal ice buckets.

Somehow, eventually, we made it to the rear: black velvet curtains guarded by a shaved-head, viper-eyed thug tattooed to the jawbone in Cyrillic. Inside, the back room was thumping with music and thick with sweat, aftershave, weed and Cohiba smoke: Armani, tracksuits, diamond and platinum Rolexes. I'd never seen so many men wearing so much gold—gold rings, gold chains, gold teeth in front. It was all like a foreign, confusing, brightly glinting dream; and I was at the uneasy stage of drunkenness where I couldn't focus my eyes or do anything but nod and weave and allow Boris to drag me around through the crowd. At some point deep in the night Myriam reappeared like a shadow; after greeting me with a kiss on the cheek that felt somber and spooky, frozen in time like some ceremonial gesture, she and Boris vanished, leaving me at a packed table of stone-drunk, chain-smoking Russian nationals all of whom seemed to know who I was ("Fyodor!") slapping me on the back, pouring me shots, offering me food, offering me Marlboros, shouting amiably at me in Russian without apparent expectation of reply—

Hand on my shoulder. Someone was removing my glasses. "Hello?" I said to the strange woman who was all of a sudden sitting in my lap.

Zhanna. Hi, Zhanna! What are you doing now? Not so much. You? Porn star, salon-tanned, surgically-augmented tits spilling out the top of her dress. Prophecy runs in my family: will you permit me to read your palm? Hey, sure: her English was pretty good though it was difficult to make out what she was saying with the racket in the club.

"I see you are philosopher by nature." Tracing my palm with the Barbie-pink point of a fingernail. "Very very intelligent. Many ups and downs—have done a bit of everything in life. But you are lonely. You dream to meet a girl to be together with for the rest of your lives, is this right?"

Then Boris reappeared, alone. He pulled up a chair and sat down. A brief, amused conversation in Ukrainian ensued between him and my new friend which ended with her putting my glasses on my face and departing, but not before bumming a cigarette from Boris and kissing him on the cheek.

"You know her?" I said to Boris.

"Never saw her in my life," said Boris, lighting up a cigarette himself. "We can go now, if you want. Gyuri's waiting outside."

viii.

BY NOW IT WAS late. The back seat of the car was soothing after all the confusion of the club (intimate glow of the console, radio turned low) and we drove around for hours with Popchik fast asleep in Boris's lap, laughing and talking—Gyuri chiming in too with hoarsely-shouted stories about growing up in Brooklyn in what he called 'the bricks' (the projects) while Boris and I drank warm vodka from the bottle and did bumps of coke from the bag that he had produced from his overcoat pocket—Boris passing it up front to Gyuri every now and then. Even though the air was on, it was burning up in the car; Boris was sweaty in the face and his ears were flaming red. "You see," he was saying—he'd already shouldered off his jacket; he was taking off his cuff links, dropping them in his pocket, rolling up his shirt sleeves—"it was your dad taught me how to dress proper. I am grateful to him for that."

"Yeah, my dad taught us both a lot of things."

"Yes," he said sincerely—vigorous nod, no irony, wiping his nose with the side of his hand. "He always looked like gentleman. Like—such a lot of these guys at the club—leather coats, velour warm-ups, straight from immigration looks like. Much better to dress plain, like your dad, nice jacket, nice watch but klássnyy—you know, simple—try to fit in."

"Right." It being my business to notice such things, I'd already noticed Boris's wristwatch—Swiss, retailing for maybe fifty thousand, a European playboy's watch—too flashy for my taste but extremely restrained compared to the jewel-set hunks of gold and platinum I'd seen at his club. There was, I saw, a blue Star of David tattooed on the inside of his forearm.

"What's that?" I said.

He held up his wrist for me to inspect. "IWC. A good watch is like cash in the bank. You can always pawn it or put it up in emergency. This is white gold but looks like stainless. Better to have watch that looks less expensive than it really is."

"No, the tattoo."

"Ah." He pushed up his sleeve and looked at his arm regretfully—but I wasn't looking at the tattoo any more. The light wasn't great in the car but I knew needle marks when I saw them. "The star you mean? Is long story."

"But—" I knew better than to ask about the marks. "You're not Jewish."

"No!" said Boris indignantly, pushing his sleeve back down. "Of course not!"

"Well then, I guess the question would be why..."

"Because I told Bobo Silver I was Jewish."

"What?"

"Because I wanted him to hire me! So I lied."

"No shit."

"Yes! I did! He came by Xandra's house a lot—snooping up and down the street, smelling for something rotten, like maybe your dad wasn't dead—and one day I made up my nerve to talk to him. Offered myself to work. Things were getting out of hand—at school there was trouble, some people had to go to rehab, others got expelled—I needed to cut ties with Jimmy, see, do something else for a while. And yes, my surname is all wrong but Boris, in Russia, is the first name of many Jews so I thought, why not? How will he know? I thought the tattoo would be a good thing—to convince him, you know, I was ok. Had a guy do it who owed me a hundred bucks. Made up big sad story, my mother Polish Jew, her family in concentration camp, boo hoo hoo—stupid me, I did not realize that tattoos were against the Jewish law. Why are you laughing?" he said defensively. "Someone like me—useful to him, you know? I speak English, Russian, Polish, Ukrainian. I am educated. Anyhow, he knew damn well I wasn't Jew, he laughed in my face, but he took me on anyway and that was very kind of him."

"How could you work for that guy who wanted to kill my dad?"

"He didn't want to kill your dad! That is not true, or fair. Only to scare him! But—yes I did work for him, almost one year."

"What did you do for him?"

"Nothing dirty, believe or not! Assistant for him only—message boy, run errands back and forth, like this. Walk his little dogs! Pick up dry-cleaning! Bobo was good and generous friend to me at bad time—father almost, I can say this hand on my heart to you and mean it. Surely father more to me than my own father. Bobo was always fair to me. More than fair. Kind. I learned a lot from him, watching him in action. So I don't mind so much wearing this star for him. And this—" he pushed his sleeve to the biceps, thorn-pierced rose, Cyrillic inscription—"this is for Katya, love of my life. I loved her more than any woman I ever knew."

"You say that about everybody."

"Yes, but with Katya, is true! Would walk through broken glass for her! Walk through Hell, through fire! Give my life, gladly! I will never love any person on the earth like Katya again—not even close. She was

the one. I would die and be happy for only one day with her. But—" pushing his sleeve back down—"you should never get a person's name tattooed
on you, because then you lose the person. I was too young to know that
when I got the tattoo."

ix.

I HADN'T DONE BLOW since Carole Lombard left town and there was no
possibility of going to sleep. At six-thirty in the morning Gyuri was spinning around the Lower East Side with Popchik in the back ("I will take
him to the deli! For a bacon egg and cheese!") and we were wired and
chattering in some dank 24-hour-a-day bar on Avenue C with graffiti-
scrawled walls and burlap tacked over the windows to keep the sunrise
out, Ali Baba Club, Three Dollar Shots, Happy Hour 10:00 AM to Noon,
trying to drink enough beer to knock ourselves out a bit.

"You know what I did in college?" I was telling him. "I took Conversational Russian for a year. Totally because of you. I did really shitty in it,
actually. Never got good enough to read it, you know, to sit down with
Eugene Onegin—you have to read it in Russian, they say, it doesn't come
through in translation. But—I thought of you so much! I used to remember little things you'd say—all sorts of things came back to me—oh, wow,
listen, they're playing 'Comfy in Nautica,' do you hear that? Panda Bear! I
totally forgot that album. Anyway. I wrote a term paper on *The Idiot* for my
Russian Literature class—Russian Literature in translation—I mean, the
whole time I was reading it I thought about you, up in my bedroom smoking my dad's cigarettes. It was so much easier to keep track of the names if I
imagined you saying them in my head…actually, it was like I heard the
whole book in your voice! Back in Vegas you were reading *The Idiot* for
like six months, remember? In Russian. For a long time it was all you did.
Remember how for a long time you couldn't go downstairs because of Xandra, I had to bring you food, it was like Anne Frank? Anyway, I read it in
English, *The Idiot,* but I wanted to get there too, to that point, you know,
where my Russian was good enough. But I never did."

"All that fucking school," said Boris, plainly unimpressed. "If you
want to speak Russian, come to Moscow with me. You will speak it in two
months."

"So, are you going to tell me what you do?"

"Like I told you. This and that. Just enough to get by." Then, kicking me under the table: "You seem better now, eh?"

"Huh?" There were only two other people in the front room with us—beautiful people, unearthly pale, a man and a woman both with short dark hair, eyes locked, and the man had the woman's hand across the table and was nibbling and chewing on the inside of her wrist. *Pippa,* I thought, with a pang of anguish. It was nearly lunchtime in London. What was she doing?

"When I ran into you, you looked on your way to jump in the river."

"Sorry, it was a rough day."

"Nice set up you've got there though," Boris was saying. He couldn't see the couple from where he was sitting. "So you guys are partners?"

"No! Not like that."

"I didn't say so!" Boris looked at me critically. "Jesus, Potter, don't be so touchy! Anyhow that was his wife, the lady, wasn't she?"

"Yes," I said restlessly, leaning back in my chair. "Well, sort of." The relationship of Hobie and Mrs. DeFrees was still a deep mystery, as was her still-extant marriage to Mr. DeFrees. "I thought she was a widow for ages but she's not. She—" I leaned forward, rubbed my nose—"see, she lives uptown and he lives downtown, but they're together all the time... she has a house in Connecticut, sometimes they go out together for the weekend. She's married—but. I never see her husband. I haven't figured it out. To tell you the truth I think they are probably just good friends. Sorry I'm going on. I really don't know why I'm telling you all this."

"And he taught you your trade! He seems like nice fellow. Real gentleman."

"Huh?"

"Your boss."

"He's not my boss! I'm his business partner." The glitter of the drugs was wearing off; blood swishing in my ears, sharp high pitch like crickets singing. "As a matter of fact I run the whole sales end of things pretty much."

"Sorry!" said Boris, holding up his hands. "No need to snap. Only I meant it when I asked you to come work with me."

"And how am I supposed to answer that?"

"Look, I want to repay you. Let you share in all the good things that have happened to me. Because," he said, interrupting me grandly, "I owe you everything. Everything good that has happened to me in life, Potter, has happened because of you."

"What? I got you in the drug-dealing business? Wow, okay," I said, lighting one of his cigarettes and pushing the pack across to him, "that's good to know, that makes me feel really great about myself, thanks."

"Drug dealing? Who said drug dealing? I want to make things up to you! For what I did. I'm telling you, it's a great life. We would have a lot of fun together."

"Are you running an escort service? Is that it?"

"Look, shall I tell you something?"

"Please."

"I am really sorry about what I did to you."

"Forget it. I don't care."

"Why should you not share in some of these good profits I've made from you? Reap some of the cream for yourself?"

"Listen, can I say something, Boris? I don't want to be involved in anything dodgy. No offense," I said, "but I'm trying hard to get out from under something and, like I said, I'm engaged now, things are different, I really don't think I want to—"

"Then why not let me help you?"

"That's not what I mean. I mean—well, I'd rather not go into it but I've done some things I shouldn't have, I want to put them right. That is, I'm trying to figure how to put them right."

"Hard to put things right. You don't often get that chance. Sometimes all you can do is not get caught."

The beautiful pair had risen to leave, hand in hand, pushing aside the beaded curtain, drifting out together into the faint cold dawn. I watched the beads clicking and undulating in the slipstream of their departure, rippling with the sway of the girl's hips.

Boris sat back. He had his eyes fixed on mine. "I've been trying to get it back for you," he said. "I wish I could."

"What?"

He frowned. "Well—this is why I came by the store. You know. Am sure you've heard, the Miami stuff. Was worried what you'd think when it hit the news—and, honest, was a little afraid they'd trace it back to you, through me, you know? Not any more, so much, but—still. Was up to my neck in it, of course—but I *knew* the set-up was bad. Should have trusted my instincts. I—" he dipped his key for another quick snort; we were the only people in the place; the little tattooed waitress, or hostess, or whoever she was, had disappeared into the sketchy back room where—from my very brief glimpse—people on yard sale sofas appeared to be gathered for a screening of some 1970s porn—"anyhow. It was terrible. I should have known. People got hurt and I've come up short, but I learned a valuable lesson from this. Always a mistake—here, wait, let me hit the other side—like I was saying, *always* a mistake to deal with people you don't know." He pinched his nose shut and passed the bag under the table to me. "It's the thing you know, that you always forget. Never deal with strangers on the big stuff! Never! People can say 'oh, this person is fine'—me, I want to believe it, it's my nature. But bad things happen like that. See—I know my friends. But my friends of my friends? Not so well! It's the way people catch AIDS, right?"

It was a mistake—I knew, even as I was doing it—to do any more blow; I'd done way too much already, jaw clenched tight and blood pounding in my temples even as the unease of the comedown had begun to steal over me, a brittleness like plate glass shivering.

"Anyway," Boris was saying. He was speaking very fast, foot tapping and jittering under the table. "Have been trying to think how to get it back. Think think think! Of course I can't use it myself any more. I've burned myself with it but good. Of course—" he shifted restlessly—"that's not why I came to see you, exactly. Partly I wanted to apologize. To say 'sorry' to you in my own voice. Because—honestly, I am. And partly, too, with all this stuff in the news—I wanted to tell you not to worry, because maybe you are thinking—well, I don't know what you're thinking. Only—I didn't like to think of you hearing all this, and being afraid, not understanding. Thinking it might be traced back to you. It made me feel very bad. And that's why I wanted to talk to you. To tell you that I've kept you out of it—no one knows of your relation with me. And moreover to tell you, that I'm really, really trying to get it back. Trying very hard. Because—" three fingertips to forehead—"I've made a fortune off it, and I would really like for you to have it all to your own again—you know, the thing itself, for old times' sake, just to have, to really be yours, keep in your closet or whatever, get out and look at, like in old days, you know? Because I know how much you loved it. I got to where I loved it myself, actually."

I stared at him. In the fresh sparkle of the drug, what he was saying had begun, at last, to sink in. "Boris, what are you talking about?"

"You know."

"No I don't."

"Don't make me say it out loud."

"Boris—"

"I tried to tell you. I begged you not to leave. I would have given it back to you if you had waited just one day."

The beaded curtain was still clicking and undulating in the draft. Sinuous glassy wavelets. Staring at him, I was transfixed with the obscure, light sensation of one dream colliding with another: clatter of silverware in the harsh noon of the Tribeca restaurant, Lucius Reeve smirking at me across the table.

"No," I said—pushing back in my chair in a cold prickle of sweat, putting my hands over my face. "No."

"What, you thought your dad took it? I was kind of hoping you thought that. Because he was so in the hole. And stealing from you already."

I dragged my hands down my face and looked at him, unable to speak.

"I switched it. Yes. It was me. I thought you knew. Look, am sorry!" he said when still I sat gaping at him. "I had it in my locker at school. Joke, you know. Well—" weakly smiling—"maybe not. Sort of joke. But—listen—" tapping the table to get my attention—"I swear, I wasn't going to keep it. That was not my plan. How was I to know about your dad? If only you had spent the night—" he threw up his arms—"I would have given it to you, I swear I would have. But I couldn't make you stay. Had to leave! Right that minute! Must go! Now, Boris, now! Wouldn't wait even till morning! Must go, must go, this very second! And I was scared to say to you what I'd done."

I stared at him. My throat was too dry and my heart had begun to pound so fast that all I could think to do was to sit very still and hope it would slow down.

"Now you are angry," said Boris resignedly. "You want to kill me."

"What are you trying to tell me?"

"I—"

"What do you mean, *switch* it?"

"Look—" glancing around nervously—"I am sorry! I knew it was not a good idea for us to get wired together. I knew this would end up coming out maybe in some ugly way! But—" leaning forward to put his palms on the table—"I have felt really bad about it, honest. Would I have come to see you, if not? Shouted your name on the street? And when I say I want to pay you back? I am serious. I am going to make it up to you. Because, you see, this picture made my fortune, it made my—"

"What's in that package I've got uptown then?"

"What?" he said, his eyebrows coming down, and then, pushing away in his chair and looking at me with his chin pulled back: "You're kidding me. All this time and you never—?"

But I couldn't answer. My lips were moving but no sound was coming out.

Boris slapped the table. "You idiot. You mean you never even opened it up? How could you not—"

When I still didn't answer him, face in hands, he reached across the table and shook me by the shoulder.

"Really?" he said urgently, trying to look me in the eye. "You did not? Never opened it to look?"

From the back room: a weak female scream, inane and empty, followed by equally inane hoots of male laughter. Then, loud as a buzz saw, a blender started up at the bar and seemed to go on for an excessively long time.

"You didn't know?" said Boris, when the racket finally stopped. In the back room, laughter and clapping. "How could you not—"

But I couldn't say a word. Multilayered graffiti on the wall, sticker tags and scribbles, drunks with crosses for eyes. In the back, a hoarse chant had risen of *go go go*. So many things were flashing in on me at once that I could hardly get my breath.

"All these years?" said Boris, half-frowning. "And you never once—?"

"Oh, God."

"Are you okay?"

"I—" I shook my head. "How did you know I even have it? How do you know that?" I repeated, when he didn't answer. "You went through my room? My things?"

Boris looked at me. Then he ran both hands through his hair and said: "You're a blackout drunk, Potter, you know that?"

"Give me a break," I said, after an incredulous pause.

"No, am serious," he said mildly. "I am alcoholic. I know it! I was

alcoholic from ten years old, when I took my first drink. But you, Potter —
you're like my dad. *He* drinks — he goes unconscious while he is walking
around, does things he can't remember. Wrecks the car, beats me up, gets
in fights, wakes up with broken nose or in whole different town maybe,
lying on bench in railway station —"

"I don't do things like that."

Boris sighed. "Right, right, but your memory goes. Just like his. And,
I'm not saying you did anything bad, or violent, you are not violent like him
but you know, like — oh, that time we went to the play pit at McDonald's,
the kid pit, and you are so drunk on the puffy thing the lady called the cops
on you, and I got you out of there fast, standing in Wal Mart half an hour
pretending to look at school pencils and then back on the bus, back to the
bus stop, and that night you don't remember any of it? Not one thing?
'McDonald's, Boris? What McDonald's?' Or," he said, sniffling lavishly,
talking over me, "or, that day you are totalled, *wrecked,* and make me go
with you for 'walk in the desert'? Okay, we go for a walk. Fine. Only you
are so drunk you can barely walk and it is a hundred and five degrees. And
you get tired of walking and lay yourself down in the sand. And ask me
that I leave you to die. 'Leave me, Boris, leave me.' Remember that?"

"Get to the point."

"What can I say? You were unhappy. Drank yourself unconscious all
the time."

"So did you."

"Yes, I remember. Passing out on the stairs, face down, remember?
Waking up on the ground, miles from home, feet sticking out from a
bush, no idea how I got there? Shit, I emailed Spirsetskaya one time in the
middle of the night, crazy drunk email, stating she is a beautiful woman
and that I love her completely, which at that time I did. Next day at school,
all hung over: 'Boris, Boris, I need to talk to you.' Well, what about? And
there she is all gentle and kind, trying to let me down easy. Email? What
email? No recollection whatsoever! Standing there red in the face while
she is giving me xerox from poetry book and telling me I need to love girls
my own age! Sure — I did plenty of stupid things. Stupider than you! But
me," he said, toying with a cigarette, "I was trying to have fun and be
happy. You wanted to be dead. It's different."

"Why do I feel like you're trying to change the subject?"

"Not trying to judge! It's just — we did crazy things back then. Things

I think maybe you don't remember. No, no!" he said quickly, shaking his head, when he saw the look on my face. "Not *that*. Although I will say, you are the only boy I have ever been in bed with!"

My laugh spluttered out angrily, as if I'd coughed or choked on something.

"With that—" Boris leaned back disdainfully in his chair, pinched his nostrils shut—"pfah. I think it happens at that age sometimes. We were young, and needed girls. I think maybe you thought it was something else. But, no, wait," he said quickly, his expression changing—I'd scraped back my chair to go—"wait," he said again, catching my sleeve, "don't, please, listen to what I'm trying to tell you, you don't at all remember the night when we were watching *Dr. No?*"

I was getting my coat from the back of my chair. But, at this, I stopped. "Do you?"

"Am I supposed to remember? Why?"

"I *know* you don't. Because I used to like test you. Mention *Dr. No*, make jokes. To see what you would say."

"What about *Dr. No?*"

"Not that long after I met you!" His knee was going up and down like crazy. "I think you weren't used to vodka—you never knew what size to pour your drink. You came in with huge glass, like so, like water glass, and I thought: shit! You don't remember?"

"There were lots of nights like that."

"You don't remember. I would clean up your vomit—throw your clothes in the wash—you would not even know I had done it. You would cry and tell me all kinds of things."

"What kind of things?"

"Like..." he made an impatient face..."oh, it was your fault your mother died...you wished it was you...if you died, you would maybe be with her, together in the darkness...no point going into it, I don't want to make you feel bad. You were a mess, Theo—fun to be with, most of time! up for anything! but a mess. Probably you should have been in hospital. Climbing on roof, jumping into the swimming pool? Could have broken your neck, it was crazy! You would lie on your back in the road at night, no streetlights, no way for anyone to see you, waiting for a car to come and run you over, I had to fight to get you up and drag you in the house—"

"I would have lain out in that godforsaken fucking street a long time before a car came by. I could have slept out there. Brought my sleeping bag."

"I am not going to go into this. You were nuts. You could have killed us both. One night you got matches and tried to set the house on fire, remember that?"

"I was just joking," I said uneasily.

"And the carpet? Big burned hole in the sofa? Was that a joke? I turned the cushions so that Xandra wouldn't see it."

"That piece of shit was so cheap it wasn't even flame-retardant."

"Right, right. Have it your way. Anyway, this one night. We are watching *Dr. No,* which I had never seen but you had, and I was liking it very much, and you are completely *v gavno,* and it's on his island, and all cool, and he presses the button and shows that picture he stole?"

"Oh, God."

Boris cackled. "You did! God help you! It was great. So drunk you are staggering—I have something to show you! Something wonderful! Best thing ever! Stepping in front of the television. No, really! Me—watching movie, best part, you wouldn't shut up. Fuck off! Anyway, off you go, mad as hell, 'fuck you,' making *all* this noise. Bang bang bang. And then, down you come with the picture, see?" He laughed. "Funny thing—was sure you were bullshitting me. World-famous museum work? give me a break. But—it was real. Anyone could see."

"I don't believe you."

"Well, is true. I *did* know. Because if possible to paint fakes that look like that? Las Vegas would be the most beautiful city in the history of earth! Anyway—so funny! Here am I, so proudly teaching you to steal apples and candy from the magazine, while you have stolen world masterpiece of art."

"I didn't steal it."

Boris chuckled. "No, no. You explained. Preserving it in safety. Big important duty in life. You're telling me," he said, leaning forward, "you really haven't opened it up and looked at it? All these years? What is the matter with you?"

"I don't believe you," I said again. "*When* did you take it?" I said when he rolled his eyes away from me. "How?"

"Look, like I said—"

"How do you expect me to believe one word of this?"

Boris rolled his eyes again. He reached in his coat pocket; he punched up a picture on his iPhone. Then he handed it across the table to me.

It was the verso of the painting. You could find a reproduction of the front anywhere. But the back was as distinctive as a fingerprint: rich drips of sealing wax, brown and red; irregular patchwork of European labels (Roman numerals; spidery, quilled signatures), which had the feeling of a steamer trunk, or some international treaty of long ago. The crumbling yellows and browns were layered with an almost organic richness, like dead leaves.

He put the phone back in his pocket. We sat for a long while in silence. Then Boris reached for a cigarette.

"Believe me now?" he said, blowing a stream of smoke out the side of his mouth.

The atoms in my head were spinning apart; the sparkle of the bump had already begun to turn, apprehension and disquiet moving in subtly like dark air before a thunderstorm. For a long, somber moment we looked at each other: high chemical frequency, solitude to solitude, like two Tibetan monks on a mountaintop.

Then I stood without a word and got my coat. Boris jumped up too.

"Wait," he said, as I shouldered past him. "Potter? Don't go angry. When I said I would make it up to you? I meant it—"

"Potter?" he called again as I stepped through the clattering bead curtain and out on to the street, into the dirty gray light of dawn. Avenue C was empty except for a solitary cab which seemed to be as glad to see me as I was to see it, and darted over to stop for me immediately. Before he could say another word I got in and drove off and left him there, standing in his overcoat by a bank of trash cans.

X.

IT WAS EIGHT-THIRTY IN the morning by the time I got to storage, with a sore jaw from grinding my teeth and a heart about to explode. Bureaucratic daylight: pedestrian morning blaring, bright with threat. By quarter of ten I was sitting on the floor of my room at Hobie's house with my mind reeling like a spun-down top wobbling and veering from side to side. Strewn on the carpet around me were a pair of shopping bags; a never-used pup tent; a beige percale pillowcase that still smelled like my bedroom in Vegas; a tin full of assorted Roxicodones and morphs I knew I ought to flush; and a snarl of packing tape into which I'd cut, painstakingly, with an X-Acto knife, twenty minutes of delicate work, pulse throbbing in my fingertips, terrified of going in too hard and nicking the painting by mistake, finally getting the side open, peeling the tape off strip by strip by careful strip, with trembling hands: only to find — sandwiched in cardboard and wrapped with newspaper — a scribbled-up Civics workbook (*Democracy, Diversity, and You!*).

Bright multicultural throng. On the cover Asian kids, Latino kids, African American kids, Native American kids, a girl in a Muslim head scarf and a white kid in a wheelchair smiled and held hands before an American flag. Inside, within the book's cheery dull world of good citizenship, where persons of different ethnicities all participated happily in their communities and inner-city kids stood around their housing project with a watering can, caring for a potted tree with branches illustrating the different branches of government, Boris had drawn daggers with his name on them, roses and hearts surrounding Kotku's initials, and a set of spying eyes, peeping slyly to one side, above a partially filled out sample test:

> Why does man need government? *to impose ideology, punish wrongdoers, and promote equality and brotherhood among peoples*
> What are some duties of an American citizen? *to vote for Congress, celebrate diversity, and fight the enemies of the state*

Hobie, thankfully, was out. The pills I'd swallowed hadn't worked, and after two hours of twisting and flopping on my bed in a torturous, falling, half-dream state — thoughts flying, exhausted from my heart beating so fast, Boris's voice still running through my mind — I forced myself to get up, clear the mess strewn round my bedroom, and shower and shave: nicking myself in the process, since my upper lip was almost dentist-chair numb from the nosebleed I'd suffered. Then I made myself a pot of coffee, found a stale scone in the kitchen and forced myself to eat it, and was down in the shop and open for business by noon — just in time to intercept the mail lady in her plastic rain poncho (looking a bit alarmed, standing well back from rheumy-eyed me with my cut lip and my bloody

Kleenex), although as she was handing the mail over to me with latex-gloved hands I realized: what was the point? Reeve could write Hobie all he wanted — phone Interpol — who cared any more.

It was raining. Pedestrians huddled and scurrying. Rain pelting hard at the window, rain beading on the plastic garbage bags at the curb. There at the desk, in my musty armchair, I tried to anchor myself or at least take some kind of comfort in the faded silks and dimness of the shop, its bittersweet gloom like rainy dark classrooms of childhood, but the dopamine slam had dropped me hard and left me with the pre-tremblings of something that felt very like death — a sadness you felt in your stomach first, beating on the inside of the forehead, all the darkness I'd shut out roaring back in.

Tunnel vision. All those years I'd drifted along too glassy and insulated for any kind of reality to push through: a delirium which had spun me along on its slow, relaxed wave since childhood, high and lying on the shag carpet in Vegas laughing at the ceiling fan, only I wasn't laughing any more, Rip van Winkle wincing and holding his head on the ground about a hundred years too late.

What way was there to make it okay? None. In a way Boris had done me a favor by taking the thing — at least, I knew that was how most people would see it; I was off the hook; no one could blame me; the greater part of my problems had been solved at a stroke but while I knew that any sane person would be relieved to have the painting off their hands, yet I'd never felt quite so scorched with despair, self-hatred, shame.

Warm weary shop. I could not stay still; I stood up and sat down, walked to the window and back again. Everything was sodden with horror. A bisque Pulcinella eyed me with spite. Even the furniture looked sickly and disproportionate. How could I have believed myself a better person, a wiser person, a more elevated and valuable and worthy-of-living person on the basis of my secret uptown? Yet I had. The painting had made me feel less mortal, less ordinary. It was support and vindication; it was sustenance and sum. It was the keystone that had held the whole cathedral up. And it was awful to learn, by having it so suddenly vanish from under me, that all my adult life I'd been privately sustained by that great, hidden, savage joy: the conviction that my whole life was balanced atop a secret that might at any moment blow it apart.

xi.

WHEN HOBIE GOT HOME, around two, he walked in off the street with a jingle of bells like a customer.

"Well, that was certainly a surprise last night." He was pink-cheeked from the rain, shrugging off his raincoat and shaking the water off; he was dressed for the auction house, Windsor-knotted tie and one of the beautiful old suits. "Boris!" He'd done well at his auction, I could tell by his mood; though he tended not to go in with strong bids he knew what he wanted and every so often in a slow session, when no one was up against him, he made off with a pile of beauties. "I gather you two made quite a night of it?"

"Ah." I was hunched in a corner, sipping tea; my headache was ferocious.

"Funny to meet him after hearing so much about him. Like meeting a character in a book. I'd always pictured him as the Artful Dodger in *Oliver* — oh you know — the little boy, the urchin, what's the actor's name. Jack something. Ragged coat. Smear of dirt along the cheek."

"Believe me, he was dirty enough back then."

"Well you know, Dickens doesn't tell us what happened to the Dodger. Grew up to be a respectable businessman, who knows? And wasn't Popper out of his mind? I've never seen an animal so happy.

"Oh and yes —" half-turning, busy with his coat; he hadn't noticed me go still at Popper's name — "before I forget, Kitsey called."

I didn't answer; I couldn't. I hadn't thought of Popper even once.

"Late-ish — ten. Told her you'd run into Boris, you'd come by, you'd gone out, hope that was all right."

"Sure," I said, after an effortful pause, struggling to collect my thoughts which were galloping in several very bad directions at once.

"*What* must I remind you." Hobie put his finger to his lips. "I was given a charge. Let me think.

"I can't remember," he said after a small start, shaking his head. "You'll have to phone her. Dinner tonight, I know, at someone's house. Dinner at eight! That I remember. But I can't remember where."

"The Longstreets," I said, my heart plunging.

"That sounds right. Anyhow, Boris! Great fun — great charmer — how long's he in town for? How long's he here for?" he repeated amiably when I didn't answer — he couldn't see my face, staring out horrified into the street. "We should have him over for dinner, don't you think? Why don't you ask him to give us a couple of nights when he's free? That is, if you like," he said, when I didn't reply. "Up to you. Let me know."

xii.

ABOUT TWO HOURS LATER—exhausted, eyes streaming with pain from my headache—I was still frantically wondering how to get Popper back while simultaneously inventing, and rejecting, explanations for his absence. I left him tied in front of a store? Someone had snatched him? An obvious lie: quite apart from the fact that it was pouring rain, Popper was so old and cranky on the leash I could hardly drag him down to the fire hydrant. Groomer? Popper's groomer, a needy-seeming old lady named Cecelia who worked out of her apartment, always had him back by three. Vet? Quite apart from the fact that Popper wasn't sick (and why wouldn't I have mentioned it if he was?) Popper went to the same vet that Hobie had known since the days of Welty and Chessie. Dr. McDermott's office was right down the street. Why would I have taken him anywhere else?

I groaned, got up, walked to the window. Again and again I ran against the same dead end, Hobie walking in befuddled, as he was bound to do in an hour or two, looking around the store: "Where's Popper? Have you seen him?" And that was it: infinite loop; no alt-tab out. You could force close, shut down the computer, start all over and run it again, and the game would still lock up and freeze at the same place. "Where's Popper?" No cheat code. Game over. There was no way past that moment.

The ragged sheets of rain had slowed to a drizzle, shining sidewalks and water dripping from the awnings, and everyone on the street seemed to have seized the moment to throw on a raincoat and dash out to the corner with the dog: dogs everywhere I looked, galumphing sheepdog, black standard poodle, terrier mutts, retriever mutts, an elderly French bulldog and a self-satisfied pair of dachshunds with their chins in the air, prissing in tandem across the street. In agitation I went back to my chair, sat down, picked up the Christie's house sale catalogue and began to leaf through it in a rattled way: horrible modernist watercolors, two thousand dollars for an ugly Victorian bronze of two buffalos fighting, absurd.

What was I going to tell Hobie? Popper was old and deaf, and some-times he fell asleep in out-of-the-way places where he didn't hear right away when we called, but soon enough it would be time for his dinner and I would hear Hobie walking around upstairs, looking for him behind the sofa and in Pippa's bedroom and all his usual places. "Popsky? Here, boy! Dinnertime!" Could I feign ignorance? Pretend to search the house too? scratch my head in puzzlement? Mysterious disappearance? Bermuda Triangle? I'd returned, with sinking heart, to the groomer idea when the shop bell jingled.

"I started to keep him."

Popper—damp, but otherwise looking none the worse for his adventure—stiffened his legs rather formally as Boris set him down on the floor and then paddled over to me, holding his head up so that I might scratch him under the chin.

"He did not miss you one bit," said Boris. "We had a very nice day together."

"What'd you do?" I said, after a long silence, because I couldn't think of anything else to say.

"Sleeped, mostly. Gyuri dropped us off—" he scrubbed his darkened eyes, and yawned—"and we had a very nice nap together, the two of us. You know—how he used to curl up? Like a fur hat on my head?" Popper had never liked to sleep with his chin on my head like that—only with Boris. "Then—we woke up, and I had a shower and I took him for a walk—not far, he did not want to go far—and I made some phone calls and we ate a bacon sandwich and drove back in. Look, I am sorry!" he said impulsively when I didn't answer, running his hand through his rumpled hair. "Really. And I am going to make it right again, and good, I will."

The silence between us was crushing.

"Did you have fun last night anyway? *I* had fun. Big night out! Not feeling so hot this morning, though. Please say something," he blurted when I didn't reply. "I have been feeling very very bad about this all day."

Popper had snuffled across the room to his water dish. Peacefully, he began to drink. For a long time there was no sound except his monoto-nous lapping and slurping.

"Really, Theo—" hand to heart—"I feel terrible. My feelings—my shame—I have no words for," he said, more gravely, when still I did not answer. "And yes, I'll admit it, part of me asks myself, 'why did you wreck everything, Boris, why did you open your big mouth.' But how could I lie and sneak? You'll give me that, at least?" he said, rubbing his hands, agitatedly. "I am not cowardly. I told you. I admitted it. I didn't want you to worry, not knowing what was going on. And I am going to make it up to you, somehow, I promise."

"Why—" Hobie was busy downstairs with the vacuum but I lowered my voice all the same, the same angry whisper when Xandra was downstairs and we didn't want her to hear us quarreling—"why—"

"Why what?"

"Why the hell did you take it?"

Boris blinked, a bit self-righteously. "Because you have Jewish Mafiya coming to your house, is why!"

"No, that's not why."

Boris sighed. "Well, is partly why—a little. Was it safe at your house? No! And not at school either. Got my old school book, wrapped it in newspaper and taped it same fatness—"

"I asked *why* did you take it."

"What can I say. I am thief."

Popper was still noisily slurping up the water. With exasperation I wondered if Boris had thought to put a bowl down for him in their so-nice day out.

"And—" lightly he shrugged—"I wanted it. Yes. Who would not?"

"Wanted it why? For money?" I said, when he didn't answer.

Boris made a face. "Of course not. Can't sell something like that. Although—must admit—one time I was in trouble, four-five years ago, I almost sold it outright, low low price, giveaway almost, just to be rid of it. Glad I did not. I was in a jam and I needed cash. But—" sniffing hard, wiping his nose—"trying to sell piece like that is the quickest way to get caught. You know that yourself. As negotiable instrument—different story! They hold it as collateral—they front you the goods. You sell the goods, whatever, return with the capital, give them their cut, picture is returned to you, game over. Understand?"

I said nothing, began to leaf through the Christie's catalogue again, which was still lying open on my desk.

"You know what they say." His voice both sad and cajoling. " 'Chance makes the thief.' Who knows that better than you? I went in your locker looking for lunch money and I thought: what? Hello? What's this? It was easy to slip it out and hide it. And then I took my old workbook to Kotku's shop class, same size, same thickness—same tape and everything! Kotku helped me do it. I didn't tell her why I was doing it though. You couldn't really tell Kotku things like that."

"I still can't believe you stole it."

"Look. Am not going to make excuses. I took it. But—" he smiled winningly—"am I dishonest? Did I lie about it?"

"Yes," I said, after a disbelieving pause. "Yes, you did lie about it."

"You never asked me straight out! If you did, I would have told you!"

"Boris, that's bullshit. You lied."

"Well, am not lying now," said Boris, looking around resignedly. "I thought you would have found out by now! Years ago! I thought that you knew it was me!"

I wandered away, to the stairs, trailed by Popchik; Hobie had shut the vacuum cleaner off, leaving a glaring silence, and I didn't want him to hear us.

"I am not too clear—" Boris blew his nose sloppily, inspected the contents of the Kleenex, winced—"but am fairly sure it is in Europe somewhere." He wadded the Kleenex and stuffed it in his pocket. "Genoa, outside chance. But my best guess is Belgium or Germany. Holland, maybe. They will be able to negotiate with it better because people are more impressed with it over there."

"That doesn't really narrow it down a lot."

"Well, listen! Be glad it is not in South America! Because then, I guarantee, no chance you would see it again."

"I thought you said it was gone."

"I am not saying anything except I think I may be able to learn where it is. *May.* That is very different from knowing how to get it back. I have not dealt with these people before at all."

"What people?"

Boris, uneasily, remained silent, casting his eyes about on the floor: iron bulldog figurines, stacked books, many little carpets.

"He doesn't pee on the antiquities?" he inquired, nodding at Popchik. "All this nice furniture?"

"Nope."

"He used to go all the time in your house. Your whole carpet down-stairs smelled like pee. I think maybe because Xandra was not so good about taking him out before we got there."

"What people?"

"Huh?"

"What people have you not dealt with."

"It's complicated. I will explain to you if you want," he added hastily, "only I think we are both tired and now is not the time. But I am going to make a few calls and tell you what I find, right? And when I do, I will come back and tell you, promise. By the way —" tapping his upper lip with his finger.

"What?" I said, startled.

"Spot there. Under your nose."

"I cut myself shaving."

"Oh." Standing there, he looked uncertain, as if he were on the verge of rushing in with some much more heated apology or outburst, but the silence that hung between us had a decidedly conclusive air, and he shoved his hands in his pockets. "Well."

"Well."

"See you later, then."

"Sure." But when he walked out the door, and I stood at the window and watched him duck the drips from the awning and saunter away — his gait loosening and lightening as soon as he thought he was out of my view — I felt there was a pretty good chance it was the last I'd see of him.

xiii.

GIVEN HOW I FELT, which was near death basically, suffering from an ugly migrainous headache and engulfed with such misery I could barely see, there was little point keeping the shop open. So though the sun had come out and people were appearing on the street, I turned around the "Closed" sign and — with Popper trundling anxiously behind me — I dragged myself upstairs, half-sick with the pain hammering behind my eyes, to pass out for a few hours before dinner.

Kitsey and I were to meet at her mother's apartment at 7:45 before heading over to the Longstreets', but I arrived a little early — partly because I wanted to see her on her own for a few minutes before we went to dinner; partly because I had something for Mrs. Barbour — a rare-ish exhibition catalogue I'd found for her in one of Hobie's estate lots, *Printmaking in the Age of Rembrandt.*

"No, no," said Etta when I went to the kitchen to ask her to knock on the door for me, "she's up and about. I took her some tea not fifteen minutes ago."

What "up and about" meant, for Mrs. Barbour, was pyjamas and puppy-chewed slippers with what looked like an old opera coat thrown over. "Oh, Theo!" she said, her face opening with a touching, unguarded plainness that made me think of Andy on the rare occasions when he was actually pleased about something — such as his Nagler 22mm telescopic eyepiece arriving in the mail or his happy discovery of the LARP (Live Action Role Play) porn site, featuring busty sword-wielding lasses getting it on with knights and wizards and so forth. "What a dear, dear duck you are!"

"You don't have it, I hope?"

"No —" leafing through it delightedly — "how perfect of you! You'll never, ever believe it but I saw this show in Boston when I was in college."

"That must have been some show," I said, settling back into an armchair. I was feeling much happier than, an hour previous, I would have thought possible. Sick over the painting, sick with headache, despairing at the thought of dinner with the Longstreets, wondering how the hell I was going to make it through an evening of hot crab dip and Forrest delivering his views on the economy when all I basically wanted to do was blow my brains out, I'd tried to call Kitsey, with the intention of begging her to plead illness with me so we could skive off and spend the evening at her apartment, in bed. But — as often happened, infuriatingly, on Kitsey's days out — my calls had gone unreturned, my texts and emails unanswered, my messages clicking straight through to voice mail — "I need to get a new phone," she'd said fretfully, when I'd complained of these all-too-frequent communication blackouts, "there's something wrong with it" — and though I'd asked her several times to walk in off the street with me to the Apple store and get a new one, she always had an excuse: lines too long, had to be somewhere, wasn't in the mood, hungry, thirsty, needed to pee, couldn't we do it another time?

Sitting on the side of my bed with eyes closed, annoyed at not being able to reach her (as I never seemed to be able to do, when I really needed to), I'd thought of calling Forrest and telling him I was ill. But as bad as I felt I still wanted to see her, even if it was only across the table at dinner with people I didn't like. Hence — to force myself out of bed, uptown, and through the most deathly part of the evening — I'd swallowed what had been, for me, in the old days, a mild dose of opiates. But though it hadn't knocked my headache out it had put me in a surprisingly good mood. I hadn't felt so well in months.

"You and Kitsey are dining out tonight?" said Mrs. Barbour, who was still happily leafing through the catalogue I'd brought. "Forrest Longstreet?"

"That's right."

"He was in your class with Andy, wasn't he?"

"Yes he was."

"He wasn't one of those boys who was so awful?"

"Well —" Euphoria had made me generous. "Not really." Forrest, oaf-ish and slow on the draw ("Sir, are trees considered plants?") had never been intelligent enough to persecute Andy and me in any kind of focused or resourceful way. "But, yes, you're right, he was part of that whole group, you know, Temple and Tharp and Cavanaugh and Scheffernan."

"Yes. Temple. I certainly remember *him*. And the Cable boy."

"What?" I said, mildly surprised.

"*He's* certainly turned out badly," she said without looking up from the catalogue. "Living on credit... can't hold a job and also some trouble with the law, I hear. Wrote some bad checks, apparently his mother had a hard time keeping the people from pressing charges. And Win Temple," she said, looking up, before I could explain that Cable hadn't really been a part of that aggressive-jock crowd. "He was the one who knocked Andy's head against the wall in the showers."

"Yes, that was him." What I mainly remembered about the showers was not so much Andy getting concussed on the tile as Scheffernan and Cavanaugh wrestling me down and trying to shove a stick of deodorant up my ass.

Mrs. Barbour — wrapped delicately in her coat, shawl over her lap as if riding in a sleigh to a Christmas party — was still leafing through her book. "Do you know what that Temple boy said?"

"Sorry?"

"The Temple boy." Her eyes were on the book; her voice was bright, as if she were speaking to a stranger at a cocktail party. "What his excuse was. When they asked why he knocked Andy unconscious."

"No, I don't know."

"He said, 'Because that kid gets on my nerves.' He's an attorney now, they tell me, I certainly hope he holds his temper a bit better in the courtroom."

"Win wasn't the worst of them," I said, after a languid pause. "Not by a long shot. Now Cavanaugh and Scheffernan—"

"The mother wasn't even listening. Texting away on her cell phone. Some terribly urgent matter with a client."

I looked at the cuff of my shirt. I'd taken care to change into a fresh one after work—if there was one thing my opiated years had taught me (not to mention my years of antiques fraud), it was that starched shirts and suits fresh from the cleaners' went a long, long way toward hiding a multitude of sins—but I'd been loopy and careless from the morphine tabs, drifting around my bedroom and humming to Elliott Smith as I dressed, *sunshine...been keeping me up for days*...and (I noticed) one of my cuffs wasn't done up properly. Moreover the knots I'd chosen weren't even a matched pair: one purple, the other blue.

"We could have sued," said Mrs. Barbour absent-mindedly. "I don't know why we didn't. Chance said he thought it would make things harder for Andy at school."

"Well—" There was no way I could inconspicuously do up my cuff again. It would have to wait for the cab. "That thing in the shower was really Scheffernan's fault."

"Yes, that's what Andy said, and the Temple boy too, but as for the actual blow, the concussion, there was no *question*—"

"Scheffernan was a sneaky guy. He pushed Andy into Temple— Scheffernan was across the locker room and laughing his head off with Cavanaugh and those guys by the time the fight started."

"Well, I don't know about that, but David—" David was Scheffernan's first name—"he wasn't a bit like the others, always perfectly nice, so polite, we had him over here a good deal, and always so good about including Andy. You know how a lot of the children were, with birthday parties—"

"Yes, but Scheffernan had it in for Andy, always. Because Scheffernan's mother was always forcing Andy down his throat. *Making* him ask Andy, *making* him come over here."

Mrs. Barbour sighed and set down her cup. The tea was jasmine; I could smell it where I sat.

"Well, goodness knows, you knew Andy better than I did," she said unexpectedly, drawing the embroidered collar of her wrap closer. "I never saw him for who he was and in some ways he was my favorite child. I wish I hadn't been always trying to make him into someone else. Certainly you were able to accept him on his own terms, more than his father and I or God knows his brother. Look," she said, in much the same tone, in the rather chilling silence that followed this. She was still leafing through the book. "Here's St. Peter. Turning the little children away from Christ."

Obediently I got up and circled behind. I knew the work, one of the great, stormy drypoints at the Morgan, the Hundred Guilder Print as it was called: the price that Rembrandt himself, according to legend, had been forced to pay to buy it back.

"He's so particular, Rembrandt. Even his religious subjects — it's as if the saints came down to model for him in the life. These two St. Peters —" she gestured to her own little pen-and-ink on the wall — "completely different works and years apart but the identical man, body and soul, you could pick him out of a line-up, couldn't you? That balding head. Same face — dutiful, earnest. Goodness written all over him and yet always that twitch of worry and disquiet. That subtle shade of the betrayer."

Though she was still gazing down at the book I found myself looking at the silver-framed photo of Andy and his father on the table beside us. It was only a snapshot but for a sense of foreshadowing, of transience and doom, no master of Dutch genre painting could have set up the composition more skillfully. Andy and Mr. Barbour against a dark background, snuffed candles in the wall sconces, Mr. Barbour's hand on a model ship. The effect could have been no more allegorical, or chilling, if he'd had his hand on a skull. Above, in lieu of the hourglass beloved by the Dutch vanitas painters, a stark and slightly sinister clock with Roman numerals. Black hands: five minutes to twelve. Time running out.

"Mommy —" It was Platt, barging in, stopping cold to see me.

"Don't bother knocking dear," said Mrs. Barbour without glancing up from her book, "you're always welcome."

"I—" Platt goggled at me. "Kitsey." He seemed rattled. He dug his hands in the bellows pockets of his field coat. "She's been held up," he said to his mother.

Mrs. Barbour looked startled. "Oh," she said. They looked at each other and some unspoken something seemed to pass between them.

"Held up?" I asked amiably, looking between them. "Where?"

There was no answer to this. Platt—gaze fixed on his mother—opened his mouth and shut it. Rather smoothly, Mrs. Barbour put her book aside and said, without looking at me: "Well, you know, I slightly think she's out there playing golf today."

"Really?" I said, mildly surprised. "Isn't it bad weather for that?"

"There's traffic," Platt said eagerly, with a glance at his mother. "She's stuck. The expressway is a mess. She's phoned Forrest," he said, turning to me, "they're holding dinner."

"Maybe," said Mrs. Barbour, thoughtfully, after a pause, "maybe you and Theo should go out and have a drink? Yes," she said decisively, to Platt, as if the matter had been settled, folding her hands. "I think that's an excellent idea. You two go out and get a drink. And you!" she said, turning to me with a smile. "What an angel you are! Thank you so much for my book," she said, reaching to clasp my hand. "The most wonderful present in the world."

"But—"

"Yes?"

"Won't she need to come back here and freshen up?" I said, after a slightly confused pause.

"Sorry?" Both of them were looking at me.

"If she's been playing golf? Won't she need to change? She won't want to go to Forrest's in her golfing clothes," I added, looking back and forth between the two of them, and then—when neither of them replied—"I don't mind waiting here."

Thoughtfully, Mrs. Barbour pursed her lips, with heavy-looking eyes—and all at once, I got it. She was tired. She hadn't been expecting to have to sit around and entertain me, only she was too polite to say so.

"Although," I said, standing up, self-consciously, "it is getting on, I could use a cocktail—"

Just then, the phone in my pocket, which had been silent all day, chimed loudly: incoming text. Clumsily—I was so exhausted I could hardly figure out where my own pocket was—I fumbled for it.

Sure enough, it was Kitsey, jingling with emoji. ♥♥ Hi Popsy ♥ runningan hour late! ⊗!✗✐✿✲❦!!! Hope I caught you! Forrest & Celia holding dinner, meet you there 9pm, love you mostest! Kits ♥✗♥✗♥✗♥

xiv.

FIVE OR SIX DAYS later, I still had not fully recovered from my evening with Boris — partly because I was busy with clients, auctions to go to, estates to look at, and partly because I had grueling events with Kitsey nearly every night: holiday parties, black-tie dinner, *Pelléas et Mélisande* at the Met, up by six every morning and bed well after midnight, one evening out until two a.m., scarcely a moment to myself and (even worse) scarcely a moment alone with her, which normally would have driven me crazy but in the circumstances kept me so submerged and embattled with fatigue that I didn't have much time to think.

All week long, I'd been looking forward to Kitsey's Tuesday with her girlfriends — not because I didn't want to see her, but because Hobie had a dinner out and I was looking forward to being on my own, eating some leftovers from the fridge and going to bed early. But at closing time, seven p.m., I still had some catching-up to do in the shop. A decorator, miraculously, had shown up to inquire about some expensive, out of fashion, and impossible-to-sell pewter that had been gathering dust atop a cabinet since Welty's day. Pewter wasn't something I knew much about, and I was looking for the article I wanted in a back number of *Antiques* when Boris dashed up from the curb and knocked on the glass door, not five minutes after I'd locked up for the day. It was pelting rain; in the ragged downpour he was a shadow in an overcoat, unrecognizable, but the cadence of his rap was distinct from the old days, when he would circle around to the patio at my dad's house and tap briskly for me to let him in.

He ducked in and shook himself violently so the water went flying. "You want to ride with me uptown?" he said without preamble.

"I'm busy."

"Yes?" he said, in a voice at once so affectionate, and exasperated, and transparently, childishly hurt, that I turned from my book shelf. "And won't you ask why? I think you might want to come."

"Uptown where?"

"I am going to talk to some people."

"And that would be about—?"

"Yes," he said brightly, sniffling and wiping his nose. "Exactly. You don't have to come, I was going to bring my boy Toly, but I thought for several reasons it might be good if you wanted to be there also—Popchyk, yes yes!" he said, stooping to pick up the dog, who had trundled up to greet him. "Glad to see you too! He likes bacon," he said to me, scratching Popper behind the ears and rubbing his own nose at the back of Popper's neck. "Do you ever cook bacon for him? Enjoys the bread too, when is soaked with grease."

"Talk to who? Who is this?"

Boris pushed the dripping hair out of his face. "Guy I know. Named Horst. Old friend of Myriam's. He got stung on this deal too—honest, I do not think he can help us, but Myriam suggested might not hurt to talk to him again? and I think maybe she is right about that."

XV.

ON THE WAY UPTOWN, in the back of the town car, rain pounding so hard that Gyuri had to shout for us to hear him ("What a dog's weather!") Boris filled me in quietly about Horst. "Sad sad story. He is German. Interesting guy, very intelligent and sensitive. Important family too...he explained to me once but I forgot. His dad was part American and left him a load of money but when his mother remarried—" here he named a world-famous industrial name, with a dark old Nazi echo. "*Millions.* I mean you can't believe how much money these people have. They are rolling in it. Money out the ass."

"Yep, that's a sad story, all right."

"Well—Horst is a bad junkie. You know me—" philosophical shrug—"I don't judge or condemn. Do what you like, I don't care! But Horst—very sad case. He fell in love with this girl who was on it and she got him on it too. Took him for everything, and when the money ran out, she left. Horst's family—they have disowned him many years ago. And still he eats his heart out for this awful rotten girl. Girl, I say—she must be nearly forty. Ulrika her name is. Every time Horst gets a little money— she comes back for a while. Then she leaves him again."

"What does he have to do with it?"

"Horst's associate Sascha set up things with this deal. I meet the guy—he seems okay—what do I know? Horst told me that he had never worked with Sascha's man in person, but I was in a hurry and I didn't go into it the way I should and—" he threw up his arms—"poof! Myriam was right—she is always right—I should have listened to her."

Water streamed down the windows, quicksilver heavy, sealing us into the car, lights winking and melting around us in a roar that reminded me of when Boris and I used to ride in the back of the Lexus in Vegas when my dad went through the car wash.

"Horst is usually a bit fussy about who he does business with, so I thought it would be okay. But—he is very restrained, you know? 'Unusual' is what he said. 'Unconventional.' Well what is that supposed to mean? Then when I get down there—these people are crazy. I mean like shooting-guns-at-chickens crazy. And situations like this—you want it calm and quiet! It was like, have they seen too much TV or something? like, this is how to act—? normally in this type situation everyone is very very polite, hush-hush, very peaceful! Myriam said—and she was right—forget about the guns! What kind of crazy thing is this for these people to keep chickens in Miami? Even a little thing like that—this is Jacuzzi neighborhood, tennis courts, you understand me—who keeps chickens? You don't want a neighbor phoning in complaint because of chicken noise in the yard! But by that time—" he shrugged—"there I was. I was in. I told myself not to worry so much, but turned out I was right."

"What happened?"

"I don't really know. I got half the goods I was promised—rest coming in a week. That's not un-typical. But then they were arrested and I didn't get the other half and I didn't get the picture. Horst—well, Horst would like to find it too, he is out some big green as well. Anyway I am hoping he has a bit more information than when we spoke last."

xvi.

GYURI LEFT US OUT in the Sixties, not far at all from the Barbours'. "This is the place?" I said, shaking the rain off Hobie's umbrella. We were out in front of one of the big limestone townhouses off Fifth—black iron doors, massive lion's-head knockers.

"Yes—it's his father's place—his other family are trying to get him out legally but good luck with that, hah."

We were buzzed in, took a cage elevator up to the second floor. I could smell incense, weed, spaghetti sauce cooking. A lanky blonde woman—short-cropped hair and a serene small-eyed face like a camel's—opened the door. She was dressed like a sort of old-fashioned street urchin or newsboy: houndstooth trousers, ankle boots, dirty thermal shirt, suspenders. Perched on the tip of her nose were a pair of wire-rimmed Ben Franklin glasses.

Without saying a word she opened the door to us and walked off, leaving us alone in a dim, grimy, ballroom-sized salon which was like a derelict version of some high-society set from a Fred Astaire movie: high ceilings; crumbling plaster; grand piano; darkened chandelier with half the crystals broken or gone; sweeping Hollywood staircase littered with cigarette butts. Sufi chants droned low in the background: *Allāhu Allāhu Allāhu Haqq. Allāhu Allāhu Allāhu Haqq.* Someone had drawn on the wall, in charcoal, a series of life-sized nudes ascending the stairs like frames in a film; and there was very little furniture apart from a ratty futon and some chairs and tables that looked scavenged from the street. Empty picture frames on the wall, a ram's skull. On the television, an animated film flickered and sputtered with epileptic vim, windmilling geometrics intercut with letters and live-action racecar images. Apart from that, and the door where the blonde had disappeared, the only light came from a lamp which threw a sharp white circle on melted candles, computer cables, empty beer bottles and butane cans, oil pastels boxed and loose, many catalogues raisonnés, books in German and English including Nabokov's *Despair* and Heidegger's *Being and Time* with the cover torn off, sketch books, art books, ashtrays and burnt tinfoil, and a grubby-looking pillow where drowsed a gray tabby cat. Over the door, like a trophy from some Schwarzwald hunting lodge, a rack of antlers cast distorted shadows that spread and branched across the ceiling with a Nordic, wicked, fairy-tale feel.

Conversation in the next room. The windows were shrouded with tacked-up bedsheets just thin enough to let in a diffuse violet glow from the street. As I looked around, forms emerged from the dark and transformed with a dream strangeness: for one thing, the makeshift room divider—consisting of a carpet sagging tenement-style from the ceiling on fishing line—was on closer look a tapestry and a good one too, eighteenth century or older, the near twin of an Amiens I'd seen at auction with an estimate of forty thousand pounds. And not all the frames on the wall were empty. Some had paintings in them, and one of them—even in the poor light—looked like a Corot.

I was just about to step over for a look when a man who could have been anywhere between thirty and fifty appeared in the door: worn-looking, rangy, with straight sandy hair combed back from his face, in black punk jeans out at the knee and a grungy British commando sweater with an ill-fitting suit jacket over it.

"Hello," he said to me, quiet British voice with a faint German bite, "you must be Potter," and then, to Boris: "Glad you turned up. You two should stay and hang out. Candy and Niall are making dinner with Ulrika."

Movement behind the tapestry, at my feet, that made me step back quickly: swaddled shapes on the floor, sleeping bags, a homeless smell.

"Thanks, we can't stay," said Boris, who had picked up the cat and was scratching it behind the ears. "Have some of that wine though, thanks."

Without a word Horst passed his own glass over to Boris and then called into the next room in German. To me, he said: "You're a dealer, right?" In the glow of the television his pale pinned gull's eye shone hard and unblinking.

"Right," I said uneasily; and then: "Uh, thanks." Another woman—bob-haired and brunette, high black boots, skirt just short enough to show the black cat tattooed on one milky thigh—had appeared with a bottle and two glasses: one for Horst, one for me.

"*Danke* darling," said Horst. To Boris he said: "You gentlemen want to do up?"

"Not right now," said Boris, who had leaned forward to steal a kiss from the dark-haired woman as she was leaving. "Was wondering though. What do you hear from Sascha?"

"Sascha—" Horst sank down on the futon and lit a cigarette. With his ripped jeans and combat boots he was like a scuffed-up version of some below-the-title Hollywood character actor from the 1940s, some minor *mitteleuropäischer* known for playing tragic violinists and weary, cultivated refugees. "Ireland is where it seems to lead. Good news if you ask me."

"That doesn't sound right."

"Nor to me, but I've talked to people and so far it checks out." He spoke with all a junkie's arrhythmic quiet, off-beat, but without the slur. "So—soon we should know more, I hope."

"Friends of Niall's?"

"No. Niall says he never heard of them. But it's a start."

The wine was bad: supermarket Syrah. Because I did not want to be anywhere near the bodies on the floor I drifted over to inspect a group of artists' casts on a beat-up table: a male torso; a draped Venus leaning against a rock; a sandaled foot. In the poor light they looked like the ordinary plaster casts for sale at Pearl Paint — studio pieces for students to sketch from — but when I drew my finger across the top of the foot I felt the suppleness of marble, silky and grainless.

"Why would they go to Ireland with it?" Boris was saying restlessly. "What kind of collectors' market? I thought everyone tries to get pieces out of there, not in."

"Yes, but Sascha thinks he used the picture to clear a debt."

"So the guy has ties there?"

"Evidently."

"I find this difficult to believe."

"What, about the ties?"

"No, about the debt. This guy — he looks like he was stealing hubcaps off the street six months ago. "

Horst shrugged, faintly: sleepy eyes, seamed forehead. "Who knows. Not sure that's correct but certainly I'm not willing to trust to luck. Would I let my hand be cut off for it?" he said, lazily tapping an ash on the floor. "No."

Boris frowned into his wine glass. "He was amateur. Believe me. If you saw him yourself you would know."

"Yes but he likes to gamble, Sascha says."

"You don't think Sascha maybe knows more?"

"I think not." There was a remoteness in his manner, as if he was talking half to himself. " 'Wait and see.' This is what I hear. An unsatisfactory answer. Stinking from the top if you ask me. But as I say, we are not to the bottom of this yet."

"And when does Sascha get back to the city?" The half-light in the room sent me straight back to childhood, Vegas, like the obscure mood of a dream lingering after sleep: haze of cigarette smoke, dirty clothes on the floor, Boris's face white then blue in the flicker of the screen.

"Next week. I'll give you a ring. You can talk to him yourself then."

"Yes. But I think we should talk to him together."

"Yes. I think so too. We'll both be smarter, in future...this need not have happened...but in any case," said Horst, who was scratching his neck slowly, absent-mindedly, "you understand I'm wary of pushing him too hard."

"That is very convenient for Sascha."

"You have suspicions. Tell me."

"I think—" Boris cut his eyes at the doorway.

"Yes?"

"I think—" Boris lowered his voice—"you are being too easy on him. Yes yes—" putting up his hands—"I know. But—all very convenient for his guy to vanish, not a clue, he knows nothing!"

"Well, maybe," Horst said. He seemed disconnected and partly elsewhere, like an adult in the room with small children. "This is pressing on me—on all of us. I want to get to the bottom of this as much as you. Though for all we know his guy was a cop."

"No," said Boris resolutely. "He was not. He was not. I know it."

"Well—to be quite frank with you, I do not think so either, there is more to this than we yet know. Still, I'm hopeful." He'd taken a wooden box from the drafting table and was poking around in it. "Sure you gentlemen wouldn't like to get into a little something?"

I looked away. I would have liked nothing better. I would also have liked to see the Corot except I didn't want to walk around the bodies on the floor to do it. Across the room, I'd noticed several other paintings propped on the wainscoting: a still life, a couple of small landscapes.

"Go look, if you want." It was Horst. "The Lépine is fake. But the Claesz and the Berchem are for sale if you're interested."

Boris laughed and reached for one of Horst's cigarettes. "He's not in the market."

"No?" said Horst genially. "I can give him a good price on the pair. The seller needs to get rid of them."

I stepped in to look: still life, candle and half-empty wineglass. "Claesz-Heda?"

"No—Pieter. Although—" Horst put the box aside, then stood beside me and lifted the desk lamp on the cord, washing both paintings in a harsh, formal glare—"this bit—" traced mid-air with the curve of a finger—"the reflection of the flame here? and the edge of the table, the drapery? Could almost be Heda on a bad day."

"Beautiful piece."

"Yes. Beautiful of its type." Up close he smelled unwashed and raunchy, with a strong, dusty import-shop odor like the inside of a Chinese box. "A bit prosaic to the modern taste. The classicizing manner. Much too staged. Still, the Berchem is very good."

"Lot of fake Berchems out there," I said neutrally.

"Yes—" the light from the upheld lamp on the landscape painting was bluish, eerie—"but this is lovely...Italy, 1655.....the ochres beautiful, no? The Claesz not so good I think, very early, though the provenance is impeccable on both. Would be nice to keep them together...they have never been apart, these two. Father and son. Came down together in an old Dutch family, ended up in Austria after the war. Pieter Claesz..." Horst held the light higher. "Claesz was so uneven, honestly. Wonderful technique, wonderful surface, but something a bit off with this one, don't you agree? The composition doesn't hold together. Incoherent somehow. Also—" indicating with the flat of his thumb the too-bright shine coming off the canvas: overly varnished.

"I agree. And here—" tracing midair the ugly arc where an over-eager cleaning had scrubbed the paint down to the scumbling.

"Yes." His answering look was amiable and drowsy. "Quite correct. Acetone. Whoever did that should be shot. And yet a mid-level painting like this, in poor condition—even an anonymous work—is worth more than a masterpiece, that's the irony of it, worth more to *me,* anyway. Landscapes particularly. Very very easy to sell. Not too much attention from the authorities...difficult to recognize from a description...and still worth maybe a couple hundred thousand. Now, the Fabritius—" long, relaxed pause—"a different calibre altogether. The most remarkable work that's ever passed through my hands, and I can say that without question."

"Yes, and that is why we would like so much to get it back," grumbled Boris from the shadows.

"Completely extraordinary," continued Horst serenely. "A still life like this one—" he indicated the Claesz, with a slow wave (black-rimmed fingernails, scarred venous network on the back of his hand)—"well, so insistently a trompe l'oeil. Great technical skill, but overly refined. Obsessive exactitude. There's a deathlike quality. A very good reason they are called natures mortes, yes? But the Fabritius..."—loose-kneed backstep—"I know the theory of *The Goldfinch,* I'm well familiar with it, people call it trompe l'oeil and indeed it can strike the eye that way from afar. But I don't care what the art historians say. True: there are passages worked like a trompe l'oeil...the wall and the perch, gleam of light on brass, and then...the feathered breast, most creaturely. Fluff and down. Soft, soft. Claesz would carry that finish and exactitude down to the death—a painter like van Hoogstraten would carry it even farther, to the last nail of the coffin. But Fabritius...he's making a pun on the genre...a masterly riposte to the whole idea of trompe l'oeil...because in other passages of the work—the head? the wing?—not creaturely or literal in the slightest, he takes the image apart very deliberately to show us how he painted it. Daubs and patches, very shaped and hand-worked, the neckline especially, a solid piece of paint, very abstract. Which is what makes him a genius less of his time than our own. There's a doubleness. You see the mark, you see the paint for the paint, and also the living bird."

"Yes, well," growled Boris, in the dark beyond the spotlight, snapping his cigarette lighter shut, "if no paint, would be nothing to see."

"Precisely." Horst turned, his face cut by shadow. "It's a joke, the Fabritius. It has a joke at its heart. And that's what all the very greatest masters do. Rembrandt. Velázquez. Late Titian. They make jokes. They amuse themselves. They build up the illusion, the trick—but, step closer? it falls apart into brushstrokes. Abstract, unearthly. A different and much deeper sort of beauty altogether. The thing and yet not the thing. I should say that that one tiny painting puts Fabritius in the rank of the greatest painters who ever lived. And with *The Goldfinch*? He performs his miracle in such a bijou space. Although I admit, I was surprised—" turning to look at me—"when I held it in my hands the first time? The weight of it?"

"Yes—" I couldn't help feeling gratified, obscurely, that he'd noted this detail, oddly important to me, with its own network of childhood dreams and associations, an emotional chord—"the board is thicker than you'd think. There's a heft to it."

"Heft. Quite. The very word. And the background—much less yellow than when I saw it as a boy. The painting underwent a cleaning—early nineties I believe. Post-conservation, there's more light."

"Hard to say. I've got nothing to compare it to."

"Well," said Horst. The smoke from Boris's cigarette, threading in from the dark where he sat, gave the floodlit circle where we stood the midnight feel of a cabaret stage. "I may be wrong. I was a boy of twelve or so when I saw it for the first time."

"Yes, I was about that age when I first saw it too."

"Well," said Horst, with resignation, scratching an eyebrow — dime-sized bruises on the backs of his hands — "that was the only time my father ever took me with him on a business trip, that time at The Hague. Ice cold boardrooms. Not a leaf stirring. On our afternoon I wanted to go to Drievliet, the fun park, but he took me to the Mauritshuis instead. And — great museum, many great paintings, but the only painting I remember seeing is your finch. A painting that appeals to a child, yes? Der Distelfink. That is how I knew it first, by its German name."

"Yah, yah, yah," said Boris from the darkness, in a bored voice. "This is like the education channel on the television."

"Do you deal any modern art at all?" I said, in the silence that followed.

"Well —" Horst fixed me with his drained, wintry eye; *deal* wasn't quite the correct verb, he seemed amused at my choice of words — "sometimes. Had a Kurt Schwitters not long ago — Stanton Macdonald-Wright — do you know him? Lovely painter. It depends a lot what comes my way. Quite honestly — do you ever deal in paintings at all?"

"Very seldom. The art dealers get there before I do."

"That is unfortunate. Portable is what matters in my business. There are a lot of mid-level pieces I could sell on the clean if I had paper that looked good."

Spit of garlic; pans clashing in the kitchen; faint Moroccan-souk drift of urine and incense. On and on flatlining, the Sufi drone, wafting and spiraling around us in the dark, ceaseless chants to the Divine.

"Or this Lépine. Quite a good forgery. There's this fellow — Canadian, quite amusing, you'd like him — does them to order. Pollocks, Modiglianis — happy to introduce you, if you'd like. Not much money in them for me, although there's a fortune to be made if one of them turned up in just the right estate." Then, smoothly, in the silence that followed: "Of older works I see a lot of Italian, but my preferences — they incline to the North as you can see. Now — this Berchem is a very fine example for what it is but of course these Italianate landscapes with the broken columns and the simple milk-maids don't so much suit the modern taste, do they? I much prefer the van Goyen there. Sadly not for sale."

"Van Goyen? I would have sworn that was a Corot."

"From here, yes, you might." He was pleased at the comparison. "Very similar painters — Vincent himself remarked it — you know that letter?

'The Corot of the Dutch'? Same tenderness of mist, that openness in fog, do you know what I mean?"

"Where—" I'd been about to ask the typical dealer's question, *where did you get it,* before catching myself.

"Marvelous painter. Very prolific. And this is a particularly beautiful example," he said, with all a collector's pride. "Many amusing details up close—tiny hunter, barking dog. Also—quite typical—signed on the stern of the boat. Quite charming. If you don't mind—" indicating, with a nod, the bodies behind the tapestry. "Go over. You won't disturb them."

"No, but—"

"No—" holding up a hand—"I understand perfectly. Shall I bring it to you?"

"Yes, I'd love to see it."

"I must say, I've grown so fond of it, I'll hate to see it go. He dealt paintings himself, van Goyen. A lot of the Dutch masters did. Jan Steen. Vermeer. Rembrandt. But Jan van Goyen—" he smiled—"was like our friend Boris here. A hand in everything. Paintings, real estate, tulip futures."

Boris, in the dark, made a disgruntled noise at this and seemed about to say something when all of a sudden a scrawny wild-haired boy of maybe twenty-two, with an old fashioned mercury thermometer sticking out of his mouth, came lurching out of the kitchen, shielding his eyes with his hand against the upheld lamp. He was wearing a weird, womanish, chunky knit cardigan that came almost to his knees like a bathrobe; he looked ill and disoriented, his sleeve was up, he was rubbing the inside of his forearm with two fingers and then the next thing I knew his knees went sideways and he'd hit the floor, the thermometer skittering out with a glassy noise on the parquet, unbroken.

"What...?" said Boris, stabbing out his cigarette, standing up, the cat darting from his lap into the shadows. Horst—frowning—set the lamp on the floor, light swinging crazily on walls and ceiling. "Ach," he said fretfully, brushing the hair from his eyes, dropping to his knees to look the young man over. "Get back," he said in an annoyed voice to the women who had appeared in the door, along with a cold, dark-haired, attentive-looking bruiser and a couple of glassy prep-school boys, no more than sixteen—and then, when they all still stood staring—flicked out a hand. "In the kitchen with you! Ulrika," he said to the blonde, *"halt sie zurück."*

The tapestry was stirring; behind it, blanket-wrapped huddles, sleepy voices: *eh? was ist los?*

"Ruhe, schlaft weiter," called the blonde, before turning to Horst and beginning to speak urgently in rapid-fire German.

Yawns; groans; farther back, a bundle sitting up, groggy American whine: "Huh? Klaus? What'd she say?"

"Shut up baby and go back *schlafen.*"

Boris had picked up his coat and was shouldering it on. "Potter," he said and then again, when I did not answer, staring horrified at the floor, where the boy was breathing in gurgles: "Potter." Catching my arm. "Come on, let's go."

"Yes, sorry. We'll have to talk later. *Schiesse,*" said Horst regretfully, shaking the boy's limp shoulder, with the tone of a parent making a not-particularly-convincing show of scolding a child. *"Dummer Wichser! Dummkopf!* How much did he take, Niall?" he said to the bruiser who had reappeared in the door and was looking on with a critical eye.

"Fuck if I know," said the Irishman, with an ominous sideways pop of his head.

"Come on Potter," said Boris, catching my arm. Horst had his ear to the boy's chest and the blonde, who had returned, had dropped to her knees beside him and was checking his airway.

As they consulted urgently in German, more noise and movement behind the Amiens, which billowed out suddenly: faded blossoms, a fête champêtre, prodigal nymphs disporting themselves amidst fountain and vine. I was staring at a satyr peeping at them slyly from behind a tree when, unexpectedly—something against my leg—I started back violently as a hand swiped from underneath and clutched my trouser cuff. From the floor, one of the dirty bundles—swollen red face just visible from under the tapestry—inquired of me in a sleepy gallant voice: "He's a margrave, my dear, did you know that?"

I pulled my trouser leg free and stepped back. The boy on the floor was rolling his head a bit and making sounds like he was drowning.

"Potter." Boris had gathered up my coat and was practically stuffing it in my face. "Come on! Let's go! *Ciao,*" he called into the kitchen with a lift of his chin (pretty dark head appearing in the doorway, a fluttering hand: *bye, Boris! Bye!*) as he pushed me ahead of him and ducked behind me out the door. *"Ciao,* Horst!" he said, making a *call me later* gesture, hand to ear.

"*Tschau* Boris! Sorry about this! We'll talk soon! Up," said Horst, as the Irishman came up and grabbed the boy's other arm from underneath; together they hoisted him up, feet limp and toes dragging and—amidst hurried activity in the doorway, the two young teenagers scrambling back in alarm—hauled him into the lighted doorway of the next room, where Boris's brunette was drawing up a syringe of something from a tiny glass bottle.

xvii.

GOING DOWN IN THE cage elevator we were suddenly encased in stillness: grinding of gears, creaking of pulleys.

Outside, the weather had cleared. "Come on," Boris said to me—nervously glancing up the street—he had his phone out of his coat pocket—"let's cross, come on—"

"What," I said—we just had the light, if we hurried—"are you calling 911?"

"No no," said Boris distractedly, wiping his nose, looking around, "I don't want to stand here waiting for the car, I'm calling him to pick us up other side of the park. We'll walk across. Sometimes some of these kids push shots that are a little too big," he said, when he saw me looking anxiously back in the direction of the townhouse. "Don't worry. He'll be fine."

"He didn't look fine."

"No, but he was breathing and Horst has Narcan. That'll bring him right out of it. Like magic, have you ever seen it? Throws you right in withdrawal. You feel like shit, but you live."

"They should take him to the ER."

"Why?" said Boris reasonably. "What will the emergency people do? Give Narcan, that's what. Horst can give it to him quicker than they can. And yes—he will come to puking himself and feeling like stabbed through the head, but better there than in ambulance, BOOM, shirt cut open, mask jammed down on him, peoples slapping his face to wake him, laws involved, everyone very harsh and judgmental—believe me, Narcan, very very violent experience, you feel bad enough when you come round without being in hospital, bright lights and everyone very disapproving and hostile, treating you like shit, 'drug addict,' 'overdose,' all these nasty looks, maybe not letting you go home when you want, psych ward maybe, social worker marching in to give you the big 'So Much to Live For' talk and maybe on top of it all, nice visit from the cops — Hang on," he said, "one moment please," and started talking in Ukrainian on the phone.

Darkness. Under the foggy corona of the street lamps, park benches slick with rain, drip drip drip, trees sodden and black. Sopping footpaths deep with leaves, a few solitary office workers hurrying home. Boris — head down, hands thrust in pockets, staring at the ground — had got off his call and was muttering to himself.

"Sorry, what?" I said, looking at him sideways.

Boris compressed his lips, tossed his head. "Ulrika," he said darkly. "That bitch. That was her that answered the door."

I wiped my brow. I felt jittery and sick and had broken out in a cold sweat. "How do you know these people?"

Boris shrugged. "Horst?" he said, kicking up a shower of leaves. "We know each other from years back. I know Myriam through him — I am grateful to him for introducing us."

"And — ?"

"What?"

"On the floor back there??"

"Him? That fell?" Boris made his old *who knows?* face. "They'll take care of him, don't worry. It happens. They're always fine. Really," he said, in a more earnest tone. "Because — listen, listen," he said, digging me in the side with his elbow. "Horst has these kids hanging around a lot — changes a lot, always a new crowd — college age, high school age. Rich kids mostly, trust fund, who might want to trade him some art or a painting they took maybe from their family? They know to come to him. Because —" tossing his head, tossing the hair from his eyes — "Horst himself, when he was a kid, you know — long time ago, nineteen eighties — he went for one year, or two, to one of these fancy-boy schools around here where they make you wear the jacket. Some place not too far away. He showed me it once, in a cab. Anyway —" he sniffed — "boy on the floor? He is not some poor boy from the street. And they will not let something happen to him. Let's hope he learns his lesson. Many of them do. He will never be so sick in his life after he gets that shot of Narcan. Besides, Candy's a nurse and she'll look after him when he comes to. Candy? The brunette?" he said, digging me in the ribs again when I didn't answer. "Did you see her?" He chortled. "Like—?" He reached down and drew a fingertip above his kneecap to simulate the line of her boots. "*She's* terrific. God, if I could get her away from that Niall guy, the Irish, I would. We went out to Coney Island one day, just the two of us, and I never had such a good time. She likes to knit sweaters, can you imagine that?" he said, looking at me slyly from the corner of his eye. "Woman like that—would you think she is woman who enjoys to knit sweaters? But she does! Offered to make me one! She was serious, too! 'Boris, I will knit you a sweater any time you like. Just tell me what color and I will do it!'"

He was trying to cheer me up but I still felt too shaken to talk. For a while we both walked with heads down and there was no noise except the two of us clicking along the park path in darkness, our footsteps seeming to echo forever and beyond the city night enormous around us, car horns and sirens sounding like they were coming from half a mile away.

"Well," said Boris presently, throwing me another sideways glance, "at least I've got it figured out now, eh?"

"What?" I said, startled. My mind was still on the boy and my own near misses: blacking out in the bathroom upstairs at Hobie's, head bloody where I'd hit it on the edge of the sink; waking up on the kitchen floor at Carole Lombard's with Carole shaking me and screaming, lucky it was four minutes, I was calling 911 if you didn't come to in five.

"Pretty sure of it. It was Sascha took the picture."

"Who?"

Boris glowered. "Ulrika's brother, funny enough," he said, folding his arms across his narrow chest. "And two boots make a pair, if you know what I mean. Sascha and Horst are pretty tight—Horst will never hear anything against him—well. Hard not to like Sascha—everyone does—he is friendlier than Ulrika, but our personalities never came together. Horst was straight as string, they all say, till he fell in with those two. Studying philosophy . . . set to go into running the dad's company . . . and here you see him now. That said, I never thought Sascha would go against Horst, not in one hundred years. You followed all that in there?"

"No."

"Well, Horst thinks Sascha's word is gold but I am not so sure. And I do not think the picture is in Ireland, either. Even Niall, the Irish, does not think it. I hate that she is back, Ulrika—I can't say plainly what I think. Because—" hands deep in pockets—"I'm a little surprised Sascha would

dare this, and I dare not say it to Horst, but I think no other explanation —
I think whole bad deal, arrest, blow-up with the cops, all that, was excuse
for Sascha to make off with painting. Horst has dozens of people living off
him — he is far too gentle and trusting — mild in his soul, you know,
believes the best of people — well, he can let Sascha and Ulrika steal from
him, fine, but I will not let them steal from me."

"Mmn." I hadn't seen very much of Horst but he hadn't seemed particularly mild in his soul to me.

Boris scowled, kicking at the puddles. "Only problem, though? Sascha's guy? The one he set me up with? Real name —? No clue. He called
himself 'Terry' which was not right — I don't use my own name either but
'Terry,' Canadian, give me a fucking break! He was from Czech Republic,
no more 'Terry White' than I am! I think he is street criminal — fresh out
of jail — know-nothing, uneducated — plain brute. I think Sascha picked
him up somewhere, to use for shill, and gave him cut in exchange for
throwing the deal — peanuts kind of cut, probably. But I know what
'Terry' looks like and I know he has connections in Antwerp and I am
going to call my boy Cherry and get him on it."

"Cherry?"

"Yes — is my boy Victor's *kliytchka,* we call him that because his nose
is red, but also because his Russian name, Vitya, is close to Russian word
for cherry. Also, there is famous soap opera in Russia, *Winter Cherry* —
well, hard to explain. I tease Vitya about this programme, it makes him
very annoyed. Anyhow — Cherry knows everyone, everything, hears all
the inside talk. Two weeks before it happens — you hear it all from
Cherry. So no need to worry about your bird, all right? I am pretty sure
we will sort it all out."

"What do you mean, 'sort it out' —?"

Boris made an exasperated noise. "Because this is closed circle, you
understand? Horst is right on the money about that. *No one is going to buy
this painting.* Impossible to sell. But — black market, barter currency? Can
be traded back and forth forever! Valuable, portable. Hotel rooms —
going back and forth. Drugs, arms, girls, cash — whatever you like."

"Girls?"

"Girls, boys, what have you. Look look," he said, holding up a hand, "I
am not involved in anything like that. I was too close to being sold myself
as a boy — these snakes are all over Ukraine, or used to be, every corner

and railway station, and I can tell you if you are young and unhappy enough it seems like good deal. Normal-seeming guy promises restaurant job in London or some such, supplies air ticket and passport—ha. Next thing you know you are waking up chained by the wrist in some basement. Would never be involved with any such. It is wrong. But it happens. And once painting is out of my hands, and Horst's—who knows what it is being traded for? This group holds it, that group holds it. Point being—" upheld forefinger—"your picture is not going to disappear in collection of oligarch art freak. It is too too famous. No one wants to buy it. Why would they? What can they do with it? Nothing. Unless cops find it—and they have *not* found it, this we know—"

"I want the cops to find it."

"Well—" Boris rubbed his nose briskly—"yes, all very noble. But for now, what I *do* know is that it *will* move, and only move in relatively small network. And Victor Cherry is great friend, and owes me big. So, cheer up!" he said, grasping my arm. "Don't look so white and ill! And we will talk soon again, I promise."

xviii.

STANDING UNDER A STREETLAMP where Boris had left me ("cannot drop you home! I am late! Somewhere to be!") I was so shaken that I had to look around to get my bearings—frothy gray façade of the Alwyn, like some lurid dementia of the Baroque—and the floodlights on the cutwork, the Christmas decorations on the door of Petrossian struck some deep-embedded memory gong: December, my mother in a snow hat: *here baby, let me run around the corner and buy some croissants for breakfast...*

I was so distracted that a man coming fast round the corner whacked straight into me: "Watch it!"

"Sorry," I said, shaking myself. Even though the accident had been the other guy's fault—too busy honking and yakking away on his cell phone to look where he was going—several people on the sidewalk had directed their disapproving looks at me. Feeling short-winded and confused, I tried to think what to do. I could catch the subway down to Hobie's, if I felt like catching the subway, but Kitsey's apartment was closer. She and her roommates Francie and Em would all be out on their Girls' Night (no point texting or calling, as I knew from experience; they usually went to a movie), but I had a key and I could let myself in and make myself a drink and lie down while I waited for her to come home.

The weather had cleared, wintry moon crisp through a gap in the storm clouds, and I began to walk east again, pausing every now and then to try and hail a cab. I wasn't in the habit of stopping by Kitsey's without phoning, mainly because I didn't care much for her roommates nor they for me. Yet despite Francie and Em and our stilted pleasantries in the kitchen, Kitsey's apartment was one of the few places I felt truly safe in New York. No one knew how to reach me at Kitsey's. There was always the sense that it was temporary; she didn't keep many clothes there and lived mostly out of a suitcase on a luggage rack at the foot of her bed; and for reasons inexplicable I liked the empty, restful anonymity of the flat, which was cheerfully but sparsely decorated with abstract-patterned rugs and modern furnishings from an affordable design store. Her bed was comfortable, the reading light was good, she had a big-screen plasma television so we could lie around and watch movies in bed if we felt like it; and the stainless-steel fridge was always well-stocked with Girl Food: hummus and olives, cake and champagne, lots of silly take-out vegetarian salads and half a dozen kinds of ice cream.

I scrabbled for the key in my pocket, then absent-mindedly unlocked the door (thinking about what I might find to eat, would I have to order up? she would have had dinner, no point waiting) and almost bumped my nose when the door caught on the chain.

I closed the door, and stood for a minute, puzzled; I opened it again so it caught with a rattle: red sofa, framed architectural prints and a candle burning on the coffee table.

"Hello?" I called and then again: "Hello?" more loudly, when I heard movement inside.

I'd been pounding hard enough to raise the neighbors when Emily, after what seemed like a very long time, came to the door and looked at me through the gap. She was wearing a ratty, at-home sweater and the kind of loudly patterned pants that made her rear end look a lot bigger. "Kitsey's not here," she said flatly without unchaining the door.

"Fine, I know," I said irritably. "That's okay."

"I don't know when she'll be back." Emily, whom I'd first met as a fat-faced nine-year-old slamming a door on me in the Barbours' apartment, had never made any secret of the fact that she didn't think I was good enough for Kitsey.

"Well, will you let me in, please?" I said, annoyed. "I want to wait for her."

"Sorry. Now's not a good time." Em still wore her wheat-brown hair in a short cut with bangs, just as she had when she was a kid, and the set of her jaw — straight out of second grade — made me think of Andy, how he'd always hated her, Emmy Phlegmmy, the Emilizer.

"This is ridiculous. Come on. Let me in," I said again, irritably, but she only stood there impassively in the crack of the door, not quite looking me in the eye but somewhere to the side of my face. "Look, Em, I just want to go back to her room and lie down—"

"I think you'd better come back later. Sorry," she said, in the incredulous silence that followed this.

"Look, I don't care what you're doing—" Francie, the other roommate, made at least a pretense of sociability — "I don't want to bother you, I just want to—"

"Sorry. I think you'd better leave. Because, because, look, I live here," she said, raising her voice above mine—

"Good grief. You can't be serious."

"—I live here," she was blinking in discomfort, "this is my place and you can't just come barging in here any time you want."

"Give me a break!"

"And, and—" she was upset too — "look, I can't help you, it's a really bad time now, I think you'd better just go. All right? Sorry." She was closing the door on me. "See you at the party."

"What?"

"Your *engagement* party?" said Emily, re-opening the door a crack and looking at me so that I saw her agitated blue eye for a moment before she shut it again.

xix.

FOR SOME MOMENTS I stood in the hallway in the abrupt stillness that had fallen, staring at the pinhole of the closed door, and in the silence I imagined I could hear Em inches away on the other side of the door and breathing just as hard as I was.

Well, that's it, you're off the bridesmaid list, I thought, turning away and clattering back down the stairs with a lot of ostentatious noise and feeling at once furious and oddly cheered by the incident, which more than confirmed every uncharitable thought I'd ever entertained about Em. Kitsey had apologized more than once for Em's 'brusqueness' but this, in Hobie's phrase, took the proverbial cake. Why wasn't she at the movies with the others? Was she with some other guy in there? Em, though thick-ankled and not very attractive, did have a boyfriend, a dud named Bill who was an executive at Citibank.

Shiny black streets. Once out of the lobby, I ducked into the doorway of the florist next door to check my messages and text Kitsey before heading downtown, just in case; if she was just getting out of her movie, I could meet her for dinner and a drink (alone, without the girlfriends: the weirdness of the incident seemed to call for it) and — definitely — a speculative and humorous talk on the behavior of Em.

Floodlit window. Mortuary glow from the cold case. Beyond the fog-condensed glass, trickling with water, winged sprays of orchids quivered in the fan's draft: ghost-white, lunar, angelic. Up front were the kinkier numbers, some of which sold for thousands of dollars: hairy and veined, freckled and fanged and blood-flecked and devil-faced, in colors ranging from corpse mold to bruise magenta — even one magnificent black orchid with gray roots snaking out its moss-furred pot. ("Please darling," Kitsey had said, correctly intuiting my plans for Christmas, "don't even think about it, they're all too gorgeous and they die the moment I touch them.")

No new messages. Quickly, I texted her (Hey call me, have to talk to you, something hilarious just happened xxxx) and just to be sure she wasn't out of the movie yet, dialed her cell again. But as it was clicking through to voice mail, I saw a reflection in the glass, in the green jungle depths in back of the shop, and — in disbelief — turned.

It was Kitsey, head down, in her pink Prada overcoat, huddled arm in arm and whispering with a man whom I recognized — I hadn't seen him in years, but I knew him instantly — same set of shoulder and loose-boned slink of a gait — Tom Cable. His crinkly brown hair was still long; he was still dressed in the same clothes that rich stoner kids had worn at our school (Tretorns, huge thick-knit Irish sweater without an overcoat) and he had a bag from the wine shop looped over his arm, the same wine shop where Kitsey and I sometimes ran together for a bottle. But what astonished me: Kitsey, who always held *my* hand at a slight distance — tugging me along behind her, winsomely swinging my arm like a child playing London Bridge — was nestled deep and sorrowfully into his side. As I watched, blank at the unfathomable sight of this — they were waiting for the light, bus whooshing past, far too wrapped up in each other to notice me — Cable, who was talking to her quietly, tousled her hair and then turned and pulled her to him and kissed her, a kiss she returned with more mournful tenderness than any kiss she'd ever given me.

Moreover, I saw — they were crossing the street; quickly I turned my back; I could see them perfectly well in the window of the lighted shop as they went into the front door of Kitsey's apartment building only a few feet away from me — Kitsey was upset, she was talking quietly, in a low voice husky with emotion, leaning into Cable with her cheek pressed against his sleeve as he reached around lovingly to squeeze her on the arm; and though I couldn't make out what she was saying, the tone of her voice was all too clear: for even in her sadness her joy in him, and his in her, was undisguisable. Any stranger on the street could have seen it. And — as they glided past me, in the dark window, a pair of affectionate ghosts leaning against each other — I saw her reach up quickly to dash a tear from her cheek, and found myself blinking in astonishment at the sight: for somehow, improbably, for the first time ever, Kitsey was crying.

XX.

I WAS AWAKE MUCH of the night; and when I went down to open the store the next day, I was so preoccupied I sat staring into space for a half an hour before I realized I'd forgotten to turn the 'Closed' sign around.

Kitsey's twice-weekly trips to the Hamptons. Strange numbers flashing, quick hang-ups. Kitsey frowning at the phone mid-dinner and shutting it off: "Oh, just Em. Oh, just Mommy. Oh, just a telemarketer, they've got me on some list." Texts coming in at the middle of the night, submarine blips, bluish sonar pulse on the walls, Kitsey jumping up bare-assed from bed to shut the thing off, white legs flashing in the dark: "Oh, wrong number. Oh, just Toddy, he's out drunk somewhere."

And, very nearly as heart-sinking: Mrs. Barbour. I was well aware of Mrs. Barbour's light touch in tricky situations — her ability to manage delicate matters behind the scenes — and while she hadn't told me a direct lie, as far as I knew, information had definitely been elided and finessed. All sorts of little things were coming back to me, such as the moment a few months before when I'd walked in on Mrs. Barbour and heard her saying in a low urgent voice to the doorman, over the intercom, in answer to a ring from the lobby: *No, I don't care, don't let him up, keep him downstairs.* And when Kitsey, not thirty seconds later, after checking her texts, had bounced up and announced unexpectedly she was taking Ting-a-Ling and Clemmy for a spin round the block! I hadn't thought a thing about it, despite the unmistakable frost of displeasure that had crossed Mrs. Barbour's face, and the renewed warmth and energy with which — when the door clicked shut after Kitsey — she had turned back to me and reached to take my hand.

We were to see each other that night: I was to accompany her to the birthday party of one of her friends, and then stop by the party of a different friend, later on. Kitsey, though she hadn't phoned, had sent me a tentative text. Theo, what's up? I'm at work. Call me. I was still staring at this uncomprehendingly, wondering if I should return the message or not — what could I possibly say? — when Boris came bursting in the front door of the shop. "I have some news."

"Oh yeah?" I said, after a moment's distracted pause.

He wiped his forehead. "We can talk here?" he said, looking around.

"Uh —" shaking my head to clear it. "Sure."

"I have a sleepy head today," he said, rubbing his eye. His hair was standing up in every direction. "Need a coffee. No, don't have time," he said blearily, raising a hand. "Can't sit, either. Can only stay one minute. But — good news — I have a good line on your picture."

"How's that?" I said, waking abruptly from my Kitsey fog.

"Well, we will soon see," he said evasively.

"Where —" struggling to focus — "is it all right? Where are they keeping it?"

"These are questions I cannot answer."

"It —" I was having a hard time collecting my thoughts; I took a deep breath, drew a line on the desktop with my thumb to compose myself, looked up —

"Yes?"

"It needs a certain temperature range and a certain humidity — you know that, right?" Someone else's voice, not mine. "They can't just be keeping it in a damp garage or any place."

Boris pursed his lips in his old derisive manner. "Believe me, Horst took care of that picture like it was his own baby. That said—" he closed his eyes—"I cannot say about these guys. I am sad to report that they are not geniuses. We will have to hope they have enough brains not to keep it behind the pizza oven or something. Joking," he said loftily, when he saw me gaping in horror. "Although, from what I hear, it is being kept in a restaurant, or near a restaurant. In same building with, anyway. We will talk about it later," he said, raising a hand.

"Here?" I said, after another disbelieving pause. "In the city?"

"Later. It can wait. But here is the other thing," he said, in an urgently hushing tone as he looked about the room and over my head. "Listen, listen. This is what I really came to tell you. Horst—he never knew your name was Decker, not until he asked me on the telephone today. You know a guy named Lucius Reeve?"

I sat down. "Why?"

"Horst says to stay away from him. Horst knows you are an antiques dealer but he didn't connect the dots with this other thing until he knew your name."

"What other thing?"

"Horst would not go into it a lot. I do not know what your involvement is with this Lucius, but Horst says to stay clear of him and I thought it important that you know it right away. He crossed Horst badly on unrelated matter and Horst got Martin after him."

"Martin?"

Boris waved a hand. "You didn't meet Martin. Believe me, you would remember if you did. Anyway, this Lucius guy is no good to be mixed up with for someone in your business."

"I know."

"What are you into him for? If I may ask?"

"I—" Again I shook my head, at the impossibility of going into it. "It's complicated."

"Well, I don't know what he has on you. If you need my help, of course you have it—I am pledging it to you—Horst too, I daresay, because he likes you. Nice to see him so involved and talkative yesterday! I do not think he knows so many persons with whom he can be himself and share his interests. It is sad for him. Very intelligent, Horst. He has a lot to give. But—" he glanced at his watch—"sorry, I do not mean to be rude, I have to be somewhere—I am feeling very hopeful about the picture! I think, possibility, we may get it back! So—" he stood, and bravely knocked his breastbone with his fist—"courage! We will speak soon."

"Boris?"

"Eh?"

"What would you do if your girl was cheating on you?"

Boris—heading out the door—did a double take. "Come again?"

"If you thought your girl was cheating on you."

Boris frowned. "Not sure? You have no proof?"

"No," I said, before realizing this wasn't strictly true.

"Then you must ask her, straight out," said Boris decisively. "In some friendly and unprotected moment when she is not expecting it. In bed maybe. If you catch her at the right moment, even if she lies—you will know it. She will lose her nerve."

"Not this woman."

Boris laughed. "Well, you have found a good one, then! A rare one! Is she beautiful?"

"Yes."

"Rich?"

"Yes."

"Intelligent?"

"Most people would say so, yes."

"Heartless?"

"A bit."

Boris laughed. "And you love her, yes. But not too much."

"Why do you say that?"

"Because you are not mad, or wild, or grieving! You are not roaring out to choke her with your own bare hands! Which means your soul is not too mixed up with hers. And that is good. Here is my experience. Stay away from the ones you love too much. Those are the ones who will kill you. What you want to live and be happy in the world is a woman who has her own life and lets you have yours."

He clapped me twice on the shoulder and then departed, leaving me to stare into the silver case with a renewed sense of despair at my dirtied-up life.

xxi.

Kitsey, when she opened the door to me that night, was not actually quite so composed as she might have been: she was talking of several things at once, new dress she wanted to buy, tried it on, couldn't decide, put it on hold, storm up in Maine—tons of trees down, old ones on the island, Uncle Harry had phoned, how sad! "Oh darling—" flittering around adorably, raising up on tiptoe to reach the wineglasses—"will you? Please?" Em and Francie, the roommates, were nowhere in evidence, as if they and their boyfriends had wisely am-scrayed before my arrival. "Oh, never mind—I've got them. Listen, I had such a good idea. Let's go have a curry before we stop by Cynthia's. I'm craving one. What's that hidey-hole on Lex you took me to—that you like? What's it called? The Mahal something?"

"You mean the fleabag?" I said stonily. I hadn't even bothered to take off my coat.

"Excuse me?"

"With the greasy rogan josh. And the old people that depressed you. The Bloomingdale's sale crowd." The Jal Mahal Restaruant (*sic*) was a shabby, tucked-away Indian on the second floor of a storefront on Lex where not a thing had changed since I was a kid: not the pappadums, not the prices, not the carpet faded pink from water damage near the windows, not even the waiters: the same heavy, beatific, gentle faces I remembered from childhood when my mother and I had gone there after the movies for samosas and mango ice cream. "Sure, why not. 'The saddest restaurant in Manhattan.' What a great idea."

She turned to me, and frowned. "Whatever. Baluchi's is closer. Or—we can do what you want."

"Oh yeah?" I stood leaning against the door frame with my hands in my pockets. Years of living with a world class liar had rendered me merciless. "What *I* want? That's rich."

"Sorry. I thought a curry might be nice. Forget it."

"That's okay. You can stop it now."

She looked up with a vacant smile on her face. "Excuse me?"

"Don't give me that. You know good and well what I'm talking about."

She said nothing. A stitch appeared in her pretty forehead.

"Maybe this will teach you to keep your phone switched on when you're with him. I'm sure she was trying to call you on the street."

"Sorry, I don't know —?"

"Kitsey, I saw you."

"Oh, please," she said, blinking, after a slight pause. "You can't be serious. You don't mean Tom, do you? Really, Theo," she said, in the deadly silence that followed, "Tom's an old friend, from way back, we're really close—"

"Yes, I gather."

"—and he's Em's friend too, and, and, I mean," blinking furiously, with an air of being unjustly persecuted, "I know how it may have seemed, I *know* you don't like Tom and you have good reason not to. Because, I know about the stuff when your mother died and sure, he behaved really badly, but he was only a kid and he feels really awful about the way he acted—"

"Feels awful?"

"—but, but he'd had some bad news last night," she continued rapidly, like an actress interrupted mid-speech, "some bad news of his own—"

"You talk about me with him? You two sit around discussing me and feeling sorry for me?"

"—and Tom, he turned up here to see us, Em and me, both of us, out of the blue, right before we were supposed to go out to the movie, that's why we stayed in and didn't go out with the others, you can ask Em if you don't believe me, he didn't have anywhere else to go, he'd had a bad upset, something personal, he only wanted someone to talk to, and what were we to—"

"You don't expect me to believe that, do you?"

"Listen. I don't know what Em told you—"

"Tell me. Does Cable's mother still have that house in East Hampton? I remember how she used to always dump him off at the country club for hours on end after she fired the babysitter, or after the babysitter quit rather. Tennis lessons, golf lessons. He probably turned out to be a pretty good golfer, no?"

"Yes," she said coldly, "yes he is pretty good."

"I could say something cheap here but I won't."

"Theo, let's not do this."

"May I run my theory by you? Do you mind? I'm sure it's wrong in a few particulars but I think this is basically it. Because I know you were see-ing Tom, Platt told me as much when I ran into him on the street, and he wasn't too thrilled about it either. And yeah," I said when she tried to inter-rupt, in a voice just as hard and dead as I felt. "Right. No need to make excuses. Girls always did like Cable. Funny guy, really entertaining when he wants to be. Even if he has been writing bad checks lately or stealing from people at the country club or any of these other things I hear—"

"—That's not true! That's a lie! He never stole anything from anybody—"

"—and Mommy and Daddy never liked Tom much, or probably at all, and then after Daddy and Andy died you couldn't keep it up, not in public anyway. Too upsetting to Mommy. And, as Platt has pointed out, numerous times—"

"I won't see him any more."

"So you're admitting it."

"I didn't think it mattered until we were married."

"Why is that?"

She brushed the hair from her eyes and said nothing.

"Didn't think it would matter? Why? You didn't think I would find out?"

Angrily she glanced up. "You're a cold fish, you know that?"

"Me?" I looked away and laughed. "I'm the one who's cold?"

"Oh, right. 'Wronged party.' 'Terribly high principles.'"

"Higher than some, it seems."

"You're thoroughly enjoying this."

"Believe me, I'm not."

"Oh no? I'd never know it from that smirk."

"And what am I supposed to do? Not say anything?"

"I've said I won't see him any more. Actually I told him I wouldn't a while back."

"But he's insistent. He loves you. He won't take no for an answer."

To my astonishment, she was blushing. "That's right."

"Poor little Kits."

"Don't be hateful."

"Poor baby," I said again, jeeringly, since I couldn't think of anything else to say.

She was scrabbling in the drawer for the corkscrew, and she turned

and regarded me bleakly. "Listen," she said. "I don't expect you to understand but it's rough to be in love with the wrong person."

I was silent. Walking in, I'd gone so cold with rage at the sight of her
that I'd tried to tell myself that she was powerless to hurt me or—God
forbid—make me feel sorry for her. But who knew better the truth of
what she was saying than me?

"Listen," she said again, putting down the corkscrew. She'd seen her
opening and she was taking it: just like on the tennis court, ruthless, watching her opponent's weak side . . .

"Get away from me."

Too heated. Wrong tone. This was going the wrong way. I wanted to
be cold and in control of things.

"Theo. Please." There she was, hand on my sleeve. Nose pinking up,
eyes pink with tears: just like poor old Andy with his seasonal allergies,
like some ordinary person you might actually feel sorry for. "I'm sorry.
Truly. With all my heart. I don't know what to say."

"Oh no?"

"No. I've done you a great disservice."

"Disservice. That's one way of putting it."

"And, I mean, I know you don't *like* Tom—"

"What does that have to do with it?"

"Theo. Does it really matter to you as much as all that? No, you know
it doesn't," she said quickly. "Not if you have to think about it. Also—"
she stopped for a moment before she plunged on—"not to put you on the
spot, but I know all about your things and I don't care."

"Things?"

"Oh, please," she said wearily. "Hang out with your sleazy friends,
take all the drugs you want. I don't care."

In the background, the radiator began to bang and set up a tremendous clatter.

"Look. We're right for each other. This marriage is absolutely the right
thing for both of us. You know it and I know it. Because—I mean, look,
I *know*. You don't have to tell me. And, I mean too—things are better for
you now since we've been seeing each other, aren't they? You've straightened up a lot."

"Oh yeah? 'Straightened up'? What's that supposed to mean."

"Look—" she sighed in exasperation—"no point pretending, Theo. Martina—Em—Tessa Margolis, remember her?"

"Fuck." I didn't think anybody knew about Tessa.

"Everyone tried to tell me. 'Stay away from him. He's darling but he's a drug addict.' Tessa told Em she stopped seeing you after she caught you snorting heroin at her kitchen table."

"It wasn't heroin," I said hotly. They'd been crushed morphine tablets and it had been a terrible idea to snort them, total waste of a pill. "And anyway, Tessa certainly didn't have any scruples about *blow,* she used to ask me to get it for her all the time—"

"Look, that's different and you know it. Mommy," she said, talking over me—

"—Oh yeah? Different?" Raising my voice over hers. "How is it different? How?"

"—Mommy, I swear—listen to me, Theo—Mommy loves you so much. *So* much. You saved her life coming along when you did. She talks, she eats, she takes an interest, she walks in the park, she looks forward to seeing you, you can't *imagine* how she was before. You're part of the family," she said, pressing her advantage. "Truly. Because, I mean, Andy—"

"Andy?" I laughed mirthlessly. Andy had entertained no illusions whatsoever about his sicko family.

"Look, Theo, don't be like this." She'd recovered now: friendly and reasonable, something of her father in her directness. "It's the right thing to do. Marrying. We're a good match. It makes sense for everyone involved, not least us."

"Oh yeah? Everyone?"

"Yes." Perfectly serene. "Don't be like that, you know what I mean. Why should we let this spoil things? After all, we're better people when we're with each other, aren't we? Both of us? And—" pale little smile; her mother, there—"we're a good couple. We like each other. We get along."

"Head not heart, then."

"If that's how you want to put it, yes," she said, looking at me with such plain pity and affection that—quite unexpectedly—I felt my anger drop out from under me: at her cool intelligence, all her own, clear as a silver bell. "Now—" stretching up on tiptoe, to kiss me on the cheek — "let's both be good, and truthful, and kind to each other, and let's be happy together and have fun always."

xxii.

So I spent the night — we ordered in, later, and then went back to bed. But though on some level it was all easy enough pretending everything was the same (because, in some way, hadn't we both been pretending all along?) on another I felt nearly suffocated by the weight of everything unknown, and unsaid, pressing down between us, and later when she lay curled against me asleep I lay awake and stared out the window feeling completely alone. The silences of the evening (my fault, not Kitsey's — even in extremis Kitsey was never at a loss for words) and the seemingly unbridgeable distance between us had reminded me very strongly of being sixteen and never having the faintest idea what to say or do around Julie, who though she definitely couldn't be called a girlfriend was the first woman I'd thought of as such. We'd met outside the liquor store on Hudson when I was standing outside money in hand wanting someone to go in and buy me a bottle of something and there she came billowing around the corner, in batlike, futuristic garb incongruous with her clumping walk and farm-girl looks, her plain-but-pleasing face of a prairie wife of the 1900s. "Hey kid —" hoisting her own wine bottle out of the bag — "here's your change. No really. Don't mention it. Are you going to stand out here in the cold and drink that?" She was twenty-seven, nearly twelve years older than me, with a boyfriend just finishing business school in California — and there was never any question that when the boyfriend came back I wasn't to come by or contact her ever again. We both knew. She hadn't had to say it. Galloping up the five flights to her studio, on the rare (to me) afternoons I was permitted to come see her, I was always bursting with words and feelings too big to contain but all the things I'd planned to say to her always vanished the instant she opened the door and instead of being able to engage in conversation for even two minutes like a normal person, I would instead hover speechless and desperate three steps behind her, hands plunged in pockets, hating myself, while she walked barefoot around the studio looking hip, talking effortlessly, apologizing for the dirty clothes on the floor and for forgetting to pick up a six-pack of beer—did I want her to run downstairs?—until at some point I would almost literally hurl myself at her mid-sentence and knock her over on the day bed, so violently sometimes my glasses flew off. It had all been so wonderful I'd thought I would die but lying awake afterward I'd been sick with emptiness, her white arm on the coverlet, streetlights coming on, dreading the eight o'clock hour which meant she would have to get up and dress for her job, at a bar in Williamsburg where I wasn't old enough to stop in and visit her. And I hadn't even loved Julie. I'd admired her, and obsessed over her, and envied her confidence, and even been a little afraid of her; but I hadn't really loved her, no more than she'd loved me. I wasn't so sure I loved Kitsey either (at least not the way I'd once wished I loved her) but still it was surprising just how bad I felt, considering I'd been through the routine before.

xxiii.

EVERYTHING WITH KITSEY HAD pushed Boris's visit temporarily from my mind but—once I went to sleep—it all came back sideways in dreams. Twice I woke and sat bolt-upright: once, from a door swinging open nightmarishly into the storage locker, while kerchiefed women fought over a pile of used clothes outside; then—drifting back asleep, into a different staging of the same dream—storage unit as flimsy curtained space open to the sky, billowing walls of fabric not quite long enough to touch the grass. Beyond was a prospect of green fields and girls in long white dresses: an image fraught (mysteriously) with such death-charged and ritualistic horror that I woke gasping.

I checked my phone: 4:00 a.m. After a miserable half hour I sat up bare-chested in bed in the dark and—feeling like a crook in a French movie—lit a cigarette and stared out at Lexington Avenue which was practically empty at that hour: cabs just coming on duty, just going off, who knew which. But the dream, which had seemed prophetic, refused to dissipate and hung like a poisonous vapor, my heart still pounding from the airy danger of it, its sense of openness and hazard.

Deserves to be shot. I'd worried enough about the painting when I believed it to be safely maintained year round (as I'd been assured, by the storage brochure, in brisk professional tones) at a conservatorially acceptable

70 degrees Fahrenheit and 50 percent humidity. You couldn't keep something like that just anywhere. It couldn't take cold or heat or moisture or direct sun. It required a calibrated environment, like the orchids in the flower shop. To imagine it shoved behind a pizza oven was enough to make my idolater's heart pound with a different, but similar, version of the terror I'd felt when I thought the driver was going to chuck poor Popper off the bus: in the rain, in the middle of nowhere, out by the side of the road.

After all: just how long had Boris had the picture? Boris? Even Horst, avowed art-lover, hadn't with that apartment of his struck me as overly particular about conservatorial issues. Disastrous possibilities abounded: Rembrandt's *Storm on the Sea of Galilee,* the only seascape he'd ever painted, according to rumor all but ruined from being stored improperly. Vermeer's masterpiece *The Love Letter,* cut off its stretchers by a hotel waiter, flaking and creased from being sandwiched under a mattress. Picasso's *Poverty* and Gauguin's *Tahitian Landscape,* water-damaged after being hidden by some numbskull in a public toilet. In my obsessive reading the story that haunted me most was Caravaggio's *Nativity with St. Francis and St. Lawrence,* stolen from the oratory of San Lorenzo and slashed from the frame so carelessly that the collector who'd commissioned the theft had burst out crying when he saw it and refused to take it.

Kitsey's phone, I'd noticed, was missing from its usual place: the charger dock on the windowsill where she always grabbed for it first thing in the morning. Sometimes I woke in the middle of the night to see the backlight glowing blue in the dark on her side of the bed, under the covers, from her secret nest of sheets. 'Oh, just checking the time,' she said, if I tumbled over drowsily to ask what she was doing. I imagined it switched off and buried deep in the alligator bag with Kitsey's usual mess of lip gloss and business cards and perfume samples and cash floating loose, crumpled twenties falling out every time she reached for her hairbrush. There, in that fragrant jumble, Cable would be calling repeatedly in the night, leaving multiple texts and voice mails for her to find when she woke in the morning.

What did they talk about? What did they say to each other? Oddly enough: it was easy to imagine their interaction. Bright chatter, a sense of sly connivance. Cable calling her silly names in bed and tickling her until she shrieked.

Grinding out my cigarette. No form, no sense, no meaning. Kitsey disliked it when I smoked in her bedroom but when she found the cigarette butt smashed out in the Limoges box on her dresser I doubted she was going to have anything to say about it. To understand the world at all, sometimes you could only focus on a tiny bit of it, look very hard at what was close to hand and make it stand in for the whole; but ever since the painting had vanished from under me I'd felt drowned and extinguished by vastness—not just the predictable vastness of time, and space, but the impassable distances between people even when they were within arm's reach of each other, and with a swell of vertigo I thought of all the places I'd been and all the places I hadn't, a world lost and vast and unknowable, dingy maze of cities and alleyways, far-drifting ash and hostile immensities, connections missed, things lost and never found, and my painting swept away on that powerful current and drifting out there somewhere: a tiny fragment of spirit, faint spark bobbing on a dark sea.

xxiv.

SINCE I COULDN'T GET back to sleep I left without waking Kitsey, in the icy black hour before sun-up, shivering as I dressed in the dark; one of the roommates had come in and was running a shower and the last thing I wanted was to bump into either of them on the way out.

By the time I got off the F train, the sky was turning pale. Dragging home in the bitter cold—depressed, dead tired, letting myself in at the side door, trudging up to my room, smudged-up glasses, reeking of smoke and sex and curry and Kitsey's Chanel No. 19, stopping to greet Popchik, who had bundled down the hall and was looping-the-loop with unusual excitement at my feet, pulling my rolled necktie out of my pocket so I could hang it on the rack on the back of the door—my blood almost froze when I heard a voice from the kitchen: "Theo? Is that you?"

Red head, poking around the corner. It was her, coffee cup in hand.

"Sorry, did I scare you? I didn't mean to." I stood transfixed, dumbfounded, as she put out her arms to me with sort of a happy crooning noise, Popchik whining and capering in excitement at our feet. She was still wearing the things she'd slept in, candy striped pyjama bottoms and a long sleeved T-shirt with an old sweater of Hobie's over it, and she still smelled like tossed bedsheets and bed: oh God, I thought, closing my eyes and pressing my face into her shoulder with a rush of happiness and fear, swift draft from Heaven, oh God.

"Lovely to see you!" There she was. Her hair—her eyes. Her. Bitten-down nails like Boris's and a pout to her lower lip like a child who'd sucked her thumb too much, red tousled head like a dahlia. "How are you? I've missed you!"

"I—" All my resolutions gone in a second. "What are you doing here?"

"I was flying to Montreal!" Harsh laugh of a much younger girl, a hoarse playground laugh. "Stopping over to see my friend Sam for a few days and then going to meet Everett in California." (Sam? I thought.) "Anyway my plane got re-routed—" she took a gulp of her coffee, word-lessly offered the cup to me, *want some? no?* another gulp—"and I was stuck at Newark, and I thought, why not, I'll take the rain check and come into the city and see you guys."

"Huh. That's great." *You guys.* I was included in that, too.

"Thought it might be fun to pop in, since I won't be here for Christmas. Also since your party's tomorrow. Married! Congratulations!" She had her fingertips on my arm and when she stretched up on tiptoe to kiss me on the cheek I felt her kiss go all through me. "When do I get to meet her? Hobie says she's a dreamboat. Are you excited?"

"I—" I was so stunned I put my hand to the place where her lips had been, where I still felt the press of them glowing, and then when I realized how it must look took it rapidly away. "Yes. Thanks."

"It's good to see you. You're looking well."

She didn't appear to notice how dumbstruck, how dizzy, how completely gobsmacked I was at the sight of her. Or maybe she did notice and didn't want to hurt my feelings.

"Where's Hobie?" I said. I wasn't asking because I cared, but because it was a little too good to be true to be alone in the house with her, and a little frightening too.

"Oh—" she rolled her eyes—"he insisted on going to the bakery. I told him not to bother but you know how he is. He likes to get me those blueberry biscuits that Mama and Welty used to buy me when I was little. Can't believe they even make them any more—they don't have them every day, he says. Sure you don't want some coffee?" moving to the stove, just the trace of a limp in her walk.

It was extraordinary—I could hardly hear a word she was saying. It was always like this when I was in the room with her, she overrode everything: her skin, her eyes, her rusty voice, flame-colored hair and a tilt to her head that sometimes gave her a look like she was humming to herself; and the light in the kitchen was all mixed up with the light of her presence, with color and freshness and beauty.

"I have some CDs I've burned for you!" Turning to look at me over her shoulder. "Wish I'd thought to bring them. Didn't know I'd be stopping though. I'll be sure and pop them in the mail when I get back home."

"And I have some CDs for you." There was a whole stack of them in my room, things I'd bought because they reminded me of her, so many I'd felt funny sending them. "And books." *And jewelry,* I neglected to say. *And scarves and posters and perfume and records on vinyl and a Make-Your-Own-Kite kit and a toy pagoda.* An eighteenth-century topaz necklace. A first edition of *Ozma of Oz.* Buying the things had been mostly a way of thinking of her, of being with her. Some of it I'd given to Kitsey but still there was no way I could come out of my room with the gigantic pile of stuff I'd actually bought for her over the years because it would look completely insane.

"Books? Oh, that's great. I finished my book on the plane, I need something else. We can swap."

"Sure." Bare feet. Blush-pink ears. The pearl white skin at the scoop neck of her T-shirt.

"*Rings of Saturn.* Everett said he thought you might like it. He says hi, by the way."

"Oh right, hi." I hated this pretense of hers, that Everett and I were friends. "I'm, er—"

"What?"

"Actually—" My hands were shaking and I wasn't even hung over. I could only hope she didn't see. "Actually I'm just going to duck in my room for a second, all right?"

She looked startled, touched her fingertips to her forehead: *silly me.* "Oh, right, sorry! I'll just be in here."

I didn't start to breathe again until I was in my room with the door shut. My suit was okay, for yesterday's, but my hair was dirty and I needed a shower. Should I shave? Change my shirt? Or would she notice? Would it look weird that I'd run in and tried to clean up for her? Could I get in the bathroom and brush my teeth without her noticing? But then suddenly I had a rush of counter-panic that I was sitting in my room with the door closed, wasting valuable moments with her.

I got up again and opened the door. "Hey," I yelled down the hall.

Her head appeared again. "Hey."

"Want to go to the movies with me tonight?"

Slight beat of surprise. "Well sure. What?"

"Documentary about Glenn Gould. Been dying to see it." In fact I'd already seen it, and had sat in the theater the whole time pretending she was with me: imagining her reaction at various parts, imagining the amazing conversation we would have about it after.

"Sounds fantastic. What time?"

"Sevenish. I'll check."

XXV.

ALL DAY, I WAS practically out-of-body with excitement at the thought of the evening ahead. Downstairs, in the store (where I was too busy with Christmas customers to devote undivided attention to my plans), I thought about what I would wear (something casual, not a suit, nothing too studied) and where I would take her to dinner—nothing too fancy, nothing that would put her on guard or seem self-conscious on my part but really special all the same, special and charming and quiet enough for us to talk and not too terribly far from Film Forum—besides which, she'd been out of the city for a while, she'd probably enjoy going someplace new ("Oh, this little place? yeah, it's great, glad you like it, a real find") but apart from all the above (and *quiet* was the main thing, more than food or location, I didn't want to be anyplace where we were going to have to yell) it was going to have to be someplace I could get us in at short notice—and then too, there was the vegetarian issue. Someplace adorable. Not too expensive to raise alarms. It couldn't look as if I was going to too much trouble; it had to seem thoughtless, unplanned. How the hell could she be living with this goofball Everett? With his bad clothes and his rabbit teeth and his always-startled eyes? Who looked as if his idea of a hot time was brown rice and seaweed from the counter at the back of the health food store?

And so the day crawled; and then it was six, and Hobie was home from his day out with Pippa, and he was poking his head in the store.

"So!" he said, after a pause, in a cheerful but cautious tone that reminded me (ominously) of the tone my mother had taken with my dad when she came home and found him buzzing about on the verge of an upswing. Hobie knew how I felt about Pippa—I'd never told him, never breathed a word of it, but he knew; and even if he hadn't, it would have been perfectly visible to him (or any stranger walking in off the street) that I practically had sparks flying out of my head. "How's everything?"

"Great! How was your day?"

"Oh wonderful!" with relief. "I was able to get us in at Union Square for lunch, we sat at the bar, wish you'd been with us. Then we went up to Moira's, and the three of us walked over to the Asia Society, and now she's out doing a bit of Christmas shopping. She says you, ah, you're meeting her later tonight?" Casual, but with the unease of a parent wondering if an erratic teenager is really going to be okay taking the car out. "Film Forum?"

"Right," I said nervously. I didn't want him to know I was taking her to the Glenn Gould movie since he knew I'd already seen it.

"She said you two are going to the Glenn Gould?"

"Well, um, I was dying to go again. Don't tell her I've been," I said impulsively; and then: "Did you, er —?"

"No no —" hastily, drawing himself up — "I didn't."

"Well, um —"

Hobie rubbed his nose. "Well, listen, I'm sure it's great. I'm dying to see it as well. Not tonight though," he added quickly. "Some other time."

"Oh —" trying hard to sound bummed-out, doing a bad job of it.

"In any case. Want me to mind the shop for you? In case you want to go upstairs for a wash and a brush-up? You should be leaving here no later than six-thirty if you plan on walking over there, you know."

xxvi.

ON THE WAY OVER, I couldn't help humming and smiling. And when I turned the corner and spotted her standing out in front of the theater I was so nervous I had to stop and compose myself for a moment before rushing in to greet her, helping her with her bags (she, laden with shopping, babbling about her day), perfect, perfect bliss of standing in line with her, huddling close because it was cold, and then inside, the red carpet and the whole evening ahead of us, clapping her gloved hands together: "oh, do you want some popcorn?" "Sure!" (me springing to the counter) "Popcorn's great here—" and then, walking into the theater together, me touching her back casually, the velvety back of her coat, perfect brown coat and perfect green hat and perfect, perfect, little red head — "here—aisle? do you like the aisle?" we'd gone to the movies just enough (five times) for me to make careful note of where she liked to sit, plus, I knew it well enough from Hobie after years of inconspicuously questioning him as much as I dared about her tastes, her likes and dislikes, her habits, slipping the questions in casually, one at a time, for almost a decade, does she like this, does she like that; and there she was, turning and smiling at me, at me! and there were way too many people in the theater because it was the seven o'clock show, way more people than I was comfortable with given my generalized anxiety and hatred of crowded places, and more people trickling in even after the film had already started but I didn't care, it could have been a foxhole in the Somme being shelled by the Germans and all that mattered was her next to me in the dark, her arm beside mine. And the music! Glenn Gould at the piano, wild-haired, ebullient, head thrown back, emissary from the realm of angels, rapt and consumed by the sublime! I kept stealing looks at her, unable to help myself; but it was at least half an hour in before I had the nerve to turn and look at her full-on—profile washed white in the glow from the screen—and realized, to my horror, that she wasn't enjoying the film. She was bored. No: she was upset.

I spent the rest of the film miserable, hardly seeing it. Or, rather, I was seeing it but in a wholly different way: not the ecstatic prodigy; not the mystic, the solitary, heroically quitting the concert stage at the height of his fame to retreat into the snows of Canada — but the hypochondriac, the recluse, the isolate. The paranoiac. The pill popper. No: the drug addict. The obsessive: glove-wearing, germ-phobic, bundled year round with scarves, twitching and racked with compulsions. The hunched nocturnal weirdo so unsure how to conduct even the most basic relations with people that (in an interview which I was suddenly finding torturous) he had asked a recording engineer if they couldn't go to a lawyer and legally be declared brothers—sort of the tragic, late-genius version of Tom Cable and me pressing cut thumbs in the darkened back-yard of his house, or—even more strangely—Boris seizing my hand, bloody at the knuckles where I'd punched him on the playground, and pressing it to his own bloodied mouth.

xxvii.

"THAT UPSET YOU," I said impulsively when we were leaving the theater. "I'm sorry."

She glanced up at me as if shocked I'd noticed. We'd come out into a bluish, dream-lit world—the first snow of the season, five inches on the ground.

"We could have left if you wanted."

In answer she only shook her head in a sort of stunned way. Snow whirling down magical, like a pure idea of North, the pure North of the movie.

"Well, no," she said reluctantly. "I mean, it's not that I didn't *enjoy* it—"

Floundering up the street. Neither of us had the proper shoes. The crunch of our feet was loud and I listened, attentively, waiting for her to continue and ready to grasp her elbow in a moment if she slipped, but when she turned to look at me all she said was: "Oh, God. We're never going to get a cab, are we?"

Mind racing. What about dinner? What to do? Did she want to go home? Fuck! "It's not that far."

"Oh, I know, but—oh, there's one!" she cried—and my heart plunged until I saw, thankfully, that someone else had grabbed it.

"Hey," I said. We were near Bedford Street—lights, cafés. "What do you say we try up here?"

"For a cab?"

"No, for something to eat." (Was she hungry? Please God: let her be hungry.) "Or a drink, at least."

xxviii.

SOMEHOW — AS IF BY pre-arrangement of the gods — the half-empty wine bar we'd ducked into, on impulse, was warm and golden and candle-lit and much, much better than any of the restaurants I'd planned for.

Tiny table. My knee to her knee — was she aware of it? Quite as aware as I was? Bloom of the candle flame on her face, flame glinting metallic in her hair, hair so bright it looked about to catch fire. Everything blazing, everything sweet. They were playing old Bob Dylan, more than perfect for narrow Village streets close to Christmas and the snow whirling down in big feathery flakes, the kind of winter where you want to be walking down a city street with your arm around a girl like on the old record cover — because Pippa was exactly that girl, not the prettiest, but the no-makeup and kind of ordinary-looking girl he'd chosen to be happy with, and in fact that picture was an ideal of happiness in its way, the hike of his shoulders and the slightly embarrassed quality of her smile, that open-ended look like they might just wander off anywhere they wanted together, and — there she was! her! and she was talking about herself, affectionate and old-shoe, asking me about Hobie and the shop and my spirits and what I was reading and what I was listening to, lots and lots of questions but seeming anxious to share her life with me too, her chilly flat expensive to heat, depressing light and damp stale smell, cheap clothes on the high street and so many American chains in London now it's like a shopping mall, and what meds are you on and what meds am I on (we both had Post Traumatic Stress Disorder, a malady that in Europe had different initials, it seemed, and got you sent to a hospital for Army vets if you weren't careful); her tiny garden, which she shared with half a dozen people, and the batty Englishwoman who'd filled it with ailing tortoises she'd smuggled from the south of France ("they all die, of cold and malnutrition — it's really cruel — she doesn't feed them properly, crum-bled bread, can you imagine, I buy them turtle food at the pet store with-out telling her") — and how terribly she wanted a dog, but of course it was hard in London with the quarantine which they had in Switzerland too, how did she always end up living in all these dog-unfriendly places? and wow, I looked better than she'd seen me in years, she'd missed me, missed the hell out of me, what an amazing evening — and we'd been there for hours, laughing over little things but being serious too, very grave, she being both generous and receptive (this was another thing about her; she listened, her attention was dazzling—I never had the feeling that other people listened to me half as closely; I felt like a different person in her company, a better one, could say things to her I couldn't say to anyone else, certainly not Kitsey, who had a brittle way of deflating serious comments by making a joke, or switching to another topic, or interrupting, or sometimes just pretending not to hear), and it was an utter delight to be with her, I loved her every minute of every day, heart and mind and soul and all of it, and it was getting late and I wanted the place never to close, never.

"No no," she was saying, running a finger around the rim of her wine glass—the shape of her hands moved me intensely, Welty's signet on her forefinger, I could stare at her hands the way I could never stare at her face without seeming like a creep. "I loved the movie, actually. And the music—" she laughed, and the laugh, for me, had all the joy of the music behind it. "Knocked the breath out of me. Welty saw him play once, at Carnegie. One of the great nights of his life, he said. It's just—"

"Yes?" The smell of her wine. Red-wine stain on her mouth. This was one of the great nights of my life.

"Well—" she shook her head—"the concert scenes. The look of those rehearsal halls. Because, you know—" rubbing her arms—"it was really, *really* hard. Practice, practice, practice—six hours a day—my arms would ache from holding the flute up—and, well, I'm sure you've heard plenty of it too, that positive-thinking crap that it's so easy for teachers and physical therapists to dole out—'oh, you can do it!' 'we believe in you!'— and falling for it and working hard and working harder and hating yourself because you're not working hard enough, thinking it's your fault you're not doing better and working even harder and then—well."

I was silent. I knew all about this from Hobie, who had spoken of it in great distress and at some length. It seemed that Aunt Margaret had been perfectly correct to send her to the wacko Swiss school with all the doctors and the therapy. Though to all normal standards she'd recovered from the accident completely, still there was a bit of neural damage, just enough to matter on the high end, slight impairment of fine motor skills. It was subtle but it was there. For almost any other vocation or avocation—singer, potter, zookeeper, any doctor apart from a surgeon—it wouldn't have mattered. But for her it did.

"And, I don't know, I listen to a lot of music at home, fall asleep with the iPod every night, but—when's the last time I went to a concert?" she said sadly.

Falling asleep with the iPod? Did that mean that she and what's-his-name weren't having sex? "And why don't you go to concerts?" I said, filing away this bit of info for later. "Audiences bother you? Crowds?"

"Knew you'd understand."

"Well, I'm sure that this has been suggested to you, because it's certainly been suggested to me—"

"What?" What was the charm of that sad smile? How could you break it down? "Xanax? Beta-blockers? Hypnosis?"

"All of the above."

"Well—if it was a panic attack, maybe. But it's not. Remorse. Grief. Jealousy—that's the worst of all. I mean—this girl Beta—that's a stupid name isn't it, Beta? Really mediocre player, I don't mean to be snotty but she could hardly keep up with the section when we were kids and she's in the Cleveland Philharmonic now and it upsets me more than I would admit to just anyone. But they don't have a drug for any of that, do they?"

"Er—" actually they did, and Jerome, up on Adam Clayton Powell, was doing a booming business in it.

"The acoustics—the audiences—it triggers something—I go home, I hate everyone, I talk to myself, have arguments with myself in different voices, I'm upset for days. And—well, I told you, teaching, I tried it, it wasn't for me." Pippa didn't have to work, thanks to Aunt Margaret's and Uncle Welty's money (Everett didn't work either, thanks to same—the 'music librarian' thing, I'd gathered, though presented originally as a striking career choice, was really more along the lines of an unpaid internship, with Pippa footing the bill). "Teenagers—well I won't even go into the torture of that, watching them head off to conservatory or to Mexico City for the summer to play in the symphony. And the younger kids aren't serious enough. I'm annoyed with them for being kids. To me—it's like they're taking it too lightly—throwing what they have away."

"Well, teaching's a shit job. I wouldn't want to do it either."

"Yes but—" gulp of wine—"if I can't play, what else is there? Because I mean—I'm around music, sort of, with Everett, and I keep going to school and keep taking courses—but quite honestly I don't like London that much, it's dark and rainy and I don't have a whole lot of friends there,

and in my flat sometimes I can hear someone crying at night, just this terrible broken weeping from next door, and I — I mean, you've found something you like to do, and I'm so glad, because sometimes I really wonder
what I'm doing with my life."

"I —" Desperately I tried to think of just the right thing to say. "Come
home."

"Home? You mean here?"

"Of course."

"What about Everett?"

I had nothing to say to this.

She looked at me critically. "You really don't like him, do you?"

"Um —" What was the point of lying? "No."

"Well — if you knew him better, you would. He's a good guy. Very
serene and even-tempered — very stable."

I had nothing to say to this, either. I was none of these things.

"Also London — I mean I've *thought* about coming back to New
York —"

"You have?"

"Of course. I miss Hobie. A lot. He jokes how he could rent me an
apartment here for what we spend on the phone — of course he's living
back in the days when long distance to London cost five dollars a minute
or whatever. Pretty much every time we speak, he tries to talk me into
coming back ... well, you know Hobie, he never says it outright, but you
know, constant hints, always tells me about jobs opening up, positions at
Columbia and stuff —"

"He does?"

"Well — on some level I can't fathom that I live so far away. Welty was
the one who took me to music lessons and to the symphony but Hobie was
the one always home, you know, who went upstairs and made me a snack
after school and helped me plant marigolds for my science project. Even
now — when I have a bad cold? when I can't remember how to cook arti-
chokes or get candle wax off the tablecloth? who do I call? Him. But —"
was it my imagination, was the wine getting her worked up a little
bit? — "tell you the truth? Know why I don't come back more? In
London —" was she about to cry? "I wouldn't tell everybody this, but in
London at least I don't think *every second* about it. 'This is the way I
walked home the day before.' 'This is where Welty and Hobie and I had

dinner the next-to-last time.' At least there I don't think quite so much: should I turn left here? Should I turn right? My whole destiny hanging on whether I take the F train or the 6. Awful premonitions. Everything petrified. When I come back here I'm thirteen again — and I mean, not in a good way. Everything stopped that day, literally. I even stopped growing. Because, did you know? I never got one inch taller after it happened, not one."

"You're a perfect size."

"Well, it's fairly common," she said, ignoring my clumsy compliment. "Injured and traumatized children — they quite often fail to grow to normal height." She went in and out, unconsciously, of her Dr. Camenzind voice — even though I'd never met Dr. Camenzind I could sense the moments when Dr. Camenzind took over, a kind of cool distancing mechanism. "Resources are diverted. The growth system shuts down. There was one girl at my school — Saudi princess who was kidnapped, when she was twelve? The guys who did it were executed. But — I met her when she was nineteen, nice girl, but tiny, like only four eleven or something, she was so traumatized that she never grew an inch past the day they snatched her."

"Wow. That underground cell girl? She was at school with you?"

"Mont-Haefeli was weird. You had girls who'd been shot at while fleeing the presidential palace, and then you had girls who got sent there because their parents wanted them to lose weight or train for the Winter Olympics."

She accepted my hand in hers, without saying anything — all bundled up, she hadn't let them take her coat. Long sleeves in summer — always swathed in half a dozen scarves, like some sort of cocooned insect wrapped in layers — protective padding for a girl who'd been broken and stitched and bolted back together again. How could I have been so blind? No wonder the film had upset her: Glenn Gould huddled year-round in heavy overcoats, pill bottles piling up, concert stage abandoned, snow growing deeper round him by the year.

"Because — I mean, I've heard you talk about it, I know you're as obsessed as I am. But I go over and over it too." The waitress had inconspicuously poured her more wine, refilled it to the top without Pippa even asking or seeming to notice: *dear waitress,* I thought, *God bless you, I'm leaving you a tip to knock your socks off.* "If only I'd signed up to audition on Tuesday, or Thursday. If only I'd let Welty take me to the museum when he wanted... he'd been trying to get me up to that show for weeks, he was determined that I see it before it came down.... But I always had something better to do. More important to go to the movies with my friend Lee Ann, whatever. Who, incidentally, vanished into thin air after my accident — never saw her again after that afternoon at the stupid Pixar film. All these tiny signs that I ignored, or didn't fully recognize — everything could have been different if only I'd been paying attention — like, Welty was trying *so* hard to get me to go earlier, he must have asked a dozen times, it was like he had a sense of it himself, something bad going to happen, it was my fault we were even there that day —"

"At least you hadn't been expelled from school."

"Were you expelled?"

"Suspended. Bad enough."

"It's weird to think — if it had never happened. If we hadn't both been there that day. We might not know each other. What do you think you would be doing now?"

"I don't know," I said, a bit startled. "I can't even imagine."

"Yeah, but you must have an idea."

"I wasn't like you. I didn't have a talent."

"What'd you do for fun?"

"Nothing that interesting. The usual. Computer games, sci-fi stuff. When people asked me what I wanted to be, I'd usually be a smart ass and say I wanted to be a blade runner or something like that."

"God, I'm so haunted by that movie. I think about Tyrell's niece a lot."

"What do you mean?"

"That scene where's she's looking at the pictures on the piano. When she's trying to figure out whether her memories belong to her or Tyrell's niece. I go back through the past too, only looking for signs, you know? Things I should have picked up on, but missed?"

"Listen, you're right, I think like that too, but, omens, signs, partial knowledge, there's no logical way you could..." why couldn't I ever get a sentence to come out right around her? "...can I just say how cuckoo it sounds? Especially when someone else says it? To blame yourself for not predicting the future?"

"Well — maybe, but Dr. Camenzind says we all do it. Accidents, catastrophes — something like seventy-five per cent of disaster victims are convinced there were warning signs they brushed off or didn't pick up on correctly, and with children under eighteen, the percentage is even higher. But that doesn't mean the signs weren't there, does it?"

"I don't think it's like that. In hindsight—sure. But I think maybe it's more like a column of figures where you add two numbers wrong at the start, and it throws the total. If you trace it back, you can see the mistake—the point where you would have had a different outcome."

"Yes, but that's almost as bad, isn't it? To see the mistake, the place where you went wrong, and not be able to go back and fix it? My audition—" large gulp of wine—"pre-college orchestra at Juilliard, my solfège teacher had told me I might get second chair but if I played really well, I might have a shot at first. And I guess it was a big deal, sort of. But Welty—" yes, definitely, tears, eyes shining in the firelight—"I knew I was wrong nagging him to come uptown with me, there was *no reason* for him to come—Welty spoiled me rotten even when my mother was alive but after she died he spoiled me more, and it was a big day for me, sure, but was it as important as I made it seem? No. Because," she was crying now, a little, "I didn't even want to go to the museum, I wanted him to come uptown with me because I knew he'd take me out to lunch before the audition, anywhere I wanted—he should have stayed home that day, he had other stuff to do, they didn't even let family sit in, he would have had to wait down the hall—"

"He knew what he was doing."

She glanced up at me as if I'd said exactly the wrong thing; only I knew it was exactly the right thing if I could voice it correctly.

"The whole time we were together, he was talking about you. And—"

"And what?"

"Nothing!" I closed my eyes, overwhelmed with the wine, with her, with the impossibility of explaining it. "It's just—his last moments on earth, you know? And the space between my life, and his, was very, very thin. There *wasn't* any space. It was like something opened up between us. Like a huge flash of what was real—what mattered. No me, no him. We were the same person. Same thoughts—we didn't have to talk. It was just a few minutes but it might have been years, we might as well still *be* there. And, um, I know this sounds weird—" in fact, it was a completely lunatic analogy, crackpot, insane, but I didn't know any other way to work around to what I wanted to say—"but you know Barbara Guibbory, who does those seminars up in Rhinebeck, those past-life-regression things?

Reincarnation and karmic ties and all that? Souls who have been together for a lot of lifetimes? I know, I *know*," I said, at her startled (and slightly alarmed) look — "every time I see Barbara she tells me I need to chant Um or Rum or whatever to heal, like, the blocked chakras — 'deficient muladhara' — I'm not kidding you, that was her diagnosis of me, 'unrooted…' 'constriction of the heart…' 'fragmented energy field…' I was just standing there having a cocktail and minding my own business and here she comes drifting up telling me all these foods I need to eat to ground myself…" I was losing her, I could see it — "sorry, I'm wandering off topic a little, it's just, well, we've had this discussion, all that stuff irritates the hell out of me. Hobie was standing there too drinking a big old Scotch and he said 'What about me, Barbara? Should I eat some root vegetables? Stand on my head?' and she just patted him on the arm and said 'oh, no worries, James, you ARE an Advanced Being.'"

That got a laugh out of her.

"But Welty — he was one too. An Advanced Being. Like — not joking. Serious. Out of the ballpark. Those stories that Barbara tells — guru What's-His-Name putting his hand on her head in Burma and in that one minute she was infused with knowledge and became a different person —"

"Well, I mean, Everett — of course he never *met* Krishnamurti but —"

"Right, right." Everett — why this annoyed quite me so much, I didn't know — had attended some sort of guru-based boarding school in the south of England where the classes had names like Care For the Earth and Thinking of Others. "But I mean — it's like Welty's energy, or force field — God that sounds so corny but I don't know what else you'd call it — it's been with me from that hour on. I was there for him and he was there for me. It's sort of permanent." I had never quite vocalized this before, to anyone, although it was something I felt very deeply. "Like — I think about him, he's present, his personality is with me. I mean — pretty much the second I came to stay with Hobie, I was up there in the shop — it reeled me in — just this instinctive thing, I can't explain it. Because — was I interested in antiques? No. Why would I be? And yet there I was. Going through his inventory. Reading his notes in the margins of auction catalogues. His world, his things. Everything up there — it drew me like a flame. Not that I was even looking for it — more that it was looking for me. And I mean, before I was eighteen, no one taught me, it was like I knew already, I was up there on my own and doing Welty's *job*. Like—" I crossed my legs, restlessly—"did you ever think how weird, that he sent me to your house? Chance—maybe. But it didn't seem like chance to me. It was like he saw who I was, and he was sending me exactly where I needed to be, to who I needed to be with. So yeah—" coming to myself a bit; I was talking a little too fast—"yeah. Sorry. Didn't mean to go off."

"That's okay."

Silence. Her eyes on mine. But unlike Kitsey—who was always at least partly somewhere else, who loathed serious talk, who at a similar turn would be looking around for the waitress or making whatever light and/or comic remark she could think of to keep the moment from getting too intense—she was listening, she was right with me, and I could see only too well how saddened she was at my condition, a sadness only worsened by the fact she truly liked me: we had a lot in common, a mental connection and an emotional one too, she enjoyed my company, she trusted me, she wished me well, she wanted above all to be my friend; and whereas some women might have preened themselves and taken pleasure at my misery, it was not amusing to her to see how torn-up I was over her.

xxix.

THE NEXT DAY — WHICH was the day of the engagement party—all the closeness of the previous evening was gone; and all that remained (at breakfast; in our quick hellos in the hallway) was the frustration of knowing I would not have her to myself again; we were awkward with each other, bumping into each other coming and going, talking a little too loudly and cheerfully, and I was reminded (all too sadly) of her visit the previous summer, four months before she'd shown up with "Everett," and the rich passionate talk we'd had out on the stoop, just the two of us, as it was getting dark: huddled side by side ("like a pair of old tramps"), my knee to her knee, my arm touching hers, and the two of us looking out at the people on the street and talking about all sorts of things: childhood, playdates in Central Park and skating at Wollman Rink (had we ever seen each other in the old days? Brushed past each other on the ice?), about *The Misfits,* which we'd just watched on TV with Hobie, about Marilyn Monroe, whom we both loved ("a little springtime ghost") and about poor ruined Montgomery

Clift walking around with handfuls of loose pills in his pockets (a detail I hadn't known, and didn't comment upon) and about the death of Clark Gable and how horribly guilty Marilyn had felt for it, how responsible— which somehow, oddly, spiraled into talk of Fate, and the occult, and fortune-telling: did birthdays have anything to do with luck, or lack of it? Bad transits; stars in unfortunate alignment? What would a palm reader say? Have you ever had your palm read? No—you? Maybe we should walk over to the Psychic Healer storefront on Sixth Avenue with the purple lights and the crystal balls, it looks like it's open twenty four hours a day— oh right, you mean the lava-lamp place where the crazy Romanian woman stands in the door belching? talking until it was so dark we could hardly see each other, whispering though there was no reason to: *do you want to go in? no, not yet,* and the fat summer moon shining white and pure overhead, and my love for her was really just that pure, as simple and steady as the moon. But then finally we had to go inside and almost the instant we did the spell was broken, and in the brightness of the hallway we were embarrassed and stiff with each other, almost as if the house lights had been turned up at the end of a play, and all our closeness exposed for what it was: make-believe. For months I had been desperate to recapture that moment; and—in the bar, for an hour or two—I had. But it was all unreal again, we were back right where we started, and I tried to tell myself it was enough, just to have had her all to myself for a few hours. Only it wasn't.

XXX.

ANNE DE LARMESSIN — KITSEY's godmother—was hosting our party at a private club which even Hobie had never set foot in, but knew all about: its history (venerable), its architects (illustrious), and its membership (stellar, running the gamut from Aaron Burr to the Whartons). "Supposed to be one of the best early Greek Revival interiors in New York State," he'd informed us with earnest delight. "The staircases—the mantels—I wonder if we'll be allowed in the reading room? The plasterwork's original, I'm told, really something to see."

"How many people will be there?" Pippa asked. She'd been forced to walk down to Morgane Le Fay and buy a dress since she hadn't packed for the party.

"Couple hundred." Of that number, maybe fifteen of the guests (including Pippa and Hobie, Mr. Bracegirdle and Mrs. DeFrees) were mine; a hundred were Kitsey's, and the remainder were people whom even Kitsey claimed not to know.

"Including," said Hobie, "the mayor. And both senators. And Prince Albert of Monaco, isn't that right?"

"They *invited* Prince Albert. I seriously doubt he's coming."

"Oh, just an intimate thing then. For the family."

"Look, I'm just showing up and doing what they tell me." It was Anne de Larmessin who had seized high command of the wedding in the "crisis" (her word) of Mrs. Barbour's indifference. It was Anne de Larmessin who was negotiating for the right church, the right minister; it was Anne de Larmessin who would work out the guest lists (dazzling) and the seating charts (unbelievably tricky) and who, in the end, it seemed, would have final say about everything from the ringbearer's cushion to the cake. It was Anne de Larmessin who had managed to get hold of just the designer for the dress, and who'd offered her estate in St. Barth's for the honeymoon; whom Kitsey phoned whenever a question arose (which it did, multiple times per day); and who had (in Toddy's phrase) firmly installed herself as Wedding Obergruppenführer. What made all this so comical and perverse was that Anne de Larmessin was so disturbed by me she could hardly stand to look at me. I was worlds from the match she had hoped for her god-daughter. Even my name was too vulgar to be spoken. "And what does *the groom* think?" "Will *the groom* be providing me with his guest list any time soon?" Clearly a marriage to someone like me (a furniture dealer!) was a fate akin — more or less — to death; hence the pomp and spectacle of the arrangements, the grim sense of ceremony, as if Kitsey were some lost princess of Ur to be feasted and decked in finery and — attended by tambourine players and handmaidens — paraded down in splendor to the Underworld.

xxxi.

SINCE I DIDN'T SEE any particular reason I needed my wits about me for the party, I made sure to get good and looped before I left, with an emergency OC tucked into the pocket of my best Turnbull and Asser just in case.

The club was so beautiful that I resented the press of guests, which made it difficult to see the architectural details, the portraits hung frame to frame — some of them very fine — and the rare books on the shelves. Red velvet swags, garlands of Christmas balsam — were those real candles on the tree? I stood in a daze at the top of the stairs, not wanting to greet or talk to people, not wanting to be there at all —

Hand on my sleeve. "What's the matter?" said Pippa.

"What?" I couldn't meet her eye.

"You look so sad."

"I am," I said, but I wasn't sure if she heard or not, I almost didn't hear myself saying it, because at exactly the same moment Hobie — sensing we'd fallen behind — had doubled back to find us in the crowd, shouting: "Ah, *there* you are..."

"Go, attend to your guests," he said, giving me a friendly parental nudge, "everyone's asking for you!" Among the strangers, he and Pippa were two of the only really unique or interesting-looking people there: she, like a fairy in her gauzy-sleeved, diaphanous green; he, elegant and endearing in his midnight blue double-breasted, his beautiful old shoes from Peal and Co.

"I —" Hopelessly, I looked around.

"Don't worry about us. We'll catch up later."

"Right," I said, steeling myself. But — leaving them to study a portrait of John Adams near the coat check, where they were waiting for Mrs. DeFrees to drop off her mink, and making my way through the crowded rooms — there was no one I recognized except Mrs. Barbour, whom I really didn't feel I could face, only she saw me before I could get by and caught me by the sleeve. She was backed in a doorway with her gin and lime, being addressed by a saturnine spritely old gentleman with a hard red face and a hard clear voice and a puff of gray hair over each ear.

"Oh, Medora," he was saying, rocking back on his heels. "Still a constant delight. Darling old girl. Rare and impressive. Nearing ninety! Her family of course of the purest Knickerbocker strain as she always likes to remind one — oh you should see her, full of ginger with the attendants —" here he permitted himself an indulgent little chuckle — "this is dreadful my dear, but so amusing, at least I think you will find it so.... they cannot now hire attendants *of color,* that's the term now, isn't it? *of color?* because Medora has such a proclivity for, shall we say, *the patois of her youth.*

Particularly when they are trying to restrain her or get her into the bathtub. Quite a fighter when the mood takes her, I hear! Got after one of the African American orderlies with a fireplace poker. Ha ha ha! Well…you know…'there but for the grace of God.' She was of what I suppose might be called the 'Cabin in the Sky' generation, Medora. And the father did have the family place in Virginia—Goochland County, was it? Mercenary marriage, if ever I saw one. Still the son—you've met the son, haven't you?—*was* rather a disappointment, wasn't he? With the drink. And the *daughter.* Bit of a social failure. Well, that's putting it delicately. Quite overweight. Collects the cats, if you know what I mean. Now Medora's brother, Owen—Owen was a dear, dear man, died of a heart attack in the locker room of the Athletic club…having a bit of an *intimate moment* in the locker room of the Athletic club if you understand me…lovely man, Owen, but he was always a bit of a lost soul, ceased to live without really finding himself, I feel."

"Theo," said Mrs. Barbour, putting her hand out to me quite suddenly as I was trying to edge away, as a person trapped in a burning car might make a last-minute clutch at rescue personnel. "Theo, I'd like for you to meet Havistock Irving."

Havistock Irving turned to fix me with a keen—and, to me, not wholly congenial—beam of interest. "Theodore Decker."

"Afraid so," I said, taken aback.

"I see." I liked his look less and less. "You are surprised I know you. Well, you see, I know your esteemed partner, Mr. Hobart. And his esteemed partner Mr. Blackwell before you."

"Is that so," I said, with resolute blandness; in the antiques trade, I had daily occasion to deal with insinuating old gents of his stripe and Mrs. Barbour, who had not let go my hand, only squeezed it tighter.

"Direct descendant of Washington Irving, Havistock is," she said helpfully. "Writing a biography of."

"How interesting."

"Yes it is rather interesting," said Havistock placidly. "Although in modern academia Washington Irving has fallen a bit out of favor. Marginalized," he said, happy to have come up with the word. "Not a distinctly American voice, the scholars say. Bit too cosmopolitan—too European. Which is only to be expected, I suppose, as Irving learned most of his craft from Addison and Steele. At any rate, my illustrious ancestor would certainly approve of my daily routine."

"Which is—?"

"Working in libraries, reading old newspapers, studying the old government records."

"Why government records?"

Airily he waved a hand. "They are of interest to me. And of even greater interest to a close associate of mine, who sometimes manages to turn up quite a lot of interesting information in the course of things...I believe you two are acquainted with each other?"

"Who is that?"

"Lucius Reeve?"

In the ensuing silence, the babble of the crowd and the clink of glasses rose to a roar, as if a gust of wind had swept through the room.

"Yes. Lucius." Amused eyebrow. Fluty, pursed lips. "Exactly. I knew his name would not be unfamiliar to you. You sold him a very interesting chest-on-chest, as you recall."

"That's right. And I'd love to buy it back if he could ever be persuaded."

"Oh, I'm sure. Only he's unwilling to sell it, as, as," he said, shushing me maliciously, "as I would be too. With the other, even more interesting piece in the offing."

"Well, I'm afraid he can forget all about that," I said pleasantly. My jolt at Reeve's name had been purely reflexive, a mindless jump from a coiled extension cord or a piece of string on the floor.

"Forget?" Havistock permitted himself a laugh. "Oh, I don't think he will forget about it."

In reply, I smiled. But Havistock only looked more smug.

"It's really very surprising the things one can find out on the computer these days," he said.

"Oh?"

"Well, you know, Lucius has quite recently managed to turn up some information on some other interesting pieces you've sold. In fact I don't think the buyers know quite how interesting they are. Twelve 'Duncan Phyfe' dining chairs, to Dallas?" he said, sipping at his champagne. "All that 'important Sheraton' to the buyer in Houston? And a great deal more of same in Los Angeles?"

I tried not to let my expression waver.

"'Museum quality pieces.' Of course —" including Mrs. Barbour in this — "we all know, don't we, that 'museum quality' really depends the sort of museum you're talking about. Ha ha! But Lucius has really done a very good job of following some of your more enterprising sales of late. And, once the holidays are over, he's been thinking of taking a trip down to Texas to — Ah!" he said, turning from me with a deft little dance-like step as Kitsey, in ice-blue satin, swept in to greet us. "A welcome and ornamental addition indeed! You look lovely, my dear," he said, leaning to kiss her. "I've just been talking to your charming husband-to-be. Really quite shocking, the friends in common we have!"

"Oh?" It was not until she actually turned to me — to look at me full-on, to peck me on the cheek — that I realized Kitsey hadn't been a hundred percent sure that I would show up. Her relief at the sight of me was palpable.

"And are you giving Theo and Mommy all the scandal?" she said, turning back to Havistock.

"Oh, Kittycat, you *are* wicked." Cozily, he slipped one arm through hers, and with the other reached over and patted her on the hand: a little Puritan-looking devil of a man, thin, amiable, spry. "Now, my dear, I see you are in need of a drink, as am I. Let's wander off on our own, shall we?" — another glance back at me — "and find a nice quiet spot so we can have a good long gossip about your fiancé."

xxxii.

"THANK HEAVENS HE'S GONE," murmured Mrs. Barbour after they had wandered away to the drinks table. "Small chatter tires me terribly."

"Same here." The sweat was pouring off me. How had he found out? All the pieces he'd mentioned I'd shipped through the same carrier. Still — I was desperate for a drink — how could he know?

Mrs. Barbour, I was aware, had just spoken. "Excuse me?"

"I said, isn't this extraordinary? I'm *astonished* by this great mob of people." She was dressed very simply — black dress, black heels, and the magnificent snowflake brooch — but black was not Mrs. Barbour's color and it only gave her a renunciate look of illness and mourning. "*Must* I mingle? I suppose I must. Oh, God, look, there's Anne's husband, what a bore. Is it very awful of me to say that I wish I were at home?"

"Who was that man just now?" I asked her.

"Havistock?" She passed her hand over her forehead. "I'm glad he is so insistent about his name or I would have had a hard time introducing you."

"I would have thought he was a dear friend of yours."

Unhappily she blinked, with a discomposure that made me feel guilty for the tone I'd taken with her.

"Well," she said resolutely. "He is very familiar. That is to say — he has a very familiar manner. He is that way with everyone."

"How do you know him?"

"Oh — Havistock does volunteer work for the New York Historical Society. Knows everything, and everyone. Although, just between us, I don't think he's a descendant of Washington Irving at all."

"No?"

"Well — he's altogether charming. That is to say, he knows absolutely everyone…claims an Astor connection as well as the Washington Irving one, and who's to say he is wrong? Some of us have found it interesting that many of the connections he invokes are dead. That said, Havistock's delightful, or *can* be. Very very good about visiting the old ladies — well, you heard him just now. Perfect trove of information about New York history — dates, names, genealogies. Before you came up, he was filling me in on the history of *every* single building up and down the street — all the old scandals — society murder in the townhouse next door, 1870s — he knows absolutely everything. That said, at a luncheon a few months ago he was regaling the table with an utterly scurrilous story about Fred Astaire which I don't feel can *possibly* be true. Fred Astaire! Cursing like a sailor, throwing a fit! Well, I don't mind telling you that I simply didn't believe it — none of us did. Chance's grandmother knew Fred Astaire back when she was working in Hollywood and she said he was simply the loveliest man alive. Never heard a whisper to the contrary. Some of the old stars were perfectly horrible, of course, and we've heard all those stories too. Oh," she said despairingly, in the same breath, "how tired and hungry I feel."

"Here —" feeling sorry for her, leading her to an empty chair — "sit down. Would you like me to get you something to eat?"

"No, please. I'd like you to stay with me. Although I suppose I shouldn't hog you to myself," she said unconvincingly. "Guest of honor."

"Honestly, it won't take a minute." My eyes sped round the room. Trays of hors d'oeuvres were going around and there was a table with food in the next room, but I urgently needed to talk to Hobie. "I'll be back as fast as I can."

Luckily Hobie was so tall — taller than virtually everyone else — that I had no difficulty spotting him, a lighthouse of safety in the crowd.

"Hey," said someone, catching my arm as I was almost to him. It was Platt, in a green velvet jacket that smelled like mothballs, looking rumpled and anxious and already half-sloshed. "Everything okay between you two?"

"What?"

"You and Kits get everything hashed out?"

I wasn't entirely sure how to answer this. After a few moments of silence he pushed a string of gray-blond hair behind one ear. His face was pink and swollen with premature middle age, and I thought, not for the first time, how there'd been no freedom for Platt in his refusal to grow up, how by slacking off too long he'd managed to destroy every last glimmer of his hereditary privilege; and now he was always going to be loitering at the margins of the party with his gin and lime while his baby brother Toddy — still in college — stood talking in a group which included the president of an Ivy League college, a billionaire financier, and the publisher of an important magazine.

Platt was still looking at me. "Listen," he said. "I know it's none of my business, you and Kits..."

I shrugged.

"Tom doesn't love her," he said impulsively. "It was the best thing that ever happened to Kitsey when you came along and she knows it. I mean, the way he treats her! She was with him, you know, that weekend Andy died? That was the big important reason why she sent Andy up to look after Daddy, even though Andy was hopeless with Daddy, why she didn't go herself. Tom, Tom, Tom. All about Tom. And yeah, apparently, he's all 'Endless Love' with her, 'My Only Love,' or so she says, but believe me it's a different story behind her back. Because—" he paused, in frustration—"the way he strung her along—leeched money constantly, went around with other girls and lied about it—it made me sick, Mommy and Daddy too. Because, basically, she's a meal ticket to him. That's how he sees her. But—don't ask me why, she was crazy for him. Completely off her head."

"Still is, it seems."

Platt made a face. "Oh, come on. It's you she's marrying."

"Cable doesn't strike me as the marrying type."

"Well—" he took a big slug of his drink —"whoever Tom *does* marry, I feel sorry for them. Kits may be impulsive but she's not stupid."

"Nope." Kitsey was far from stupid. Not only had she arranged for the marriage that would most please her mother; she was sleeping with the person she really loved.

"It would never have panned out. Like Mommy said. 'Utter infatuation.' 'A rope of sand.'"

"She told me she loved him."

"Well, girls always love assholes," said Platt, not bothering to dispute this. "Haven't you noticed?"

No, I thought bleakly, *untrue.* Else why didn't Pippa love me?

"Say, you need a drink, pal. Actually—" knocking the rest of his back —"I could use another myself."

"Look, I just have to go and speak to someone. Also, your mother—" I turned and pointed in the direction where I'd seated her —"she needs a drink too and something to eat."

"Mommy," said Platt, looking like I'd just reminded him of a kettle he'd left boiling on the stove, and hurried off.

xxxiii.

"Hobie?"

He seemed startled at the touch of my hand on his sleeve, turned quickly. "Everything all right?" he said immediately.

I felt better just standing next to him—just to breathe in the clean air of Hobie. "Listen," I said, glancing round nervously, "if we could just have a quick—"

"Ah, and is this the groom?" interjected a woman in his eagerly hovering group.

"Yes, congratulations!" More strangers, pressing forward.

"How young he looks! How very young you look." Blonde lady, mid fifties, pressing my hand. "And how handsome!" turning to her friend. "Prince Charming! Can he be a moment over twenty-two?"

Courteously, Hobie introduced me around the circle — gentle, tactful, unhurried, a social lion of the mildest sort.

"Um," I said, looking around the room, "sorry to drag you away, Hobie, I hope you won't think me rude if —"

"Word in private? Certainly. You'll excuse me?"

"Hobie," I said, as soon as we were in a relatively quiet corner. The hair at my temples was damp with sweat. "Do you know a man named Havistock Irving?"

The pale brows came down. "Who?" he said, and then, looking at me more closely, "Are you sure you're all right?"

His tone, and his expression, made me realize that he knew more about my mental state than he'd been letting on. "Sure," I said, pushing my glasses up on the bridge of my nose. "I'm fine. But — listen, Havistock Irving, does that name ring a bell?"

"No. Should it?"

Somewhat erratically — I was dying for a drink; it had been foolish of me not to stop at the bar on the way over — I explained. As I spoke, Hobie's face grew blanker and blanker.

"What," he said, scanning over the heads of the crowd. "Do you see him?"

"Um —" throngs milling by the buffet, beds of cracked ice, gloved servers shucking oysters by the bucketful — "there."

Hobie — shortsighted without his glasses — blinked twice and squinted. "What," he said shortly, "him with the —" he brought his hands up to the sides of his head to simulate the two puffs of hair.

"Yes that's him."

"Well." He folded his arms, with a rough, unpracticed ease that made me see for a flash the alternate Hobie: not the tailor-fitted antiquaire but the cop or tough priest he might have been in his old Albany life.

"You know him? Who is he?"

"Ah." Hobie, uncomfortably, patted his breast pocket for a cigarette he wasn't allowed to smoke.

"Do you know him?" I repeated more urgently, unable to stop myself glancing over at the bar in Havistock's direction. Sometimes it was hard to get information out of Hobie on touchy matters — he tended to change the subject, clam up, drift into vagueness, and the worst possible place to ask him anything was a crowded room where some genial party was apt to wander up and interrupt.

"Wouldn't say know. We've had dealings. What's he doing here?"

"Friend of the bride," I said — and received a startled look at the tone in which I'd said this. "How do you know him?"

Rapidly he blinked. "Well," he said, somewhat reluctantly, "don't know his real name. Welty and I knew him as Sloane Griscam. But his true name — something else entire."

"Who is he?"

"Knocker," said Hobie curtly.

"Right," I said, after an off-balance pause. A knocker, in the trade, was a shark who charmed his way into old people's homes: to cheat them of valuables and sometimes to rob them outright.

"I —" Hobie rocked on his heels, looked awkwardly away — "rich pickings for him here, that's for sure. First-class swizzler — him and his partner as well. Smart as Satan, those two."

A radiantly smiling bald man in a clerical collar was threading his way toward us; I folded my arms and tried to angle myself away from him, blocking his approach, hoping Hobie wouldn't see and cut his story short to welcome him.

"Lucian Race. At least, that was the name he went by. Oh, they were a pretty pair. See — Havistock, or Sloane, or whatever he's calling himself now, would chat up the old ladies and old gents too, get to know where they lived, drop in to visit... he'd hunt them out at benefit dinners, funerals, Important Americana auctions, all over the place. Anyway —" studying his drink — "he'd turn up to visit with his delightful friend, Mr. Race, and while the old dears were occupied... really, it was dreadful. Jewelry, paintings, watches, silver, whatever they could lay their hands on. Well," he said on an altered note. "Long time ago."

I wanted a drink so badly it was difficult for me not to keep glancing in the direction of the bar. Already I could see Toddy pointing me out to an elderly couple who were smiling expectantly at me, like they were about to totter over and introduce themselves, and obstinately I turned my back. "Old folks?" I repeated to Hobie, hoping to get a little more out of him.

"Yes — sorry to say it, but they preyed on some pretty helpless people. Anyone that let them in the door. And a lot of the old folks didn't have much, they'd clean them out in one go but if there was real loot for the taking —? oh, they'd keep up the fruit baskets and the confidential talks and the hand-patting for weeks —"

The priest, or minister, or whoever he was, had seen that I was engaged and had held up a friendly hand—later!—as he edged past in the crowd, and I threw him a grateful smile. Was he the Episcopal bishop, Father What's His Name, who was supposed to be marrying us? Or one of the Catholic priests from St. Ignatius that Mrs. Barbour had taken up with after Andy and Mr. Barbour died?

"Very very smooth. Sometimes they'd pretend to be furniture appraisers, offering free valuations, that's how they'd get the foot in. Or, with the really dire cases—bedridden, daffy—they'd con the home health nurses, pretend to be family. Still and all—" Hobie shook his head. "Have you had anything to eat?" he asked in his changing-the-subject voice.

"Yeah," I said, though I hadn't, "thanks, but say—"

"Oh, good!" with relief. "There's oysters over there, and caviar. The crab thing was good too. You never came up for lunch today. I left a plate of beef stew for you, some green beans and salad—you didn't eat it, I saw it was still in the fridge—"

"What did you and Welty have to do with him?"

Hobie blinked. "Sorry?" he said, in his distracted way. "Oh—" nodding his head in Griscam's direction—"him?"

"Right." The holiday brightness of the room—lights, mirrors, fireplaces ablaze and chandeliers glittering—had given me a nightmarish feeling of being pressed in upon and observed from all sides.

"Well—" he looked away—they'd just brought out a fresh bowl of caviar; he was already half turned toward the buffet—and then relented. "He turned up in the shop with a load of jewelry and silver to sell, years back now, didn't he. Family stuff, he claimed. Only, one salt-cellar—it was early, important, and Welty knew it because he knew the lady he'd sold it to. And he knew she'd been swizzled by a pair of knocker boys who'd conned their way in pretending to collect old books for charity. Anyhow Welty took the pieces on consignment and called the old lady and called the police. And me, well, on my end—" blotting his forehead with the flowered Liberty square from his pocket; his voice was so quiet I could barely hear him but I didn't dare ask him to speak up—"eighteen months earlier I'd bought an *estate* from the guy, I should have known something was wrong, but—nothing I could put my finger on, not quite. Brand new building in the East Eighties—odd collection of Americana piled harum-scarum in the middle of the room, tea chests, banjo clocks, whalebone figurines, Windsor chairs enough to start a school with—but no rugs, no sofa, nothing to *eat* from, no place to *sleep*—well, I'm sure you would have had it figured before me. No estate, no auntie. Just a flat he'd rented on the fly to warehouse his ill-gotten gains. And the thing was too, and this is what threw me, I knew him by reputation because at the time he had his own little shop, just a storefront, real little bandbox actually on Madison not far from the old Parke-Burnet, very pretty place, appointment only. Chevallet Antiques. Some really first rate French stuff—not my bailiwick. Every time I ever went by there, it was closed, always used to look in at the window. Never knew who owned it until he contacted me about this estate."

"And?" I said, turning my back yet again, telepathically willing Platt to stay away from me with the head of his publishing house whom he was triumphantly leading over to meet me.

"And—" he sighed—"long story short, it went to court, and Welty and I gave statements. Sloane—the *delapidateur* as Welty called him— had vanished into thin air by that time—shop cleared out overnight, 'renovation,' never opened again of course. But Race, I believe, went to jail."

"When was this?"

Hobie bit the side of his forefinger and thought. "Oh, goodness, has to be—thirty years ago? Thirty-five, even?"

"And Race?"

His brow came down. "Is *he* here?" Scanning the crowd again.

"Not that I've seen."

"Hair like this." Hobie measured it with a fingertip, down below the nape of his neck. "Over the collar. Like the English wear it. English of a certain age."

"White hair?"

"Not then. Maybe now. And little, mean mouth—" he puckered up his lips—"like so."

"That's him."

"Well—" He fished in his pocket for his magnifying light, before seeming to realize that the occasion didn't require it. "You offered him his money back. So if it really *is* Race—I don't understand why he's pressing, because he's absolutely in no position to cause trouble or make demands, is he?"

"No," I said, after a long pause, though this was such a big lie that I could hardly force the word out of my mouth.

"Well then, don't look so worried," said Hobie, clearly relieved to be off the subject. "This is absolutely the last thing that should spoil your evening. Although—" clapping me on the shoulder; he was looking across the room, for Mrs. Barbour—"you should certainly warn Samantha. She shouldn't be letting that scoundrel in her house. For any reason whatsoever. Hello!" he said, turning to find the elderly couple who had finally managed to dodder over and were smiling expectantly behind us. "James Hobart. May I introduce you to the groom?"

xxxiv.

THE PARTY WAS FROM six to nine. I smiled, sweated, tried to make my way to the bar only to get waylaid and cut off and sometimes physically dragged back by the arm like Tantalus, dying of thirst while in very sight of relief—"And *here* he is, man of the hour!" "The beamish boy!" "Congratulations!" "Here, Theodore, you *must* meet Harry's cousin Francis—the Longstreets and the Abernathys are related on the father's side, Boston branch of the family, Chance's grandfather, you see was the first cousin of—Francis? oh, you two know each other? Perfect! And here is…Oh, Elizabeth, there you are, let me steal you away for a moment, *don't* you look delightful, that blue suits you beautifully, I'd very much like to introduce you to…" At last I gave up on the idea of drink (and food) and—hemmed-in amongst the ever-shifting press of strangers—stood snatching flutes of champagne from the waiters who happened by, every now and then an hors d'oeuvre, tiny quiche lorraine, miniature blini with caviar, strangers coming and going, locked-in and nodding politely amidst the crowds of well-born, wealthy, powerful…

(*never forget you arent one of them,* my junkie pal from Accounts had whispered in my ear when he'd seen me socializing among important clients at an Impressionist and Modern Art sale…)

…freezing and turning to smile with random groups when the photographer swept in, captive to ambient scraps of mind-numbing conversation about golf games, politics, children's sports, children's schools, third and fourth and fifth homes in Hyères and Hyannis and Paris and London and Jackson Hole and Jupiter and wasn't it hideous how *terribly built up* Vail had become, remember when it was just a darling little village....where do you ski, Theo? *Do* you ski? Why then, *definitely* you and Kitsey must come out with us to our house in the...

Though I had an eye out for Hobie and Pippa, I scarcely saw them. Playfully, Kitsey dragged people over to introduce to me and then vanished as quickly as a bird flying from a windowsill. Havistock, thankfully, was nowhere in evidence. At last things began to clear out, but not much; people had started moving toward the coat check and the waiters were starting to remove the cake and the dessert dishes from the buffet when — trapped in conversation with a group of Kitsey's cousins — I glanced across the room for Pippa (as I'd been doing, compulsively, all night long, trying to catch sight of her red head, the only interesting or important thing in the room) — and, much to my surprise, espied her with Boris. Conversing with animation. He was all over her, loosely draped arm, unlit cigarette dangling from his fingers. Whispering. Laughing. Was he biting her ear?

"Excuse me," I said, and made my way quickly across the room to them by the fireplace — where, in perfect unison, they turned and held their arms out to me.

"Hello!" said Pippa. "We were just talking about you!"

"Potter!" said Boris, throwing his arm around me. Though he was dressed for the occasion, in a blue chalk-stripe suit (it had often struck me, the hordes of rich Russians in the Ralph Lauren shop on Madison), there was somehow no cleaning him up: his smudged eyes made him look stormy and disreputable, and though his hair wasn't technically dirty it gave the impression of dirtiness. "Am happy to see you!"

"Same here." I'd asked Boris never dreaming he would show — it not being in the nature of Boris to remember pesky things like dates, or addresses, or to turn up on time if he did. "You know who this is, don't you?" I said, turning to Pippa.

"Of course she knows me! Knows all about me! We are now dearest of friends! Now—" to me, with a mock show of officiousness — "small word in private. You'll excuse us please?" he said to Pippa.

"More private conversations?" Kicking my shoe playfully with her ballet slipper.

"Don't worry! I will bring him back! Goodbye to you!" Blowing a kiss.

Then to me, in my ear, as we walked away: "She is lovely. God, but I love a redhead."

"So do I, but she's not the one I'm marrying."

"No?" He looked surprised. "But she greeted me! By my name! Ah," he said, looking at me more closely, "are you blushing! Yes you are, Potter!" he crowed. "Blushing! Like a little girl!"

"Shut up," I hissed, glancing back for fear she'd heard.

"Not her then? Not Little Red? Too bad, huh." He was looking round the room. "Which one, then?"

I pointed her out. "There."

"Ah! In the sky-blue?" He pinched me affectionately on the arm. "My God, Potter! *Her?* Loveliest woman in the room! Divine! A goddess!" making as if to prostrate himself on the floor.

"No, no—" grabbing him by the arm, hastily pulling him up.

"An angel! Straight from paradise! Pure as a baby's tear! *Much* too good for the likes of you—"

"Yes, I think that's the general opinion."

"—although—" he reached for my vodka glass and took a big slug before handing it back to me—"a bit icy to look at, no? I like the warmer ones myself. She—she is a lily, a snowflake! Less frosty in private, I hope?"

"You'd be surprised."

His eyebrows went up. "Ah. And…she is the one…."

"Yes."

"She admitted it?"

"Yes."

"And so you are not standing with her. You are annoyed."

"More or less."

"Well"—Boris ran his hand through his hair—"you must go and speak to her now."

"Why?"

"Because we have to leave."

"Leave? Why?"

"Because I need you to take a walk with me."

"Why?" I said, looking around the room, wishing he hadn't dragged me away from Pippa, desperate to find her again. The candles, the orange gleam of firelight where she'd been standing made me think of the warmth of the wine bar, as if the light itself might be a passageway back to the night before and the little wooden table where we had sat knee to knee, her face washed with the same orange-tinged light. There had to be some way I could walk across the room and grab her hand and pull her back to that moment.

Boris threw the hair out of his eyes. "Come on. You will feel fantastic when you hear what I have to say! But you will need to go home. Get your passport. And there is a question of cash, too."

Over Boris's shoulder: imperturbable faces of strange, cold women. Mrs. Barbour in profile, slightly turned to the wall, clutching the hand of the jolly cleric who didn't look quite so jolly any more.

"What? Are you listening to me?" Shaking my arm. The same voice that had pulled me back to earth many times, from fractal glue-sniffing skies where I laid open-eyed and insensate on the bed, gazing at the impressive blue-white explosions on the ceiling.

"Come on! Talk in the car. Let's go. I have a ticket for you—"

Go? I looked at him. It was all I heard.

"I will explain. Don't look at me like that! Everything is good. No worries. But—first off—you must arrange to be gone for a couple of days. Three days. Tops. So"—flicking a hand—"go, go arrange with Snowflake and let's get out of here. I can't smoke in here, can I?" he said, looking around. "No one is smoking?"

Get out of here. They were the only words anyone had said to me all night that made sense.

"Because you must go home *immediately.*" He was endeavoring to catch my eye in a familiar way. "Get your passport. And—money. How much cash do you have on hand?"

"Well, in the bank," I said, pushing my glasses up on the bridge of my nose, oddly sobered by his tone.

"I am not talking about the bank. Or tomorrow. I am talking about on hand. Now."

"But—"

"I can get it back, I'm telling you. But we can't stand around here any longer. We must go now. Right away. Off with you, go," he said, with a friendly little kick in the shin.

XXXV.

"THERE YOU ARE DARLING," said Kitsey, slipping her arm through my elbow and stretching on tiptoe to kiss me on the cheek—a kiss caught, simultaneously, by the photographers circling her: one from the social pages, the other hired for the evening by Anne. "Isn't this glorious? Are you exhausted? I hope my family hasn't been too overwhelming! Annie dear"—extending a hand to Anne de Larmessin, stiff blonde hair, stiff taffeta dress, wrinkled neckline that did not match the tautness of her chiseled face—"listen, it's been absolute heaven...do you suppose we can get a family snap? Just you, me and Theo? We three?"

"Listen," I said impatiently, as soon as our awkward photo op was over and Anne de Larmessin (who clearly didn't consider me anything even approaching family) had drifted away to say goodbye to some other, more important guests. "I'm going."

"But—" she looked confused—"I think Anne's booked a table somewhere—"

"Well, you'll have to make an excuse for me. That shouldn't be a problem for you, should it?"

"Theo, please don't be hateful."

"Because your *mother* isn't going, I'm sure of it." It was almost impossible to get Mrs. Barbour to go out to a restaurant for dinner, unless it was some place she felt sure she wouldn't run into someone she knew. "Say I've taken her home. Say she's been taken ill. Say *I've* been taken ill. Use your imagination. You'll think of something."

"Are you vexed with me?" Family language: *vexed.* A word Andy had used when we were children.

"Vexed? No." Now that it had settled, and I was used to the idea (Cable? Kitsey?) it was almost like some scurrilous bit of gossip that had nothing to do with me. She was wearing my mother's earrings, I noticed—which was weirdly moving since she was absolutely right, they didn't suit her at all—and with a pang I reached out and touched them, and then her, on the cheek.

"Ahhh," cried some onlookers in the background—pleased to finally see some affection between the happy couple. Kitsey—catching to it instantly—seized my hand and kissed it, prompting another battery of snaps.

"All right?" I said in her ear as she leaned close. "If anyone asks, I'm away on business. Old lady's called me to look at an estate."

"Certainly." You had to hand it to her: she was as cool as dammit. "When will you be back?"

"Oh, soon," I said, not very convincingly. I would have been happy to walk out of that room and keep walking for days and months until I was on some beach in Mexico maybe, some isolated shore where I could wander alone and wear the same clothes till they rotted off me and be the crazy gringo in the horn rimmed glasses who repaired chairs and tables for a living. "Look after yourself. And keep this Havistock out of your mother's house."

"Well —" her voice so low I could scarcely hear her — "he's been rather a pest recently. Phones *constantly,* wanting to drop in, bring flowers, chocolates, poor old thing. Mum won't see him. Feel a bit guilty about putting him off."

"Well, don't. Keep him away. He's a sharper. Now, bye," I said loudly, smacking her on the cheek (more clicking of cameras; this was the shot the photographers had been waiting for all evening), and went to tell Hobie (happily inspecting a portrait, leaning forward with his nose inches from the canvas) that I was leaving for a bit.

"Okay," he said cautiously, turning away. The whole time I'd worked with him I'd scarcely taken a vacation, certainly never to go out of town. "You and —" he nodded at Kitsey.

"No."

"Everything all right?"

"Sure."

He looked at me; he looked across the room at Boris. "You know, if you need anything," he said unexpectedly. "You can always ask."

"Right, yes," I said — taken aback, not quite sure what he meant, or how to respond — "thanks."

He shrugged, in seeming embarrassment, and turned self-consciously back to the portrait. Boris was at the bar drinking a glass of champagne and gobbling leftover blinis with caviar. Seeing me, he drained the rest of his glass and ticked his head at the door: *let's get out of here!*

"See you," I said to Hobie, shaking his hand (which was not something I ordinarily did) and leaving him to stare after me in some perplexity. I wanted to say goodbye to Pippa but she was nowhere in sight. Where was she? The library? The loo? I was determined to catch another glimpse of her — just one more — before I left. "Do you know where she is?" I said to Hobie, after making a quick tour around; but he only shook his head. So I stood anxiously by the coat check for several minutes, waiting for her to return, until finally Boris — mouth full of hors d'oeuvres — grabbed me by the arm and pulled me down the staircase and out the door.

V.

We have art in order not to die from the truth.

— NIETZSCHE

Chapter 11.

The Gentleman's Canal

i.

THE LINCOLN TOWN CAR was circling the block — but when the driver stopped for us, it was not Gyuri but a guy I'd never seen, with a haircut that looked like someone had administered it to him in the drunk tank and piercing, polar-blue eyes.

Boris introduced us in Russian. *"Privet! Myenya zovut Anatoly,"* said the guy, extending a hand slurred with indigo crowns and starbursts like the patterns on Ukrainian Easter eggs.

"Anatoly?" I said cautiously. *"Ochyen' priyatno?"* A stream of Russian followed, of which I understood not a word, and I turned to Boris in despair.

"Anatoly," Boris said pleasantly, "does not speak one stitch of English. Do you, Toly?"

In answer Anatoly gazed at us seriously in the rear view mirror and made another speech. His knuckle tattoos, I was pretty sure, had jailhouse significance: inked bands indicating time sentenced, time served, time marked in accretions like rings on a tree.

"He says you are pretty speaker," said Boris ironically. "Well-schooled in politeness."

"Where is Gyuri?"

"Oh — he flew over yesterday," Boris said. Scrabbling in the breast pocket of his jacket.

"Fly? Fly where?"

"Antwerp."

"My painting's there?"

"No." Boris had retrieved two sheets of paper from his pocket, which he scanned in the weak light before passing one to me. "But my flat is in

Antwerp, and my car. Gyuri is picking up the car and some things and driving to meet us."

Holding the paper to the light, I saw that it was a printout of an electronic ticket:

CONFIRMED

DECKER/THEODORE DL2334

NEWARK LIBERTY INTL **(EWR)** TO AMSTERDAM, NETHERLANDS **(AMS)**

BOARDING TIME **12:45A**

TOTAL TRAVEL TIME 7 HRS 44 MINS

"From Antwerp to Amsterdam is only three hours' drive," said Boris. "We will arrive at Schiphol about same time—me, maybe an hour after you—I had Myriam book us on different planes. Mine connects through Frankfurt. Yours is direct."

"Tonight?"

"Yes—well, as you see, it does not leave us much time—"

"And why am I going?"

"Because I may need some help, and do not want to bring anyone else in on this. Well—Gyuri. But I did not tell even Myriam purpose of our trip. Oh, oh, I *could* have," he said, interrupting me. "It's only—fewer people know of this, the better. Anyway you must run in and get your passport and what cash you can lay hands on. Toly will drive us to Newark. I—" he patted the carry-on, which I had only just noticed in the back seat—"I am all ready. Will wait in the car for you."

"And the money?"

"What you have."

"You should have told me earlier."

"No need. The cash—" he was rooting around for a cigarette—"well, I would not kill yourself with that. Whatever you have, whatever's convenient—? Because, is not important. Is mostly for show."

I took my glasses off, polished them on my sleeve. "Excuse me?"

"Because—" knocking himself with the knuckles on the side of his head, gesture of old, *blockhead*— "because I plan to pay them, but not the full amount requested. *Reward* them for stealing from me? Because why then won't they rob and steal from me whenever they want? What kind of a lesson is this? 'This man is weak.' 'We can do what we like to him.'

But—" crossing his legs spasmodically, patting himself down for a light—
"I want them to think we are willing to pay the whole thing. Possibly you
want to stop at a machine and get money—we can do that on the way, or
at the airport maybe. They will look nice, the new bills. I think you are
only allowed to bring ten thousand currency in, to EU—? But I will
rubber-band the extra and carry in my case. Also—" offering me a
cigarette—"I do not think it is fair for you to come up with the whole sum.
I will supply more cash once we get there. My gift to you. And bank draft,
as well—at any rate, bad paper for bank draft—bad deposit slip, bad
check. Brass-plate bank down in the Caribbean. Looks very good, very
legitimate. I do not know how well that part is going to work out. We will
have to play it by ear. No one with any brains is going to accept bank draft
instead of cash for something like this! But I think they are inexperienced,
and desperate, so—" he crossed his fingers—"I am hopeful. We will see!"

ii.

WHILE ANATOLY CIRCLED THE block, I ran into the shop and grabbed all
the unbanked cash to hand without counting it, somewhere in the neighborhood of sixteen thousand. Then I ran upstairs and—while Popper
paced and circled, whining with anxiety—threw a few things into my
bag: passport, toothbrush, razor, socks, underwear, first pair of suit trousers I found, couple of extra shirts, sweater. The Redbreast Flake tin was
at the bottom of my sock drawer and I grabbed it up too and then dropped
it and shut the drawer on it, quick.

As I hurried down the hall, dog at my heels, Pippa's Hunter boots standing outside her bedroom door brought me up sharply: their bright summer
green fused in my mind with her and with happiness. For a moment I
paused, uncertain. Then I went back to my room, got the first edition of
Ozma of Oz and dashed off a note so quickly I didn't have time to second-
guess. *Safe trip. I love you. No kidding.* This I blew dry and tucked in the
book, which I placed on the floor by her boots. The resulting tableau on the
carpet (Emerald City, green wellies, Ozma's color) was almost as if I'd stumbled on a haiku or some other perfect combination of words to explain to
her what she was to me. For a moment I stood in perfect stillness—ticking
clock, submerged memories from childhood, doors opening to bright old

daydreams where we walked together on summer lawns—before, resolutely, going back to my room for the necklace which had called to me in an auction house showroom with her name: lifting it from its midnight velvet box and, carefully, draping it over one of the boots so a splash of gold caught the light. It was topaz, eighteenth century, a necklace for a fairy queen, girandôle with diamond bow and huge, clear, honey-colored stones: just the shade of her eyes. As I turned away, averting my gaze from the wall of her photos opposite, and hurried down the stairs, it was almost with the old childhood terror and exhilaration of having thrown a rock through a window. Hobie would know exactly how much the necklace had cost. But by the time Pippa found it, and the note, I would be long gone.

iii.

WE WERE LEAVING FROM different terminals, so we said our goodbyes on the curb where Anatoly dropped me. The glass doors slid with a breathless gasp. Inside, past security, on the shiny floors of the predawn concourse, I consulted the monitors and walked past dark shops with the metal gates pulled down, Brookstone, Tie Rack, Nathan's hot dogs, bright seventies music drifting into consciousness (*love... love will keep us together... think of me babe whenever...*) past chilly ghost gates that were roped and empty except for college kids sprawled full-length and drowsing across four seats at a time, past the lone bar that was still open, the lone yogurt hut, the lone Duty Free where, as Boris had repeatedly and with some urgency advised me to do, I stopped for a fifth of vodka ("better safe than sorry... booze only available in the state controlled shops... maybe you want to get two") and then all the way to the end to my own (crowded) gate filled with dead-eyed ethnic families, backpackers cross-legged on the floor, and stale, oily-faced businessmen on laptops who looked like they were used to the drill.

The plane was full. Shuffling on, crowds in the aisle (economy, middle of the row, five across), I wondered how Myriam had managed to get me a seat at all. Luckily I was too tired to wonder about much else; and I was asleep almost before the seat belt light went off—missing drinks, missing dinner, missing the in-flight movies—waking only when the shades were pulled up and light flooded the cabin and the stewardess came pushing her cart through with our pre-packaged breakfasts: chilled twig of grapes; chilled cup of juice; lardy, yolk-yellow, cellophane-wrapped croissant; and our choice of coffee or tea.

We'd arranged to meet in baggage claim. Businessmen silently grabbed up their cases and fled—to their meetings, their marketing plans, their mistresses, who knew? Loudly shouting stoner kids with rainbow patches on their backpacks jostled each other and tried to snatch duffels that weren't theirs and argued about which was the best wake-and-bake coffeeshop to hit in the morning—"oh, guys, the Bluebird, *definitely*—"

"no, wait—Haarlemmerstraat? no, I'm serious, I wrote it down? It's on this paper? no, wait, listen guys, we should just go straight there? because I can't remember the name but it opens early and they have awesome *breakfasts?* And you can get your pancakes and OJ and your Apollo 13 and vape up right at the table?"

Off they trooped—fifteen or twenty of them, carefree, lustroushaired, laughing, hoisting their backpacks and arguing about the cheapest way to get into town. Despite the fact that I had no checked baggage, I stood in the claim area for well over an hour, watching a heavily taped suitcase circle round and round forlornly on the belt until Boris came up behind me and greeted me by throwing his arm around my neck in a choke hold and trying to step on the back of my shoes.

"Come on," he said, "you look awful. Let's get something to eat, and talk! Gyuri's got the car outside."

iv.

WHAT I SOMEHOW HADN'T expected was a city prinked-up for Christmas: fir boughs and tinsel, starburst ornaments in the shop windows and a cold stiff wind coming off the canals and fires and festival stalls and people on bicycles, toys and color and candy, holiday confusion and gleam. Little dogs, little children, gossipers and watchers and package bearers, clowns in top hats and military greatcoats and a little dancing jester in Christmas clothes à la Avercamp. I still wasn't quite awake and none of it seemed to have any more reality than the fleeting dream of Pippa I'd had on the plane where I'd spotted her in a park with many tall fountains and a Saturn-ringed planet hanging low and majestic in the sky.

"Nieuwmarkt," said Gyuri as we came out on a big circle with a tur-reted fairytale castle and — around it — an open air market, cut evergreens lightly frosted with snow, mittened vendors stamping, an illustration from a children's book. "Ho, ho, ho."

"Always a lot of police here," said Boris gloomily, sliding into the door as Gyuri took the turn hard.

For various reasons I was apprehensive about accommodations, and ready to make my excuses in case they involved anything like squatter conditions or sleeping on the floor. Luckily Myriam had booked me a hotel in a canal house in the old part of town. I dropped my bags, locked the cash in the safe, and went back out to the street to meet Boris. Gyuri had gone to park the car.

He dropped his cigarette on the cobblestones and dashed it under his heel. "I've not been here in a while," he said, his breath coming out white, as he looked round appraisingly at the soberly clad pedestrians on the street. "My flat in Antwerp — well it is for business reasons I am in Ant-werp. Beautiful city too — same sea clouds, same light. Someday we will go there. But I always forget how much I like it here as well. Starving to death, you?" he said, punching me in the arm. "Mind walking a bit?"

Down narrow streets we wandered, damp alleys too narrow for cars, foggy little ochreous shops filled with old prints and dusty porcelains. Canal footbridge: brown water, lonely brown duck. Plastic cup half-submerged and bobbing. The wind was raw and wet with blown pin-pricks of sleet and the space around us felt close and dank. Didn't the canals freeze in winter? I asked.

"Yes, but —" wiping his nose — "global warming, I suppose." In his overcoat and suit from the previous night's party he looked both com-pletely out of place and completely at home. "What a dog's weather! Shall we duck in here? Do you think?"

The dirty canal-side bar, or café, or whatever it was, had dark wood and a maritime theme, oars and life preservers, red candles burning low even in the daytime and a desolate foggy feel. Smoky, muggy light. Water droplets condensed on the inside of the windowpane. No menus. In back was a chalkboard scrawled with foods unintelligible to me: *dagsoep, draad-jesvlees, kapucijnerschotel, zuurkoolstamppot.*

"Here, let me order," said Boris, and proceeded to do so, surprisingly, in Dutch. What arrived was a typically Boris meal of beer, bread, sausages, and potatoes with pork and sauerkraut. Boris — happily gobbling — was reminiscing about his first and only attempt to ride a bicycle in the city (wipeout, disaster) and also how much he enjoyed the new herring in Amsterdam, which fortunately wasn't in season since apparently you ate it by holding it up by the tail fin and dangling it down into your mouth, but I was too disoriented by my surroundings to listen very closely and with almost painfully heightened senses I stirred at the potato mess with my fork and felt the strangeness of the city pressing in all around me, smells of tobacco and malt and nutmeg, café walls the melancholy brown of an old leather-bound book and then beyond, dark passages and brackish water lapping, low skies and old buildings all leaning against each other with a moody, poetic, edge-of-destruction feel, the cobblestoned loneliness of a city that felt — to me, anyway — like a place where you might come to let the water close over your head.

Before long Gyuri joined us, red-cheeked and breathless. "Parking — bit of a problem here," he said. "Sorry." He extended his hand to me. "Glad to see you!" he said, embracing me with a genuine-seeming warmth that startled me, as if we were old friends long separated. "Everything is okay?"

Boris, on his second pint by now, was holding forth a bit about Horst. "I do not know why he does not move to Amsterdam," he said, gnawing happily on a hunk of sausage. "Constantly he complains about New York! Hate hate hate! And all the holy while —" waving a hand at the canal outside the fogged window — "everything he loves is here. Even the language is same as his. If he really wanted to be happy in the world, Horst? To have any kind of joyful or happy life? He should pay twenty grand to go back to his rapid detox place and then come here and smoke Buddha Haze and stand in a museum all day long."

"Horst —?" I said, looking from one to the other.

"Sorry?"

"Does he know you're here?"

Boris gulped his beer. "Horst? No. He does not. It is going to be much, much easier if Horst learns about all this after. Because —" licking a dab of mustard off his finger — "my suspicions are correct. Fucking Sascha who stole the thing. *Ulrika's brother*," he said urgently. "Which with Ulrika puts Horst in bad position. So — much better if I take care of it on my own, see? I am doing Horst a favor this way — favor he won't forget."

"What do you mean, 'take care of it'?"

Boris sighed. "It —" he looked around to make sure no one was listening, even though we were the only people in the place —"well, it is complicated, I could talk for three days, but I can also tell you in three lines what has happened."

"Does Ulrika know he took it?"

Rolled eyes. "Search me." A phrase I had taught Boris years ago, horsing around at my house after school. *Search me. Cut it out.* Smoky desert twilight, shades drawn. *Make up your mind. Let's face it. No way.* Same shadows on his face. Gold light glinting off the doors by the pool.

"I think Sascha would have to be very stupid to tell Ulrika," said Gyuri, with a worried expression on his face.

"I don't know what Ulrika knows or does not know. Has no relevance. She has loyalty to her brother over Horst, as she has shown many and many times over. You would think —" grandly signalling the waitress to bring Gyuri a pint— "you would think Sascha had sense to sit on it for a while, at least! But no. He can't get a loan on it in Hamburg or Frankfurt because of Horst —because Horst would hear of it in one second. So he has brought it here."

"Well look, if you know who has it we should just call the police."

The silence, and blank looks that followed this, were as if I'd produced a can of gasoline and suggested lighting ourselves on fire.

"Well, I mean," I said defensively, after the waitress had arrived with Gyuri's beer, set it down, left again, and neither Gyuri nor Boris had spoken a word. "Isn't that the safest? And easiest? If the cops recover it and you have nothing to do with it?"

Ding of a bicycle bell, woman clattering by on the sidewalk, rattle of spokes, witchy black cape flying behind.

"Because —" glancing between them — "when you think of what this picture has gone through —what it *must* have gone through —I don't know if you understand, Boris, how much care has to be taken even to *ship* a painting? Just to *pack* it properly? Why take any chances?"

"This is my feeling exactly."

"An anonymous call. To the art-crimes people. They're not like the normal cops —no connections with the normal cops —the picture is all they care about. They'll know what to do."

Boris leaned back in his chair. He looked around. Then he looked at me.

"No," he said. "That is not a good idea." His tone was that of someone addressing a five year old. "And, do you want to know why?"

"Think about it. It's the easiest way. You wouldn't have to do a thing."

Boris set his beer glass down carefully.

"They'd have the best chance of getting it back unharmed. Also, if *I* do it — if *I* call them — shit, I could have Hobie call them —" hands to head — "any way you look at it, you wouldn't be putting yourselves at risk. That is to say" — I was too tired, disoriented; two pairs of Dremel-drill eyes, I couldn't think — "if *I* did it, or someone else not a part of your, um, organization —"

Boris let out a shout of laughter. "*Organization?* Well —" shaking his head so vigorously the hair fell in his eyes — "I suppose we count as organization, of sorts, since we are three or more —! But we are not very large or very organized as you can see."

"You should eat something," said Gyuri to me, in the tense pause that followed, looking at my untouched plate of pork and potato. "He should eat," he said to Boris. "Tell him to eat."

"Let him starve if he wants. Anyway," said Boris, grabbing a chunk of pork off my plate and popping it in his mouth —

"One call. I'll do it."

"No," said Boris, glowering suddenly and pushing back in his chair. "You will not. No, no, fuck you, shut up, you *won't,*" he said, lifting his chin aggressively when I tried to talk over him — Gyuri's hand on my wrist very suddenly, a touch I knew very well, the old forgotten Vegas language of when my dad was in the kitchen ranting about whose house it was? and who paid for what? —

"And, and," said Boris imperiously, taking advantage of a lull in my response he was not expecting, "I want you to stop talking this stupid 'call' business right away. 'Call, call,'" he said, when he got no answer from me, waving his hand back and forth ridiculously in the air as if "call" were some absurd kiddie word that meant 'unicorn' or 'fairyland.' "I know you are trying to help but this is not helpful suggestion on your part. So forget it. No more 'call.' Anyway," he said amiably, pouring part of his own beer into my half-empty glass. "As I was explaining to you. Since Sascha is in so big hurry? Is he thinking clearly? Is he playing more than one, or maybe two moves ahead? No. Sascha is out of towner. His connections here are poisonous to him. He needs money. And he is working so hard to stay clear of Horst that he has wandered smack into me."

I said nothing. It would be easy enough to phone the police myself. There was no reason to involve Boris or Gyuri at all.

"Amazing stroke of luck, no? And our friend the Georgian—very rich man, but so far from Horst's world and so far from art collector, he did not even know of picture by name. Just a bird—little yellow bird. But Cherry believes he is telling the truth that he saw it. Very powerful guy in terms of real estate? Here and in Antwerp? Plenty of paper and father to Cherry almost, but not person of great education if you understand me."

"Where is it now?"

Boris rubbed his nose vigorously. "I do not know. They are not going to tell us that, are they? But Vitya has got in touch to say he knows of a buyer. And a meeting has been set up."

"Where?"

"Not settled yet. They have already changed the location half a dozen times. Paranoid," he said, making a screw-loose gesture at the side of his head with his hand. "They may make us wait a day or two. We may know only an hour before."

"Cherry," I said, and stopped. Vitya was short for Cherry's Russian name, Viktor—Victor, the Anglicized version—but Cherry was only a nickname and I didn't know a thing about Sascha: not his age, not his surname, not what he looked like, nothing at all except that he was Ulrika's brother—and even this was uncertain in the literal sense, given how loosely Boris threw around the word.

Boris sucked a bit of grease off his thumb. "My idea was—set up something at your hotel. You know, you, American, big shot, interested in the picture. They"—he lowered his voice as the waitress switched his empty pint for a full one, Gyuri nodding politely, leaning in—"they would come to your room. That's how is done usually. All very businesslike. But"—minimal shrug—"they are new at this, and paranoid. They want to call their own location."

"Which is?"

"Don't know yet! Didn't I just say? They keep changing their mind. If they want us to wait—we wait. We have to let them think they are boss.

Now, sorry," he said, stretching and yawning, rubbing a dark-circled eye with a fingertip, "I am tired! Want a nap!" He turned and said something to Gyuri in Ukrainian, and then turned back to me. "Sorry," he said, leaning in and slinging his arm around my shoulder. "You can find your way back to your hotel?"

I tried to disengage myself without seeming to. "Right. Where are you staying?"

"Girlfriend's flat — Zeedijk."

"Near Zeedijk," said Gyuri, rising purposefully, with a polite and vaguely military air. "Chinese quarter of the old times."

"What's the address?"

"Cannot remember. You know me. I cannot remember addresses in my head and like that. But —" Boris tapped his pocket — "your hotel."

"Right." Back in Vegas, if we ever got separated — running from the mall cops, pockets full of stolen gift cards — my house was always the rendezvous point.

"So — I'll meet you back there. And you have my phone number, and I have yours. Will call you when I know something more. Now —" slapping me on the back of the head — "stop worrying, Potter! Don't stand there and look so unhappy! If we lose, we win, and if we win, we win! Everything is good! You know which way to go to get back, don't you? Just up this way, and left when you get to the Singel. Yes, there. We will speak soon."

v.

I TOOK A WRONG turn on the way to the hotel and for several hours wandered aimlessly, shops decorated with glass baubles and gray dream alleys with unpronounceable names, gilded buddhas and Asian embroideries, old maps, old harpsichords, cloudy cigar-brown shops with crockery and goblets and antique Dresden jars. The sun had come out and there was something hard and bright by the canals, a breathable glitter. Gulls plunged and cried. A dog ran by with a live crab in its mouth. In my lightheadedness and fatigue, which made me feel drastically cut off from myself and as if I were observing it all at a remove, I walked past candy shops and coffee shops and shops with antique toys and Delft tiles from the 1800s, old mirrors and silver glinting in the rich, cognac-colored light, inlaid French cabinets and tables in the French court style with garlanded carvings and veneerwork that would have made Hobie gasp with admiration — in fact the entire foggy, friendly, cultivated city with its florists and bakeries and antiekhandels reminded me of Hobie, not just for its antique-crowded richness but because there was a Hobie-like wholesomeness to the place, like a children's picture book where aproned tradespeople swept the floors and tabby cats napped in sunny windows.

But there was much too much to see, and I was overwhelmed and exhausted and cold. Finally, by accosting strangers for directions (rosy housewives with armloads of flowers, tobacco-stained hippies in wire-rimmed glasses), I retraced my path over canal bridges and back through narrow fairy-lit streets to my hotel, where I immediately changed some dollars at the front desk, went up for a shower in the bathroom which was all curved glass and voluptuous fixtures, hybrid of the Art Nouveau and some icy, pod-based, science fiction future, and fell asleep face down on the bed — where I was awakened, hours later, by my cell phone spinning on the bed table, the familiar chirrup making me think, for a moment, I was at home.

"Potter?"

I sat up and reached for my glasses. "Um —" I hadn't drawn the curtains before I fell asleep and reflections of the canal wavered across the ceiling in the dark.

"What's wrong? Are you high? Don't tell me you went to a coffee shop."

"No, I —" Dazedly I slid an eye around — dormers and beams, cupboards and slants and — out the window, when I stood, rubbing my head — canal bridges lighted in tracework, arched reflections on black water.

"Well I'm coming up. You don't have a girl up there, do you?"

vi.

MY ROOM WAS TWO different elevators and a walk from the front desk, so I was surprised how quickly the knock came. Gyuri, discreetly, went to the window and stood with his back to us while Boris looked me over. "Get dressed," he said. I was barefoot, in the hotel robe and my hair standing on end from falling asleep straight out of the shower. "You need to clean up. Go—comb your hair and shave."

When I emerged from the bathroom (where I'd left my suit hanging to let the wrinkles fall out) he pursed his lips critically and said: "Don't you have anything better than that?"

"This is a Turnbull and Asser suit."

"Yes but it looks like you slept in it."

"I've been wearing it a while. I have a better shirt."

"Well put it on." He was opening a briefcase on the foot of the bed. "And get your money and bring it here."

When I came back in, doing up my cufflinks, I stopped dead in the middle of the room to see him standing head bent at the bedside, intent upon assembling a pistol: snapping a pin with a clear-eyed competence like Hobie at work in the shop, pulling back the slide with a forceful true-to-life quality, click.

"Boris," I said, "what the mother fuck."

"Calm down," he said to me, with a sideways glance. Patting his pockets, taking out a magazine and popping it in: snick. "Is not what you think. Not at all. Is just for show!"

I looked at Gyuri's broad back, perfectly impassive, the same professional deafness I sometimes turned away to assume, in the shop, when couples were bickering over whether to buy a piece of furniture or not.

"It is just—" He was snapping something back and forth on the gun, expertly, testing it, then bringing it up to his eye and sighting it, surreal gestures from some deep underlayer of the brain where the black and white movies flickered twenty-four hours a day. "We are meeting them on their own ground, and they will be three. Well, really only two. Two that *count*. And I can tell you now—I was a little worried Sascha might be here. Because then I couldn't go with you. But everything has worked out perfectly, and here I am!"

"Boris—" standing there, it had crashed in on me all at once, in a sick rush, what a dumb fucking thing I'd stepped into—

"No worries! I have done the worrying for you. Because—" patting me on the shoulder—"Sascha is too nervous. He is afraid to show his face in Amsterdam—afraid it will get back to Horst. For good reason. And this is very very good news for us.

"So." He snapped the gun shut: chrome silver, mercury black, with a smooth density that blackly distorted the space around it like a drop of motor oil in a glass of water.

"Don't tell me you're taking that," I said, in the incredulous silence that followed.

"Well, yes. For holster—to keep in holster *only*. But wait, wait," he said, lifting a palm, "before you start—" although I wasn't talking, I was only standing there blank with horror—"how many times do I have to say it? Is only for looks."

"You've got to be kidding."

"Dress-up," he said briskly, as if I had not spoken. "Pure make-believe. So they will be worried to try something if they see it on me, okay?" he added, when I still stood staring. "Safety measure! Because, because," he said over me, "you are the rich man, and we are the bodyguards and this is how it is. They will expect it. All very civilized. And if we move our coat just so—" he had a concealed-carry holster at his waist—"they will be respectful and not try anything. *Much* more dangerous to wander in like—" he rolled his eyes around the room in the manner of a daffy girl.

"Boris." I felt ashen and woozy. "I can't do this."

"Can't what?" He pulled back his chin and looked at me. "Can't get out of car and stand with me for five minutes while I get your fucking picture for you? What?"

"No, I mean it." The gun was lying on the bedspread; the eye was drawn to it; it seemed to crystallize and magnify all the bad energy humming in the air. "I can't. Seriously. Let's just forget it."

"Forget?" Boris made a face. "Don't do this! You have brought me over here for nothing and now I am in a pinch. And now—" flinging out an arm—"last minute, you start making conditions and saying 'unsafe, unsafe' and telling me how to do things? Don't you trust me?"

"Yes, but—"

"Well, then. Trust me on this, please. You're the buyer," he said impatiently, when I didn't answer. "That's the story. It's been set up."

"We should have talked about this earlier."

"Oh, come on," he said in exasperation, picking the gun off the bed and sticking it into the holster. "Please do not argue with me, we are going to be late. You would never have seen it at all, if you stayed in the bathroom two minutes longer! Never known I had a weapon on me at all! Because—Potter, listen to me. Will you listen, please? Here is all that will happen. We walk in, five minutes, stand stand stand, we do all the talking, talk *only,* you get your picture, everyone is happy, we leave and we go get some dinner. Okay?"

Gyuri, who had moved over from the window, was looking me up and down. With a worried frown, he said something to Boris in Ukrainian. An obscure exchange followed. Then Boris reached to his wrist and began to unbuckle his watch.

Gyuri said something else, shaking his head vigorously.

"Right," said Boris. "You are right." Then, to me, with a nod: "Take his."

Platinum Rolex President. Diamond-crusted dial. I was trying to think of some polite way to refuse when Gyuri pulled the whopping bevel-cut diamond off his pinky and — hopefully, like a child presenting a home-made gift — held them both to me on his open hands.

"Yes," said Boris when I hesitated. "He is right. You do not look rich enough. I wish we had some different shoes for you," he said, looking critically at my black monk straps, "but those will have to work. Now, we will put the money in this bag here" — leather grip, full of stacked bills — "and go." Working quickly, clever hands, like a hotel maid making a bed. "Biggest bills on top. All these nice hundreds. Very pretty."

vii.

OUT ON THE STREET: holiday splendor and delirium. Reflections danced and shimmered on black water: laced arcades above the street, garlands of light on the canal boats.

"This is all going to be very easy and comfortable," said Boris, who was clicking around on the radio past Bee Gees, past news in Dutch, in French, trying to find a song. "I am counting on the fact that they want this money quick. Sooner they get rid of the picture — less chance running crossways of Horst. They will not be looking too closely at that bank draft or deposit slip. That six hundred thousands figure is all they will see."

I was sitting alone in the back seat with the bag of money. ("Because, you must accustom yourself, sir, to being distinguished passenger!" Gyuri had said when he circled around and opened the back door of the car for me to get in.)

"You see — what I hope will fool him — deposit slip is perfectly legitimate," Boris was saying. "So is bank draft. It is just from bad bank. Anguilla. Russians in Antwerp—here too, on P. C. Hooftstraat—they come here to invest, wash money, buy art, ha! This bank was fine six weeks ago but it is not fine now."

We were past the canals, past the water. On the street: multicolored neon angels, in silhouette, leaning out from the tops of the buildings like ship figureheads. Blue spangles, white spangles, tracers, cascades of white lights and Christmas stars, blazing, impenetrable, no more to do with me than the implausible pinky diamond glittering on my hand.

"See, what I have to tell you," said Boris, forgetting the radio and turning to address me in the back seat, "I want to tell you not to worry. With all my heart," he said, knitting his eyebrows and reaching out encouragingly to shake my shoulder. "Everything is fine."

"Piece of cake!" said Gyuri, and beamed in the rear view mirror, happy to have produced the phrase.

"Here is plan. Do you want to know the plan?"

"I guess I'm supposed to say yes."

"We are dropping the car off. Out of the city a bit. Then Cherry will meet us at location, and drive us to meeting in *his* car."

"And this is all going to be peaceful."

"Absolutely. And because why? You have the cash! That's all they want. And even with fake bank draft—good deal for them. Forty thousand dollars for no work? Not much! Afterwards—Cherry will leave us back off at the garage, with the picture—and then—we go out! we celebrate!"

Gyuri muttered something.

"He is complaining about the garage. Just so you know. He thinks it is a bad idea. But—I do not want to go in my own car, and last thing we need is to get hit with a parking ticket."

"Where is the meeting?"

"Well—bit of a headache. We have to drive out of the city and then back in. They insisted on their own place and Cherry agreed because—well, really, it is better. At least, on their ground, we can count on no interference from the cops."

We had gotten to a lonelier stretch of road, straight and desolate, where the traffic was sparse and the streetlamps were farther apart, and the bracing crack and sparkle of the old city, its lighted tracery, its hidden design—

silver skates, happy children beneath the tree—had given way to a more familiar urban bleakness: Fotocadeau, Locksmith Sleutelkluis, signs in Arabic, Shoarma, Tandoori Kebab, gates down, everything closed.

"This is the Overtoom," said Gyuri. "Not very interesting or nice."

"This is my boy Dima's parking garage. He has put out the Full sign for tonight so no one to bother us. We will be in the long term—ah," he screamed, *"blyad,"* as a honking van cut in front of us from nowhere, forcing Gyuri to swerve and slam on the brakes.

"Sometimes people here are little bit aggressive for no reason," said Gyuri gloomily as he put on his blinker and made the turn into the garage.

"Give me your passport," Boris said.

"Why?"

"Because, am going to lock it in the glove box for when we get back. Better not to have it on you, just in case. I am putting in mine, too," he said, holding it up for me to see. "And Gyuri's. Gyuri is honest born American citizen—yes," he said, over Gyuri's laughing interjection, "all very nice for you, but for me? very very hard to get an American passport and I really do not want to lose this thing. You know, don't you Potter," he said, looking at me, "that you are required now by law in Netherlands to carry ID at all times? Random street checks—non-compliance punished. I mean—Amsterdam? What kind of police state thing is this? Who would believe it? *Here?* Me—never. Not in one hundred years. Anyway"—shutting and locking the glove box—"better a fine and talk our way out of it than the real thing on us if we are stopped."

viii.

INSIDE THE PARKING GARAGE, which vibrated depressingly with olive-green light, there were a number of empty spaces in the long-term area despite the Full sign. As we nosed into the space a man in a sports coat lounging against a white Range Rover threw his cigarette in a spit of orange cinders and walked toward the car. His receding hairline, his tinted aviators and his taut military torso gave him the wind-whipped look of an ex-pilot, a man who monitored delicate instruments at some test site in the Urals.

"Victor," he said, when we got out of the car, crushing my hand in his. Gyuri and Boris received a thump on the back. After terse preliminaries in Russian, a baby-faced curly-headed teenager climbed out of the driver's seat and was greeted, by Boris, with a slap on the cheek and a jaunty seven note whistle: *On the Good Ship Lollipop.*

"This is Shirley T," he said to me, rumpling the corkscrew curls. "Shirley Temple. We all call him that—why? Can you guess?"—laughing as the kid, unable to help it, smiled in embarrassment, displaying deep dimples.

"Do not be deceived by looks," said Gyuri to me quietly. "Shirley looks like baby but he has as much onions as any of us here."

Politely, Shirley nodded at me—did he speak English? it didn't seem so—and opened the back door of the Range Rover for us and the three of us climbed in—Boris, Gyuri, and me—while Victor Cherry sat up front and talked to us from the passenger seat.

"This should be easy," he said to me formally as we pulled out of the garage and back out onto the Overtoom. "Straightforward pawn." Up close his face was broad and knowing, with a small prim mouth and a wry alertness that made me feel somewhat less agitated about the logic of the evening, or the lack of it: the car changes, the lack of direction and information, the nightmare foreignness. "We are doing Sascha a favor and because of that? He is going to behave nice to us."

Long low buildings. Disjointed lights. There was a sense that it wasn't happening, that it was happening to someone who wasn't me.

"Because can Sascha walk in bank and get a loan on the painting?" Victor was saying, pedantically. "No. Can Sascha walk in a pawn shop and get a loan on the painting? No. Can Sascha due to circumstances of theft go to any of his usual connections from Horst and get a loan on the painting? No. Therefore Sascha is extremely glad of the appearance of mystery American—you—who I have hooked him up with."

"Sascha shoots heroin the way that you and I breathe," said Gyuri to me quietly. "One stitch of money and he is out buying big load of drugs like clockwork."

Victor Cherry adjusted his glasses. "Exactly. He is not art lover and he is not particular. He is utilizing picture like high interest credit card or so he thinks. Investment for you—cash for him. You front him the money—you hold the painting as security—he buys schmeck, keeps half, steps on the rest and sells it, and returns with double your money in one month to pick up the painting. And if? In one month he does not return with double your money? The painting is yours. Like I said. Simple pawn."

"Except not so simple—" Boris stretched, and yawned—"because when you vanish? and bank draft is bad? What can he do? If he runs to Horst and calls for help on this one he will have his neck broken for him."

"I am glad they have changed the meeting place so many times. It is a little bit ridiculous. But it helps because today is Friday," said Victor, taking off his aviators and polishing them on his shirt. "I made them think you were backing out. Because they kept cancelling and changing the plan— you did not even arrive until today, but they do not know that—because they kept changing the plan I told them you were tired and nervous of sitting around Amsterdam with suitcase of green waiting to hear from them, you'd re-banked your moneys and were flying back to U.S. They did not like to hear that. So—" he nodded at the bag—"here it is the weekend, and banks are closed, and you are bringing what cash you have, and— well, they have been talking to me plenty, lots of time on the phone and I have met with them once already down in a bar in the Red Light, but they have agreed to bring the painting and make the exchange tonight without prior meeting of you, because I have told them your plane leaves tomorrow, and because they have fucked around on their end it is bank draft for the balance or nothing. Which—well, they did not like, but they accepted as proper explanation for bank draft. Makes things easier."

"Much easier," said Boris. "I was not sure how bank draft was going to go over. Better if they think the bank draft is their own fault for dicking around."

"What's the place?"

"Lunchcafe." He pronounced it as one word. "De Paarse Koe."

"That means 'the Purple Cow' in Dutch," said Boris helpfully. "Hippie place. Close to the Red Light."

Long lonely street—shut-up hardware stores, stacks of brick by the side of the road, all of it important and hyper-significant somehow even though it was speeding by in the dark much too fast to see.

"Food is so awful," said Boris. "Sprouts and some hard old wheat toast. You would think hot girls go there but is just old gray-head women and fat."

"Why there?"

"Because quiet street in the evening," said Victor Cherry. "Lunchcafe is closed, after hours, but because semi-public nothing will get out of control, see?"

Everywhere: strangeness. Without noticing it I'd left reality and crossed the border into some no-man's-land where nothing made sense. Dreaminess, fragmentation. Rolled wire and piles of rubble with the plastic sheeting blown to the side.

Boris was speaking to Victor in Russian; and when he realized I was looking at him, he turned to me.

"We are only saying, Sascha is in Frankfurt tonight," he said, "hosting party at a restaurant for some friend of his just got out of jail, and we are all of us confirmed on this from three different sources, Shirley too. He thinks he is being smart, staying out of town. If it gets back to Horst what has happened here tonight he wants to be able to throw up his hands and say, 'Who, me? I had nothing to do with it.'"

"You," said Victor to me, "you are based in New York. I have said you are an art dealer, arrested for forgery, and now run an operation like Horst's— much smaller scale in terms of paintings, much larger in terms of money."

"Horst—God bless him," said Boris. "Horst would be the richest man in New York except he gives it all away, every cent. Always has. Supports many many persons besides himself."

"Bad for business."

"Yes. But he enjoys company."

"Junkie philanthropist, ha," said Victor. He pronounced it philan*throp*ist. "Good they die off time to time or who knows how many schmeckheads crammed in that dump with him. Anyway—less you say in there, the better. They will not be expecting polite conversation. This is all business. It will be fast. Give him the bank draft, Borya."

Boris said something sharp in Ukrainian.

"No, he should produce it himself. It should be from his hand."

Both bank draft, and deposit slip, were printed with the words Farruco Frantisek, Citizen Bank Anguilla, which only increased the sense of dream trajectory, a track speeding up too fast to slow down.

"Farruco Frantisek? I'm him?" Under the circumstances it felt like a meaningful question—as if I might be somehow disembodied or at least had passed beyond a certain horizon where I was freed of basic facts like identity.

"I did not choose the name. I had to take what I could get."

"I'm supposed to introduce myself as this?" There was something wrong with the paper, which was too flimsy, and the fact that the slips said Citizen Bank and not Citizen's Bank made them look all wrong.

"No, Cherry will introduce you."

Farruco Frantisek. Silently I tried the name out, turned my tongue around it. Even though it was a hard name to remember, it was just strong and foreign enough to carry the lost-in-space hyperdensity of the black streets, tram tracks, more cobblestones and neon angels — back in the old city now, historic and unknowable, canals and bicycle racks and Christmas lights shaking on the dark water.

"When were you going to tell him?" Victor Cherry was asking Boris. "He needs to know what his name is."

"Well now he knows."

Unknown streets, incomprehensible turns, anonymous distances. I'd stopped even trying to read the street signs or keep track of where we were. Of everything around me — of all I could see — the only point of reference was the moon, riding high above the clouds, which though bright and full seemed weirdly unstable somehow, void of gravity, not the pure anchoring moon of the desert but more like a party trick that might pop out at a conjurer's wink or else float away into the darkness and out of sight.

ix.

THE PURPLE COW WAS on an untravelled one-way street just wide enough for a car to go through. All the other businesses around — pharmacy, bakery, bike shop — were shut tight, everything but an Indonesian restaurant on the far end. Shirley Temple let us off out front. On the opposite wall, graffiti: smiley face and arrows, Warning Radioactive, stenciled lightning bolt with the word Shazam, dripping horror-movie letters, *keep it nice!*

I looked in through the glass door. The place was long and narrow, and — at first glance — empty. Purple walls; stained glass ceiling lamp; mismatched tables and chairs painted kindergarten colors and the lights low except for a grillside counter area and a lighted cold case glowing in back. Sickly house plants; signed black-and-white photo of John and Yoko;

bulletin board shaggy with leaflets and flyers for satsangs and yoga classes and varied holistic modalities. On the wall was a mural of the Tarot arcana and, in the window, a flimsy computer-printed menu featuring a number of Everett-style wholefoods: carrotsoup, nettlesoup, nettlemash, lentil-nutspie—nothing very appetizing, but it made me remember that the last honest-to-God, more-than-a-few-bites meal I'd eaten had been the take-out curry in bed back at Kitsey's.

Boris saw me looking at it. "I am hungry too," he said, rather formally. "We will go get a really good dinner together. Blake's. Twenty minutes."

"You're not going in?"

"Not yet." He was standing slightly to the side, out of view of the glass doors, looking up and down the street. Shirley Temple was circling the block. "Don't be here talking to me. Go with Victor and Gyuri."

The man who sloped up to the glass door of the cafe was a scrawny, sketchy, twitchy-looking guy in his sixties, with a long narrow face and long freak hair past his shoulders and a peaked denim cap straight from Soul Train 1973. He stood there with his ring of keys and looked past Victor to me and Gyuri and seemed undecided whether to let us in. His close-set eyes, his brushy gray eyebrows and his puffy gray moustache gave him the look of a suspicious old schnauzer dog. Then another guy appeared, much much younger and much much bigger, half a head taller even than Gyuri, Malaysian or Indonesian with a face tattoo and eyepopping diamonds in his ears and a black topknot on the crown of his head that made him look like one of the harpooners from *Moby Dick*, if one of the harpooners from *Moby Dick* had happened to be wearing velvet track pants and a peach satin baseball jacket.

The old tweaker was making a call on his mobile. He waited, his eyes cagily on us the whole while. Then he made another call and turned his back and walked away into the depths of the lunchcafe, talking, palm pressed to cheek and ear in the manner of a hysterical housewife while the Indonesian stood in the glass door and watched us, unnaturally still. There was a brief exchange and then the old tweaker returned and with wrinkled brow and seeming reluctance began fumbling with the key ring, turning the key in the lock. The minute we were in he began yammering to Victor Cherry and throwing his arms about, while the Indonesian strolled over and leaned against the wall with his arms folded, listening.

Some disturbance, definitely. Discomfort. What language were they speaking? Romanian? Czech? What it was about I had not a clue but Victor Cherry seemed cold and annoyed while the old gray-head tweaker grew more and more agitated—angry? no: irritable, frustrated, wheedling even, a whine climbing in his voice, and all the time the Indonesian kept his eyes on us with the unsettling stillness of an anaconda. I stood about ten feet away and—despite Gyuri, with moneybag, pressing in on me much too close—put on a self-consciously blank expression and pretended to examine the signs and slogans on the wall: Greenpeace, Fur-Free Zone, Vegan Friendly, Protected by Angels! Having bought enough drugs in enough dodgy situations (cockroach apartments in Spanish Harlem, piss-smelling stairwells in the St. Nicholas projects), I knew enough not to be interested, since—in my experience anyway—transactions of this nature were mostly the same. You acted relaxed and disengaged, didn't talk unless you had to and spoke in a monotone when you did, and—as soon as you got what you came for—left.

"Protected by angels, my ass," said Boris, in my ear, having sidled up noiselessly on my other side.

I said nothing. Even all these years later, it was all too easy for us to fall into the habit of whispering with our heads together like in Spirsetskaya's class, which seemed like not a good dynamic in the situation.

"We are on time," said Boris. "But one of their men has not shown. That is why Grateful Dead here is so jumpy. They want us to wait till he comes. It is their own fault for changing the meeting place so often."

"What's going on over there?"

"Let Vitya handle it," he said, poking his shoe at a desiccated furball on the floor—dead mouse? I thought, with a start, before realizing it was a chewed-up cat toy, one of several strewn across the floor beside a clumped and piss-darkened cat tray which lay half-hidden, turds and all, at the base of a table for four.

I was wondering how a dirty cat tray placed where diners were likely to step in it was possibly convenient in terms of food-service logistics (not to mention attractive, or healthful, or even legal) when I realized the talking had stopped and the two of them had turned to Gyuri and me—Victor Cherry, the old tweaker with a wary expectant look, stepping forward, his eyes darting from me to the bag in Gyuri's hand. Obligingly Gyuri stepped forward, opened it, set it down with a servile bow of his head, and stepped away for the old guy to look at it.

The old guy peered in, nearsightedly; his nose wrinkled. With some peevish exclamation he looked up at Cherry, who remained impassive. Another obscure exchange ensued. The grayhair seemed discontented. Then he closed the bag and stood up and looked at me, eyes darting.

"Farruco," I said nervously, having forgotten my last name and hoping I would not be required to produce it.

Cherry gave me a look: *the papers.*

"Right, right," I said, reaching in the top inside pocket of my jacket for the bank draft and the deposit slip—unfolding them, in what I hoped was a casual way, checking them out before I handed them over—

Frantisek. But just as I was extending my hand—bam, it happened like a gust of wind that blows through the house and slams a door loudly in a direction where you aren't expecting it—Victor Cherry stepped fast behind the grayhair and whacked him on the back of the head with the pistol butt so hard his cap flew off and his knees buckled and down he went with a grunt. The Indonesian, still in his wall-slouch, seemed as startled by this as I was: he stiffened, our eyes connected in a sharp *what the fuck?* jolt that was almost like a glance between friends, and I couldn't understand why he wasn't moving away from the wall until I looked behind me and saw to my horror that Boris and Gyuri both had guns on him: Boris neatly resting the butt of the pistol in the cup of his left palm and Gyuri, one-handed, with the bag of money, backing out the front door.

Disconnected flash, someone flitting from the kitchen in back: young-ish Asian woman—no, a boy; white skin, blank frightened eyes sweeping the room, Ikat print scarf, long hair flying, just as quickly gone.

"Someone's in back," I said rapidly, looking around, every direction, room wheeling around me like a carnival ride and heart beating so wildly I couldn't make the words come out quite right, I wasn't sure if anyone heard me say it—or if Cherry heard, at any rate, since he was hauling the grayhair up by the back of his jeans jacket, catching him in a chokehold, pistol at his temple, screaming at him in whatever Eastern-European tongue and jostling him to the rear as the Indonesian un-slouched himself from the wall, gracefully and carefully, and looked at Boris and me for what seemed like a long time.

"You cunts are going to be sorry for this," he said quietly.

"Hands, hands," said Boris cordially. "Where I can see them."

"I don't got a weapon."

"Right there anyway."

"Right you are," said the Indonesian, just as cordially. He looked me up and down with his hands in the air — memorizing my face, I realized with a chill, image straight to data file — and then he looked at Boris.

"I know who you are," he said.

Submarine glow of the fruit juice cooler. I could hear my own breath going in and out, in and out. Clang of metal in the kitchen. Indistinct cries.

"Down, if you please," said Boris, nodding at the floor.

Obligingly the Indonesian got to his knees and — very slowly — stretched himself full length. But he didn't seem rattled or afraid.

"I know you," he said again, voice slightly muffled.

Fast darting movement in the corner of my eye, so fast I started: a cat, devil black, like a living shadow, darkness flying to darkness.

"And who am I then?"

"Borya-from-Antwerp, innit?" It wasn't true that he didn't have a weapon; even I could see it bulging at his armpit. "Borya the Polack? Giggleweed Borya? Horst's mate?"

"And so if I am?" said Boris genially.

The man was silent. Boris, tossing the hair out of his eyes with a flick of his head, made a derisive noise and seemed about to say something sarcastic but just then Victor Cherry came out of the back, alone, pulling what looked like a set of flexcuffs out of his pocket — and my heart skipped to see, under his arm, a package of the correct size and thickness, wrapped in white felt and tied with baker's twine. He dropped a knee in the Indonesian's back and began to fumble with the cuffs at his wrists.

"Get out," said Boris to me, and then, again — my muscles had locked up and hardened; he gave me a little push — "Go! get in the car."

Blankly I looked around — I couldn't see the door, there wasn't a door — and then there it was and I scrambled out so fast I slipped and nearly fell on a cat toy, out to the Range Rover puffing at the curb. Gyuri was keeping watch out front, on the street, in the light drizzle which had just begun to fall — "In, in," he hissed, sliding into the back seat and waving me to come in after him, just as Boris and Victor Cherry burst out of the restaurant and hopped in too and off we drove, at a sedate and anticlimactic speed.

X.

IN THE CAR, OUT on the main road again, all was jubilation: laughter, high fives, while my heart was slamming so hard I could barely breathe. "What's going on?" I rasped, several times—gulping for breath and looking back and forth between them and then, when they kept ignoring me, babbling in a percussive mix of Russian and Ukrainian, all four of them including Shirley Temple: *"Angliyski!"*

Boris turned to me, wiping his eyes, and slung his arm around my neck. "Change of plans," he said. "That was all on the fly—improvised. We could have asked for nothing better. Their third man didn't show."

"Catching them short-handed."

"Flatfooted."

"Pants down! On the crapper!"

"You"—I had to gasp to get the words out—"you said no guns."

"Well, no one got hurt, did they? What difference does it make?"

"Why didn't we just pay?"

"Because we lucked out!" Throwing up his arms. "Once in a lifetime chance! We had the opportunity! What were they going to do? They were two—we were four. If they had any sense, they should never have let us inside. And—yes, I know, only forty thousand, but why should I pay them one cent if I don't have to? For stealing my own property?" Boris chortled. "Did you see the look on his face? Grateful Dead? When Cherry whipped him back of the dome?"

"You know what he was complaining about, the old goat?" said Victor, turning to me jubilantly. "Wanted it in Euros! 'What, dollars?'" imitating his peevish expression. "'You brought me dollars?'"

"Bet he wishes he had those dollars now."

"I bet he wishes he kept his mouth shut."

"I'd like to hear that phone call to Sascha."

"I wish I knew the name of the guy. That stood them up. Because I would like to buy him a drink."

"Wonder where he is?"

"He is probably at home in the shower."

"Studying his Bible lesson."

"Watching 'Christmas Carol' on television."

"Waiting at the wrong place, most like."

"I—" My throat was so constricted I had to swallow to speak. "What about that kid?"

"Eh?" It was raining, light rain pattering on the windshield. Streets black and glistening.

"What kid?"

"Boy. Girl. Kitchen boy. Whatever."

"What?" Cherry turned—still winded, breathing hard. "I didn't see anyone."

"I didn't either."

"Well, I did."

"What'd she look like?"

"Young." I could still see the freeze-frame of the young ghostly face, mouth slightly open. "White coat. Japanese-looking."

"Really?" said Boris curiously. "You can tell apart by looking? Like where they are from? Japan, China, Vietnam?"

"I didn't get a good look. Asian."

"He, or she?"

"I think is all girls that work in the kitchen there," said Gyuri. "Macrobyotik. Brown rice and like that."

"I—" Now I really wasn't sure.

"Well—" Cherry ran his hand over the top of his close-cropped hair—"glad she ran, whoever, because you know what else I found back there? Sawed-off Mossberg 500."

Laughter and whistles at this.

"Shit."

"Where was it? Grozdan didn't—?"

"No. In a—" he gestured, to indicate a sling—"what do you call it. Hanging under the table, in some cloth like. Just happened to see it when I was down on the floor. Like—looked up. There it was, right over my head."

"You didn't leave it there, did you?"

"No! I wouldn't have minded to take it except was too big and had my hands full. Unscrewed it and knocked the pin out and threw it in the alley. Also—" he pulled a silver snub-nosed pistol out of his pocket, which he passed over to Boris—"this!"

Boris held it up to the light and looked at it.

"Nice little conceal-carry J-frame. Ankle holster in those bell bottom jeans! But to his misfortune he was not quick enough."

"Flexcuffs," said Gyuri to me, with slightly inclined head. "Vitya thinks ahead."

"Well—" Cherry wiped the sweat from his broad forehead—"they are light and slim to carry, and they have saved me many times shooting people. I do not like to hurt anyone if I don't have to."

Medieval city: crooked streets, lights draped on bridges and shining off rain-peppered canals, melting in the drizzle. Infinity of anonymous shops, twinkling window displays, lingerie and garter belts, kitchen utensils arrayed like surgical instruments, foreign words everywhere, Snel bestellen, Retro-stijl, Showgirl-Sexboetiek.

"Back door was open to the alley," said Cherry, elbowing off his sports coat and swigging from a bottle of vodka which Shirley T. had produced from under the front seat—hands a bit shaky and his face, the nose particularly, glowing a flagrant, stressed-out, Rudolph red. "They must have left it open for him—their third man—to come in at the back. I closed it and locked it—made Grozdan close and lock it, gun to his head, he was snivel and crying like baby—"

"That Mossberg," Boris said to me, accepting the bottle passed over the front seat. "Evil dirty thing. Sawed off—? sprays pellets here to Hamburg. Aim it way the fuck away from everyone and still you will hit half the people in the room."

"Good trick, no?" said Victor Cherry philosophically. "To say your third man is not there? 'Wait five minutes, please'? 'Sorry, mix up'—? 'He will be here any moment'? While he is all the time in back with the shotgun. Good double cross, if they had thought of it—"

"Maybe they did think of it. Why else have the gun back there?"

"I think we had a narrow miss, is what I think—"

"There was one car pulled up front, scared Shirley and me," said Gyuri, "while you were all in there, two guys, we thought we were in the shit but was only two gays, French guys, looking for restaurant—"

"—but no one in the back, thank God, I got Grozdan on the floor and cuffed him to radiator," Cherry was saying. "Ah, but—!" he held up the felt-wrapped package—"first. This. For you."

He handed it over the seat to Gyuri, who—gingerly, with his fingertips, as if it were a tray he might spill—passed it to me. Boris—downing his slug, wiping his mouth with the back of his hand—chucked me gaily in the arm with the bottle while humming *we wish you a merry Christmas we wish you a merry Christmas*

Package on my knees. Running my hands all around the edge. The felt was so thin that I sensed the rightness of it immediately with my fingertips, the texture and weight were perfect.

"Go on," said Boris, nodding, "better open it, make sure it's not the Civics book this time! Where was it?" he asked Cherry as I began to fumble with the string.

"Dirty little broom closet. Piece-of-shit plastic briefcase. Grozdan took me right to it. I thought he might fuck around a bit but burner at the head was all it took. No sense getting popped when all that good space cake still around for the taking."

"Potter," said Boris, trying to get my attention; and then again: "Potter."

"Yes?"

Lifting the briefcase. "This 40 rocks is going to Gyuri and Shirley T. Keeping them green. For services rendered. Because it is thanks to these two that we did not pay Sascha *one cent* for the favor of stealing your property. And Vitya—" reaching across to clasp his hand—"we are more than equal now. The debt is mine."

"No, I can never repay what I owe you, Borya."

"Forget it. Is nothing."

"Nothing? *Nothing?* Not true, Borya, because this very night I carry my life because of you, and every night until the last night…"

It was an interesting story he was telling, if I'd had ears to listen to it—someone had fingered Cherry for some unspecified but apparently very serious crime which he had not committed, nothing to do with, perfectly innocent, the guy had rolled for reduced prison time and unless Cherry, in turn, wanted to roll on his higher-ups ("unwise to do, if I wish to keep breathing"), he was looking at ten sticks and Boris, Boris had saved the day because Boris had tracked down the slimebag, in Antwerp and out on bail, and the story of how he had done this was very involved and enthusiastic and Cherry was getting choked up and sniffing a bit and there was more and it seemed to involve arson and bloodshed and something to do with a power saw but by that point I wasn't hearing a word because I'd gotten the string untied and streetlights and watery rain reflections were rolling over the surface of my painting, my goldfinch, which—I knew incontrovertibly, without a doubt, before even turning to look at the verso — was real.

"See?" said Boris, interrupting Vitya right in the heat of his story. "Looks good, no, your *zolotaia ptitsa?* I told you we took care of it, didn't I?"

Running my fingertip incredulously around the edges of the board, like Doubting Thomas across the palm of Christ. As any furniture dealer knew, or for that matter St. Thomas: it was harder to deceive the sense of touch than sight, and even after so many years my hands remembered the painting so well that my fingers went to the nail marks immediately, at the bottom of the panel, the tiny holes where (once upon a time, or so it was said) the painting was nailed up as a tavern sign, part of a painted cabinet, no one knew.

"He still alive back there?" Victor Cherry.

"Think so." Boris dug an elbow in my ribs. "Say something."

But I couldn't. It was real; I knew it, even in the dark. Raised yellow streak of paint on the wing and feathers scratched in with the butt of the brush. One chip on the upper left edge that hadn't been there before, tiny mar less than two millimeters, but otherwise: perfect. I was different, but it wasn't. And as the light flickered over it in bands, I had the queasy sense of my own life, in comparison, as a patternless and transient burst of energy, a fizz of biological static just as random as the street lamps flashing past.

"Ah, beautiful," said Gyuri amiably, leaning in to look at my right side. "So pure! Like a daisy. You know what I am trying to express?" he said, nudging me, when I did not answer. "Plain flower, alone in a field? It's just —" he gestured, *here it is! amazing!* "Do you know what I am saying?" he asked, nudging me again, only I was still too dazed to reply.

Boris in the meantime was murmuring half in English and half Russian to Vitya about the *ptitsa* as well as something else I couldn't quite catch, something about mother and baby, lovely love. "Still wishing you had phoned the art cops, eh?" he said, slinging his arm around my shoulder with his head close to mine, exactly as when we were boys.

"We can *still* phone them," said Gyuri, with a shout of laughter, punching me on the other arm.

"That's right, Potter! Shall we? No? Maybe not such a good idea any more, eh?" he said across me, to Gyuri, with a raised eyebrow.

xi.

When we turned in to the garage and got out of the car everyone was still high and laughing and recounting bits and pieces of the ambush in multiple languages — everyone except me, blank and echoing with shock, fast cuts and sudden movements still reverberating from the dark at me and too stunned to speak a word.

"Look at him," said Boris, breaking short from what he was saying and knocking me in the arm. "He looks like he just had the best blow job of his life."

They were all laughing at me, even Shirley Temple, the whole world was laughter bouncing fractal and metallic off the tiled walls, delirium and phantasmagorica, a sense of the world growing and swelling like some fabulous blown balloon floating and billowing away to the stars, and I was laughing too and I wasn't even sure what I was laughing at since I was still so shaken I was trembling all over.

Boris lit a cigarette. His face was greenish in the subterranean light. "Wrap that thing up," he said affably, nodding at the painting, "and then we will stick it in the hotel safe and go and get you a real blow job."

Gyuri frowned. "I thought we were going to eat first?"

"You are right. I am starving. Dinner first, then blow job."

"Blake's?" said Cherry, opening the passenger door of the Land Rover. "An hour, say?"

"Sounds good."

"Hate to go like this," Cherry said, plucking at the collar of his shirt, which was transparent and stuck to him with sweat. "Then again I could use a cognac. Some of the hundred-euro stuff. I could install about a quart right now. Shirley — Gyuri —" he said something in Ukrainian.

"He is saying," said Boris, in the burst of laughter that followed, "he is telling Shirley and Gyuri that they are buying the dinner tonight. With —" Gyuri triumphantly hoisting the bag.

Then — a pause. Gyuri looked troubled. He said something to Shirley Temple, and Shirley — laughing at him, deep peachy dimples — waved him off, waved off the bag that Gyuri tried to offer, and rolled his eyes when Gyuri offered it again.

"*Ne syeiychas,*" said Victor Cherry irritably. "Not now. Divide it later."

"Please," said Gyuri, offering the bag one more time.

"Oh, come on. Divide it later or we'll be here all night."

Ya khochu chto-by Shirli prinyala eto, said Gyuri, a sentence so plain and so earnestly enunciated that even I, with my lousy Russki, understood it. *I want that Shirley takes it.*

"No way!" said Shirley, in English, and—unable to resist—darted a glance at me to make sure I'd heard him say it, like a kid proud of knowing the answer in school.

"Come *on.*" Boris—hands on hips—looked aside in exasperation. "Does it matter who carries in their car? One of you is going to make off with it? No. We are all friends here. What will you do?" he said, when neither of them made a move. "Leave it on the floor for Dima to find? One of you decide please."

There was a long silence. Shirley, standing with arms folded, shook his head firmly at Gyuri's repeated insistence and then, with a worried look, asked Boris a question.

"Yes, yes, fine with me," said Boris impatiently. "Go ahead," he said to Gyuri. "You three go together."

"Are you sure?"

"I am positive. You have worked enough for tonight."

"You'll manage?"

"No," said Boris, "we will two of us walk! of course, of course," he said, shushing Gyuri's objection, "we can manage, go on," and we were all laughing as Vitya and Shirley and Gyuri too waved us goodbye (*Davaye!*) and hopped in the Range Rover and drove away, up the ramp and out to the Overtoom again.

xii.

"AH, WHAT A NIGHT," said Boris, scratching his stomach. "Starving! Let's get out of here. Although—" he glanced back, knotted brow, at the Range Rover driving off—"well, no matter. We will be fine. Short hop. Blake's is easy walk from your hotel. And you," he said to me, nodding—"careless! You should tie that thing up again! Don't just carry it wrapped with no string."

"Right," I said, "right," and I circled to the front of the car so I could rest it on the hood while I fumbled for the baker's twine in my pocket.

"May I see?" said Boris, coming up behind me.

I drew back the felt, and the two of us stood awkwardly for a moment like a pair of minor Flemish noblemen hovering at the margin of a nativity painting.

"Lot of trouble —" Boris lit a cigarette, blew the smoke in a sidestream away from the picture — "but worth it, yes?"

"Yes," I said. Our voices were joking but subdued, like boys uneasy in church.

"I had it longer than anyone," said Boris. "If you count the days." And then, in a different tone: "Remember — if you feel like, I can always arrange something for money. Only one deal, and you could retire."

But I only shook my head. I couldn't have put into words what I felt, though it was something deep and primary that Welty had shared with me, and I with him, in the museum all those years ago.

"Was just kidding. Well — sort of. But no, seriously," he said, rubbing his knuckles on my sleeve, "is yours. Free and clear. Why don't you keep for a while and enjoy, before you return to museum people?"

I was silent. I was already wondering how exactly I was going to get it out of the country.

"Go on, wrap it up. We need to get out of here. Look at it later all you want. Oh, give it here," he said, snatching the string from my clumsy hands; I was still fumbling, trying to find the ends — "come on, let me do it, we'll be here all night."

xiii.

THE PAINTING WAS WRAPPED and tied, and Boris had tucked it under his arm and — taking a last draw on his cigarette — had stepped around to the driver's side and was about to get in the car when, behind us, a casual and friendly-sounding American voice said, "Merry Christmas."

I turned. There were three of them, two lazy-walking middle-aged men drifting along a bit bemusedly with the air of having come to do us a favor — it was Boris they were addressing, not me, they seemed glad to see him—and, skittering slightly in front of them, the Asian boy. His white coat was not a kitchen worker's coat at all but some asymmetrical thing made out of white wool about an inch thick; and he was shivering and practically blue-lipped with fright. He was unarmed, or seemed to be, which was good, because what I mainly noticed about the other two— big guys, all business—was blued handgun metal glinting in the sleazy fluorescents. Even then, I didn't get it—the friendly voice had thrown me; I thought they'd caught the boy and were bringing him to us—until I looked over at Boris and saw how still he'd gone, chalk-white.

"Sorry to do this to you," said the American to Boris, though he didn't sound sorry—if anything, pleased. He was broadshouldered and bored-looking, in a soft gray coat, and despite his age there was something petu-lant and cherubic about him, overly ripe, soft white hands and a soft managerial blandness.

Boris—cigarette in mouth—stood frozen. "Martin."

"Yeah, hey!" said Martin genially, as the other guy—gray blond thug in a pea coat, coarse features out of Nordic folklore—ambled straight up to Boris, and, after grappling around at Boris's waistband, took his gun and passed it over to Martin. In my confusion I looked at the boy in the white coat but it was like he'd been struck on the head with a hammer, he didn't seem any more amused or edified by any of this than I was.

"I know this sucks for you," said Martin—"but. Wow." The low key voice was a shocking contrast to the eyes, which were like a puff adder's. "Hey. Sucks for me too. Frits and I were at Pim's, we weren't expecting to get out. Nasty weather, eh? Where's our white Christmas?"

"What are you doing here?" said Boris, who despite his overly still air was as afraid as I'd ever seen him.

"What do you think?" Jocular shrug. "I'm surprised as you, if it makes any difference. Never would have thought Sascha had the balls to call in Horst on this. But—hey, fuck-up like this, who else could he call, I guess? Let's have it," he said, with an affable tick of the gun, and with a rush of horror I realized he was pointing the gun at Boris, gesturing with the gun at the felt-wrapped package in Boris's hands. "Come on. Give it over."

"No," said Boris sharply, shaking the hair from his eyes.

Martin blinked, with a sort of befuddled whimsy. "What's that you say?"

"No."

"What?" Martin laughed. "No? Are you kidding me?"

"Boris! Give it to them!" I stammered, as I stood frozen in horror, as the one named Frits put his pistol to Boris's temple and then caught Boris by the hair and pulled his head back so sharply he groaned.

"I know," said Martin amicably, with a collegial glance at me, as if to say: *hey, these Russians—nuts, am I right?* "Come on," he said to Boris. "Let's have it."

Again Boris moaned, as the guy yanked his hair once more, and from across the car threw me an unmistakeable look—which I understood just as plainly as if he'd spoken the words aloud, an urgent and very specific cut of the eyes straight from our shoplifting days: *run for it, Potter, go.*

"Boris," I said, after a disbelieving pause, "please, just give it to them," but Boris only moaned again, despairingly, as Frits jammed the gun hard under his chin and Martin stepped forward to take the painting from him.

"Excellent. Thanks for that," he said bemusedly, tucking his gun under his arm and beginning to pluck and fumble with the string, which Boris had tied in an obstinate little knot. "Cool." His fingers weren't working very well, and up close, when he'd reached to take the painting, I'd seen why: he was high as a kite. "Anyway—" Martin glanced behind him, as if wanting to include absent friends on the joke, then back with another bemused shrug—"sorry. Take them over there, Frits," he said, still busy with the painting, nodding at a shadowy, dungeon-like corner of the garage, darker than the rest, and when Frits turned partly from Boris to gesture at me with the gun—*come on, come on, you too*—I realized, cold with horror, what Boris had known was going to happen from the moment he saw them: why he'd wanted me to run for it, or at least to try.

But in the half-moment as Frits was motioning to me with the gun, we'd all lost track of Boris, whose cigarette flew out in a shower of sparks. Frits screamed and slapped his cheek, then stumbled back grappling at his collar where it had lodged against his neck. In the same instant Martin—distracted with the painting, directly across from me—looked up, and I was still looking at him blankly across the roof of the car when I heard it, to my right, three fast cracks which made us both turn quickly to the side. With the fourth (flinching, eyes closed) a warm spray of blood thumped across the car roof and struck me in the face and when I opened my eyes again the Asian kid was stepping back horrified and drawing a hand down his front in a bloody smear like a butcher's apron and I was staring at a lighted sign **Beetaalautomaat op** where Boris's head had been; blood was pouring from under the car and Boris was on the ground on his elbows, feet going, he was trying to scramble up from the floor, I couldn't tell if he was hurt or not and I must have run around to him without thinking because the next thing I knew I was on the other side of the car and trying to help him up, blood everywhere, Frits was a mess, slumped against the car with a baseball-sized hole in the side of his head, and I'd just noticed Frits's gun lying on the ground when I heard Boris exclaim sharply and there was Martin, tight-eyed with blood on his sleeve, hand clamped to his arm and fumbling to bring up his gun

It had happened before it even happened, like a skip in a DVD throwing me forward in time, because I have no memory at all of picking the pistol off the floor, only of a kick so hard it threw my arm in the air, I didn't really hear the bang until I felt the kick and the casing flew back and hit me in the face and I shot again, eyes half-closed against the noise and my arm jolting with every shot, the trigger had a resistance to it, a stiffness, like pulling some too-heavy door latch, car windows popping and Martin with an arm coming up, exploding safety glass and chunks of concrete flying out a pillar and I'd got Martin in the shoulder, the soft gray cloth was drenched and dark, a spreading dark stain, cordite smell and deafening echo that drove me so deep inside my skull that it was less like actual sound striking my eardrums than a wall slamming down hard in my mind and driving me back into some hard internal blackness from childhood, and Martin's viper eyes met mine and he was slumped forward with the gun propped on the roof of the car when I shot again and hit him above the eye, red burst that made me flinch and then, somewhere behind me, I heard the sound of running feet slapping on concrete — the boy, white coat running to the exit ramp with the painting under his arm, he was running up the ramp to the street, echoes reverberating in the tiled space and I almost shot at him only somehow it was a completely different moment and I was facing away from the car, I was doubled over with my hands on my knees and the gun was on the ground, I had no memory of dropping it although the sound was there, it was clattering to the floor and it kept on clattering and I was still hearing the echoes and feeling the vibration of the gun up my arm, retching and doubled over, with Frits's blood crawling and curling on my tongue.

Out of the darkness the sound of feet running, and again I could not see, or move, everything black at the edges and I was falling even though I wasn't because somehow I was sitting on a low stretch of tiled wall with my head between my knees looking down at clear red spit, or vomit, on the shiny, epoxy-painted concrete between my shoes and Boris, there was Boris, winded and breathless and bloody, running back in, his voice was coming from a million miles off, Potter, are you all right? he's gone, I couldn't catch him, he got away

I drew my palm down my face and looked at the red smear on my hand. Boris was still talking to me with some urgency but even though he was shaking my shoulder it was mostly mouth movements and nonsense through soundproof glass. The smoke from the fired gun was oddly the same bracing ammonia smell of Manhattan thunderstorms and wet city pavements. Robin's egg speckles on the door of a pale blue Mini. Nearer, creeping dark from under Boris's car, a glossy satin pool three feet wide was spreading and inching forward like an amoeba, and I wondered how long before it reached my shoe and what I would do when it did.

Hard, but without anger, Boris cuffed me with his closed fist on the side of the head: an impersonal clout, no heat about it at all. It was as if he were performing CPR.

"Come on," he said. "Your specs," he said with a short nod.

My glasses — blood-smeared, unbroken — lay on the ground by my foot. I didn't remember them falling off.

Boris picked them up himself, wiped them on his own sleeve, and handed them to me.

"Come on," he said, catching my arm, pulling me up. His voice was level and soothing although he was splattered with blood and I could feel his hands shaking. "All over now. You saved us." The gunshot had set off my tinnitus like a swarm of locusts buzzing in my ears. "You did good. Now — over here. Hurry."

He led me behind the glassed-in office, which was locked and dark. My camel's-hair coat had blood on it, and Boris took it off me like an attendant at a coat check, and turned it inside out and draped it over a concrete post.

"You will have to get rid of this thing," he said, with a violent shudder. "Shirt too. Not now — later. Now —" opening a door, crowding in behind me, flipping on a light — "come on."

Dank bathroom, stinking of urinal cakes and urine. No sink, only a bare water spigot and a drain in the floor.

"Quick, quick," said Boris, turning the faucet full pressure. "Not perfection. Just—yeow!" grimacing as he stuck his head under the spout, splashing his face, scrubbing it palm down—

"Your arm," I found myself saying. He was holding it wrong.

"Yes yes—" cold water flying everywhere, coming up for air— "he winged me, not bad, only a nick—oh God—" spitting and spluttering—"I should have listened to you. You tried to say! Boris, you said, someone back there! In the kitchen! But did I listen to you? Pay attention? No. That little fucker—the Chinese kid—that was Sascha's boyfriend! Woo, Goo, I cannot remember his name. Aah—" sticking his head under the faucet again, burbling for a moment as the water streamed over his face—"—bloo! you saved us Potter, I thought we were dead...."

Standing back, he scrubbed his hands over his face, bright red and dripping. "Okay," he said, wiping the water out of his eyes, slinging it away, then steering me to the pounding faucet, "now, you. Head under— yes yes, cold!" Pushing me under when I flinched. "Sorry! I know! Hands, face—"

Water like ice, choking, it was going up my nose, I'd never felt anything so cold but it brought me around a bit.

"Quick, quick," said Boris, hauling me up. "Suit—dark—doesn't show. Nothing we can do about the shirt, collar up, here, let me do it. Scarf is in the car, yes? You can wind it around your neck? No no—forget it—" I was shivering, grabbing for my coat, teeth ringing with cold, my whole upper body was soaked through—"well, go ahead, you'll freeze, just keep it turned to lining side out."

"Your arm." Though his coat was dark and the light was bad I saw the burnt skid at his bicep, black wool sticky with blood.

"Forget it. Is nothing. My God, Potter—" starting back to the car— half running, me hurrying to keep up, panicked at the thought of losing him, of being left. "Martin! That bastard is a bad diabetic, I have been hoping he would die for years. Grateful Dead, I owe you too!" he said, tucking the snub nose in his pocket, then—from the handkerchief pocket of his suit—drawing a bag of white powder which he opened and tossed down in a spray.

"There," he said, dusting his hands off with a lurching back step; he was ash white, his pupils were fixed and even when he looked up at me, he seemed not to see me. "That is all they will be looking for. Martin will be carrying too, all junked up, did you notice? That was why he was so slow—him and Frits too. They were not expecting that call—not expecting to go to work tonight. *God*—" squeezing his eyes shut—"we were lucky." Sweaty, dead pale, wiping his forehead. "Martin knows me, he knows what I carry, he was not expecting me to have that other gun and you—they were not thinking of you at all. Get in the car," he said. "No no—" catching my arm; I was following him to the driver's side like a sleepwalker—"not there, it's a mess. Oh—" stopping, cold, an eternity passing in the flickering greenish light—before wobbling around for his own gun on the floor, which he wiped clean with a cloth from his pocket and—holding it carefully, between the cloth—dropped on the ground.

"Whew," he said, trying to catch his breath. "That will confuse them. They will be trying to trace that thing for years." He stopped, holding his nicked arm with one hand: he looked me up and down. "Can you drive?"

I couldn't answer. Glazed, dizzy, trembling. My heart, after the collision and freeze of the moment, had begun to pound with hard, sharp, painful blows like a fist striking in the center of my chest.

Quickly, Boris shook his head, made a *tch tch* sound. "Other side," he said, when I, feet moving of their own accord, followed him again. "No no—" leading me back around, opening the front passenger door and giving me a little shove.

Drenched. Shivering. Nauseated. On the floor: pack of Stimorol gum. Road map: Frankfurt Offenbach Hanau.

Boris had circled around to the car, checking it out. Then, gingerly, he came back to the driver's side—weaving a bit; trying not to step in blood—and sat behind the wheel and held it with both hands and took a deep breath.

"Okay," he said, on a long exhale, talking to himself like a pilot about to take off on a mission. "Buckle up. You too. Brake lights working? Tail lights?" Patting his pockets, sliding up the seat, turning the heater up to High. "Plenty of gas—good. Heated seats too—will warm us up. We can't be stopped," he explained. "Because I cannot drive."

All sorts of tiny noises: creak of seat leather, water ticking from my wet sleeve.

"Can't drive?" I said, in the intense ringing silence.

"Well, I *can*." Defensively. "I *have*. I—" starting up the car, backing out with his arm along the seat—"well, why do you think I have a driver?

Am I this fancy? No. I *do* have—" upheld forefinger—"drunk-driving conviction."

I closed my eyes to keep from seeing the slumped bloody mass as we drove past it.

"So, you see, if they stop me they will run me in and this is what we do not want to happen." I could barely hear what he was saying over the fierce buzzing in my head. "You will have to help me out. Like—watch for street signs and keep me from driving in bus lanes. The cycle paths are red here, you are not supposed to drive on them either so help me watch for those too."

On the Overtoom again, heading back into Amsterdam: Locksmith Sleutelkluis, Vacatures, Digitaal Printen, Haji Telecom, Onbeperkt Genieten, Arabic letters, lights streaking, it was like a nightmare, I was never going to get off this fucking road.

"God, I better slow down," said Boris somberly. He looked glassy and wrecked. "Trajectcontrole. Help me watch for signs."

Blood smear on my cuff. Big fat drops.

"Trajectcontrole. That means some machine tells the police you are speeding. They drive unmarked cars, a lot of them, and sometimes they will follow a while before they stop you although—we are lucky—not much traffic out this way tonight. Weekend, I guess, and holiday. This is not exactly Happy Christmas neighborhood out here if you get me. You understand what just happened, don't you?" said Boris, heaving for breath and scrubbing his nose hard with a gasping sound.

"No." Somebody else talking, not me.

"Well—Horst. Both those guys were Horst's. Frits is maybe only person in Amsterdam he knew to call on such short notice but Martin—fuck." He was speaking very fast and erratically, so fast he could barely get the words out, and his eyes were flat and staring. "Who even knew Martin was in town? You know how Horst and Martin met, don't you?" he said, half-glancing at me. "Mental home! Fancy California mental home! 'Hotel California,' Horst used to call it! That was back when Horst's family was still talking to him. Horst was in for rehab but Martin was in because he is really, truly nuts. Like, eyestabber kind of nuts. I have seen Martin do things I really do not like to talk about. I—"

"Your arm." It was hurting him; I could see the tears glittering in his eyes.

Boris made a face. "Nyah. This is zero. This is nothing. Aah," he said, lifting his elbow up so I could wrap the phone charger cable around his arm—I'd yanked it out, wrapped it twice above the wound, tied it tight as I could—"smart you. Good precaution. Thanks! Although, no need really. Just a graze—more bruised than anything, I think. Good this coat is so thick! Clean it out—some antibyotic and something for pain—I'll be fine. I—" deep shuddering breath—"I need to find Gyuri and Cherry. I hope they went straight to Blake's. Dima—Dima needs a heads-up too, about the mess in there. He will not be happy—there will be cops, big headache—but it will look random. There is nothing to tie him to this."

Headlights sweeping past. Blood pounding in my ears. There weren't many cars on the road but every one that passed made me flinch.

Boris moaned and dragged his palm across his face. He was saying something, very speedy and agitated. "What?"

"I said—this is a mess. I am still figuring it out." Voice staccato and cracked. "Because this is what I am wondering now—maybe I am wrong, maybe I am paranoid—but maybe Horst knew all along? That Sascha took the picture? Only Sascha brought the picture out of Germany and tries to borrow money on it behind Horst's back. And then when things go wrong—Sascha panics—who else could he call? of course, I am just thinking out loud, maybe Horst *didn't* know Sascha took it, maybe he would never have known if Sascha hadn't been so careless and dumb as to—Goddamn this fucking ring road," said Boris suddenly. We had gotten off the Overtoom and were circling around. "Which is the direction I want? Turn on the Nav."

"I—" fumbling around, incomprehensible words, menu I couldn't read, Geheugen, Plaats, turning the dial, different menu, Gevarieerd, Achtergrond.

"Oh, hell. We will try this one. God, that was close," said Boris, taking the turn a little too fast and sloppy. "You have some minerals, Potter. Frits—Frits was out of it, nodding practically, but Martin, my God. Then you—? Coming around so brave? Hurrah! I did not even think of you there. But there you were! Say you never handled a firearm before?"

"No." Wet black streets.

"Well, let me tell you something that will maybe sound funny? But— is a compliment. You shoot like a girl. You know why is a compliment? Because," said Boris, with a giddy, feverish slur in his voice, "in situation of threat, male who never fired weapon before and female who never fired weapon before? The female — so Bobo used to say — is much more likely to drop her mark. Most men? want to look tough, have seen too much movies, get too impatient and pop their shot off too fast — Shit," said Boris suddenly, slamming on the brakes.

"What?"

"We don't want this."

"Don't want what?"

"This street is closed." Throwing the car in reverse. Backing down the street.

Construction. Fences with bulldozers behind them, empty buildings with blue plastic tarps in the windows. Stacks of piping, cement blocks, graffiti in Dutch.

"What are we going to do?" I said, in the paralyzed silence that followed, after we'd turned down a different street that seemed to have no streetlights at all.

"Well — no bridge here that we can cross. And that's a dead end, so..."

"No, I mean what are we going to *do*."

"About what?"

"I —" My teeth were chattering so hard I could barely get the words out. "Boris, we're fucked."

"No! We are not. Grozdan's gun —" awkwardly he patted his coat pocket — "I'll drop it in the canal. They can't trace it back to me, if they can't trace it back to him? And — nothing else to tie us. Because my gun? Clean. No serial. Even the car tires are new! I'll get the car to Gyuri and he'll change them tonight. Look here," said Boris, when I didn't answer, "don't worry! We are safe! Shall I say it again? S-A-F-E" (spelling it out clumsily on four fingers).

Hitting a pothole, I flinched, unconsciously, a startle reaction, hands flying up to my face.

"And why, more than anything? Because we are old friends — because we trust each other. And because — oh God, there's a cop, let me slow down."

Staring at my shoes. Shoes shoes shoes. All I could think, when I'd put them on a few hours before I hadn't killed anybody.

"Because — Potter, Potter, think about this. Listen for one moment please. What if I was a stranger — someone you did not know or trust? If you were driving from garage now with stranger? Then your life would be chained with a stranger's forever. You would need to be very very careful with this person, long as you live."

Cold hands, cold feet. Snackbar, Supermarkt, spotlit pyramids of fruit and candy, Verkoop Gestart!

"Your life — your freedom — resting on a stranger's loyalty? In that case? Yes. Worry. Absolutely. You would be in very big trouble. But — no one knows of this thing but us. Not even Gyuri!"

Unable to speak, I shook my head vigorously at this, trying to catch my breath.

"Who? China Boy?" Boris made a disgusted noise. "Who's he going to tell? He is underage and not here legally. He does not speak any proper language."

"Boris" — leaning forward slightly; I felt like I was going to pass out — "he's got the painting."

"Ah." Boris grimaced with pain. "*That* is gone, I'm afraid."

"What?"

"For good, maybe. I am sick over that — sick in my heart. Because, I hate to say it — Woo, Goo, what's his name? After what he saw — ? All he will think about is himself. Scared to death! People dead! Deportation! He does not want to be involved. Forget about the picture. He has no idea of its true value. And if he finds himself in any kind of fix with the cops? Rather than spend one day in jail even? All he will want is to get rid of it. So —" he shrugged woozily — "let's hope he *does* get away, the little shit. Otherwise very good chance the *ptitsa* will end up thrown in canal — burned."

Streetlights glinting off the hoods of parked cars. I felt disincarnate, cut loose from myself. How it would feel to be back in my body again I couldn't imagine. We were back in the old city, cobblestone rattle, nocturne monochrome straight out of Aert van der Neer with the seventeenth century pressing close on either side and silver coins dancing on black canal water.

"Ach, this is closed," groaned Boris, jerking to a stop again, backing up the car, "we must find another way."

"Do you know where we are?"

"Yes — of course," said Boris, with a sort of scary disconnected cheerfulness. "That's your canal over there. The Herengracht."

"Which canal?"

"Amsterdam is an easy city to get around," Boris said, as if I hadn't spoken. "In the old city all you have to do is follow the canals until—Oh, God, they closed this off too."

Tonal gradations. Weirdly enlivened darks. The small ghostly moon above the bell gables was so tiny it looked like the moon of a different planet, hazed and occult, spooky clouds lit with just the barest tinge of blue and brown.

"Don't worry, this happens all the time. They are always building something here. Big construction messes. All this—I think is for a new subway line or something. Everyone is annoyed by it. Many accusations of fraud, yah yah. Same in every city, no?" His voice was so blurry he sounded drunk. "Roadwork everywhere, politicians getting rich? That is why everyone rides a bike, it is quicker, only, I am sorry, I am not riding a bicycle anywhere one week before Christmas. Oh no—" narrow bridge, dead halt behind a line of cars—"are we moving?"

"I—" We were stopped on a pedestrian footbridge. Visible pink drops on the rain-splashed windows. People walking back and forth not a foot away.

"Get out of the car and look. Oh, hang on," he said impatiently before I could pull myself together; throwing the car into Park, getting out himself. I saw his floodlit back in the headlights, formal and staged-looking amidst billows of exhaust.

"Van," he said, throwing himself back in the car. Slamming the door. Taking a deep breath, bracing his arms out straight against the steering wheel.

"What is he doing?" Glancing side to side, panicked, half expecting some random pedestrian to notice the bloodstains, rush at the car, bang at the windows, throw open the door.

"How should I know? There are too many cars in this fucking city. Look," said Boris—sweating and pale in the lurid tail lights of the car in front of us; more cars had pulled up behind, we were trapped—"who knows how long we will be here. We are only few blocks from your hotel. Better you should get out and walk."

"I—" Was it the lights of the car in front of us that made the water drops on the windshield look quite so red?

He made an impatient flicking movement of the hand. "Potter, just go," he said. "I don't know what is going on with this van up here. I'm afraid the traffic police will show up. Better for us both if we are not together just now. Herengracht—you cannot miss it. The canals here run in circles, you know that, don't you? Just go that way—" he pointed—"you will find it."

"What about your arm?"

"It's nothing! I'd take off my coat to show you except is too much trouble. Now go. I have to talk to Cherry." Pulling his cell phone from his pocket. "I may have to leave town for a little while—"

"What?"

"—but if we don't speak for a bit, don't worry, I know where you are. Best if you don't try to call me or get in touch. I'll be back soon as I can. Everything will be okay. Go—clean up—scarf around the neck, up high—we will speak soon. Don't look so pale and ill! Do you have anything on you? Do you need something?"

"What?"

Scrabbling in his pocket. "Here, take this." Glassine envelope with a smeared stamp. "Not too much, it is very very pure. Size of a match head. No more. And when you wake up, it will not be quite so bad. Now, remember—" dialing his phone; I was very conscious of his heavy breathing—"keep your scarf high up at your neck and walk on the dark side of the street as much as you can. Go!" he shouted when still I sat there, so loudly that I saw a man on the pedestrian walk of the bridge turn to look. "Hurry up! *Cherry,*" he said, slumping back in his seat in visible relief and beginning to babble hoarsely in Ukrainian as I exited the car—feeling lurid and exposed in the ghastly wash of headlights from the stalled vehicles—and walked back over the bridge, the way we'd come. My last sight of him, he was talking on the phone with the window rolled down and leaning out, in extravagant clouds of auto fume, to see what was going on with the stalled van ahead.

xiv.

THE SUBSEQUENT HOUR, OR hours, of wandering the canal rings hunting for my hotel were as miserable as any in my life, which is saying something. The temperature had plunged, my hair was wet, my clothes were soaked, my teeth were chattering with cold; the streets were just dark enough that they all looked alike and yet not nearly dark enough to be roaming around in clothes bloodied from a man I'd just killed. Down the black streets I walked, fast, with oddly confident-sounding heel taps, feeling as uneasy and conspicuous as a dreamer wandering naked in a nightmare, staying out of the streetlights and trying hard to reassure myself, with dwindling success, that my inside-out coat looked perfectly normal, nothing unusual about it at all. There were pedestrians on the street, but not many. Afraid of being recognized, I'd removed my glasses since I knew from experience that my glasses were my most distinctive feature — what people noticed first, what people remembered — and though this was unhelpful in terms of finding my way it also gave me an irrational sense of safety and concealment: illegible street signs and fogged streetlamp coronas floating up isolated out of the dark, blurred car lights and holiday tracers, a feeling of being viewed by pursuers with an out-of-focus lens.

What had happened was: I'd overshot my hotel by a couple of blocks. Moreover: I was not used to European hotels where you had to ring to get in after a certain hour, and when at last I splashed up sneezing and bonechilled to find the glass door locked, I stood for some indefinite time rattling the handle like a zombie, back and forth, back and forth, with a rhythmic, locked-in, metronome dumbness, too stupefied with cold to understand why I couldn't get in. Dismally, through the glass, I gazed through the lobby at the sleek, black desk: empty.

Then — hurrying from the back, startled eyebrows — neat darkhaired man in dark suit. There was an awful flash where his eyes met mine and I realized how I must look, and then he was looking away, fumbling with the key.

"Sorry, sir, we lock the door after eleven," he said. Still averting his eyes. "It's for the safety of the customers."

"I got caught in the rain."

"Of course, sir." He was — I realized — staring at the cuff of my shirt, splatted with a browned blood drop the size of a quarter. "We have umbrellas at the desk should you require them."

"Thanks." Then, nonsensically: "I spilled chocolate sauce on myself."

"Sorry to hear that, sir. We'll be happy to try to get it out in the laundry if you like."

"That'd be great." Couldn't he smell it on me, the blood? In the heated lobby I reeked of it, rust and salt. "My favorite shirt too. Profiteroles." *Shut up, shut up.* "Delicious though."

"Happy to hear it sir. We'll be happy to book you a table at a restaurant tomorrow night if you like."

"Thanks." Blood in my mouth, the smell and taste of it everywhere, I could only hope he couldn't smell it quite so strongly as me. "That'd be great."

"Sir?" he said as I was starting off to the elevator.

"Sorry?"

"I believe you need your key?" Moving behind the desk, selecting a key from a pigeonhole. "Twenty-seven, is it?"

"Right," I said, at once thankful he'd told me my room number and alarmed that he'd known it so readily, off the top of his head.

"Good night sir. Enjoy your stay."

Two different elevators. Endless hallway, carpeted in red. Coming in, I threw on all the lights—desk lamp, bed lamp, chandelier blazing; shrugged my coat on the floor, and headed straight for the shower, unbuttoning my bloodied shirt as I went, stumbling like Frankenstein's monster before pitchforks. I wadded the sticky mess of cloth and threw it into the bottom of the bathtub and turned on the water as hard and hot as it would go, rivulets of pink streaming beneath my feet, scrubbing myself with the lily scented bath gel until I smelled like a funeral wreath and my skin was on fire.

The shirt was a loss: brown stains scalloped and splotched at the throat long after the water ran clean. Leaving it to soak in the tub, I turned to the scarf and then the jacket—smeared with blood, though too dark to show it—and then, turning it right side out, as gingerly as I could (why had I worn the camel's-hair to the party? why not the navy?) the coat. One lapel was not so bad and the other very bad. The wine-dark splash carried a blatting animation that threw me back into the energy of the shot all over again: the kick, the burst, trajectory of droplets. I stuffed it under the tap in the sink and poured shampoo on it and scrubbed and scrubbed with a shoebrush from the closet; and after the shampoo was gone, and the bath gel too, I rubbed bar soap on the spot and scrubbed some more, like some hopeless servant in a fairy tale doomed to complete an impossible task before dawn, or die. At last, hands trembling from fatigue, I turned to my toothbrush and toothpaste straight from the tube—which, oddly enough, worked better than anything I'd tried, but still didn't do the job.

Finally I gave it up for useless, and hung the coat to drip in the bathtub: sodden ghost of Mr. Pavlikovsky. I'd taken care to keep blood off the towels; with toilet paper, which I compulsively wadded and flushed every few moments, I mopped up, laboriously, the rusty smears and drips on the tile. Taking my toothbrush to the grout. Clinical whiteness. Mirrored walls glittering. Multiple reflecting solitudes. Long after the last tinge of pink was gone, I kept going—rinsing and re-washing the hand towels I'd sullied, which still had a suspicious flush—and then, so tired I was reeling, got in the shower with water so hot I could barely stand it and scrubbed myself down all over again, head to toe, grinding the bar of soap in my hair and weeping at the suds that ran into my eyes.

XV.

I WAS AWAKENED, AT some indeterminate hour, by a bell buzzing loudly at my door which made me leap up as if I'd been scalded. The sheets were tangled and drenched with sweat and the blackout shades were down so I had no idea what time it was or even if it was day or night. I was still half asleep. Throwing on my robe, cracking the door on the chain I said: "Boris?"

Moist-faced, uniformed woman. "Laundry, sir."

"Sorry?"

"Front desk, sir. They said you asked for laundry pickup this morning."

"Er—" I glanced down at the doorknob. How, after everything, could I have neglected to put out the Do Not Disturb sign? "Hang on."

From my case I retrieved the shirt I'd worn to Anne's party—the one Boris said wasn't good enough for Grozdan's. "Here," I said, passing it to her through the door and then: "Wait."

Suit jacket. Scarf. Both black. Did I dare? They were wrecked-looking and wet to the touch but when I switched on the desk lamp and examined them minutely—specs on, with my Hobie-trained eye, nose inches from the cloth—no blood to be seen. With a piece of white tissue, I dabbed in several places to see if it came away pink. It did—but only the faintest bit.

She was still waiting and in a way it was a relief, having to hurry: quick decision, no hesitating. From the pockets I retrieved my wallet, the damp-but-amazingly-intact Oxycontin which I'd slipped into my pocket before the de Larmessin party (Did I ever think I'd be grateful for that hard time-release matrix? No) and Boris's fat glassine envelope before handing suit and scarf over as well.

Closing the door, I was suffused with relief. But not thirty seconds later a murmur of worry crept in, worry which rose to a shrieking crescendo in moments. Snap judgment. Insane. What had I been thinking?

I lay down. I got up. I lay back down and tried to go to sleep. Then I sat up in bed and in a dreamlike rush, unable to help myself, found myself dialing the front desk.

"Yes Mr. Decker, how can I help you?"

"Er —" squeezing my eyes shut tight; why had I paid for the room with a credit card? "I was just wondering — I just sent a suit out to be dry cleaned, and I wonder if it's still on premises?"

"Sorry?"

"Do you send the laundry out to be done? Or is it done on site?"

"We send it out, sir. The company we use is very reliable."

"Is there any way you could see if it's gone out yet? I just realized that I need it for an event tonight."

"I'll just check sir. Hang on."

Hopelessly, I waited, staring at the bag of heroin on the nightstand, which was stamped with a rainbow skull and the word **AFTERPARTY**. In a moment the desk clerk came back on. "What time will you be needing the suit, sir?"

"Early."

"I'm afraid it's already gone out. The truck just left. But our dry cleaning is same-day service. You'll have it this afternoon by five, guaranteed. Will there be anything more, sir?" he asked, in the silence that followed.

xvi.

BORIS WAS RIGHT ABOUT his dope, how pure it was — pure white, a normal sized bump knocked me cockeyed, so that for an indeterminate interlude I drifted in and out pleasantly on the verge of death. Cities, centuries. In and out I glided of slow moments, delightful, shades drawn, empty cloud dreams and evolving shadows, a stillness like Jan Weenix's gorgeous trophy pieces, dead birds with bloodstained feathers hanging from a foot, and in whatever wink of consciousness that remained to me I felt I understood the secret grandeur of dying, all the knowledge held back from all humankind until the very end: no pain, no fear, magnificent detachment, lying in state upon the death barge and receding into the grand immensities like an emperor, gone, gone, observing all the distant scurryers on shore, freed from all the old human pettiness of love and fear and grief and death.

When the doorbell shrilled into my dreams, hours later, it might have been hundreds of years, I didn't even flinch. Amiably I got up — swaying happily on air, supporting myself on bits of furniture as I walked — and smiled at the girl in the door: blonde, shy-seeming, offering me my clothes wrapped in plastic.

"Your laundry, Mr. Decker." As all the Dutch did, or seemed to do, she pronounced my surname "Decca," as in Decca Mitford, once-upon-a-time acquaintance of Mrs. DeFrees. "Our apologies."

"What?"

"I hope there's been no inconvenience." Adorable! Those blue eyes! Her accent was charming.

"Excuse me?"

"We promised them to you at five p.m. The desk said not to put it on your bill."

"Oh, that's fine," I said, wondering if I should tip her, realizing that money, and counting, was much too much to think about, and then — closing the door, dropping the clothes on the foot of the bed and making my unsteady way to the night table — checked Gyuri's watch: six-twenty, which made me smile. To contemplate the face-clawing worry the dope had saved me — an hour and twenty minutes of anguish! Frantic, phoning the front desk! envisioning cops downstairs! flooded me with Vedic serenity. Worry! What a waste of time. All the holy books were right. Clearly 'worry' was the mark of a primitive and spiritually unevolved person. What was that line from Yeats, about the bemused Chinese sages? All things fall and are built again. Ancient glittering eyes. This was wisdom. People had been raging and weeping and destroying things for centuries and wailing about their puny individual lives, when — what was the point? All this useless sorrow? *Consider the lilies of the field.* Why did anyone ever worry about anything? Weren't we, as sentient beings, put upon the earth to be happy, in the brief time allotted to us?

Absolutely. Which was why I didn't fret about the snippy pre-printed note Housekeeping had slid under my door (*Dear Guest, we made an attempt to service your room but were unfortunately unable to gain access to…*), why I was more than happy to venture into the hall in my bathrobe and waylay the chambermaid with a sinister armload of waterlogged towels — every towel in the room was soaked, I'd rolled my coat in them to help press the water out, pinkish marks on some of them that I hadn't really noticed before I — fresh towels? Certainly! oh, you forgot your key sir? you're locked out? Oh, one moment, shall I let you back in? and why, even after that, I didn't think twice about ordering up from room service, indulgently permitting the bellboy to enter the room and wheel the table *right to the foot of the bed* (tomato soup, salad, club sandwich, chips, most of which I managed to throw right back up again half an hour later, the pleasantest vomit in the world, so much fun it made me laugh: whoopsy! Best dope ever!) I was sick, I knew it, hours of wet clothes in zero-fahrenheit weather had given me a high fever and chills, and yet I was much too grandly removed from it to care. This was the body: fallible, subject to malady. Illness, pain. Why did people get so worked up about it? I put on every piece of clothing in my suitcase (two shirts, sweater, extra trousers, two pairs of socks) and sat sipping coca-cola from the minibar and — still high and coming down — fell in and out of vivid waking dreams: uncut diamonds, glittering black insects, one particularly vivid dream of Andy, sopping wet, tennis shoes squelching, trailing water into the room behind him something not quite right about him something weird looking little bit off what's up Theo?

not much, you?

not much hey I heard you and Kits were getting married Daddy told me

cool

yeah cool, we can't come though, Daddy's got an event at the yacht club

hey that's too bad

and then we were going somewhere together Andy and me with heavy suitcases we were going by boat, on the canal, only Andy was like no way am I getting in that boat and I was like sure I understand, so I took apart the sailboat screw by screw, and put the pieces in my suitcase, we were carrying it overland, sails and all, this was the plan, all you had to do was follow the canals and they'd take you right where you wanted to go or maybe just right back where you started but it was a bigger job than I'd thought, disassembling a sailboat, it was different than taking apart a table or chair and the pieces were too big to fit in the luggage and there was a huge propeller I was trying to jam in with my clothes and Andy was bored and off to the side playing chess with someone I didn't like the looks of and he said well if you can't plan it out ahead of time, you'll just have to work it out as you go along

xvii.

I WOKE WITH A snap of the head, nauseated and itching all over like ants were crawling under my skin. With the drug leaving my system the panic had roared back twice as strong since clearly I was sick, fever and sweats, no denying it any more. After staggering to the bathroom and throwing up again (this, not a fun junkie throw-up, but the usual misery), I came back in my room and contemplated my suit and scarf in plastic at the foot of the bed and thought, with a shiver, how lucky I was. It had all turned out okay (or had it?) but it mightn't have.

Awkwardly, I removed suit and scarf from the plastic—the floor underneath me had a drowsy, nautical roll that made me grab for the wall to steady myself—and reached for my glasses and sat on the bed to examine them under the light. The cloth looked worn but otherwise okay. Then again, I couldn't tell. The cloth was too black. I saw spots, and then I didn't. My eyes still weren't working quite right. Maybe it was a trick—maybe if I went down to the lobby I'd find cops waiting for me—but no—beating this thought back—ridiculous. They'd keep the clothes if they'd found anything suspicious on them, wouldn't they? Certainly they wouldn't return them pressed and cleaned.

I was still out of the world halfway: not myself. Somehow my dream of the sailboat had bled through and infected the hotel room, so it was a room but also the cabin of a ship: built-in cupboards (over my bed and under the eaves) neatly fitted with countersunk brass and enamelled to a high nautical gloss. Ship's carpentry; deck swaying, and lapping outside, the black canal water. Delirium: unmoored and drifting. Outside, the fog was thick, not a breath of wind, streetlights burning through with a diffuse, haggard, ashen stillness, softened and blurred to haze.

Itching, itching. Skin on fire. Nausea and splitting headache. The more sumptuous the dope, the deeper the anguish—mental and physical—when it wore off. I was back to the chunk spewing out of Martin's forehead only on a more intimate level, inside it almost, every pulse and spurt, and—even worse, a deeper freezing point entirely—the painting, gone. Bloodstained coat, the feet of the running-away kid. Blackout. Disaster. For humans—trapped in biology—there was no mercy: we lived a while, we fussed around for a bit and died, we rotted in the ground like garbage. Time destroyed us all soon enough. But to destroy, or lose, a deathless thing—to break bonds stronger than the temporal—was a metaphysical uncoupling all its own, a startling new flavor of despair.

My dad at the baccarat table, in the air-conditioned midnight. *There's always more to things, a hidden level.* Luck in its darker moods and manifestations. Consulting the stars, waiting to make the big bets when Mercury was in retrograde, reaching for a knowledge just beyond the known. Black his lucky color, nine his lucky number. Hit me again pal. *There's a pattern and we're a part of it.* Yet if you scratched very deep at that idea of pattern (which apparently he had never taken the trouble to do), you hit an emptiness so dark that it destroyed, categorically, anything you'd ever looked at or thought of as light.

Chapter 12.

The Rendezvous Point

THE DAYS LEADING TO Christmas were a blur, since thanks to illness and what amounted to solitary confinement I soon lost track of time. I stayed in the room; the Do Not Disturb sign stayed on the door; and television — instead of providing even a false hum of normalcy — only racketed-up the variform confusion and displacement: no logic, no structure, what was on next, you didn't know, could be anything, *Sesame Street* in Dutch, Dutch people talking at a desk, more Dutch people talking at a desk, and though there was Sky News and CNN and BBC none of the local news was in English (nothing that mattered, nothing pertaining to me or the parking garage) though at one point I had a bad start when, flipping through the channels past an old American cop show, I stopped astonished at the sight of my twenty-five-year-old father: one of his many non-speaking roles, a yes-man hovering behind a political candidate at a press conference, nodding at the guy's campaign promises and for one eerie blink glancing into the camera and straight across the ocean and into the future, at me. The multiple ironies of this were so layered and uncanny that I gaped in horror. Except for his haircut and his heavier build (bulked up from lifting weights: he'd been going to the gym a lot in those days) he might have been my twin. But the biggest shock was how straightforward he looked — my already (circa 1985) criminally dishonest and sliding-into-alcoholism father. None of his character, or his future, was visible in his face. Instead he looked resolute, attentive, a model of certainty and promise.

After that I switched the television off. Increasingly, my main contact with reality was room service, which I ordered up only in the blackest pre-dawn hours when the delivery boys were slow and sleepy. "No, I'd like Dutch papers, please," I said (in English) to the Dutch-speaking bellhop who brought up the *International Herald Tribune* with my Dutch rolls and coffee, my ham and eggs and chef's assortment of Dutch cheeses. But since he kept turning up with the *Tribune* anyway, I went down the back stairs before sunrise for the local papers, which were conveniently fanned on a table just off the staircase where I didn't have to pass the front desk.

Bloedend. Moord. The sun didn't seem to rise until about nine in the morning and even then it was hazed and gloomy, casting a low, weak, purgatorial light like a stage effect in some German opera. Apparently the toothpaste I'd used on the lapel of my coat had contained peroxide or some other bleaching agent since the scrubbed spot had faded to a white halo the size of my hand, chalky at the outer edges, ringing the just-visible ghost of Frits's cranial plasma. At about three thirty in the afternoon the light began to go; by five p.m. it was black out. Then, if there weren't too many people on the street, I turned up the lapels of my coat and tied my scarf tight at the neck and—taking care to keep my head down—ducked out in the dark to a tiny, Asian-run market a few hundred yards from the hotel where with my remaining euros I bought pre-wrapped sandwiches, apples, a new toothbrush, cough drops and aspirin and beer. *Is alles?* said the old lady in broken-sounding Dutch. Counting my coins with infuriating slowness. Click, click, click. Though I had credit cards I was determined not to use them—another arbitrary rule in the game I'd devised for myself, a completely irrational precaution because who was I kidding? what did it matter, a couple of sandwiches at a convenience shop, when they already had my card at the hotel?

It was partly fear and partly illness that clouded my judgment, since whatever cold or chill I'd caught wasn't going away. With every hour, it seemed, my cough got deeper and my lungs hurt more. It was true about the Dutch and cleanliness, Dutch cleaning products: the market had a bewildering selection of never-before-seen items and I returned to the room with a bottle featuring a snow white swan against a snow-topped mountain and a skull-and-crossbones label on the back. But though it was strong enough to leach the stripes out of my shirt it wasn't strong enough to lift the stains at the collar, which had faded from liver-dark blobs to sinister, overlapping outlines like bracket fungi. For the fourth or fifth time I rinsed it, eyes streaming, then wrapped it and tied it in plastic bags and pushed it to the back of a high cupboard. Without something to weigh it down, I knew it would float if I dropped it in the canal and I was afraid to take it to the street and shove it in a rubbish bin — someone would see me, I'd be caught, this was how it would happen, I knew it deeply and irrationally like knowledge in a dream.

A little while. What was a little while? Three days tops, Boris had said at Anne de Larmessin's. But then he hadn't factored in Frits and Martin.

Bells and garlands, Advent stars in the shop windows, ribbons and gilded walnuts. At night I slept with socks, stained overcoat, polo-neck sweater in addition to coverlet since the counterclockwise turn of radiator knob as advertised in the leather-bound hotel booklet didn't warm the room enough to help my fever aches and chills. White goosedown, white swans. The room reeked of bleach like a cheap Jacuzzi. Could the chambermaids smell it in the hall? They wouldn't give you more than ten years for art theft but with Martin I'd crossed the border into a different country — one way, no return.

Yet somehow I'd developed a workable way of thinking about Martin's death, or thinking around it, rather. The act — the eternity of it — had thrown me into such a different world that to all practical purposes I was already dead. There was a sense of being past everything, of looking back at land from an ice floe drifted out to sea. What was done could never be undone. I was gone.

And that was fine. I didn't matter much in the scheme of things and Martin didn't either. We were easily forgotten. It was a social and moral lesson, if nothing else. But for all foreseeable time to come — for as long as history was written, until the icecaps melted and the streets of Amsterdam were awash with water — the painting would be remembered and mourned. Who knew, or cared, the names of the Turks who blew the roof off the Parthenon? the mullahs who had ordered the destruction of the Buddhas at Bamiyan? Yet living or dead: their acts stood. It was the worst kind of immortality. Intentionally or no: I had extinguished a light at the heart of the world.

An act of God: that was what the insurance companies called it, catastrophe so random or arcane that there was otherwise no taking the measure of it. Probability was one thing, but some events fell so far outside the actuarial tables that even insurance underwriters were compelled to haul in the supernatural in order to explain them — *rotten luck,* as my father had said mournfully one night out by the pool, dusk falling hard, smoking Viceroy after Viceroy to keep the mosquitoes away, one of the few times he'd tried to talk to me about my mother's death, why do bad things happen, why me, why her, wrong place wrong time, just a fluke kid, one in a million, not an evasion or cop-out in any way but—I recognized, coming from him—a profession of faith and the best answer he had to give me, on a par with Allah Has Written It or It's the Lord's Will, a sincere bowing of the head to Fortune, the greatest god he knew.

If he were in my shoes. It almost made me laugh. I could imagine him holed up and pacing all too clearly, trapped and prowling, relishing the drama of the predicament, a framed cop in a jail cell as portrayed by Farley Granger. But I could imagine just as well his second-hand fascination at my plight, its turns and reversals as random as any turn of the cards, could imagine only too well his woeful shake of the head. *Bad planets. There's a shape to this thing, a larger pattern. If we're just talking story, kid, you got it.* He'd be doing his numerology or whatever, looking at his Scorpio book, flipping coins, consulting the stars. Whatever you said about my dad, you couldn't say he didn't have a cohesive world view.

The hotel was filling up for the holidays. Couples. American servicemen talking in the halls with a military flatness, rank and authority audible in their voices. In bed, in my opiated fevers, I dreamed of snowy mountains, pure and terrifying, alpine vistas from newsreel films of Berchtesgaden, great winds that crossfaded and blew with the windwhipped seas in the oil painting above my desk: tiny tossed sailboat, alone in dark waters.

My father: Put down that remote control when I'm talking to you.

My father: Well, I won't say disaster, but failure.

My father: Does he have to eat with us, Audrey? Does he have to sit at the table with us every fucking night? Can't you make Alameda feed him before I get home?

Uno, Battleship, Etch-A-Sketch, Connect Four. Some green army figures and creepy-crawly rubber insects I'd got in my Christmas stocking.

Mr. Barbour: Two flag signal. Victor: Require Assistance. Echo: I am altering my course to starboard.

The apartment on Seventh Avenue. Rainy-day gray. Many hours spent blowing in and out monotonously on a toy harmonica, in and out, in and out.

On Monday, or maybe it was Tuesday, when I finally worked up the nerve to pull up the blackout shade, so late in the afternoon that the light was going, there was a television crew on the street outside my hotel waylaying Christmas tourists. English voices, American voices. Christmas concerts at Sint Nicolaaskerk and seasonal stalls selling oliebollen. "Almost got hit by a bicycle but apart from that it's been a fun time." My chest hurt. I drew the blackouts again and stood in a hot shower with the water beating down until my skin was sore. The whole neighborhood sparkled with fairy-lit restaurants, beautiful shops displaying cashmere topcoats and heavy, hand-knit sweaters and all the warm clothes I'd neglected to pack. But I didn't even dare phone down for a pot of coffee thanks to the Dutch-language newspapers I'd been thrashing through since well before sunrise that morning, one featuring a front page photo of the parking garage with police tape across the exit.

The papers were spread on the floor on the far side of my bed, like a map to some horrible place I didn't want to go. Repeatedly, unable to help myself, in between drowsing off and falling into feverish conversations I wasn't having, with people I wasn't having them with, I went back and scoured them over and over for Dutch-English cognates which were few and far between. *Amerikaan dood aangetroffen.* Heroïne, cocaïne. *Moord:* mortality, mordant, morbid, murder. *Drugsgerelateerde criminaliteit:* Frits Aaltink afkomstig uit Amsterdam en Mackay Fiedler Martin uit Los Angeles. *Bloedig:* bloody. *Schotenwisseling:* who could say, although, *schoten:* could that mean shots? *Deze moorden kwamen als en schok voor* — what?

Boris. I walked to the window and stood, and then walked back again. Even in the confusion on the bridge I remembered him instructing me not to call, he'd been very firm on the point though we'd parted in such haste I wasn't sure he'd explained why I was supposed to wait for him to contact me, and in any case I wasn't sure it mattered any more. He'd also been very firm on the point that he wasn't hurt, or so I kept reminding myself, though in the swamp of unwanted memories that bombarded me from that evening I kept seeing the burnt hole in the arm of his coat, sticky black wool in the roll of the sodium lamps. For all I knew, the traffic police had caught him on the bridge and hauled him in for driving without a license: an admittedly shitty break, if indeed the case, but a lot better than some of the other possibilities I could think of.

Twee doden bij bloedige... It didn't stop. There was more. The next day, and the next, along with my Traditional Dutch Breakfast, there was more about the killings on the Overtoom: smaller column inches but denser information. *Twee dodelijke slachtoffers. Nog een of meer betrokkenen. Wapengeweld in Nederland.* Frits's photograph, along with the photos of some other guys with Dutch names and a longish article I had no hope of reading. *Dodelijke schietpartij nog onopgehelderd*...It worried me that they'd stopped talking about drugs—Boris's red herring—and had moved on to other angles. I'd set this thing loose, it was out in the world, people were reading about it all over the city, talking about it in a language that wasn't mine.

Huge Tiffany ad in the *Herald Tribune*. Timeless Beauty and Craftsmanship. Happy Holidays from Tiffany & Co.

Chance plays tricks, my dad had liked to say. Systems, spread breakdowns.

Where was Boris? In my fever haze I tried, unsuccessfully, to amuse or at least divert myself with thoughts of how very likely he was to show up at just the moment you didn't expect him. Cracking his knuckles, making the girls jump. Turning up half an hour after our state issued Proficiency Exam had begun, widespread classroom laughter at his puzzled face through the wire reinforced glass of the locked door: *hah, our bright future,* he'd said scornfully when on the way home I'd tried to explain to him about standardized tests.

In my dreams I couldn't get to where I needed to be. There was always something keeping me from where I needed to go.

He had texted me his number before we left the States, and though I was afraid to text him back (not knowing his circumstances, or if the text could be traced to me somehow), I reminded myself continually that I could reach him, if I had to. He knew where I was. Yet, hours into the night, I lay awake arguing with myself: relentless tedium, back and forth, what if, what if, what harm could it do? At last, at some disoriented point—night light burning, half-dreaming, out of it—I broke down and reached for the phone on the nightstand and texted him anyway before I had the chance to think better of it: Where are you?

Over the next two or three hours I lay awake in a state of barely controlled anxiety, lying with my forearm over my face to keep the light out even though there wasn't any light. Unfortunately, when I woke from my sweat-soaked sleep, somewhere around dawn, the phone was stone dead because I'd forgotten to switch it off, and—reluctant to negotiate the front desk, to ask if they had chargers for loan—I hesitated for hours until finally, mid-afternoon, I broke down.

"Certainly, sir," said the desk clerk, hardly looking at me. "United States?"

Thank God, I thought, trying not to hurry too much as I walked upstairs. The phone was old, and slow, and after I plugged it in and stood for a while, I got tired of waiting for the Apple logo to come up and went to the minibar and got myself a drink and came back and stared at it a bit more until at last the lock screen came up, old school photo I'd scanned in as a joke, never had I been so glad to see a picture, ten year old Kitsey flying midair at the penalty kick. But just as I was about to type in the pass code, the home screen popped off, then fizzed for about ten seconds, bands of black and gray that shifted and broke into particles before the sad face came on and clicked with a queasy down-whir to black.

Four-fifteen p.m. The sky was turning ultramarine over the bell gables across the canal. I was sitting on the carpet with my back against the bed and the charger cord in my hand, having methodically, twice, tried all the sockets in the room—I'd switched the phone on and off a hundred times, held it to the lamp to see if maybe it was on and the display had just gone dark, tried to re-set it, but the phone was fried: nothing happening, cold black screen, dead as a doornail. Clearly I'd short-circuited it; the night of the garage it had gotten wet—drops of water on the screen when I took it from my pocket—but though I'd had a bad minute or two waiting for it to come on, it had seemed to be working just fine, right up until the moment I tried to put a charge in it. Everything was backed up on my laptop at home, apart from the only thing I needed: Boris's number, which he'd texted me in the car on the way to the airport.

Water reflections wavering on the ceiling. Outside, somewhere, tinny Christmas carillon music and off-key carolers singing. *O Tannenbaum, O Tannenbaum, wie treu sind deine Blätter.*

I didn't have a return ticket. But I had a credit card. I could take a cab to the airport. *You can take a cab to the airport,* I told myself. Schiphol. First plane out. Kennedy, Newark. I had money. I was talking to myself like a child. Who knew where Kitsey was—out in the Hamptons, for all I knew—but Mrs. Barbour's assistant, Janet (who still had her old job despite the fact that Mrs. Barbour had nothing much she needed assisting with, any more), was the kind of person who could get you on a plane out of anywhere with a few hours' notice, even on Christmas Eve.

Janet. The thought of Janet was absurdly reassuring. Janet who was an efficient mood system all her own, Janet fat and rosy in her pink shetlands and madras plaids like a Boucher nymph as dressed by J. Crew, Janet who said *excellent!* in answer to everything and drank coffee from a pink mug that said *Janet*.

It was a relief to be thinking straight. What good was it doing Boris, or anyone, me waiting around? The cold and damp, the unreadable language. Fever and cough. The nightmare sense of constraint. I didn't want to leave without Boris, without knowing if Boris was okay, it was the war-movie confusion of running on and leaving a fallen friend with no idea what worse hell you were running into, but at the same time I wanted out of Amsterdam so badly I could imagine falling to my knees upon disembarkation at Newark, touching my forehead to the concourse floor.

Telephone book. Pencil and paper. Only three people had seen me: the Indonesian, Grozdan, and the Asian kid. And while it was quite possible Martin and Frits had colleagues in Amsterdam looking for me (another good reason to get out of town), I had no reason to think the police were looking for me at all. There was no reason they would have flagged my passport.

Then — it was like being struck in the face — I flinched. For whatever reason I'd been thinking that my passport was downstairs, where I'd had to present it at check-in. But in truth I hadn't thought of it at all, not since Boris had taken it away from me to lock in the glove box of his car.

Very very calmly, I set down the phone book, making an effort to set it down in a manner that would look casual and unstudied to some neutral observer. In a normal situation it was straightforward enough. Look up the address, find the office, figure out where to go. Stand in line. Await my turn. Speak courteously and patiently. I had credit cards, photo ID. Hobie could fax my birth certificate. Impatiently, I tried to beat back an anecdote Toddy Barbour had told at dinner — how, upon losing his passport (in Italy? Spain?) he'd been required to haul in a flesh-and-blood witness to vouch for his identity.

Bruised inky skies. It was early in America. Hobie just breaking for lunch, walking over to Jefferson Market, maybe picking up groceries for the lunch he was hosting on Christmas Day. Was Pippa in California still?

I imagined her tumbling over in a hotel bed and reaching sleepily for the telephone, eyes still closed, Theo is that you, is something wrong?

Better a fine and talk our way out of it in case we are stopped.

I felt ill. To present myself at the consulate (or whatever) for a round of interviews and paperwork was asking for far more trouble than I needed. I hadn't put a time limit on waiting, on how long I would wait, and yet any movement—random movement, senseless movement, insect-buzzing-around-a-jar movement—seemed preferable to being cooped up in the room even one minute more, seeing shadow people out of the corner of my eye.

Another huge Tiffany ad in the *Tribune,* bringing me Season's Greetings. Then on the opposite page a different ad, for digital cameras, scrawled in artsy letters and signed Joan Miró:

> You can look at a picture for a week and never think of it again. You can also look at a picture for a second and think of it all your life

Centraal Station. European Union, no passport control at the borders. Any train, anywhere. I pictured myself riding in aimless circles through Europe: Rhine falls and Tyrolean passes, cinematic tunnels and snowstorms.

Sometimes it's about playing a poor hand well, I remembered my dad saying drowsily, half asleep on the couch.

Staring at the telephone, lightheaded with fever, I sat very still and tried to think. Boris, at lunch, had spoken of taking the train from Amsterdam to Antwerp (and Frankfurt: I didn't want to go anywhere near Germany) but, also, to Paris. If I went to a consulate in Paris to apply for a new passport: maybe less likelihood of connection with the Martin stuff. But there was no getting away from the fact that the Chinese kid was an eyewitness. For all I knew I was on every law-enforcement computer in Europe.

I went to the bathroom to splash water on my face. Too many mirrors. I switched off the water and reached for a towel to pat my face dry. Methodical actions, one by one. It was after nightfall when my mood always darkened, when I began to be afraid. Glass of water. Aspirin for my fever. That too always began to climb after dark. Simple actions. I was working myself up and I knew it. I didn't know what warrants Boris had out on him but though it was worrying to think he'd been arrested, I was a lot more worried that Sascha's people had sent someone else after him. But this was yet another thought I could not allow myself to follow.

ii.

THE NEXT DAY — CHRISTMAS Eve — I forced myself to eat a huge room-service breakfast even though I didn't want it, and threw away the newspaper without looking at it since I was afraid if I saw the words *Overtoom* or *Moord* one more time there was no way I could make myself do what I had to. After I'd eaten, stolidly, I gathered the week's accumulation of newspapers on and around my bed and rolled them up and put them in the trash basket; retrieved from the cupboard my bleach-rotted shirt and — after checking to see the bag was tied tight — slipped it into another bag from the Asian market (leaving it open, for carrying ease, also in case I happened to spot a helpful brick). Then, after turning up my coat collar and tying my scarf over it, I turned around the sign for the chambermaid, and left.

The weather was rotten, which helped. Wet sleet, blowing in sideways, drizzled over the canal. I walked for about twenty minutes — sneezing, miserable, chilled — until I happened upon a rubbish bin on a particularly deserted corner with no cars or foot traffic, no shops, only blind-looking houses shuttered tight against the wind.

Quickly I shoved the shirt in and walked on, with a burst of exhilaration that sped me four or five streets along very rapidly, despite chattering teeth. My feet were wet; the soles of my shoes were too thin for the cobblestones and I was very cold. When did they pick up the garbage? No matter.

Unless — I shook my head to clear it — the Asian market. The plastic bag had the name of the Asian market on it. Only a few blocks from my hotel. But it was ridiculous to think this way and I tried to reason myself out of it. Who had seen me? No one.

Charlie: Affirmative. Delta: I am proceeding with Difficulty.

Stop it. Stop it. No going back.

Not knowing where a taxi stand was, I trudged along aimlessly for twenty minutes or more until finally I managed to flag down a taxi on the street. "Centraal Station," I told the Turkish cab driver.

But when he left me off in front, after a drive through haunted gray streets like old newsreel footage, I thought for a moment he'd taken me to the wrong place since the building from the front looked more like a museum: red-brick fantasia of gables and towers, bristling Dutch Victoriana. In I wandered, amidst holiday crowds, doing my best to look as if I belonged and ignoring the police who seemed to be standing around nearly everywhere I looked and feeling bewildered and uneasy as the great democratic world swept and surged around me once more: grandparents, students, weary young-marrieds and little kids dragging backpacks; shopping bags and Starbucks cups, rattle of suitcase wheels, teenagers collecting signatures for Greenpeace, back in the hum of human things. There was an afternoon train to Paris but I wanted the latest one they had.

The lines were endless, all the way back to the news kiosk. "This evening?" said the clerk when I finally got to the window: a broad, fair, middle aged woman, pillowy at the bosom and impersonally genial like a procuress in a second rate genre painting.

"That's right," I said, hoping I didn't quite look as sick as I felt.

"How many?" she said, hardly looking at me.

"Just one."

"Certainly. Passport please."

"Just a—" voice husky with illness, patting myself down; I'd hoped they wouldn't ask — "ah. Sorry, I don't have it on me, it's in the safe back at the hotel—but—" producing my New York State ID, my credit cards, my Social Security card, pushing them through the window. "Here you go."

"You require a passport to travel."

"Oh, sure." Doing my best to sound reasonable, knowledgeable. "But I'm not leaving till tonight. See—?" indicating the empty floor at my feet: no luggage. "I'm seeing my girlfriend off, and since I'm here I thought I'd go ahead and get in line and buy the ticket if that's all right."

"Well—" the clerk glanced at her screen — "you have plenty of time. I'd suggest you wait and purchase your ticket when you return this evening."

"Yes—" pinching my nose, so I wouldn't sneeze — "but I'd like to purchase it now."

"I'm afraid that's not possible."

"Please. It'd be a huge help. I've been standing here for forty-five minutes and I don't know what the lines will be like tonight." From Pippa—who had gone all over Europe by rail—I was fairly sure I remembered hearing they didn't check passports for the train. "All I want is to buy it now so I have time to run all my errands before I come back this evening."

The clerk looked hard at my face. Then she picked up the ID and looked at the picture, then again at me.

"Look," I said, when she hesitated, or seemed to hesitate: "You can see it's me. You have my name, my Social Security card—here," I said, reaching in my pocket for pen and paper. "Let me duplicate the signature for you."

She compared the two, side by side. Again she looked at me, and the card—and then, all at once, seemed to make up her mind. "I can't accept this documentation." Pushing my cards back to me through the window.

"Why not?"

The line behind me was growing.

"Why?" I repeated. "It's perfectly legitimate. It's what I use in lieu of passport to fly in the U.S. The signatures match," I said, when she didn't answer, "can't you see?"

"Sorry."

"You mean—" I could hear the desperation in my voice; she was meeting my gaze aggressively, as if defying me to argue. "You're telling me I've got to come all the way back here tonight and stand in line all over again?"

"Sorry, sir. Can't help you. Next," said the clerk, looking over my shoulder at the next passenger.

As I was walking away—pushing and bumping my way through crowds—someone said behind me: "Hey. Hey, mate?"

At first, disoriented from the ticket window, I thought I was hallucinating the voice. But when, uneasily, I turned, I saw a ferret-faced teenager with pink-rimmed eyes and a shaved head, bouncing up and down on the toes of his gigantic sneakers. From his darting side-to-side glance I thought he was going to offer to sell me a passport but instead he leaned forward and said: "Don't try it."

"What?" I said uncertainly, glancing up at the policewoman standing about five feet behind him.

"Listen, mate. Back and forth a hundred times when I had the thing, and they never checked once. But the one time I didn't have it? Crossing into France? They locked me up, didn't they, France immigration jail, twelve hours with they rubbish food and rubbish attitude, horrible. Horrible dirty police cell. Trust me — you want your documents in order. And no funny shit in your case either."

"Hey, right," I said. Sweating in my coat, which I didn't dare unbutton. Scarf I didn't dare untie.

Hot. Headache. Walking away from him, I felt the furious gaze of a security camera burning into me; and I tried not to look self-conscious as I threaded through the crowds, floating and woozy with fever, grinding the phone number of the American consulate in my pocket.

It took me a while to find a pay phone — all the way at the other end of the station, in an area packed with sketchy teenagers sitting in quasi-tribal council on the floor — and it took even longer for me to figure out how to make the actual call.

Buoyant stream of Dutch. Then I was greeted by a pleasant American voice: welcome to the United States consulate of the Netherlands, would I like to continue in English? More menus, more options. Press 1 for this, press 2 for that, please hold for operator. Patiently I followed the instructions and stood gazing out at the crowd until I realized maybe it wasn't such a great idea to let people see my face and turned back to the wall.

The telephone rang so long I'd drifted off into a dissociated fog when suddenly the line clicked on, easy American voice sounding fresh off the beach in Santa Cruz: "Good morning, American Consulate of the Netherlands, how may I help you?"

"Hi," I said, relieved. "I —" I'd debated giving a false name, just to get the information I wanted, but I was too faint and exhausted to bother — "I'm afraid I'm in a jam. My name is Theodore Decker and my passport's been stolen."

"Hey, sorry to hear that." She was keying in something, I could hear her on the other end. Christmas music playing in the background. "Bad time of year for it — everyone travelling, you know? Did you report to the authorities?"

"What?"

"Stolen passport? Because you have to report it immediately. The police need to know right away."

"I —" cursing myself; why had I said it was stolen? — "no, sorry, it just happened. Centraal Station"—I looked around—"I'm calling from a pay phone. To tell you the truth I'm not sure it was stolen, I think it fell out of my pocket."

"Well—" more keyboarding—"lost or stolen, you still have to make a police report."

"Yeah, but I was just about to catch a train, see, and now they won't let me on. And I have to be in Paris tonight."

"Hang on a sec." There were too many people in the train station, damp wool and muggy crowd smells blooming horribly in the overheated warmth. In a moment she clicked back on. "Now—let me get some information from you—"

Name. Date of birth. Date and city of passport issue. Sweating in my overcoat. Humid breathing bodies all around.

"Do you have documentation establishing your citizenship?" she was saying.

"Sorry—?"

"An expired passport? Birth or naturalization certificate?"

"I have a Social Security card. And a New York State ID. I can have a copy of my birth certificate faxed from the States."

"Oh, great. That should be sufficient."

Really? I stood motionless. Was that all?

"Do you have access to a computer?"

"Um—" computer at the hotel? — "sure."

"Well—" she gave me a web address. "You'll need to download, print, and fill out an affidavit regarding lost and stolen passport and bring it here. To our offices. We're near the Rijksmuseum. Do you know where?"

I was so relieved that I could only stand there and let the crowd noises babble and stream over me in a psychedelic blur.

"So—this is what I need from you," California Girl was saying, her crisp voice recalling me from my varicolored fever reverie. "The affidavit. The faxed documents. Two copies of a 5x5 centimeter photograph with a white background. Also, don't forget, copy of the police report."

"Sorry?" I said, jarred.

"Like I was saying. With lost or stolen passports we require you to file a police report?"

"I—" Staring at an eerie convergence of veiled Arabic women, gliding past silently in head-to-toe black. "I won't have time for that."

"What do you mean?"

"It's not like I'm flying to America today. It's just that—" it took me a moment to recover; my coughing fit had brought tears to my eyes— "my train to Paris leaves in two hours. So, I mean—I don't know what to do. I'm not sure I can get all this paperwork done and make it to the police station too."

"Well"—regretfully—"hey, actually you know, our offices are only open for another forty-five minutes."

"What?"

"We close early today. Christmas Eve, you know? And we're gone tomorrow, and the weekend. But we'll be open again at eight-thirty a.m. on the Monday after Christmas."

"Monday?"

"Hey, I'm sorry," she said. She sounded resigned. "It's a process."

"But it's an emergency!" Voice rasping with illness.

"Emergency? Family or medical?"

"I—"

"Because, in certain very rare situations we do supply emergency after-hours support." She wasn't so friendly any more; she was rushed, reciting from her script, I could hear another call ringing in the background like a radio phone-in show. "Unfortunately this is confined to urgent situations of life or death and our staff has to determine that domestic emergency is warranted before we issue a passport waiver. So unless circumstances of death or critical illness require you to travel to Paris this afternoon, and unless you can supply information establishing the critical emergency such as an affidavit with attending physician, clergy, or funeral director—"

"I—" Monday? Fuck! I didn't even want to think about the police report—"hey, sorry, listen—" she was trying to ring off—

"That's right. You get it all together by Monday the twenty-eighth. And then, yes, once the application is in we'll process it for you as quickly as we can—sorry, will you excuse me a second?" Click. Her voice, fainter. "Good morning, United States Consulate of the Netherlands, will you please hold?" Immediately the phone began to ring again. Click. "Good morning, United States Consulate of the Netherlands, will you please hold?"

"How fast can you have it for me?" I said, when she came back on.

"Oh, once you get the application in we should actually have it for you within ten working days, tops. That's working days. Like — normally I'd do my best to rush it through for you in seven? but with the holidays, I'm sure you understand, the office is a little backed up right now, and our hours are really irregular until New Year's. So — hey, sorry," she added, in the stunned silence that had fallen, "it may be a while. Rotten news, I know."

"What am I supposed to do?"

"Do you need traveller's assistance?"

"I'm not sure what that means." Sweat pouring off me. Rank heated air, heavy with crowd odors, barely breathable.

"Money wired? Temporary accommodations?"

"How am I supposed to get home?"

"You're a resident of Paris?"

"No, United States."

"Well with a temporary passport — a temporary passport doesn't even have the chip you need to enter the United States so I'm not sure that there are really any short cuts that will get you there a whole lot faster than I can get you there by —" Ring ring, ring ring. "Just a moment, sir, will you please hold?

"Now, my name is Holly. Would you like me to give you my extension number, just in case you run into any problems or need any assistance during your stay?"

iii.

My FEVER, FOR WHATEVER reason, tended to spike at nightfall. But after so long on my feet in the cold, it had begun to shoot up in ragged jumps that had the jerky quality of a heavy object being hauled by fits and starts up the side of a tall building, so that on the walk home I hardly understood why I was moving or why I didn't fall down or indeed how I was proceeding forward at all, a sort of groundless gliding unconsciousness that carried me high above myself on rainy canal side-streets and up into disembodied lofts and drafts where I seemed to be looking down on myself from above; it had been a mistake not to get a cab back at the station, I kept seeing the plastic bag in the garbage bin and the shiny pink face of the ticket clerk and Boris with tears in his eyes and blood on his hand, clutching at the burnt place on his sleeve; and the wind roared and my head burned and at irregular intervals I flinched at dark epileptic flutters at elbow's edge: black splashes, false starts, no one there, in fact no one on the street at all except—every now and then—a cyclist dim and hunched in the drizzle.

Heavy head, bad throat. When, finally, I managed to flag down a cab on the street, I was only a few minutes from the hotel. The one good thing, when I got upstairs—bonechilled and shaking—was that they'd cleaned the room and restocked the bar, which I'd drunk clear down to the Cointreau.

I retrieved both mini-bottles of gin and mixed them with hot water from the tap and sat in the brocade chair by the window, glass dangling from my fingertips, watching the hours slide: barely awake, a half-dreaming state, solemn winter light tilting from wall to wall in parallelograms that slipped to the carpet and narrowed until they faded out to nothing and it was dinnertime, and my stomach ached and my throat was raw with bile and there I still sat, in the dark. It was nothing I hadn't thought of, plenty, and in far less taxing circumstances; the urge shook me grandly and unpredictably, a poisonous whisper that never wholly left me, that on some days lingered just on the threshold of my hearing but on others roared up uncontrollably into a sort of lurid visionary frenzy, why I wasn't sure, sometimes even a bad movie or a gruesome dinner party could trigger it, short term boredom and long term pain, temporary panic and permanent desperation striking all at once and flaring up in such an ashen desolate light that I saw, really saw, looking back down the years and with all clear-headed and articulate despair, that the world and everything in it was intolerably and permanently fucked and nothing had ever been good or okay, unbearable claustrophobia of the soul, the windowless room, no way out, waves of shame and horror, *leave me alone,* my mother dead on a marble floor, *stop it stop it,* muttering aloud to myself in elevators, in cabs, *leave me alone, I want to die,* a cold, intelligent, self-immolating fury that had—more than once—driven me upstairs in a resolute fog to swallow indiscriminate combos of whatever booze and pills I happened to have on hand: only tolerance and ineptitude that I'd botched it, unpleasantly surprised when I woke up though relieved for Hobie that he hadn't had to find me.

Black birds. Disastrous lead-colored skies out of Egbert van der Poel.

I stood and snapped on the desk light, swaying in the weak, urine-colored glow. There was waiting. There was running away. But these were not so much choices as endurance measures: the useless scurries and freezes of a mouse in a snake tank, serving only to prolong discomfort and suspense. And there was also a third choice: since for various reasons I felt that a consulate member would be fairly speedy to return my call if I left an after-hours message stating that I was an American citizen wishing to turn myself in for capital murder.

Act of rebellion. Life: vacant, vain, intolerable. What loyalty did I owe it? None whatsoever. Why not beat Fate to the punch? Throw the book on the fire and be done with it? There was no end in sight to the present horror, plenty of external, empirical horror to line up with my own endogenous supply; and, given enough dope (inspecting the bag: less than half left), I would happily have set up a fat line and toppled right over: great-souled darkness, explosion of stars.

But there wasn't enough to be sure of finishing myself off. I didn't want to waste what I had on a few hours of oblivion only to wake up again in my cage (or, worse: in a Dutch hospital with no passport). Then again my tolerance was down and I was pretty sure I had enough to do the job if I got good and drunk first and topped it off with my emergency pill.

Bottle of chilled white in the mini-bar. Why not? I drank the rest of my gin and uncorked it, feeling resolute and jubilant — I was hungry, they'd restocked the crackers and cocktail snacks but this was all going to work a lot better on an empty stomach.

The relief was immense. Quiet dismissal. Perfect, perfect joy of throwing it all away. I found a classical station on the radio — Christmas plainchant, somber and liturgical, less melody than a spectral commentary on it — and thought about running myself a bath.

But that could wait. Instead I opened the desk and found a folder of hotel stationery. Gray cathedral stone, minor hexachords. Rex virginum amator. Between fever, and canal water lapping outside, the space around me had fallen quietly into haunted doubleness, a border zone which was both hotel room and the cabin of a gently tossing ship. Life on the high seas. Death by water. Andy, when we were kids, telling me in his eerie

Martian-boy voice that he'd heard on the Learning Channel that Mary protected sailors, that one of the protections of the Rosary was that you would never die by drowning. Mary Stella Maris. Mary Star of the Sea.

I thought of Hobie at midnight mass, kneeling in the pew in his black suit. Gilding wears away naturally. On a cabinet door, on the flap of a bureau, there are often a quantity of tiny indentations.

Objects seeking out their rightful owners. They had human qualities. They were shifty or honest or suspicious or fine.

Really remarkable pieces do not appear on the scene from nowhere.

The hotel pen wasn't great, I wished I had a better one, but the paper was creamy and thick. Four letters. Hobie's and Mrs. Barbour's would have to be the longest, as they were the persons who most deserved an explanation and also because they were the only persons who, if I died, would actually care. But I would write to Kitsey as well—to assure her that it wasn't her fault. Pippa's letter would be the shortest. I wanted her to know just how much I loved her while also letting her know that she bore not one particle of blame for not loving me back.

But I wouldn't say that. It was rosepetals I wanted to throw, not a poison dart. The point was to let her know, briefly, how happy she had made me while leaving out all the more obvious part.

When I shut my eyes, I was struck by clinically sharp flashes of memory that the fever brought bursting up from nowhere, like tracer rounds going off in the jungle, lurid flares of highly detailed and emotionally complex material. Harpstrings of light through the barred windows of our old apartment on Seventh Avenue, scratchy sisal matting and the red waffled texture it left in my hands and knees when I was playing down on the floor. A tangerine party dress of my mother's with shiny things on the skirt I always wanted to touch. Alameda, our old housekeeper, mashing plantains in a glass bowl. Andy, saluting me before stumbling down the gloomy hall of his parents' apartment: *Aye, Captain.*

Medieval voices, austere and otherworldly. The gravity of unadorned song.

I didn't actually feel upset, that was the thing. Instead it was more like the last and worst of my root canals when the dentist had leaned in under the lamps and said *almost done.*

December 24

Dear Kitsey,

I'm terribly sorry about this but I want you to know that it has nothing to do with you, and nothing to do with any of your family. Your mother will be receiving a separate letter which will have a bit more information but in the meantime I want to assure you, privately, that my course of action has not been influenced by anything that has happened between us, especially events of late.

Where this stiff voice, and unnaturally stiff handwriting had come from — incongruous with the cloudbursts of memory and hallucination crashing in on me from all sides — I did not know. The wet sleet pelting against the windowpanes had a kind of deep historical weight to it, starvation, armies marching, a never-ending drizzle of sadness.

As you well know, and have pointed out to me yourself, I have numerous problems that began long before I met you, and none of these problems are your fault. If your mother has questions for you about your role in recent events, I should urge you to refer her to Tessa Margolis, or — even better — Em, who will be more than delighted to share her views on my character. Also — completely unrelated matter, but I also urge you not to let Havistock Irving into your apartment again, ever.

Kitsey as a child. Fine hair straggling in her face. Shut up you goofballs. Cut it out or I'll tell.

Last but not least —

(my pen hovering over this line)

last but not least I want to tell you how beautiful you looked at the party and how touched I was that you wore my mother's earrings. She was crazy about Andy — she would have loved you too, and would have loved for us to be together. I'm sorry it didn't work out. But I do hope things work out for you. Really.

Best love,
Theo

Sealed; addressed; put aside. They'd have stamps at the front desk.

Dear Hobie,

This is a hard letter to write and I'm sorry to be writing it.

Alternate sweats and frosts. I was seeing green spots. My fever was so high the walls seemed to be shrinking.

This isn't about the bad pieces I've sold. I expect you'll hear soon enough what it's about.

Nitric acid. Lampblack. Furniture, like all living things, acquired marks and scars over the course of time.
The effects of time, visible and invisible.

and, I don't quite know how to say this but I guess what I'm thinking about is this sick puppy my mother and I found on the street in China-town. She was lying in a space between two garbage cans. She was a baby pit bull. Smelly, dirty. Skin and bones. Too weak to stand up. People just walking by her. And I got upset and my mother promised me that we'd pick her up if she was still there when we finished eat-ing. And when we got out of the restaurant, there she still was. So we hailed a cab, I carried her in my arms, and when we got her home my mother made her a box in the kitchen and she was so happy and licked our faces and drank a ton of water and ate the dog food we bought her and threw it all right back up.
   Well to make a long story short, she died. It wasn't our fault. We felt like it was. We took her in to the vet, and bought her special food, but she only got sicker and sicker. We were both really fond of her by

this time. And my mother took her in again, to a specialist at the Animal Medical Center. And the vet said — this dog has a disease, which I forget the name of, and she had it when you found her, and I know this is not what you want to hear but it is going to be a whole lot kinder if you euthanize her right now

My hand had been flying in reckless jerks and starts across the paper. But at the end of the page while reaching for another, I stopped, appalled. What I'd experienced as weightlessness, a sort of sweeping, last-chance glide, was not at all the eloquent and affecting farewell I'd imagined. The handwriting sloped and slopped all over the place and was not intelligent or coherent or even legible. There had to be some much briefer, and simpler, way to thank Hobie and say what I had to say: namely, that he shouldn't feel bad, he'd always been good to me and done his best to help me, just as my mother and I had done our best to help this baby pit bull, who — it was actually a pertinent point, only I didn't want to spin the story out too long — for all her sweet-tempered qualities had been incredibly destructive in the days leading to her death, she'd pretty much destroyed the whole apartment and ripped our sofa to pieces.

Maudlin, self-indulgent, tasteless. My throat felt as if the lining had been scraped out with a razor.

Off comes the upholstery. Look here: we have woodworm. We'll have to treat it with Cuprinol.

The night I'd overdosed in Hobie's upstairs bathroom, expecting not to wake up and waking up anyway with my cheek on the trippy old hexagonal floor tile, I'd been amazed at exactly how radiant a pre-war bathroom with plain white fittings could be when you were looking at it from the afterlife.

The beginning of the end? Or the end of the end?

Fabelhaft. Having the best fun ever.

One thing at a time. Aspirins. Cold water from the minibar. The aspirins rasped and stuck in my chest, like swallowing gravel, and I pounded trying to get them down, the booze had made me feel a whole lot sicker, thirsty, confused, fish hooks in my throat, water trickling absurdly down my cheeks, gasping and wheezing, I'd opened the wine as a treat (supposedly) but it was going down like turpentine, burning and razoring around in my stomach, should I run a bath, should I call down for something hot, something simple, broth or tea? No: the thing was simply to finish the wine or maybe just go right ahead and start in on the vodka; somewhere online I'd read that only two per cent of attempted suicides by overdose were successful, which seemed like an absurdly low number although one unfortunately borne out by previous experience. *It aint gonna rain no mo'.* That was somebody's suicide note. *It was only a farce.* Jean Harlow's husband, who killed himself on their wedding night. George Sanders's had been the best, an Old Hollywood classic, my father had known it by heart and liked to quote from it. *Dear World, I am leaving because I am bored.* And then, Hart Crane. Pivot and drop, shirt ballooning as he fell. *Goodbye everybody!* A shouted farewell, jumping off ship.

I no longer considered my body my own. It had ceased to belong to me. My hands, moving, felt separate, floating of their own accord, and when I stood it was like operating a marionette, unfolding myself, rising jerkily on strings.

Hobie had told me that when he was a young man he drank Cutty Sark because it was Hart Crane's whiskey. Cutty Sark means Short Skirt.

Pale green walls in the piano room, palm trees and pistachio ices.

Ice-coated windows. Unheated rooms of Hobie's childhood.

The Old Masters, they were never wrong.

What did I think, what did I feel?

It hurt to breathe. The packet of heroin was in the night table on the other side of the bed. But though my dad, with his unflagging love for showbiz hell, would have adored the whole set up—dope, dirty ashtray, booze and all—I couldn't quite bear the thought of being found sprawled out in my complimentary hotel robe like a has-been lounge singer. The thing to do was clean up, shower and shave and put on my suit so I didn't look too seedy when they found me and only then, at the last, after the night chambermaids were off duty, take the Do Not Disturb sign off the door: better if they found me first thing, I didn't want them to find me from the smell.

It felt like a lifetime had come and gone since my night with Pippa and I thought how happy I'd been, rushing to meet her in the sharp-edged winter darkness, my elation at spotting her under a streetlamp out in front of Film Forum and how I'd stood on the corner to savor it—the joy of watching her watch for me. Her expectant watching-the-crowd face. Me she was watching for: me. And the heart-shock of believing, for only a moment, that you might just have what could never be yours.

Suit from the closet. Shirts all dirty. Why hadn't I thought to send one out? My shoes were waterlogged and wrecked which added a final sorry note to the picture — but no (pausing muddled in the middle of the room), was I going to lay myself out fully dressed, shoes and all, like a corpse on a slab? I'd broken out in a cold sweat, shivers and chills again, the whole routine. I needed to sit down. Maybe I was going to have to re-think the whole presentation. Tear up the letters. Make it look like an accident. Much nicer if it looked like I was on my way to some mysterious dress-up party, just having a bump on the way out — sitting on the edge of the bed, little too much, black sparklers and fizz-pops, keeling over deliciously. Whoops.

White wings of tumult. Running jump into the infinite.

Then — at a blare of trumpets — I started. The liturgical chant had given way to a burst of inappropriately festive orchestration. Melodic, brassy. A wave of frustration boiled up in me. Nutcracker Suite. All wrong. All wrong. A full-blooded Seasonal Extravaganza wasn't at all the note to go out on, dashing orchestral number, March of the Something Something, and all at once my stomach heaved, violent pitch right into my throat, it felt like I'd swallowed a quart of lemon juice and the next thing I knew almost before I could lurch for the wastebasket it was all coming up in a clear acid gush, wave after wave after yellowy wave.

After it was over, I sat on the carpet with my forehead resting on the sharp metal edge of the can and the kiddie-ballet music sparkling along irritatingly in the background: not even drunk, that was the hell of it, just sick. In the hallway I could hear a gaggle of Americans, couples, laughing, saying their loud goodbyes as they parted for their respective rooms: old college friends, jobs in the financial sector, five-plus years of corporate law and Fiona entering first grade in the fall, all's well in Oaklandia, well goodnight then, God we love you guys, a life I might have had myself except I didn't want it. That was the last thing I remember thinking before I made it swaying to my feet and switched the annoying music off and — stomach roiling — threw myself face down on the bed like throwing myself off a bridge, every lamp in the room still blazing as I sank away from the light, blackness closing over my head.

iv.

WHEN I WAS A boy, after my mother died, I always tried hard to hold her in my mind as I was falling asleep so maybe I'd dream of her, only I never did. Or, rather, I dreamed of her constantly, only as absence, not presence: a breeze blowing through a just-vacated house, her handwriting on a note-pad, the smell of her perfume, streets in strange lost towns where I knew she'd been walking only a moment before but had just vanished, a shadow moving away against a sunstruck wall. Sometimes I spotted her in a crowd, or in a taxicab pulling away, and these glimpses of her I treasured despite the fact that I was never able to catch up with her. Always, ulti-mately, she eluded me: I'd always just missed her call, or misplaced her phone number; or run up breathless and gasping to the place where she was supposed to be, only to find her gone. In adult life these chronic near misses pulsed with a messier and much more painful anxiety: I would be stricken with panic to learn, or remember, or be told by some implausible party that she was living across town in some terrible slum apartment where for reasons inexplicable I had not gone to see her or contacted her in years. Usually I was frantically trying to hail a cab or make my way to her when I woke up. These insistent scenarios had a repetitive and borderline-brutal quality that reminded me of the wound-up Wall Street husband of one of Hobie's clients who, when he got in a certain mood, liked to tell the same three stories of his Vietnam war experience over and over with the same mechanical wording and gestures: same rat-a-tat of gunfire, same chopping hand, always in the exact same spot. Everyone's face got very still over the after-dinner drinks when he spieled off into his routine, which we'd all seen a million times and which (like my own ruthless loop of searching for my mother, night after night, year after year, dream after dream) was rigid and invariable. He was always going to stumble and fall over the same tree root; he would never make it to his friend Gage in time, just as I would never manage to find my mother.

But that night, finally, I did find her. Or more accurately: she found me. It felt like a one off, although maybe some other night, some other dream, she'll come to me like that again — maybe when I'm dying, though it seems almost too much to wish for. Certainly I would be less frightened of death (not just my own death but Welty's death, Andy's death, Death in general) if I thought a familiar person came to meet us at the door, because — writing this now, I'm close to tears — I think how poor Andy told me, with terror on his face, that my mother was the only person he'd known, and liked, who'd ever died. So — maybe when Andy washed up spitting and coughing into the country on the far side of the water, maybe my mother was the very one who knelt down by his side to greet him on the foreign shore. Maybe it's stupid to even articulate such hopes. But, then again, maybe it's more stupid not to.

Either way — one-off or not — it was a gift; and if she had only one visit, if that's all they allowed her, she saved it for when it mattered. Because all of a sudden, there she was. I was standing in front of a mirror and looking at the room reflected behind me, which was an interior much like Hobie's shop, or, rather, a more spacious and eternal-seeming version of the shop, cello-brown walls and an open window which was like an entry point into some much larger, unimaginable theater of sunlight. The space behind me in the frame was not so much a space in the conventional sense as a perfectly composed harmony, a wider, more real-seeming reality with a deep silence around it, beyond sound and speech; where all was stillness and clarity, and at the same time, as in a backward-run movie, you could also imagine spilled milk leaping back into the pitcher, a jumping cat flying backward to land silently upon a table, a waystation where time didn't exist or, more accurately, existed all at once in every direction, all histories and movements occurring simultaneously.

And when I looked away for a second and then looked back, I saw her reflection behind me, in the mirror. I was speechless. Somehow I knew I wasn't allowed to turn around — it was against the rules, whatever the rules of the place were — but we could see each other, our eyes could meet in the mirror, and she was just as glad to see me as I was to see her. She was herself. An embodied presence. There was psychic reality to her, there was depth and information. She was between me and whatever place she had stepped from, what landscape beyond. And it was all about the moment when our eyes touched in the glass, surprise and amusement, her beautiful blue eyes with the dark rings around the irises, pale blue eyes with a lot of light in them: hello! Fondness, intelligence, sadness, humor. There was motion and stillness, stillness and modulation, and all the charge and magic of a great painting. Ten seconds, eternity. It was all a circle back to her. You could grasp it in an instant, you could live in it forever: she existed only in the mirror, inside the space of the frame, and though she wasn't alive, not exactly, she wasn't dead either because she wasn't yet born, and yet never not born — as somehow, oddly, neither was I. And I knew that she could tell me anything I wanted to know (life, death, past, future) even though it was already there, in her smile, the answer to all questions, the before-Christmas smile of someone with a secret too wonderful to let slip, just yet: *well, you'll just have to wait and see, won't you?* But just as she was about to speak — drawing an affectionate exasperated breath I knew very well, the sound of which I can hear even now — I woke up.

V.

WHEN I OPENED MY eyes, it was morning. All the lamps in the room were still blazing and I was under the covers with no memory of how I'd gotten under them. Everything was still bathed and saturated with her presence — higher, wider, deeper than life, a shift in optics that had produced a rainbow edge, and I remember thinking that this must be how people felt after visions of saints — not that my mother was a saint, only that her appearance had been as distinct and startling as a flame leaping up in a dark room.

Still half sleeping, I drifted in the bedclothes, buoyed by the sweetness of the dream washing quietly about me. Even the ambient morning sounds in the hallway had taken on the atmosphere and color of her presence; for if I listened hard, in my half-dreaming state, it seemed that I could hear the specific light, cheerful sound of her footsteps mixed up with the clank of the room service trays up and down the hall and the rattle of elevator cables, the opening and closing of elevator doors: a very urban sound, a sound I associated with Sutton Place, and her.

Then, suddenly, bursting into the last wisps of bioluminescence still trailing from the dream, the bells of the nearby church broke out in such violent clangor that I bolted upright in a panic, fumbling for my glasses. I had forgotten what day it was: Christmas.

Unsteadily, I got up and went to the window. Bells, bells. The streets were white and deserted. Frost glittered on tiled rooftops; outside, on the Herengracht, snow danced and flew. A flock of black birds was cawing and swooping over the canal, the sky was hectic with them, great sideways sweeps and undulations as a single, intelligent body, eddying to and fro, and their movement seemed to pass into me on almost a cellular level, white sky and whirling snow and the fierce gusting wind of poets.

First rule of restorations. Never do what you can't undo.

I took a shower, shaved and dressed. Then, quietly, I cleared up and packed my things. Somehow I would have to get Gyuri's ring and watch back to him, assuming he was still alive, which I was increasingly doubtful he was: the watch alone was a fortune—a BMW 7 series, a down payment on a condo. I would FedEx them to Hobie for safekeeping and leave his name for Gyuri at the front desk, just in case.

Frosted panes, snow ghosting the cobblestones, deep and speechless, no traffic on the streets, centuries superimposed, 1940s by way of 1640s.

It was important not to think too deeply. The important thing was to ride the energy of the dream that had followed me into waking. Since I didn't speak Dutch, I would go to the American consulate and have the consulate phone the Dutch police. Spoiling some consulate member's Christmas, the festive family meal. But I didn't trust myself to wait. Possibly a good idea to go down and look at the State Department's website and apprise myself of my rights as an American citizen—certainly there were many worse places in the world to be in jail than the Netherlands and maybe if I was up front about everything I knew (Horst and Sascha, Martin and Frits, Frankfurt and Amsterdam) they could run the painting down.

But who knew how it would play. I was certain of nothing except that evasive action was over. Whatever happened, I would not be like my father, dodging and scheming up until the very moment of flipping the car and crashing in flames; I would stand forward and take what was coming to me; and, to that point, I went straight to the bathroom and flushed the glassine stamp down the toilet.

And that was that: fast as Martin, and just as irrevocable. What was it my dad liked to say? *Face the music.* Not something he'd ever done.

I had been to every corner of the room, done all there was to do except for the letters. Even the handwriting made me wince. But—the consciousness made me start back—I *did* have to write Hobie: not the self-pitying wobbles of drunkenness but a few businesslike lines, whereabouts of checkbook, ledger, deposit-box key. Probably just as well if I admitted, in writing, the furniture fraud, and made it crystal-clear he'd had no knowledge of it. Maybe I could have it witnessed and notarized at the American consulate; maybe Holly (or whoever) would take pity and call someone in to do it before they phoned the police. Grisha could back me up on a lot of it without incriminating himself: we'd never discussed it, he'd never questioned me but he'd known it wasn't kosher, all those hush-hush trips out to the storage unit.

That left Pippa and Mrs. Barbour. God, the letters I'd written Pippa and never sent! My best effort, my most creative, after the disastrous visit with Everett, had begun, and ended, with what I felt was the light, affecting line: *Leaving for a while.* As a would-be suicide note it had seemed at the time, in terms of concision anyway, a minor masterpiece. Unfortunately I'd miscalculated the dose and awakened twelve hours later with vomit all over the bedspread and had to stagger downstairs still sick as a dog for a ten a.m. meeting with the IRS.

That said: a going-to-jail note was different, and best left unwritten. Pippa wasn't fooled by who I was. I had nothing to offer her. I was illness, instability, everything she wanted to get away from. Jail would only confirm what she knew. The best thing I could do was break off contact. If my father had really loved my mother — really loved her the way he said he had, once upon a time — wouldn't he have done the same?

And then — Mrs. Barbour. It was sinking-ship knowledge, the sort of extremely surprising thing you don't realize about yourself until the absolute last ditch, until the lifeboats are lowered and the ship is in flames — but, in the end, when I thought of killing myself she was the one I really couldn't bear to do it to.

Leaving the room — going down to inquire about FedEx and to look at the State Department's website before I called the consulate — I stopped. Tiny ribbon-wrapped bag of candies over the doorknob, a hand-written note: *Merry Christmas!* Somewhere people were laughing and a delicious smell of strong coffee and burnt sugar and freshly baked bread from room service was floating up and down the hall. Every morning I'd been ordering up the hotel breakfasts, grimly plowing through them — wasn't Holland meant to be famous for its coffee? Yet I'd been drinking it every day and not even tasting it.

I slipped the bag of candy in the pocket of my suit and stood in the hallway breathing deep. Even condemned men were allowed to choose a last meal, a topic of discussion which Hobie (indefatigable cook, joyous eater) had more than once introduced at the end of the evening over Armagnac while he was scrambling around for empty snuffboxes and extra saucers to serve as impromptu ashtrays for his guests: for him it was a metaphysical question, best considered on a full stomach after all the desserts were cleared and the final plate of jasmine caramels was being passed, because — really looking at the end of it, at the end of the night, closing your eyes and waving goodbye to Earth — what would you actually choose? Some comforting reminder of the past? Plain chicken dinner from some lost Sunday in boyhood? Or — last grasp at luxury, the far end of the horizon — pheasant and cloudberries, white truffles from Alba? As for me: I hadn't even known I was hungry until I'd stepped into the hallway, but at that moment, standing there with a rough stomach and a bad taste in my mouth and the prospect of what would be my last freely chosen meal, it seemed to me that I'd never smelled anything quite so delicious as that sugary warmth: coffee and cinnamon, plain buttered rolls from the Continental breakfast. Funny, I thought, going back into the room and picking up the room service menu: to want something so easy, to feel such appetite for appetite itself.

Vrolijk Kerstfeest! said the kitchen boy half an hour later — a stout, disheveled teenager straight from Jan Steen with a wreath of tinsel on his head and a sprig of holly behind one ear.

Lifting the silver tops of the trays with a flourish. "Special Dutch Christmas bread," he said, pointing it out ironically. "Just for today." I'd ordered the "Festive Champagne Breakfast" which included a split of champagne, truffled eggs and caviar, a fruit salad, a plate of smoked salmon, a slab of pâté, and half a dozen dishes of sauce, cornichons, capers, condiments, and pickled onions.

He had popped the champagne and left (after I'd tipped him with most of my remaining euros) and I'd just poured myself some coffee and was tasting it carefully, wondering if I could stomach it (I was still queasy and it smelled not quite so delicious, up close), when the telephone rang.

It was the desk clerk. "Merry Christmas Mr. Decker," he said rapidly. "I'm sorry but I'm afraid you've got someone on the way up. We tried to stop them at the desk —"

"What?" Frozen. Cup halfway to mouth.

"On the way up. Now. I tried to stop them. I asked them to wait but they wouldn't. That is — my colleague asked him to wait. He started up before I could telephone —"

"Ah." Looking around the room. All my resolve gone in an instant.

"My colleague —" muffled aside — "my colleague just started up the stairs after him — it was all very sudden, I thought I should —"

"Did he give a name?" I asked, walking to the window and wondering if I could break it with a chair. I wasn't on a high floor and it was a short jump, maybe twelve feet.

"No he didn't sir." Speaking very fast. "We couldn't — that is to say he was very determined — he slipped right by the desk before —"

Commotion in the hall. Some shouted Dutch.

"— we're short-staffed this morning, as I'm sure you understand —"

Determined pounding at the door — coarse nervous jolt, like the never-ending burst spraying out of Martin's forehead, that sent my coffee flying. Fuck, I thought, looking at my suit and shirt: wrecked. Couldn't they have waited until after breakfast? Then again, I thought — dabbing my shirt with a napkin, starting grimly to the door: Maybe it was Martin's guys. Maybe it would be quicker than I thought.

But instead, when I threw open the door — I could scarcely believe it — there stood Boris. Rumpled, red-eyed, battered-looking. Snow in his hair, snow on the shoulders of his coat. I was too startled to be relieved. "What," I said, as he embraced me, and then to the determined-looking clerk in the hallway, striding rapidly toward us: "No, it's okay."

"You see? Why should I wait? Why should I wait?" he said angrily, flinging out an arm at the clerk, who had stopped dead to stare. "Didn't I say? I told you I knew where his room was! How would I know, if not my friend?" Then, to me: "I don't know why this big production. Ridiculous! I was standing there forever and no one at desk. No one! Sahara Desert!" (glaring at clerk). "Waiting, waiting. Rang the bell! Then, the second I start up — 'wait wait sir —'" whiny baby voice — "'come back' — here *he* comes chasing me —"

"Thank you," I said to the clerk, or his back rather, since after several moments of looking between us in surprise and annoyance he had quietly turned to walk away. "Thanks a lot. I mean it," I called down the hall after him; it was good to know they stopped people charging upstairs on their own.

730 | DONNA TARTT

"Of course sir." Not bothering to look around. "Merry Christmas."

"Are you going to let me in?" said Boris, when finally the elevator doors closed and we were alone. "Or shall we stand here tenderly and gaze?" He smelled rank, as if he hadn't showered in days, and he looked both faintly contemptuous and very pleased with himself.

"I —" my heart was pounding, I felt sick again — "for a minute, sure."

"A minute?" Disdainful look up and down. "You have some place to go?"

"As a matter of fact, yes."

"Potter —" half-humorously, putting down his bag, feeling my forehead with his knuckles — "you look bad. You are fevered. You look like you just dug the Panama Canal."

"I feel great," I said curtly.

"You don't look great. You are white as a fish. Why are you all dressed up? Why did you not answer my calls? What's this?" he said — looking past me, espying the room service table.

"Go ahead. Help yourself."

"Well if you don't mind, I will. What a week. Been driving all fucking night. Shitty way to spend Christmas Eve —" shouldering his coat off, letting it fall on the floor — "well, truth told, I've spent many worse. At least no traffic on the motorway. We stopped at some awful place on the road, only place open, petrol station, frankfurters with mustard, usually I like them, but oh my God, my stomach —" He'd gotten a glass from the bar, was pouring himself some champagne.

"And you, here." Flicking a hand. "Living it up, I see. Lap of luxury." He'd kicked off his shoes, wiggling wet sock feet. "Christ, my toes are frozen. Very slushy on the streets — snow is all turning to water." Pulling up a chair. "Sit with me. Eat something. Very good timing." He'd lifted the cover of the chafing dish, was sniffing the plate of truffled eggs. "Delicious! Still hot! What, what is this?" he said, as I reached in my coat pocket and handed him Gyuri's watch and ring. "Oh, yes! I forgot. Never mind about that. You can give them back yourself."

"No, you can do it for me."

"Well, we should phone him. This is feast enough for five people. Why don't we call down —" he lifted up the champagne, looked at the level as if studying a table of troubling financials — "why don't we call for another of these, full bottle, or maybe two, and send down for more coffee or some

tea maybe? I —" pushing his chair in closer —"I am starving! I'll ask
him —" lifting up a piece of smoked salmon, dangling it to his mouth to
gobble it before reaching in his pocket for his cell phone —"ask him to
dump the car somewhere and walk over, shall I?"

"Fine." Something in me had gone dead at the sight of him, almost
like with my dad when I was a kid, long hours alone at home, the involuntary wave of relief at his key in the lock and then the immediate heart-
sink at the actual sight of him.

"What?" Licking his fingers noisily. "You don't want Gyuri to come?
Who's been driving me all night? Who went without sleep? Give him
some breakfast at least." He'd already started in on the eggs. "A lot has
happened."

"A lot has happened to me too."

"Where are you going?"

"Order what you want." Fishing the key card out of my pocket, handing it to him. "I'll leave the total open. Charge it to the room."

"Potter —" throwing down the napkin, starting after me then stopping mid-step and —much to my surprise —laughing. "Go then. To your
new friend or activity so important!"

"A lot has happened to me."

"Well —" smugly —"I don't know what happened to *you,* but I
can say that what happened to *me* is at least five thousand times more.
This has been some week. This has been one for the books. While you
have been luxuriating in hotel, I —" stepping forward, hand on my
sleeve —"hang on." The phone had rung; he turned half away, spoke rapidly in Ukrainian before breaking off and hanging up very suddenly at
the sight of me heading out the door.

"Potter." Grabbing me by the shoulders, looking hard into my pupils,
then turning me and steering me around, kicking the door shut behind
him with one foot. "What the fuck? You are like Night of the Zombie.
What was that movie we liked? The black and white? Not Living Dead,
but the poetry one —?"

"*I Walked with a Zombie.* Val Lewton."

"That's right. That's the one. Sit down. Weed is very very strong here,
even if you are used to it, I should have warned you —"

"I haven't smoked any weed."

"—because I tell you, when I came here first, age twenty maybe, at the

time smoking trees every day, I thought I could handle anything and—
oh my God. My own fault—I was an ass with the guy at the coffeeshop.
'Give me strongest you have.' Well he did! Three hits and I couldn't walk!
I couldn't stand! It was like I forgot to move my feet! Tunnel vision, no
control of muscles. Total disconnection from reality!" He had steered me
to the bed; he was sitting beside me with his arm around my shoulders.
"And, I mean, you know me but—never! Fast pounding heart, like running and running and whole time sitting still—no comprehension of my
locale—terrible darkness! All alone and crying a little, you know, speaking to God in my mind, 'what did I do,' 'why do I deserve this.' Don't
remember leaving the place! Like a horrible dream. And this is weed,
mind you! Weed! Came to on the street, all jelly legs, clutching onto a bike
rack near Dam Square. I thought traffic was driving up on the sidewalk
and going to wreck into me. Finally found my way to my girl's flat in the
Jordaan and layed around for a long time in a bath with no water in it.
So—" He was looking suspiciously at my coffee-splattered shirt front.

"I didn't smoke any weed."

"I know, you said! Was just telling you a story. Thought it was a little
interesting to you maybe. Well—no shame," he said. "Whatever." The
ensuing silence was endless. "I forgot to say—I forgot to say"—he was
pouring me a glass of mineral water—"after this time I told you? Wandering on the Dam? I felt wrong for three days after. My girl said, 'Let's
go out, Boris, you can't lie here any more and waste the whole weekend."
Vomited in the van Gogh museum. Nice and classy."

The cold water, hitting my sore throat, threw me into goosebumps
and into a visceral bodily memory from boyhood: painful desert sunlight,
painful afternoon hangover, teeth chattering in the air-conditioned chill.
Boris and I so sick we kept retching, and laughing about retching, which
made us retch even harder. Gagging on stale crackers from a box in my
room.

"Well—" Boris stealing a glance at me sideways—"something going
around maybe. If was not Christmas Day, I would run down and get
something to help your stomach. Here here—" dumping some food on a
plate, shoving it at me. He picked up the champagne bottle from the ice
bucket, looked at the level again, then poured the remainder of the split
into my half-empty orange juice glass (half empty, because he had drunk
it himself).

"Here," he said, raising his champagne glass to me. "Merry Christmas to you! Long life to us both! Christ is born, let us glorify Him! Now —" gulping it down — he'd turned the rolls on the tablecloth, was heaping out food to himself in the ceramic bread dish — "I am sorry, I know you want to hear about everything, but I am hungry and must eat first."

Pâté. Caviar. Christmas bread. Despite everything, I was hungry too, and I decided to be grateful for the moment and for the food in front of me and began to eat and for a while neither of us said anything.

"Better?" he said presently, throwing me a glance. "You are exhausted." Helping himself to more salmon. "There is a bad flu going round. Shirley has it too."

I said nothing. I had only just begun to adjust myself to the fact that he was in the room with me.

"I thought you were out with some girl. Well — here is where Gyuri and I have been," he said, when I didn't answer. "We have been in Frankfurt. Well — this you know. Some crazy time it's been! But —" downing his champagne, walking to the minibar and squatting down to look inside —

"Do you have my passport?"

"Yes I have your passport. Wow, there is some nice wine in here! And all these nice baby Absoluts."

"Where is it?"

"Ah —" Loping back to the table with a bottle of red wine under his arm, and three minibar bottles of vodka which he stuck in the ice bucket. "Here you go." Fishing it from his pocket, tossing it carelessly onto the table. "Now" — sitting down — "shall we drink a toast together?"

I sat on the edge of the bed without moving, my half-eaten plate of food still in my lap. My passport.

In the long silence that followed, Boris reached across the table and flicked the edge of my champagne glass with middle finger, sharp crystalline ting like a spoon on an after dinner goblet.

"May I have your attention, please?" he inquired ironically.

"What?"

"Toast?" Tipping his glass to me.

I rubbed my hand over my forehead. "And you are what, here?"

"Eh?"

"Toasting what, exactly?"

"Christmas Day? Graciousness of God? Will that do?"

The silence between us, while not exactly hostile, took on as it grew a distinctly glaring and unmanageable tone. Finally Boris fell back in his chair and nodded at my glass and said: "Hate to keep asking, but when you are through with staring at me, do you think we can—?"

"I'm going to have to figure all this out at some point."

"What?"

"I guess I'll have to sort this all out in my mind some time. It's going to be a job. Like, this thing over there...that over here. Two different piles. Three different piles maybe."

"Potter, Potter, Potter—" affectionate, half-scornful, leaning forward— "you are a blockhead. You have no sense of gratitude or beauty."

"'No sense of gratitude.' I'll drink to that, I guess."

"What? Don't you remember our happy Christmas that one time? Happy days gone by? Never to return? Your dad—" grand flinging gesture—"at the restaurant table? Our feast and joy? Our happy celebration? Don't you honor that memory in your heart?"

"For God's sake."

"Potter—" arrested breath—"you are something. You are worse than a woman. 'Hurry, hurry.' 'Get up, go.' Didn't you read my texts?"

"What?"

Boris—reaching for his glass—stopped cold. Quickly he glanced at the floor and I was, suddenly, very aware of the bag by his chair.

In amusement, Boris stuck his thumbnail between his front teeth. "Go ahead."

The words hovered over the wrecked breakfast. Distorted reflections in the domed cover of the silver dish.

I picked up the bag and stood; and his smile faded when I started to the door.

"Wait!" he said.

"Wait what?"

"You're not going to open it?"

"Look —" I knew myself too well, didn't trust myself to wait; I wasn't letting the same thing happen twice —

"What are you doing? Where are you going?"

"I'm taking this downstairs. So they can lock it in the safe." I didn't even know if there was a safe, only that I didn't want the painting near me — it was safer with strangers, in a cloakroom, anywhere. I was also going to phone the police the moment Boris left, but not until; there was no reason dragging Boris into it.

"You didn't even open it! You don't even know what it is!"

"Duly noted."

"What the hell is that supposed to mean?"

"Maybe I don't need to know what it is."

"Oh no? Maybe you do. It's not what you think," he added, a bit smugly.

"No?"

"No."

"How do you know what I think?"

"Of course I know what you think it is! And — you are wrong. Sorry. But —" raising his hands — "is something much, much better than."

"Better than?"

"Yes."

"How can it be *better* than?"

"It just is. Lots lots better. You will just have to believe me on this. Open and see," he said, with a curt nod.

"What is this?" I said after about thirty stunned seconds. Lifting out one brick of hundreds — dollars — then another.

"That is not all of it." Rubbing the back of his head with the flat of his hand. "Fraction of."

I looked at it, then at him. "Fraction of what?"

"Well —" smirking — "thought more dramatic if in cash, no?"

Muffled comedy voices floating from next door, articulated cadences of a television laugh track.

"Nicer surprise for you! That is not all of it, mind you. U.S. currency, I thought, more convenient for you to return with. What you came over with — a bit more. In fact they have not paid yet — no money has yet come through. But — soon, I hope."

"They? Who hasn't paid? Paid what?"

"This money is mine. Own personal. From the house safe. Stopped in Antwerp to get it. Nicer this way — nicer for you to open, no? Christmas morning? Ho Ho Ho? But you have a lot more coming."

I turned the stack of money over and looked at it: forward and back. Banded, straight from Citibank.

" 'Thank you Boris.' 'Oh, no problem,' " he answered, ironically, in his own voice. "Glad to do it.' "

Money in stacks. Outside the event. Crisp in the hand. There was some kind of obvious content or emotion to the whole thing I wasn't getting.

"As I say — fraction of. Two million euro. In dollars much much more. So — merry Christmas! My gift to you! I can open you an account in Switzerland for the rest of it and give you a bank book and that way — what?" he said, recoiling almost, when I put the stack of bills in the bag, snapped it shut, and shoved it back at him. "No! It's yours!"

"I don't want it."

"I don't think you understand! Let me explain, please."

"I said I don't want it."

"Potter —" folding his arms and looking at me coldly, the same look he'd given me in the Polack bar — "a different man would walk out laughing now and never come back."

"Then why don't you?"

"I —" looking around the room, as if at a loss for a reason why — "I will tell you why not! For old times' sake. Even though you treat me like a criminal. And because I want to make things up to you —"

"Make what up?"

"Sorry?"

"What, exactly? Will you explain it to me? Where the hell did this money come from? How does this fix a fucking thing?"

"Well, actually, you should not be so quick to jump to —"

"I don't care about the money!" I was half-screaming. "I care about the painting! Where's the painting?"

"If you would just wait a second and not fly off the —"

"What's this money for? Where's it from? From what source, exactly? Bill Gates? Santa Claus? The Tooth Fairy?"

"Please. You are like your dad with the drama."

"Where is it? What'd you do with it? It's gone, isn't it? Traded? Sold?"

"No, of course I — hey —" scraping his chair back hastily — "Jesus, Potter, calm down. Of course I didn't sell it. Why would I do any such?"

"I don't know! How should I know? What was all this for? What was the point of any of this? Why did I even come here with you? Why'd you have to drag me into it? You thought you'd bring me over here to help you kill people? Is that it?"

"I've never killed anybody in my life," said Boris haughtily.

"Oh, God. Did you just say that? Am I supposed to laugh? Did I really just hear you say you never—"

"That was self defense. You know it. I do not go around hurting people for the fun of it but I will protect myself if I have to. And you," he said, talking imperiously over me, "with Martin, apart from the fact I would not be here now and most likely you neither—"

"Will you do me a favor? If you won't shut up? Will you maybe go over there and stand for a minute? Because I really don't want to see you or look at you now."

"—with Martin the police, if they knew, they would give you a medal and so would many others, innocent, not now living, thanks to him. Martin was—"

"Or, actually, you could leave. That's probably better."

"Martin was a devil. Not all human. Not all his fault. He was born that way. No feelings, you know? I have known Martin to do much worse things to people than shooting them. Not to *us*," he said, hastily, waving his hand, as if this were the point of all misunderstanding. "Us, he would have shot out of courtesy, and none of his other badness and evil. But— was Martin a good man? A proper human being? No. He was not. Frits was no flower, either. So—this remorse and pain of yours—you must view it in a different light. You must view it as heroism in service of higher good. You cannot always take such a dark perspective of life all the time, you know, it is very bad for you."

"Can I ask you just one thing?"

"Anything."

"Where's the painting?"

"Look—" Boris sighed, and looked away. "This was the best I could do. I know how much you wanted it. I did not think you would be quite so upset not to have it."

"Can you just tell me where it is?"

"Potter—" hand on heart—"I'm sorry you are so angry. I was not expecting this. But you said you weren't going to keep it anyway. You were going to give it back. Isn't that what you said?" he added when I kept on staring at him.

"How the hell is this the right thing?"

"Well, I'll tell you! If you would shut up and let me talk! Instead of ranting back and forth and frothing at mouth and spoiling our Christmas!"

"What are you talking about?"

"Idiot." Rapping his temple with his knuckles. "Where do you think this money came from?"

"How the fuck should I know?"

"This is the reward money!"

"Reward?"

"Yes! For safe return of!"

It took a moment. I was standing. I had to sit down.

"Are you angry?" said Boris carefully.

Voices in the hallway. Dull winter light glinting off the brass lampshade.

"I thought you would be pleased. No?"

But I had not recovered sufficiently to speak. All I could do was stare, in dumbfoundment.

At my expression, Boris shook the hair out of his face and laughed. "You gave me the idea yourself. I don't think you knew how great it was! Genius! I wish had thought of it myself. 'Call the art cops, call the art cops.' Well—crazy! So I thought at the time. You're a bit nuts on this subject to be perfectly honest. Only then—" he shrugged—"unfortunate events took course, as you only too well know, and after we parted on the bridge I spoke to Cherry, what to do, what to do, wringing our hands a bit, and we did a little nosing around, and—" lifting his glass to me—"well in fact, a genius idea! Why should I doubt you? Ever? You are the brains of all this from the start! While I am in Alaska—walking five miles to petrol station to steal a Nestlé bar—well, look at you. Mastermind! Why should I ever doubt you? Because—I look into it, and—" throwing up his arms—"you were right. Who would have thought? Over million dollars for your picture out there in reward money! Not even picture! Information leading to recovery of picture! No questions asked! Cash, free and clear—!"

Outside, snow was flying against the window. Next door, someone was coughing hard, or laughing hard, I couldn't tell which.

"Back and forth, back and forth, all these years. A game for suckers. Inconvenient, dangerous. And—question I am asking myself now—why did I even bother? with all this legal money straight-up for the claiming? Because—you were right—straight business thing for them. No questions asked whatever. All they cared about was getting the picture back." Boris lit a cigarette and dropped the match with a hiss in his water glass. "I did not see it myself, I wish I had—did not think a good idea to stick around if you get me. German SWAT team! Vests, guns. Drop everything! Lie down! Great commotion and crowd in the street! Ah, I would have loved to see the look on Sascha's face!"

"You phoned the cops?"

"Well not me personally! My boy Dima—Dima is furious at the Germans because of the shooting in his garage. Completely unnecessary, and a big headache for him. See—" restlessly, he crossed his legs, blew out a big cloud of smoke—"I had an idea where they had the picture. There's an apartment in Frankfurt. Used to belong to an old girlfriend of Sascha's. People keep stuff there. But no way in hell could I get in, even with half a dozen guys. Keys, alarms, cameras, passcode. Only problem—" yawning, wiping his mouth with the back of his hand—"well, two problems. First one is that police need probable cause to search the apartment. You can not just call with name of thief, anonymous citizen being helpful if you know what I mean. And second problem—I could not remember the exact address of the place. Very very secretive—I have only been there once—late at night, and not in best of condition. Knew roughly the neighborhood...used to be squats, now is very nice...had Gyuri drive me up the streets and down, up the streets and down. Took for fucking ever. Finally—? I had it pinned to a row of houses but was not one hundred percent sure which. So I got out and walked it. Scared as I was, to be on that street—afraid to be seen—I got out of the car and walked it. With my own two feet. Eyes closed halfway. Hypnotized myself a bit, you know, trying to remember number of steps? Trying to feel it in my body? Anyway—I am getting ahead of myself. Dima—?" he was picking assiduously through the breads on the tablecloth—"Dima's cousin's sister in law, ex-sister in law actually, married a Dutchman, and they have a son named Anton—twenty-one maybe, twenty-two, squeaky clean, surname van den Brink—Anton is Dutch citizen and has grown up speaking Dutch so this is helpful for us too if you get me. Anton—" nibbling on a roll: making a face, spitting a rye seed between his teeth—"Anton works in a bar where many rich people go, off P. C. Hooftstraat, fancy Amsterdam—Gucci Street, Cartier street. Good kid. Speaks English,

Dutch, only two words maybe of Russian. Anyway Dima had Anton
phone the police and report that he had seen two Germans, one of which
answers to precise description of Sascha — granny glasses, 'Little House
on the Prairie' shirt, tribal tattoo on his hand which Anton is able to draw
exactly, from photograph we supplied — anyway, Anton telephoned the
art police and told them he had seen these Germans drunk as gods in his
bar, arguing, and they are so angry and upset they had left behind —
what? A folder! Well of course it is a doctored folder. We were going to do
a phone, a doctored phone, but none of us were nerd enough to be sure we
did it totally untraceable. So — I printed out some photos…photo I
showed you, plus some others that I happened to have on my phone…
finch along with relatively recent issue of newspaper to date it, you know.
Two years old newspaper but — no matter. Anton just happened to find
this folder, see, under a chair, with some other documents from the Miami
thing, you know, to connect to prior sighting. Frankfurt address conveniently inserted, as well as Sascha's name. All this is Myriam's idea, she
deserves the credit, you should buy Myriam big drink when you get back
home. FedExed some things from America — very very convincing. It has
Sascha's name, it has —"

"Sascha's in jail?"

"Indeed he is." Boris cackled. "We get the ransom, museum gets the
painting, cops get to close the case, insurance company gets its money
back, public is edified, everyone wins."

"Ransom?"

"Well, reward, ransom, whatever you want to call it."

"Who paid this money out?"

"I don't know." Boris made an irritated gesture. "Museum, government, private citizen. Does it matter?"

"It matters to me."

"Well it shouldn't. You should shut up and be grateful. Because," he
said, lifting his chin, speaking over me, "you know what, Theo? Know
what? Guess! Guess how lucky we were! Not only do they have your bird
in there, but — who would have guessed it? Many other stolen pictures!"

"What?"

"Two dozens, or more! Missing for many years, some of them! And —
not all of them are as lovely or beautiful as yours, in fact most of them are
not. This is my own personal opinion. But there are big rewards out on

four or five of them all the same — bigger than for yours. And even some
of the not-so-famous ones — dead duck, boring picture of fat-faced man
you don't know — even these have smaller rewards — fifty thousand,
hundred thousand here and there. Who would think? 'Information leading to recovery of.' It adds up. And I hope," he said, with some austerity,
"that maybe you can forgive me for that?"

"What?"

"Because — they are saying, 'one of great art recoveries of history.' And
this is the part I hoped would please you — maybe not, who knows, but I
hoped. Museum masterworks, returned to public ownership! Stewardship
of cultural treasure! Great joy! All the angels are singing! But it would
never have happened, if not for you."

I sat in silent amazement.

"Of course," Boris added, nodding at the bag open on the bed, "this is
not all of it. Nice Christmas present in it for Myriam and Cherry and
Gyuri. And I gave Anton and Dima a thirty per cent cut right off the top.
Fifteen per cent each. Anton did all the work really, so in my opinion he
should have got twenty and Dima ten. But this is a lot of money for Anton
so he is happy."

"Other paintings they recovered. Not just mine."

"Yes, did you not just hear me say —?"

"What other paintings?"

"Oh, some very celebrated and famous ones! Missing for years!"

"Such as —?"

Boris made an irritated sound. "Oh, I do not know the names, you
know not to ask me that. Few modern things — very important and
expensive, everyone very excited although I will be frank, I do not
understand why the big deal on some of them. Why does it cost so much,
a thing like from kindergarten class? 'Ugly Blob.' 'Black Stick with Tan-
gles.' But then too — multiple works of historic greatness. One was a
Rembrandt."

"Not a seascape?"

"No — people in a dark room. Little bit boring. Nice van Gogh,
though, of a sea shore. And then . . . oh, I don't know . . . usual thing, Mary,
Jesus, many angels. Some sculptures even. And Asian artworks too. They
looked to me worth nothing but I guess they were a lot." Boris stabbed out
his cigarette vigorously. "Which reminds me. He got away."

"Who?"

"Sascha's China boy." He had gone to the minibar, returned with corkscrew and two glasses. "He was not at apartment when the cops came, lucky for him. And—if he is smart, which he is—he will not be coming back." Holding up crossed fingers. "He will find some other rich man to live off of. That is what he does. Good work if you can get it. Anyway—" biting his lip as he pulled out the cork, pop! — "I wish I had thought of it myself, years ago! One big easy check! Legal Tender! Instead of this Follow the Bouncing Ball, so many years. Back and forth—" wagging the corkscrew, tick, tock—"back and forth. Nervewracking! All this time, all this headache, and all this easy, government money right under my nose! I will tell you—" crossing over, pouring me out a noisy glug of red—"in some ways, Horst is probably just as glad it fell out like this as you. He likes to make a dollar same as anyone but he also has guilt, same ideas of public good, cultural patrimony, blah blah blah."

"I don't understand how Horst fits into this."

"No, nor do I, and we will never know," said Boris firmly. "It's all very careful and polite. And, yes yes—" impatiently, taking a quick sneaky gulp of his wine—"and yes, I am angry at Horst, a bit, maybe I don't trust him so much as formerly, maybe in fact I don't trust him so much at all. But—Horst is saying he wouldn't have sent Martin if he knew it was us. And maybe he's telling the truth. 'Never, Boris—I would never.' Who can know? To be quite honest—just between us—I think he may be saying it only to save face. Because once it fell to pieces with Martin and Frits, what else could he do? Except gracefully back away? Claim no knowledge? I do not know this for a fact, mind you," he said. "This is just my theory. Horst has his own story."

"Which is—?"

"Horst is saying—" Boris sighed—"Horst says he didn't know that Sascha took the picture, not until we snatched it ourselves and Sascha phoned from clear blue sky asking Horst's help to get it back. Pure coincidence that Martin was in town—here from LA for the holidays. For druggies, Amsterdam is fairly popular Christmas spot. And yes, that part—" he rubbed his eye—"well, I am pretty sure Horst is telling the truth. That call from Sascha *was* a surprise. Throwing himself on Horst's mercy. No time to talk. Had to act quick. How was Horst to know it was us? Sascha wasn't even in Amsterdam—he was hearing it all at second hand, from

Chinky, whose German is not that great—Horst was hearing it at third. It all lines up if you look at it the right way. That said—" he shrugged.

"What?"

"Well—Horst definitely didn't know the painting was in Amsterdam, nor that Sascha was trying to get a loan on it, not until Sascha panicked and called him when we took it. Of that? I am confident. But: did Horst and Sascha collude to make painting vanish in the first place, to Frankfurt, with bad Miami deal? Possibly. Horst liked that picture very very much. *Very* much. Did I tell you—he knew what it was, first time he saw it? Like, off the top of his head? Name of painter and everything?"

"It's one of the most famous paintings in the world."

"Well—" Boris shrugged—"like I said, he is educated. He grew up around beauty. That said, Horst does not know that it was me cooked up the folder. He might not be so happy. And yet—" he laughed aloud—"would it ever occur to Horst? I wonder. All the time, all this reward sitting there? Free and legal! Shining in plain sight, like the sun! I know I never thought of it—not until now. Worldwide happiness and joy! Lost masterworks recovered! Anton the big hero—posing for photos, talking on Sky News! Standing ovation at the press conference last night! Everyone loves him—like that man who landed the plane in the river a few years back and saved everyone, remember him? But, in my mind, is not Anton the people are clapping for—really is you."

There were so many things to say to Boris, I could say none of them. And yet I could only feel the most abstract gratitude. Maybe, I thought—reaching in the bag, taking out a stack of money and looking it over—maybe good luck was like bad luck in that it took a while to sink in. You didn't feel anything at first. The feeling came later on.

"Pretty nice, no?" said Boris, clearly relieved I'd come round. "You are happy?"

"Boris, you need to take half this."

"Believe me, I took care of myself. I have enough now that I can not do anything I don't feel like for a while. Who knows—maybe go into bar business even, in Stockholm. Or—maybe not. Little bit boring. But you—that's all yours! And more to come. Remember that time your dad gave us the five hundred each? Flying like feathers! Very noble and grand! Well—to me then? Hungry half the time? Sad and lonely? Nothing to my name? That was a fortune! More money than I had ever seen! And you—" his nose had grown pink; I thought he was about to sneeze—"always decent and good, shared with me everything you had, and—what did I do?"

"Oh, Boris, come on," I said uneasily.

"I stole from you—that's what I did." Alcoholic glitter in his eyes. "Took your dearest possession. And how could I treat you so badly, when I wished you only well?"

"Stop it. No—really, stop," I said, when I saw he was crying.

"What can I say? You asked me why I took it? and what can I reply? Only that—it's never the way it seems—all good, all bad. So much easier if it was. Even your dad...feeding me, talking with me, spending time, sheltering me in his roof, giving me clothes off his back...you hated your dad so much but in some ways he was good man."

"I wouldn't say good."

"Well I would."

"Well, you would be the only one. You would be wrong."

"Look. I am more tolerance than you," said Boris, invigorated by the prospect of a disagreement and sniffing up his tears in a gulp. "Xandra—your dad—always you wanted to make them so evil and bad. And yes... your dad was destructive...irresponsible...a child. His spirit was huge. It pained him terribly! But he hurt himself worse than he ever hurt anyone else. And yes—" he said theatrically, over my objection—"yes, he stole from you, or tried to, I know it, but do you know what? I stole from you too and got away with it. Which is worse? Because I'm telling you—" prodding the bag with his toe—"the world is much stranger than we know or can say. And I know how you think, or how you like to think, but maybe this is one instance where you can't boil down to pure 'good' or pure 'bad' like you always want to do—? Like, your two different piles? Bad over here, good over here? Maybe not quite so simple. Because—all the way driving here, driving all night, Christmas lights on the motorway and I'm not ashamed to tell you, I got choked up—because I was thinking, couldn't help it, about the Bible story—? you know, where the steward steals the widow's mite, but then the steward flees to far country and invests the mite wisely and brings back thousandfold cash to widow he stole from? And with joy she forgave him, and they killed the fatted calf, and made merry?"

"I think that's maybe not all the same story."

"Well—Bible school, Poland, it was a long time ago. Still. Because, what I am trying to say—what I was thinking in the car from Antwerp last night—good doesn't always follow from good deeds, nor bad deeds result from bad, does it? Even the wise and good cannot see the end of all actions. Scary idea! Remember Prince Myshkin in *The Idiot*?"

"I'm not really up for an intellectual talk right now."

"I know, I know, but hear me out. You read *The Idiot*, right? Right. Well, 'Idiot' was very disturbing book to me. In fact it was so disturbing I have never really read very many fictions after, apart from Dragon Tattoo kind of thing. Because"—I was trying to interject—"well, maybe you can tell me about that later, what you thought, but let me tell you why I found it disturbing. Because all Myshkin ever did was good...unselfish... he treated all persons with understanding and compassion and what resulted from this goodness? Murder! Disaster! I used to worry about this a lot. Lie awake at night and worry! Because—why? How could this be? I read that book like three times, thinking I wasn't understanding right. Myshkin was kind, loved everyone, he was tender, always forgave, he never did a wrong thing—but he trusted all the wrong people, made all bad decisions, hurt everyone around him. Very dark message to this book. 'Why be good.' But—this is what took hold on me last night, riding here in the car. What if—is more complicated than that? What if maybe opposite is true as well? Because, if bad can sometimes come from good actions—? where does it ever say, anywhere, that only bad can come from bad actions? Maybe sometimes—the wrong way is the right way? You can take the wrong path and it still comes out where you want to be? Or, spin it another way, sometimes you can do everything wrong and it still turns out to be right?"

"I'm not sure I see your point."

"Well—I have to say I personally have never drawn such a sharp line between 'good' and 'bad' as you. For me: that line is often false. The two are never disconnected. One can't exist without the other. As long as I am acting out of love, I feel I am doing best I know how. But you—wrapped up in judgment, always regretting the past, cursing yourself, blaming yourself, asking 'what if,' 'what if.' 'Life is cruel.' 'I wish I had died instead of.' Well—think about this. What if all your actions and choices, good or bad, make no difference to God? What if the pattern is pre-set? No no— hang on—this is a question worth struggling with. What if our badness and mistakes are the very thing that set our fate and bring us round to good? What if, for some of us, we can't get there any other way?"

"Get where?"

"Understand, by saying 'God,' I am merely using 'God' as reference to long-term pattern we can't decipher. Huge, slow-moving weather system rolling in on us from afar, blowing us randomly like—" eloquently, he batted at the air as if at a blown leaf. "But—maybe not so random and impersonal as all that, if you get me."

"Sorry but I'm not really appreciating your point here."

"You don't need a point. The point is maybe that the point is too big to see or work round to on our own. Because—" up went the batwing eyebrow—"well, if you didn't take picture from museum, and Sascha didn't steal it back, and I didn't think of claiming reward—well, wouldn't all those dozens of other paintings remain missing too? Forever maybe? Wrapped in brown paper? Still shut in that apartment? No one to look at them? Lonely and lost to the world? Maybe the one had to be lost for the others to be found?"

"I think this goes more to the idea of 'relentless irony' than 'divine providence.'"

"Yes—but why give it a name? Can't they both be the same thing?"

We looked at each other. And it occurred to me that despite his faults, which were numerous and spectacular, the reason I'd liked Boris and felt happy around him from almost the moment I'd met him was that he was never afraid. You didn't meet many people who moved freely through the world with such a vigorous contempt for it and at the same time such odd-ball and unthwartable faith in what, in childhood, he had liked to call "the Planet of Earth."

"So—" Boris downed the rest of his wine, and poured himself some more—"what are your so-big plans?"

"As regards what?"

"A moment ago, you were tearing off. Why not stay here a while?"

"Here?"

"No—I didn't mean *here* here—not in Amsterdam—I will agree with you that it is a very good idea for us probably to get out of town, and as for myself I will not care to be coming back for a while. What I meant was, why not relax a bit and hang out before flying back? Come to Antwerp with me. See my place! Meet my friends! Get away from your girl problems for a bit."

"No, I'm going home."

"When?"

"Today, if I can."

"So soon? No! Come to Antwerp! There is this fantastic service — not like red light — two girls, two thousand euro and you have to call two days in advance. Everything is two. Gyuri can drive us — I'll sit up front, you can stretch out and sleep in the back. What do you say?"

"Actually, I think maybe you should drop me at the airport."

"Actually — I think I should better not. If I was selling the tickets? I would not even let you on a plane. You look like you have bird flu or SARS." He was unlacing his waterlogged shoes, trying to jam his feet into them. "Ugh! Will you answer me this question? Why —" holding up the ruined shoe — "tell me why do I buy these so-fancy Italian leathers when I wreck them in one week? When — my old desert boots — you remember? Good for running away fast! Jumping out of windows! Lasted me years! I don't care if they look crap with my suits. I will find me some more boots like that, and then I will wear them for rest of my life. Where," he said, frowning at his watch, "where did Gyuri get to? He should not be having so much problems parking on Christmas Day?"

"Did you call him?"

Boris slapped his head. "No, I forgot. Shit! He probably ate breakfast already. Or else he is in the car, freezing to death." Draining the rest of his wine, pocketing the mini-bottles of vodka. "Are you packed? Yes? Fantastic. We can go then." He was, I noticed, wrapping up leftover bread and cheese in a cloth napkin. "Go down and pay up. Although —" he looked disapprovingly at the stained coat thrown over the bed — "you really need to get rid of that thing."

"How?"

He nodded at the murky canal outside the window.

"Really —?"

"Why not? No law against throwing a coat in the canal, is there?"

"I would have thought so, yes."

"Well — who knows. Not very widely enforced law, if you ask me. You should see some of the shit I saw floating in that thing during the

garbage strike. Drunk Americans puking in, you name it. Although—"
glancing out the window—"I am with you, rather not do it in broad daylight. We can take it back to Antwerp in the trunk of the car and throw it
down the incinerator. You'll like my flat a lot." Fishing for his phone; dialing the number. "Artist's loft, without the art! And we'll walk out and buy
you a new overcoat when the shops are open."

vi.

I FLEW HOME ON the red-eye two nights later (after a Boxing Day in Antwerp involving neither party nor escort service, but canned soup, a peni-
cillin injection, and some old movies on Boris's couch) and got back to
Hobie's about eight in the morning, breath coming out in white clouds,
letting myself in through the balsam-decked front door, through the parlor with its darkened Christmas tree mostly empty of presents, all the way
to the back of the house where I found a swollen-faced and sleepy-eyed
Hobie, in bathrobe and slippers, standing on a kitchen ladder to put
away the soup tureen and punch bowl he'd used for his Christmas lunch.
"Hi," I said, dropping my suitcase—occupied with Popchik who was
pacing round my feet in staunch geriatric figure eights of greeting—and
only when I glanced up at him climbing down from the ladder did I notice
how resolute he looked: troubled, but with a firm, defensive smile fixed on
his face.

"And you?" I said, straightening up from the dog, unshouldering my
new overcoat and draping it over a kitchen chair. " Anything going on?"

"Not much." Not looking at me.

"Merry Christmas! Well—a little late. How *was* Christmas?"

"Fine. Yours?" he inquired stiffly a few moments later.

"Actually, not so bad. I was in Amsterdam, " I added, when he didn't
say anything.

"Oh really? That must have been nice." Distracted, unfocused.

"How'd your lunch go?" I asked after a cautious pause.

"Oh, very well. We had a bit of sleet but otherwise it was a good gathering." He was trying to collapse the kitchen ladder and having a bit of a
problem with it. "Few presents for you still under the tree in there, if you
feel like opening them."

"Thanks. I'll open them tonight. I'm pretty beat. Can I help you with that?" I said, stepping forward.

"No, no. No thanks." Whatever was wrong was in his voice. "I've got it."

"Okay," I said, wondering why he hadn't mentioned his gift: a child's needlework sampler, vine-curled alphabet and numerals, stylized farm animals worked in crewel, *Marry Sturtevant Her Sample-r Aged 11 1779.* Hadn't he opened it? I'd unearthed it in a box of polyester granny pants at the flea market — not cheap for the flea market, four hundred bucks, but I'd seen comparable pieces sell at Americana auctions for ten times as much. In silence I watched him pottering around the kitchen on autopilot — wandering in circles a bit, opening the refrigerator door, closing it without getting anything out, filling the kettle for tea, and all the time wrapped in his cocoon and refusing to look at me.

"Hobie, what's going on?" I said at last.

"Nothing." He was looking for a spoon but he'd opened the wrong drawer.

"What, you don't want to tell me?"

He turned to look at me, flash of uncertainty in his eyes, before he turned to the stove again and blurted: "It was really inappropriate for you to give Pippa that necklace."

"What?" I said, taken aback. "Was she upset?"

"I —" Staring at the floor, he shook his head. "I don't know what's going on with you," he said. "I don't know what to think any more. Look, I don't want to be censorious," he said, when I sat motionless. "Really I don't. In fact I'd rather not talk about it at all. But —" He seemed to search for words. "Do you not see that it's distressing and unsuitable? To give Pippa a thirty thousand dollar necklace? On the night of your engagement party? Just leave it in her shoe? Outside her door?"

"I didn't pay thirty thousand for it."

"No, I dare say you would have paid seventy-five if you'd bought it at retail. And also, for another thing —" Very suddenly he pulled out a chair and sat down. "Oh, I don't know what to do," he said miserably. "I've no idea how to begin."

"Sorry?"

"Please tell me all this other business has nothing to do with you."

"Business?" I said cautiously.

"Well." Morning classical on the kitchen transistor, meditative piano sonata. "Two days before Christmas, I had a fairly extraordinary visit from your friend Lucius Reeve."

The sense of fall was immediate, the swiftness and depth of it.

"Who had some fairly startling accusations to make. Above and beyond the expected." Hobie pinched his eyes shut between thumb and forefinger, and sat for a moment. "Let's leave aside the other matter for a moment. No, no," he said, waving my words away when I tried to speak. "First things first. About the furniture."

There rolled between us an unbearable silence.

"I understand that I haven't made it exactly easy for you to come to me. And I understand too, that I'm the very one who put you in this position. But—" he looked around—"two million dollars, Theo!"

"Listen, let me say something—"

"I should have made notes—he had photocopies, bills of shipping, pieces we never sold and never had to sell, pieces at the Important Americana level, nonexistent, I couldn't add it all in my head, at some point I just stopped counting. Dozens! I had no idea the extent of it. And you lied to me about the planting. That's not what he wants at all."

"Hobie? Hobie, listen." He was looking at me without quite looking at me. "I'm sorry you had to find out this way, I was hoping I could straighten it up first but—it's taken care of, okay? I can buy it all back now, every stick."

But instead of seeming relieved, he only shook his head. "This is terrible, Theo. How could I let this happen?"

If I'd been a little less shaken, I would have pointed out that he'd committed only the sin of trusting me and believing what I told him, but he seemed so genuinely bewildered that I couldn't bring myself to say anything at all.

"How did it go so far? How can I not have known? He had—" Hobie looked away, shook his head again quickly in disbelief—"Your handwriting, Theo. Your signature. Duncan Phyfe table…Sheraton dining chairs…Sheraton sofa out to California…I made that very sofa, Theo, with my own two hands, you saw me make it, it's no more Sheraton than that shopping bag from Gristede's over there. All new frame. Even the arm supports are new. Only two of the legs are original, you stood there and watched me reeding the new ones—"

"I'm sorry Hobie — the IRS was phoning every day — I didn't know what to do —"

"I know you didn't," he said, though there seemed to be a question in his eyes even as he said this. "It was the Children's Crusade down there. Only —" he pushed back in his chair, rolled his eyes at the ceiling — "why didn't you stop? Why'd you keep on with it? We've been spending money we don't have! You've dug us halfway to China! It's been going on for years! Even if we could cover it all, which we absolutely can't and you know it —"

"Hobie, first of all, I *can* cover it and second —" I needed coffee, I wasn't awake, but there wasn't any on the stove and it really wasn't the moment to get up and make it — "second, well, I don't want to say it's okay, because, absolutely it's not, I was only trying to tide us over and get some debts settled, I don't know how I let it get so far out of hand. But — no, no, listen," I said urgently; I could see him drifting away, fogging over, as my mother had been apt to do when being forced to sit still and suffer through some complicated and improbable lie of my dad's. "Whatever he said to you, and I don't know, I've got the money now. It's all fine. Okay?"

"I suppose I don't dare ask where you got it." Then, sadly, leaning back in his chair: "Where were you really? If you don't mind my asking?"

I crossed and re-crossed my legs, smeared my hands over my face. "Amsterdam."

"Why Amsterdam?" Then, as I fumbled over my answer: "I didn't think you were coming back."

"Hobie —" afire with shame; I'd always worked so hard to screen my double-dealing self from him, to show him only the improved-and-polished version, never the shameful threadbare self I was so desperate to hide, deceiver and coward, liar and cheat —

"Why *did* you come back?" He was speaking fast, and miserably, as if all he wanted was to get the words out of his mouth; and in his agitation he got up and began to walk around, his heel-less shoes slapping on the floor. "I thought we'd seen the last of you. All last night — the last few nights — lying awake trying to think what to do. Shipwreck. Catastrophe. All over the news about these stolen paintings. Some Christmas. And you — nowhere to be found. Not answering your phone — no one knew where you were —"

"Oh, God," I said, honestly appalled. "I'm sorry. And listen, listen," I said—his mouth was thin, he was shaking his head as if he'd already detached himself from what I was saying, no point in even listening—"if it's the furniture you're worried about—"

"Furniture?" Placid, tolerant, conciliatory Hobie: rumbling like a boiler about to explode. "Who said anything about furniture? Reeve said you'd bolted, made a run for it but—" he stood blinking rapidly, attempting to compose himself—"I didn't believe it of you, I couldn't, and I was afraid it was something much worse. Oh, you know what I mean," he said half-angrily when I didn't respond. "What was I to think? The way you tore off from the party...Pippa and I, you can't imagine it, there was a bit of a huff with the hostess, 'where is the groom,' sniff sniff, you left so suddenly, we weren't invited to the after-party so we legged it—and then—imagine how I felt coming home to find the house unlocked, door standing open practically, cash drawer ransacked...never mind the necklace, that note you left Pippa was so strange, she was just as worried as I was—"

"She was?"

"Of course she was!" Flinging out an arm. He was practically shouting. "What were we to think? And then, this terrible visit from Reeve. I was in the middle of making pie crust—should never have gone to the door, I thought it was Moira—nine a.m. and standing there gaping at him with flour all over me—Theo, why did you do it?" he said despairingly.

Not knowing what he meant—I'd done so much—I had no choice but to shake my head and look away.

"It was so preposterous—how could I possibly believe it? As a matter of fact I *didn't* believe it. Because I understand," he said, when I didn't respond, "look, I understand about the furniture, you did what you had to, and believe me, I'm grateful, if not for you I'd be working for hire somewhere and living in some ratty little bed-sit. But—" digging his fists into the pocket of his bathrobe—"all this other malarkey? Obviously I can't help wondering where you fit into all that. Especially since you'd hared off with hardly a word, with your pal—who, I hate to say it, very charming boy but he looks like he's seen the inside of a jail cell or two—"

"Hobie—"

"Oh, Reeve. You should have heard him." All the energy seemed to have left him; he looked limp and defeated. "The old serpent. And—I want you to know, as far as that went—art theft? I took up for you in no uncertain terms. Whatever else you'd done—I was certain you hadn't done *that*. And then? Not three days later? What turns up in the news? What very painting? Along with how many others? Was he telling the truth?" he said, when I still didn't answer. "Was it you?"

"Yes. Well, I mean, technically no."

"Theo."

"I can explain."

"Please do," he said, grinding the heel of his hand into his eye.

"Sit down."

"I—" Hopelessly he looked around, as if he was afraid of losing all his resolve if he sat down at the table with me.

"No, you should sit. It's a long story. I'll make it short as I can."

vii.

HE DIDN'T SAY A WORD. He didn't even answer the telephone when it rang. I was bone-tired and aching from the plane, and though I steered clear of the two dead bodies, I gave him the best account of the rest of it that I could: short sentences, matter of fact, not trying to justify or explain. When I was finished he sat there—me shaken by his silence, no noise in the kitchen except the flatline hum of the old fridge. But, at last, he sat back and folded his arms.

"It does all swing around strangely sometimes, doesn't it?" he said.

I was silent, not knowing what to say.

"I mean only—" rubbing his eye—"I only understand it, as I get older. How funny time is. How many tricks and surprises."

The word *trick* was all I heard, or understood. Then, abruptly, he stood up—all six foot five of him, something stern and regretful in his posture or so it seemed to me, ancestral ghost of the beatwalking cop or maybe a bouncer about to toss you out of the pub.

"I'll go," I said.

Rapidly he blinked. "What?"

"I'll write you a check for the whole amount. Just hold it until I tell you it's okay to cash it, that's all I ask. I never meant you any harm, I swear."

With a full-armed gesture of old, he swatted away my words. "No, no. Wait here. I want to show you something."

He got up and creaked into the parlor. He was gone a while. And — when he came back — it was with a falling-to-pieces photo album. He sat down. He leafed through it for several pages. And — when he got to a certain page — he pushed it across the table to me. "There," he said.

Faded snapshot. A tiny, beaky, birdlike boy smiled at a piano in a palmy Belle Époque room: not Parisian, not quite, but Cairene. Twinned jardinières, many French bronzes, many small paintings. One — flowers in a glass — I dimly recognized as a Manet. But my eye tripped and stopped at the twin of a much more familiar image, one or two frames above.

It was, of course, a reproduction. But even in the tarnished old photograph, it glowed in its own isolated and oddly modern light.

"Artist's copy," said Hobie. "The Manet too. Nothing special but —" folding his hands on the table — "those paintings were a huge part of his childhood, the happiest part, before he was ill — only child, petted and spoiled by the servants — figs and tangerines and jasmine blossoms on the balcony — he spoke Arabic, as well as French, you knew that, right? And —" Hobie crossed his arms tight, and tapped his lips with a forefinger — "he used to speak of how with very great paintings it's possible to know them deeply, inhabit them almost, even through copies. Even Proust — there's a famous passage where Odette opens the door with a cold, she's sulky, her hair is loose and undone, her skin is patchy, and Swann, who has never cared about her until that moment, falls in love with her because she looks like a Botticelli girl from a slightly damaged fresco. Which Proust himself only knew from a reproduction. He never saw the original, in the Sistine Chapel. But even so — the whole novel is in some ways about that moment. And the damage is part of the attraction, the painting's blotchy cheeks. Even through a copy Proust was able to re-dream that image, re-shape reality with it, pull something all his own from it into the world. Because — the line of beauty is the line of beauty. It doesn't matter if it's been through the Xerox machine a hundred times."

"No," I said, though I wasn't thinking of the painting but of Hobie's changelings. Pieces enlivened by his touch and polished until they looked as if they'd had pure, golden Time poured over them, copies that made you love Hepplewhite, or Sheraton, even if you'd never looked at or thought about a piece of Hepplewhite or Sheraton in your life.

"Well — I'm just an old copyist talking myself. You know what Picasso says. 'Bad artists copy, good artists steal.' Still with real greatness, there's a jolt at the end of the wire. It doesn't matter how often you grab hold of the line, or how many people have grabbed hold of it before you. It's the same line. Fallen from a higher life. It still carries some of the same shock. And these copies —" leaning forward with hands folded on the table — "these artists' copies he grew up with were lost when the house in Cairo burned, and to tell you the truth they were lost to him earlier, when he was crippled and they sent him back to America, but — well, he was a person like us, he got attached to objects, they had personalities and souls to him, and though he lost almost everything else from that life, he never lost those paintings because the originals were still out in the world. Made several trips to see them — matter of fact, we took the train all the way to Baltimore to see the original of his Manet when it was exhibited here, years ago, back when Pippa's mother was still living. Quite a journey for Welty. But he knew he'd never make it back to the Musée d'Orsay. And the day he and Pippa went up to the Dutch exhibition? What picture do you think he was taking her specially to see?"

The interesting thing, in the photograph, was how the fragile little knock-kneed boy — smiling sweetly, pristine in his sailor suit — was also the old man who'd clasped my hand while he was dying: two separate frames, superimposed upon each other, of the same soul. And the painting, above his head, was the still point where it all hinged: dreams and signs, past and future, luck and fate. There wasn't a single meaning. There were many meanings. It was a riddle expanding out and out and out.

Hobie cleared his throat. "Ask you something?"

"Of course."

"How'd you store it?"

"In a pillowcase."

"Cotton?"

"Well — is percale cotton?"

"No padding? Nothing to protect it?"

"Just paper and tape. Yep," I said, when his eyes blurred with alarm.

"You should have used glassine and bubble wrap!"

"I know that now."

"Sorry." Wincing; putting a hand to his temple. "Still trying to get my

head around it. You flew with that painting in checked baggage on Continental Airlines?"

"Like I said. I was thirteen."

"Why didn't you just tell me? You could have done," he said, when I
shook my head.

"Oh, sure," I said, a little too quickly, though I was remembering the
isolation and terror of that time: my constant fear of Social Services; the
soap-heavy smell of my un-lockable bedroom, the drastic chill of the
stone-gray reception area where I waited to see Mr. Bracegirdle, my fear of
being sent away.

"I'd have figured out something. Although, when you tipped up here
homeless like you did ... well, I hope you don't mind my saying so but even
your own lawyer — well, you know it as well as I do, the situation made
him nervous, he was pretty anxious to get you out of here and then on my
end, as well, several very old friends said, 'James, this is absolutely too
much for you ...' well you can understand why they'd think it," he added
hastily, when he saw the look on my face.

"Oh, sure, of course." The Vogels, the Grossmans, the Mildebergers,
while always polite, had always managed to silently convey (to me, anyway) their Hobie-has-quite-enough-to-deal-with philosophy.

"On some level it was mad. I know how it looked. And yet — well — it
seemed a plain message, how Welty had sent you here, and then there you
were, like a little insect, coming back and coming back —" He thought a
moment, brow furrowed, a deeper version of his perpetual worried
expression — "I'll tell you what I'm trying a bit clumsily to say, after my
mother died I'd walk and walk, that awful dragging summer. Walk all
the way from Albany to Troy sometimes. Standing under awnings of
hardware stores in the rain. Anything to keep from going home to that
house without her in it. Floating around like a ghost. I'd stay in the library
until they kicked me out and then get on the Watervliet bus and ride and
then wander some more. I was a big kid, twelve years old and tall as a
man, people thought I was a tramp, housewives chased me with brooms
from their doorsteps. But that's how I ended up at Mrs. De Peyster's — she
opened the door when I was sitting on her porch and said: You must be
thirsty, would you like to come in? Portraits, miniatures, daguerreotypes,
old Aunt This, old Uncle Thus and So. That spiral staircase coming
down. And there I was — in my lifeboat. I'd found it. You had to pinch

yourself in that house sometimes to remind yourself it wasn't 1909. Some of the most beautiful American Classical pieces I've ever seen to this day, and, my God, that Tiffany glass — this was in the days before Tiffany was so special, people didn't care for it, it wasn't the thing, probably it was already commanding big prices in the city but back then you could find it in upstate junk shops for next to nothing. Soon enough I started prowling those junk shops myself. But this — this had all come down in her family. Every piece had a story. And she was delighted to show you just where to stand, at what hour, to catch each piece in the best light. In the late afternoon, when the sun wheeled round the room —" he splayed his fingers, *pop, pop!* — "they'd fire up one by one like firecrackers on a string."

From my chair I had a clear view of Hobie's Noah's Ark: paired elephants, zebras, carven beasts marching two by two, clear down to tiny hen and rooster and the bunnies and mice bringing up the rear. And the memory was located there, beyond words, a coded message from that first afternoon: rain streaming down the skylights, the homely file of creatures lined on the kitchen counter waiting to be saved. Noah: the great conservator, the great caretaker.

"And —" he'd gotten up to make some coffee — "I suppose it's ignoble to spend your life caring so much for *objects* —"

"Who says?"

"Well —" turning from the stove — "it's not as if we're running a hospital for sick children down here, let's put it that way. Where's the nobility in patching up a bunch of old tables and chairs? Corrosive to the soul, quite possibly. I've seen too many estates not to know that. Idolatry! Caring too much for objects can destroy you. Only — if you care for a thing enough, it takes on a life of its own, doesn't it? And isn't the whole point of things — beautiful things — that they connect you to some larger beauty? Those first images that crack your heart wide open and you spend the rest of your life chasing, or trying to recapture, in one way or another? Because, I mean — mending old things, preserving them, looking after them — on some level there's no rational grounds for it —"

"There's no 'rational grounds' for anything I care about."

"Well, no, nor me either," he said reasonably. "But" — peering nearsightedly into the coffee jar, spooning ground coffee into the pot — "well, sorry to maunder on, but from here, from where I'm standing, it looks like a bit of a fix, doesn't it?"

"What?"

He laughed. "What's to say? Great paintings—people flock to see them, they draw crowds, they're reproduced endlessly on coffee mugs and mouse pads and anything-you-like. And, I count myself in the following, you can have a lifetime of perfectly sincere museum-going where you traipse around enjoying everything and then go out and have some lunch. But—" crossing back to the table to sit again "—if a painting really works down in your heart and changes the way you see, and think, and feel, you don't think, 'oh, I love this picture because it's universal.' 'I love this painting because it speaks to all mankind.' That's not the reason anyone loves a piece of art. It's a secret whisper from an alleyway. *Psst, you. Hey kid. Yes you.*" Fingertip gliding over the faded-out photo—the conservator's touch, a touch-without-touching, a communion wafer's space between the surface and his forefinger. "An individual heart-shock. Your dream, Welty's dream, Vermeer's dream. You see one painting, I see another, the art book puts it at another remove still, the lady buying the greeting card at the museum gift shop sees something else entire, and that's not even to mention the people separated from us by time—four hundred years before us, four hundred years after we're gone—it'll never strike anybody the same way and the great majority of people it'll never strike in any deep way at all but—a really great painting is fluid enough to work its way into the mind and heart through all kinds of different angles, in ways that are unique and very particular. *Yours, yours. I was painted for you.* And—oh, I don't know, stop me if I'm rambling..." passing a hand over his forehead.... "but Welty himself used to talk about fateful objects. Every dealer and antiquaire recognizes them. The pieces that occur and recur. Maybe for someone else, not a dealer, it wouldn't be an object. It'd be a city, a color, a time of day. The nail where your fate is liable to catch and snag."

"You sound like my dad."

"Well—let's put it another way. Who was it said that coincidence was just God's way of remaining anonymous?"

"Now you *really* sound like my dad."

"Who's to say that gamblers don't really understand it better than anyone else? Isn't everything worthwhile a gamble? Can't good come around sometimes through some strange back doors?"

...
viii.

AND YES. I SUPPOSE it can. Or—to quote another paradoxical gem of my dad's: sometimes you have to lose to win.

Because it's almost a year later now and I've been travelling almost the whole time, eleven months spent largely in airport lounges and hotel rooms and other walk-through places, Stow for Taxi, Take-off, and Landing, plastic trays and stale air through the shark-gill cabin vents—and even though it's not quite Thanksgiving the lights are up already and they're starting to play easy-listening Christmas standards like Vince Guaraldi's "Tannenbaum" and Coltrane's "Greensleeves" at the airport Starbucks; and among the many, many things I've had time to think about (such as what's worth living for? what's worth dying for? what's completely foolish to pursue?) I've been thinking a lot about what Hobie said: about those images that strike the heart and set it blooming like a flower, images that open up some much, much larger beauty that you can spend your whole life looking for and never find.

And it's been good for me, my time alone on the road. A year is how long it's taken me to quietly wander round on my own and re-purchase the frauds still out, a delicate proceeding which I've found is best conducted in person: three or four trips a month, New Jersey and Oyster Bay and Providence and New Canaan, and—further afield—Miami, Houston, Dallas, Charlottesville, Atlanta, where at the invitation of my lovely client Mindy, the wife of an auto-parts magnate named Earl, I spent three fairly congenial days in the guest house of a spanking new coral-stone château featuring its own billiard parlour, "gentleman's pub" (with authentic, imported, English-born barkeep), and indoor shooting range with custom track mounted target system. Some of my dot-com and hedge fund clients have second homes in exotic places, exotic to me anyway, Antigua and Mexico and the Bahamas, Monte Carlo and Juan-les-Pins and Sintra, interesting local wines and cocktails on terraced gardens with palm trees and agaves and white umbrellas whipping out by the pool like sails. And in between, I've been in a kind of bardo state, flying around in a gray roar, climbing with drop-spattered windows to laddered sunlight, descending to rainclouds and rain and escalators down and down to a tumble of faces in baggage claim, eerie kind of afterlife, the space between earth and not-earth, world and not-world, highly polished floors and glass-roof cathedral echoes and the whole anonymous concourse glow, a mass identity I don't want to be a part of and indeed am not a part of, except it's almost as if I've died, I feel different, I *am* different, and there's a certain benumbed pleasure in moving in and out of the group mind, napping in molded plastic chairs and wandering the gleaming aisles of Duty Free and of course everyone perfectly nice when you touch down, indoor tennis courts and private beaches and — after the obligatory tour, all very nice, admiring the Bonnard, the Vuillard, light lunch out by the pool — a hefty check and a taxi ride back to the hotel again a good deal poorer.

It's a big shift. I don't know quite how to explain it. Between wanting and not wanting, caring and not caring.

Of course it's a lot more than that too. Shock and aura. Things are stronger and brighter and I feel on the edge of something inexpressible. Coded messages in the in-flight magazines. Energy Shield. Uncompromising Care. Electricity, colors, radiance. Everything is a signpost pointing to something else. And, lying on my bed in some frigid biscuit-colored hotel room in Nice, with a balcony facing the Promenade des Anglais, I watch the clouds reflected on sliding panes and marvel how even my sadness can make me happy, how wall to wall carpet and fake Biedermeier furniture and a softly murmuring French announcer on Canal Plus can all somehow seem so necessary and right.

I'd just as soon forget, but I can't. It's kind of the hum of a tuning fork. It's just there. It's here with me all the time.

White noise, impersonal roar. Deadening incandescence of the boarding terminals. But even these soul-free, sealed-off places are drenched with meaning, spangled and thundering with it. Sky Mall. Portable stereo systems. Mirrored isles of Drambuie and Tanqueray and Chanel No. 5. I look at the blanked-out faces of the other passengers — hoisting their briefcases, their backpacks, shuffling to disembark — and I think of what Hobie said: beauty alters the grain of reality. And I keep thinking too of the more conventional wisdom: namely, that the pursuit of pure beauty is a trap, a fast track to bitterness and sorrow, that beauty has to be wedded to something more meaningful.

Only what is that thing? Why am I made the way I am? Why do I care about all the wrong things, and nothing at all for the right ones? Or, to tip it another way: how can I see so clearly that everything I love or care about is illusion, and yet—for me, anyway—all that's worth living for lies in that charm?

A great sorrow, and one that I am only beginning to understand: we don't get to choose our own hearts. We can't make ourselves want what's good for us or what's good for other people. We don't get to choose the people we are.

Because—isn't it drilled into us constantly, from childhood on, an unquestioned platitude in the culture—? From William Blake to Lady Gaga, from Rousseau to Rumi to *Tosca* to Mister Rogers, it's a curiously uniform message, accepted from high to low: when in doubt, what to do? How do we know what's right for us? Every shrink, every career counselor, every Disney princess knows the answer: "Be yourself." "Follow your heart."

Only here's what I really, really want someone to explain to me. What if one happens to be possessed of a heart that can't be trusted—? What if the heart, for its own unfathomable reasons, leads one willfully and in a cloud of unspeakable radiance away from health, domesticity, civic responsibility and strong social connections and all the blandly-held common virtues and instead straight towards a beautiful flare of ruin, self-immolation, disaster? Is Kitsey right? If your deepest self is singing and coaxing you straight toward the bonfire, is it better to turn away? Stop your ears with wax? Ignore all the perverse glory your heart is screaming at you? Set yourself on the course that will lead you dutifully towards the norm, reasonable hours and regular medical check-ups, stable relationships and steady career advancement, the New York Times and brunch on Sunday, all with the promise of being somehow a better person? Or— like Boris—is it better to throw yourself head first and laughing into the holy rage calling your name?

It's not about outward appearances but inward significance. A grandeur *in* the world, but not *of* the world, a grandeur that the world doesn't understand. That first glimpse of pure otherness, in whose presence you bloom out and out and out.

A self one does not want. A heart one cannot help.

Though my engagement isn't off, not officially anyway, I've been given to understand—gracefully, in the lighter-than-air manner of the Barbours—that no one is holding me to anything. Which is perfect. Nothing's been said and nothing *is* said. When I'm invited for dinner (as I am, often, when I'm in town) it's all very pleasant and light, voluble even, intimate and subtle while not at all personal; I'm treated like a family member (almost), welcome to turn up when I want; I've been able to coax Mrs. Barbour out of the apartment a bit, we've had some pleasant afternoons out, lunch at the Pierre and an auction or two; and Toddy, without being impolitic in the least, has even managed to let casually and almost accidentally drop the name of a very good doctor, with no suggestion whatever that I might possibly need such a thing.

[As for Pippa: though she took the Oz book, she left the necklace, along with a letter I opened so eagerly I literally ripped through the envelope and tore it in half. The gist — once I got on my knees and fit the pieces together — was this: she'd loved seeing me, our time in the city had meant a lot to her, who in the world could have picked such a beautiful necklace for her? it was perfect, more than perfect, only she couldn't accept it, it was much too much, she was sorry, and — maybe she was speaking out of turn, and if so she hoped I forgave her, but I shouldn't think she didn't love me back, because she did, she did. (You do? I thought, bewildered.) Only it was complicated, she wasn't thinking only of herself but me too, since we'd both been through so many of the same things, she and I, and we were an awful lot alike — too much. And because we'd both been hurt so badly, so early on, in violent and irremediable ways that most people didn't, and couldn't, understand, wasn't it a bit...precarious? A matter of self-preservation? Two rickety and death-driven persons who would need to lean on each other quite so much? not to say she wasn't doing well at the moment, because she was, but all that could change in a flash with either of us, couldn't it? the reversal, the sharp downward slide, and wasn't that the danger? since our flaws and weaknesses were so much the same, and one of us could bring the other down way too quick? and though this was left to float in the air a bit, I realized instantly, and with some considerable astonishment, what she was getting at. (Dumb of me not to have seen it earlier, after all the injuries, the crushed leg, the multiple surgeries; adorable drag in the voice, adorable drag in the step, the arm-hugging and the pallor, the scarves and sweaters and multiple layers of clothes, slow drowsy smile: she herself, the dreamy childhood her, was sublimity and disaster, the morphine lollipop I'd chased for all those years.)

But, as the reader of this will have ascertained (if there ever is a reader) the idea of being Dragged Down holds no terror for me. Not that I care to drag anyone else down with me, but—can't *I* change? Can't *I* be the strong one? Why not?]

[You can have either of those girls you want, said Boris, sitting on the sofa with me in his loft in Antwerp, cracking pistachios between his rear molars as we were watching Kill Bill.

No I can't.

And why can't you? I'd pick Snowflake myself. But if you want the other, why not?

Because she has a boyfriend?

So? said Boris.

Who lives with her?

So?

And here's what I'm thinking too: So? What if I go to London? So?

And this is either a completely disastrous question or the most sensible one I've ever asked in all my life.]

I've written all this, oddly, with the idea that Pippa will see it someday—which of course she won't. No one will, for obvious reasons. I haven't written it from memory: that blank notebook my English teacher gave me all those years ago was the first of a series, and the start of an erratic if lifelong habit from age thirteen on, beginning with a series of formal yet curiously intimate letters to my mother: long, obsessive, home-sick letters which have the tone of being written to a mother alive and anxiously waiting for news of me, letters describing where I was "staying" (never living) and the people I was "staying with," letters detailing exhaustively what I ate and drank and wore and watched on television, what books I read, what games I played, what movies I saw, things the Barbours did and said and things Dad and Xandra did and said—these epistles (dated and signed, in a careful hand, ready to be torn out of the notebook and mailed) alternating with miserable bursts of I Hate Everyone and I Wish I was Dead, months grinding by with a disjointed scribble or two, B's house, haven't been to school in three days and it's Friday already, my life in haiku, I am in a state of semi-zombie, God we got so trashed last night like I whited out sort of, we played a game called Liar's Dice and ate cornflakes and breath mints for dinner.

And yet even after I got to New York, I kept writing. "Why the hell is it so much colder here than I remember, and why does this stupid fucking desk lamp make me so sad?" I described suffocating dinner parties; I recorded conversations and wrote down my dreams; I took many careful notes of what Hobie taught me below stairs in the shop.

> eighteenth century mahogany easier to match than walnut—eye fooled by the darker wood
> When artificially done—too evenly executed!
>
> 1. bookcase will show wear on bottom rails where dusted and touched, but not on top
> 2. on items that lock, look for dents and scratches below the keyhole, where wood will have been struck by opening the lock with a key on a bunch

Interspersed throughout this, and notes of auction results from Important Americana sales ("Lot 77 Fed. part ebz. girandôle cvx mirror $7500") and—increasingly—sinister charts and tables which I somehow thought would be incomprehensible to a person picking up the notebook but in fact are perfectly clear:

Dec. 1–8	320.5 mg
Dec. 9–15	202.5 mg
Dec. 16–22	171.5 mg
Dec. 23–30	420.5 mg

... pervading this daily record, and raising it above itself, is the secret visible only to me: blooming in the darkness and never once mentioned by name.

Because: if our secrets define us, as opposed to the face we show the world: then the painting was the secret that raised me above the surface of life and enabled me to know who I am. And it's there: in my notebooks, every page, even though it's not. Dream and magic, magic and delirium. The Unified Field Theory. A secret about a secret.

[That little guy, said Boris in the car on the way to Antwerp. You know the painter *saw* him—he wasn't painting that bird from his mind, you know? That's a real little guy, chained up on the wall, there. If I saw him mixed up with dozen other birds all the same kind, I could pick him out, no problem.]

And he's right. So could I. And if I could go back in time I'd clip the chain in a heartbeat and never care a minute that the picture was never painted.

Only it's more complicated than that. Who knows why Fabritius painted the goldfinch at all? A tiny, stand-alone masterpiece, unique of all its kind? He was young, celebrated. He had important patrons (although unfortunately almost none of the work he did for them survives). You'd imagine him like the young Rembrandt, flooded with grandiose commissions, his studios resplendent with jewels and battle axes, goblets and furs, leopard skins and costume armor, all the power and sadness of earthly things. Why this subject? A lonely pet bird? Which was in no way characteristic of his age or time, where animals featured mainly dead, in sumptuous trophy pieces, limp hares and fish and fowl, heaped high and bound for table? Why does it seem so significant to me that the wall is plain — no tapestry or hunting horns, no stage decoration — and that he took such care to inscribe his name and the year with such prominence, since he can hardly have known (or did he?) that 1654, the year he made the painting, would also be the year of his death? There's a shiver of premonition about it somehow, as if perhaps he had an intimation that this tiny mysterious piece would be one of the very few works to outlive him. The anomaly of it haunts me on every level. Why not something more typical? Why not a seascape, a landscape, a history painting, a commissioned portrait of some important person, a low-life scene of drinkers in a tavern, a bunch of tulips for heaven's sake, rather than this lonely little captive? Chained to his perch? Who knows what Fabritius was trying to tell us by his choice of tiny subject? His presentation of tiny subject? And if what they say is true — if every great painting is really a self-portrait — what, if anything, is Fabritius saying about himself? A painter thought so surpassingly great by the greatest painters of his day, who died so young, so long ago, and about whom we know almost nothing? About himself as a painter: he's saying plenty. His lines speak on their own. Sinewy wings; scratched pinfeather. The speed of his brush is visible, the sureness of his hand, paint dashed thick. And yet there are also half-transparent passages rendered so lovingly alongside the bold, pastose strokes that there's tenderness in the contrast, and even humor; the underlayer of paint is visible beneath the hairs of his brush; he wants us to feel the downy breast-fluff, the softness and texture of it, the brittleness of the little claw curled about the brass perch.

But what does the painting say about Fabritius himself? Nothing about religious or romantic or familial devotion; nothing about civic awe or career ambition or respect for wealth and power. There's only a tiny heartbeat and solitude, bright sunny wall and a sense of no escape. Time that doesn't move, time that couldn't be called time. And trapped in the heart of light: the little prisoner, unflinching. I think of something I read about Sargent: how, in portraiture, Sargent always looked for the animal in the sitter (a tendency that, once I knew to look for it, I saw everywhere in his work: in the long foxy noses and pointed ears of Sargent's heiresses, in his rabbit-toothed intellectuals and leonine captains of industry, his plump owl-faced children). And, in this staunch little portrait, it's hard not to see the human in the finch. Dignified, vulnerable. One prisoner looking at another.

But who knows what Fabritius intended? There's not enough of his work left to even make a guess. The bird looks out at us. It's not idealized or humanized. It's very much a bird. Watchful, resigned. There's no moral or story. There's no resolution. There's only a double abyss: between painter and imprisoned bird; between the record he left of the bird and our experience of it, centuries later.

And yes — scholars might care about the innovative brushwork and use of light, the historical influence and the unique significance in Dutch art. But not me. As my mother said all those years ago, my mother who loved the painting only from seeing it in a book she borrowed from the Comanche County Library as a child: the significance doesn't matter. The historical significance deadens it. Across those unbridgeable distances — between bird and painter, painting and viewer — I hear only too well what's being said to me, a *psst* from an alleyway as Hobie put it, across four hundred years of time, and it's really very personal and specific. It's there in the light-rinsed atmosphere, the brush strokes he permits us to see, up close, for exactly what they are — hand worked flashes of pigment, the very passage of the bristles visible — and then, at a distance, the miracle, or the joke as Horst called it, although really it's both, the slide of transubstantiation where paint is paint and yet also feather and bone. It's the place where reality strikes the ideal, where a joke becomes serious and anything serious is a joke. The magic point where every idea and its opposite are equally true.

And I'm hoping there's some larger truth about suffering here, or at least my understanding of it—although I've come to realize that the only truths that matter to me are the ones I don't, and can't, understand. What's mysterious, ambiguous, inexplicable. What doesn't fit into a story, what doesn't have a story. Glint of brightness on a barely-there chain. Patch of sunlight on a yellow wall. The loneliness that separates every living creature from every other living creature. Sorrow inseparable from joy.

Because—what if that particular goldfinch (and it is very particular) had never been captured or born into captivity, displayed in some household where the painter Fabritius was able to see it? It can never have understood why it was forced to live in such misery: bewildered by noise (as I imagine), distressed by smoke, barking dogs, cooking smells, teased by drunkards and children, tethered to fly on the shortest of chains. Yet even a child can see its dignity: thimble of bravery, all fluff and brittle bone. Not timid, not even hopeless, but steady and holding its place. Refusing to pull back from the world.

And, increasingly, I find myself fixing on that refusal to pull back. Because I don't care what anyone says or how often or winningly they say it: no one will ever, ever be able to persuade me that life is some awesome, rewarding treat. Because, here's the truth: life is catastrophe. The basic fact of existence—of walking around trying to feed ourselves and find friends and whatever else we do—is catastrophe. Forget all this ridiculous 'Our Town' nonsense everyone talks: the miracle of a newborn babe, the joy of one simple blossom, Life You Are Too Wonderful To Grasp, &c. For me—and I'll keep repeating it doggedly till I die, till I fall over on my ungrateful nihilistic face and am too weak to say it: better never born, than born into this cesspool. Sinkhole of hospital beds, coffins, and broken hearts. No release, no appeal, no "do-overs" to employ a favored phrase of Xandra's, no way forward but age and loss, and no way out but death. ["Complaints bureau!" I remember Boris grousing as a child, one afternoon at his house when we had got off on the vaguely metaphysical subject of our mothers: why they—angels, goddesses—had to die? while our awful fathers thrived, and boozed, and sprawled, and muddled on, and continued to stumble about and wreak havoc, in seemingly indefatigable health? "They took the wrong ones! Mistake was made! Everything is unfair! Who do we complain to, in this shitty place? Who is in charge here?"]

And—maybe it's ridiculous to go on in this vein, although it doesn't matter since no one's ever going to see this—but does it make any sense at all to know that it ends badly for all of us, even the happiest of us, and that we all lose everything that matters in the end—and yet to know as well, despite all this, as cruelly as the game is stacked, that it's possible to play it with a kind of joy?

To try to make some meaning out of all this seems unbelievably quaint. Maybe I only see a pattern because I've been staring too long. But then again, to paraphrase Boris, maybe I see a pattern because it's there.

And I've written these pages, on some level, to try to understand. But—on another level I don't want to understand, or try to understand, for by doing so I'll be false to the fact. All I can really say for sure is that I've never felt the mystery of the future so much: sense of the hourglass running out, fast-running fever of time. Forces unknown, unchosen, unwilled. And I've been travelling so long, hotels before dawn in strange cities, so long on the road that I feel the jet-speed vibration in my bones, in my body, a sense of constant motion across continents and time zones that continues long after I'm off the plane and swaying at yet another check-in desk, Hi my name is Emma/Selina/Charlie/Dominic, welcome to the So-and-So! exhausted smiles, signing in with shaky hands, pulling down another set of black-out shades, lying on another strange bed with another strange room rocking around me, clouds and shadows, a sickness that's almost exhilaration, a feeling of having died and gone to heaven.

Because—only last night I dreamed of a journey and of snakes, striped ones, poisonous, with arrow-shaped heads, and though they were quite near I wasn't afraid of them, not at all. And in my head a line I heard from somewhere: *We being round thee, forget to die.* These are the lessons that come to me in shadowed hotel rooms with radiantly lit minibars and foreign voices in the hallway, where the boundary between the worlds grows thin.

And as an ongoing prospect, after Amsterdam, which was really my Damascus, the way station and apogee of my Conversion as I guess you'd call it, I continue to be immensely moved by the impermanence of hotels: not in any mundane Travel-and-Leisure way but with a fervor bordering on the transcendent. Some time in October, right around Day of the Dead actually, I stayed in a Mexican seaside hotel where the halls flowed with blown curtains and all the rooms were named after flowers. The Azalea Room, the Camellia Room, the Oleander Room. Opulence and splendor, breezy corridors that swept into something like eternity and each room with its different colored door. Peony, Wisteria, Rose, Passion Flower. And who knows — but maybe that's what's waiting for us at the end of the journey, a majesty unimaginable until the very moment we find ourselves walking through the doors of it, what we find ourselves gazing at in astonishment when God finally takes His hands off our eyes and says: Look!

[Do you ever think about quitting? I asked, during the boring part of *It's a Wonderful Life,* the moonlight walk with Donna Reed, when I was in Antwerp watching Boris with spoon and water from an eyedropper, mixing himself what he called a "pop."

Give me a break! My arm hurts! He'd already shown me the bloody skid mark — black at the edges — cutting deep into his bicep. *You* get shot at Christmas and see if you want to sit around swallowing aspirin!

Yeah, but you're crazy to do it like that.

Well — believe it or not — for me not so much a problem. I only do it special occasions.

I've heard that before.

Well, is true! Still a chipper, for now. I've known of people chipped three-four years and been ok, long as they kept it down to two-three times a month? That said, Boris added somberly — blue movie light glinting off the teaspoon — I *am* alcoholic. Damage is done, there. I'm a drunk till I die. If anything kills me — nodding at the Russian Standard bottle on the coffee table — that'll be it. Say you never shot before?

Believe me, I had problems enough the other way.

Well, big stigma and fear, I understand. Me — honest, I prefer to sniff most times — clubs, restaurants, out and about, quicker and easier just to duck in men's room and do a quick bump. This way — always you crave it. On my death bed I will crave it. Better never to pick it up. Although — really very irritating to see some bone head sitting there smoking out of a crack pipe and make some pronouncement about how dirty and unsafe, they would never use a needle, you know? Like they are so much more sensible than you?

Why did you start?

Why does anyone? My girl left me! Girl at the time. Wanted to be all bad and self-destructive, hah. Got my wish.

Jimmy Stewart in his varsity sweater. Silvery moon, quavery voices. Buffalo Gals won't you come out tonight, come out tonight.

So, why not stop then? I said.

Why should I?

Do I really have to say why?

Yeah, but what if I don't feel like it?

If you can stop, why wouldn't you?

Live by the sword, die by the sword, said Boris briskly, hitting the button on his very professional-looking medical tourniquet with his chin as he was pushing up his sleeve.]

And as terrible as this is, I get it. We can't choose what we want and don't want and that's the hard lonely truth. Sometimes we want what we want even if we know it's going to kill us. We can't escape who we are. (One thing I'll have to say for my dad: at least he *tried* to want the sensible thing — my mother, the briefcase, me — before he completely went berserk and ran away from it.)

And as much as I'd like to believe there's a truth beyond illusion, I've come to believe that there's no truth beyond illusion. Because, between 'reality' on the one hand, and the point where the mind strikes reality, there's a middle zone, a rainbow edge where beauty comes into being, where two very different surfaces mingle and blur to provide what life does not: and this is the space where all art exists, and all magic.

And — I would argue as well — all love. Or, perhaps more accurately, this middle zone illustrates the fundamental discrepancy of love. Viewed close: a freckled hand against a black coat, an origami frog tipped over on its side. Step away, and the illusion snaps in again: life-more-than-life, never-dying. Pippa herself is the play between those things, both love and not-love, there and not-there. Photographs on the wall, a balled-up sock under the sofa. The moment where I reached to brush a piece of fluff from her hair and she laughed and ducked at my touch. And just as music is the space between notes, just as the stars are beautiful because of the space between them, just as the sun strikes raindrops at a certain angle and throws a prism of color across the sky — so the space where I exist, and want to keep existing, and to be quite frank I hope I die in, is exactly this middle distance: where despair struck pure otherness and created something sublime.

And that's why I've chosen to write these pages as I've written them. For only by stepping into the middle zone, the polychrome edge between truth and untruth, is it tolerable to be here and writing this at all.

Whatever teaches us to talk to ourselves is important: whatever teaches us to sing ourselves out of despair. But the painting has also taught me that we can speak to each other across time. And I feel I have something very serious and urgent to say to you, my non-existent reader, and I feel I should say it as urgently as if I were standing in the room with you. That life — whatever else it is — is short. That fate is cruel but maybe not random. That Nature (meaning Death) always wins but that doesn't mean we have to bow and grovel to it. That maybe even if we're not always so glad to be here, it's our task to immerse ourselves anyway: wade straight through it, right through the cesspool, while keeping eyes and hearts open. And in the midst of our dying, as we rise from the organic and sink back ignominiously into the organic, it is a glory and a privilege to love what Death doesn't touch. For if disaster and oblivion have followed this painting down through time — so too has love. Insofar as it is immortal (and it is) I have a small, bright, immutable part in that immortality. It exists; and it keeps on existing. And I add my own love to the history of people who have loved beautiful things, and looked out for them, and pulled them from the fire, and sought them when they were lost, and tried to preserve them and save them while passing them along literally from hand to hand, singing out brilliantly from the wreck of time to the next generation of lovers, and the next.

Thanks to:

Robbert Ammerlaan, Ivan Nabokov, Sam Pace, Neal Guma. I could not have written this novel without any of you. Thanks as well to my editor Michael Pietsch; my agents Amanda Urban and Gill Coleridge; and to Wayne Furman, David Smith, and Jay Barksdale of the New York Public Library.

I must also thank Michelle Aielli, Hanan Al-Shaykh, Molly Atlas, Kate Bernheimer, Richard Beswick, Paul Bogaards, Pauline Bonnefoi, Skye Campbell, Kevin Carty, Alfred Cavallero, Rowan Cope, Simon Costin, Sjaak de Jong, Doris Day, Alice Doyle, Matt Dubov, Greta Edwards-Anthony, Phillip Feneaux, Edna Golding, Alan Guma, Matthew Guma, Marc Harrington, Dirk Johnson, Cara Jones, James Lord, Bjorn Linnell, Lucy Luck, Louise McGloin, Jay McInerney, Malcolm Mabry, Victoria Matsui, Hope Mell, Antonio Monda, Claire Nozieres, Ann Patchett, Jeanine Pepler, Alexandra Pringle, Rebecca Quinlan, Tom Quinlan, Eve Rabinovits, Marius Radieski, Peter Reydon, Georg Reuchlein, Laura Robinson, Tracy Roe, Jose Rosada, Rainer Schmidt, Elizabeth Seelig, Susan de Soissons, George Sheanshang, Jody Shields, Louis Silbert, Jennifer Smith, Maggie Southard, Daniel Starer, Synthia Starkey, Hector Tello, Mary Tondorf-Dick, Robyn Tucker, Karl Van Devender, Paul van der Lecq, Arjaan van Nimwegen, Leland Weissinger, Judy Williams, Jayne Yaffe Kemp, and the staff of Hotel Ambassade and the former Helmsley Carlton House Hotel.

Donna Tartt was born in Greenwood, Mississippi, and is a graduate of Bennington College. She is the author of the novels *The Secret History* and *The Little Friend,* which have been translated into thirty languages.

Martin, Shauna 8/12

Project Management

Seventh Edition

The Library & Learning Centre
Abingdon Campus
Wootton Road
Abingdon OX14 1GG
01235 216240
library@abingdon-witney.ac.uk

This book is due for return on or before the last
date shown below.

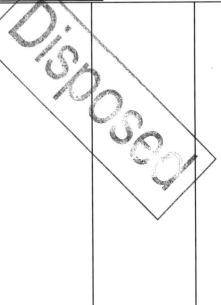

Please note a fine will be charged for overdues